Murderous Schemes:

An Anthology of Classic Detective Stories

Murderous Schemes:

An Anthology of Classic Detective Stories

In association with

The International Association of Crime Writers

Edited by

Donald E. Westlake

Consulting Editor, J. Madison Davis

Oxford University Press
Oxford New York

Oxford University Press

Oxford New York
Athens Auckland Bangkok Bogotá Bombay
Calcutta Cape Town Dar es Salaam Delhi
Florence Hong Kong Istanbul Karachi
Kuala Lumpur Madras Madrid Melbourne
Mexico City Nairobi Paris Singapore
Taipei Tokyo Toronto Warsaw

and associated companies in
Berlin Ibadan

First published by Oxford University Press, Inc., 1996

First issued as an Oxford University Press paperback, 1998

Library of Congress Cataloging-in-Publication Data
Murderous Schemes: An Anthology of Classic Detective Stories/
edited by Donald E. Westlake
p. cm.
ISBN: 0-19-510321-1
ISBN: 0-19-510487-0 (pbk.)
1. Detective and mystery stories, American.
2. Detective and mystery stories, English.
I. Westlake, Donald E.
PR1309.D4M876 1996
813'.087208--dc20 96-19121

1 3 5 7 9 8 6 4 2

Printed in the United States of America

CONTENTS

Murderous Schemes:

An Anthology of Classic Detective Stories

INTRODUCTION

Donald E. Westlake

The major flaw with the genre under consideration is that no one knows quite what to call it. Many people call it the "mystery story," though that doesn't take into account all those stories firmly within the genre which are *not* mysteries, such as heist novels, in which we follow the crooks before, during, and after a crime, usually a robbery: *The Asphalt Jungle*, for instance, or "Don't Know Much About Art," in the current collection. "Mystery story" also leaves out all those murder stories in which the identity of the murderer is known to the reader/audience from the beginning: the *Columbo* series on television, as one example, or *Payment Deferred*, or the charmingly self-referential "The Man Who Read John Dickson Carr" within.

"Crime story" certainly covers the possibilities, but somehow in terms of this genre the phrase "crime story" has lost its generality and has come to mean almost exclusively stories about professional criminals, leaving out all those wife murderers and greedy heirs. The British, and briefly also the Americans, tried to call our genre the "thriller," but that never quite took, sounding more like fantasy or horror before settling where the "thriller" resides today, as a definition of a story combining spies with technology, meaning in most cases a story more than usually devoid of thrills.

"Suspense" is also used sometimes as a name for the genre, but suspense is not a kind of story, it's an element in *all* story, it's the element that creates the desire to know what happens next, which is to say, the desire to be told the story. Suspense is the nicotine of storytelling, the drug that brings us back. Suspense began when Eve reached for that apple, which was a long long time ago. We can't co-opt the word for one single genre, as though to say there's no suspense in it when the rustler cuts through the barbed wire or the paratrooper jumps out of the airplane over the combat zone.

My own preference for a name for this genre is "detective story," even though I personally have almost never written about detectives, and in fact most of my characters, when confronted by a detective, do their level best to blend in with the wallpaper. But I like the term "detective story," and will use it from here on in this essay, mostly because it is a term of disparagement.

Well, yes, it is. I can no longer count the times I have been at a cocktail party and heard someone say, "I never have any time for serious/good/real novels any more. When I want to unwind, I just go to bed with a detective story." That is the context in which the phrase "detective story" is now used, and right now, at this exact moment when you are reading this sentence, the phrase "detective story" is being spoken in exactly that same familiar, easy, disparaging way at least forty times somewhere on the planet.

Who are these speakers? They are intelligent, they are educated, they are usually in the professions (though sometimes in the arts). They are precisely the people any writer would be delighted to count among his readership, and I *am* delighted, and I am willing to accept the barb that comes with it.

Because I know what they really mean, and they don't. Consider: When it comes time for them to unwind, do they unwind by fooling with the Etch-a-Sketch? No. Do they unwind by watching *I Love Lucy* reruns on cable television? No. They don't even unwind with western stories or biographies. Every reader I've ever heard speak in this fashion unwinds with "detective stories."

What they are seeming to say, these people, when they assure us they "just" read detective stories, is that they unwind by insulting their own intelligence. Their brains and educations and wide-ranging intellects, they would like us to know, better fit them for better books, the serious praiseworthy novels they would certainly be reading if they hadn't tired themselves out at the office.

The mistake is that too many people are confused about what reading fiction is *for*. They believe you're supposed to read novels to be improved, to be present at the clash of great ideas, to be challenged by new and profound ways to look at life. And then it turns out, they're too tired.

Oh, they buy the books, the serious award winners, described by publisher and critic alike as important, ground-breaking, even deeply disturbing. They pay their dues. But when the moment comes, once again they fail. Just for now, just as a stopgap, sheepishly they slink off, inadvertently to read fiction for the right reason: Because it's fun. Just for now, they'll read detective stories.

What are these detective stories, that so enthrall people who should be spending their time on more worthy pursuits? What is this drug anyway?

The purpose of this anthology, assembled and annotated with J. Madison Davis, is to answer that question by showing it has many answers, that the sundry schemes and proliferating variations have been the norm in detective stories from the beginning. Whether examining psychological coercion in the category I Confess! or exploring the undeniable attraction of evil in Come Into My Parlor, the detective story is protean, adapting itself to the manifold purposes of its practitioners, so that to define it is a slippery prospect at best.

Which is why we have chosen something better than definition. We have chosen to describe the detective story in terms of its categories, and to let the categories themselves spread as they will. And when we do that, we see that nitty-gritty realism belongs in the detective story, as shown in "Tang" herein, and formal puzzles do, like "The Secret Garden," and comedy does (I'm happy to say), and social commentary, and regional realism, and just about anything you can think of in fiction of any kind at all. About the only constant in every detective story is crime; they all contain some sort of crime.

Why is that? Why is the element of crime so useful to the storyteller and such a magnet to the reader? I'd like to try to answer that by borrowing from the classical description of theater: One character on a stage is a speech, two characters an argument, three characters drama. The variant I would propose begins with society. When you have only society, you have predictability and order; life in an anthill. When you have society and the individual, you have conflict, because the greater good of society is never exactly the same as the greater good of any one individual within it. When you have society and a crime, you have a rent in the fabric, a distortion away from predictability and order; but to no effect, it's merely disordered. When you have all three, society and the individual and a crime, you have all the multiple possibilities of drama, plus all the multiple possibilities of free will; that is, life. Society and crime are in unending opposition, but the individual is in a shifting relationship to the other two, depending on how *this* individual feels about *this* crime in *this* society.

That's why there are detective stories about cops, but also detective stories about robbers; detective stories in which virtue is triumphant, and detective stories in which virtue is trampled in the dust; detective stories hinged on professional expertise, and detective stories hinged on amateur brilliance; detective stories in which we root for the hero, and detective stories in which we root for the villain.

Because the reach of the detective story is so long, and its field so wide, there is I think a natural tendency to want to categorize it, to make some order out of this protean disorder. Critics speak of police procedurals and private eyes and so on, though acknowledging that all these cousins live inside the same large tent (to borrow, only this once, an image from the political world). In this anthology, we look beyond the typical organization of stories by subgenre and delve into a variety of recurring plot devices. This unique and innovative arrangement shows how various writers throughout the ages have shaped the basic story structures. But in doing so we have also demonstrated the impossibility of doing so, because the detective story just doesn't fit into neat pigeonholes.

Take the very first category in this volume, The Locked Room. The four stories collected under that heading could not be more unalike, while they certainly all fit the category, to demonstrate how even an apparently simple and constricting discipline can permit great latitude. But then move on, and the very first story in the section entitled Only One Among You, "The Secret Garden," while it certainly belongs in that category, is also a locked room mystery! And very different from the preceding four.

But that isn't all. In The Caper, the third category, "The Impossible Theft" is both a caper and a locked room story. In the next section, The Armchair Detective, "The Blue Geranium" is certainly an armchair detective story, but it is also—no surprise—a locked room story.

The varieties flow into one another, feed one another, feed the underlying concept of story. But in this process, when we first sort the stories into category, and then see how they are not fully confined by those neat labels, we come to an understanding of the entire field of the detective story in a way we could not have done if we'd merely left it all an unexamined jumble.

When we see the relationships between the stories, and between the categories, when we see how the best writers have made personal use of the traditional schemes and the limitless variations, and when we see at the same time how free this field of the detective story leaves its practitioners to explore their own imaginative concerns, we can understand why the detective story has not only attracted so many readers for so long, but has also been such a magnet to the best writers. Beginning from that basic triumvirate, society and the individual and a crime, writers of every stamp, attracted to different categories within the field, have been exploring the schemes and variations, measuring the possibilities, expanding the territory of the detective story, since . . .

Well, there's some dispute about that. There are those who will tell you the story of Cain and Abel is the first murder mystery, and we can only nod and agree, while saying that doesn't help us much. The modern detective story essentially began with Edgar Allan Poe, who invented most of it, including the first consulting detective, C. Auguste Dupin, out of whom was bred Sherlock Holmes and then, by eccentric fits and starts, various progeny leading at last to today's private eye.

Poe started others of our plots spinning as well. Tales told by brooding murderers (today mostly of the bran-enriched serial kind) come slouching out of Poe's "The Imp of the Perverse," and Indiana Jones is a direct descendant of William LeGrand in "The Gold Bug." The Poe story in this volume, " 'Thou Art the Man,' " introduces both the amateur detective and the unjustly accused innocent who must struggle to clear himself.

Since Poe, the detective story has, like a tree, grown tall and fruitful, with many branches sprouting from those original roots, but with all of them holding to the original recipe: a heightened mixture of intellect and emotion, wedded to the triumvirate of society/individual/crime. Some of Poe's offspring he himself might have trouble recognizing, but the lineage is clear.

In the century and a half since Poe started it all, the detective story has gone through greater and lesser phases of semi-respectability (never full respectability, thank God), and has attracted writers gifted with every degree of talent and art from the idiosyncratic genius of a Damon Runyon or a Chester Himes (both represented in these pages) to cookie-cutter hacks who couldn't rise above formula with the aid of a hydraulic lift (none of them represented herein).

The hacks have always outnumbered the geniuses, but that's true everywhere, and the entire community of writers, from the most brilliantly original to the most ploddingly imitative, do all feed the genre, help to keep it alive, to reassure the reader that, whenever there's unwinding to be done, there will always be another new detective story, unread, unsavored, unsolved, very near to hand.

And these readers, after all, are still intelligent and discriminating, even when all they want is "just" a detective story. As they read, they can tell the good from the better, and the better from the best. Then, as time, the great winnower, moves on, the also-rans fall away and the geniuses remain, to segue into literary history, and become objects of study and interpretation. You'll find a number of their names on the contents page herein.

But a dangerous trend has become evident within the last two decades. The scholars have grown less patient, less content to wait for a detective story writer to be safely tucked away on the inactive shelf before they turn their serious eyes on him. This very volume might be considered a part of this trend: if so, I apologize to my fellow entertainers. The last thing we want is for our readers to think of us as more than "just" detective story writers. If they thought there was any meat in that stew, they'd flee at once. They don't want to be harassed. They want to unwind.

On the other hand, where would they flee? If driven from the detective story by perceived seriousness, where could the unwinders go? Not to eco-politics-riddled science fiction. Not to biography, which reverses the satisfying pattern of the detective story; where the detective story begins (often) with a death, a biography by its very nature ends with one. Hardly bedside reading, that.

Even the movies aren't safely frivolous any more.

No, I'm sorry, we're still, if not the only, the best game in town. For the intelligent, educated reader who, despite his or her best efforts to remain serious and responsible twenty-four hours a day, nevertheless inadvertently reads fiction for the right reason (because it's fun), the detective story still is, as Goldilocks said about Baby Bear's porridge, "*just* right."

The tales in this book are all detective stories, just detective stories, some of the best work by some of the best writers in the field. Welcome aboard. Enjoy. It is, after all, better to be read than dead.

The Locked Room

A CRIME IS COMMITTED IN A ROOM, SEALED FROM THE INSIDE OR under constant scrutiny. How did the criminal get in, commit the crime, and then escape? The puzzle of the locked room has been a tradition since the mystery genre's inception in the nineteenth century, though the basic premise appears as early as the Book of Bel and the Dragon (c. 100 B.C.), in which the prophet Daniel proves that the priests of Baal are using a secret passage to steal food sealed up for their god. Edgar Allan Poe's "The Murders in the Rue Morgue" (1841) is usually considered the first locked room mystery; since then, dozens of authors have used the scheme. Israel Zangwill (1864–1926), a writer who vividly depicted the Jewish community of East London and often wrote about crime there, is frequently credited with the first locked room novel, *The Big Bow Mystery* (1892). Though its status as the first is debated, this work still is generally thought one of the best. Arthur Conan Doyle's exercise in the form, "The Adventure of the Speckled Band," is one of the most famous of the Sherlock Holmes stories, despite the liberties the author takes with the details about snakes that make the murder possible. Numerous other writers of the puzzle mystery were attracted to the locked room, including Gaston Leroux, Baroness Orczy, Edgar Wallace, S. S. Van Dine, and Ellery Queen. John Dickson Carr made the form his specialty and had his character, Dr. Gideon Fell, catalog the possible ways to commit such crimes. The philosophical underpinnings of the locked room mystery are very much part of the nineteenth century's preoccupation with the scientific method. "I cannot paint an angel because I have never seen one," remarked artist Gustave Courbet, reflecting the realist trend. Similarly, all phenomena in mystery fiction were required to have a rational explanation: walls, floors, and locked doors had impenetrable mass, and crimes could not be committed by ghosts and demons oozing through walls. By the end of the century, writers and social scientists would assert that the thin line separating appropriate moral and social behavior from crime was drawn by predetermined causes such as economics, childhood trauma, and genetics. The locked room mystery has perhaps been popular exactly because of the reassurance it offers. At least in the world of stories, the madly irrational can be demonstrated to be logical, as long as one is clever enough to interpret detailed observations.

JOHN DICKSON CARR

(1906–1977)

Once described as the American who chose to be an Englishman, John Dickson Carr was born in Uniontown, Pennsylvania, and duly trundled off to school to become an attorney like his father. Carr rebelled and was constantly in trouble. An enthusiastic reader of Arthur Conan Doyle, Gaston Leroux, and Jacques Futrelle, he wrote a number of stories while editing The Haverfordian, *the student literary magazine of Haverford College. He tried writing his first novel while spending a year in Paris, but discarded it. Shortly after his return to the United States, he published* It Walks by Night *(1930), featuring detective Henri Bencolin. Two years later he married, and then moved to his wife's homeland, England, because he believed the best mystery writers were English. Though he often returned to America when he objected to the government in power in Britain, he was inspired by the surroundings. He wrote some seventy novels before his death, numerous short stories, radio plays for the BBC, and a biography of Conan Doyle. He created two major series characters besides Bencolin: Dr. Gideon Fell and Sir Henry Merrivale, the latter in novels published under the transparent pseudonym of Carter Dickson. He also wrote several nonseries novels and used the pseudonyms of Carr Dickson and Roger Fairbairn. Elected president of the Mystery Writers of America, he won several awards, including the Grandmaster for lifetime achievement. The locked room, or "impossible," mystery was Carr's special forte. He developed a unique approach in which intimations of the occult and supernatural would hang in the atmosphere of page upon page until the detective would prove that the events were possible and rational. This obsession with the locked room may have led to a gradual exhaustion of ideas for Carr; however, no one explored the possibilities of the form more thoroughly. In the following, his first locked room mystery and his first use of Bencolin, young Carr in 1926 begins his lifelong preoccupation.*

THE SHADOW OF THE GOAT

It was a thoughtful room, and tobacco smoke clung round the edges of the lamp. The two men who sat there were thoughtful, but that was not the only point of similarity between them. They had the same worried look of persons too much interested in other men's affairs. Sir John Landervorne had once come from that vague section of London known as Whitehall, and he had been possibly the only man in the city who might have given police orders to Scotland Yard. If M. Henri Bencolin was only one of France's eighty-six prefects of police, he was not the least important of them.

Fog had made London medieval again, a place of towers and footsteps and dim figures. It blurred the windows of the room in Fontain Court, the backwater of Fleet Street where the barristers sometimes walk in their ghostly wigs, swinging canes like swords. In the room the two men, sitting opposite each other with white shirt fronts bulging exactly alike, smoked similar cigars—Bencolin with his black beard, Landervorne's beard gray as the cigar ash. It gave one a weird feeling: picture of a detective at thirty, then a picture of him at sixty. Their eyes were somber.

"If you tell me your story," said Sir John, "you will have to tell it to Billy Garrick, because these are his rooms, and he will be in presently. But it will be safe; he was there last night too."

Bencolin nodded. He spoke rather wearily.

"I know it, my friend. Of course, I did not telephone you officially—I am not connected officially with the matter. Well! Last night near Worksop, in Nottinghamshire, M. Jules Fragneau was murdered. That is why I wanted to see you."

"Then," said the Englishman, "I shall have to tell you a story which will not interest you, unless you believe in sorcery. Because, you see, the only man who might have killed Fragneau walked through a pair of locked shutters at ten o'clock last night."

"The report is true, then. Oh, the devil!" Bencolin fretted.

"The report is fantastic, and true. I saw Cyril Merton go into a room that had only one door, which was bolted and which I was watching. The room had only one window, barred, with locked shutters. There was no fireplace, nor was there any secret means of egress; the walls were stone. Exactly that. It was a stone box. But I tell you Merton went into the place—and vanished. Lord Brandon and Garrick, who were with me when we searched it both before and after the disappearance, will verify what I say. Afterwards an even stranger thing occurred. For surely Merton killed Fragneau, and then he very nearly committed another murder, at which time I saw him evaporate before my eyes. That, my dear sir, is witchcraft, and," he added thoughtfully, "I am a sane man. At least, I think I am a sane man."

M. Bencolin got up. Fog had crept in and mingled with the tobacco smoke; the Frenchman shivered. He looked small and shrunken, and very tired. With the cigar protruding ludicrously from his mouth, he began to wander about the room.

"My friend, I am beaten. Name of God!" he said fiercely. "I am beaten! I thought that I had enough impossible riddles in my case. But unless we can prove he made a phantom of himself a third time, and got into a locked house, a poor stupid fellow named Fulke will be indicted for murder. Of course these events are connected! Tell me the whole story, please."

Sir John sat back in his chair. His face was pinched with thought.

"Very well. There's a preface, you see, about Cyril Merton. Give Merton a wig and a sword, and he would be your seventeenth-century swashbuckler—but you must grant him a wig. For though he was tall, and rather strangely handsome with a thin luminous face in which you saw every emotion as through glass, the man's head was shaven. He had studied in Germany before he became an actor, and his ugly nature got him into duels with the saber, which left scars on his head. The scars were so hideous that hair only made them worse. So he kept his head shaven, criss-crossed white. But the beauty of his face, with the short dark beard, kept him from being ridiculous.

"He was our greatest actor. If you saw him in any of the old romantic plays you know the medieval soul of the man. He could turn himself into any sort of character; that was his genius. The man's hobby was sorcery and the deadly arts, in pursuit of which he had a library stuffed with forgotten books—the works of Hermes the Egyptian, Lillius, Geber, James Stuart, Cotton Mather, all of them. He belonged in a day when they burned such men.

"That was why he bought the place. Bell House is on a tract of ground that was once a part of Sherwood Forest, about thirty miles from where Fragneau lived. Bell House! You can see the tower of the bell lifted over the trees, with a hill of silver birches white in the moonlight, and the wind moving them. It was built when William the Norman darkened England with a hurricane of swords, and there are clanking ghosts in its halls. That was a dirty, snarling age—church and the devil frightening the soul out of people, big men in armor, faces caked with blood, butchering in nameless filth—the very bogey house of history. Why, the moat around Bell House is twenty feet deep.

"I have to tell you about a dinner Cyril Merton gave. There was the banquet hall, with pointed windows of painted glass, and the candles shining on them; I remember the white shirt fronts, the cigar smoke, the flashing teeth when people laughed. One gets a series of impressions in a shadowy place like that. For example, I remember the picture of Billy Garrick with Madeline—maybe because Madeline is my daughter—on the staircase after dinner; on the staircase under the dark portraits, and the candles. They are both yellow-haired, handsome as old Saxons. It was an absurd gesture on his part, but the place for it: he kissed her hand.

"They are in love, and I have an especial interest in Garrick for that reason. I was worried about him that evening. Billy is a nephew of Jules Fragneau. Because the old man had been rather more than his father, and made him his heir, Fragneau's enemies were Billy's enemies. Which was the reason why Merton, who hated Fragneau almost to the point of idiocy, never got along with the lad. He had been forced to invite him because Billy was my guest, and I was too close a neighbor to be omitted. For the same reason Billy had been forced to accept. All through the evening I felt uneasy.

"It all culminated in a foolish argument in the smoking room. The men had assembled there by a big blazing fireplace, with stags' heads, and all that. Having just come away from Madeline, Billy was in an exultant, swaggering mood. He smoked cigarettes and laughed at Merton, who was holding forth on his hobby of medieval magic against Lord Brandon and Mr. Julian Arbor. He was standing against the mantelpiece, black beard, shaven head, using that smile with which he argues.

" 'I was telling you,' said Merton, 'about the book of Gersault de Brilliers, published by Meroit, Paris, in 1697 'Contes du Diable,' with a subhead: 'Avec L'Histoire de L'Homme Qui Savait S'Evanouir.' One of the accounts deals with a man who walked into a locked room and vanished utterly. De Brilliers put it down to sorcery, which is possible. But a perfectly practicable kind of sorcery.'

"Mr. Julian Arbor protested. Arbor is a strange sort of English gentleman; doesn't at all object to helping out people who are financially in a hole—at tremendous interest. Just a polished form of moneylender. The man looks kindly, but he has a hard glaze on him like a tombstone. He protested gently: 'My dear fellow—'

" 'Bosh!' struck in Billy Garrick. 'Bosh, Merton!'

"It was a typical gathering, with a mass of stuffy landed proprietors who always have the look of just having eaten too much. Bald and florid and oratorical as the elder Pitt. Lord Brandon is one of these.

" 'This, sir,' observed Lord Brandon, 'strikes me as being a great deal of foolishness.' He waddled to the fire, waving his hands.

" 'Nevertheless, it happened,' the actor replied. 'It can happen again.'

"Billy was just a bit drunk. He protested furiously:

" 'Look here, Merton, you're usually so aloof that nobody contradicts you. And this grand superiority complex of yours is making me tired! If you can stand there and talk solemn stuff like that—'

" 'It can be done,' said Merton quietly. 'I can do it myself.'

"He was always one to play to an audience, and he enjoyed the consternation he created among that group of squires, smiling at his cigar.

" 'You mean, Merton, that you can walk into a locked room—a real locked room—and disappear?' asked Julian Arbor.

" 'Trap doors!' snapped Billy instantly.

" 'There are no trap doors. I say that I can go into a stone room here at the castle, have you lock doors and windows, and I can vanish. Just that.'

" 'Bosh!' repeated Billy.

" 'See here,' said Merton, 'if you want my opinion, even a host's opinion, your talk is damned impertinence.'

" 'And if you want mine,' said Billy, 'yours is damned nonsense.'

"Merton was furious; the glass face lit like fire.

" 'We'll drop your gutter behavior for the present; it can be argued later. Garrick, do you want to wager me a thousand pounds that I can't do what I say, eh?'

" 'Oh, I say!' cried Julian Arbor. 'Don't be a fool!' He turned to Billy in alarm. 'Surely you won't—Merton, I refuse to allow—'

" 'What have you got to do with it?' demanded Billy, who was angry too. 'Keep out of this, sir! Merton, I shall be glad to see you make an ass of yourself. I accept your wager.'

" 'If Mr. Merton will allow me, I accept it too,' Lord Brandon interposed.

"Merton laughed.

" 'Are there any other takers, gentlemen?' he said casually."

Sir John paused. Bencolin had sat down, and was staring at him. The Englishman lighted another cigar before he resumed.

"Well, the thing was fantastic, but it was done. Only Mr. Julian Arbor would not remain to see the wager carried out. He said he had to catch a night train for London, departing with somewhat jarring abruptness—"

"For *London?*" demanded Bencolin. "London? Pardon me; go on."

The words had been rather like a yelp. Sir John smiled.

"I was surprised, I must confess, but there were other matters on my mind. Merton was carrying off the affair with theatrical grace. We had to tell the ladies, who suspected some sort of joke, but insisted on following us. And yet the big halls, the weird unnaturalness of the place, got their nerves on edge; Madeline enjoyed it. The others began a shrill rush of talk, which gradually slowed and stopped like a run-down gramophone. Anything was better than the unnatural sound of those voices.

"Merton took us upstairs. We were a solemn company, parading the halls with candles. That castle was too big for us, and the moon was too far—it followed us along every hall, peering through the windows. Once Merton paused by a window, the silhouette of him with the moon behind his head; his face jumped suddenly out of the dark as he lighted a cigarette by the candleflame, and then it vanished. The silhouette contorted as though the man were dancing.

"He led us to an immense room, quite bare, so that you could see only the aimless candles moving under people's faces. At its far end was a door, which Merton threw open. It communicated with a flight of steps, walled with stone and having at the top another door. On the threshold Merton paused, with a kind of bluish glow behind him.

" 'This,' he said, 'is the room itself. I should prefer that the ladies did not enter. Come along, Lord Brandon, Sir John, Garrick too—examine it. I shall go in here. You will bolt the door at the bottom of the steps on the outside, and watch it. First go over this staircase to be sure there is no other exit.'

"Somebody laughed a bit nervously. Merton finished his cigarette while we moved around the flight of steps. Then—"

"Wait!" Bencolin interrupted. "Please don't describe it; don't describe the room. I am going to see it, and I want to form my own impressions. It might lead me astray if I heard too many details. But one thing: was there a washstand in the place?"

Sir John's heavy eyes flashed open.

"Yes! Why do you ask? That washstand was a curious thing to see there. . . ."

"Go on, my friend."

"We will say, then, that the room was large and odd. Garrick, Lord Brandon and I went over every foot of it. Intact! A window in a big stone embrasure was firmly barred. We closed and locked the shutters. Then we pronounced ourselves satisfied, Lord Brandon red and puzzled. As we were going out, Merton stopped us. He stood by the table in the light of a lamp of blue glass, but only his absolutely pallid hand protruded from the shadow, toying with a little ebony figure of . . . a goat. Garrick, as tall and threatening as he, said: 'Anything more?'

" 'Lord Brandon,' Merton answered, ignoring him, 'I am doing a dangerous thing. If I make a mistake, if you have any cause to think that such is the case, at the end of fifteen minutes come up here instantly! You promise me that?'

"Brandon promised—"

"One moment," said the Frenchman. "Did you look in all the table drawers?"

"My dear fellow," Sir John returned petulantly, "a man can't hide in a table drawer, or escape through it."

"Of course not. Well?"

"The last thing I remember was Merton standing by the table, playing with the tiny goat's figure. It was as though he were deliberately trying to call our attention to that image.

"He was. He may have been trying to give you a clue."

"Oh, come! What do you mean by that?"

"I don't know; it merely struck me as curious. You went downstairs?"

"We went downstairs, yes. I bolted the lower door on the outside. Then it began. We found that we had left all but two of the candles in Merton's room. There we were, a blundering, half-frightened crowd in a gulf of a place, candles tossing. Nervous laughter, figures moving about us. I had one of the lights, and kept it on my watch. Fifteen minutes—dragging. And women talking, and talking. But I never lost sight of the door, nor did Lord Brandon, who was standing in front of it. Somewhere in the house I thought I heard hurrying footsteps, and once the sound of water running. Finally there occurred the thing that broke our nerves like somebody jumping on you in the dark.

"It was an explosion, the terrific noise a pistol makes when it is fired indoors. Brandon and his following would have rushed the door even had not somebody shouted, 'Time's up!' The cry ripped into a screech of the bolt and a rush of feet up the stairs, but I remained in the background to make sure nobody slipped past those who entered. Nobody did! I went up slowly, examining the stairs, and joined the group at the door when I was certain of it—"

Suddenly Sir John crashed his fist down on the chair arm.

"Merton was gone! No one left the top door; the others stood guard while Brandon, Garrick and I searched the whole apartment. We were in a kind of frenzy. Shutters fastened, bars untouched; as a matter of fact, there was dust on the bars. No Merton, no hidden door. Some sort of weapon had been fired there, for a faint tang of powder was in the air, but we found no weapon. The blue glass lamp burned dully, fixing our eyes like a crucible, and a bit of smoke hovered over it like waving hands . . . But in spite of it all, I know that before we came nobody had either entered or left that door!"

And, as later events proved, Sir John spoke the absolute truth.

II

Lamplight had made the thickening smoke in the room a yellow haze. Both Bencolin and Sir John Landervorne looked weirdly unnatural. Bencolin said:

"That statement, my friend, would be ridiculed in a court of law. We can prove nothing on the man now—don't you see? Under the circumstances of Fragneau's death, either the man Fulke or myself, the only other occupants of his house, must have killed him. Fragneau was stabbed about twelve o'clock last night. Merton disappeared at ten, easily in time for him to have gone thirty miles by motor. There is nothing more inconspicuous than the driver of an automobile at night. Now, then, at twelve-fifteen, or thereabouts, I telephoned you at your home, because I knew that you lived close to Merton. It was no burglar's work, because nothing had been stolen at Fragneau's home; the only person who might have killed Fragneau was Merton, and I wanted to check up on his whereabouts instantly. There would be no possibility of his servants lying as to his movements if I communicated with *you*. Your butler told me that you were at Merton's, and had not returned. I left a message for you to call—"

"At twelve-fifteen," interrupted the Englishman, "Madeline, Garrick and I were returning to my home. In that interval Merton had not appeared. The question being: if he was perpetrating a joke, why did he not return? We waited two hours before we reassured the servants and left. But in the vicinity of one-thirty, Merton *did* come back. We will connect that up with the story later. Tell me about Fragneau."

"The very devilish simplicity of it, my friend, is that I have no story. You know Fragneau. His hobby was astronomy; I will not say astrology, because it was there that the Merton-Fragneau feud began. Every time I have visited his house he has shown me some new device to keep out burglars. He had a big glass dome of an observatory on the roof, an open place, so that in this fanatical fear of intruders there was an iron fence, ten feet high and electrically charged, around the entire roof. The house being small, every window had its own protective fastening. On each of the two doors was a lock for which no duplicate key could be made! Imagine it—the place was a fortress. Fulke, a big, awkward, red-haired fellow, was his new servant. I remember his wooden face at the door when I arrived, hair tilted over its side like a vivid wig—and the white-lit dome uncanny up against the night sky, with Fragneau's shadow flickering over it.

"Facts, these. At eleven o'clock Fragneau went over the place, adjusted all his devices, locked his doors. We had been talking, but he insisted on working in his laboratory as a nightly ritual. I was not interested, and went to my room to read. It overlooked the front stairs. At twelve I grew tired of reading, at which time I started for the observatory to bring him down for a final cigar. . . .

"Fragneau sat before the telescope with a stupid grin on his face. His chest was heavy with blood where he had been stabbed with a bone-handled knife a very few minutes before. The glare of light, the white-pointed face like a goat's, the yellow shaft protruding from his chest, all calm as sleep.

"I summoned Fulke; the house was searched, the doors and windows found locked. Neither of us had heard an intruder. We calmly went about questioning each other; then I put in two telephone messages, to you and to the local police. That is all, except for one point. At twelve-thirty a man rang the doorbell and asked to see Fragneau. . . . Once," added the Frenchman abruptly, "when I learned that Fulke was a new servant, I conceived a theory as to the assassination. Now it is all dark, considering what you say, unless . . ." He paused, and smiled.

"Unless what?"

"Unless, in a manner of speaking, Cyril Merton washed himself down the drain. To give you more than an indication—"

"Bencolin," demanded the Englishman, "are you insane? Great God!"

"Wait! Please wait! You should be insulted if I continued. My friend, I think the motive in this affair is money. Do you know who rang the doorbell half an hour after the murder? It was Mr. Julian Arbor."

III

A gust of colder air blew in from the foggy corridor as the door opened. Bencolin was still straining forward, elbow on the table, the fingers of his hand crooked toward Sir John. And as a third figure, lean and tall in its greatcoat, came toward them, they had the appearance of people in a storm. The newcomer took off his hat, displaying eyes of a rather brilliant vivid blue in a face glistening like wax. The eyes struck Bencolin with the suddenness of rifle shots; they had a wretched, terrible appeal.

"Hello, Sir John," he said hoarsely, croaking with a cold. "This the M. Bencolin you came to see? My name's Garrick, sir. Well, every dragnet in England is out for that damned murdering— Start a fire, will you?"

He sat down, shivering, and threw off his coat. His arm was in a sling.

"I—I just left Madeline. She was crying. . . ."

There was an odd strained silence. Then Sir John got up blunderingly and began to heap wood in the fireplace.

"He didn't suffer," said Bencolin. "I mean . . ."

"I am glad to hear it," replied the young man. They did not see his face.

"My friend," the Frenchman began, "God willing, we will find Merton."

He paused, but the words had something like the ring of an oath. Then he looked at Garrick's arm. "The second victim! When did he attack?"

"It was about one-thirty. Sir, the thing is too incredible! Are you sure Merton is a *man*?"

"Steady!" warned sir John.

"Well . . . I had gone to bed. It was bright moonlight in the room, hard and clear as glass. I was fuming about Merton, just drifting to sleep, when I heard someone cry out."

Sir John paused with a lighted match in his hand.

"I was at one window across the quadrangle," he interposed. "My room. I could not sleep. Then I saw a shadow move. The moon shone on a head that was perfectly white. Something began climbing the ivy toward a window on the second floor, and when I realized whose window, I knew who that person was. I could not help screaming to warn Garrick—"

"It saved my life," the other said calmly. "When I sat up in bed, a silhouette reared up over the windowsill, but I saw the white head. And then," he rushed on, "it came at a kind of bound, like a goat. The light from the open window was blocked as it got me; I felt the tangle of the bedclothes, the rip into my arm of a pain, blinding and sickish like ether. My arm began to grow hot, but I fought him. Somehow he tore away—Sir John, are you *sure* nobody left by the door?"

"I would swear to it. Listen, Bencolin, for your final riddle. After I cried out, I ran out of my room. In the central hallway I met Dorset, the butler who took your message. I didn't explain, but I told him to hurry outside and stop anybody who came out by a window. Don't you see? If we were in time, we had Merton trapped! Doors were banging open in the house, lights flashing on. When I reached Garrick's door the lights in the corridor were blazing. Behind the door was the furious wheezing and thudding of a fight; a chair clattered over; somebody began to run. The door was bolted, but it was flimsy wood. I battered it until the bolt ripped out. Billy almost ran into me—and before him there was a shadow. I switched on the lights, standing in the door, and for one instant the picture was hideous and sharp and motionless as waxworks. Billy, full white on the square of gray moonlight, with a sheet trailing him, his arm running red as though it were alive. The intruder was gone! We hunted the room over, after which I called to Dorset. He answered that nobody had left by the window."

"He was going for the door!" Garrick cried excitedly. "Then you opened it in my face. And yet I touched him a moment before!"

Bencolin sat with his head between his hands; Sir John was standing by the fireplace without moving, and held the charred curl of a match. Fog had seeped into the room until the lamplight was all but obscured.

IV

Bencolin had not slept for twenty-four hours. If the man who had listened to the amazing recitals of Sir John Landervorne and Billy Garrick the night before had been neat, correct as a picture, then it was somewhat of an apparition which went stamping about Bell House the next day. Unshaven, with a battered hat stuck on his head like a helmet, the man resembled a conception of an early Goth. He had been seen early in the morning standing against a red tattered sky among the mists at the edge of the moat, and he was poking in the water with a walking stick.

This was no England of the sort called merrie, of Robin Hood and warm leaves and gray goose feather. It was stern as the Norman. And the work which presently occupied the constables under Bencolin's direction was sterner still. Through the November morning they were wading in the moat.

When, after a while, he entered the big silent house, there were only a few servants for him to question. Their employer had not returned, and yet they were fearful to leave. While he explored every dusty corner, he could hear the solemn tramp of feet. Finally he went upstairs to the tower room. It was there, in the afternoon, that those he had summoned found him.

The afternoon sun, an ugly rose color, shot across the room like a spotlight from the window embrasure. It rested on the closed door of a closet, which Bencolin had earlier in the day explored and found empty. In the middle of the apartment stood the table with its tiny goat's statue, so that the sun outlined on the closet door a monstrous figure of a goat. When Sir John Landervorne opened the door to the room, he saw only that shaft of light in shadows, beyond which was the glow of Bencolin's eternal cigar. The Englishman shuddered, fumbling at his beard.

"That you, Bencolin?" he asked. "Ugh! What a place! Shall we come in?"

"I see no reason," protested a voice behind him, "for dragging us up here from London! I told you everything you wanted to know last night." It was Julian Arbor, who pushed past Sir John; though he seemed angry, not a muscle in his big white face moved.

"The matter is serious," Bencolin responded. "Will the rest of you come in? Lord Brandon? Thank you. And Mr. Garrick. Who's that?" His nerves were jumpy, and he leaned suddenly out into the light at the sound of another voice.

"Madeline insisted—" said Sir John.

"I did!" a little voice confirmed him, laughing. The girl looked light as though she might be blown by a wind, with a sort of half beauty in her face that was rather better than loveliness. Whiteclad, she moved forward. "Mayn't I stay? You've promised us a solution, and I want to hear it."

"Sir John, this is impossible!" the Frenchman snapped.

"I won't go," said the girl. "I have as much right to be here as anyone."

Bencolin stared at her; at the sight of his face a movement went through the watchers. They knew why. In that room was terror.

"Merton is here!" said Bencolin.

That was it—terror. Sir John began thickly, nervously.

"Go out, Madeline; please go out. My God, what are you saying?"

"He is here," went on the Frenchman, "he is in this room. Lord Brandon, stand in front of that door. The rest of you sit down, and whatever happens, do not move."

In the half darkness somebody stumbled a little. Bencolin had stepped in front of the window. Against the reddish light they saw his profile with the high hooked nose and bearded jaw. The energy had gone out of him; his shoulders were stooped, and he stared out thoughtfully into the sky.

"It's an odd case," he said. "It's the only case on record in which a man proves an alibi for his murderer. And it shows many curious things. For example, there is that appearance of Mr. Julian Arbor at Fragneau's house after the murder—"

"Look here," snapped Arbor, and he came into the light with his big white face intent. "I told you I was there, I admitted it. But what does that mean? It doesn't show that I killed Fragneau, if that's what you think! It doesn't show that I had any criminal intent—"

"Of course not," said the Frenchman, "but what does it show? I mean, you have been telling me what it doesn't show; now I ask you what it does show." He did not turn from the window, but he went on rapidly: "And what does the white head of this midnight prowler show?"

"Why, that it was Merton." Sir John stared at him oddly.

"You are wrong. The white head shows that it was *not* Merton."

"Then you say," Sir John cried, "that Merton did not stab Garrick?"

"Not at all. Merton did stab Garrick."

"Well, why didn't Merton come in the window, then?"

"Because he was dead," said Bencolin quietly.

There was a sudden silence like the stroke of a gong. They all looked at Bencolin as though he had gone mad and were gabbling calm nonsense.

"You will find Merton's body in the closet behind you, Sir John," continued the Frenchman. He turned full about, and he did not raise his voice when he spoke again, but it had a horrible sound of finality:

"Open the closet, Garrick. One of your victims is inside."

V

Garrick stood looking stupidly before him, his hand moving in a tiny futile gesture. The others were perfectly motionless.

"We got his body out of the moat this morning," Bencolin said with dull flat monotony, "where you threw it. Open the door!"

A tiny space separated Garrick from collapse. He looked down at his feet. There was a trickle of water crawling from under the door.

"I—can't," muttered Billy Garrick.

"Listen! You killed Fragneau."

"Yes. I killed Fragneau." The reply was mechanical. Sir John suddenly sat down, with his head between his hands.

"Shall I tell them how it happened?"

"No!"

"But I will, Garrick. You and Merton were in debt to Julian Arbor. You arranged this impersonation, you and Merton, so that by following your own example, Lord Brandon and others would wager five thousand pounds. Really, some sort of plot was obvious when I knew that no such book as 'Contes du Diable' exists! Julian Arbor did not know, which was why he protested against a wager in which either of you two must lose. You are exactly the same height as Merton—Sir John said so—and of his build. When he went to his room he put into effect the genius at impersonation that Sir John has mentioned. He shaved off his beard, he wore a wig which he had prepared in that table drawer, and cosmetic touches under the lights completed the effect. It was his genius! Remember: candlelight! Nobody could detect it. There might have been a slip only in the *voice*, but you had a cold, the same cold you have now, and hence it was easy. After the door had been bolted on the outside and Merton had completed his preparations, he went to the stairs and waited, flat against the wall by the lower door. On his way down he fired a blank cartridge, which was the one thing that would send the watchers flying pell-mell through the door. It was dark; Brandon had no candle, and could see nothing before or behind him except the lighted door at the top of the stairs. Those who came through the door felt only jostling bodies—Merton mingled with them and went upstairs again *as you*. You had already slipped down into the house and out of it; remember that Sir John did not see you from the time he left the tower room until after he had entered it again in search of Merton, and that he heard footsteps in the house. Nobody was watching any door except the one behind which Merton had locked himself. Nobody saw you go out. For the space of the next three hours *Merton was yourself.*

"But you had a deeper motive when you connived with Merton for this impersonation. Ostensibly it was a mere matter of winning the money bet by Lord Brandon and dividing it; that was how you obtained Merton's assistance. Your real motive was murder. Your real motive was in establishing an alibi for your presence at Bell House while you motored to Fragneau's home. Diabolical cleverness of it! You could not conceivably be accused of the crime when all unknowingly Merton had proved you to be at Bell House while Fragneau was being killed. And you meant Merton to be accused of the deed instead!" He turned to Sir John. "Think, my friend! Who would be the only person in the world who would have a key to that Fragneau house? Why, the man Fragneau trusted, the man who was his heir! Did that never strike you as logical? Fulke did not know, because Fulke was a new servant, and I nearly overlooked the possibility because you, Sir John, had sworn Garrick was at Bell House the entire evening. Garrick needed money; therefore Fragneau, he reasoned, must die. The winning of a fortune, and Merton punished for the act. But because Merton had established his alibi, Merton too must die, or otherwise the plan would be revealed.

"What does he do? He lets himself into Fragneau's house, kills him, and returns. Meanwhile Merton, masquerading as Garrick, has been forced to go home with Sir John. He retires immediately, lets himself out of the window, and goes back to Bell House, where he has arranged to meet Garrick that they may change identities again before daylight destroys the complete reality of the make-up. At the edge of the moat Garrick meets him. Ah, don't you see it? The struggle by the water, where Merton, almost wresting the knife from Garrick before the latter stabs him, wounds Garrick in the arm. Then Merton's death, the sack filled with stones into which the body is stuffed, the disappearance into the water. It is done! For though police authorities might search Bell House for a living Merton, they would never search the moat for a dead one.

"Garrick, wounded, returns from Bell House to Sir John's residence. As he crosses the lawn Sir John sees him, but imagines very naturally that it is Merton, whom he has no grounds to suspect dead. Yellow hair in the moonlight makes an excellent 'white head;' try the effect of it for yourself. Garrick hears Sir John's warning cry; he knows that he is trapped unless . . .

"Then," cried the Frenchman, "what occurs to this master sorcerer? Why, Sir John has fancied that Merton is attacking him; why not pretend that such was the case, else otherwise Garrick could never explain the wound in his arm? It dovetailed perfectly! Garrick strips off his clothing, dons pajamas, and tears the bandage from his arm, allowing the blood to flow. Something like four minutes elapsed before Sir John came to the room. Garrick scuffles with himself in the dark, invents an ingenious story which is the only thing that will save him from discovery. Out of near catastrophe he has produced another attack that will be ascribed to Merton!"

VI

The tensity had gone out of them all, and there remained only the ruin of tragedy. False emotional stimulant left a sickish after-feeling. Arbor and Sir John had moved away from Garrick. All the elaborate mummery that had been gone into seemed cheap and tawdry as a music hall illusion. Here was simply a felon.

Bencolin made a little gesture of weariness.

"Eh, bien!" he murmured. "You do not find it pleasant, you do not find it even clever. It upsets every beautiful tradition of a story; not only have we shattered our hero, but there is not enough of the theatrical in him to follow a story formula and kill himself. Because reality is infinitely more childish than the stories about it. Messieurs, you have lived an allegory. What do you make of it? And how do you explain the chance that made Mr. Arbor, irritated by this blind wager of those who could not afford it, leave Bell House and go to Fragneau's to demand recompense for his nephew's debts?"

Rather absently Sir John put on his hat.

"Well . . ." he said without looking at Garrick. Lord Brandon opened the door. He had not spoken. There was nothing in his face but contempt.

Julian Arbor muttered, "You gutter rat!" somewhat incredulously. A constable had come into the darkling room and was going toward Garrick. The latter's nerves were entirely gone; he had slid down to the floor, and Bencolin thought he heard him moan just once. The Frenchman was speaking softly:

"We should none of us fancy that we are devils. Merton did, because he could take any form at will, like Satan, who appeared at the witches' sabbath in the form of a goat (that was why he kept calling your attention to the goat). . . . Somewhere we people of the old school thought that there was faith, and honor, and loyalty. We do not believe it now, Sir John. We have seen the other side of youth. . . . It is our last illusion, as the impersonation was Merton's. . . . We do not think it now, Sir John. . . ."

It was almost dark in the room now. The others were all at the door, except Madeline Landervorne. She had come up steadily, and she was bending over the man on the floor, and as she knelt, her eyes glittered with tears.

"Billy," she said, "I don't believe them. I don't believe them!"

DAMON RUNYON

(1884–1946)

Alfred Damon Runyon is one of those rare writers whose style and imaginative world was so distinctive that, as with Joyce and Kafka, an adjective was coined to describe it: Runyonesque. His unique mixture of petty criminal slang, overblown metaphors, and curiously formal locutions is instantly recognizable, and if humor were not often treated as a stepchild of literature, Runyon might be regarded as a more significant writer. He was born in Manhattan, Kansas, and reared in Colorado. *Even before he enlisted in the army at age fourteen, he had written for local newspapers. After serving in the Spanish-American War, he practiced journalism in the West before moving on to the New York* American *in 1911. Initially a sportswriter, he went to Europe as a World War I correspondent for the Hearst papers, then returned as a columnist. His humorous portrayal of the colorful characters of Broadway and of the New York underworld caused many to label him a "realist" along with other American crime writers of the 1920s and 1930s. However, his language and exaggerations make for an unusual form of realism at best, and his achievement in creating setting, tone, atmosphere, and character is often dismissed as mere colorfulness. Though most of his stories deal with crime, as did his only play (*A Slight Case of Murder, *1935), he is not usually thought of as a crime writer. The delightful musical* Guys and Dolls *was based on his short stories and revived interest in his writings, especially when the motion picture with Frank Sinatra and Marlon Brando was released in 1955. In the following story, Runyon mocks theater critics and parodies both the locked room mystery and the truism that the butler, as least likely suspect, must have done it. Parody succeeds only if its subjects are familiar. These devices were already over-ripe when this story was published in* Blue Plate Special *in 1934.*

WHAT, NO BUTLER?

To look at Ambrose Hammer, the newspaper scribe, you will never suspect that he has sense enough to pound sand in a rat hole, but Ambrose is really a pretty slick guy. In fact, Ambrose is a great hand for thinking, and the way I find this out makes quite a story.

It begins about seven o'clock one May morning when I am standing at the corner of Fiftieth Street and Broadway, and along comes Ambrose with his neck all tied up as if he has a sore throat, and he gives me a large hello in a hoarse tone of voice.

Then we stand there together, speaking of the beautiful sunrise, and one thing and another, and of how we wish we have jobs that will let us enjoy the daylight more, although personally I do not have any job to begin with, and if there is one thing I hate and despise it is the daylight, and the chances are this goes for Ambrose, too.

In fact, in all the years I know Ambrose, I never catch him out in the daylight more than two or three times, and then it is when we are both on our way home and happen to meet up as we do this morning I am talking about. And always Ambrose is telling me what a tough life he leads, and how his nerves are all shot to pieces, although I hear the only time Ambrose's nerves really bother him is once when he goes to Florida for a vacation, and has a nervous breakdown from the quiet that is around and about those parts.

This Ambrose Hammer is a short, chubby guy, with big, round, googly eyes, and a very innocent expression, and in fact it is this innocent expression that causes many guys to put Ambrose away as slightly dumb, because it does not seem possible that a guy who is around Broadway as long as Ambrose can look so innocent unless he is dumb.

He is what is called a dramatic critic by trade, and his job is to write pieces for the paper about the new plays that somebody is always producing on Broadway, and Ambrose's pieces are very interesting, indeed, as he loves to heave the old harpoon into actors if they do not act to suit him, and as it will take a combination of Katherine Cornell, Jimmy Durante and Lillian Gish to really suit Ambrose, he is generally in there harpooning away very good.

Well, while we are standing on the corner boosting the daylight, who comes along but a plain-clothes copper by the name of Marty Kerle, and he stops to give us a big good-morning. Personally, I have no use for coppers, even if they are in plain clothes, but I believe in being courteous to them at all times, so I give Marty a big good-morning right back at him, and ask him what he is doing out and about at such an hour, and Marty states as follows:

"Why," Marty says, "some doll who claims she is housekeeper for Mr. Justin Veezee just telephones the station that she finds Mr. Justin Veezee looking as if he is very dead in his house over here in West Fifty-sixth Street, and I am going there to investigate this rumor. Maybe," Marty says, "you will wish to come along with me."

"Mr. Justin Veezee?" Ambrose Hammer says. "Why, my goodness gracious, this cannot be true, because I hear he is in the Club Soudan only a few hours ago watching the Arabian acrobatic dancer turn flip-flops, and one thing and another, although personally," Ambrose says, "I do not think she is any more Arabian than Miss Ethel Barrymore."

But of course if Mr. Justin Veezee is dead, it is a nice item of news for Ambrose Hammer to telephone in to his paper, so he tells Marty he will be delighted to go with him, for one, and I decide to go too, as I will rather be looking at a dead guy than at guys hurrying to work at such an hour.

Furthermore, I am secretly hoping that the housekeeper does not make any mistake, as I can think of nothing nicer than seeing Mr. Justin Veezee dead, unless maybe it is two or three Mr.

Justin Veezees dead, for personally I consider Mr. Justin Veezee nothing but an old stinker.

In fact, everybody in this town considers Mr. Justin Veezee nothing but an old stinker, because for many years he is along Broadway, in and out, and up and down, and always he is on the grab for young dolls such as work in night clubs and shows, and especially young dolls who do not have brains enough to realize that Mr. Justin Veezee is nothing but an old stinker. And of course there is always a fresh crop of such dolls coming to Broadway every year, and in fact it is getting so nowadays that there are several crops per year.

But although it is well known to one and all that Mr. Justin Veezee is nothing but an old stinker, nobody ever dasts speak of this matter out loud, as Mr. Justin Veezee has plenty of potatoes, which come down to him from his papa, and it is considered very disrespectful along Broadway to speak of a guy with plenty of potatoes as an old stinker, even if he is as tight with his potatoes as Mr. Justin Veezee, which is very, very, very, very tight, indeed.

Now, the house in West Fifty-sixth Street where Mr. Justin Veezee lives is between Fifth and Sixth avenues, and is once the private home of the Veezee family when there is quite a raft of Veezees around, but it seems that these Veezees all die off one by one, except Mr. Justin Veezee, and so he finally turns the old home into an apartment house.

It is a very nice-looking building, maybe four or five stories high, with apartments on each floor, and Mr. Justin Veezee's apartment is on the first floor above the street, and takes in the whole floor, although this does not mean so much space at that, as the house is very narrow.

It is one of these apartment houses where you push a button at the front door on the street floor, and this push rings a bell in the apartment you are after, and then somebody in the apartment pushes a button up there, and this unlocks the front door, and you walk up the stairs to where you are going, as there is no elevator, and no doorman, either.

Well, anyway, it is in the front room of Mr. Justin Veezee's apartment that we see Mr. Justin Veezee himself. He is sitting straight up in a big easy-chair beside a table on which there is a stack of these pictures called etchings, and he has on evening clothes, and his eyes are wide open and bugging out of his head, as if he is totally amazed at something he sees, and the chances are he is, at that.

There is no doubt whatever but that Mr. Justin Veezee is very dead, indeed, and Marty Kerle says we are not to touch anything until the medical examiner has a peek, although by the time he says this, Ambrose Hammer is looking the etchings over with great interest, as Ambrose is such a guy as dearly loves to look at works of art.

The housekeeper who calls up the station is present when we arrive, but she turns out to be nothing but an old tomato by the name of Mrs. Swanson, who does not live in Mr. Justin Veezee's house, but who comes every morning at an early hour to clean up the joint. And this Mr. Swanson states that she finds Mr. Justin Veezee just as he is when she comes in on this particular morning, although she says that usually he is in the hay pounding his ear at such an hour.

She thinks maybe he falls asleep in the chair, and tries to roust him out, but as Mr. Justin Veezee does not say aye, yes, or no, she figures the chances are he is dead, and so she gives the gendarmes a buzz.

"Well," I say to Ambrose Hammer, "this is a most ghastly scene, indeed. In fact, Mr. Justin Veezee looks worse dead than he does alive, which I will never consider possible. The chances are this guy dies of old age. He must be fifty, if he is a day," I say.

"No," Ambrose says, "he does not die of old age. The way I look at it, this is a case of homicide. Somebody gets in here and cools off Mr. Justin Veezee, and it is a very dirty trick if you ask me, because," Ambrose says, "they do not give Mr. Justin Veezee a chance to change into something more comfortable than a dinner jacket."

Well, Ambrose says he will look around and see if he can locate any clues, and while he is snooping around the joint in comes a guy from the medical examiner's office and takes a gander at Mr. Justin Veezee. And the guy states at once that Mr. Justin Veezee is positively dead, although nobody is giving him any argument on this point, and he further states that what kills Mr. Justin Veezee is nothing but a broken neck.

Right away this broken neck becomes a very great mystery, because it does not stand to reason that a guy can break his own neck sitting down, unless maybe he is practicing to be a contortionist, and nobody figures it possible that Mr. Justin Veezee is practicing to be a contortionist at his age.

Furthermore, the medical guy finds certain marks on Mr. Justin Veezee's neck which he claims show that somebody grabs Mr. Justin Veezee by the guzzle and cracks his neck for him as if he is nothing but a goose, and the medical guy says it must be somebody with very strong dukes to play such a prank on Mr. Justin Veezee.

Well, Ambrose Hammer seems to be all heated up about this whole matter, although personally I cannot see where it is any of his put-in. The way I look at it, Mr. Justin Veezee is no price any way you take him when he is alive and kicking, and his death does not change the betting any as far as I am concerned, because I know from the things I see of Mr. Justin Veezee, and the things I hear of him, that he is still an old stinker, in spades.

Ambrose tells me that he is certainly going to solve this mystery in the interests of justice, and I tell him that the only way to solve a murder mystery is to suspect everybody in town, beginning with the old tomato who discovers the remains of Mr. Justin Veezee, and winding up with the gendarmes who investigate the case.

"But," I say to Ambrose Hammer, "you do not pin the foul deed on any of these parties, but on the butler, because this is the way these things are done in all the murder-mystery movies and plays I ever see, and also in all the murder-mystery books I ever read."

Well, at this Marty Kerle, the plain-clothes copper, states that the only trouble with my idea is that there is no butler connected with Mr. Justin Veezee's establishment in any way, shape, manner, or form, and when I tell Ambrose that maybe we can hire a butler to double in murder for us, Ambrose becomes very indignant, and speaks to me as follows:

"No butler commits this murder," Ambrose says, "and, furthermore, I do not consider your remarks in good taste, no matter if you are joking, or what. I am convinced that this crime is the work of nobody but a doll, because of certain clues I encounter in my survey of the premises."

But Ambrose will not tell me what these clues are, and personally I do not care, because the way I look at it, even if some doll does give Mr. Justin Veezee the business, it is only retribution for what Mr. Justin Veezee does to other dolls in his time.

Well, the scragging of Mr. Justin Veezee is a very great sensation, and the newspapers make quite a lot of it, because there is no doubt but what it is the greatest mystery in this town in several weeks. Furthermore, anybody that ever as much as speaks to Mr. Justin Veezee in the past twenty years becomes very sorry for it when the newspapers commence printing their names and pictures, and especially any dolls who have any truck with Mr. Justin Veezee in the past, for naturally the newspaper scribes and the gendarmes are around asking them where they are at such and such an hour on such and such a date, and it is quite amazing how few guys and dolls can remember this offhand, especially dolls.

In fact, pretty soon the scragging of Mr. Justin Veezee becomes one of the most embarrassing propositions that ever comes off east of the Mississippi River, and many citizens are thinking of going out and scragging somebody else just to take the attention of the scribes and the gendarmes away from Mr. Justin Veezee.

As near as anybody can find out, the last party to see Mr. Justin Veezee alive the morning he is scragged is a red-headed doll at the Club Soudan by the name of Sorrel-top, and who is by no means a bad-looking doll, if you like them red-headed. This Sorrel-top is in charge of the check-room where one and all are supposed to check their hats and coats on entering the Club Soudan, and to tip Sorrel-top a shilling or two when they go out for keeping cases on these articles.

It seems that Sorrel-top always remembers when Mr. Justin Veezee leaves the Club Soudan, because he never stakes her to as much as a thin dime when he calls for his kady, and naturally Sorrel-top is bound to remember such a guy, especially as he is the only guy in the United States of America who dasts pass up Sorrel-top in this manner.

So she remembers that Mr. Justin Veezee leaves the Club Soudan on the morning in question around three bells, and the chances are he walks home, as none of the taxi jockeys who hang out in front of the Club Soudan remember seeing him, and, anyway, it is only a few blocks from the club to Mr. Justin Veezee's house, and it is a cinch he is never going to pay money to ride in a taxi just a few blocks.

Now it comes out that there are only two entrances to Mr. Justin Veezee's apartment, and one entrance is the front door, but the other entrance is a back door, but the back door is locked and barred on the inside when Mr. Justin Veezee is found, while the front door is locked with a patent snap lock, and Mrs. Swanson, the old tomato who does the housekeeping for Mr. Justin Veezee, states that she and Mr. Justin Veezee have the only two keys in the world to this lock that she knows of, although of course the parties who live in the other apartments in the house have keys to the street door, and so has the old tomato.

Furthermore, the windows of Mr. Justin Veezee's apartment are all locked on the inside, and there seems to be no way whatever that anybody except Mr. Justin Veezee and the old tomato can get in this apartment, and the gendarmes begin looking at the old tomato very suspiciously, indeed, until she digs up a milkman by the name of Schmalz, who sees her going into the apartment house about six-thirty in the morning, and then sees her a few minutes later come tearing out of the joint yelling watch, murder, police, and the medical guys say there is no chance she can guzzle Mr. Justin Veezee in this time, unless she is a faster worker than anybody they ever hear of in all their days.

Anyway, nobody can figure a motive for the old tomato to guzzle Mr. Justin Veezee, although a couple of the newspaper scribes try to make out that maybe she is an ever-loving sweetheart of Mr. Justin Veezee in the long ago, and that he does her dirt. Personally, I consider this proposition reasonable enough, because it is a sure thing that if the old tomato is ever Mr. Justin Veezee's sweetheart, he is just naturally bound to do her dirt. But the old tomato seems so depressed over losing a customer for her housekeeping that finally nobody pays any more attention to her, and one and all go looking around for someone else who may have a motive for giving Mr. Justin Veezee the business.

Well, it comes out that there are a large number of parties, including both male and female, in this part of the country who figure to have a motive for giving Mr. Justin Veezee the business, but they are all able to prove they are some place else when this matter comes off, so the mystery keeps getting more mysterious by the minute, especially as the gendarmes say there is no chance that robbery is the motive, because Mr. Justin Veezee has all his jewelry on him and plenty of potatoes in his pockets when he is found, and nothing in the apartment seems disturbed.

Furthermore, they find no fingerprints around and about, except some that turn out to belong to Ambrose Hammer, and at that Ambrose has a tough time explaining that he makes these fingerprints after Mr. Justin Veezee is found, and not before. They find most of Ambrose's fingerprints on the etchings, and personally I am glad I am not around fingering anything while I am in the joint, as the gendarmes may not listen to my explanations as easy as they listen to Ambrose.

Well, I do not see Ambrose for several nights, but it seems that this is because there are some shows opening around town and Ambrose is busy harpooning the actors. Finally one night he comes looking for me, and he states that as I am with him when he starts working on the mystery of who gives Mr. Justin Veezee the business, it is only fair that I be present when he exposes the party who commits this dastardly deed. And, Ambrose says, the hour now arrives, and although I do my best to show Ambrose that there can be no percentage for him in hollering copper on anybody in this matter, nothing will do but I must go with him.

And where does he take me but to the Club Soudan, and as it is early in the evening there are very few customers in the joint when we arrive, as the Club Soudan does not heat up good until along about midnight. Furthermore, I judge that the customers are strangers in the city, as they seem to be partaking of food, and nobody who is not a stranger in the city will think of partaking of food in the Club Soudan, although the liquor there is by no means bad.

Well, Ambrose and I get to talking to a character by the name of Flat-wheel Walter, who has a small piece of the joint, and who is called by this name because he walks with a gimp on one side, and by and by Ambrose asks for the Arabian acrobatic dancer, and Flat-wheel says she is at this time in her dressing-room making up for her dance. So Ambrose takes me up a flight of stairs to a little room, which is one of several little rooms along a hallway, and sure enough, there is this Arabian acrobatic dancer making up.

And the way she is making up is by taking off her clothes, because it seems that an Arabian acrobatic dancer cannot dance with anything on except maybe a veil or two, and personally I am somewhat embarrassed by the spectacle of a doll taking off her clothes to make up, especially an Arabian. But Ambrose Hammer does not seem to mind, as he is greatly callused to such scenes because of his experience with the modern stage, and, anyway, the Arabian manages to get a few veils around her before I can really find any grounds for complaint. But I wish to say that I am greatly surprised when I hear this Arabian dancer speak in very good English, and in fact with a Brooklyn accent, and as follows:

"Oh, Ambrose," she says, "I am so glad to see you again."

With this she makes out as if to put her arms around Ambrose Hammer, but then she remembers just in time that if she does this she will have to let go her hold of the veils and, anyway, Ambrose pulls away from her and stands looking at her with a very strange expression on his kisser.

Well, I will say one thing for Ambrose Hammer, and this is that he is at all times very gentlemanly, and he introduces me to the Arabian acrobatic dancer, and I notice that he speaks of her as Miss Cleghorn, although I remember that they bill her in lights in front of the Club Soudan as Illah-Illah, which is maybe her first name.

Now Ambrose gazes at Miss Cleghorn most severely, and then he speaks:

"The game is up," Ambrose says. "If you wish to confess to me and this party, well and good, otherwise you will tell your story to the gendarmes. I know you kill Mr. Justin Veezee, and," Ambrose says, "while you may have an excellent excuse, it is against the law."

Well, at this Miss Cleghorn turns very pale, indeed, and begins trembling so she almost forgets to hold on to her veils, and then she sits down in a chair and breathes so hard you will think she just finishes a tough tenth round. Naturally, I am somewhat surprised by Ambrose's statement, because up to this time I am not figuring Miss Cleghorn as such a doll as will harm a flea, although of course I will never lay a price against this proposition on any doll without having something of a line on her.

"Yes," Ambrose says, speaking very severely, indeed, to Miss Cleghorn, "you make an appointment to go to Mr. Justin Veezee's apartment the other morning after you get through with your Arabian acrobatic dancing here, to look at his etchings. I am surprised you fall for etchings, but I am glad you do, at that, because it gives me my first clue. No guy is hauling out etchings at four o'clock in the morning to look at them by himself," Ambrose says. "It is one of the oldest build-ups of a doll in the world," he says.

"Well," Ambrose goes on, "you look at Mr. Justin Veezee's etchings. They are very bad. In fact, they are terrible. But never mind this. Presently you struggle. You are very strong on account of your Arabian acrobatic dancing. Yes," Ambrose says, "you are very, very, very strong. In this struggle you break Mr. Justin's Veezee's neck, and now he is extremely dead. It is all very sad," Ambrose says.

Now, I wish to state that I am greatly mortified at being present at this scene, because if I know what Ambrose Hammer says he knows about Miss Cleghorn, I will keep my trap closed, especially as there is no reward offered for any information leading to the apprehension of the party who gives Mr. Justin Veezee the business, but Ambrose is undoubtedly a very law-abiding guy, and the chances are he feels he is only doing his duty in this matter, and, furthermore, he may get a nice item for his paper out of it.

But when he tells Miss Cleghorn that she is guilty of this unladylike conduct toward Mr. Justin Veezee, she gets up out of her chair, still holding onto her veils, and speaks to Ambrose Hammer like this:

"No, Ambrose," she says, "you are wrong. I do not kill Mr. Justin Veezee. I admit I go to his apartment, but not to see his etchings. I go there to have a bite to eat with him, because Mr. Justin Veezee swears to me that his housekeeper will be present, and I do not know he is deceiving me until after I arrive there. Mr. Justin Veezee gets out his etchings later when he can think of nothing else. But even Mr. Justin Veezee is not so old-fashioned as to believe any doll will go to his apartment just to look at etchings nowadays. I admit we struggle, but," Miss Cleghorn says, "I do not kill him."

"Well," Ambrose says, "if you do not think Mr. Justin Veezee is dead, a dollar will win you a trip around the world."

"Yes," Miss Cleghorn says, "I know he is dead. He is dead when I leave the apartment. I am very, very sorry for this, but I tell you again I do not kill him."

"Well," Ambrose says, "then who does kill Mr. Justin Veezee?"

"This I will never, never tell," Miss Cleghorn says.

Now, naturally, Ambrose Hammer becomes very indignant at this statement, and he tells Miss Cleghorn that if she will not tell him she will have to tell the gendarmes, and she starts in to cry like I do not know what, when all of a sudden the door of the dressing-room opens, and in comes a big, stout-built, middle-aged-looking guy, who does not seem any too well dressed, and who speaks as follows:

"Pardon the intrusion, gentlemen," the guy says, "but I am waiting in the next room and cannot help overhearing your conversation. I am waiting there because Miss Cleghorn is going to draw enough money off her employers to get me out of this part of the country. My name," the guy says, "is Riggsby. I am the party who kills Mr. Justin Veezee."

Well, naturally Ambrose Hammer is greatly surprised by these remarks, and so am I, but before either of us can express ourselves, the guy goes on like this:

"I am a roomer in the humble home of Mrs. Swanson in Ninth Avenue," he says. "I learn all about Mr. Justin Veezee from her. I sneak her key to the street door of Mr. Justin Veezee's house, and her key to the door of Mr. Justin Veezee's apartment one day and get copies of them made, and put the originals back before she misses them. I am hiding in Mr. Justin Veezee's apartment the other morning waiting to stick him up.

"Well," the guy says, "Mr. Justin Veezee comes in alone, and I am just about to step out on him and tell him to get them up, when in comes Miss Cleghorn, although of course I do not know at the time who she is. I can hear everything they say, and I see at once from their conversation that Miss Cleghorn is there under false pretenses. She finally wishes to leave, and Mr. Justin Veezee attacks her. She fights valiantly, and in just a straightaway hand-to-hand struggle, I will relish a small bet on her against Mr. Justin Veezee, or any other guy. But Mr. Justin Veezee picks up a bronze statuette and is about to bean her with it, so," the middle-aged guy says, "I step into it.

"Well," he says, "I guess maybe I am a little rougher with Mr. Justin Veezee than I mean to be, because I find myself putting a nice flying-mare hold on him and hurling him across the room. I fear the fall injures him severely. Anyway, when I pick him up he seems to be dead. So I sit him up in a chair, and take a bath towel and wipe out any chance of fingerprints around and about, and then escort Miss Cleghorn to her home.

"I do not intend to kill Mr. Justin Veezee," the middle-aged-looking guy says. "I only intend to rob him, and I am very sorry he is no longer with us, especially as I cannot now return and carry out my original plan. But," he says, "I cannot bear to see you hand Miss Cleghorn over to the law, although I hope and trust she will never be so foolish as to go visiting the apartments of such characters as Mr. Justin Veezee again."

"Yes," Ambrose Hammer says to Miss Cleghorn, "why do you go there in the first place?"

Well, at this Miss Cleghorn begins crying harder than ever, and between sobs she states to Ambrose Hammer as follows:

"Oh, Ambrose," she says, "it is because I love you so. You do not come around to see me for several nights, and I accept Mr. Justin Veezee's invitation hoping you will hear of it, and become jealous."

So of course there is nothing for Ambrose Hammer to do but take her in his arms and start whispering to her in such terms as guys are bound to whisper under these circumstances, and I motion the middle-aged-looking guy to go outside, as I consider this scene far too sacred for a stranger to witness.

Then about this time, Miss Cleghorn gets a call to go downstairs and do a little Arabian acrobatic dancing for the customers of the Club Soudan, and so she leaves us without ever once forgetting in all this excitement to keep a hold on her veils, although I am watching at all times to remind her in case her memory fails her in this respect.

And then I ask Ambrose Hammer something that is bothering me no little, and this is how he comes to suspect in the first place that Miss Cleghorn may know something about the scragging of Mr. Justin Veezee, even allowing that the etchings give him a clue that a doll is present when the scragging comes off. And I especially wish to know how he can ever figure Miss Cleghorn even as much as an outside chance of scragging Mr. Justin Veezee in such a manner as to break his neck.

"Why," Ambrose Hammer says, "I will gladly tell you about this, but only in strict confidence. The last time I see Miss Cleghorn up to tonight is the night I invite her to my own apartment to look at etchings, and they are better etchings than Mr. Justin Veezee shows her, at that. And," Ambrose says, "maybe you remember I am around with my neck tied up for a week."

Well, the middle-aged-looking guy is waiting for us outside the Club Soudan when we come out, and Ambrose Hammer stakes him to half a C and tells him to go as far as he can on this, and I shake hands with him, and wish him luck, and as he is turning to go, I say to him like this:

"By the way, Mr. Riggsby," I say, "what is your regular occupation, anyway, if I am not too nosey?"

"Oh," he says, "until the depression comes on, I am for years rated one of the most efficient persons in my line in this town. In fact, I have many references to prove it. Yes," he says, "I am considered an exceptionally high-class butler."

EDWARD D. HOCH

(b. 1930)

After brief stints in the army, at the Rochester (New York) Public Library, and with Pocket Books, Edward D. Hoch worked for fourteen years at an advertising firm. He published his first story in 1955, and in 1968 decided to become a professional author. He never looked back, and by 1996 was almost certainly the sole surviving full-time writer of mystery short stories in the United States and probably the world. Though he published four novels between 1969 and 1976 and a juvenile book in 1978, his impressively steady creation of short stories, both under his own name and under several pseudonyms, is where his reputation lies. His publications number in the high hundreds and the list continues to lengthen. Hoch, a fixture in the monthly Ellery Queen's Mystery Magazine, *received an award from the publisher for his unbroken string of appearances. He has accomplished his prodigious output by means of fifteen series, the most celebrated being stories with Nick Velvet, the thief of objects of no value, and Captain Leopold, a city policeman; but Hoch has not limited himself to series stories. He has also developed stories focused on Western settings, the 1920s, spy situations, and many others. Hoch particularly favors the fair-play puzzle, in which all the clues are presented to the reader as well as to the detective, a form codified during the golden age of the 1920s and 1930s and particularly practiced by Ellery Queen. Hoch has explored almost every traditional mystery device and made many visits to the locked room. In the following story, one of his best, he varies the traditional formula by having a character other than the victim locked inside the room. It isn't hard to identify the prime suspect when he's sealed in with the body.*

THE LEOPOLD LOCKED ROOM

Captain Leopold had never spoken to anyone about his divorce, and it was a distinct surprise to Lieutenant Fletcher when he suddenly said, "Did I ever tell you about my wife, Fletcher?"

They were just coming up from the police pistol range in the basement of headquarters after their monthly target practise, and it hardly seemed a likely time to be discussing past marital troubles. Fletcher glanced at him sideways and answered, "No, I guess you never did, Captain."

They had reached the top of the stairs and Leopold turned in to the little room where the coffee, sandwich, and soft-drink machines were kept. They called it the lunchroom, but only by the boldest stretch of the imagination could the little collection of tables and chairs qualify as such. Rather it was a place where off-duty cops could sit and chat, which was what Leopold and Fletcher were doing now.

Fletcher bought the coffee and put the steaming paper cups on the table between them. He had never seen Leopold quite this open and personal before, anxious to talk about a life that had existed far beyond the limits of Fletcher's friendship. "She's coming back," Leopold said simply, and it took Fletcher an instant to grasp the meaning of his words.

"Your wife is coming back?"

"My ex-wife."

"Here? What for?"

Leopold sighed and played with the little bag of sugar that Fletcher had given him with his coffee. "Her niece is getting married. Our niece."

"I never knew you had one."

"She's been away at college. Her name is Vicki Nelson, and she's marrying a young lawyer named Moore. And Monica is coming back east for the wedding."

"I never even knew her name," Fletcher observed, taking a sip of his coffee. "Haven't you seen her since the divorce?"

Leopold shook his head. "Not for fifteen years. It was a funny thing. She wanted to be a movie star, and I guess fifteen years ago lots of girls still thought about being movie stars. Monica was intelligent and very pretty—but probably no prettier than hundreds of other girls who used to turn up in Hollywood every year back in those days. I was just starting on the police force then, and the future looked pretty bright for me here. It would have been foolish of me to toss up everything just to chase her wild dream out to California. Well, pretty soon it got to be an obsession with her, really bad. She'd spend her afternoons in movie theaters and her evenings watching old films on television. Finally, when I still refused to go west with her, she just left me."

"Just walked out?"

Leopold nodded. "It was a blessing, really, that we didn't have children. I heard she got a few minor jobs out there—as an extra, and some technical stuff behind the scenes. Then apparently she had a nervous breakdown. About a year later I received the official word that she'd divorced me. I heard that she recovered and was back working, and I think she had another marriage that didn't work out."

"Why would she come back for the wedding?"

"Vicki is her niece and also her godchild. We were just married when Vicki was born, and I suppose Monica might consider her the child we never had. In any event, I know she still hates me, and blames me for everything that's gone wrong with her life. She told a friend once a few years ago she wished I were dead."

"Do you have to go to this wedding, too, Captain?"

"Of course. If I stayed away it would be only because of her. At least I have to drop by the reception for a few minutes." Leopold smiled ruefully. "I guess that's why I'm telling you all this, Fletcher. I want a favor from you."

"Anything, Captain. You know that."

"I know it seems like a childish thing to do, but I'd like you to come out there with me. I'll tell them I'm working, and that I can only stay for a few minutes. You can wait outside in the car if you want. At least they'll see you there and believe my excuse."

Fletcher could see the importance of it to Leopold, and the effort that had gone into the asking. "Sure," he said. "Be glad to. When is it?"

"This Saturday. The reception's in the afternoon, at Sunset Farms."

Leopold had been to Sunset Farms only once before, at the wedding of a patrolman whom he'd especially liked. It was a low rambling place at the end of a paved driveway, overlooking a wooded valley and a gently flowing creek. If it had ever been a farm, that day was long past; but for wedding receptions and retirement parties it was the ideal place. The interior of the main building was, in reality, one huge square room, divided by accordion doors to make up to four smaller square rooms.

For the wedding of Vicki Nelson and Ted Moore three-quarters of the large room was in use, with only the last set of accordion doors pulled shut its entire width and locked. The wedding party occupied a head table along one wall, with smaller tables scattered around the room for the families and friends. When Leopold entered the place at five minutes of two on Saturday afternoon, the hired combo was just beginning to play music for dancing.

He watched for a moment while Vicki stood, radiant, and allowed her new husband to escort her to the center of the floor. Ted Moore was a bit older than Leopold had expected, but as the pair glided slowly across the floor, he could find no visible fault with the match. He helped himself to a glass of champagne punch and stood ready to intercept them as they left the dance floor.

"It's Captain Leopold, isn't it?" someone asked. A face from his past loomed up, a tired man with a gold tooth in the front of his smile. "I'm Immy Fontaine, Monica's stepbrother."

"Sure," Leopold said, as if he'd remembered the man all along. Monica had rarely mentioned Immy, and Leopold recalled meeting him once or twice at family gatherings. But the sight of him now, gold tooth and all, reminded Leopold that Monica was somewhere nearby, that he might confront her at any moment.

"We're so glad you could come," someone else said, and he

turned to greet the bride and groom as they came off the dance floor. Up close, Vicki was a truly beautiful girl, clinging to her new husband's arm like a proper bride.

"I wouldn't have missed it for anything," he said.

"This is Ted," she said, making the introductions. Leopold shook his hand, silently approving the firm grip and friendly eyes.

"I understand you're a lawyer," Leopold said, making conversation.

"That's right, sir. Mostly civil cases, though. I don't tangle much with criminals."

They chatted for a few more seconds before the pressure of guests broke them apart. The luncheon was about to be served, and the more hungry ones were already lining up at the buffet tables. Vicki and Ted went over to start the line, and Leopold took another glass of champagne punch.

"I see the car waiting outside," Immy Fontaine said, moving in again. "You got to go on duty?"

Leopold nodded. "Just this glass and I have to leave."

"Monica's in from the west coast."

"So I heard."

A slim man with a mustache jostled against him in the crush of the crowd and hastily apologized. Fontaine seized the man by the arm and introduced him to Leopold. "This here's Dr. Felix Thursby. He came east with Monica. Doc, I want you to meet Captain Leopold, her ex-husband."

Leopold shook hands awkwardly, embarrassed for the man and for himself. "A fine wedding," he mumbled. "Your first trip east?"

Thursby shook his head. "I'm from New York. Long ago."

"I was on the police force there once," Leopold remarked.

They chatted for a few more minutes before Leopold managed to edge away through the crowd.

"Leaving so soon?" a harsh unforgettable voice asked.

"Hello, Monica. It's been a long time."

He stared down at the handsome, middle-aged woman who now blocked his path to the door. She had gained a little weight, especially in the bosom, and her hair was graying. Only the eyes startled him, and frightened him just a bit. They had the intense wild look he'd seen before on the faces of deranged criminals.

"I didn't think you'd come. I thought you'd be afraid of me," she said.

"That's foolish. Why should I be afraid of you?"

The music had started again, and the line from the buffet

tables was beginning to snake lazily about the room. But for Leopold and Monica they might have been alone in the middle of a desert.

"Come in here," she said, "where we can talk." She motioned toward the end of the room that had been cut off by the accordion doors. Leopold followed her, helpless to do anything else. She unlocked the doors and pulled them apart, just wide enough for them to enter the unused quarter of the large room. Then she closed and locked the doors behind them, and stood facing him. They were two people, alone in a bare unfurnished room.

They were in an area about thirty feet square, with the windows at the far end and the locked accordion doors at Leopold's back. He could see the afternoon sun cutting through the trees outside, and the gentle hum of the air conditioner came through above the subdued murmur of the wedding guests.

"Remember the day we got married?" she asked.

"Yes. Of course."

She walked to the middle window, running her fingers along the frame, perhaps looking for the latch to open it. But it stayed closed as she faced him again. "Our marriage was as drab and barren as this room. Lifeless, unused!"

"Heaven knows I always wanted children, Monica."

"You wanted nothing but your damned police work!" she shot back, eyes flashing as her anger built.

"Look, I have to go. I have a man waiting in the car."

"Go! That's what you did before, wasn't it? *Go, go!* Go out to your damned job and leave me to struggle for myself. Leave me to—"

"You walked out on me, Monica. Remember?" he reminded her softly. She was so defenseless, without even a purse to swing at him.

"Sure I did! Because I had a career waiting for me! I had all the world waiting for me! And you know what happened because you wouldn't come along? You know what happened to me out there? They took my money and my self-respect and what virtue I had left. They made me into a tramp, and when they were done they locked me up in a mental hospital for three years. Three years!"

"I'm sorry."

"Every day while I was there I thought about you. I thought about how it would be when I got out. Oh, I thought. And planned. And schemed. You're a big detective now. Sometimes your cases even get reported in the California papers." She was pacing back and forth, caged, dangerous. "Big detective. But I can still destroy you just as you destroyed me!"

He glanced over his shoulder at the locked accordion doors, seeking a way out. It was a thousand times worse than he'd imagined it would be. She was mad—mad and vengeful and terribly dangerous. "You should see a doctor, Monica."

Her eyes closed to mere slits. "I've seen doctors." Now she paused before the middle window, facing him. "I came all the way east for this day, because I thought you'd be here. It's so much better than your apartment, or your office, or a city street. There are one hundred and fifty witnesses on the other side of those doors."

"What in hell are you talking about?"

Her mouth twisted in a horrible grin. "You're going to know what I knew. Bars and cells and disgrace. You're going to know the despair I felt all those years."

"Monica—"

At that instant perhaps twenty feet separated them. She lifted one arm, as if to shield herself, then screamed in terror. "No! Oh, God, no!"

Leopold stood frozen, unable to move, as a sudden gunshot echoed through the room. He saw the bullet strike her in the chest, toppling her backward like the blow from a giant fist. Then somehow he had his own gun out of its belt holster and he swung around toward the doors.

They were still closed and locked. He was alone in the room with Monica.

He looked back to see her crumple on the floor, blood spreading in a widening circle around the torn black hole in her dress. His eyes went to the windows, but all three were still closed and unbroken. He shook his head, trying to focus his mind on what had happened.

There was noise from outside, and a pounding on the accordion doors. Someone opened the lock from the other side, and the gap between the doors widened as they were pulled open. "What happened?" someone asked. A woman guest screamed as she saw the body. Another toppled in a faint.

Leopold stepped back, aware of the gun still in his hand, and saw Lieutenant Fletcher fighting his way through the mob of guests. "Captain, what is it?"

"She . . . Someone shot her."

Fletcher reached out and took the gun from Leopold's hand—carefully, as one might take a broken toy from a child. He put it to his nose and sniffed, then opened the cylinder to inspect the bullets. "It's been fired recently, Captain. One shot." Then his eyes seemed to cloud over, almost to the point of tears. "Why the hell did you do it?" he asked, "Why?"

Leopold saw nothing of what happened then. He only had vague and splintered memories of someone examining her and saying she was still alive, of an ambulance and much confusion. Fletcher drove him down to headquarters, to the Commissioner's office, and he sat there and waited, running his moist palms up and down his trousers. He was not surprised when they told him she had died on the way to Southside Hospital. Monica had never been one to do things by halves.

The men—detectives who worked under him—came to and left the Commissioner's office, speaking in low tones with their heads together, occasionally offering him some embarrassed gesture of condolence. There was an aura of sadness over the place, and Leopold knew it was for him.

"You have nothing more to tell us, Captain?" the Commissioner asked. "I'm making it as easy for you as I can."

"I didn't kill her," Leopold insisted again. "It was someone else."

"Who? How?"

He could only shake his head. "I wish I knew. I think in some mad way she killed herself, to get revenge on me."

"She shot herself with *your* gun, while it was in *your* holster, and while *you* were standing twenty feet away?"

Leopold ran a hand over his forehead. "It couldn't have been my gun. Ballistics will prove that."

"But your gun had been fired recently, and there was an empty cartridge in the chamber."

"I can't explain that. I haven't fired it since the other day at target practise, and I reloaded it afterwards."

"Could she have hated you that much, Captain?" Fletcher asked. "To frame you for her murder?"

"She could have. I think she was a very sick woman. If I did that to her—if I was the one who made her sick—I suppose I deserve what's happening to me now."

"The hell you do," Fletcher growled. "If you say you're innocent, Captain, I'm sticking by you." He began pacing again, and finally turned to the Commissioner. "How about giving him a paraffin test, to see if he's fired a gun recently?"

The Commissioner shook his head. "We haven't used that in years. You know how unreliable it is, Fletcher. Many people have nitrates or nitrites on their hands. They can pick them up from dirt, or fertilizers, or fireworks, or urine, or even from simply handling peas or beans. Anyone who smokes tobacco can have deposits on his hands. There are some newer tests for the presence of barium or lead, but we don't have the necessary chemicals for those."

Leopold nodded. The Commissioner had risen through the ranks. He wasn't simply a political appointee, and the men had always respected him. Leopold respected him. "Wait for the ballistics report," he said. "That'll clear me."

So they waited. It was another 45 minutes before the phone rang and the Commissioner spoke to the ballistics man. He listened, and grunted, and asked one or two questions. Then he hung up and faced Leopold across the desk.

"The bullet was fired from your gun," he said simply. "There's no possibility of error. I'm afraid we'll have to charge you with homicide."

The routines he knew so well went on into Saturday evening, and when they were finished Leopold was escorted from the courtroom to find young Ted Moore waiting for him. "You should be on your honeymoon," Leopold told him.

"Vicki couldn't leave till I'd seen you and tried to help. I don't know much about criminal law, but perhaps I could arrange bail."

"That's already been taken care of," Leopold said. "The grand jury will get the case next week."

"I—I don't know what to say. Vicki and I are both terribly sorry."

"So am I." He started to walk away, then turned back. "Enjoy your honeymoon."

"We'll be in town overnight, at the Towers, if there's anything I can do."

Leopold nodded and kept on walking. He could see the reflection of his guilt in young Moore's eyes. As he got to his car, one of the patrolmen he knew glanced his way and then quickly in the other direction. On a Saturday night no one talked to wife murderers. Even Fletcher had disappeared.

Leopold decided he couldn't face the drab walls of his office, not with people avoiding him. Besides, the Commissioner had been forced to suspend him from active duty pending grand jury action and the possible trial. The office didn't even belong to him anymore. He cursed silently and drove home to his little apartment, weaving through the dark streets with one eye out for a patrol car. He wondered if they'd be watching him, to prevent his jumping bail. He wondered what he'd have done in the Commissioner's shoes.

The eleven o'clock news on television had it as the lead item, illustrated with a black-and-white photo of him taken during a case last year. He shut off the television without listening to their comments and went back outside, walking down to the corner for an early edition of the Sunday paper. The front-page headline was as bad as he'd expected: *Detective Captain Held in Slaying of Ex-Wife.*

On the way back to his apartment, walking slowly, he tried to remember what she'd been like—not that afternoon, but before the divorce. He tried to remember her face on their wedding day, her soft laughter on their honeymoon. But all he could remember were those mad vengeful eyes. And the bullet ripping into her chest.

Perhaps he had killed her after all. Perhaps the gun had come into his hand so easily he never realized it was there.

"Hello, Captain."

"I—Fletcher! What are you doing here?"

"Waiting for you. Can I come in?"

"Well . . ."

"I've got a six-pack of beer. I thought you might want to talk about it."

Leopold unlocked his apartment door. "What's there to talk about?"

"If you say you didn't kill her, Captain, I'm willing to listen to you."

Fletcher followed him into the tiny kitchen and popped open two of the beer cans. Leopold accepted one of them and dropped into the nearest chair. He felt utterly exhausted, drained of even the strength to fight back.

"She framed me, Fletcher," he said quietly. "She framed me as neatly as anything I've ever seen. The thing's impossible, but she did it."

"Let's go over it step by step, Captain. Look, the way I see it there are only three possibilities: either you shot her, she shot herself, or someone else shot her. I think we can rule out the last one. The three windows were locked on the outside and unbroken, the room was bare of any hiding place, and the only entrance was through the accordion doors. These were closed and locked, and although they could have been opened from the other side you certainly would have seen or heard it happen. Besides, there were one hundred and fifty wedding guests on the other side of those doors. No one could have unlocked and opened them and then fired the shot, all without being seen.

Leopold shook his head. "But it's just as impossible that she could have shot herself. I was watching her every minute. I never looked away once. There was nothing in her hands, not even a purse. And the gun that shot her was in my holster, on my belt. I never drew it till *after* the shot was fired."

Fletcher finished his beer and reached for another can. "I didn't look at her close, Captain, but the size of the hole in her dress and the powder burns point to a contact wound. The Medical Examiner agrees, too. She was shot from no more than an inch or two away. There were grains of powder in the wound itself, though the bleeding had washed most of them away."

"But she had nothing in her hand," Leopold repeated. "And there was nobody standing in front of her with a gun. Even I was twenty feet away."

"The thing's impossible, Captain."

Leopold grunted. "Impossible—unless I killed her."

Fletcher stared at his beer. "How much time do we have?"

"If the grand jury indicts me for first-degree murder, I'll be in a cell by next week."

Fletcher frowned at him. "What's with you, Captain? You almost act resigned to it! Hell, I've seen more fight in you on a routine holdup!"

"I guess that's it, Fletcher. The fight is gone out of me. She's drained every drop of it. She's had her revenge."

Fletcher sighed and stood up. "Then I guess there's really nothing I can do for you, Captain. Good night."

Leopold didn't see him to the door. He simply sat there, hunched over the table. For the first time in his life he felt like an old man.

Leopold slept late Sunday morning, and awakened with the odd sensation that it had all been a dream. He remembered feeling the same way when he'd broken his wrist chasing a burglar. In the morning, on just awakening, the memory of the heavy cast had always been a dream, until he moved his arm. Now, rolling over in his narrow bed, he saw the Sunday paper where he's tossed it the night before. The headline was still the same. The dream was a reality.

He got up and showered and dressed, reaching for his holster out of habit before he remembered he no longer had a gun. Then he sat at the kitchen table staring at the empty beer cans, wondering what he would do with his day. With his life.

The doorbell rang and it was Fletcher. "I didn't think I'd be seeing you again," Leopold mumbled, letting him in.

Fletcher was excited, and the words tumbled out of him almost before he was through the door. "I think I've got something, Captain! It's not much, but it's a start. I was down at headquarters first thing this morning, and I got hold of the dress Monica was wearing when she was shot."

Leopold looked blank. "The dress?"

Fletcher was busy unwrapping the package he'd brought. "The Commissioner would have my neck if he knew I brought this to you, but look at this hole!"

Leopold studied the jagged, blood-caked rent in the fabric. "It's large," he observed, "but with a near-contact wound the powder burns would cause that."

"Captain, I've seen plenty of entrance wounds made by a .38 slug. I've even caused a few of them. But I never saw one that looked like this. Hell, it's not even round!"

"What are you trying to tell me, Fletcher?" Suddenly something stirred inside him. The juices were beginning to flow again.

"The hole in her dress is much larger and more jagged than the corresponding wound in her chest, Captain. That's what I'm telling you. The bullet that killed her couldn't have made this hole. No way! And that means maybe she wasn't killed when we thought she was."

Leopold grabbed the phone and dialed the familiar number of the Towers Hotel. "I hope they slept late this morning."

"Who?"

"The honeymooners." He spoke sharply into the phone, giving the switchboard operator the name he wanted, and then waited. It was a full minute before he heard Ted Moore's sleepy voice answering on the other end. "Ted, this is Leopold. Sorry to bother you."

The voice came alert at once. "That's all right, Captain. I told you to call if there was anything—"

"I think there is. You and Vicki between you must have a pretty good idea of who was invited to the wedding. Check with her and tell me how many doctors were on the invitation list."

Ted Moore was gone for a few moments and then he returned. "Vicki says you're the second person who asked her that."

"Oh? Who was the first?"

"Monica. The night before the wedding, when she arrived in town with Dr. Thursby. She casually asked if he'd get to meet any other doctors at the reception. But Vicki told her he was the only one. Of course we hadn't invited him, but as a courtesy to Monica we urged him to come."

"Then after the shooting, it was Thursby who examined her? No one else?"

"He was the only doctor. He told us to call an ambulance and rode to the hospital with her."

"Thank you, Ted. You've been a big help."

"I hope so, Captain."

Leopold hung up and faced Fletcher. "That's it. She worked it with this guy Thursby. Can you put out an alarm for him?"

"Sure can," Fletcher said. He took the telephone and dialed the unlisted squadroom number. "Dr. Felix Thursby? Is that his name?"

"That's it. The only doctor there, the only one who could help Monica with her crazy plan of revenge."

Fletcher completed issuing orders and hung up the phone. "They'll check his hotel and call me back."

"Get the Commissioner on the phone, too. Tell him what we've got."

Fletcher started to dial and then stopped, his finger in mid-air. What *have* we got, Captain?"

The Commissioner sat behind his desk, openly unhappy at being called to headquarters on a Sunday afternoon, and listened bleakly to what Leopold and Fletcher had to tell him. Finally he spread his fingers on the desktop and said, "The mere fact that this Dr. Thursby seems to have left town is hardly proof of his guilt, Captain. What you're saying is that the woman wasn't killed until later—that Thursby killed her in the ambulance. But how could he have done that with a pistol that was already in Lieutenant Fletcher's possession, tagged as evidence? And how could he have fired the fatal shot without the ambulance attendants hearing it?"

"I don't know," Leopold admitted.

"Heaven knows, Captain, I'm willing to give you every reasonable chance to prove your innocence. But you have to bring me more than a dress with a hole in it."

"All right," Leopold said. "I'll bring you more."

"The grand jury gets the case this week, Captain."

"I know," Leopold said. He turned and left the office, with Fletcher tailing behind.

"What now?" Fletcher asked.

"We go to talk to Immy Fontaine, my ex-wife's stepbrother."

Though he'd never been friendly with Fontaine, Leopold knew where to find him. The tired man with the gold tooth lived in a big old house overlooking the Sound, where on this summer Sunday they found him in the back yard, cooking hot dogs over a charcoal fire.

He squinted into the sun and said, "I thought you'd be in jail, after what happened."

"I didn't kill her," Leopold said quietly.

"Sure you didn't."

"For a stepbrother you seem to be taking her death right in stride," Leopold observed, motioning toward the fire.

"I stopped worrying about Monica fifteen years ago."

"What about this man she was with? Dr. Thursby?"

Immy Fontaine chuckled. "If he's a doctor I'm a plumber! He has the fingers of a surgeon, I'll admit, but when I asked him about my son's radius that he broke skiing, Thursby thought it was a leg bone. What the hell, though, I was never one to judge Monica's love life. Remember, I didn't even object when she married you."

"Nice of you. Where's Thursby staying while he's in town?"

"He was at the Towers with Monica."

"He's not there any more."

"Then I don't know where he's at. Maybe he's not even staying for her funeral."

"What if I told you Thursby killed Monica?"

He shrugged. "I wouldn't believe you, but then I wouldn't particularly care. If you were smart you'd have killed her fifteen years ago when she walked out on you. That's what I'd have done."

Leopold drove slowly back downtown, with Fletcher grumbling beside him. "Where are we, Captain? It seems we're just going in circles."

"Perhaps we are, Fletcher, but right now there are still too many questions to be answered. If we can't find Thursby I'll have to tackle it from another direction. The bullet, for instance."

"What about the bullet?"

"We're agreed it could not have been fired by my gun, either while it was in my holster or later, while Thursby was in the ambulance with Monica. Therefore, it must have been fired earlier. The last time I fired it was at target practise. Is there any possibility—any chance at all—that Thursby or Monica could have gotten one of the slugs I fired into that target?"

Fletcher put a damper on it. "Captain, we were both firing at the same target. No one could sort out those bullets and say which came from your pistol and which from mine. Besides, how would either of them gain access to the basement target range at police headquarters?"

"I could have an enemy in the department," Leopold said.

"Nuts! We've all got enemies, but the thing is still impossible. If you believe people in the department are plotting against you, you might as well believe that the entire ballistics evidence was faked."

"It was, somehow. Do you have the comparison photos?"

"They're back at the office. But with the narrow depth of field you can probably tell more from looking through the microscope yourself."

Fletcher drove him to the lab, where they persuaded the Sunday-duty officer to let them have a look at the bullets. While Fletcher and the officer stood by in the interests of propriety, Leopold squinted through the microscope at the twin chunks of lead.

"The death bullet is pretty battered," he observed, but he had to admit that the rifling marks were the same. He glanced at the identification tag attached to the test bullet: *Test slug fired from Smith & Wesson .38 Revolver, serial number* 2420547.

Leopold turned away with a sigh, then turned back.

2420547.

He fished into his wallet and found his pistol permit. *Smith & Wesson* 2421622.

"I remembered those two's on the end," he told Fletcher. "That's not my gun."

"It's the one I took from you, Captain. I'll swear to it!"

"And I believe you, Fletcher. But it's the one fact I needed. It tells me how Dr. Thursby managed to kill Monica in a locked room before my very eyes, with a gun that was in my holster at the time. And it just might tell us where to find the elusive Dr. Thursby."

By Monday morning Leopold had made six long-distance calls to California, working from his desk telephone while Fletcher used the squadroom phone. Then, a little before noon, Leopold,

Fletcher, the Commissioner, and a man from the District Attorney's office took a car and drove up to Boston.

"You're sure you've got it figured?" the Commissioner asked Leopold for the third time. "You know we shouldn't allow you to cross the state line while awaiting grand jury action."

"Look, either you trust me or you don't," Leopold snapped. Behind the wheel Fletcher allowed himself a slight smile, but the man from the D.A.'s office was deadly serious.

"The whole thing is so damned complicated," the Commissioner grumbled.

"My ex-wife was a complicated woman. And remember, she had fifteen years to plan it."

"Run over it for us again," the D.A.'s man said.

Leopold sighed and started talking. "The murder gun wasn't mine. The gun I pulled after the shot was fired, the one Fletcher took from me, had been planted on me some time before."

"How?"

"I'll get to that. Monica was the key to it all, of course. She hated me so much that her twisted brain planned her own murder in order to get revenge on me. She planned it in such a way that it would have been impossible for anyone but me to have killed her."

"Only a crazy woman would do such a thing."

"I'm afraid she was crazy—crazy for vengeance. She set up the entire plan for the afternoon of the wedding reception, but I'm sure they had an alternate in case I hadn't gone to it. She wanted some place where there'd be lots of witnesses."

"Tell them how she worked the bullet hitting her," Fletcher urged.

"Well, that was the toughest part for me. I actually saw her shot before my eyes. I saw the bullet hit her and I saw the blood. Yet I was alone in a locked room with her. There was no hiding place, no opening from which a person or even a mechanical device could have fired the bullet at her. To you people it seemed I must be guilty, especially when the bullet came from the gun I was carrying.

"But I looked at it from a different angle—once Fletcher forced me to look at it at all! I *knew* I hadn't shot her, and since no one else physically could have, I knew no one did! If Monica was killed by a .38 slug, it must have been fired *after* she was taken from that locked room. Since she was dead on arrival at the hospital, the most likely time for her murder—to me, at least—became the time of the ambulance ride, when Dr. Thursby must have hunched over her with careful solicitousness."

"But you *saw* her shot!"

"That's one of the two reasons Fletcher and I were on the phones to Hollywood this morning. My ex-wife worked in pictures, at times in the technical end of movie-making. On the screen there are a number of ways to simulate a person being shot. An early method was a sort of compressed-air gun fired at the actor from just off-camera. These days, especially in the bloodiest of the Western and war films, they use a tiny explosive charge fitted under the actor's clothes. Of course the body is protected from burns, and the force of it is directed outward. A pouch of fake blood is released by the explosion, adding to the realism of it."

"And this is what Monica did?"

Leopold nodded. "A call to her Hollywood studio confirmed the fact that she worked on a film using this device. I noticed when I met her that she'd gained weight around the bosom, but I never thought to attribute it to the padding and the explosive device. She triggered it when she raised her arm as she screamed at me."

"Any proof?"

"The hole in her dress was just too big to be an entrance hole from a .38, even fired at close range—too big and too ragged. I can thank Fletcher for spotting that. This morning the lab technicians ran a test on the bloodstains. Some of it was her blood, the rest was chicken blood."

"She was a good actress to fool all those people."

"She knew Dr. Thursby would be the first to examine her. All she had to do was fall over when the explosive charge ripped out the front of her dress."

"What if there had been another doctor at the wedding?"

Leopold shrugged. "Then they would have postponed it. They couldn't take that chance."

"And the gun?"

"I remembered Thursby bumping against me when I first met him. He took my gun and substituted an identical weapon—identical, that is, except for the serial number. He'd fired it just a short time earlier, to complete the illusion. When I drew it I simply played into their hands. There I was, the only person in the room with an apparently dying woman, and a gun that had just been fired."

"But what about the bullet that killed her?"

"Rifling marks on the slugs are made by the lands in the rifled barrel of a gun causing grooves in the lead of a bullet. A bullet fired through a smooth tube has no rifling marks."

"What in hell kind of gun has a smooth tube for a barrel?" the Commissioner asked.

"A home-made one, like a zip gun. Highly inaccurate, but quite effective when the gun is almost touching the skin of the victim. Thursby fired a shot from the pistol he was to plant on me, probably into a pillow or some other place where he could retrieve the undamaged slug. Then he reused the rifled slug on another cartridge and fired it with his home-made zip gun, right into Monica's heart. The original rifling marks were still visible and no new ones were added."

"The ambulance driver and attendant didn't hear the shot?"

"They would have stayed up front, since he was a doctor riding with a patient. It gave him a chance to get the padded explosive mechanism off her chest, too. Once that was away, I imagine he leaned over her, muffling the zip gun as best he could, and fired the single shot that killed her. Remember, an ambulance on its way to a hospital is a pretty noisy place—it has a siren going all the time."

They were entering downtown Boston now, and Leopold directed Fletcher to a hotel near the Common. "I still don't believe the part about switching the guns," the D.A.'s man objected. "You mean to tell me he undid the strap over your gun, got out the gun, and substituted another one—all without your knowing it?"

Leopold smiled. "I mean to tell you only one type of person could have managed it—an expert, professional pickpocket. The type you see occasionally doing an act in night clubs and on television. That's how I knew where to find him. We called all over Southern California till we came up with someone who knew Monica and knew she'd dated a man named Thompson who had a pickpocket act. We called Thompson's agent and discovered he's playing a split week at a Boston lounge, and is staying at this hotel."

"What if he couldn't have managed it without your catching on? Or what if you hadn't been wearing your gun?"

"Most detectives wear their guns off-duty. If I hadn't been, or if he couldn't get it, they'd simply have changed their plan. He must have signaled her when he'd safely made the switch."

"Here we are," Fletcher said. "Let's go up."

The Boston police had two men waiting to meet them, and they went up in the elevator to the room registered in the name of Max Thompson. Fletcher knocked on the door, and when it opened the familiar face of Felix Thursby appeared. He no longer wore the mustache, but he had the same slim surgeon-like fingers that Immy Fontaine had noticed. Not a doctor's fingers, but a pickpocket's.

"We're taking you in for questioning," Fletcher said, and the Boston detectives issued the standard warnings of his legal rights.

Thursby blinked his tired eyes at them, and grinned a bit when he recognized Leopold. "She said you were smart. She said you were a smart cop."

"Did you have to kill her?" Leopold asked.

"I didn't. I just held the gun there and she pulled the trigger herself. She did it all herself, except for switching the guns. She hated you that much."

"I know," Leopold said quietly, staring at something far away. "But I guess she must have hated herself just as much."

WILLIAM BRITTAIN

(b.1930)

Like his fellow short story specialist Edward D. Hoch, William Brittain was born in Rochester, New York. Educated at Colgate University, Brockport State Teachers College, and Hofstra University, Brittain had a long career as an English teacher at Lawrence Junior High School, retiring in 1986. He claimed to get many of his ideas from ordinary occurrences during his work day. Writing as William Brittain and as James Knox, in the mystery genre he has confined himself to short stories. As Bill Brittain, however, he has published over a half dozen juvenile novels. The Wish Giver *(1984) earned him a Newbery Honor Book award. His familiarity with the high school milieu is vivid in his Mr. Strang series. Strang teaches at Aldershot High School (which Brittain asserts is quite a bit livelier than his own) and solves various crimes. In "Mr. Strang Takes a Field Trip," for example, his students are accused of stealing a mask from a museum and Strang proves them innocent. In another, his car is stolen and used in a robbery. The general tone is light, and the emphasis is on the puzzle. Brittain's other series is a tribute to celebrated crime writers and began in 1966 with "The Man Who Read John Dickson Carr" (the following selection) and "The Man Who Read Ellery Queen." Other titles in the series include "The Woman Who Read Rex Stout" and "The Boy Who Read Agatha Christie." Other authors treated are Arthur Conan Doyle, Dashiell Hammett, Georges Simenon, John Creasey, G. K. Chesterton, and Isaac Asimov. Early on Brittain even wrote "The Man Who Didn't Read." In the following selection, Brittain turns his acquaintance with the locked room mysteries of John Dickson Carr and the readers' familiarity with the form into an amusing trick story, pointing up the one essential ingredient in any locked room mystery.*

THE MAN WHO READ JOHN DICKSON CARR

Although he did not realize it at the time, Edgar Gault's life first gained purpose and direction when, at the age of twelve, he idly picked up a copy of John Dickson Carr's *The Problem of the Wire Cage* at his neighborhood lending library. That evening after supper he sat down with the book and read until bedtime. Then, smuggling the book into his room, he finished it by flashlight under the sheets.

He returned to the library the following day for another of Carr's books, *The Arabian Nights Murder,* which took him two days to finish—Edgar's governess had confiscated the flashlight. Within a week he read every John Dickson Carr mystery the library had on its shelves. His gloom on the day he finished reading the last one turned to elation when he learned that his favorite author also wrote under the pseudonym of Carter Dickson.

In the course of the next ten years Edgar accompanied Dr. Gideon Fell, Sir Henry Merrivale, et al. through every locked room in the Carr-Dickson repertoire. He was exultant the day his knowledge of an elusive point in high school physics allowed him to solve the mystery of *The Man Who Could Not Shudder* before the author saw fit to give his explanation. It was probably then that Edgar made his momentous decision.

One day he, Edgar Gault, would commit a locked-room murder which would mystify the master himself.

An orphan, Edgar lived with his uncle in a huge rambling house in a remote section of Vermont. The house was not only equipped with a library—that boon to mystery writers, but something few modern houses possess—but the library had barred windows and a two-inch-thick oak door which, opening into the room, could be locked only by placing a ponderous wooden bar into iron carriers bolted solidly to the wall on both sides of the door. There were no secret passages. The room, in short, would have pleased any of Carr's detectives, and it suited Edgar perfectly.

The victim, of course, would be Edgar's Uncle Daniel. Not only was he readily available, but he was a believer in Ralph Waldo Emerson's philosophy of self-reliance, and in order to help Edgar achieve that happy condition, Uncle Daniel had decided to cut the youth out of his will in the near future.

Since Edgar was perfectly prepared to wallow in his uncle's filthy lucre all the days of his life, it was up to him to do the old man in before the will could be changed.

All of which serves only to explain why Edgar, one bright day in early spring, was standing inside the library fireplace, covered with soot and scrubbing the inside of the chimney until it gleamed.

The chimney, of course, was Edgar's means of escape from his locked room. It was just large enough to accommodate his slim body and had an iron ladder which ran up the inside for the convenience of a chimney sweep. The necessity of escape by chimney somewhat disappointed Edgar, since Dr. Gideon Fell had ruled it out during his famous locked-room lecture in *The Three Coffins*. But it was the only exit available, and Edgar had devised a scheme to make use of it that he was sure even John Dickson Carr would approve of. Maybe Edgar would even get a book written about his crime—like Carr's *The Murder of Sir Edmund Godfrey*.

It didn't worry Edgar that he would be immediately suspected of the crime. Nobody saw his preparations—Uncle Daniel was away on business, and the cook and gardener were on vacation. And at the time the crime would actually be committed, Edgar would have two unimpeachable witnesses to testify that neither he—nor, for that matter, any other human being—could possibly have been the murderer.

Finishing his scrubbing, Edgar carried the pail of water to the kitchen and emptied it down the drain. Then, after a thorough shower to rid his body of soot, he went to the linen closet, took out a newly washed bedsheet, and returned to the library. Wrapping the sheet around him, he got back into the fireplace and began to climb the iron ladder. Reaching the top, he came down again, purposely rubbing the sheet against the stones at frequent intervals.

Stepping back into the library, he walked to a window, removed the sheet, and held it up to the sunlight. Although wrinkled, it had remained gleamingly white. Edgar smiled as he put the sheet into a hamper. Then, going upstairs, he unlocked the window of a storeroom beside which the chimney rose. After that, in his own room, he dressed in clothing chosen especially for the crime—white shirt, white trousers, and white tennis shoes. Finally, he removed a long cavalry saber from the wall, took it to the library, and stood it in a shadowy corner.

His preparations were nearly complete.

Early that evening, from his chair in the music room, Edgar heard his uncle's return. "Edgar? You home?" The nasal New England twang of Uncle Daniel's voice bespoke two hundred years of unbroken Vermont ancestry.

"I'm in here, Uncle Daniel—in the music room."

"Ayah," said Daniel, looking in through the door. "That's the trouble with you, young fella. You think more o' strummin' that guitar than you do about gettin' ahead in the world. Business first, boy—that's the only ticket for success."

"Why, Uncle, I've been working on a business arrangement most of the day. I just finished about an hour ago."

"Well, I meant what I said about my will, Edgar," Uncle Daniel continued. "In fact, I'm going to talk to Stoper about it tonight when he comes over for cards."

Even the weekly game of bridge, in which Edgar was usually a reluctant fourth to Uncle Daniel, Lemuel Stoper, and Dr. Harold Crowley, was a part of The Plan. Even the perfect crime needs witnesses to its perfection.

Later, as Edgar arranged the last of three armloads of wood in the library fireplace—and added to the kindling a small jar from his pocket—he heard the heavy knocker of the front door bang three times. He took the opportunity to set his watch. Exactly seven o'clock.

"Take the gentlemen to the music room and make them comfortable," said Uncle Daniel. "Give 'em a drink and get the card table ready. I'll be in presently."

"Why must they always wait for you, Uncle?" asked Edgar, his assumed frown almost a smirk.

"They'll wait forever for me and like it, if that's what I want. They know where the biggest part of their earnings comes from, all right." And still another part of Edgar's plan dropped neatly into place.

Entering the old house, Lemuel Stoper displayed, as always, an attitude of disdain toward everything not directly involved with Uncle Daniel's considerable fortune. "White, white, and more white," he sneered, looking at Edgar's clothing. "You look like a waiter in a restaurant."

"Don't let him get to you, boy," said a voice from outside. "You look fine. Been playin' tennis?" Dr. Crowley, who reminded Edgar of a huge lump of clear gelatine, waddled in and smiled benignly.

"No need to butter the boy up any more," said Stoper. "Dan'l's changin' his will tonight."

"Oh," said Crowley, surprised. "That's too bad, boy—uh—Edgar."

"Yes, Uncle has already spoken to me about his decision," said Edgar. "I'm in complete agreement with it." No sense in providing *too* much in the way of a motive.

In a small but important change from the usual routine Edgar led the men to the door of the library on the way to the music room. "Uncle," he called. "Dr. Crowley and Mr. Stoper are here."

"I know they're here," growled Daniel. "Wait in the music room. I'll be along in a few minutes."

The two men had seen Uncle Daniel alive and well. Everything was now ready.

In the music room Edgar poured drinks and set up the card table. Then he snapped his fingers and raised his eyebrows—the perfect picture of a man who has just remembered something.

"I must have left the cards upstairs," he said. "I'll go and find them." And before his guests could answer, he left the room.

Once through the door, Edgar's pace quickened. He reached the door of the library eight seconds later. Ignoring his uncle's surprised expression, Edgar took the saber from its corner and strode to the desk where Daniel sat, a newspaper still in his hand.

"Edgar, what in—" Without a word Edgar thrust the sword violently at his uncle. The point entered Daniel's wattled neck just below the chin and penetrated the neck to the back of the chair, pinning the old man to his place. Edgar chuckled, recalling a similar scene in Carr's *The Bride of Newgate.*

He held the sword in place for several seconds. Then he felt carefully for a pulse. None. The murder had been carried off exactly as planned—in seventy seconds.

Hurrying to the fireplace, Edgar picked up the small jar he had placed there earlier. Then, shuffling his feet through the generous supply of paper among the kindling and wood, he pulled the tall fire screen into place and began to climb up the chimney. Reaching the top, he glanced at his watch. Two minutes had gone by since he had left Stoper and Crowley.

Standing on the roof beside the chimney, Edgar removed several small pieces of blank paper from the jar. He had prepared the paper himself from a formula in a book on World War II sabotage operations. These "calling cards" were designed to burst into flame shortly after being exposed to the air. During the war they had been dropped from planes to start fires in fields of enemy grain. Edgar, who had shortened the time needed to make them ignite, knew the pieces of paper would start a fire in the library fireplace.

Dropping the papers down the chimney, he waited a few seconds, and finally was rewarded with a blast of warm air coming up through the opening. Three minutes and ten seconds. Right on schedule.

Edgar moved along the slanted roof to a large decorative gable in which was set the storeroom window. Carefully inching along the edge of the roof, he raised the window and scrambled inside, taking care not to get dust or dirt on his clothing. He went to his own room, took a fresh deck of cards he had left there earlier, then trotted loudly down the stairs to the music room. He rejoined the two guests a little less than five minutes after he had left them—again exactly as planned.

Edgar apologized for his short absence, privately gloating over the unsullied whiteness of his clothing. Surely he could not just have climbed up the inside of a chimney from which smoke was now issuing.

Soon Stoper became restless. "I wonder what's keepin' Dan'l?" he grumbled.

"Mebbe we'd better fetch him," said Crowley.

As they rose, Edgar attempted a yawn while his heart pounded wildly. "I believe I'll wait here," he said, trying to act nonchalant.

John Dickson Carr would be proud of me, thought Edgar as Stoper and Crowley left the room. He hoped that the investigation of his crime would not include any theories involving the supernatural. He remembered his disappointment at the ending in *The Burning Court* with its overtones of witchcraft.

Odd, he thought, that there was no shouting, no crashing sounds as the two old men tried to batter down the heavy library door. But there was no need to worry. The plan was perfect, foolproof. It was—

In the doorway of the music room appeared the figure of Lemuel Stoper, looking tired and beaten. In his hand he held a revolver from Uncle Daniel's desk.

"Did his money mean that much to you, boy?" Stoper asked, his voice trembling with shock and rage. "Is that why you did it?"

For only a moment Edgar wondered how Mr. Stoper had got into the library so fast. And then suddenly he knew. For a fleeting instant he wondered if a plea of insanity would help. But then nobody would appreciate the perfect crime he had devised. What would Dr. Fell think of him now? What would H. M. think? What would John Dickson Carr himself think?

What could anyone think of a locked-room murder in which the murderer had forgotten to lock the door?

Only One Among You

THE CHORUS OF SHAKESPEARE'S *HENRY V* APOLOGIZES FOR CONfining "mighty men" to the "little room" of a stage. Yet, as Aristotle warned in his *Poetics*, the action (plotline) of a drama must be of a magnitude that can be readily grasped. All forms of storytelling, whether drama or fiction, limit the multiplicity of possibilities in reality. In daily life the sources of misfortune often seem to be infinite. People are unpredictably victimized at any hour, by strangers or loved ones with motives that are obscure or ridiculous or hardly motives at all. In storytelling, the clutter of our world is reduced to a finite number of possibilities. Thus, in the Bible, when Solomon is asked to identify which of the two contending women is the mother of the infant, the reader assumes it can be only one of the two, and not a third who has gone unmentioned. As with all fiction, mysteries entertain us with their manipulation of a limited number of characters in a finite space. However, there are additional implications when it is assumed that one of those present *must* be the criminal. The only one among you formula is really a mirror image of the locked room. The suspects—by contrivance, the only possible perpetrators of the crime—are contained within the site rather than excluded from it. As in the locked room mystery, truth is illuminated and verified by careful physical observation and logical thought. Again there is comfort in believing that false leads can be eliminated and a single, absolute solution revealed. Various contrivances have been used to limit the number of possible suspects: a mansion is cut off by a storm, or the crime occurs on a ship, an airplane, or a train. Possible explanations implying the guilt of each character are provided. The device of confining a group of suspects to a limited space is more common in novels, where there is sufficient space to create a variety of suspects, and to elaborate on their motives, but it is also standard fare in short stories. Four likely suspects of this story type have been gathered in the following pages.

G. K. CHESTERTON

(1874–1936)

Literary scholars respect Gilbert Keith Chesterton primarily as an essayist and literary critic, but in the world of mystery and detection he is revered as the creator of one of the greatest amateur detectives, Father Brown. Born in London and educated at the Slade School of Art, Chesterton did some work as an illustrator, but turned to writing and became one of the most prolific authors in our century, publishing more than a hundred books. Father Brown was based on Father John O'Connor of St. Cuthbert's, Bradford, an eccentric parish priest who converted Chesterton to Catholicism and finally brought him into the Church in 1922. Like O' Connor, Father Brown is seemingly distracted and out of touch with the details of everyday life, which ought to be catastrophic for a detective. Yet, Father Brown solves crimes not by the scientific empiricism of his contemporary fictional detectives but through psychological insight. Criticized for not introducing enough of the standard stuff of puzzle mysteries of the time—the placement of the furniture, the details of the locks, the cigarette ashes on the rug—Chesterton instead used obvious clues whose meaning could only be deciphered by an understanding of the motivation, behavior, and mentality of the suspects. The form of fiction was not what Chesterton found compelling. He was interested in the moral and social insight that could be drawn from the tale and is frequently described (both favorably and unfavorably) as a man full of ideas. The Father Brown stories have led to a host of lesser imitators and a loose subgenre of clerical mysteries. From Ralph McInerny's Father Dowling to Harry Kemelman's Rabbi Small, Chesterton's footprints are obvious. Agatha Christie's Jane Marple, as well as every other underestimated eccentric crime-solver, owes a great deal to Father Brown. In one of the best Father Brown stories, included here, a decapitation in a locked garden provides a limited number of suspects. How can the odd little priest explain two heads and one body?

THE SECRET GARDEN

Aristide Valentin, Chief of the Paris Police, was late for his dinner, and some of his guests began to arrive before him. These were, however, reassured by his confidential servant, Ivan, the old man with a scar and a face almost as grey as his moustaches, who always sat at a table in the entrance hall—a hall hung with weapons. Valentin's house was perhaps as peculiar and celebrated as its master. It was an old house, with high walls and tall poplars almost overhanging the Seine; but the oddity—and perhaps the police value—of its architecture was this: that there was no ultimate exit at all except through this front door, which was guarded by Ivan and the armoury. The garden was large and elaborate, and there were many exits from the house into the garden. But there was no exit from the garden into the world outside; all round it ran a tall, smooth unscalable wall with special spikes at the top; no bad garden, perhaps, for a man to reflect in whom some hundred criminals had sworn to kill.

As Ivan explained to the guests, their host had telephoned that he was detained for ten minutes. He was, in truth, making some last arrangements about executions and such ugly things; and though these duties were rootedly repulsive to him, he always performed them with precision. Ruthless in the pursuit of criminals, he was very mild about their punishment. Since he had been supreme over French—and largely over European—police methods, his great influence had been honourably used for the mitigation of sentences and the purification of prisons. He was one of the great humanitarian French freethinkers; and the only thing wrong with them is that they make mercy even colder than justice.

When Valentin arrived he was already dressed in black clothes and the red rosette—an elegant figure, his dark beard already streaked with grey. He went straight through his house to his study, which opened on the grounds behind. The garden door of it was open, and after he had carefully locked his box in its official place, he stood for a few seconds at the open door looking out upon the garden. A sharp moon was fighting with the flying rags and tatters of a storm, and Valentin regarded it with a wistfulness unusual in such scientific natures as his. Perhaps such scientific natures have some psychic prevision of the most tremendous problem of their lives. From any such occult mood, at least, he quickly recovered, for he knew he was late and that his guests had already begun to arrive. A glance at his drawing-room when he entered it was enough to make certain that his principal guest was not there, at any rate. He saw all the other pillars of the little party: he saw Lord Galloway, the English Ambassador—a choleric old man with a russet face like an apple, wearing the blue ribbon of the Garter. He saw Lady Galloway, slim and thread-like, with silver hair and a face sensitive and superior. He saw her daughter, Lady Margaret Graham, a pale and pretty girl with an elfish face and copper-coloured hair. He saw the Duchess of Mont St. Michel, black-eyed and opulent, and with her her two daughters, black-eyed and opulent also. He saw Dr. Simon, a typical French scientist, with glasses, a pointed brown beard, and a forehead barred with those parallel wrinkles which are the penalty of superciliousness, since they come through constantly elevating the eyebrows. He saw Father Brown of Cobhole, in Essex, whom he had recently met in England. He saw—perhaps with more interest than any of those— a tall man in uniform, who had bowed to the Galloways without receiving any very hearty acknowledgment, and who now advanced alone to pay his respects to his host. This was Commandant O'Brien, of the French Foreign Legion. He was a slim yet somewhat swaggering figure, clean-shaven, dark-haired, and blue-eyed, and as seemed natural in an officer of that famous regiment of victorious failures and successful suicides, he had an air at once dashing and melancholy. He was by birth an Irish gentleman, and in boyhood had known the Galloways—especially Margaret Graham. He had left his country after some crash of debts, and now expressed his complete freedom from British etiquette by swinging about in uniform, sabre and spurs. When he bowed to the Ambassador's family, Lord and Lady Galloway bent stiffly, and Lady Margaret looked away.

But for whatever old causes such people might be interested in each other, their distinguished host was not specially interested in them. No one of them at least was in his eyes the guest of the evening. Valentin was expecting, for special reasons, a man of world-wide fame, whose friendship he had secured during some of his great detective tours and triumphs in the United States. He was expecting Julius K. Brayne, that multi-millionaire whose colossal and even crushing endowments of small religions have occasioned so much easy sport and easier solemnity for the American and English papers. Nobody could quite make out whether Mr. Brayne was an atheist or a Mormon, or a Christian Scientist; but he was ready to pour money into any intellectual vessel, so long as it was an untried vessel. One of his hobbies was to wait for the American Shakespeare—a hobby more patient than angling. he admired Walt Whitman, but thought that Luke P. Tanner, of Paris, Pa., was more "progressive" than Whitman any day. He liked anything that he thought "progressive." He thought Valentin "progressive," thereby doing him a grave injustice.

The solid appearance of Julius K. Brayne in the room was as decisive as a dinner bell. He had this great quality, which very few of us can claim, that his presence was as big as his absence. He was a huge fellow, as fat as he was tall, clad in complete evening black, without so much relief as a watch-chain or a ring. His hair was white and well brushed back like a German's; his face was red, fierce and cherubic, with one dark tuft under the lower lip that threw up that otherwise infantile visage with an effect theatrical and even Mephistophelean. Not long, however, did that *salon* merely stare at the celebrated American; his lateness had already become a domestic problem, and he was sent with all speed into the dining-room with Lady Galloway upon his arm.

Except on one point the Galloways were genial and casual enough. So long as Lady Margaret did not take the arm of that adventurer O'Brien her father was quite satisfied; and she had not done so; she had decorously gone in with Dr. Simon. Nevertheless, old Lord Galloway was restless and almost rude. He was diplomatic enough during dinner, but when, over the cigars, three of the younger men—Simon the doctor, Brown the priest, and the detrimental O'Brien, the exile in a foreign uniform—all melted away to mix with the ladies or smoke in the conservatory, then the English diplomatist grew very undiplomatic indeed. He was stung every sixty seconds with the thought that the scamp O'Brien might be signalling to Margaret somehow; he did not attempt to imagine how. He was left over the coffee with Brayne, the hoary Yankee who believed in all religions, and Valentin, the grizzled Frenchman who believed in none. They could argue with each other, but neither could appeal to him. After a time this "progressive" logomachy had reached a crisis of tedium; Lord Galloway got up also and sought the drawing-room. He lost his way in long passages for some six or eight minutes: till he heard the high-pitched, didactic voice of the doctor, and then the dull voice of the priest, followed by general laughter. They also, he thought with a curse, were probably arguing about "science and religion." But the instant he opened the *salon* door he saw only one thing—he saw what was not there. He saw that Commandant O'Brien was absent, and that Lady Margaret was absent, too.

Rising impatiently from the drawing-room, as he had from the dining-room, he stamped along the passage once more. His notion of protecting his daughter from the Irish-Algerian ne'er-do-well had become something central and even mad in his mind. As he went towards the back of the house, where was Valentin's study, he was surprised to meet his daughter, who swept past with a white, scornful face, which was a second enigma. If she had been with O'Brien, where was O'Brien? If she had not been with O'Brien, where had she been? With a sort of senile and passionate suspicion he groped his way to the dark back parts of the mansion, and eventually found a servants' entrance that opened on to the garden. The moon with her scimitar had now ripped up and rolled away all the storm-wrack. The argent light lit up all four corners of the garden. A tall figure in blue was striding across the lawn towards the study door; a glint of moonlit silver on his facings picked him out as Commandant O'Brien.

He vanished through the French windows into the house, leaving Lord Galloway in an indescribable temper, at once virulent and vague. The blue-and-silver garden, like a scene in a theatre, seemed to taunt him with all that tyrannic tenderness against which his worldly authority was at war. The length and grace of the Irishman's stride enraged him as if he were a rival instead of a father; the moonlight maddened him. He was trapped as if by magic into a garden of troubadours, a Watteau fairyland; and, willing to shake off such amorous imbecilities by speech, he stepped briskly after his enemy. As he did so he tripped over some tree or stone in the grass; looked down at it first with irritation and then a second time with curiosity. The next instant the moon and the tall poplars looked at an unusual sight—an elderly English diplomatist running hard and crying or bellowing as he ran.

His hoarse shouts brought a pale face to the study door, the beaming glasses and worried brow of Dr. Simon, who heard the nobleman's first clear words. Lord Galloway was crying: "A corpse in the grass—a blood-stained corpse." O'Brien at least had gone utterly from his mind.

"We must tell Valentin at once," said the doctor, when the other had brokenly described all that he had dared to examine. "It is fortunate that he is here;" and even as he spoke the great detective entered the study, attracted by the cry. It was almost amusing to note his typical transformation; he had come with the common concern of a host and a gentleman, fearing that some guest or servant was ill. When he was told the gory fact, he turned with all his gravity instantly bright and business-like; for this, however abrupt and awful, was his business.

"Strange, gentlemen," he said, as they hurried out into the garden, "that I should have hunted mysteries all over the earth, and now one comes and settles in my own backyard. But where is the place?" They crossed the lawn less easily, as a slight mist had begun to rise from the river; but under the guidance of the shaken Galloway they found the body sunken in deep grass—the body of a very tall and broad-shouldered man. He lay face downwards, so they could only see that his big shoulders were clad in black cloth, and that his big head was bald, except for a wisp or two of brown hair that clung to his skull like wet seaweed. A scarlet serpent of blood crawled from under his fallen face.

"At least," said Simon, with a deep and singular intonation, "he is none of our party."

"Examine him, doctor," cried Valentin rather sharply. "He may not be dead."

The doctor bent down. "He is not quite cold, but I am afraid he is dead enough," he answered. "Just help me to lift him up."

They lifted him carefully an inch from the ground, and all doubts as to his being really dead were settled at once and frightfully. The head fell away. It had been entirely sundered from the body; whoever had cut his throat had managed to sever the neck as well. Even Valentin was slightly shocked. "He must have been as strong as a gorilla," he muttered.

Not without a shiver, though he was used to anatomical abortions, Dr. Simon lifted the head. It was slightly slashed about the neck and jaw, but the face was substantially unhurt. It was a ponderous, yellow face, at once sunken and swollen, with a hawk-like nose and heavy lids—the face of a wicked Roman emperor, with, perhaps, a distant touch of a Chinese emperor. All present seemed to look at it with the coldest eye of ignorance. Nothing else could be noted about the man except that, as they had lifted his body, they had seen underneath it the white gleam of a shirtfront defaced with a red gleam of blood. As Dr. Simon said, the man had never been of their party. But he might very well have been trying to join it, for he had come dressed for such an occasion.

Valentin went down on his hands and knees and examined with his closest professional attention the grass and ground for some twenty yards round the body, in which he was assisted less skillfully by the doctor, and quite vaguely by the English lord. Nothing rewarded their grovellings except a few twigs, snapped or chopped into very small lengths, which Valentin lifted for an instant's examination, and then tossed away.

"Twigs," he said gravely; "twigs, and a total stranger with his head cut off; that is all there is on this lawn."

There was an almost creepy stillness, and then the unnerved Galloway called out sharply:

"Who's that? Who's that over there by the garden wall?"

A small figure with a foolishly large head drew waveringly near them in the moonlit haze; looked for an instant like a goblin, but turned out to be the harmless little priest whom they had left in the drawing-room.

"I say," he said meekly, "there are no gates to this garden, do you know."

Valentin's black brows had come together somewhat crossly, as they did on principle at the sight of the cassock. But he was far too just a man to deny the relevance of the remark. "You are right," he said. "Before we find out how he came to be killed, we may have to find out how he came to be here. Now listen to me, gentlemen. If it can be done without prejudice to my position and duty, we shall all agree that certain distinguished names might well be kept out of this. There are ladies, gentlemen, and there is a foreign ambassador. If we must mark it down as a crime, then it must be followed up as a crime. But till then I can use my own discretion. I am the head of the police; I am so public that I can afford to be private. Please Heaven, I will clear every one of my own guests before I call in my men to look for anybody else. Gentlemen, upon your honour, you will none of you leave the house till to-morrow at noon; there are bedrooms for all. Simon, I think you know where to find my man, Ivan, in the front hall; he is a confidential man. Tell him to leave another servant on guard and come to me at once. Lord Galloway, you are certainly the best person to tell the ladies what has happened, and prevent a panic. They also must stay. Father Brown and I will remain with the body."

When this spirit of the captain spoke in Valentin he was obeyed like a bugle. Dr. Simon went through to the armoury and routed out Ivan, the public detective's private detective. Galloway went to the drawing-room and told the terrible news tactfully enough, so that by the time the company assembled there the ladies were already startled and already soothed. Meanwhile the good priest and the good atheist stood at the head and foot of the dead man motionless in the moonlight, like symbolic statues of their two philosophies of death.

Ivan, the confidential man with the scar and the moustaches, came out of the house like a cannon ball, and came racing across the lawn to Valentin like a dog to his master. His livid face was quite lively with the glow of this domestic detective story, and it was with almost unpleasant eagerness that he asked his master's permission to examine the remains.

"Yes; look, if you like, Ivan," said Valentin, "but don't be long. We must go in and thrash this out in the house."

Ivan lifted his head, and then almost let it drop.

"Why," he gasped, "it's—no, it isn't; it can't be. Do you know this man, sir?"

"No," said Valentin indifferently; "we had better go inside."

Between them they carried the corpse to a sofa in the study, and then all made their way to the drawing-room.

The detective sat down at a desk quietly, and even with hesitation; but his eye was the iron eye of a judge at assize. He made a few rapid notes upon paper in front of him, and then said shortly: "Is everybody here?"

"Not Mr. Brayne," said the Duchess of Mont St. Michel, looking round.

"No," said Lord Galloway, in a hoarse, harsh voice. "And not Mr. Neil O'Brien, I fancy. I saw that gentleman walking in the garden when the corpse was still warm."

"Ivan," said the detective, "go and fetch Commandant O'Brien and Mr. Brayne. Mr. Brayne, I know, is finishing a cigar in the dining-room; Commandant O'Brien, I think, is walking up and down the conservatory. I am not sure."

The faithful attendant flashed from the room, and before anyone could stir or speak Valentin went on with the same soldierly swiftness of exposition.

"Everyone here knows that a dead man has been found in the garden, his head cut clean from his body. Dr. Simon, you have examined it. Do you think that to cut a man's throat like that would need great force? Or, perhaps, only a very sharp knife?"

"I should say that it could not be done with a knife at all," said the pale doctor.

"Have you any thought," resumed Valentin, "of a tool with which it could be done?"

"Speaking within modern probabilities, I really haven't," said the doctor, arching his painful brows. "It's not easy to hack a neck through even clumsily, and this was a very clean cut. It could be done with a battle-axe or an old headsman's axe, or an old two-handed sword."

"But, good heavens!" cried the Duchess, almost in hysterics; "there aren't any two-handed swords and battle-axes round here."

Valentin was still busy with the paper in front of him. "Tell me" he said, still writing rapidly, "could it have been done with a long French cavalry sabre?"

A low knocking came at the door, which for some unreasonable reason, curdled everyone's blood like the knocking in *Macbeth*. Amid that frozen silence Dr. Simon managed to say: "A sabre—yes, I suppose it could."

"Thank you," said Valentin. "Come in, Ivan."

The confidential Ivan opened the door and ushered in Commandant Neil O'Brien, whom he had found at last pacing the garden again.

The Irish officer stood disordered and defiant on the threshold. "What do you want with me?" he cried.

"Please sit down," said Valentin in pleasant, level tones. "Why, you aren't wearing your sword! Where is it?"

"I left it on the library table," said O'Brien, his brogue deepening in his disturbed mood. "It was a nuisance, it was getting——"

"Ivan," said Valentin: "please go and get the Commandant's sword from the library." Then, as the servant vanished: "Lord Galloway says he saw you leaving the garden just before he found the corpse. What were you doing in the garden?"

The Commandant flung himself recklessly into a chair. "Oh," he cried in pure Irish; "admirin' the moon. Communing with Nature, me boy."

A heavy silence sank and endured, and at the end of it came again that trivial and terrible knocking. Ivan reappeared, carrying an empty steel scabbard. "This is all I can find," he said.

"Put it on the table," said Valentin, without looking up.

There was an inhuman silence in the room, like that sea of inhuman silence round the dock of the condemned murderer. The Duchess's weak exclamations had long ago died away. Lord Galloway's swollen hatred was satisfied and even sobered. The voice that came was quite unexpected.

"I think I can tell you," cried Lady Margaret, in that clear, quivering voice with which a courageous woman speaks publicly. "I can tell you what Mr. O'Brien was doing in the garden, since he is bound to silence. He was asking me to marry him. I refused; I said in my family circumstances I could give him nothing but my respect. He was a little angry at that; he did not seem to think much of my respect. I wonder," she added, with rather a wan smile, "if he will care at all for it now. For I offer it him now. I will swear anywhere that he never did a thing like this."

Lord Galloway had edged up to his daughter, and was intimidating her in what he imagined to be an undertone. "Hold your tongue, Maggie," he said in a thunderous whisper. "Why should you shield the fellow? Where's his sword? Where's his confounded cavalry——"

He stopped because of the singular stare with which his daughter was regarding him, a look that was indeed a lurid magnet for the whole group.

"You old fool!" she said, in a low voice without pretence of piety; "what do you suppose you are trying to prove? I tell you this man was innocent while with me. But if he wasn't innocent, he was still with me. If he murdered a man in the garden, who was it who must have seen—who must at least have known? Do you hate Neil so much as to put your own daughter——"

Lady Galloway screamed. Everyone else sat tingling at the

touch of those satanic tragedies that have been between lovers before now. They saw the proud, white face of the Scotch aristocrat and her lover, the Irish adventurer, like old portraits in a dark house. The long silence was full of formless historical memories of murdered husbands and poisonous paramours.

In the centre of this morbid silence an innocent voice said: "Was it a very long cigar?"

The change of thought was so sharp that they had to look round to see who had spoken.

"I mean," said little Father Brown, from the corner of the room. "I mean that cigar Mr. Brayne is finishing. It seems nearly as long as a walking-stick."

Despite the irrelevance there was assent as well as irritation in Valentin's face as he lifted his head.

"Quite right," he remarked sharply. "Ivan, go and see about Mr. Brayne again, and bring him here at once."

The instant the factotum had closed the door, Valentin addressed the girl with an entirely new earnestness.

"Lady Margaret," he said, "we all feel, I am sure, both gratitude and admiration for your act in rising above your lower dignity and explaining the Commandant's conduct. But there is a hiatus still. Lord Galloway, I understand, met you passing from the study to the drawing-room, and it was only some minutes afterwards that he found the garden and the Commandant still walking there."

"You have to remember," replied Margaret, with a faint irony in her voice, "that I had just refused him, so we should scarcely have come back arm in arm. He is a gentleman, anyhow; and he loitered behind—and so got charged with murder."

"In those few moments," said Valentin gravely, "he might really——"

The knock came again, and Ivan put in his scarred face.

"Beg pardon, sir," he said, "but Mr. Brayne has left the house."

"Left!" cried Valentin, and rose for the first time to his feet.

"Gone. Scooted. Evaporated," replied Ivan, in humorous French. "His hat and coat are gone, too; and I'll tell you something to cap it all. I ran outside the house to find any traces of him, and I found one, and a big trace, too."

"What do you mean?" asked Valentin.

"I'll show you," said his servant, and reappeared with a flashing naked cavalry sabre, streaked with blood about the point and edge. Everyone in the room eyed it as if it were a thunderbolt; but the experienced Ivan went on quite quietly:

"I found this," he said, "flung among the bushes fifty yards up the road to Paris. In other words, I found it just where your respectable Mr. Brayne threw it when he ran away."

There was again a silence, but of a new sort. Valentin took the sabre, examined it, reflected with unaffected concentration of thought, and then turned a respectful face to O'Brien. "Commandant," he said, "we trust you will always produce this weapon if it is wanted for police examination. Meanwhile," he added, slapping the steel back in the ringing scabbard, "let me return you your sword."

At the military symbolism of the action the audience could hardly refrain from applause.

For Neil O'Brien, indeed, that gesture was the turning-point of existence. By the time he was wandering in the mysterious garden again in the colours of the morning the tragic futility of his ordinary mien had fallen from him; he was a man with many reasons for happiness. Lord Galloway was a gentleman, and had offered him an apology. Lady Margaret was something better than a lady, a woman at least, and had perhaps given him something better than an apology, as they drifted among the old flower-beds before breakfast. The whole company was more lighthearted and humane, for though the riddle of the death remained, the load of suspicion was lifted off them all, and sent flying off to Paris with the strange millionaire—a man they hardly knew. The devil was cast out of the house—he had cast himself out.

Still, the riddle remained; and when O'Brien threw himself on a garden seat beside Dr. Simon, that keenly scientific person at once resumed it. He did not get much talk out of O'Brien, whose thoughts were on pleasanter things.

"I can't say it interests me much," said the Irishman frankly, "especially as it seems pretty plain now. Apparently Brayne hated this stranger for some reason; lured him into the garden, and killed him with my sword. Then he fled to the city, tossing the sword away as he went. By the way, Ivan tells me the dead man had a Yankee dollar in his pocket. So he was a countryman of Brayne's, and that seems to clinch it. I don't see any difficulties about the business."

"There are five colossal difficulties," said the doctor quietly; "like high walls within walls. Don't mistake me. I don't doubt that Brayne did it; his flight, I fancy, proves that. But as to how he did it. First difficulty: Why should a man kill another man with a great hulking sabre, when he can almost kill him with a pocket knife and put it back in his pocket? Second difficulty: Why was there no noise or outcry? Does a man commonly see another come up waving a scimitar and offer no remarks? Third difficulty: A servant watched the front door all the evening; and a rat cannot get into Valentin's garden anywhere. How did the dead man get into the garden? Fourth difficulty: Given the same conditions, how did Brayne get out of the garden?"

"And the fifth," said Neil, with eyes fixed on the English priest, who was coming slowly up the path.

"Is a trifle, I suppose," said the doctor, "but I think an odd one. When I first saw how the head had been slashed, I supposed the assassin had struck more than once. But on examination I found many cuts across the truncated section; in other words, they were struck *after* the head was off. Did Brayne hate his foe so fiendishly that he stood sabring his body in the moonlight?"

"Horrible!" said O'Brien, and shuddered.

The little priest, Brown, had arrived while they were talking, and had waited, with characteristic shyness, till they had finished. Then he said awkwardly:

"I say, I'm sorry to interrupt. But I was sent to tell you the news!"

"News?" repeated Simon, and stared at him rather painfully through his glasses.

"Yes, I'm sorry," said Father Brown mildly. "There's been another murder, you know."

Both men on the seat sprang up, leaving it rocking.

"And, what's stranger still," continued the priest, with his dull eyes on the rhododendrons, "it's the same disgusting sort; it's another beheading. They found the second head actually bleeding in the river, a few yards along Brayne's road to Paris; so they suppose that he——"

"Great Heaven!" cried O'Brien. "Is Brayne a monomaniac?"

"There are American vendettas," said the priest impassively. Then he added: "They want you to come to the library and see it."

Commandant O'Brien followed the others towards the inquest, feeling decidedly sick. As a soldier, he loathed all this secretive carnage; where were these extravagant amputations going to stop? First one head was hacked off, and then another; in this case (he told himself bitterly) it was not true that two heads were better than one. As he crossed the study he almost staggered at a shocking coincidence. Upon Valentin's table lay the coloured picture of yet a third bleeding head; and it was the head of Valentin himself. A second glance showed him it was only a Nationalist paper, called *The Guillotine,* which every week showed one of its political opponents with rolling eyes and writhing features just after execution; for Valentin was an anti-clerical of some note. But O'Brien was an Irishman, with a kind of chastity even in his sins; and his gorge rose against that great brutality of the intellect which belongs only to France. He felt Paris as a whole, from the grotesque on the Gothic churches to the gross caricatures in the newspapers. He remembered the gigantic jests of the Revolution. He saw the whole city as one ugly energy, from the sanguinary sketch lying on Valentin's table up to where, above a mountain and forest of gargoyles, the great devil grins on Notre Dame.

The library was long, low, and dark; what light entered it shot from under low blinds and had still some of the ruddy tinge of morning. Valentin and his servant Ivan were waiting for them at the upper end of a long, slightly-sloping desk, on which lay the mortal remains, looking enormous in the twilight. The big black figure and yellow face of the man found in the garden confronted them essentially unchanged. The second head, which had been fished from among the river reeds that morning, lay streaming and dripping beside it; Valentin's men were still seeking to recover the rest of this second corpse, which was supposed to be afloat. Father Brown, who did not seem to share O'Brien's sensibilities in the least, went up to the second head and examined it with his blinking care. It was little more than a mop of wet, white hair, fringed with silver fire in the red and level morning light; the face, which seemed of an ugly, empurpled and perhaps criminal type, had been much battered against trees or stones as it tossed in the water.

"Good morning, Commandant O'Brien," said Valentin, with quiet cordiality. "You have heard of Brayne's last experiment in butchery, I suppose?"

Father Brown was still bending over the head with white hair, and he said, without looking up:

"I suppose it is quite certain that Brayne cut off this head, too."

"Well, it seems common sense," said Valentin, with his hands in his pockets. "Killed in the same way as the other. Found within a few yards of the other. And sliced by the same weapon which we know he carried away."

"Yes, yes; I know," replied Father Brown, submissively. "Yet, you know, I doubt whether Brayne could have cut off this head."

"Why not?" inquired Dr. Simon, with a rational stare.

"Well, doctor," said the priest, looking up blinking, "can a man cut off his own head? I don't know."

O'Brien felt an insane universe crashing about his ears; but the doctor sprang forward with impetuous practicality and pushed back the wet, white hair.

"Oh, there's no doubt it's Brayne," said the priest quietly. "He had exactly that chip in the left ear."

The detective, who had been regarding the priest with steady and glittering eyes, opened his clenched mouth and said sharply: "You seem to know a lot about him, Father Brown."

"I do," said the little man simply. "I've been about with him for some weeks. He was thinking of joining our church."

The star of the fanatic sprang into Valentin's eyes; he strode towards the priest with clenched hands. "And, perhaps," he cried, with a blasting sneer: "perhaps he was also thinking of leaving all his money to your church."

"Perhaps he was," said Brown stolidly; "it is possible."

"In that case," cried Valentin, with a dreadful smile: "you may indeed know a great deal about him. About his life and about his——"

Commandant O'Brien laid a hand on Valentin's arm. "Drop that slanderous rubbish, Valentin," he said: "or there may be more swords yet."

But Valentin (under the steady, humble gaze of the priest) had already recovered himself. "Well," he said shortly: "people's private opinions can wait. You gentlemen are still bound by your promise to stay; you must enforce it on yourselves—and on each other. Ivan here will tell you anything more you want to know; I must get to business and write to the authorities. We can't keep this quiet any longer. I shall be writing in my study if there is any more news."

"Is there any more news, Ivan?" asked Dr. Simon, as the chief of police strode out of the room.

"Only one more thing, I think, sir," said Ivan, wrinkling up his grey old face; "but that's important, too, in its way. There's that old buffer you found on the lawn," and he pointed without pretence of reverence at the big black body with the yellow heard. "We've found out who he is, anyhow."

"Indeed!" cried the astonished doctor; "and who is he?"

"His name was Arnold Becker," said the under-detective, "though he went by many aliases. He was a wandering sort of scamp, and is known to have been in America; so that was where Brayne got his knife into him. We didn't have much to do with him ourselves, for he worked mostly in Germany. We've communicated, of course, with the German police. But, oddly enough, there was a twin brother of his, named Louis Becker, whom we had a great deal to do with. In fact, we found it necessary to guillotine him only yesterday. Well, it's a rum thing, gentlemen, but when I saw that fellow flat on the lawn I had the greatest jump of my life. If I hadn't seen Louis Becker guillotined with my own eyes, I'd have sworn it was Louis Becker lying there in the grass. Then, of course, I remembered his twin brother in Germany, and following up the clue——"

The explanatory Ivan stopped, for the excellent reason that nobody was listening to him. The Commandant and the doctor were both staring at Father Brown, who had sprung stiffly to his feet, and was holding his temples tight like a man in sudden and violent pain.

"Stop, stop, stop!" he cried; "stop talking a minute, for I see half. Will God give me strength? Will my brain make the one jump and see all? Heaven help me! I used to be fairly good at thinking. I could paraphrase any page in Aquinas once. Will my head split—or will it see? I see half—I only see half."

He buried his head in his hands, and stood in a sort of rigid torture of thought or prayer, while the other three could only go on staring at this last prodigy of their wild twelve hours.

When Father Brown's hands fell they showed a face quite fresh and serious, like a child's. He heaved a huge sigh, and said: "Let us get this said and done with as quickly as possible. Look here, this will be the quickest way to convince you all of the truth." He turned to the doctor. "Dr. Simon," he said, "you have a strong head-piece, and I heard you this morning asking the five hardest questions about this business. Well, if you will now ask them again, I will answer them."

Simon's pince-nez dropped from his nose in his doubt and wonder, but he answered at once. "Well, the first question, you know, is why a man should kill another with a clumsy sabre at all when a man can kill with a bodkin?"

"A man cannot behead with a bodkin," said Brown, calmly, "And for *this* murder beheading was absolutely necessary."

"Why?" asked O'Brien, with interest.

"And the next question?" asked Father Brown.

"Well, why didn't the man cry out or anything?" asked the doctor; "sabres in gardens are certainly unusual."

"Twigs," said the priest gloomily, and turned to the window which looked on the scene of death. "No one saw the point of the twigs. Why should they lie on that lawn (look at it) so far from any tree? They were not snapped off; they were chopped off. The murderer occupied his enemy with some tricks with the sabre, showing how he could cut a branch in mid-air, or what not. Then, while his enemy bent down to see the result, a silent slash, and the head fell."

"Well," said the doctor slowly, "that seems plausible enough. But my next two questions will stump anyone."

The priest still stood looking critically out of the window and waited.

"You know how all the garden was sealed up like an air-tight chamber," went on the doctor. "Well, how did the strange man get into the garden?"

Without turning round, the little priest answered: "There never was any strange man in the garden."

There was a silence, and then a sudden cackle of almost childish laughter relieved the strain. The absurdity of Brown's remark moved Ivan to open taunts.

"Oh!" he cried; "then we didn't lug a great fat corpse on to a sofa last night? He hadn't got into the garden, I suppose?"

"Got into the garden?" repeated Brown reflectively. "No, not entirely."

"Hang it all," cried Simon, "a man gets into a garden, or he doesn't."

"Not necessarily," said the priest, with a faint smile. "What is the next question, doctor?"

"I fancy you're ill," exclaimed Dr. Simon sharply; "but I'll ask the next question if you like. How did Brayne get out of the garden?"

"He didn't get out of the garden," said the priest, still looking out of the window.

"Didn't get out of the garden?" exploded Simon.

"Not completely," said Father Brown.

Simon shook his fists in a frenzy of French logic. "A man gets out of a garden, or he doesn't," he cried.

"Not always," said Father Brown.

Dr. Simon sprang to his feet impatiently. "I have no time to spare on such senseless talk," he cried angrily. "If you can't understand a man being on one side of the wall or the other, I won't trouble you further."

"Doctor," said the cleric very gently, "we have always got on very pleasantly together. If only for the sake of old friendship, stop and tell me your fifth question."

The impatient Simon sank into a chair by the door and said briefly: "The head and shoulders were cut about in a queer way. It seemed to be done after death."

"Yes," said the motionless priest, "it was done so as to make you assume exactly the one simple falsehood that you did assume. It was done to make you take for granted that the head belonged to the body."

The borderland of the brain, where all the monsters are made, moved horribly in the Gaelic O'Brien. He felt the chaotic presence of all the horse-men and fish-women that man's unnatural fancy has begotten. A voice older than his first feathers seemed saying in his ear: "Keep out of the monstrous garden where grows the tree with double fruit. Avoid the evil garden where died the man with two heads." Yet, while these shameful symbolic shapes passed across the ancient mirror of his Irish soul, his Frenchified intellect was quite alert, and was watching the odd priest as closely and incredulously as all the rest.

Father Brown had turned round at last, and stood against the window with his face in dense shadow; but even in that shadow they could see it was pale as ashes. Nevertheless, he spoke quite sensibly, as if there were no Gaelic souls on earth.

"Gentlemen," he said; "you did not find the strange body of Becker in the garden. You did not find any strange body in the garden. In face of Dr. Simon's rationalism, I still affirm that Becker was only partly present. Look here!" (pointing to the black bulk of the mysterious corpse); "you never saw that man in your lives. Did you ever see this man?"

He rapidly rolled away the bald-yellow head of the unknown, and put in its place the white-maned head beside it. And there, complete, unified, unmistakable, lay Julius K. Brayne.

"The murderer," went on Brown quietly, "hacked off his enemy's head and flung the sword far over the wall. But he was too clever to fling the sword only. He flung the *head* over the wall also. Then he had only to clap on another head to the corpse, and (as he insisted on a private inquest) you all imagined a totally new man."

"Clap on another head!" said O'Brien, staring. "What other head? Heads don't grow on garden bushes, do they?"

"No," said Father Brown huskily, and looking at his boots; "there is only one place where they grow. They grow in the basket of the guillotine, beside which the Chief of Police, Aristide Valentin, was standing not an hour before the murder. Oh, my friends, hear me a minute more before you tear me in pieces. Valentin is an honest man, if being mad for an arguable cause is honesty. But did you ever see in that cold, grey eye of his that he is mad? He would do anything, *anything,* to break what he calls the superstition of the Cross. He has fought for it and starved for it, and now he has murdered for it. Brayne's crazy millions had hitherto been scattered among so many sects that they did little to alter the balance of things. But Valentin heard a whisper that Brayne, like so many scatter-brained sceptics, was drifting to us; and that was quite a different thing. Brayne would pour supplies into the impoverished and pugnacious Church of France; he would support six Nationalist newspapers like *The Guillotine*. The battle was already balanced on a point, and the fanatic took flame at the risk. He resolved to destroy the millionaire, and he did it as one would expect the greatest of detectives to commit his only crime. He abstracted the severed head of Becker on some criminological excuse, and took it home in his official box. He had that last argument with Brayne, that Lord Galloway did not hear the end of; that failing, he led him out into the sealed garden, talked about swordsmanship, used twigs and a sabre for illustration, and——"

Ivan of the Scar sprang up. "You lunatic," he yelled; "you'll go to my master now, if I take you by——"

"Why, I was going there," said Brown heavily; "I must ask him to confess, and all that."

Driving the unhappy Brown before them like a hostage or sacrifice, they rushed together into the sudden stillness of Valentin's study.

The great detective sat at his desk apparently too occupied to hear their turbulent entrance. They paused a moment, and then something in the look of that upright and elegant back made the doctor run forward suddenly. A touch and a glance showed him that there was a small box of pills at Valentin's elbow, and that Valentin was dead in his chair; and on the blind face of the suicide was more than the pride of Cato.

DOROTHY L. SAYERS

(1893–1957)

Dorothy Leigh Sayers was a forceful and opinionated figure in the Detection Club and the golden age of mystery in the 1930s. She grew up in Oxford and East Anglia, taught in Yorkshire, and worked in France and London, meticulously using the atmosphere and details of those settings in her best work. Scenes from her detective Lord Peter Wimsey's cases in the Bloomsbury district of London, Oxford, and other locations can be readily identified. Churches, streets, buildings, even the common surnames of the area are incorporated in the stories. One of the greatest detective characters, Wimsey is firmly in the tradition of Sherlock Holmes, the intellectual gentleman detective with more than a few personal foibles. Many critics credit Sayers in her later Wimsey writings with pushing crime writing away from its obsession with puzzles toward a more literary interest in character, with the psychology of motive becoming more significant than the mathematics of means and opportunity. She even gave Wimsey a love interest in Harriet Vane and had them marry, something very unusual in the classic detective story. Like Holmes's creator, Sayers aspired to a more significant literary form and grew tired of her creation. In the last twenty years of her life, she almost entirely abandoned Lord Peter in order to write on religious subjects. Although she is usually grouped with Agatha Christie, Margery Allingham, and other golden age "cozy" writers and although she criticized the trend toward sensationalism in the American detective story, her own stories are often startling in their ingenious grotesqueness. In one novel the victim is killed by the pealing of bells. In another story a man wills his heir his entire alimentary canal, from throat to rectum. In the following selection, Lord Peter attends an eccentric Christmas feast. One of the guests, of course, is up to no good, and it is up to Wimsey to winnow the criminal from the guest list.

THE NECKLACE OF PEARLS

Sir Septimus Shale was accustomed to assert his authority once in the year and once only. He allowed his young and fashionable wife to fill his house with diagrammatic furniture made of steel; to collect advanced artists and anti-grammatical poets; to believe in cocktails and relativity and to dress as extravagantly as she pleased; but he did insist on an old-fashioned Christmas. He was a simple-hearted man, who really liked plum-pudding and cracker mottoes, and he could not get it out of his head that other people, "at bottom," enjoyed these things also. At Christmas, therefore, he firmly retired to his country house in Essex, called in the servants to hang holly and mistletoe upon the cubist electric fittings; loaded the steel sideboard with delicacies from Fortnum & Mason; hung up stockings at the heads of the polished walnut bedsteads; and even, on this occasion only, had the electric radiators removed from the modernist grates and installed wood fires and a Yule log. He then gathered his family and friends about him, filled them with as much Dickensian good fare as he could persuade them to swallow, and, after their Christmas dinner, set them down to play "Charades" and "Clumps" and "Animal, Vegetable, and Mineral" in the drawing-room, concluding these diversions by "Hide-and-Seek" in the dark all over the house. Because Sir Septimus was a very rich man, his guests fell in with this invariable programme, and if they were bored, they did not tell him so.

Another charming and traditional custom which he followed was that of presenting to his daughter Margharita a pearl on each successive birthday—this anniversary happening to coincide with Christmas Eve. The pearls now numbered twenty, and the collection was beginning to enjoy a certain celebrity, and had been photographed in the Society papers. Though not sensationally large—each one being about the size of a marrow-fat pea—the pearls were of very great value. They were of exquisite colour and perfect shape and matched to a hair's-weight. On this particular Christmas Eve, the presentation of the twenty-first pearl had been the occasion of a very special ceremony. There was a dance and there were speeches. On the Christmas night following, the more restricted family party took place, with the turkey and the Victorian games. There were eleven guests, in addition to Sir Septimus and Lady Shale and their daughter, nearly all related or connected to them in some way: John Shale, a brother, with his wife and their son and daughter Henry and Betty; Betty's fiancé, Oswald Truegood, a young man with parliamentary ambitions; George Comphrey, a cousin of Lady Shale's, aged about thirty and known as a man about town; Lavinia Prescott, asked on George's account; Joyce Trivett, asked on Henry Shale's account; Richard and Beryl Dennison, distant relations of Lady Shale, who lived a gay and expensive life in town on nobody precisely knew what resources; and Lord Peter Wimsey, asked, in a touching spirit of unreasonable hope, on Margharita's account. There were also, of course, William Norgate, secretary to Sir Septimus, and Miss Tomkins, secretary to Lady Shale, who had to be there because, without their calm efficiency, the Christmas arrangements could not have been carried through.

Dinner was over—a seemingly endless succession of soup, fish, turkey, roast beef, plum-pudding, mince-pies, crystallized fruit, nuts, and five kinds of wine, presided over by Sir Septimus, all smiles, by Lady Shale, all mocking deprecation, and by Margharita, pretty and bored, with the necklace of twenty-one pearls gleaming softly on her slender throat. Gorged and dyspeptic and longing only for the horizontal position, the company had been shepherded into the drawing-room and set to play "Musical Chairs" (Miss Tomkins at the piano), "Hunt the Slipper" (slipper provided by Miss Tomkins), and "Dumb Crambo" (costumes by Miss Tomkins and Mr. William Norgate). The back drawing-room (for Sir Septimus clung to these old-fashioned names) provided an admirable dressing-room, being screened by folding doors from the large drawing-room in which the audience sat on aluminum chairs, scrabbling uneasy toes on a floor of black glass under the tremendous illumination of electricity reflected from a brass ceiling.

It was William Norgate who, after taking the temperature of the meeting, suggested to Lady Shale that they should play at something less athletic. Lady Shale agreed and, as usual, suggested bridge. Sir Septimus, as usual, blew the suggestion aside.

"Bridge? Nonsense! Nonsense! Play bridge every day of your lives. This is Christmas time. Something we can all play together. How about 'Animal, Vegetable, and Mineral?' "

This intellectual pastime was a favourite with Sir Septimus; he was rather good at putting pregnant questions. After a brief discussion, it became evident that this game was an inevitable part of the programme. The party settled down to it, Sir Septimus undertaking to "go out" first and set the thing going.

Presently they had guessed among other things Miss Tomkins's mother's photograph, a gramophone record of "I want to be happy" (much scientific research into the exact composition of records, settled by William Norgate out of the *Encyclopaedia Britannica*), the smallest stickleback in the stream at the bottom of the garden, the new planet Pluto, the scarf worn by Mrs. Dennison (very confusing, because it was not silk, which would be animal, or artificial silk, which would be vegetable, but made of spun glass—mineral, a very clever choice of subject), and had failed to guess the Prime Minister's wireless speech—which was voted not fair, since nobody could decide whether it was animal by nature or a kind of gas. It was decided that they should do one more word and then go on to "Hide-and-Seek." Oswald Truegood had retired into the back room and shut the door behind him while the party discussed the next subject of examination, when suddenly Sir Septimus broke in on the argument by calling to his daughter:

"Hullo, Margy! What have you done with your necklace?"

"I took it off, Dad, because I thought it might get broken in 'Dumb Crambo.' It's over here on this table. No, it isn't. Did you take it, mother?"

"No, I didn't. If I'd seen it, I should have. You are a careless child."

Sir Septimus denied the accusation with some energy. Everybody got up and began to hunt about. There were not many places in that bare and polished room where a necklace could be hidden. After ten minutes' fruitless investigation, Richard Dennison, who had been seated next to the table where the pearls had been placed, began to look rather uncomfortable.

"Awkward, you know," he remarked to Wimsey.

At this moment, Oswald Truegood put his head through the folding-doors and asked whether they hadn't settled on something by now, because he was getting the fidgets.

This directed the attention of the searchers to the inner room. Margharita must have been mistaken. She had taken it in there, and it had got mixed up with the dressing-up clothes somehow. The room was ransacked. Everything was lifted up and shaken. The thing began to look serious. After half an hour of desperate energy it became apparent that the pearls were nowhere to be found.

"They must be somewhere in these two rooms, you know," said Wimsey. "The back drawing-room has no door and nobody could have gone out of the front drawing-room without being seen. Unless the windows—"

No. The windows were all guarded on the outside by heavy shutters which it needed two footmen to take down and replace. The pearls had not gone out that way. In fact, the mere suggestion that they had left the drawing-room at all was disagreeable. Because—because—

It was William Norgate, efficient as ever, who coldly and boldly, faced the issue.

"I think, Sir Septimus, it would be a relief to the minds of everybody present if we could all be searched."

Sir Septimus was horrified, but the guests, having found a leader, backed up Norgate. The door was locked, and the search was conducted—the ladies in the inner room and the men in the outer.

Nothing resulted from it except some very interesting information about the belongings habitually carried about by the average man and woman. It was natural that Lord Peter Wimsey should possess a pair of forceps, a pocket lens, and a small folding foot-rule—was he not a Sherlock Holmes in high life? But that Oswald Truegood should have two liver-pills in a screw of paper and Henry Shale a pocket edition of *The Odes of Horace* was unexpected. Why did John Shale distend the pockets of his dress-suit with a stump of red sealing-wax, an ugly little mascot, and a five-shilling piece? George Comphrey had a pair of folding scissors, and three wrapped lumps of sugar, of the sort served in restaurants and dining-cars—evidence of a not uncommon form of kleptomania; but that the tidy and exact Norgate should burden himself with a reel of white cotton, three separate lengths of string, and twelve safety-pins on a card seemed really remarkable till one remembered that he had superintended all the Christmas decorations. Richard Dennison, amid some confusion and laughter, was found to cherish a lady's garter, a powder-compact, and half a potato; the last-named, he said, was a prophylactic against rheumatism (to which he was subject), while the other objects belonged to his wife. On the ladies' side, the more striking exhibits were a little book on palmistry, three invisible hair-pins, and a baby's photograph (Miss Tomkins); a Chinese trick cigarette-case with a secret compartment (Beryl Dennison); a *very* private letter and an outfit for mending stocking-ladders (Lavinia Prescott); and a pair of eyebrow tweezers and a small packet of white powder, said to be for headaches (Betty Shale). An agitating moment followed the production from Joyce Trivett's handbag of a small string of pearls—but it was promptly remembered that these had come out of one of the crackers at dinner-time, and they were, in fact, synthetic. In short, the search was unproductive of anything beyond a general shamefacedness and the discomfort always produced by undressing and re-dressing in a hurry at the wrong time of the day.

It was then that somebody, very grudgingly and haltingly, mentioned the horrid word "Police". Sir Septimus, naturally, was appalled by the idea. It was disgusting. He would not allow it. The pearls must be somewhere. They must search the rooms again. Could not Lord Peter Wimsey, with his experience of—er—mysterious happenings, do something to assist them?

"Eh?" said his lordship. "Oh, by Jove, yes—by all means, certainly. That is to say, provided nobody supposes—eh, what? I mean to say, you don't know that I'm not a suspicious character, do you, what?"

Lady Shale interposed with authority.

"We don't think *anybody* ought to be suspected," she said, "but, if we did, we'd know it couldn't be you. You know *far* too much about crimes to want to commit one."

"All right," said Wimsey. "But after the way the place has been gone over—" He shrugged his shoulders.

"Yes, I'm afraid you won't be able to find any footprints," said Margharita. "But we may have overlooked something."

Wimsey nodded.

"I'll try. Do you all mind sitting down on your chairs in the outer room and staying there. All except one of you—I'd better have a witness to anything I do or find. Sir Septimus—you'd be the best person, I think."

He shepherded them to their places and began a slow circuit of the two rooms, exploring every surface, gazing up to the polished brazen ceiling, and crawling on hands and knees in the approved fashion across the black and shining desert of the floors. Sir Septimus followed, staring when Wimsey stared, bending with his hands upon his knees when Wimsey crawled, and puffing at intervals with astonishment and chagrin. Their progress rather resembled that of a man taking out a very inquisitive puppy for a very leisurely constitutional. Fortunately, Lady Shale's taste in furnishing made investigation easier; there were scarcely any nooks or corners where anything could be concealed.

They reached the inner drawing-room, and here the dressing-up clothes were again minutely examined, but without result. Finally, Wimsey lay down flat on his stomach to squint under a steel cabinet which was one of the very few pieces of furniture with possessed short legs. Something about it seemed to catch his attention. He rolled up his sleeve and plunged his arm into the cavity, kicked convulsively in the effort to reach farther than was humanly possible, pulled out from his pocket and extended his folding foot–rule, fished with it under the cabinet, and eventually succeeded in extracting what he sought.

It was a very minute object—in fact, a pin. Not an ordinary pin, but one resembling those used by entomologists to impale extremely small moths on the setting-board. It was about three-quarters of an inch in length, as fine as a very fine needle, with a sharp point and a particularly small head.

"Bless my soul!" said Sir Septimus. "What's that?"

"Does anybody here happen to collect moths or beetles or anything?" asked Wimsey, squatting on his haunches and examining the pin.

"I'm pretty sure they don't," replied Sir Septimus. "I'll ask them."

"Don't do that." Wimsey bent his head and stared at the floor, from which his own face stared meditatively back at him.

"I see," said Wimsey presently. "That's how it was done. All right, Sir Septimus. I know where the pearls are, but I don't know who took them. Perhaps it would be as well—for everybody's satisfaction—just to find out. In the meantime they are perfectly safe. Don't tell anyone that we've found this pin or that we've discovered anything. Send all these people to bed. Lock the drawing-room door and keep the key, and we'll get our man—or woman—by breakfast-time."

"God bless my soul," said Sir Septimus, very much puzzled.

Lord Peter Wimsey kept careful watch that night upon the drawing-room door. Nobody, however, came near it. Either the thief suspected a trap or he felt confident that any time would do to recover the pearls. Wimsey, however, did not feel that he was wasting his time. He was making a list of people who had been left alone in the back drawing-room during the playing of "Animal, Vegetable, and Mineral." The list ran as follows:

Sir Septimus Shale
Lavinia Prescott
William Norgate
Joyce Trivett and Henry Shale (together, because they had claimed to be incapable of guessing anything unaided)
Mrs. Dennison
Betty Shale
George Comphrey
Richard Dennison
Miss Tomkins
Oswald Truegood

He also made out a list of the persons to whom pearls might be useful or desirable. Unfortunately, this list agreed in almost all respects with the first (always excepting Sir Septimus) and so was not very helpful. The two secretaries had both come well recommended, but that was exactly what they would have done had they come with ulterior designs; the Dennisons were notorious livers from hand to mouth; Betty Shale carried mysterious white powders in her handbag, and was known to be in with a rather rapid set in town; Henry was a harmless dilettante, but Joyce Trivett could twist him round her little finger and was what Jane Austen liked to call "expensive and dissipated;" Comphrey speculated; Oswald Truegood was rather frequently present at Epsom and Newmarket—the search for motives was only too fatally easy.

When the second housemaid and the under-footman appeared in the passage with household implements, Wimsey abandoned his vigil, but he was down early to breakfast. Sir Septimus with his wife and daughter were down before him, and a certain air of tension made itself felt. Wimsey, standing on the hearth before the fire, made conversation about the weather and politics.

The party assembled gradually, but, as though by common consent, nothing was said about pearls until after breakfast, when Oswald Truegood took the bull by the horns.

"Well now!" said he. "How's the detective getting along? Got your man, Wimsey?"

"Not yet," said Wimsey easily.

Sir Septimus, looking at Wimsey as though for his cue, cleared his throat and dashed into speech.

"All very tiresome" he said, "All very unpleasant. Hr'rm. Nothing for it but the police, I'm afraid. Just at Christmas, too. Hr'rm. Spoilt the party. Can't stand seeing all this stuff about the place." He waved his hand towards the festoons of evergreens and coloured paper that adorned the walls. "Take it all down, eh, what? No heart in it. Hr'rm. Burn the lot."

"What a pity, when we worked so hard over it," said Joyce.

"Oh, leave it, Uncle," said Henry Shale. "You're bothering too much about the pearls. They're sure to turn up."

"Shall I ring for James?" suggested William Norgate.

"No," interrupted Comphrey, "let's do it ourselves. It'll give us something to do and take our minds off our troubles."

"That's right," said Sir Septimus. "Start right away. Hate the sight of it."

He savagely hauled a great branch of holly down from the mantelpiece and flung it, crackling, into the fire.

"That's the stuff," said Richard Dennison. "Make a good old blaze!" He leapt up from the table and snatched the mistletoe from the chandelier. "Here goes! One more kiss for somebody before it's too late."

"Isn't it unlucky to take it down before the New Year?" suggested Miss Tomkins.

"Unlucky be hanged. We'll have it all down. Off the stairs and out of the drawing-room too. Somebody go and collect it."

"Isn't the drawing-room locked?" asked Oswald.

"No. Lord Peter says the pearls aren't there, wherever else they are, so it's unlocked. That's right, isn't it, Wimsey?"

"Quite right. The pearls were taken out of these rooms. I can't tell yet how, but I'm positive of it. In fact, I'll pledge my reputation that wherever they are, they're not up there."

"Oh, well," said Comphrey, "in that case, have at it! Come along, Lavinia—you and Dennison do the drawing-room and I'll do the back room. We'll have a race."

"But if the police are coming in," said Dennison, "oughtn't everything to be left just as it is?"

"Damn the police!" shouted Sir Septimus. "They don't want evergreens."

Oswald and Margharita were already pulling the holly and ivy from the staircase, amid peals of laughter. The party dispersed. Wimsey went quietly upstairs and into the drawing-room, where the work of demolition was taking place at a great rate, George having bet the other two ten shillings to a tanner that they would not finish their part of the job before he finished his.

"You mustn't help," said Lavinia, laughing to Wimsey. "It wouldn't be fair."

Wimsey said nothing, but waited till the room was clear. Then he followed them down again to the hall, where the fire was sending up a great roaring and spluttering, suggestive of Guy Fawkes' night. He whispered to Sir Septimus, who went forward and touched George Comphrey on the shoulder.

"Lord Peter wants to say something to you, my boy," he said.

Comphrey started and went with him a little reluctantly, as it seemed. He was not looking very well.

"Mr. Comphrey," said Wimsey, "I fancy these are some of your property." He held out the palm of his hand, in which rested twenty-two fine, small-headed pins.

"Ingenious," said Wimsey, "but something less ingenious would have served his turn better. It was very unlucky, Sir Septimus, that you should have mentioned the pearls when you did. Of course, he hoped that the loss wouldn't be discovered till we'd chucked guessing games and taken to 'Hide-and-Seek.' Then the pearls might have been anywhere in the house, we shouldn't have locked the drawing-room door, and he could have recovered them at his leisure. He had had this possibility in his mind when he came here, obviously, and that was why he brought the pins, and Miss Shale's taking off the necklace to play 'Dumb Crambo' gave him his opportunity.

"He had spent Christmas here before, and knew perfectly well that 'Animal, Vegetable, and Mineral' would form part of the entertainment. He had only to gather up the necklace from the table when it came to his turn to retire, and he knew he could count on at least five minutes by himself while we were all arguing about the choice of a word. He had only to snip the pearls from the string with his pocket-scissors, burn the string in the grate, and fasten the pearls to the mistletoe with the fine pins. The mistletoe was hung on the chandelier, pretty high—it's a lofty room—but he could easily reach it by standing on the glass table, which wouldn't show footmarks, and it was almost certain that nobody would think of examining the mistletoe for extra berries. I shouldn't have thought of it myself if I hadn't found that pin which he had dropped. That gave me the idea that the pearls had been separated and the rest was easy. I took the pearls off the mistletoe last night—the clasp was there, too, pinned among the holly-leaves. Here they are. Comphrey must have got a nasty shock this morning. I knew he was our man when he suggested that the guests should tackle the decorations themselves and that he should do the back drawing-room—but I wish I had seen his face when he came to the mistletoe and found the pearls gone."

"And you worked it all out when you found the pin?" said Sir Septimus.

"Yes; I knew then where the pearls had gone to."

"But you never even looked at the mistletoe."

"I saw it reflected in the black glass floor, and it struck me then how much the mistletoe berries looked like pearls."

DASHIELL HAMMETT

(1894–1961)

Samuel Dashiell Hammett was born in Maryland and, like Raymond Chandler (the writer to whom he is most often linked), had various occupations before becoming a writer. His popular reputation rests primarily upon the novels The Maltese Falcon *(1930) and the influential (if less critically respected)* The Thin Man *(1934), though* Red Harvest *(1929),* The Glass Key *(1931), and his short stories have had many critical enthusiasts. In total he wrote only six novels. One view is that he wasted his considerable talent working in Hollywood as a screenwriter, only to be blacklisted and jailed for contempt of Congress when he refused to inform on suspected Communists during the 1950s. Another view is that a writer who has changed the history of his genre can hardly be termed a failure, no matter how little he produced. The importance of Hammett and the lesser-known founders of the "hard-boiled" school is that they invented a new way to tell detective stories, in a distinctly American idiom. Until the hard-boiled style's decline into repetitive parody of itself in the 1950s, it was also distinctively realistic. Hammett's prose style is blunt and powerful, reflecting the language he learned on the streets in his experiences as a Pinkerton detective. The terseness of* The Maltese Falcon *is often compared to the distinct modern style Ernest Hemingway developed, and the character Sam Spade has many traits that link him to the tradition of the antihero. Intellectuals such as Robert Graves and André Gide admired Hammett's work. While helping to create a new school of American crime writing, Hammett remained attracted to the more conventional detective story. The following story uses the traditional devices of the mansion fully stocked with potentially murderous heirs, hidden clues, and the criminal's trickery. The style, however, almost makes one overlook these standard elements.*

THEY CAN ONLY HANG YOU ONCE

Samuel Spade said, "My name is Ronald Ames. I want to see Mr. Binnett—Mr. Timothy Binnett."

"Mr. Binnett is resting now, sir," the butler replied hesitantly.

"Will you find out when I can see him? It's important." Spade cleared his throat. "I'm—uh—just back from Australia, and it's about some of his properties there."

The butler turned on his heel while saying, "I'll see, sir," and was going up the front stairs before he had finished speaking.

Spade made and lit a cigarette.

The butler came downstairs again.

"I'm sorry; he can't be disturbed now, but Mr. Wallace Binnett—Mr. Timothy's nephew—will see you."

Spade said, "Thanks," and followed the butler upstairs.

Wallace Binnett was a slender, handsome, dark man of about Spade's age—thirty-eight—who rose smiling from a brocaded chair, said, "How do you do, Mr. Ames?" waved his hand at another chair, and sat down again. "You're from Australia?"

"Got in this morning."

"You're a business associate of Uncle Tim's?"

Spade smiled and shook his head. "Hardly that, but I've some information I think he ought to have—quick."

Wallace Binnett looked thoughtfully at the floor, then up at Spade. "I'll do my best to persuade him to see you, Mr. Ames, but, frankly, I don't know."

Spade seemed mildly surprised. "Why?"

Binnett shrugged. "He's peculiar sometimes. Understand, his mind seems perfectly all right, but he has the testiness and eccentricity of an old man in ill health and—well—at times he can be difficult."

Spade asked slowly, "He's already refused to see me?"

"Yes."

Spade rose from his chair. His blond satan's face was expressionless.

Binnett raised a hand quickly.

"Wait, wait," he said, "I'll do what I can to make him change his mind. Perhaps if—" His dark eyes suddenly became wary. "You're not simply trying to sell him something, are you?"

"No."

The wary gleam went out of Binnett's eyes. "Well, then, I think I can—"

A young women came in crying angrily, "Wally, that old fool has—"

She broke off with a hand to her breast when she saw Spade.

Spade and Binnett had risen together.

Binnett said suavely, "Joyce, this is Mr. Ames. My sister-in-law, Joyce Court."

Spade bowed.

Joyce Court uttered a short, embarrassed laugh and said, "Please excuse my whirlwind entrance."

She was a tall, blue-eyed, dark woman of twenty-four or -five with good shoulders and a strong, slim body. Her features made up in warmth what they lacked in regularity. She wore wide-legged, blue satin pajamas.

Binnett smiled good-naturedly at her and asked:

"Now what's all the excitement?"

Anger darkened her eyes again and she started to speak. Then she looked at Spade and said:

"But we shouldn't bore Mr. Ames with our stupid domestic affairs. If—" She hesitated.

Spade bowed again. "Sure," he said, "certainly."

"I won't be a minute," Binnett promised, and left the room with her.

Spade went to the open doorway through which they had vanished and, standing just inside, listened. Their footsteps became inaudible. Nothing else could be heard.

Spade was standing there—his yellow-gray eyes dreamy—when he heard the scream. It was a woman's scream, high and shrill with terror. Spade was through the doorway when he heard the shot.

It was a pistol shot, magnified, reverberated by walls and ceilings.

Twenty feet from the doorway Spade found a staircase, and went up it three steps at a time. He turned to the left. Halfway down the hallway a woman lay on her back on the floor.

Wallace Binnett knelt beside her, fondling one of her hands desperately, crying in a low, beseeching voice, "Darling, Molly, darling!"

Joyce Court stood behind him and wrung her hands while tears streaked her cheeks.

The woman on the floor resembled Joyce Court but was older, and her face had a hardness the younger one's had not.

"She's dead, she's been killed," Wallace Binnett said incredulously, raising his white face toward Spade.

When Binnett moved his head Spade could see the round hole in the woman's tan dress over her heart and the dark stain which was rapidly spreading below it.

Spade touched Joyce Court's arm.

"Police, emergency hospital—phone," he said.

As she ran toward the stairs he addressed Wallace Binnett: "Who did—"

A voice groaned feebly behind Spade.

He turned swiftly. Through an open doorway he could see an old man in white pajamas lying sprawled across a rumpled bed. His head, a shoulder, an arm dangled over the edge of the bed. His other hand held his throat tightly. He groaned again and his eyelids twitched, but did not open.

Spade lifted the old man's head and shoulders and put them up on the pillows. The old man groaned again and took his hand from his throat. His throat was red with half a dozen bruises. He was a gaunt man with a seamed face that probably exaggerated his age.

A glass of water was on a table beside the bed. Spade put water on the old man's face and, when the old man's eyes twitched again, leaned down and growled softly:

"Who did it?"

The twitching eyelids went up far enough to show a narrow

strip of bloodshot gray eyes. The old man spoke painfully, putting a hand to his throat again:

"A man—he—" He coughed.

Spade made an impatient grimace. His lips almost touched the old man's ear.

"Where'd he go?" His voice was urgent.

A gaunt hand moved weakly to indicate the rear of the house and fell back on the bed.

The butler and two frightened female servants had joined Wallace Binnett beside the dead woman in the hallway.

"Who did it?" Spade asked them.

They stared at him blankly.

"Somebody look after the old man," he growled, and went down the hallway.

At the end of the hallway was a rear staircase. He descended two flights and went through a pantry into the kitchen. He saw nobody. The kitchen door was shut but, when he tried it, not locked. He crossed a narrow back yard to a gate that was shut, not locked. He opened the gate. There was nobody in the narrow alley behind it.

He sighed, shut the gate, and returned to the house.

Spade sat comfortably slack in a deep leather chair in a room that ran across the front second story of Wallace Binnett's house. There were shelves of books and the lights were on. The window showed outer darkness weakly diluted by a distant street lamp.

Facing Spade, Detective Sergeant Polhaus—a big, carelessly shaven, florid man in dark clothes that needed pressing—was sprawled in another chair; Lieutenant Dundy—smaller, compactly built, square-faced—stood with legs apart, head thrust a little forward, in the center of the room.

Spade was saying:

"—and the doctor would only let me talk to the old man a couple of minutes. We can try it again when he's rested a little, but it doesn't look like he knows much. He was catching a nap and he woke up with somebody's hands on his throat dragging him around the bed. The best he got was a one-eyed look at the fellow choking him. A big fellow, he says, with a soft hat pulled down over his eyes, dark, needing a shave. Sounds like Tom." Spade nodded at Polhaus.

The detective sergeant chuckled, but Dundy said, "Go on," curtly.

Spade grinned and went on:

"He's pretty far gone when he hears Mrs. Binnett scream at the door. The hands go away from his throat and he hears the shot and just before passing out he gets a flash of the big fellow heading for the rear of the house and Mrs. Binnett tumbling down on the hall floor. He says he never saw the big fellow before."

"What size gun was it?" Dundy asked.

"Thirty-eight. Well, nobody in the house is much more help. Wallace and his sister-in-law, Joyce, were in her room, so they say, and didn't see anything but the dead woman when they ran out, though they think they heard something that could've been somebody running downstairs—the back stairs.

"The butler—his name's Jarboe—was in here when he heard the scream and shot, so he says. Irene Kelly, the maid, was down on the ground floor, so she says. The cook, Margaret Finn, was in her room—third floor back—and didn't even hear anything, so she says. She's deaf as a post, so everybody else says. The back door and gate were unlocked, but are supposed to be kept locked, so everybody says. Nobody says they were in or around the kitchen or yard at the time." Spade spread his hands in a gesture of finality. "That's the crop."

Dundy shook his head. "Not exactly," he said. "How come you were here?"

Spade's face brightened.

"Maybe my client killed her," he said. "He's Wallace's cousin, Ira Binnett. Know him?"

Dundy shook his head. His blue eyes were hard and suspicious.

"He's a San Francisco lawyer," Spade said, "respectable and all that. A couple of days ago he came to me with a story about his uncle Timothy, a miserly old skinflint, lousy with money and pretty well broken up by hard living. He was the black sheep of the family. None of them had heard of him for years. But six or eight months ago he showed up in pretty bad shape every way except financially—he seems to have taken a lot of money out of Australia—wanting to spend his last days with his only living relatives, his nephews Wallace and Ira.

"That was all right with them. 'Only living relatives' meant 'only heirs' in their language. But by and by the nephews began to think it was better to be an heir than to be one of a couple of heirs—twice as good, in fact—and started fiddling for the inside track with the old man. At least, that's what Ira told me about Wallace, and I wouldn't be surprised if Wallace would say the same thing about Ira, though Wallace seems to be the harder up of the two. Anyhow, the nephews fell out, and then Uncle Tim, who had been staying at Ira's, came over here. That was a couple of months ago, and Ira hasn't seen Uncle Tim since, and hasn't been able to get in touch with him by phone or mail.

"That's what he wanted a private detective about. He didn't think Uncle Tim would come to any harm here—oh, no, he went to a lot of trouble to make that clear—but he thought maybe undue pressure was being brought to bear on the old boy, or he was being hornswoggled somehow, and at least being told lies about his loving nephew Ira. He wanted to know what was what. I waited until today, when a boat from Australia docked, and came up here as a Mr. Ames with some important information for Uncle Tim about his properties down there. All I wanted was fifteen minutes alone with him."

Spade frowned thoughtfully. "Well. I didn't get them. Wallace told me the old man refused to see me. I don't know."

Suspicion had deepened in Dundy's cold blue eyes.

"And where is this Ira Binnett now?" he asked.

Spade's yellow-gray eyes were as guileless as his voice. "I wish I knew. I phoned his house and office and left word for him to come right over, but I'm afraid—"

Knuckles knocked sharply twice on the other side of the room's one door.

The three men in the room turned to face the door.

Dundy called, "Come in."

The door was opened by a sunburned blond policeman whose left hand held the right wrist of a plump man of forty or forty-five in well-fitting gray clothes. The policeman pushed the plump man into the room.

"Found him monkeying with the kitchen door," he said.

Spade looked up and said, 'Ah!" His tone expressed satisfaction. "Mr. Ira Binnett, Lieutenant Dundy, Sergeant Polhaus."

Ira Binnett said rapidly, "Mr. Spade, will you tell this man that—"

Dundy addressed the policeman: "All right. Good work. You can leave him."

The policeman moved a hand vaguely toward his cap and went away.

Dundy glowered at Ira Binnett and demanded, "Well?"

Binnett looked from Dundy to Spade. "Has something—"

Spade said, "Better tell him why you were at the back door instead of the front."

Ira Binnett suddenly blushed. He cleared his throat in embarrassment.

He said, "I—uh—I should explain. It wasn't my fault, of course, but when Jarboe—he's the butler—phoned me that Uncle Tim wanted to see me he told me he'd leave the kitchen door unlocked, so Wallace wouldn't have to know I'd—"

"What'd he want to see you about?" Dundy asked.

"I don't know, he didn't say. He said it was very important."

"Didn't you get my message?" Spade asked.

Ira Binnett's eyes widened. "No. What was it? Has anything happened? What is—"

Spade was moving toward the door.

"Go ahead," he said to Dundy. "I'll be right back."

He shut the door carefully behind him and went up to the third floor.

The butler Jarboe was on his knees at Timothy Binnett's door with an eye to the keyhole. On the floor beside him was a tray holding an egg in an egg-cup, toast, a pot of coffee, china, silver, and a napkin.

Spade said, "Your toast's going to get cold."

Jarboe, scrambling to his feet, almost upsetting the coffeepot in his haste, his face red and sheepish, stammered:

"I—er—beg your pardon, sir. I wanted to make sure Mr. Timothy was awake before I took this in." He picked up the tray, "I didn't want to disturb his rest if—"

Spade, who had reached the door, said "Sure, sure," and bent over to put his eye to the keyhole. When he straightened up he said in a mildly complaining tone, "You can't see the bed—only a chair and part of the window."

The butler replied quickly, "Yes, sir, I found that out."

Spade laughed.

The butler coughed, seemed about to say something, but did not. He hesitated, then knocked lightly on the door.

A tired voice said, "Come in."

Spade asked quickly in a low voice, "Where's Miss Court?"

"In her room, I think, sir, the second floor on the left," the butler said.

The tired voice inside the room said petulantly, "Well, come on in."

The butler opened the door and went in. Through the door, before the butler shut it, Spade caught a glimpse of Timothy Binnett propped up on pillows in his bed.

Spade went to the second door on the left and knocked. The

door was opened almost immediately by Joyce Court. She stood in the doorway, not smiling, not speaking.

He said, 'Miss Court, when you came into the room where I was with your brother-in-law you said, 'Wally, that old fool has—' Meaning Timothy?"

She stared at Spade for a moment. Then: "Yes."

"Mind telling me what the rest of the sentence would have been?"

She said slowly, "I don't know who you really are or why you ask, but I don't mind telling you. It would have been 'sent for Ira.' Jarboe had just told me."

"Thanks."

She shut the door before he had turned away.

He returned to Timothy Binnett's door and knocked on it.

"Who is it now?" the old man's voice demanded.

Spade opened the door. The old man was sitting up in bed. Spade said, "This Jarboe was peeping through your keyhole a few minutes ago," and returned to the library.

Ira Binnett, seated in the chair Spade had occupied, was saying to Dundy and Polhaus, "And Wallace got caught in the crash, like most of us, but he seems to have juggled accounts trying to save himself. He was expelled from the Stock Exchange."

Dundy waved a hand to indicate the room and its furnishings. "Pretty classy layout for a man that's busted."

"His wife has some money," Ira Binnett said, "and he always lived beyond his means."

Dundy scowled at Binnett. "And you really think he and his missus weren't on good terms?"

"I don't think it," Binnett replied evenly. "I know it."

Dundy nodded. "And you know he's got a yen for the sister-in-law, this Court?"

"I don't know that. But I've heard plenty of gossip to the same effect."

Dundy made a growling noise in his throat, then asked sharply. "How does the old man's will read?"

"I don't know. I don't know whether he's made one." He addressed Spade, now earnestly: "I've told everything I know, every single thing."

Dundy said, "It's not enough." He jerked a thumb at the door. "Show him where to wait Tom, and let's have the widower in again."

Big Polhaus said, "Right," went out with Ira Binnett, and returned with Wallace Binnett, whose face was hard and pale.

Dundy asked, "Has your uncle made a will?"

"I don't know," Binnett replied.

Spade put the next question, softly: "Did your wife?"

Binnett's mouth tightened in a mirthless smile. He spoke deliberately:

"I'm going to say some things I'd rather not have to say. My wife, properly, had no money. When I got into financial trouble some time ago I made some property over to her, to save it. She turned it into money without my knowing about it till afterward. She paid our bills—our living expenses—out of it, but she refused to return it to me and she assured me that in no event—whether she lived or died or we stayed together or were divorced—would I ever be able to get hold of a penny of it. I believed her, and still do."

"You wanted a divorce?" Dundy asked.

"Yes."

"Why?"

"It wasn't a happy marriage."

"Joyce Court?"

Binnett's face flushed. He said stiffly, "I admire Joyce Court tremendously, but I'd've wanted a divorce anyway."

Spade said, "And you're sure—still absolutely sure—you don't know anybody who fits your uncle's description of the man who choked him?"

"Absolutely sure."

The sound of the doorbell ringing came faintly into the room. Dundy said sourly, "That'll do."

Binnett went out.

Polhaus said, "That guy's as wrong as they make them. And—"

From below came the heavy report of a pistol fired indoors. The lights went out.

In darkness the three detectives collided with one another going through the doorway into the dark hall.

Spade reached the stairs first. There was a clatter of footsteps below him, but nothing could be seen until he reached a bend in the stairs. Then enough light came from the street through the open front door to show the dark figure of a man standing with his back to the open door.

A flashlight clicked in Dundy's hand—he was at Spade's heels—and threw a glaring white beam of light on the man's face.

He was Ira Binnett. He blinked in the light and pointed at something on the floor in front of him.

Dundy turned the beam of his light down on the floor. Jarboe lay there on his face, bleeding from a bullet hole in the back of his head.

Spade grunted softly.

Tom Polhaus came blundering down the stairs. Wallace Binnett close behind him. Joyce Court's frightened voice came from farther up:

"Oh, what's happened? Wally, what's happened?"

"Where's the light switch?" Dundy barked.

"Inside the cellar door, under these stairs," Wallace Binnett said. "What is it?"

Polhaus pushed past Binnett toward the cellar door.

Spade made an inarticulate sound in his throat and, pushing Wallace Binnett aside, sprang up the stairs. He brushed past Joyce court and went on, heedless of her startled scream. He was halfway up the stairs to the third floor when the pistol went off up there.

He ran to Timothy Binnett's door. The door was open. He went in.

Something hard and angular struck him above his right ear, knocking him across the room, bringing him down on one knee. Something thumped and clattered on the floor just outside the door.

The lights came on.

On the floor, in the center of the room, Timothy Binnett lay on his back bleeding from a bullet wound in his left forearm. His pajama jacket was torn. His eyes were shut.

Spade stood up and put a hand to his head. He scowled at the old man on the floor, at the room, at the black automatic pistol lying on the hallway floor.

He said, "Come on, you old cutthroat. Get up and sit on a chair and I'll see if I can stop that bleeding till the doctor gets here."

The man on the floor did not move.

There were footsteps in the hallway and Dundy came in, followed by the two younger Binnetts. Dundy's face was dark and furious.

"Kitchen door wide open," he said in a choked voice. "They run in and out like—"

"Forget it," Spade said. "Uncle Tim is our meat." He paid no attention to Wallace Binnett's gasp, to the incredulous looks on

Dundy's and Ira Binnett's faces. "Come on, get up," he said to the old man on the floor, "and tell us what it was the butler saw when he peeped through the keyhole."

The old man did not stir.

"He killed the butler because I told him the butler had peeped," Spade explained to Dundy. "I peeped, too, but didn't see anything except that chair and the window, though we'd made enough racket by then to scare him back to bed. Suppose you take the chair apart while I go over the window."

He went to the window and began to examine it carefully. He shook his head, put a hand out behind him, and said, "Give me the flashlight."

Dundy put the flashlight in his hand.

Spade raised the window and leaned out, turning the light on the outside of the building. Presently he grunted and put his other hand out, tugging at a brick a little below the sill. Presently the brick came loose. He put it on the window sill and stuck his hand into the hole its removal had made. Out of the opening, one at a time, he brought an empty black pistol holster, a partially filled box of cartridges, and an unsealed manila envelope.

Holding these things in his hands, he turned to face the others.

Joyce Court came in with a basin of water and a roll of gauze and knelt beside Timothy Binnett.

Spade put the holster and cartridges on a table and opened the manila envelope. Inside were two sheets of paper, covered on both sides with boldly penciled writing. Spade read a paragraph to himself, suddenly laughed, and began at the beginning again, reading aloud:

" 'I, Timothy Kieran Binnett, being sound of mind and body, do declare this to be my last will and testament. To my dear nephews, Ira Binnett and Wallace Bourke Binnett, in recognition of the loving kindness with which they have received me into their homes and attended my declining years, I give and bequeath, share and share alike, all my worldly possessions of whatever kind, to wit, my carcass and the clothes I stand in.

" 'I bequeath them, furthermore, the expense of my funeral and these memories: First, the memory of their credulity in believing that the fifteen years I spent in Sing Sing were spent in Australia; second, the memory of their optimism in supposing that those fifteen years had brought me great wealth, and that if I lived on them, borrowed from them, and never spent any of my own money, it was because I was a miser whose hoard they would inherit; and not because I had no money except what I shook them down for; third, for their hopefulness in thinking that I would leave either of them anything if I had it; and, lastly, because their painful lack of any decent sense of humor will keep them from ever seeing how funny this has all been. Signed and sealed this—' "

Spade looked up to say, "There is no date, but it's signed Timothy Kieran Binnett with flourishes."

Ira Binnett was purple with anger.

Wallace's face was ghastly in its pallor and his whole body was trembling.

Joyce Court had stopped working on Timothy Binnett's arm.

The old man sat up and opened his eyes. He looked at his nephews and began to laugh. There was in his laughter neither hysteria nor madness: it was sane, hearty laughter, and subsided slowly.

Spade said, "All right, now you've had your fun. Let's talk about the killings."

"I know nothing more about the first one than I've told you," the old man said, "and this one's not a killing, since I'm only—"

Wallace Binnett, still trembling violently, said painfully through his teeth:

"That's a lie. You killed Molly. Joyce and I came out of her room when we heard Molly scream, and heard the shot and saw her fall out of your room, and nobody came out afterward."

The old man said calmly, "Well, I'll tell you: it was an accident. They told me there was a fellow from Australia here to see me about some of my properties there. I knew there was something funny about that somewhere"—he grinned—"not ever having been there. I didn't know whether one of my dear nephews was getting suspicious and putting up a game on me or what, but I knew that if Wally wasn't in on it he'd certainly try to pump the gentleman from Australia about me and maybe I'd lose one of my free boarding houses."

He chuckled.

"So I figured I'd get in touch with Ira so I could go back to his house if things worked out bad here, and I'd try to get rid of this Australian. Wally's always thought I'm half-cracked"—he leered at his nephew—"and's afraid they'll lug me off to a madhouse before I could make a will in his favor, or they'll break it if I do. You see, he's got a pretty bad reputation, what with that Stock Exchange trouble and all, and he knows no court would appoint him to handle my affairs if I went screwy—not as long as I've got another nephew"—he turned his leer on Ira—"who's a respectable lawyer. So now I know that rather than have me kick up a row that might wind me up in the madhouse, he'll chase this visitor, and I put on a show for Molly, who happened to be the nearest one to hand. She took it too seriously, though.

"I had a gun and I did a lot of raving about being spied on by my enemies in Australia and that I was going down and shoot this fellow. But she got too excited and tried to take the gun away from me, and the first thing I knew it had gone off, and I had to make these marks on my neck and think up that story about the big dark man."

He looked contemptuously at Wallace.

"I didn't know he was covering me up. Little as I thought of him, I never thought he'd be low enough to cover up his wife's murderer—even if he didn't like her—just for the sake of money."

Spade said "Never mind that. Now about the butler?"

"I don't know anything about the butler," the old man replied, looking at Spade with steady eyes.

Spade said, "You had to kill him quick, before he had time to do or say anything. So you slip down the back stairs, open the kitchen door to fool people, go to the front door, ring the bell, shut the door, and hide in the shadow of the cellar door under the front steps. When Jarboe answered the doorbell you shot him—the hole was in the back of his head—pulled the light switch, just inside the cellar door, and ducked up the back stairs in the dark and shot yourself carefully in the arm. I got up there too soon for you; so you smacked me with the gun, chucked it through the door, and spread yourself on the floor while I was shaking pinwheels out of my noodle."

The old man sniffed again. "You're just—"

"Stop it," Spade said patiently. "Don't let's argue. The first killing was an accident—all right. The second couldn't be. And it ought to be easy to show that both bullets, and the one in your arm, were fired from the same gun. What difference does it make which killing we can prove first-degree murder on? They can only hang you once." He smiled pleasantly. "And they will."

STUART M. KAMINSKY

(b.1934)

Stuart Melvin Kaminsky's multiple talents surfaced early in his life. Born in Chicago, he received a bachelor's degree in journalism (1957), a master's degree in English (1959), and a doctoral degree in speech (1972). In 1973, he began an academic career at Northwestern University in the speech department and by 1979 became head of the film division, later moving on to direct the film school at Florida State University. His work in film and film criticism is extensive. He was a scriptwriter for Sergio Leone's epic gangster film Once Upon a Time in America *(1984) and for several other projects. He has also published several volumes of film criticism including books on Clint Eastwood, John Huston, Gary Cooper, and director Don Siegel. He has taught a number of successful writers, including Sara Paretsky, and created the series character Porfiry Petrovich Rostnikov, a Russian detective. He is best known, however, for creating Toby Peters, a private eye of the 1930s and 1940s. In many respects there is nothing extraordinary about Peters as a detective. Money rarely comes his way, but he takes cases and bulls his way to the solution through the mean streets of Hollywood. Several elements in the novels make Kaminsky's works more than pastiches of the hard-boiled detective novel and thereby more appealing. Though tough and honest, Peters is no man of steel, which humanizes him. He has oddball friends. Most important, however, are the appearances of legendary movie figures in the novels: John Wayne, Mae West, Bela Lugosi, the Marx Brothers, and others. These cameo roles exploited the "camp" and pop art sensibilities of the 1970s but have not become dated. In the following story, Toby Peters must discover who among the dinner guests at a D. W. Griffith dinner party is a murderer.*

BUSTED BLOSSOMS

Darkness. I couldn't see, but I could hear someone shouting at me about Adolf Hitler. I opened my eyes. I still couldn't see. Panic set in before memory told me where I was. I pushed away the jacket covering my head. After a good breath of stale air, I realized where I was, who I was, and what I was doing there.

It was 1938, February, a cool Sunday night in Los Angeles, and I was Toby Peters, a private investigator who had been hired to keep an eye on a washed-up movie director who had come in from out of town and picked up a few death threats. I was getting fifteen dollars a day, for which I was expected to stay near the target and put myself in harm's way if trouble came up. I was not being paid to fall asleep.

My mouth tasted like ragweed pollen. I reached over to turn off the radio. When I had put my head back to rest on the bed and pulled my suede zipped jacket over me, Jeanette MacDonald had been singing about Southern moons. I woke up to the news that Reichsführer Hitler had proclaimed himself chief of national defense and had promoted Hermann Wilhelm Göring, minister of aviation, to field marshal. I was just standing when the door opened and D. W. Griffith walked in.

"Mr. Peters," he said, his voice deep, his back straight, and, even across the room, his breath dispensing the Kentucky fumes of bourbon.

"I was on my way down," I said. "I was listening to the news."

Griffith eyed me from over his massive hawk of a nose. He was about five-ten, maybe an inch or so taller than me, though I guessed he weighed about 180, maybe twenty pounds more than I did. We both seemed to be in about the same shape, which says something good for him or bad for me. I was forty-one, and he was over sixty. He was wearing a black suit over a white shirt and thin black tie.

"I have something to tell you," Griffith said.

So, I was canned. It had happened before, and I had a double sawbuck in my wallet.

"I really was coming down," I said, trying to get some feeling in my tongue.

"You were not," Griffith said emphatically. "But that is of little consequence. A man has been murdered."

"Murdered?" I repeated.

I am not the most sophisticated sight even when I'm combed, shaved, and operating on a full stomach. My face is dark and my nose mush, not from business contacts, but from an older brother who every once in a while thought I needed redefinition. I sold that tough look to people who wanted a bodyguard. Most of my work was for second-rate clothing stores that had too much shoplifting, hard-working bookies whose wives had gone for Chiclets and never came back, and old ladies who had lost their cats, who were always named Sheiba. That's what I usually did, but once in a while I spent a night or a few days protecting movie people who got themselves threatened or were afraid of getting crushed in a crowd. D.W. had no such fears. No one was looking for his autograph anymore. No one was hiring him. He seemed to have plenty of money and a lot of hope; that was why he had driven up from Louisville. He hoped someone would pick up the phone and call him to direct a movie, but in the week I had worked for him, no one had called, except the guy who threatened to lynch him with a Ku Klux Klan robe. D.W. had explained that such threats had not been unusual during the past two decades since the release of *Birth of a Nation,* which had presented the glories of the Ku Klux Klan. D.W. had tried to cover his prejudice with *Intolerance* and a few more films, but the racism of *Birth* wouldn't wash away.

"Mr. Peters." He tried again, his voice now loud enough to be heard clearly in the back row if we were in a Loews theater. "You must rouse yourself. A man has been murdered downstairs."

"Call the police," I said brilliantly.

"We are, you may recall, quite a distance from town," he reminded me. "A call has been placed, but it will be some time before the constabulary arrives."

Constabulary. I was in a time warp. But that was the way I had felt since meeting Griffith, who now touched his gray sideburns as if he were about to be photographed for *Click* magazine.

"Who's dead?" I asked.

"Almost everyone of consequence since the dawn of time," Griffith said, opening the door. "In this case, the victim is Jason Sikes. He is sitting at the dinner table with a knife in his neck."

"Who did it?" I began.

"That, I fear, is a mystery," Griffith said. "Now let us get back to the scene."

I walked out the door feeling that I was being ushered from act one to act two. I didn't like the casting. Griffith was directing the whole thing, and I had the feeling he wanted to cast me as the detective. I wanted to tell him that I had been hired to protect his back, not find killers. I get double time for finding killers. But one just didn't argue with Dave Griffith. I slouched ahead of him, scratched an itch on my right arm, and slung my suede jacket over my shoulder so I could at least straighten the wrinkled striped tie I was wearing.

What did I know? That I was in a big house just off the California coast about thirty miles north of San Diego. The house belonged to a producer named Korites, who Griffith hoped would give him a directing job. Korites had gathered his two potential stars, a comic character actor, and a potential backer, Sikes, to meet the great director. I had come as Griffith's "associate." D.W. had left his young wife back at the Roosevelt Hotel in Los Angeles, and we had stopped for drinks twice on the way in his chauffeur-driven Mercedes. In the car Griffith had talked about Kentucky, his father, his mother, who had never seen one of his films—"She did not approve of the stage," he explained—and about his comeback. He had gone on about his youthful adventures as an actor, playwright, boxer, reporter, and construction worker. Then, about ten minutes before we arrived, he had clammed up, closed his eyes, and hadn't said another word.

Now we were going silently down the stairs of the house of Marty Korites, stepping into a dining room, and facing five well-dressed diners, one of whom lay with his face in a plate of Waldorf salad with a knife in his back.

The diners looked up when we came in. Korites, a bald, jowly man with Harold Lloyd glasses, was about fifty and looked every bit of it and more. His eyes had been resting angrily on the dead guest, but they shot up to us as we entered the room. On one side of the dead guy was a woman, Denise Giles, skinny as ticker tape, pretty, dark, who knows what age. I couldn't even tell from the freckles on her bare shoulders. On the other side of the dead guy was an actor named James Vann, who looked like the lead in a road-show musical, blond, young, starched, and confused. He needed someone to feed him lines. Griffith was staring at the corpse. The great director looked puzzled. The last guest sat opposite the dead man. I knew him, too, Lew Dollard, a frizzy-haired comedian turned character actor who was Marty Korites' top name, which gives you an idea of how small an operator Marty was and what little hope Griffith had if he had traveled all the way here in the hope of getting a job from him.

"Mr. Griffith says you're a detective, not a film guy," Korites said, his eyes moving from the body to me for an instant and then back to the body. I guessed he didn't want the dead guy to get away when he wasn't looking.

"Yeah, I'm a detective," I said. "But I don't do windows and I don't do corpses."

Dollard, the roly-poly New York street comic in a rumpled suit, looked up at me.

"A comedy writer," he said with a smile showing big teeth. I had seen one of Dollard's movies. He wasn't funny.

"Someone killed Sikes," Korites said with irritation.

"Before the main course was served, too," I said. "Some people have no sense of timing. Look. Why don't we just sit still, have a drink or two, and wait till the police get here. We can pass the time by your telling me how someone can get killed at the dinner table and all of you not know who did it. That must have been some chicken liver appetizer."

"It was," said Griffith, holding his open palm toward the dead man, "like a moment of filmic chicanery, a magic moment from Méliès. I was sipping an aperitif and had turned to Miss Giles to answer a question. And then, a sound, a groan. I turned, and there sat Mr. Sikes."

We all looked at Sikes. His face was still in the salad.

"Who saw what happened?" I asked.

They all looked up from the corpse and at each other. Then they looked at me. Dollard had a cheek full of something and a silly grin on his face. He shrugged.

"A man gets murdered with the lights on with all of you at

the table and no one knows who did it?" I asked. "That's a little hard to believe. Who was standing up?"

"No one," said Vann, looking at me unblinking.

"No one," agreed Griffith.

There was no window behind the body. One door to the room was facing the dead man. The other door was to his right. The knife couldn't have been thrown from either door and landed in his back. The hell with it. I was getting paid to protect Griffith, not find killers. I'd go through the motions till the real cops got there. I had been a cop back in Glendale before I went to work for Warner Brothers as a guard and then went into business on my own. I knew the routine.

"Why don't we go into the living room?" Korites said, starting to get up and glancing at the corpse. "I could have Mrs. Windless—"

"Sit down," I said. "Mrs. Windless is . . .?"

"Housekeeper," Korites said. "Cook."

"Was she in here when Sikes was killed?"

I looked around. All heads shook no.

"Anyone leave the room before or after Sikes was killed?" I went on.

"Just Mr. Griffith," said Vann. The woman still hadn't said anything.

"We stay right here till the police arrive. Anyone needs the toilet, I go with them, even the dragon lady," I said, trying to get a rise out of Denise Giles. I got none.

"What about you?" said Dollard, rolling his eyes and gurgling in a lousy imitation of Bert Lahr.

"I wasn't in the room when Sikes took his dive into the salad," I said. "Look, you want to forget the whole thing and talk about sports? Fine. You hear that Glenn Cunningham won the Wanamaker mile for the fifth time yesterday?"

"With a time of 4:11," said Denise Giles, taking a small sip of wine from a thin little glass.

I looked at her with new respect. Griffith had sat down at the end of the table, the seat he had obviously been in when murder interrupted the game. Something was on his mind.

"Who was Sikes?" I asked, reaching down for a celery stick.

"A man of means," said Griffith, downing a slug of bourbon.

"A backer," said Korites. "He was thinking of bankrolling a movie D. W. would direct and I would produce."

"With Vann here and Miss Giles as stars?" I said.

"Right," said Korites.

"Never," said Griffith emphatically.

"You've got no choice here," Korites shouted back. "You take the project the way we give it to you or we get someone else. Your name's got some curiosity value, right, but it doesn't bring in any golden spikes."

"A man of tender compassion," sighed Griffith, looking at me for understanding. "It was my impression that the late Mr. Sikes had no intention of supplying any capital. On the contrary, I had the distinct impression that he felt he was in less than friendly waters and had only been lured here with the promise of meeting me, the wretched director who had once held the industry in his hand, had once turned pieces of factory-produced celluloid into art. As I recall, Sikes also talked about some financial debt he expected to be paid tonight."

"You recall?" Korites said with sarcasm, shaking his head. "You dreamed it up. You're still back in the damn nineteenth century. Your movies were old-fashioned when you made them. You don't work anymore because you're an anachronism."

"Old-fashioned?" said Griffith with a smile. "Yes, old-fashioned, a romantic, one who respects the past. I would rather die with my Charles Dickens than live with your Hemingway."

Dollard finished whatever he had in his mouth and said, "You think it would be sacrilegious to have the main course? Life goes on."

"Have a celery stick," I suggested.

"I don't want to eat a celery stick," he whined.

"I wasn't suggesting that you put it in your mouth," I said.

This was too much for Dollard. He stood up, pushing the chair back.

"I'm the comic here," he said. "Tell him."

He looked around for someone to tell me. The most sympathetic person was Sikes, and he was dead.

"So that's the way it is," Dollard said, looking around the room. "You want me to play second banana."

"This is a murder scene," shouted Korites, taking his glasses off, "not a night club, Lew. Try to remember that." His jowls rumbled as he spoke. He was the boss, but not mine.

"Someone in this room murdered the guy in the salad," I reminded them.

"My father," said Griffith.

"Your father killed Sikes?" I asked, turning to the great director. Griffith's huge nose was at the rim of his almost empty glass. His dark eyes were looking into the remaining amber liquid for an answer.

"My father," he said without looking up, "would have known how to cope with this puzzle. He was a resourceful man, a gentleman, a soldier."

"Mine was a grocer," I said.

"This is ridiculous," said Denise Giles throwing down her napkin.

"Not to Sikes," I said. Just then the door behind me swung open. I turned to see a rail of a woman dressed in black.

"Are you ready for the roast?" she asked.

"Yes," said Dollard.

"No," said Korites, "we're not having any more food."

"I have rights here," Dollard insisted.

Now I had it. This was an Alice in Wonderland nightmare and I was Alice at the Mad Hatter's tea party. We'd all change places in a few seconds and the Dormouse, Sikes, would have to be carried.

"What," demanded Mrs. Windless, "am I to do with the roast?"

"You want the punch line or can I have it?" Dollard said to me.

"Sikes already got the punch line," I reminded him.

Mrs. Windless looked over at Sikes for the first time.

"Oh my God," she screamed. "That man is dead."

"Really?" shouted Dollard leaping up. "Which one?"

"Goddamn it," shouted Korites. "This is serious." His glasses were back on now. He didn't seem to know what to do with them.

Griffith got up and poured himself another drink.

"We know he's dead, Mrs. Windless," Korites said. "The police are on the way. You'll just have to stick all the food in the refrigerator and wait."

"What happened?" Mrs. Windless asked, her voice high, her eyes riveted on Sikes. "who did this? I don't want anything to do with murder."

"You don't?" said Dollard. "Why didn't you tell us that before we killed him? We did it for you." He crossed his eyes but didn't close them in time to block out the wine thrown in his face by the slinky Denise.

Dollard stood up sputtering and groped for a napkin to wipe his face. Purple tears rolled down his cheeks.

"Damn it," he screamed. "What the hell? What the hell?"

His hand found a napkin. He wiped his eyes. The stains were gone, but there was now a piece of apple from the Waldorf salad on his face.

"Mrs. Windless," said D.W., standing and pointing at the door. "You will depart and tell my driver, Mr. Reynolds, that Mr. Peters and I will be delayed. Mr. Dollard. You will sit down and clean your face. Miss Giles, you will refrain from outbursts, and Mr. Vann, you will attempt to show some animation. It is difficult to tell you from Mr. Sikes. Mr. Peters will continue the inquiry."

Vann stood up now, kicking back his chair. Griffith rose to meet him. They were standing face to face, toe to toe. Vann was about thirty years younger, but Griffith didn't back away.

"You can't tell us what to do. You can't tell anyone what to do. You're washed up," Vann hissed.

"As Bluebeard is rumored to have said," whispered Griffith, "I'm merely between engagements."

"See, see," grouched Dollard, pointing with his fork at the two antagonists. "Everyone's a comic. I ask you."

I sighed and stood up again.

"Sit down," I shouted at Vann and Griffith. The room went silent. The mood was ruined by my stomach growling. But they sat and Mrs. Windless left the room. "Who called the police?"

"I did," said Korites.

"I thought no one left the room but Griffith?" I said.

"Phone is just outside the door, everyone could see me call. I left the door open," Korites said. He pushed his dirty plate away from him and then pulled it back. "What's the difference?"

"Why didn't you all start yelling, panic, accuse each other?" I asked.

"We thought it was one of Jason's practical jokes," said Denise Giles. "He was fond of practical jokes."

"Rubber teeth, joy buzzers ink in the soup," sighed Dollard. "A real amateur, a putz. Once pretended he was poisoned at a lunch in . . ."

"Lew," shouted Korites. "Just shut up."

"All right you people," I said. "None of you liked Sikes, is that right?"

"Right," Korites said, "but that's a far cry from one of us . . ."

"How about hate?" I tried. "Would hate be a good word to apply to your feelings about the late dinner guest?"

"Maybe," said Korites, "there was no secret about that among our friends. I doubt if anyone who knew Jason did anything less than hate him. But none of us murdered him. We couldn't have."

"And yet," Griffith said, "one of you had to have done the deed. In *The Birth of a Nation*—"

"This is death, not birth," hissed Vann. "This isn't a damn movie."

Griffith drew his head back and examined Vann over his beak of a nose.

"Better," said Griffith. "Given time I could possibly motivate you into a passable performance. Even Richard Barthelmess had something to learn from my humble direction."

There was a radio in the corner. Dollard had stood up and turned it on. I didn't stop him. We listened to the radio and watched Sikes and each other while I tried to think. Griffith was drawing something on the white tablecloth with his fork.

Dollard found the news, and we learned that Hirohito had a cold but was getting better, King Farouk of Egypt had just gotten married, Leopold Stokowski was on his way to Italy under an assumed name, probably to visit Greta Garbo, and a guy named Albert Burroughs had been found semi-conscious in a hotel room in Bloomington, Illinois. The room was littered with open cans of peas. Burroughs managed to whisper to the ambulance driver that he had lived on peas for nine days even though he had $77,000 in cash in the room.

I got up and turned off the radio.

"You tell a story like that in a movie," said Korites, "and they say it isn't real."

"If you tell it well, they will believe anything," said Griffith, again doodling on the cloth.

The dinner mess, not to mention Sikes' corpse, was beginning to ruin the party.

"Things are different," Griffith said, looking down at what he had drawn. He lifted a long-fingered hand to wipe out the identations in the tablecloth.

"Things?" I asked, wondering if he was going to tell us tales about his career, his father, or the state of the universe.

"I am an artist of images," he explained, looking up, his eyes moving from me to each of the people around the table. "I kept the entire script of my films, sometimes 1,500 shots, all within my head." He pointed to his head in case we had forgotten where it was located.

"This scene," he went on, "has changed. When I left this room to find Mr. Peters, Mr. Sikes had a knife in his neck, not his back, and it was a somewhat different knife."

"You've had three too many D.W.," Dollard said with a smile.

I got up and examined Sikes. There was no hole in his neck or anywhere else on his body that I could find.

"No cuts, bruises, marks . . ." I began, and then it hit me. My eyes met Giffith's. I think it hit him at the same moment.

"We'll just wait for the police," Korites said, removing his glasses again.

"Go on Mr. G.," I said. "Let's hear your script."

Griffith stood again, put down his glass, and smiled. He was doing either Abe Lincoln or Sherlock Holmes.

"This scene was played for me," he said. "I was not the director. I was the audience. My ego is not fragile, at least not too fragile to realize that I have witnessed an act. I can see each of you playing your roles, even the late Mr. Sikes. Each of you in an iris, laughing, silently enigmatic, attentive. And then the moment arrives. The audience is distracted by a pretty face in close-up. Then a cut to body, or supposed body, for Sikes was not dead when I left this room to find Mr. Peters."

"Come on . . ." laughed Dollard.

"Of all . . ." sighed Denise Giles.

"You're mad . . ." counterpointed Vann.

But Korites sat silent.

"He wasn't dead," I said again, picking up for Griffith, who seemed to have ended his monologue. All he needed was applause. He looked good, but he had carried the scene as far as he could. It was mine now.

"Let's try this scenario," I said. "Sikes was a practical joker, right?"

"Right," Dollard agreed, "but—"

"What if you all agreed to play a little joke on D.W.? Sikes pretends to be dead with a knife in his neck when Denise distracts Griffith. Sikes can't stick the fake knife in his back. He can't reach his own back. He attaches it to his neck. Then you all discover the body, Griffith comes for me, Sikes laughs. You all laugh, then one of you, probably Korites, moves behind him and uses a real knife to turn the joke into fact. You're all covered. Someone did it. The police would have a hell of a time figuring out which one, and meanwhile, it would make a hell of a news story. Griffith a witness. All of you suspects. Probably wind up with a backer who'd cash in on your morbid celebrity."

"Ridiculous," laughed Korites.

"I was the audience," Griffith repeated with a rueful laugh.

"Even if this were true," said Denise Giles, "you could never prove it."

"Props," I said. "You didn't have time to get rid of that fake knife, at least not to get it hidden too well. D.W. was with me for only a minute or two, and you didn't want to get too far from this room in case we came running back here. No, if we're right, that prop knife is nearby, where it can be found, somewhere in this room or not far from it."

"This is ridiculous," said Vann, standing up. "I'm not staying here for any more of this charade." He took a step toward the door behind Griffith, giving me a good idea of where to start looking for the prop knife, but the director was out of his chair and barring his way.

"Move," shouted Vann.

"Never," cried Griffith.

Vann threw a punch, but Griffith caught it with his left and came back with a right. Vann went down. Korites started to rise, looked at my face, and sat down again.

"We can work something out here," he said, his face going white.

A siren blasted somewhere outside.

"Hell of a practical joke," Dollard said, dropping the radish in his fingers. "Hell of a joke."

No one moved while we waited for the police. We just sat there, Vann on the floor, Griffith standing. I imagined a round iris closing in on the scene, and then a slow fade to black.

The Caper

Surpassing normal physical and social limits is a recurring human fantasy. In mythology, Daedalus made wings to fly and Prometheus stole fire from the gods. In more recent times, the exploits of Jesse James and Willie Sutton draw admiration. Even Mafiosi and serial killers have become mythic figures, despite the sordidness of their reality. The Romantic poet Samuel Taylor Coleridge understood the appeal of the rebel in asserting that the hero of John Milton's *Paradise Lost* is Satan, as a character far more interesting than the angels who side with God and even more interesting, as a character, than God. Similarly, the criminal hero has been a staple of the mystery since its beginnings during the Romantic period. The wildly improbable memoirs of Eugène-François Vidocq, a thief who turned undercover cop and became head of the Sûreté, were a major influence on Poe, as well as on Victor Hugo and Balzac. French writers led the way with criminal heroes: Pierre Alexis de Pouson created Rocambole; Maurice Leblanc, Arsène Lupin; and Pierre Souvestre and Marcel Allain, Fantômas. The evil mastermind is an enduring cliché of crime fiction also, from Professor Moriarty to Madame Sara to Fu-Manchu to Hannibal Lector, all properly counterbalanced by a righteous pursuer who is often much less interesting than the criminal. Caper stories largely avoid the menace of an evil mastermind by focussing on theft, whereas most other crime fiction is about murder. The pleasure in the caper resembles that of the locked room and other puzzle mysteries. There is meticulous attention to the means by which thieves are to be foiled: dogs, locks, alarms, watchmen, and complicated traps. In this approach, the question becomes how the hero will get into a locked room, rather than how the criminal got out. The puzzle exists before the crime is committed. The victims are rarely seriously harmed, except in pride, and their humiliation is justified by their own greed, cruelty, or excessive power. By contrast, the thief is usually clever, charming, and witty. There is a certain moral comment in most caper stories: an underdog gives the rich and arrogant a well-deserved comeuppance, thus avenging common people and reminding us that pride cometh before a fall. In many tales, thievery serves justice when legal methods have been exhausted. All these things palliate the sneaking suspicion that the reader's joy is indecently celebrating antisocial behavior.

E. W. HORNUNG

(1866–1922)

Strangely, three of the world's most celebrated fictional characters had ties to Arthur Conan Doyle. He created Sherlock Holmes; his friend Bram Stoker created Dracula; and Ernest William Hornung, Doyle's brother-in-law, invented the gentleman thief A. J. Raffles. As an eighteen-year-old, Hornung went to Australia for health reasons and tutored at a remote school. He began writing there and created some memorable stories of outlaws and bush life, but he would be forgotten were it not for Raffles. In an odd way Hornung was flattering his brother-in-law. Raffles is based upon Holmes, but is a criminal. His loyal companion, Bunny Manders, is the narrator of the tales but is more the fool than John Watson and not nearly as tough. Bunny (the silly name is apt) will suffer any humiliation for Raffles. What makes Raffles interesting is the contrast between his gentlemanly behavior and the ungentlemanly thieving he practices. Conan Doyle himself complained about the practice of making a criminal the hero, but somehow Raffles is so charming, readers wickedly delight in his escapades. Raffles's sheer joy in befuddling the police and tweaking the nose of the pompous infects the reader and is balanced by Raffles's patriotism, wit, and refinement. Unlike his predecessor criminal heroes, such as Eugène-François Vidocq, Fantômas, and Arsène Lupin, Raffles comes across as a vivid, living personality, which is why he has had so many incarnations in film and television. Under the pseudonym Barry Perowne, Philip Atkey (1908–1985) continued the character in many stories beginning in the 1930s. Although in the Hornung stories Raffles rarely steals for the sake of justice, Atkey and later screenwriters regularly coerced Raffles (and characters imitating him) to do so in order to make him more morally acceptable. In our selection Raffles steals from a man who clearly deserves it, uses his skills as a master of disguise, and hooks us with the recurring question of the stories, "How will he get out of this predicament?" Why, with style, of course!

A COSTUME PIECE

London was just then talking of one whose name is already a name and nothing more. Reuben Rosenthall had made his millions on the diamond fields of South Africa, and had come home to enjoy them according to his lights; how he went to work will scarcely be forgotten by any reader of the halfpenny evening papers, which revelled in endless anecdotes of his original indigence and present prodigality, varied with interesting particulars of the extraordinary establishment which the millionaire set up in St. John's Wood. Here he kept a retinue of Kaffirs, who were literally his slaves; and hence he would sally with enormous diamonds in his shirt and on his finger, in the convoy of a prize-fighter of heinous repute, who was not, however, by any means the worst element in the Rosenthall *ménage*. So said common gossip; but the fact was sufficiently established by the interference of the police on at least one occasion, followed by certain magisterial proceedings which were reported with justifiable gusto and huge headlines in the newspapers aforesaid. And this was all one knew of Reuben Rosenthall up to the time when the Old Bohemian Club, having fallen on evil days, found it worth its while to organise a great dinner in honour of so wealthy an exponent of the club's principles. I was not at the banquet myself, but a member took Raffles, who told me all about it that very night.

"Most extraordinary show I ever went to in my life," said he.

"As for the man himself—well, I was prepared for something grotesque, but the fellow fairly took my breath away. To begin with, he's the most astounding brute to look at, well over six feet, with a chest like a barrel, and a great hook-nose, and the reddest hair and whiskers you ever saw. Drank like a fire-engine, but only got drunk enough to make us a speech that I wouldn't have missed for ten pounds. I'm only sorry you weren't there too, Bunny, old chap."

I began to be sorry myself, for Raffles was anything but an excitable person, and never had I seen him so excited before. Had he been following Rosenthall's example? His coming to my rooms at midnight, merely to tell me about his dinner, was in itself enough to excuse a suspicion which was certainly at variance with my knowledge of A. J. Raffles.

"What did he say?" I inquired mechanically, divining some subtler explanation of this visit, and wondering what on earth it could be.

"Say?" cried Raffles. "What did he not say! He boasted of his rise, he bragged of his riches, and he blackguarded society for taking him up for his money and dropping him out of sheer pique and jealousy because he had so much. He mentioned names, too, with the most charming freedom, and swore he was as good a man as the Old Country had to show—*pace* the Old Bohemians. To prove it he pointed to a great diamond in the middle of his shirt-front with a little finger loaded with another just like it: which of our bloated princes could show a pair like that? As a matter of fact, they seemed quite wonderful stones, with a curious purple gleam to them that must mean a pot of money. But old Rosenthall swore he wouldn't take fifty thousand pounds for the two, and wanted to know where the other man was who went about with twenty-five thousand in his shirt-front, and another twenty-five on his little finger. He didn't exist. If he did, he wouldn't have the pluck to wear them. But he had—he'd tell us why. And before you could say Jack Robinson he had whipped out a whacking great revolver!"

"Not at the table?"

"At the table! In the middle of his speech! But it was nothing to what he wanted to do. He actually wanted us to let him write his name in bullets on the opposite wall to show us why he wasn't afraid to go about in all his diamonds! That brute Purvis, the prize-fighter, who is his paid bully, had to bully his master before he could be persuaded out of it. There was quite a panic for the moment; one fellow was saying his prayers under the table, and the waiters bolted to a man."

"What a grotesque scene!"

"Grotesque enough, but I rather wish they had let him go the whole hog and blaze away. He was as keen as knives to show us how he could take care of his purple diamonds; and, do you know, Bunny, I was as keen as knives to see."

And Raffles leant towards me with a sly, slow smile that made the hidden meaning of his visit only too plain to me at last.

"So you think of having a try for his diamonds yourself?"

He shrugged his shoulders.

"It is horribly obvious, I admit. But—yes, I have set my heart upon them! To be quite frank, I have had them on my conscience for some time; one couldn't hear so much of the man, and his prize-fighter, and his diamonds, without feeling it a kind of duty to have to go for them; but when it comes to brandishing a revolver and practically challenging the world, the thing becomes inevitable. It is simply thrust upon one. I was fated to hear that challenge, Bunny, and I, for one, must take it up. I was only sorry I couldn't get on my hind legs and say so then and there."

"Well," I said, "I don't see the necessity as things are with us; but, of course, I'm your man."

My tone may have been half-hearted. I did my best to make it otherwise. But it was barely a month since our bond Street exploit, and we certainly could have afforded to behave ourselves for some time to come. We had been getting along so nicely: by his advice I had scribbled a thing or two; inspired by Raffles, I had even done an article on our own jewel robbery; and for the moment I was quite satisfied with this sort of adventure. I thought we ought to know when we were well off, and could see no point in our running fresh risks before we were obliged. On the other hand, I was anxious not to show the least disposition to break the pledge that I had given a month ago. But it was not on my manifest disinclination that Raffles fastened.

"Necessity, my dear Bunny? Does the writer only write when the wolf is at the door? Does the painter paint for bread alone? Must you and I be driven to crime like Tom of Bow and Dick of Whitechapel? You pain me, my dear chap; you needn't laugh, because you do. Art for art's sake is a vile catchword, but I confess it appeals to me. In this case my motives are absolutely pure, for I doubt if we shall ever be able to dispose of such peculiar stones. But if I don't have a try for them—after to-night—I shall never be able to hold up my head again."

His eye twinkled, but it glittered too.

"We shall have our work cut out," was all I said.

"And do you suppose I should be keen on it if we hadn't?" cried Raffles. "My dear fellow, I would rob St. Paul's Cathedral if I could, but I could no more scoop a till when the shopwalker wasn't looking than I could bag apples out of an old woman's basket. Even that little business last month was a sordid affair, but it was necessary, and I think its strategy redeemed it to some extent. Now there's some credit, and more sport, in going where they boast they're on their guard against you. The Bank of England, for example, is the ideal crib; but that would need half a dozen of us with years to give to the job; and meanwhile Reuben Rosenthall is high enough game for you and me. We know he's armed. We know how Billy Purvis can fight. It'll be no soft thing. I grant you. But what of that, my good Bunny—what of that? A man's reach must exceed his grasp, dear boy, or what the dickens is a heaven for?"

"I would rather we didn't exceed ours just yet," I answered laughing, for his spirit was irresistible, and the plan was growing upon me, despite my qualms.

"Trust me for that," was his reply; "I'll see you through. After all I expect to find that the difficulties are nearly all on the surface. These fellows both drink like the devil, and that should simplify matters considerably. But we shall see, and we must take our time. There will probably turn out to be a dozen different ways in which the thing might be done, and we shall have to choose between them. It will mean watching the house for at least a week in any case; it may mean lots of other things that will take much longer; but give me a week, and I will tell you more. That's to say if you're really on?"

"Of course I am," I replied indignantly. "But why should I give you a week? Why shouldn't we watch the house together?"

"Because two eyes are as good as four, and take up less room. Never hunt in couples unless you're obliged. But don't you look offended, Bunny; there'll be plenty for you to do when the time comes, that I promise you. You shall have your share of the fun, never fear, and a purple diamond all to yourself—if we're lucky."

On the whole, however, this conversation left me less than lukewarm, and I still remember the depression which came upon me when Raffles was gone. I saw the folly of the enterprise to which I had committed myself—the sheer, gratuitous, unnecessary folly of it. And the paradoxes in which Raffles revelled, and the frivolous casuistry which was nevertheless half sincere, and which his mere personality rendered wholly plausible at the moment of utterance, appealed very little to me when recalled in cold blood. I admired the spirit of pure mischief in which he seemed prepared to risk his liberty and his life, but I did not find it an infectious spirit on calm reflection. Yet the thought of withdrawal was not to be entertained for a moment. On the contrary, I was impatient of the delay ordained by Raffles; and, perhaps, no small part of my secret disaffection came of his galling determination to do without me until the last moment.

It made it no better that this was characteristic of the man and of his attitude towards me. For a month we had been, I suppose, the thickest thieves in all London, and yet our intimacy was curiously incomplete. With all his charming frankness, there was in Raffles a vein of capricious reserve which was perceptible enough to be very irritating. He had the instinctive secretiveness of the inveterate criminal. He would make mysteries of matters of common concern; for example, I never knew how or where he disposed of the Bond Street jewels, on the proceeds of which we were both still leading the outward lives of hundreds of other young fellows about town. He was consistently mysterious about that and other details, of which it seemed to me that I had already earned the right to know everything. I could not but remember how he had led me into my first felony, by means of a trick, while yet uncertain whether he could trust me or not. That I could no longer afford to resent, but I did resent his want of confidence in me now. I said nothing about it, but it rankled every day, and never more than in the week that succeeded the Rosenthall dinner. When I met Raffles at the club he would tell me nothing; when I went to his rooms he was out, or pretended to be. One day he told me he was getting on well, but slowly; it was a more ticklish game than he had thought; but when I began to ask questions he would say no more. Then and there, in my annoyance, I took my own decision. Since he would tell me nothing of the result of his vigils, I determined to keep one on my own account, and that very evening found my way to the millionaire's front gates.

The house he was occupying is, I believe, quite the largest in the St. John's Wood district. It stands in the angle formed by two broad thoroughfares, neither of which, as it happens, is a 'bus route, and I doubt if many quieter spots exist within the four-mile radius. Quiet also was the great square house, in its garden of grass-plots and shrubs; the lights were low, the millionaire and his friends obviously spending their evening elsewhere. The garden walls were only a few feet high. In one there was a side door opening into a glass passage; in the other two five-barred, grained-and-varnished gates, one at either end of the little semi-circular drive, and both wide open. So still was the place that I had a great mind to walk boldly in and learn something of the premises; in fact, I was on the point of doing so, when I head a quick, shuffling step on the pavement behind me. I turned round and faced the dark scowl and the dirty clenched fists of a dilapidated tramp.

"You fool!" said he. "You utter idiot!"

"Raffles!"

"That's it," he whispered savagely; "tell all the neighbourhood—give me away at the top of your voice!"

With that he turned his back upon me, and shambled down the road, shrugging his shoulders and muttering to himself as though I had refused him alms. A few moments I stood astounded, indignant, at a loss; then I followed him. His feet trailed, his knees gave, his back was bowed, his head kept nodding; it was the gait of a man eighty years of age. Presently he waited for me midway between two lamp-posts. As I came up he was lighting rank tobacco, in a cutty pipe, with an evil-smelling match, and the flame showed me the suspicion of a smile.

"You must forgive my heat, Bunny, but it really was very foolish of you. Here am I trying every dodge—begging at the door one night—hiding in the shrubs the next—doing every mortal thing but stand and stare at the house as you went and did. It's a costume piece, and in you rush in your ordinary clothes. I tell you they're on the look-out for us night and day. It's the toughest nut I ever tackled!"

"Well," said I, "if you had told me so before I shouldn't have come. You told me nothing."

He looked hard at me from under the broken rim of a battered billycock.

"You're right," he said at length. "I've been too close. It's become second nature with me, when I've anything on. But here's an end of it, Bunny, so far as you're concerned. I'm going home now, and I want you to follow me; but for heaven's sake keep your distance, and don't speak to me again until I speak to you. There—give me a start." And he was off again, a decrepit vagabond, with his hands in his pockets, his elbows squared, and frayed coat-tails swinging raggedly from side to side.

I followed him to the Finchley Road. There he took an Atlas omnibus, and I sat some rows behind him on the top, but not far enough to escape the pest of his vile tobacco. That he could carry his character-sketch to such a pitch—he who would only smoke one brand of cigarettes! It was the last, least touch of the insatiable artist, and it charmed away what mortification there still remained in me. Once more I felt the fascination of a comrade who was for ever dazzling one with a fresh and unsuspected facet of his character.

As we neared Piccadilly I wondered what he would do. Surely he was not going into the Albany like that? No, he took another omnibus to Sloane Street, I sitting behind him as before. At Sloane Street we changed again, and were presently in the long lean artery of the King's Road. I was now all agog to know our destination, nor was I kept many more minutes in doubt. Raffles got down. I followed. He crossed the road and disappeared up a dark turning. I pressed after him, and was in time to see his coat-tails as he plunged into a still darker flagged alley to the right. He was holding himself up and stepping out like a young man once more; also, in some subtle way, he already looked less disreputable. But I alone was there to see him; the alley was absolutely deserted, and desperately dark. At the further end he opened a door with a latchkey, and it was darker yet within.

Instinctively I drew back and heard him chuckle. We could no longer see each other.

"All right, Bunny! There's no hanky-panky this time. These are studios, my friend, and I'm one of the lawful tenants."

Indeed, in another minute we were in a lofty room with skylight, easels, dressing-cupboard, platform, and every other adjunct save the signs of actual labour. The first thing I saw, as Raffles lit the gas, was its reflection in his silk hat on the pegs beside the rest of his normal garments.

"Looking for the works of art?" continued Raffles, lighting a cigarette and beginning to divest himself of his rags. "I'm afraid you won't find any, but there's the canvas I'm always going to make a start upon. I tell them I'm looking high and low for my ideal model. I have the stove lit on principle twice a week, and look in and leave a newspaper and a smell of Sullivans—how good they are after shag! Meanwhile I pay my rent, and am a good tenant in every way; and it's a very useful little *pied-à-terre*—there's no saying how useful it might be at a pinch. As it is, the billycock comes in and the topper goes out, and nobody takes the slightest notice of either; at this time of night the chances are that there's not a soul in the building except ourselves."

"You never told me you went in for disguises," said I, watching him as he cleansed the grime from his face and hands.

"No, Bunny, I've treated you very shabbily all round. There was really no reason why I shouldn't have shown you this place a month ago, and yet there was no point in my doing so, and circumstances are just conceivable in which it would have suited us both for you to be in genuine ignorance of my whereabouts. I have something to sleep on, as you perceive, in case of need, and, of course, my name is not Raffles in the King's Road. So you will see that one might bolt further and fare worse."

"Meanwhile you use the place as a dressing-room?"

"It's my private pavilion," said Raffles. "Disguises? In some cases they're half the battle, and it's always pleasant to feel that, if the worst comes to the worst, you needn't necessarily be convicted under your own name. Then they're indispensable in dealing with the fences. I drive all my bargains in the tongue and raiment of Shoreditch. If I didn't there'd be the very devil to pay in blackmail. Now, this cupboard's full of all sorts of toggery. I tell the woman who cleans the room that it's for my models when I find 'em. By the way, I only hope I've got something that'll fit you, for you'll want a rig for to-morrow night."

"To-morrow night!" I exclaimed. "Why, what do you mean to do?"

"The trick," said Raffles. "I intended writing to you as soon as I got back to my rooms, to ask you to look me up to-morrow afternoon; then I was going to unfold my plan of campaign, and take you straight into action then and there. There's nothing like putting the nervous players in first; it's the sitting with their pads on that upsets their applecart; that was another of my reasons for being so confoundedly close. You must try to forgive me. I couldn't help remembering how well you played up last trip, without any time to weaken on it beforehand. All I want is for you to be as cool and smart to-morrow night as you were then; though, by Jove, there's no comparison between the two cases.

"I thought you would find it so."

"You were right. I have. Mind you, I don't say this will be the tougher job all round; we shall probably get in without any difficulty at all; it's the getting out again that may flummox us. That's the worst of an irregular household!" cried Raffles, with quite a burst of virtuous indignation. "I assure you, Bunny, I spent the whole of Monday night in the shrubbery of the garden next door, looking over the wall, and, if you'll believe me, somebody was about all night long! I don't mean the Kaffirs. I don't believe they ever get to bed at all, poor devils! No, I mean Rosenthall himself, and that pasty-faced beast Purvis. They were up and drinking from midnight, when they came in, to broad daylight, when I cleared out. Even then I left them sober enough to slang each other. By the way, they very nearly came to blows in the garden, within a few yards of me, and I heard something that might come in useful and make Rosenthall shoot crooked at a critical moment. You know what an IDB is?"

"Illicit Diamond Buyer?"

"Exactly. Well, it seems that Rosenthall was one. He must have let it out to Purvis in his cups. Anyhow, I heard Purvis taunting him with it, and threatening him with the breakwater at Capetown; and I begin to think our friends are friend and foe. But about to-morrow night; there's nothing subtle in my plan. It's simply to get in while these fellows are out on the loose, and to lie low till they come back, and longer. If possible, we must doctor the whisky. That would simplify the whole thing, though it's not a very sporting game to play; still, we must remember Rosenthall's revolver; we don't want him to sign his name on us. With all those Kaffirs about, however, it's ten to one on the whisky, and a hundred to one against us if we go looking for it. A brush with the heathen would spoil everything, if it did no more. Besides, there are the ladies—"

"The deuce there are!"

"Ladies with an eye, and the very voices for raising Cain. I fear, I fear the clamour! It would be fatal to us. *Au contraire,* if we can manage to stow ourselves away unbeknown, half the battle will be won. If Rosenthall turns in drunk, it's a purple diamond apiece. If he sits up sober, it may be a bullet instead. We will hope not, Bunny; and all the firing wouldn't be on one side; but it's on the knees of the gods."

And so we left it when we shook hands in Piccadilly—not by any means as much later as I could have wished. Raffles would not ask me to his rooms that night. He said he made it a rule to have a long night before playing cricket and—other games. His final word to me was framed on the same principle.

"Mind, only one drink to-night, Bunny. Two at the outside—as you value your life—and mine!"

I remember my abject obedience, and the endless, sleepless night it gave me; and the roofs of the houses opposite standing out at last against the blue-grey London dawn. I wondered whether I should ever see another, and was very hard on myself for that little expedition which I had made on my own wilful account.

It was between eight and nine o'clock in the evening when we took up our position in the garden adjoining that of Reuben Rosenthall; the house itself was shut up, thanks to the outrageous libertine next door, who, by driving away the neighbours, had gone far towards delivering himself into our hands. Practically secure from surprise on that side, we could watch our house under cover of a wall just high enough to see over, while a fair margin of shrubs in either garden afforded us additional protection. Thus entrenched we had stood an hour, watching a pair of lighted bow-windows with vague shadows flitting continually across the blinds, and listening to the drawing of corks, the clink of glasses, and a gradual crescendo of coarse voices within. Our luck seemed to have deserted us: the owner of the purple diamonds was dining at home, and dining at undue length. I thought it was a dinner-party. Raffles differed; in the end he proved right. Wheels grated in the drive, a carriage and pair stood at the steps; there was a stampede from the dining-room, and the loud voices died away, to burst forth presently from the porch.

Let me make our position perfectly clear. We were over the wall, at the side of the house, but a few feet from the dining-room windows. On our right, one angle of the building cut the back lawn in two diagonally; on our left, another angle just permitted us to see the jutting steps and the waiting carriage. We saw Rosenthall come out—saw the glimmer of his diamonds before anything. Then came the pugilist; then a lady with a head of hair like a bath sponge; then another, and the party was complete.

Raffles ducked and pulled me down in great excitement.

"The ladies are going with them," he whispered. "This is great!"

"That's better still."

"The Gardenia!" the millionaire had bawled.

"And that's best of all," said Raffles, standing upright as hoofs and wheels crunched through the gates and rattled off at a fine speed.

"Now what?" I whispered, trembling with excitement.

"They'll be clearing away. Yes, here come their shadows. The drawing-room windows open on the lawn. Bunny, it's the psychological moment. Where's that mask?"

I produced it with a hand whose trembling I tried in vain to still, and could have died for Raffles when he made no comment on what he could not fail to notice. His own hands were firm and cool as he adjusted my mask for me, and then his own.

"By Jove, old boy!" he whispered cheerily, "you look about the greatest ruffian I ever saw! These masks alone will down a negro, if we meet one. But I'm glad I remembered to tell you not to shave. You'll pass for Whitechapel if the worst comes to the worst and you don't forget to talk the lingo. Better sulk like a mule if you're not sure of it, and leave the dialogue to me; but, please our stars, there will be no need. Now, are you ready?"

"Quite."

"Got your gag?"

"Yes."

"Shooter?"

"Yes."

"Then follow me."

In an instant we were over the wall, in another on the lawn behind the house. There was no moon. The very stars in their courses had veiled themselves for our benefit. I crept at my leader's heels to some French windows opening upon a shallow verandah. He pushed. They yielded.

"Luck again," he whispered; "nothing but luck! Now for a light."

And the light came!

A good score of electric burners glowed red for the fraction of a second, then rained merciless white beams into our blinded eyes. When we found our sight four revolvers covered us, and between two of them the colossal frame of Reuben Rosenthall shook with a wheezy laughter from head to foot.

"Good-evening, boys," he hiccoughed. "Glad to see ye at last! Shift foot or finger, you on the left, though, and you're a dead boy. I mean you, you greaser!" he roared out at Raffles. "I know you. I've been waitin' for you. I've been watchin' you all this week! Plucky smart you thought yerself, didn't you? One day beggin', next time shammin' tight, and next one o' them old pals from Kimberley what never come when I'm in. But you left the same tracks everyday, you buggins, an' the same tracks every night, all round the blessed premises."

"All right, guv'nor," drawled Raffles; "don't excite. It's a fair cop. We don't sweat to know 'ow you brung it orf. On'y don't you go for to shoot, 'cos we 'aint awmed, s'help me Cord!"

"Ah, you're a knowin' one," said Rosenthall, fingering his triggers. "But you've struck a knowin'er."

"Ho, yuss, we know all abaht thet! Set a thief to catch a thief—ho, yuss."

My eyes had torn themselves from the round black muzzles, from the accursed diamonds that had been our snare, the pasty pig-face of the overfed pugilist, and the flaming cheeks and hook nose of Rosenthall himself. I was looking beyond them at the doorway filled with quivering silk and plush, black faces, white eye-balls, woolly pates. But a sudden silence recalled my attention to the millionaire. And only his nose retained its colour.

"What d'ye mean?" he whispered with a hoarse oath. "Spit it out, or, by Christmas, I'll drill you!"

"Whort price thet brikewater?" drawled Raffles coolly.

"Eh?"

Rosenthall's revolvers were describing widening orbits.

"What price thet brikewater—old IDB?"

"Where in hell did you get hold o' that?" asked Rosenthall with a rattle in his thick neck meant for mirth.

"You may well arst," says Raffles. "It's all over the plice w'ere I come from."

"Who can have spread such rot?"

"I dunno," says Raffles; 'arst the gen'leman on yer left; p'raps 'e knows."

The gentleman on his left had turned livid with emotion. Guilty conscience never declared itself in plainer terms. For a moment his small eyes bulged like currants in the suet of his face; the next, he had pocketed his pistols on a professional instinct, and was upon us with his fists.

"Out o' the light—out o' the light!" yelled Rosenthall in a frenzy.

He was too late. No sooner had the burly pugilist obstructed his fire than Raffles was through the window at a bound; while I, for standing still and saying nothing, was scientifically felled to the floor.

I cannot have been many moments without my senses. When I recovered them there was a great to-do in the garden, but I had the drawing-room to myself. I sat up. Rosenthall and Purvis were rushing about outside, cursing the Kaffirs and nagging at each other.

"Over that wall, I tell yer!"

"I tell you it was this one. Can't you whistle for the police?"

"Police be damned! I've had enough of the blessed police."

"Then we'd better get back and make sure of the other rotter."

"Oh, make sure o' yer skin. That's what you'd better do.—Jala, you black hog, if I catch you skulkin' . . ."

I never heard the threat. I was creeping from the drawing-room on my hands and knees, my own revolver swinging by its steel ring from my teeth.

For an instant I thought that the hall also was deserted. I was wrong, and I crept upon a Kaffir on all fours. Poor devil, I could not bring myself to deal him a base blow, but I threatened him most hideously with my revolver, and left the white teeth chattering in his black head as I took the stairs three at a time. Why I went upstairs in that decisive fashion, as though it were my only course, I cannot explain. But garden and ground floor seemed alive with men, and I might have done worse.

I turned into the first room I came to. It was a bedroom—empty, though lit up; and never shall I forget how I started as I entered, on encountering the awful villain that was myself at full length in a pier-glass! Masked, armed, and ragged, I was indeed fit carrion for a bullet or the hangman, and to one or the other I made up my mind. Nevertheless, I hid myself in the wardrobe behind the mirror, and there I stood shivering and seeing my fate, my folly, and Raffles most of all—Raffles first and last—for I dare say half an hour. Then the wardrobe door was flung suddenly open; they had stolen into the room without a sound; and I was hauled downstairs, an ignominious captive.

Gross scenes followed in the hall. The ladies were now upon the stage, and at sight of the desperate criminal they screamed with one accord. In truth I must have given them fair cause, though my mask was now torn away and hid nothing but my left ear. Rosenthall answered their shrieks with a roar for silence; the woman with the bath-sponge hair swore at him shrilly in return; the place became a Babel impossible to describe. I remember wondering how long it would be before the police appeared. Purvis and the ladies were for calling them in and giving me in charge without delay. Rosenthall would not hear of it. He swore that he would shoot man or woman who left his sight. He had had enough of the police. He was not going to have them coming there to spoil sport; he was going to deal with me in his own way. With that he dragged me from all other hands, flung me against a door, and sent a bullet crashing through the wood within an inch of my ear.

"You drunken fool! It'll be murder!" shouted Purvis, getting in the way a second time.

"Wha' do I care? He's armed, isn't he? I shot him in self-defence. It'll be a warning to others. Will you stand aside, or d'ye want it yourself?"

"You're drunk," said Purvis, still between us. "I saw you take a neat tumblerful since you came in, and it's made you drunk as a fool. Pull yourself together, old man. You ain't a-going to do what you'll be sorry for."

"Then I won't shoot at him, I'll only shoot roun' and' roun' the beggar. You're quite right, ole feller. Wouldn't hurt him. Great mishtake. Roun' an' roun'. There—like that!"

His freckled paw shot up over Purvis's shoulder, mauve lightning came from his ring, a red flash from his revolver, and shrieks from the women as the reverberations died away. Some splinters lodged in my hair.

Next instant the prize-fighter disarmed him; and I was safe from the devil, but finally doomed to the deep sea. A policeman was in our midst. He had entered through the drawing-room window; he was an officer of few words and creditable promptitude. In a twinkling he had the handcuffs on my wrist, while the pugilist explained the situation, and his patron reviled the force and its representative with impotent malignity. A fine watch they kept; a lot of good they did; coming in when all was over and the whole household might have been murdered in their sleep. The officer only deigned to notice him as he marched me off.

"We know all about you, sir," said he contemptuously, and he refused the sovereign Purvis proffered. "You will be seeing me again, sir, at Marylebone."

"Shall I come now?"

"As you please, sir. I rather think the other gentleman requires you more, and I don't fancy this young man means to give much trouble."

"Oh, I'm coming quietly," I said.

And I went.

In silence we traversed perhaps a hundred yards. It must have been midnight. We did not meet a soul. At last I whispered:

"How on earth did you manage it?"

"Purely by luck," said Raffles. "I had the luck to get clear away through knowing every brick of those back-garden walls, and the double luck to have these togs with the rest over at Chelsea. The helmet is one of a collection I made up at Oxford; here it goes over this wall, and we'd better carry the coat and belt before we meet a real officer. I got them once for a fancy ball—ostensibly—and thereby hangs a yarn. I always thought they might come in useful a second time. My chief crux to-night was getting rid of the hansom that brought me back. I sent him off to Scotland Yard with ten bob and a special message to good old Mackenzie. The whole detective department will be at Rosenthall's in about half an hour. Of course I speculated on our gentleman's hatred of the police—another huge slice of luck. If you'd got away, well and good; if not, I felt he was the man to play with his mouse as long as possible. Yes, Bunny, it's been more of a costume piece than I intended, and we've come out of it with a good deal less credit. But, by Jove, we're jolly lucky to have come out of it at all!"

JOHN F. SUTER

(b. 1914)

John F. Suter was born in Lancaster, Pennsylvania, and moved to Charleston, West Virginia, at age ten. Except for his college years, when he earned a bachelor of science degree in chemistry from Franklin and Marshall College, he has resided in Charleston. A Union Carbide research chemist, Suter began writing when he heard an episode of CBS radio's Suspense *(a popular show from 1942 to 1962) and thought he could do better. He found a book in the public library on how to write for radio and proceeded to write "Short Order," for which he was later paid a modest sum. Airing the day after V-J Day, this show must have been one of the least-heard shows ever broadcast. He wrote a few more for the series, but television was on the ascendant. Writing for television would have required that Suter move to California (the* Suspense *television series was broadcast live from there). As a result, he decided to try fiction, entering a short story in the annual Ellery Queen contest. His entries in the first three years all won prizes. Suter has had more than fifty stories published since then, and his work has appeared in more than thirty anthologies and in a textbook. Most of his stories are nonseries; however, he wrote some fifteen stories continuing fellow West Virginian Melville Davisson Post's character of Uncle Abner (who appears elsewhere in this volume). Suter has also created a series of stories involving a heavy equipment operator, who in the course of his work discovers and solves various crimes. He has written several stories with variations on the locked room, including one in which a child disappears into a fairy ring. He has said he set out with the following story to reverse the situation, having his main character locked in, rather than out. In doing this, Suter clearly demonstrates the affinity of the locked room mystery to the caper in a tale about a brilliantly simple theft.*

THE IMPOSSIBLE THEFT

Robert Chisholm's palms were faintly damp. He had less confidence in his ability to persuade than in the probability of his accomplishing the theft. Still, he hoped that theft would be unnecessary.

Donald Tapp looked up at him sardonically as he turned the second key to the double-locked room.

"Robert," he said in a voice that had been hoarse all his life, "you still haven't told me how you found out about my collection."

Chisholm's shrug was the smooth, practiced action of a man who knows and controls every muscle. He permitted his smile to be open and frank, instead of the faintly diabolical one which his lean face wore on certain occasions.

"I told you," he said. "A mutual friend. He just doesn't want to be identified."

Tapp reached around the metal doorframe and pressed a switch. Fluorescent lights hesitated, blinked, then came on.

He pursed his thick lips. "Mutual friend? I don't advertise what I own. There is always a clamor to have such items as these placed in a museum. Time enough for that when I'm dead." He studied Chisholm quizzically. "Would it have been Perry?"

Chisholm became poker-faced. "Sorry, Don."

Tapp still waited before ushering him into the room.

"Robert, I haven't seen you in—how many years? Even though we played together as boys and went to school together—clear through college. Now you arrive in town for a convention and after all these years you look me up. I'm delighted, Robert, delighted. I don't see old friends much any more. Chiefly my own fault. But, Robert, you arrive and make small talk and then, in the middle of it, you ask to see the collection."

Chisholm said, just a shade too casually, "If you'd rather not—"

Ask yourself, Don, he thought; *when you were a kid and somebody asked, "Whatcha got?" you'd always hide it, make a big secret of it.*

Tapp stepped away from the door, lifting a stubby right hand. "Come in and look. I'll be honest and say I'm particular. Not everybody can get into this room. But you're an old friend. At least, you were never grabby like the other kids."

If you only knew, Chisholm thought, entering the strongroom which Tapp devoted to his collection of rare historical documents.

It was a windowless room, about 12 feet by 20, lighted only by two rows of fluorescent tubes overhead. The only door was at the end of one long wall. To the left, on entering, the wall was decorated with a large rectangular mirror in a gilded frame. The borders of the glass itself were worked in elaborate scrolls and tracery. Ranged against the two long walls and the far end of the room were nine exhibition cases, four along each wall, one at the end. The cases were of beautifully grained wood, with glass tops.

Tapp beckoned Chisholm across the room.

"We'll begin here." He snapped a switch on the side of one cabinet, and the interior became evenly illuminated, showing a frayed yellowed paper on a background of black velvet.

As Chisholm bent his lean shoulders to look at the descriptive card, Tapp began to explain, "The last page of a letter by James Garfield. Identity of recipient unknown, but signature authenticated. Can you read it? It says, *As to your wish that I make a Fourth of July address in your community, this would give me the greatest of pleasure. I must defer my answer, however, because I feel that there is some prior commitment which I cannot identify at this moment. Should this prove to be only faulty memory, I shall be pleased to accept* . . . Of course, when you realize this was written just prior to that fatal July 2, it makes for interesting speculation, doesn't it?"

As Chisholm murmured an appropriate reply, Tapp switched off the light and moved to the right. "In this cabinet I have a receipt from William Tecumseh Sherman to Braxton Bragg for money that Bragg asked Sherman to invest for him in San Francisco in 1854, when Sherman was in the banking business. The accompanying letters have great historical significance."

Chisholm stared with a fascination he did not need to pretend as Tapp led him from case to case, showing him exceptionally valuable documents signed by George Washington, Abraham Lincoln, Andrew Johnson, Alexander Graham Bell, John C. Fremont, William H. Seward, and Carry Nation. This last brought a chuckle from Tapp.

"Simple, isn't it? *No truce with Demon Rum! Carry Nation.*"

He snapped off the light in the eighth case and turned toward the last one, at the end of the room. He paused and glanced at Chisholm.

"Robert, what was it you told me you were doing these days?"

"Area man for Shaw and Pontz Lock Company." Chisholm reached toward his left lapel with supple, slender fingers and tapped the identity tag which was stuck to his coat by the adhesive on the back of the tag. "The convention is one of hardware dealers. I'm showing a new line of passage sets."

Tapp shrugged off a faint air of perplexity. "Well! Let's look at my prize exhibit." He illuminated the last cabinet.

In it lay a scrap of paper no bigger than the palm of the average-sized hand. It was even more yellowed than the other documents, the ink slightly more faded. It was charred along the top edge.

Tapp said nothing. Chisholm bent to look closely.

"Some kind of register or ledger?"

"That's right. From an inn."

"Three names. James—Allen? Samuel Green. That one's clear. But—*Button Gwinnett?*"

Tapp rubbed his stubborn chin with his solid-fleshed left hand. The tip of his broad nose wrinkled in amusement.

"You're amazed, Robert. Yes, the rarest of all signatures in United States history. Your amazement is justified. But it's genuine, I assure you—absolutely genuine."

"But how did you—? Where did you—?"

Tapp shook his head. "When I am dead, all information on

these documents will be released to the museum which will inherit them. In the meantime, that information is my secret."

Chisholm glanced around the room. "I hope you have these well protected. And adequately insured."

"Both, you may be sure."

"What protection, Don? This interests me, since I'm in the lock business." He bent over the case containing the Button Gwinnett signature.

"I'm satisfied with it," said Tapp bluntly.

"Are you?" Chisholm drew a key ring from his pocket. It bristled with keys—and other odd-looking objects. His supple fingers gripped something which Tapp could not see, and he inserted it quickly into the lock on the edge of the glass top. Something clicked and he lifted the lid of the case. "You see?"

Instantly a clamor began somewhere in the big house.

"I see. And do you hear?" Tapp gave his old friend an exasperated look. "Come on. I'll have to shut off the alarm."

"Might I remain here, Don? I'd like to look some more. I promise I won't touch anything."

Tapp shook his head. "Nobody looks unless I'm here. But if you don't want to come with me, you may stand by the door, outside, until I come back."

After Tapp had locked both locks from the outside, Chisholm stood by the door thinking about the strongroom. All the cases were obviously wired to alarms. He had seen no wires. This meant that the wiring probably went through the legs of the cases, where it would be difficult to reach. Did each case activate a separate alarm, or trip a separate indicator, to show exactly which cabinet a burglar had attacked? Probably.

And the mirror on the left wall? What was a mirror doing in a room of this sort?

Tapp came bustling back, his chunky frame still radiating annoyance.

"Now, Robert," he said, unlocking the door for the second time, "I ask you, *please* don't try to sell me any locks—not this time."

"We have some things which would help you, if you'd let me demonstrate," Chisholm said, as he began to scan the room closely on re-entering.

"All right, all right—but show me a little later. In my den or in my office. Of course, I'm always interested in improving my safeguards. But not just now."

Chisholm moved slowly from case to case, keeping up a running conversation to distract Tapp's attention. But he could discover nothing other than the alarms and the puzzling mirror. There were, of course, the two locks in the door—which would be impossible to jimmy, or to pick. Then two tiny air passages, high in the end walls, protected by a fine, strong mesh caught his roving eye; but he dismissed them as irrelevant.

Finally he straightened and looked directly at Tapp.

"There's a lot of money represented here, Don."

Tapp nodded soberly. "I'd hate to tell you how much, Robert."

"And you'll put even more documents in this room, won't you?"

"If something good comes along."

"This, of course, means that you have the money to spend."

Tapp's expression grew pained. "You're being a bit ingenuous, Robert. Of course I have the money."

"Have you ever considered putting some of that money into something more worthwhile?"

Tapp grinned without humor. "I should have known there was more to this visit than a chat with an old friend. Now comes the touch. How much do you need?"

Chisholm shook his head. "The need isn't mine, Don. It's Green Meadows Hospital. A check for $50,000 from you would put their new equipment drive over the top."

Tapp grimaced. "Green Meadows! I've heard their pitch. A corny one, too. Green Meadows—even the name's corny. No, thanks, Robert. Why did you have to spoil our first meeting in years?"

Chisholm said seriously, "I don't consider geriatric problems corny, Don. Are you sure you just don't like to think of the kind of future any one of us might have to face? Look here: I've contributed $20,000 myself, and believe me, it'll hurt for a while. If I could give twenty, surely you can give fifty?"

Tapp grimaced again. "I don't like people telling me what I can or can't give to charity."

"It would be a deduction on your income tax return."

"Thanks. I know all the possible deductions upside down and backwards."

"Is there any way I can reach you on this, Don? Could I tell you some details of their program—"

Tapp shook his head firmly. "No way at all—not even for an old buddy. Especially not for an old buddy. I can't stand corn."

Chisholm's eyes narrowed, and his brows slanted up in a manner familiar to many people who had met him.

"All right, Don. You won't listen to a rational argument, so I'll make you an irrational proposition. Is your gambling blood still what it used to be?"

Tapp's smile was grim. "If it's a sure thing, I'll still bet."

"Would you bet a check for $50,000 that I can't steal something of value from this room?"

Shock and amazement crossed Tapp's heavy features. "Why, that's idiotic. I won't listen."

Chisholm held out a restraining hand. "No, wait. You have complete confidence in your safeguards. Let's see just how good they are. I don't know a thing about them except there are locks on the door and alarms connected with the cabinets. Yet I am willing to bet I can beat your system."

Tapp pondered. "There's nothing in the world which can't stand improvement. But $50,000—"

Chisholm pressed on. "Here's what I propose: shut me in this room for fifteen minutes—no more. In that short time I guarantee to steal one of these documents—*and get it out of here in spite of all your safeguards.* If I get that paper *out* of this room, you'll make the contribution to the hospital."

"And if you fail? What is your stake?"

"I'll guarantee to increase the efficiency of your safeguards one hundred per cent."

"That's hardly worth fifty thousand."

"I own a quarter interest in my company. I'll assign it to you."

Tapp eyed him shrewdly. "You seem pretty confident."

"I might be betting on a sure thing, Don. The way you like to do. Or I might be willing to take a bigger risk than you."

Tapp mused, "Fifteen minutes. And you have to get it *out* of the room by the end of that time. You know, I could just leave you locked in here."

"No, you must come and let me out. But I must agree to let you search me or put any reasonable restrictions on me until it's absolutely clear that you've lost."

"When do you want to do this?"

"Right now."

Tapp studied Chisholm speculatively. "Chisel—remember how we used to call you that?—when we were kids a lot of the others had contempt for me because I wouldn't take chances. I've done pretty well in life because of caution. But don't be misled: I *will* take a risk. I'll take this one."

Chisholm smiled broadly, but this time his smile had a Mephistophelian look. "Fine. Shall we begin?"

Tapp held out his wrist silently and they compared watches.

"Fifteen minutes from the time you close the door," said Chisholm.

Tapp went out. As he pushed the door shut, he called through the narrowing crack, "Not that I think you have a snowball's chance, Chisel."

The door had scarcely closed before Chisholm was examining the mirror on the long wall with minute attention. He would have to proceed as though it were a two-way mirror, with only a thin layer of silver. He doubted that this was true, but he could not ignore the possibility. Finally he located what he was looking for: a circular loop in the border decoration on the glass. The glass within the loop looked subtly different.

His smile grew even more diabolical. He quickly stripped the convention badge from his left lapel and pasted it over the circle in the glass.

He then turned swiftly to the cases, taking out his keyring. Before he started to use it, he took a pair of thin rubber gloves from another pocket and put them on. Then, at a pace only a little slower than a walk, he went from case to case and opened the locks, which he had studied while looking at the documents the second time.

When he had lifted all the lids, he laughed at the thought of nine alarms ringing simultaneously in Tapp's ears, or nine position lights flashing at one time in Tapp's face. He then went from case to case and reached inside each. All his movements were swift. Most of them were intended as pure misdirection.

Finally he had what he wanted. Now all he had to do was to make sure—doubly sure—that he was not being observed. To provide a cloak, he removed his jacket and slipped it over his shoulders backward, with the back of the jacket hanging in front of him and concealing his hands. His fingers made several rapid movements beneath the protection of the jacket. Then he suddenly reversed the process and put the coat back in its normal position.

He looked at his watch. Only eight minutes had passed.

For the remainder of the time Chisholm lounged against the doorframe singing slightly ribald songs in a clear, but not overloud, voice.

Precisely at the end of fifteen minutes, first one, then the other of the door locks was opened. The door itself, which was covered with a paneling of steel, swung back.

As Tapp stepped in, his glance already darting around the room, Chisholm clapped him lightly on the back.

"I hope you brought the check with you, Don."

Tapp half turned, and Chisholm felt a hard object bore into his ribs. He looked down. Tapp had shoved a pistol into his side.

"I have the check, Chisel, but you're going to earn it—if you get it at all. Step back."

Chisholm obeyed.

"Now, go over there to the opposite wall and sit on the floor by that first case. Extend your arms so that one is on either side of the leg of the case. Very good."

Chisholm, from his position on the floor, saw Tapp take a pair of handcuffs from his pocket. Warily, the shorter man approached him.

"Wrists out, Chisel. Good."

Tapp leaned over and snapped the cuffs on Chisholm's wrists. The tall diabolical-looking man had not ceased to smile.

"A lot of trouble, Don, just to find out what I did take. A lot of trouble to keep me from confusing you even more while you look. But I'll be glad to tell you without all this melodrama."

"Just be quiet, Chisel." Tapp said calmly "If you aren't, I'll slug you with the butt of this gun."

"Violence wasn't in our agreement, Don."

"You were not completely honest with me, Chisel. After you put all your misdirections into action, the hunch I'd had about you came out into the open. I remembered your hobby when you were a boy. I made one phone call to a local convention delegate I happen to know, and he told me you still practice your hobby. You're still an amateur magician, aren't you, Chisel?"

Chisholm shrugged. "I do a little routine to catch the buyer's attention, then I work it into a sales talk for our products. It often helps."

"Spare me," Tapp muttered, peering into cases. His face darkened. "You lied to me, Chisel. You said you would take only one document. I count three of them: the Garfield letter we read, the Seward I mentioned, and the Button Gwinnett."

"I didn't lie," Chisholm replied calmly. "Figure it out for yourself."

"Misdirection again." Tapp turned and stared at him, but it

was clear that his thoughts were elsewhere. In a moment he turned back to the cabinets and carefully lifted the velvet in the bottom of each. He found nothing.

He stood in thought for a few more minutes.

"The Garfield and the Alexander Graham Bell are the same size, and so are the Seward and the Lincoln. The Button Gwinnett doesn't match any, but it is *smaller* . . ."

Once more he went from case to case, this time lifting each of the remaining documents. When he had finished, he was smiling. He had found two of the missing papers carefully placed beneath others of the same size. He restored the Garfield and Seward documents to their proper cases.

"That leaves only the Button Gwinnett, Chisel. But this was what you had in mind all along. It's obvious. And if you're worth your salt as a magician, its hiding place won't be obvious. So let's eliminate the commonplace."

Tapp went over the cases carefully, first lifting out all the documents, then each piece of velvet. When he had replaced everything, he closed and locked the cases. Then he dropped to his knees and inspected the under sides of the cabinets.

He found nothing.

He walked to each end of the room in turn and reached up to the tiny air passages. The mesh in both was still firmly in place, and he could not budge it at either opening.

Then his eye caught the mirror.

"Oh, and another thing—" He walked to the mirror and stripped off the convention tag. "You're a sharp fellow, Robert."

Chisholm laughed. "Was my guess right? Closed-circuit TV? Did I cover the lens?"

"You put a patch on its eye, I must admit."

"No two-way mirror?"

"I considered it, but with several receivers on the TV, I can be at any one of several places in the house. A two-way mirror would only restrict me."

He walked over and stood in front of Chisholm. "Two possibilities still remain. One is that you might have slipped it into my own pocket at the door. So I'll check that out now."

He searched through all his pockets, but found nothing which had not been in them before.

He now stooped and unlocked the handcuffs, but made no move to take them from Chisholm's wrists.

"Drop the cuffs there, get up, and go to that corner," he said, motioning with the gun to the bare corner farthest away from the door.

Chisholm obeyed. When he had moved, Tapp inspected the area where the magician had been sitting.

"All right. Now take off your clothes—one garment at a time—and throw them over to me."

Chisholm complied, beginning with his coat jacket, until he stood completely stripped.

Tapp went over each item minutely, crushing cloth carefully, listening for the crackle of paper, inspecting shoes for false heels and soles and the belt for a secret compartment. From Chisholm's trousers he extracted a handkerchief and an ordinary keyring. In the pockets of the coat jacket he found a larger collection. The inside breast pocket yielded a wallet and two used envelopes with jottings on the back. The outside pockets contained the unusual keyring, the rubber gloves, a nearly full pack of cigarettes, a crumpled cigarette package, a ballpoint pen, and a rubber band.

Tapp examined all these things with intense concentration. In the wallet he found money, a driver's license, a miscellany of credit and indentification cards, and a small receipt for the purchase of a shirt at a local department store. He searched for a hidden compartment in the wallet, but found none. He then shook the cigarettes from the pack, but neither the pack itself nor the individual cigarettes was the least out of the ordinary. Replacing them, he then smoothed out the crumpled pack. Several items inside it he dumped on the top of one of the cases: a twist of cellophane; two wadded bits of brownish, waxy-looking paper; a fragment of wrapper from a roll of peppermints; and part of a burned match. He snorted and swept this trash back into its container.

He drew in his breath with an angry hiss. "All right, Chisel, let's look *you* over. Turn around. Raise your arms. All right, now sit down on the floor and raise your feet."

"Nothing on the soles of my feet except dust from the floor. You should clean this place oftener," said Chisholm, leaning back on his arms.

Tapp's only answer was a growl.

"Have you checked the ceiling?" Chisholm asked.

Tapp looked up involuntarily. The ceiling was bare.

"See, you wouldn't have thought of that, would you?" Chisholm mocked.

Tapp leaned against one of the cabinets and aimed the pistol at Chisholm's midriff.

"Chisel, playtime is over. I want that Button Gwinnett back."

"Or else, eh? You forget a number of things. We haven't yet established whether the paper is in this room or out of it. We haven't exchanged your check for $50,000 for the stolen document. I haven't even put my clothes back on. And, incidentally, I give you my word: the missing paper isn't in my clothing."

Tapp tossed the clothing to Chisholm. "It doesn't matter. You're going to tell me where that piece of paper is."

Chisholm began to dress. "How do you propose to make me tell? Shoot me? On the grounds that I broke into your house to steal? A respected businessman like me—steal? If you killed me, then you'd never find your paper. If you only wounded me, I'd refuse to talk. So where are we, old friend?"

Tapp said grimly, "This bet of yours is just a stall. Once you get out of this room you'll take off with that signature to certain other collectors I could name. Why else won't you admit who told you about my collection? Only a handful of people know about it."

Chisholm was tempted to yield on this point and reveal to Tapp that it was the district manager of Tapp's own insurance company who had mentioned the collection to him in strict confidence. Had he not wished to show even the slightest sign of weakness, he would have told this.

"The whole thing was strictly honorable," Chisholm said. "This stunt was my own idea."

"And my idea," said Tapp heavily, "is to lock you in here without food and water until you return that paper. When you finally get out, I could always claim that I thought you had left the house and had locked you in without knowing."

Chisholm shook his head. "I had more respect for you, Don. If you did that, you'd either have to leave the other documents with me—and risk my destroying them—or take them out and have their absence disprove your story."

Inwardly, Chisholm was beginning to have qualms. If Tapp should abandon reason in favor of a collector's passion, as he seemed about to do, anything might happen. The best course was an immediate distraction.

"How do you know," he said challengingly, "that the paper isn't *already* outside the room?"

Tapp snorted. "Impossible!"

"Is it, now? There is a small trick I often do at dinner gatherings *which depends entirely on the victim's being too close to me to see what my hands are really doing.* I move a handkerchief or tissue from hand to hand near the victim's face, then throw it over his shoulder when my hand is too close for him to see exactly what I've done."

Tapp said warily, "But at no time were you outside this room."

"I didn't have to be."

Suddenly Tapp understood. "You mean when I came in!" He moved back and reached behind him to open the door. "Stay where you are." He stepped out and pushed the door shut again.

Chisholm waited tensely.

The door opened to a pencil-wide crack. "There's nothing out here, Chisel."

Chisholm answered evenly. "I didn't say there was. But if you'll use the brains I've always given you credit for, you'll realize that I don't *want* to steal your precious piece of paper. If I had, why make the bet? Let me out of here and give me the $50,000 check for the hospital, and I'll tell you where the Button Gwinnett signature is."

A silence followed his words. Seconds dragged by. Minutes.

Finally Tapp spoke. "You swear that this will end here? That you won't even tell anyone about this incident? I used to think your word could be relied on, Chisel."

"I'll swear on anything you name."

"That won't be necessary." The door opened wide. "Now, where is it?"

Chisholm smiled and shook his head. "First, the $50,000 check."

Tapp eyed him shrewdly. "I don't know that the paper is out of the room. I don't owe you anything unless it *is* outside, and you're still *inside*. But you agreed to tell me where it is."

Chisholm kept smiling. "I'll swear again, if you like. The paper is outside the room, according to the conditions of our bet.'

Tapp studied him. "Very well, come up to my den and I'll give you the check. You have my word that I'll keep my part of the bargain. Now—*where is that paper?*"

Chisholm stepped to Tapp's side and clapped him affectionately on the back. Then he held out his right hand.

"Here."

As Tapp all but snatched the document from him, Chisholm fished in his own jacket pocket. He took out the crumpled cigarette pack, opened it, and shook out the contents.

"Remember the convention badge I stuck over your TV camera lens? Such badges are only strips of cardboard coated on the back with a permanently tacky adhesive—the way surgical adhesive tape is coated." From the cigarette pack he took the two scraps of brownish, waxy paper. "That gave me the idea. It's easy to obtain tape with such an adhesive on *both* front and back. This brown paper protects the adhesive until it's peeled off, making the tape ready for use. In this case I kept a small bit of such tape in my pocket, removed the Button Gwinnett signature from the cabinet, exposed the adhesive on one side of the tape, and stuck the Button Gwinnett to that exposed side. Then I made the other side of the tape ready and palmed the whole thing."

Chisholm repeated an earlier gesture. A look of comprehension spread over Tapp's face.

"When you came into the room at the end of the fifteen minutes," Chisholm explained, "I simply put the Button Gwinnett paper in the one place you couldn't see—*on your back!*"

SIMON BRETT

(b. 1945)

The wit and charm of Simon Brett are legendary among his writing colleagues. His incisive parodies of fiction and drama never fail to draw large and enthusiastic audiences at professional conventions. His novels and short stories exude the same sharp humor and have made him a popular writer around the world. Born in Surrey, England, he was educated at Dulwich College and received a bachelor of arts degree in English with honors from Wadham College at Oxford University. Brett was rewarded for his interest in theater soon after graduation. He went to work for the BBC as a radio producer and by 1970 had a one-act play, Mrs. Gladys Moxon, *produced in London. Later he wrote a musical, and several television and radio plays, and became a producer for London Weekend Television. He also wrote several books, including* The Childowner's Handbook *(1983).* Cast, in Order of Disappearance *(1975) introduced the world to Brett's highly original detective, Charles Paris. Paris is a drunkard and a second-rate actor who takes whatever roles he can, even playing the corpse in a mystery production. In* What Bloody Man Is That? *(1987), for example, Paris assumes the minor roles of murdered cast members in a production of* Macbeth *until so many have died that, in order for the show to go on he would have had to play opposite himself. Brett's hilarious satires of theater people are interwoven with his murder plots, and though it may be implausible that a drunken actor like Paris would be sharp enough mentally to solve cases, Brett makes it credible. In the following story, Brett employs a similarly unimpressive main character, comparable to Brett's more famous hero. The unlikely hero of the tale outwits both the law and the criminal mastermind in the theft of a painting and is revealed to be much more intelligent than his initial thuggishness makes him seem. A devil-may-care tone, common in many caper stories, is well suited to Brett's particular talents.*

DON'T KNOW MUCH ABOUT ART

I have been described as not very bright. Partly, I reckon it's my size. People who look like me have appeared as dumb villains in too many movies and television series. And if you've had a background as a professional wrestler, you find the general public doesn't have too many expectations of you as an intellect.

Also, I have to face it, there have been one or two unfortunate incidents in my past. Jobs that didn't turn out exactly like they was planned. Like when I was in the getaway car outside the bank and I drove off with the wrong passengers. Or when I got muddled after that bullion robbery and delivered it all back to the security firm. Or when I wrote my home address on that ransom demand. OK, silly mistakes, sort of thing anyone could do in the heat of the moment, but I'm afraid it's the kind of thing that sticks in people's minds and I have got a bit of a reputation in the business as a dumbo.

Result of it all is, most of the jobs I get tend to be—to put it mildly—intellectually undemanding. In fact, the approach of most of the geezers who hire me seems to be, "We couldn't find a blunt instrument, so you'll have to do."

Now, of course, my own view of my mental capacity doesn't exactly coincide with that, but a chap has to live, and a recession isn't the time you can afford to be choosy. I mean, you read all this about rising crime figures, but you mustn't get the impression from that that villains are doing well. No, we feel the pinch like anyone else. For a start, there's a lot more blokes trying to muscle in. Side-effect of unemployment, of course, and most of them are really amateurs, but they do queer the pitch for us professionals. They undercut our rates and bring into the business a kind of dishonesty that I'm sure wasn't there when I started. The cake isn't that much bigger than it ever was, and there's a hell of a lot more blokes trying to get slices.

Result is, I take anything I'm offered . . . driving, bouncing, frightening, looming (often booked for looming I am, on account of my size). No, I'll do anything. Short of contract killing. Goes against my principles, that and mugging old ladies. As I say, it's no time to be choosy. When this country's got more than three million unemployed, you just got to put off your long-term ambitions, forget temporarily about career structure, and be grateful you got a job of any sort.

So when I was offered the Harbinger Hall job, never crossed my mind to turn it down. Apart from anything else, it sounded easy and the pay was bloody good. Five grand for a bit of petty larceny . . . well, that can't be bad, can it? Sure there was always the risk of getting nicked, but didn't look like there'd be any rough stuff. Mind you, never be quite sure in stately homes. Tend to be lots of spears and shotguns and that stuck on the walls, so there's always the danger that someone might have a fit of temperament and cop hold of one of those.

Still, five grand for a weekend's work in a slow autumn was good money.

The initial contact come through Wally Clinton, which I must say surprised me. It was Wally I was driving to Heathrow after that jeweller's job the time I ran out of petrol, so I didn't think I was exactly his Flavour of the Month. Still, shows how you can misjudge people. Here he was letting bygones be bygones and even putting a nice bit of work my way. Take back all that I said about him at the Black Dog last New Year's Eve.

Anyway, so Wally gets in touch, asks if I'm in the market and when I says yes, tells me to go and meet this bloke, "Mr. Loxton," in this sauna club off St. Martin's Lane.

Strange sauna club it was. Not a girl in sight. I think it actually must've been for geezers who wanted to have saunas. All neat and tidy, no little massage cubicles with plastic curtains, no funny smell, no nasty bits of screwed-up tissue on the floor. Most peculiar.

Bloke on the door was expecting me. Give me a big white towel and showed me into a changing-room that was all very swish with pine and clean tiles. He told me to take my clothes off, put on the towel and go into the sauna. Mr. Loxton would join me shortly.

Don't mind telling you, I felt a bit of a grapefruit sitting on this wooden shelf with nothing on but this towel. When I first went in I sat on the top shelf, but blimey it was hot. Soon realised it got cooler the lower you went, so I went to the bottom one. Still uncomfortably hot, mind. Geezer my size really sweats when he sweats.

I tried to work out why Mr. Loxton had chosen this place for the meet. I mean, a sauna's good if you're worried the opposition might've got shooters. Isn't anywhere you can put one when you've got your clothes off. Nowhere comfortable, anyway. But this wasn't that kind of encounter.

On the other hand, it wasn't bad if you didn't want to be identified. The lights in the sauna was low and it was a bit steamy. Also, people don't look the same when they're starkers. Oh, I know they do lots of corpse identification from secret birthmarks and moles on the body and that, but the average bloke without clothes on doesn't look like himself. For a start, next time you see him, chances are he'll be dressed, and you'd be surprised how many clues you get to what a person's like from what they wear. I reckoned Mr. Loxton was meeting there to maintain the old incog.

I felt even more sure of that when he come in. He had a big towel round him under his armpits like me, but he also got a small one draped over his head like a boxer. He didn't turn his face towards me, but immediately went over to a wooden bucket in the corner, picked out a ladleful of water and poured it over this pile of stones. Well, that really got the steam going, and when he did turn towards me, he wasn't no more than a blur.

"You are Billy Gorse."

I admitted it. Wasn't spoken like a question, anyway, more a statement.

"Thank you for coming. Wally Clinton recommended you for a job that needs doing."

He might have hid his face with all the towels and the steam, but he had a voice that was really distinctive. Private school, you know, and a bit prissy. I'm good with voices. Knew I'd recognise his if I ever heard it again.

I stayed stumm, waiting for the details, and he went on. "What I want you to do, Gorse, is to steal a painting."

"Blimey," I said, "I don't know much about art."

"You don't need to."

"But surely . . . paintings . . . I mean specialist work, isn't it? Not like walking in and nicking someone's video. If a painting's any good, it's got security systems all round it. And then finding a fence who'll handle them sort of goods—"

"All that side is taken care of. All I said I wanted you to do was to steal a painting."

"You mean I'd be, like, part of a gang?"

"There's no need for you to know anything about anyone else involved. All you have to do is to follow instructions without question."

"I can do that."

"Good. Wally said you could. You do the job on the last weekend of October."

"Where?"

"Have you heard of Harbinger Hall?"

I shook my head.

"Then I suppose you haven't heard of the Harbinger Madonna either."

"Who's she?"

" 'She' is the painting you are going to steal."

"Oh. Well, like I said, I don't know much about art."

"No." His voice sounded sort of pleased with that. Smug.

He asked me where he could send my instructions. I nearly gave him my home address, but something told me to hold my horses, so I give him the name of Red Rita's gaff. She often holds mail for me, on account of services rendered what I needn't go into here.

Then Mr. Loxton reached into his towel and pulled out a polythene bag. Thought of everything, he did. Didn't want the notes to get damp.

"Five hundred in there. Two thousand when you get your instructions. Second half on completion of the job." He rose through the steam. "Stay here another ten minutes. If you appear in the changing room before I've left the building, the contract's cancelled." He reached for the door handle.

"Oh, Mr. Loxton . . ."

His reaction was that half-second slow, which confirmed that he wasn't using his real name. No great surprise. Very few of the geezers I deal with do. Not for me, that. Always stick to "Billy Gorse." Only time I tried anything different, I forgot who I was half-way through the job.

"What did you want, Mr. Gorse?"

I'd got what I wanted, but I said, "Oh, just to say thank you for the job, Mr. Loxton."

He done a sort of snort and walked out the sauna.

Long ten minutes it was in that heat. When I come out I was sweating like a Greek cheese.

Instructions come the following week as per. I went down Red Rita's for reasons that aren't any of your business, and after a bit she give me this thick brown envelope. Just my name on it. No stamps, nothing like that. Just come through her letterbox. She didn't see who dropped it.

I didn't open it till I got back to my place next morning. First I counted the money. Fifties, forty of them all present and correct. Then there was this postcard of some bird in blue with this nipper on her knee. That was presumably the picture I was going to nick. I didn't take much notice of it, but unfolded the typewritten sheet of instructions.

No mention of my name and they wasn't signed either. Plain paper, no other clues to where it might've come from. It was all typed in capital letters, which I must say got my goat a bit. Reckon Wally Clinton'd been casting aspersions on my literacy, the cheeky devil. Anyway, what I had to do was spelled out very clear.

> FIRST—FILL IN THE ENCLOSED BOOKING FORM, BOOKING YOURSELF INTO THE "STATELY HOME WEEKEND" AT HARBINGER HALL FOR THE 29TH AND 30TH OCTOBER. SEND THE FULL PAYMENT BY MONEY ORDER. (ALL YOUR EXPENSES WILL BE REPAID.)
>
> SECOND—THIS FRIDAY, 21ST OCTOBER, TRAVEL DOWN TO HARBINGER HALL AND TAKE THE CONDUCTED TOUR OF THE BUILDING (THESE RUN EVERY HOUR ON THE HOUR BETWEEN 10 A.M. AND 4 P.M.). WHEN YOU REACH THE GREAT HALL, LOOK CAREFULLY AT THE PAINTING OF THE MADONNA, NOTING THE VISIBLE SECURITY ARRANGEMENTS AROUND IT.
>
> WHEN THE TOUR REACHES THE END OF THE LONG GALLERY UPSTAIRS, LINGER BEHIND THE GROUP. AS THE REST OF THEM GO INTO THE BLUE BEDROOM, OPEN THE DOOR LABELLED "PRIVATE" AT THE END OF THE GALLERY. YOU WILL FIND YOURSELF AT THE TOP OF A SMALL STAIRCASE. GO DOWN THIS QUICKLY AND YOU WILL FIND YOURSELF IN A SMALL LOBBY. ON THE WALL OPPOSITE THE FOOT OF THE STAIRS YOU WILL SEE THE BOXES CONTROLLING THE BUILDING'S ALARM SYSTEM. THESE ARE OPERATED BY A KEY,

BUT YOU WILL SEE THE WIRES WHICH COME OUT OF THE TOP OF THE BOXES. WHEN YOU ACTUALLY COME TO STEAL THE MADONNA, YOU WILL CUT THROUGH THESE WIRES. HAVING SEEN THEIR POSITION, RETURN AS QUICKLY AS POSSIBLE UP THE STAIRS AND REJOIN YOUR GROUP. COMPLETE THE REST OF THE TOUR AND RETURN HOME WITHOUT FURTHER INVESTIGATION.

FURTHER INSTRUCTIONS WILL FOLLOW NEXT WEEK. MEMORISE THE DETAILS IN THESE SHEETS AND THEN BURN THEM.

I done like I was told and before the Friday I got a confirmation of my booking on this "Stately Home Weekend." I read the brochure on that and I must say it didn't really sound my scene. Tours of the grounds, lectures on the history of the place, full mediaeval banquet on the Saturday night, farewell tea with Lord Harbinger on the Sunday. I mean, my idea of a fun weekend is going down Southend with a few mates and putting back a few beers. Still, I'd put up with a lot for five grand.

So, the Friday I do as I'm told. Get the train out to Limmerton, and from there they've got this courtesy bus takes you out to Harbinger Hall.

Not a bad little gaff old Lord Harbinger's got, I'll say that for him. Don't know any more about architecture than I do about art, but I can tell it's old. Don't build places like that nowadays, not with blooming great pillars in front of the door and all them windows and twiddly bits on the roof.

Nice position and all. It's high, like on top of this hill, looking out over all the rest of the countryside. That's how you first see it in the bus from the station. As you get nearer, you lose sight for a bit, because it's a really steep hill with trees. So you sort of zigzag up this drive, which is really a bit hairy and makes you glad the old bus's got decent brakes. And then suddenly you come out the top and you're right in front of the house and it's blooming big. And there's car parks off to the right and left, but the bus drops you pretty well by the front door.

I looked around as I got out. You know, some of these stately homes've got sort of zoos and funfairs and that, you know, a bit of entertainment. And, since I had to spend a whole weekend there, I thought it'd be nice to know there'd be something interesting to do. But no such luck. Place hadn't been developed like that. Maybe the grounds wasn't big enough.

In fact, not only hadn't the place been developed, it looked a bit tatty. I mean that sort of gaff isn't my style. Blimey, if I owned it, I'd knock it down and put up a nice executive Regency-style townhouse with double garage and Italian suite bathroom. But even I could tell this one needed a few grand spending on it.

And if my busload was anything to go by, the few grand wasn't going to come very quickly from tourists. OK, end of the season and that, but there wasn't many of us. Had to wait around till a few more come from the car parks before they'd start our guided tour, and then it was only about a dozen of us. Well, at a couple of sovs a head, takes you a long time to make money that way.

The guide what took us round had done the trip a few thousand times and obviously hadn't enjoyed it much even the first time. The spiel come out like a recording, jokes and all. Didn't look a happy man.

And what he said was dead boring. I never got on with history at school, couldn't see the percentage in it, so all his cobblers about what Duke built which bit and when didn't do a lot for me. And to think that I'd got a whole weekend of lectures on it coming up. I began to think I was going to earn my five grand.

Anyway, eventually we get to the Great Hall, and I see this picture all the fuss is about. Didn't go on it much in the postcard; the real thing's just the same, only bigger. Not big, though, compared to some of the numbers they got on the walls. I don't know, two foot by eighteen inches maybe. Don't know why they wanted to nick this one. Some of them was ten times the size, must've been worth a lot more. Still, not my decision. And a good thing, come to think of it, that they didn't want me to walk out with one of the twenty-foot numbers under my arm.

So the picture's just this Mum and her sprog. Frame was nice, mind. All gold and wiggly, like my brother-in-law's got round the cocktail bar in his lounge. And at the bottom of the frame there's this little brass plate nailed on. It says:

MADONNA AND CHILD
Giacomo Palladino
Florentine
(1473–1539)

Never heard of the git myself.

Anyway, I'd memorised my instructions like a good boy, so I have a good butchers at the pic. Can't see a lot in the way of security. I mean, there's a sort of purple rope strung between uprights to keep the punters six feet away from the wall, but that isn't going to stop anyone. Of course, there might be some photo-electric beam or some rocker device what sounds the alarm if you actually touch the thing. I step over the rope to take a closer look.

"Art-lover, are we, sir?" asks this sarcastic voice behind me.

I turn round and see this bloke in uniform. Not the guide, he's up the other end blathering about some king or other. No, this geezer's just some sort of security guard I noticed hanging around when we arrived.

"No," I says, with what people have described as my winning smile. "Don't know a blind thing about art."

"Then why are you studying the Madonna so closely?"

I'm about to say that I'm just interested in what security arrangements she got, and then I twig that this might not be so clever, so I do this big shrug and step back over the rope and join up with the other punters. I glance back as we're leaving the hall and this guard's giving me a really beady look.

Upstairs I follow the instructions without sweat. Dawdle doing the old untied shoe-lace routine while the rest troop in to hear the history of the Blue Bedroom, quick look round to see if I'm on my own in the gallery, then through the old "Private" door and down the stairs.

It's just like they said it would be. These big metal-covered boxes opposite me with coloured lights and chrome keyholes on them. And at the top the wires. Not that thick. Quick snip with the old metal-cutters. No prob.

I think for a minute. I know some of these systems got a sort of fail-safe so's they sound off if anyone tampers with the wiring. For a moment I wonder if someone's trying to set me up. Certainly are one or two geezers what I have sort of inadvertently offended in the course of my varied career, but this'd be a bloody elaborate way of getting their own back. Anyway, there's the two and a half grand I already got. Nobody's going to spend that kind of bread just to fix me. I hurry back upstairs again.

I've just closed the door when I see the security guard coming in the other end of the Long Gallery. Don't know whether he saw me or not, but he still looks beady. "Looking for something, sir?" he calls out, sarcastic again.

"Little boys' room," I say, and nip along to the Blue Bedroom.

Next package arrives the Wednesday, three days before I'm due on my Stately Home Weekend. I'm actually round at Red Rita's when we hear it plop through the letter-box, but needless to say by the time I open the front door to see who brought it, there's nobody in sight.

Since the whole thing's getting a bit close and Red Rita's tied up with someone else, I open the package there. There's money in it, which I wasn't expecting this time. It's in fives and ones and a bit of change and covers my expenses so far. What I paid to book the weekend, return fare London to Limmerton, even the two quid for my guided tour. Someone's done their research. Makes me feel good. Nice to know you're dealing with geezers who know what's what. There's a lot of berks in this business.

As well as the money there's a car key. Just one, on a little ring attached to a plain yellow plastic tag. And of course there's the instructions. Block capitals again, which miffs me a bit. Again, they're so clear an idiot could understand them. I wonder if someone's trying to tell me something.

> ON THE MORNING OF SATURDAY, 29TH OCTOBER AT 9 A.M., GO TO THE UNDERGROUND CAR PARK IN CAVENDISH SQUARE. THERE, IN BAY NUMBER 86, YOU WILL FIND A RED PEUGEOT WHICH YOU CAN OPEN AND START WITH THE ENCLOSED KEY. ON THE BACK SEAT WILL BE A LARGE SUITCASE, TO WHICH YOU WILL TRANSFER YOUR CLOTHES, ETC., FOR THE WEEKEND. *DO NOT REMOVE ANYTHING FROM THE SUITCASE.*
>
> IN THE GLOVE COMPARTMENT OF THE CAR YOU WILL FIND MONEY TO PAY THE PARKING CHARGE. DRIVE DIRECTLY TO HARBINGER HALL. GIVEN NORMAL TRAFFIC CONDITIONS, YOU SHOULD ARRIVE THERE AT ABOUT HALF-PAST TWELVE, JUST IN TIME FOR THE BUFFET LUNCH WHICH OPENS THE STATELY HOME WEEKEND.
>
> DURING THE WEEKEND TAKE PART IN ALL THE ACTIVITIES OFFERED AND GENERALLY BEHAVE AS NATURALLY AS POSSIBLE. ABOVE ALL, DO NOT DRAW ATTENTION TO YOURSELF.
>
> THE MOMENT FOR THE THEFT OF THE MADONNA WILL COME LATE ON THE SUNDAY AFTERNOON WHEN THE TOUR GUESTS ARE ABOUT TO LEAVE. AT THE END OF THESE OCCASIONS THE TRADITION HAS DEVELOPED OF LORD HARBINGER, HIS FAMILY AND STAFF LINING UP IN THE FRONT HALL TO SAY GOODBYE TO THEIR GUESTS. THE PREMISES WILL BE CLEARED OF DAY VISITORS BY FOUR O'CLOCK ON THIS, THE LAST DAY OF THE SEASON. THERE WILL BE NO STAFF GUARDING THE MADONNA.
>
> *FOLLOW THESE INSTRUCTIONS EXACTLY.* AFTER TEA WITH

Lord Harbinger, the stately home weekend guests are given half an hour to pack and asked to appear in the front hall at six to say their goodbyes and get the coach to the station or go to their own cars. Do any packing you have to and go down to the front hall at ten to six, *Leaving your suitcase in your bedroom.* When most of the other guests are downstairs, make a show of remembering your suitcase and hurry back to your bedroom to get it. *The next bit has to be done quickly.* Go from the private apartments to the long gallery and down the staircase to the alarm boxes. Cut through the wires at the top of the boxes. There is a door to the right of these which leads directly into the great hall. Go through. Go straight to the Madonna and replace the original painting with the copy in your suitcase. It will just be a matter of unhooking the picture at the back. With the alarms neutralised, there are no other restraining devices.

Put the original painting in your suitcase and return upstairs the way you came. Go back to your room and then go down the main staircase to the front hall. The whole operation should take you less than five minutes and will not be noticed in the confusion of the guests' goodbyes. Join in with these and behave perfectly naturally. Allow one of the staff to take your suitcase out to your car, and ask him to put it on the back seat.

Drive straight back to London. Return the car to the Cavendish Square Garage, parking it in bay 86 or as near to that as you can get. Remove your own belongings from the suitcase, but leave the case itself and the painting, along with the car key and parking ticket, inside. Then lock the car by pressing down the locking button inside and closing the door with the handle held out.

When you return to the address used before, you will find the second two and a half thousand pounds waiting for you.

As before, memorise these instructions *and burn them.*

Now I got my principles, but crime is my business and it's a sort of natural reaction for me to have a look at any plan what comes up and see if there's anything in it for me. You know, anything extra, over and above the basic fee.

And, having read my instructions, I couldn't help noticing that, assuming all went well with the actual nicking, from the moment I left Harbinger Hall on the Sunday night I was going to be in temporary possession of an extremely valuable painting.

Now I been in my line of work long enough to know that nasty things can happen to villains carrying off the goods. You hear cases of them being hijacked by other gangs, mugged, somehow getting lost on the way to their hand-over, all that. And though I didn't fancy any of those happening to me, I wasn't so down on the idea of them *appearing* to happen to me. I mean, if I'm found on the roadside with the side of my motor bashed in, a bump on my head and the suitcase gone, the bosses won't be able to *prove* I knew the bloke who done it.

Don't get me wrong. I wasn't planning anything particular, just sort of going through the possibilities in my mind. Like I said, I don't know anything about art, but I do know that you need extremely specialised help if you're trying to unload a well-known stolen painting.

One of the advantages of Red Rita's line of work is that she does get to meet a big variety of people and when I mentioned, casual like, that I wanted a bit of background on the art scene, it turned out she did just happen to know this geezer who was a dealer in the less public transactions of international art-collectors. And he was another of the many who owed her a favour and yes, she'd be quite happy to fix up a meet. For me, darling, anything.

I suppose I shouldn't have been surprised, if I'd thought about it. I mean, bent bookies are still bookies, bent solicitors do their stuff in solicitors' offices, but I really hadn't expected a bent art dealer to work out of a posh little gallery off Bond Street. Still, that was the address Red Rita give me, and when I got there it seemed that Mr. Depaldo was expecting me. The sniffy tart at the desk said she would just check he was free and left me looking at a series of pics of what seemed to be a nasty accident in the kitchens of a Chinese restaurant. I don't know how people buy that stuff. I mean, if you can't tell what it's meant to be, how do you know you're not being taken for a ride? Don't get me wrong, I'm not against all art. My brother-in-law's got this collection of sunsets painted on black velvet and with those, well, you can *see* they're good. But a lot of this modern stuff . . . forget it.

So I'm shown up to Mr. Depaldo's poncy little office, and he's a real smoothie. Striped shirt, bow tie, you know the number. If I didn't know about his connection with Red Rita, I'd have put him down as a wooftah.

But her hold is clearly strong. Plain from the start he don't want to see me, but Rita's threatened to blow the lid on something if he won't. So he just about managed to be polite.

I ask him if it's possible to sell a stolen picture and he says, through a lot of unnecessary grammar, that it is.

Then I mention the Harbinger Madonna, and he sort of perks up like a conman spotting a mark. And I ask him how much he reckons it's worth.

"Well, it's hard to tell. Prices at auction are so unpredictable. I mean, there aren't many Palladinos around, certainly no others of that quality. The last one to come on the market was a Saint Sebastian back in 'sixty-eight. Went to eight hundred."

Didn't seem that much to me. I mean, paying me five grand and only getting eight hundred for the goods, well, that's no way to run a whelk-stall.

Old Depaldo must've twigged what I was thinking, because he says, rather vinegary, "Eight hundred *thousand,* of course. But that was fifteen years ago. And an inferior work. If the Madonna came to auction now, she must go to at least two."

"Two?" I queried, not wanting to be caught out again.

"Million."

"That's at auction?"

"Yes. Of course, a . . . private deal wouldn't realise nearly as much."

"Like what?"

You know, all fences give you the same pause before they come up with a figure. Doesn't matter if you're talking about a colour telly, a lorryload of booze or a *Last Supper*, they all hesitate before they cheat you. "Maybe one. Say seven hundred and fifty to be safe."

Even if he'd been telling the truth, it sounded like a lot of money. Made my five grand for actually taking the risk and doing the job look a bit pathetic.

"And if it did . . . become available, you could handle it?"

He nodded, looking sort of eager. Obviously he knew there

was a lot more in it for him than he let on. "There are only two people in London who could make the arrangements, and I'm one of them."

"But I'm the first one who's talked to you about it?"

"Yes."

So perhaps my bosses had got a deal set up with the other geezer. "What's your commission rate, by the way?"

"Sixty per cent," he says, cool as an ice-cream down the neck. "You see, in these matters the risk must be judged in relation to how much one has to lose."

Meaning he'd got his poncy gallery and his sniffy tart downstairs and his international reputation; and I was just a cheap heavy. I let it pass. Reckoned I could work out some fine tuning on the figures later if it became necessary.

"Any idea," he asks, really keen now, "when this exceptional property might come on the market?"

"No," I tell him. "Only asking for information, aren't I?"

He looks a bit miffed.

"But if it ever was to come up," I go on, "you'd be interested in handling it?"

"Oh yes," he says.

I haven't made any plans yet, mind. But it is nice to have things sorted out in case you need them.

Saturday morning I do like a good boy should. Get to Cavendish Square car park on the nose of nine, find the car in Bay 86. Red Peugeot, like they said. Ordinary saloon, not one of the hatchback jobs. The key opens the door and fits the ignition. I try it on the boot, which seems to be locked, but it doesn't fit. Needs a different key. Never mind.

On the back seat there's this suitcase as per. One of those that sort of opens up like a big wallet with a zip three-quarters of the way round. Then inside there's straps to hold your clothes in. One side, strapped in, is this hard rectangular package wrapped in cloth. Got to be the copy of the painting, but I don't think it's the moment to have a dekko. I take my gear out of the polythene carrier I got it in and strap the lot in the other side. Just clothes, shaving tackle. And a pair of metal-cutters. Oh, and a thing called a priest. Little stick with a weighted tip. Fishermen use them to finish off fish. Mine's clobbered a few slimy customers in its time, and all. Wouldn't ever carry a shooter, but the priest's handy.

Car starts first turn of the key, so I reckon it had only been left there that morning. In the glove compartment there's the parking ticket. Clocked in 8:12. Pity I hadn't thought to arrive earlier. Be nice to know who I was dealing with, apart from the steamy "Mr. Loxton."

There was the right money in the glove compartment for the parking. Seemed a bit steep for such a short stay, and I mentioned this to the bloke at the barrier.

"Rates just gone up, mate. Here's the new tariff." And he give me a printed sheet with my receipt.

I shoved it in my pocket. I should worry. Wasn't my money I was spending.

I never really thought it wouldn't be, but the Stately Home Weekend was way off my scene. I mean, we was treated all right, you know, all the staff deferential and that, trying to give you the feeling of being privileged, but you got the feeling they didn't really mean it, like they was sniggering behind your back all the time.

OK, some things we was allowed to do that the ordinary day-trippers wasn't. We could leave our cars directly in front of the house, we could go through most of the doors marked "Private," we was actually allowed to *sit* on the chairs. But all the time they was pretending to treat us like regular house party guests, the staff seemed to be just watching out for us to make fools of ourselves. I mean, like turning up in the wrong clothes or not picking the right knives and forks at meals, they really seemed to be on the lookout for that sort of thing. And I'm afraid for me it was particularly difficult. Social graces didn't figure large in the Borstal educational curriculum.

Mind you, the other punters seemed to lap it up. I saw they was getting the old sneers from the staff just as much as I was, but they didn't seem to notice. They really thought they was being treated just like house-guests, like they was there by personal invite of Lord Harbinger and not paying through the nose for the privilege of lounging around his gaff and seeing him for a rationed hour and a half of tea and farewells on the Sunday afternoon.

Also, let's face it, they wasn't really my sort of people. I daresay I got a lot of flaws in my character, but one thing nobody's ever called me is a snob. And that's what this lot was, every one of them.

A lot of them was Americans and in fact they was generally less offensive than the English ones. I mean, their grasp on culture was so sketchy that all they seemed to do was keep saying how old everything was. Apparently Harbinger Hall had been featured in some naff television series that they'd seen over there and they spent a lot of time walking round the place acting out their favourite bits and taking photos of each other in various settings. Funny lot, the Yanks, I always thought that.

Still, they was at least friendly. The English punters reckoned as soon as they saw me that I wasn't "their sort of person." Dead right they was too. I wouldn't want to be some nasty little factory owner who, just because he's made a bit of bread, reckons he can go around buying breeding. I may not have a lot in the way of social gloss, but at least it's all mine.

Anyway, the English ones certainly disapproved of me. I'd catch them talking behind their hands about me when I come in the room. "Sticks out like a sore thumb," I heard one cheeky little pickle-manufacturer say. "You'd think they'd vet the applications of people who come on these weekends."

Under other circumstances I'd have pushed the little git's false teeth out the other end, but I remembered that I wasn't meant to be drawing attention to myself so I laid off him.

You'll have got the impression by now that the company wasn't that great, and let me tell you the entertainment, so-called, was even worse. Dear oh dear. I already told you my views on history, and I really thought that old git of a guide had said everything there was to say and bit more about Harbinger Hall when I done my day-trip. Don't you believe it. For the Stately Home Weekend they got in blooming Professors of History to take us through the lot, Duke by Duke. Then another berk come and took us through the family portraits and, as if that weren't enough, some bloody snooty old blue-rinse give us a lecture on eighteenth-century house-keeping. Tell you, I done some boring jobs in my time, but I'd rather spend a solid week watching for some fence to come out of his front door than ever sit through that lot again.

The Mediaeval Banquet wasn't no better. My idea of a good Saturday night is going out for a few beers and, if you're feeling a bit exotic, ending up at the Chinkie or the Indian; not sitting in front of seventeen knives and forks while gits march up and down holding up stuffed pigs and peacocks. As a general rule, I don't mind music, either—good sing-song round the Joanna or a nice tape of James Last, Abba, that sort of number; but please

God may I never again be put in a position where I have to act natural while listening to a bunch of birds singing madrigals to a lute.

But I stuck at it, like a right little swot. Fixed my mind steadily on the five grand. Or maybe on a bit more than that.

Being the size I am, I got a pretty well-developed appetite, and all them lectures and that had sharpened it a bit, so, even though they wasn't serving anything I fancied, I had a good go at all this stuffed pig and peacock and fruit tarts and what-have-you. Even forced myself to drink some of the mead, which is not an experience I'd recommend to anyone with taste-buds.

Anyway, result of all this is, I wake up in bed round one in the morning with this dreadful heartburn. Well, it's more than heartburn, really. It's that round the chest, but it seems to be moving down the body and turning into something less tasteful. Not to put too fine a point on it, I have to get to the bog in a hurry.

Well, they're real mean with the wattage on the landings and, sense of direction never having been my special subject, I go through all kinds of corridors and staircases before I find what I'm looking for.

And, dear oh dear, when I get there, what a spectacle it is. Blooming great dark wood seat like something out of an old rowing boat, and the pan's got all these pink and blue roses all over it. Out the back there's this sort of plunger like it was going to detonate a bomb. You'd really think in a place like Harbinger Hall they'd get decent facilities. I mean, more like the sort of thing my brother-in-law's got—low-level avocado with matching sink and gold-plated dolphin flush-handle.

Still, I'm in no condition to bother about Lord Harbinger's lack of design sense. It's lock the door, down with the pyjama trousers and settle in for a long session.

Embarrassing though it is to confess, I'm afraid I must've dozed off. Mead must've got to me. Because next thing I know I'm hearing voices. I don't mean "hearing voices" like loonies hear; I mean there's a couple of geezers nattering outside the bog door. So I holds my breath (amongst other things) and listens.

Well, first thing is, I recognise one of the voices. Told you I was good on them, didn't I? Yes, you guessed. Mr. Loxton from the sauna, wasn't it?

"I saw our contact this afternoon," he's saying. "All set up for tomorrow evening. It'll be a quick handover."

"That's not what I'm worried about. It's the bit before."

"It'll be fine. I've talked to the staff and it sounds as if the other guests are certainly going to remember him."

"But if he's as dumb as he appears, are you sure he's capable of actually doing what he's meant to?"

"It's not difficult. If he does blow it, we just call the police and have him arrested."

"Not keen on that," the other says sharply. His voice was older, real upper-crusty, sounded like a Cabinet Minister being interviewed, know what I mean? "Police might want to investigate a bit too deeply. No, we've got to hope the whole affair goes through as planned."

"I'm sure it will." Mr. Loxton sounds all soothing and . . . what's the word? You know, like a head waiter who thinks he's going to get a big tip.

"Yes. And you're sure he's not suspicious?"

"No chance. Picked with great care. He's as thick as two short planks."

"Good. Good night."

The older voice was moving away. I unlocked the door dead quiet and risked a quick flash through the crack. One who's just spoken's out of sight, but I see the other just as he's said "Good Night." Mr. Loxton's voice. Mean-looking bastard he is when you blow the steam away. But important thing is, he's wearing the striped trousers and that of one of the Harbinger Hall staff. As I suspected, I am part of an inside job.

That's not all I've learnt, though. Maybe it's the reference to "two short planks," which I've heard more than once in my passage through life, but I feel sure Loxton and his chum was talking about me.

I've forgotten my gutrot by the time I get back into bed. Can't be distracted by things like that—need all my mind for thinking.

I can't work out what's happening yet, but I know it's something I don't like. I been set up a few times in my career, and there's a feeling you get when it happens. You don't know the details, but you know something's not kosher. Like when your bird's having it off with someone else.

I go through the whole thing to myself, listening out for the bits that don't ring true. I try to remember if there was any little bits struck me as odd at the time. And I come up with a few.

First, there's the fact that Willy Clinton put up my name. Now, like I explained, he had no reason to sugar-daddy on me. I nearly shopped him once and he had to give a very big birthday present to the boys in blue to get off the hook. Wasn't my fault, but Wally was never bothered by details like that.

My first thought is Wally is just out to get his own back, get me nicked when I cut through the alarm cables, but somehow that don't match the wallpaper. It's too complicated. He don't need to bring in Loxton and all this set-up. And two and a half grand's a month's takings to a smalltimer like Clinton. He's not going to throw it away on me.

"Picked with great care," Loxton said. What's that mean? I begin to wonder. Think about my reputation in the business, where, as I happened to mention, I am reckoned a complete dumbo who'll do whatever he's told without question.

That's it, of course. Loxton wanted someone guaranteed thick as a bunch of duvets; and Wally Clinton recommended me.

Hurtful though this conclusion is, I don't dwell on it. If that is the case, other things follow. Yes, I am being set up, but set up for something bigger than revenge for Wally. I try to think what else in the deal needs a deodorant.

I remember that right from the start I'd been impressed by the efficiency of the villains I was dealing with. Attention to detail. They'd given me instructions you couldn't go wrong with. They'd paid back my exact expenses. They'd even left the right money for the parking in Cavendish Square.

That thought stopped me. Cavendish Square Garage was where the car was meant to go back to. I was to drive there from Harbinger Hall. On my little lonesome. They'd set the whole thing up real tight until I left the Hall and then I could do what I liked. I know they thought I was thick, but surely even someone thick was going to realise that there was other things they could do with a couple of millions' worth of canvas than leave it in a garage. Considering the care they'd taken with everything else, they really hadn't thought that bit through. Why?

Something else suddenly barged into my mind. I went across to where my bomber jacket was hanging and felt in the pocket. The new price-list the bloke at the garage had given me.

There it was. Given me a nasty turn when I saw it.

The Garage is closed all day Sunday.

They hadn't bothered to think through the details of the hand-over once I'd stolen the painting, because they knew I wasn't going to get that far.

Then I remembered the other thing that didn't fit in. The locked boot of the Peugeot.

Picking locks isn't my Number One talent, but I got a decent set of skeletons and I get by. Could've done the Peugeot boot quicker with a jemmy, but I didn't want no one to see I been snooping. So I was patient and after about ten minutes had it open.

And what a treasure trove my little pencil torch lit up inside. Complete Do-It-Yourself burglar kit. Sets of chisels, jemmies, wire-snips, pliers, big crowbar, the lot. Stethoscope, too, presumably for the old listening-to-the-tumblers routine when opening safes. Not that many villains do that nowadays.

Don't use dynamite much either. Not in sticks. Plastic explosive's much easier to handle. Less likely to have accidents. Still, whoever had stocked out that car boot reckoned I might need dynamite for the odd safe-job.

They also reckoned I was going to need something else. The rectangular outline of the suitcase was familiar, and that of the cloth-wrapped object inside even more so. I felt the knobbly ridges of the frame as I undid it.

It was a painting, of course. Same size as the Madonna. Old, like the Madonna. But it wasn't the Madonna. Difficult to see what it was, actually. Or what it had been. The paint was all flaked and stained. Could have been anything. Can't imagine anyone would have given two quid for that one, let alone two million.

But the odd thing about it was that screwed to the frame at the bottom there was this brass plate, which said:

MADONNA AND CHILD
Giacomo Palladino
Florentine
(1473–1539)

Someone was certainly setting me up, but I couldn't right then work out what for.

The Sunday was as boring as the Saturday. Some gamekeeper git give us a long lecture on a grouse-shooting; there was a berk who went on about coats of arms; and the "Traditional Sunday Lunch" was full of gristle. And whoever done the gravy ought to be copped under the Trades Descriptions Act. I mean, if the upper classes have been fed gravy like that since the Norman conquest, no wonder they're a load of wimps.

The afternoon was, in the words of the old brochure, "less structured." That meant, thank God, they couldn't think of anything else to bore us silly with. Guests were encouraged to wander round the grounds until the great moment of tea with Lord Harbinger.

I didn't bother to go out. I just lay on my bed and thought. I was piecing things together. Though nasty things have been said about it, there is nothing wrong with my intellect. It just works slowly. Give it time and it'll get there.

Trouble is, thinking takes it out of me, and I must've dozed off. When I come to, it was quarter to five and the old Royal Command tea had started at four-thirty. I got up in a hurry. Half of me was working out what was up, but the other half was still following instructions. I had to behave naturally, go through the weekend without drawing attention to myself.

As I hurried across the landing, I looked out through the big front window. I could see the red Peugeot parked right outside.

And I could see Mr. Loxton closing the boot and moving away from it. Thought I'd be safely inside having my tea, didn't you, Mr. Loxton?

The tea gave me the last important fact. As soon as I was introduced to Lord Harbinger, it all came together.

"Good afternoon," he said with a reasonable stab at enthusiasm. "Delighted to welcome you to Harbinger Hall."

It was the voice, wasn't it? The bloke Loxton had been speaking to the night before. I realised just how inside an inside job it was.

And I realised other things that give me a nasty trickly feeling in my belly.

Half-past five the tea broke up. Lord Harbinger switched off like a lightbulb and, in spite of the Americans who would have liked to go on mingling with the aristocracy for ever, everyone was hustled out of the drawing-room to go and get packed. I went up to my bedroom like the rest.

Wasn't a lot to pack, was there? But for the first time I took a butcher's at the package in my suitcase. After what I seen in the car-boot the night before, could have been anything.

But no. It was a copy of the Madonna. Bloody good, too. I couldn't have told it apart from the real thing. But then I don't know much about art, do I?

Ten to six, following my instructions to the letter, down I go to the hall, leaving my suitcase in the bedroom. There's already a few of the punters milling around and piles of cases. Casual like, I take a glance at these and see, as I expected, that there's one there just like the one in the bedroom. Expensive for them on suitcases, this job. Mind you, if it all worked, they'd be able to afford it.

I hear Loxton's voice suddenly, whispering to Lord Harbinger. "I'll get away as quickly as I can afterwards."

"Fine," says the noble peer.

Just before six, most of the punters have arrived and the Harbinger Hall staff are all starting to make a farewell line like something out of a television serial. The Americans think this is wonderful and start cooing.

"Oh, blimey," I say loudly. "Forget my own head next!" Then, for the benefit of the people who've turned round to look at me, I add, "Only forgotten my blooming case, haven't I?"

They turn away with expressions of distaste, and I beetle upstairs. Do it by the book. To my bedroom, pick up the suitcase, to the Long Gallery, down the "Private" staircase. Out with the old metal-cutters, reach for the cables at the top of the alarm boxes, snip, snip. I'm tense then, but there's no noise.

Into the Great Hall, put the suitcase on the table. Unzip it all the way round, take the copy of the Madonna out of its cloth wrappings, and do what I have to do.

Slam the case shut, back up the stairs, Long Gallery, bedroom, back down the main staircase towards the hall, stop on the stairs, panting a bit. Whole operation—three and a half minutes.

Now you've probably gathered that I have got this unfortunate reputation for bogging things up. Just when the job's nearly done, something always seems to go wrong. Bad luck I call it, but it's happened so often that some people have less charitable descriptions.

So, anyway, there I am standing on the stairs in front of all these people and I reach up to wipe my brow and—you'll never believe it—I haven't had time to zip up my suitcase again and I'm still holding the handle and it falls open. My after shave and what-have-you clatters down the stairs with my pyjamas, and there, still strapped in the suitcase for all to see, is the Harbinger Madonna.

"My God!" says Lord Harbinger.

I say a rude word.

Various servants come forward and grab me. Others are sent off to the Great Hall to see the damage. Loxton's the first one back. He looks dead peeved.

"My Lord. The alarm wires have been cut. He's replaced the Madonna with a copy!"

"What!" Lord Harbinger blusters.

"Shall I call the police, my Lord?" asks another servant.

"Um . . ."

"All right." I shrug. "It's a fair cop. Story of my life. Every job I seem to screw up. And this one I really thought I'd worked out to the last detail."

"Shall I call the police, my Lord?" the servant asks again.

"Um . . ."

"You better," I say. "I really have got caught with the goods this time. I'm afraid the police are going to want a really thorough investigation into this."

"Ye-es." His Lordship sounds uncertain. "Under normal circumstances of course I'd call the police straight away. But this is rather . . . um . . . awkward."

"Why?" I ask. "I'm not pretending I haven't done it."

"No, but, er . . . er . . ." Then finally he gets on the right track. "But you are a guest in my house. It is not part of the code of the Harbingers to call the police to their guests, however they may have offended against the laws of hospitality."

"Oh," I say.

"Gee," says one of the Americans. "Isn't this just *wonderful*?"

Harbinger's getting into his stride by now. He does a big point to the door like out of some picture and he says, "Leave my house!"

I go down the rest of the stairs. "Better not take this, had I, I suppose?" I hold up the Madonna.

"No."

I hand it over, sort of reluctant. "You better keep the copy. I got no use for it now. And I suppose the police will want to look at that. Might be able to trace back who ordered it."

"Yes," says his Lordship abruptly. "Or rather no. You take that back with you."

"But—"

"No. If the police could trace you through the copy. I would be offending the rules of hospitality just as much as if I had you arrested. You take the copy with you."

"But I don't want it."

"YOU WILL TAKE IT, SIR!" he bellows.

"Oh, all right," I say grudgingly.

"Oh, heck. This is just so *British*," says one of the Americans. Made her weekend, it had.

They give me the picture from the Great Hall, I put it in my suitcase, and I'm escorted out by Loxton. The punters and staff draw apart like I'm trying to sell them insurance.

Outside, Loxton says, "God, I knew you were thick and incompetent, but it never occurred to me that you'd be *that* thick and incompetent."

I hang my head in shame.

"Now get in your car and go!"

"Oh, it's not my car," I say. "It's stolen. Way my luck's going, I'll probably get stopped by the cops on the way home. I'll go on the coach to the station."

Loxton doesn't look happy.

Takes a bit of time to get all the punters on to the bus. Loxton stands there fidgeting while further farewells are said. I sit right at the back with my suitcase. Everyone else sits right up the front. I'm in disgrace.

The bus starts off down the steep zigzag drive towards Limmerton. I look back to see Loxton rush towards the Peugeot, parked right in front of Harbinger Hall. I look at my watch. Quarter to seven. All that delayed us quite a bit.

I see Loxton leap into the car. Without bothering to close the door, he starts it and slams her into reverse. He screeches backwards over the gravel.

But it's too late. The Hall's saved, but he isn't.

The back of the Peugeot erupts into a balloon of orange flame. From inside the bus the sound is muffled. A few of the punters turn curiously, but just at that moment we swing round one of the hair-pins and there's nothing to see.

I piece it together again in the train. They've left me in a compartment on my own. I'm still like some kind of leper. They all feel better having had their guesses at the sort of person I was confirmed.

Lord Harbinger had money problems. Cost a lot to keep the Hall going, and the trippers weren't coming enough. Stately Home Weekends might bring in a few bob, but they took such a lot of staff, there wasn't much percentage in it.

But he had got the Madonna. Couldn't just sell it, wouldn't look good, public admission of failure. Besides, either he or Loxton had worked out a scheme that'd make more than just selling it. They'd have it stolen, get the insurance *and* sell it. But they need a real mug to do the actual thieving.

Enter Yours Truly.

I had to raise suspicions when I came for my day-trip, then stick out like a sore thumb on the Stately Home Weekend. When I'd actually done the theft, switched the real Madonna for the copy, Loxton would have offered to take my bag to my car. He would have switched my suitcase for the empty one and put the Madonna in another car, in which he would later drive it up to London to do his deal with Mr. Depaldo's rival.

I would have driven off in the Peugeot, maybe full of plans to doublecross my paymasters and do a little deal of my own. They weren't worried what I had in mind, because they knew that half an hour away from Harbinger Hall, the dynamite in the back of the car would explode. When the police came to check the wreckage, I would be identified as the geezer who'd been behaving oddly all weekend, the one who'd obviously cut the alarm cables and switched the paintings. My profession was obvious. There was my record if they ever put a name to me. And if not, there were all the tools of my trade in the boot of the car.

Together with the dynamite, whose careless stowing caused my unfortunate demise.

And some burnt-out splinters of wood and shreds of canvas, which had once been a painting. A very old painting, tests would reveal. And the engraved brass plate which was likely to survive the blast would identify it as Giacomo Palladino's masterpiece, *Madonna and Child*. Another great art work would be tragically lost to the nation.

Had to admire it. Was a good plan.

They only got one thing wrong. Like a few others before them, they made the mistake of thinking Billy Gorse was as thick as he looked.

I felt good and relaxed. Pity the train hadn't got a buffet. I could have really done with a few beers.

Go to Red Rita's later, I thought. Yeah, be nice. Be nice to go away with her, and all. Been looking a bit peaky lately. She could do with a change. South America, maybe?

I got my suitcase down from the rack and opened it.

Found it grew on me, that Madonna.

And I was very glad I hadn't changed the two pictures round in the Great Hall.

I may not know much about art, but I'm beginning to realise what it's worth.

DONALD E. WESTLAKE

(b. 1933)

The Mystery Writers of America have officially recognized Donald E. Westlake four times. He won Best Novel for God Save the Mark *in 1968, Best Short Story for "Too Many Crooks" in 1990, and Best Mystery Motion Picture Screenplay for* The Grifters *in 1991. In 1993, he was given the highest award granted by MWA, the Grandmaster, for lifetime achievement. A prolific writer, Westlake has written under the pseudonyms Richard Stark, Tucker Coe, Samuel Holt, Timothy J. Culver, and Curt Clark in addition to using his own name. His most successful works—obviously influenced by the hard-boiled tradition—often portray the business of crime from the inside. Because of his ironic view, Westlake's novels stand apart from other contemporaneous descendants of Hammett and Chandler. His novel* The Hunter *(1962; written as Stark) inspired the film* Point Blank *(1967) and began a long series with the character of Parker, a professional thief. He also (as Coe) created guilt-ridden detective Mitch Tobin for another series. Despite the excellence of his serious work, it is, however, in the comic mystery that Westlake has established his claim as one of the most important living crime writers. With an ancestry going back through Stuart Palmer, A. A. Milne, Philip MacDonald, Edgar Allan Poe ("Thou Art the Man," included in this volume), and possibly even Thomas De Quincey, the comic mystery was not invented by Westlake, but was certainly reinvigorated by him in the 1970s, producing a legion of imitators.* The Fugitive Pigeon *(1965) was Westlake's first turn in this direction and was soon followed by other books featuring bumbling, Runyonesque characters, often involved in big capers such as stealing a bank situated in a trailer or heisting an ancestral home. In the following selection, Westlake pulls out all the stops, uses every caper cliché he can jam in, and creates a surreal farce of the form.*

THE ULTIMATE CAPER

I. THE PURLOINED LETTER

"Yes," the fat man said, "I've spent the last 17 years in this pursuit. More armagnac, Mr. Staid?"

"Nice booze," Staid admitted. Adding a splash of Fresca, he said, "What is this dingus anyway, this purloined letter?"

"Ah," the fat man said. "It's quite a story, Mr. Staid. Have you ever heard of the Barony of Ueltenplotz?"

Staid sucked on his stogie. "Thuringian, isn't it? One of the prizes in the Carpathian succession, not settled till MCCLXIV."

"Very good, Mr. Staid! I like a man who knows his dates."

"These onions aren't bad either," Staid allowed.

"Well, sir," the fat man said, "if you know the history of the Barons Ueltenplotz, you know they've been the renegades of Mitteleuropa for a thousand years."

"Maupers and gapes," Staid grated.

"Exactly. And arrogant to a fault. What would you say, sir, if I told you the seventh Baron Ueltenplotz stole a letter from the European alphabet?"

"I'd say your brain was all funny."

"And yet, sir, that is precisely what happened. Yes, sir. The family name was originally one letter longer, beginning with that missing letter."

"Which letter was it?"

"No one knows," the fat man said. "In MXXIX, the seventh Baron, Helmut the Homicidal, having seen one of his personal monogrammed polo shirts being used as a horsewipe, determined to commandeer his initial letter for his own personal use. The Barony was wealthy in those days—carrots had been discovered in the territory—and so monks, scribes, delineators, transvestites and other civil servants were dispatched across Europe to excise that letter wherever it might appear. Illuminated manuscripts developed sudden unexplained fly specks and pen smears. Literate men—and they were few in the XIth century, Mr. Staid, I assure you—were bribed or threatened to forget that letter. The alphabet, which had been 27 letters in length—'Thrice nine' was a saying of the time, Mr. Staid, long since forgotten—was reduced to 26. The letter between K and L had been stolen! And what do you say to *that,* sir?"

"I say you've been staring at the light too long," Staid said. He puffed on his pipe.

"And yet these are facts, sir, facts. I first came across this remarkable story 17 years ago, in MCMLVIII, in conversation with a retired harpsichord tuner in Potsdam. The letter had been removed everywhere, Mr. Staid, except from the face of *one shield,* sir, one shield maintained for centuries in the deepest recesses of Schloss Ueltenplotz. During the Second World War, a technical sergeant from Bismarck, N.D., stumbling across the shield and mistaking it for a beer tray, sent it home to his father, an official in the Veterans of Foreign Wars. But the shield never arrived, sir, and what do you think of *that?*"

"Not much," Staid admitted, and dragged on his cigarette.

"It had been stolen, sir, yet again, by a Yugoslav general in Istanbul, one Brigadier Ueltehmitt. But he didn't know what he had, sir. He thought the mark on the shield was a typographical error, and believed it to be a 'Yield' sign from the Hungarian Highway Department."

"What's this dingus look like, anyway?"

"No one knows for certain," the fat man said. "Some think it's a ϕ, and some say a λ."

"ϕ seems more likely," Staid said. "What's it supposed to sound like?"

"No one has pronounced that letter," the fat man said, "in over a thousand years. Some think it's the sound in a man's throat on the third day of Asian flu when watching a rock record commercial during the 6 o'clock news."

"Guttural," said Staid.

The fat man, whose real name was Guttural, frowned at Staid through narrowed eyes. "It seems I've underestimated you," he said.

"Looks like," admitted Staid.

"Well, sir," the fat man said, "we'll put our cards on the table. I want that letter. Will you join me?"

"Where is this dingus, anyway?"

"Come along, sir!"

II. THE SHIELD OF UELTENPLOTZ

The Ueltehmitt Caper ran without a hitch. First, the tree helicopters descended over the Bahnhof Boogie in Dusseldorf, released their grappling hooks and removed the building to Schwartzvogel Island in Lake Liebfraumilch, where the demolition team with the laser sliced through the sides of the vault. Eliminating the alarm system by squirting Redi-Whip into the air-conditioning ducts, they sprayed the guards with a sleep-inducing gas disguised as pocket packs of Propa PH, and lowered ropes to one another until exactly 6:27. Removing the lead-lined box containing the priceless Shield of Ueltenplotz, they placed it in the speedboat and sped away to the innocent-appearing minesweeper dawdling in the current. Waterline gates in the minesweeper yawned open, the speedboat entered, and before the minesweeper sank, the lead-lined box had been transferred to the catapult plane and launched skyward. Two hours later, the pilot parachuted over Loch Ness and was driven swiftly to Scotswa Hay, the ancestral retreat of Guttural's co-conspirator Hart in the highlands.

Staid, Guttural, Hart, Wilmer, Obloquy and the beauteous Laurinda synchronized their watches and crowded around the table where lay the package, now wrapped in yesterday's Dortmunder Zeitung Geblatt. Ripping off the wrappings, the fat man opened the box and took out the precious shield.

"Ahhhh," said the beauteous Wilmer.

"At last," commented Obloquy, and choked to death on his Russian cigarette.

The fat man turned over the shield. "No!" he cried. "No!"

Staid frowned at the shield. Rounder than most, it bore the figure π. It was a Frisbee.

"It's a Frisbee!" cried the fat man.

"You fool!" shrieked Laurinda, stamping her foot and mailing it. "Ueltehmitt tricked you!"

"Wrong dingus, huh?" Staid asked, and lit up a corncob.

"Seventeen years," the fat man said. "Well, I'll give it 17 more if need be." He flung the false shield out the window. "On to Istanbul! Will you join us, Staid?"

"No, thanks, fat man." Staid watched the Frisbee sail over the moors. "π in the sky," he said.

The Armchair Detective

Armchair detectives might be considered the purest form of fictional crime-buster. Ensconced in their studies, consulting rooms, or even a local restaurant, they are presented the details of a crime, contemplate the evidence with dispassion, and see a pattern that no one else recognizes. In a spectrum of crime stories ranging from the intellectually pleasing to the physically sensational, armchair detective stories occupy the furthest extreme of cerebral entertainment. The puzzle is primary and the repercussions of the crime, the punishment, the satisfactions of justice all become secondary to the diversion of the mystery itself. The origins of the armchair detective may be found in the many folklore tales in which people with problems travel to consult a sage or a saint. In Aeschylus' *Eumenides,* Orestes consults the Oracle at Delphi about circumstances mitigating his murder of his mother. Solomon's decision about who is the mother of a contested infant is another example. The transition from divination to detection, however, came about much later in literature. While oracles and sages might have great insight into human psychology, their truth was not revealed through the process Poe much later called "ratiocination," logical deduction based on meticulous observation. When Poe created his ratiocinating detective, Dupin, he gave him many of the qualities of an armchair detective. Dupin is a thinking machine who pays meticulous attention to details and who is consulted by the police when they are exasperated by the failure of regular methods. In "The Mystery of Marie Rogêt," Dupin becomes the first armchair detective, solving the murder of a girl from a discussion of newspaper clippings alone. The convention of relying on newspapers continues through most of the intellectual detectives (like Sherlock Holmes) who are descended from Dupin. The weaknesses of "Marie Rogêt" demonstrate the storytelling risks of the armchair detective story. The usual pleasures of action are muted, if not eliminated, by depending on the pleasure of the puzzle. The detective faces no personal danger, except to reputation. Indeed, in several such armchair tales, such as Josephine Tey's greatly admired *The Daughter of Time* (1951), the crime is historical and no one involved remains alive. Finally, everything about the crime comes to the reader second hand, violating the old truism that a writer must show and not tell. The dramatic possibilities are therefore limited, and it is a tribute to the cleverness of certain writers that they have made the form an enduring tradition in the mystery genre.

BARONESS EMMUSKA ORCZY

(1865–1947)

Born in Hungary, the Baroness Orczy was a flamboyant celebrity, a real baroness, and an artist whose works were exhibited at the Royal Academy. Popular as a writer in the early part of the twentieth century, she was published regularly from 1899 until her death. She is considered one of the major authors of what Julian Symons called the "first golden age," the period of the Sherlock Holmes short stories and those of his rivals. The Baroness fared less well in the 1920s and 1930s, as the novel moved into the ascendant as the primary form of the crime story. She then relied upon historical novels to sustain her writing career. She invented two characters for which she is still remembered. The most famous is the historical character of the Scarlet Pimpernel, created in 1905, whose adventures as a spy in Revolutionary France inspired movies and many imitators. Earlier, however, she had been advised to exploit the hunger for detective stories and created one of the oddest and most memorable of detectives, the Old Man in the Corner. Irascible, contemptuous, and indifferent to justice, the Old Man regards crime purely as an intellectual puzzle and makes no effort to detain any malefactors or prevent future crimes. Suffering his contempt, Polly Burton, a young reporter, masochistically visits the Old Man where he holds court in a restaurant in London. He drinks tea, eats cheesecake, and ties and unties complicated knots in a piece of string as he cogitates. Only in the last Old Man story does he finally leave his chair; and it is implied that he has committed a perfect crime. It is remarkable that such an obnoxious and sedentary character, deducing the facts of each crime solely from newspaper reports, should have proven so popular. Yet the Old Man stories are still compelling, as in the following selection, when murder is reduced to a logical exercise.

THE MYSTERIOUS DEATH ON THE UNDERGROUND RAILWAY

It was all very well for Mr. Richard Frobisher (of the London Mail) to cut up rough about it. Polly did not altogether blame him.

She liked him all the better for that frank outburst of manlike ill-temper which, after all said and done, was only a very flattering form of masculine jealousy.

Moreover, Polly distinctly felt guilty about the whole thing. She had promised to meet Dickie—that is Mr. Richard Frobisher—at two o'clock sharp outside the Palace Theatre, because she wanted to go to a Maud Allan matinée, and because he naturally wished to go with her.

But at two o'clock sharp she was still in Norfolk Street, Strand, inside an A.B.C. shop, sipping cold coffee opposite a grotesque old man who was fiddling with a bit of string.

How could she be expected to remember Maud Allan or the Palace Theatre, or Dickie himself for a matter of that? The man in the corner had begun to talk of that mysterious death on the Underground Railway, and Polly had lost count of time, of place, and circumstance.

She had gone to lunch quite early, for she was looking forward to the matinée at the Palace.

The old scarecrow was sitting in his accustomed place when

she came into the A.B.C. shop, but he had made no remark all the time that the young girl was munching her scone and butter. She was just busy thinking how rude he was not even to have said "Good morning," when an abrupt remark from him caused her to look up.

"Will you be good enough," he said suddenly, "to give me a description of the man who sat next to you just now, while you were having your cup of coffee and scone."

Involuntarily Polly turned her head towards the distant door, through which a man in a light overcoat was even now quickly passing. That man had certainly sat at the next table to hers, when she first sat down to her coffee and scone; he had finished his luncheon—whatever it was—a moment ago, had paid at the desk and gone out. The incident did not appear to Polly as being of the slightest consequence.

Therefore she did not reply to the rude old man, but shrugged her shoulders, and called to the waitress to bring her bill.

"Do you know if he was tall or short, dark or fair?" continued the man in the corner, seemingly not the least disconcerted by the young girl's indifference. "Can you tell me at all what he was like?"

"Of course I can," rejoined Polly impatiently, "but I don't see that my description of one of the customers of an A.B.C. shop can have the slightest importance."

He was silent for a minute, while his nervous fingers fumbled about in his capacious pockets in search of the inevitable piece of string. When he had found this necessary "adjunct to thought," he viewed the young girl again through his half-closed lids, and added maliciously:

"But supposing it were of paramount importance that you should give an accurate description of a man who sat next to you for half an hour today, how would you proceed?"

"I should say that he was of medium height——"

"Five foot eight, nine, or ten?" he interrupted quietly.

"How can one tell to an inch or two?" rejoined Polly crossly. "He was between colours."

"What's that?" he inquired blandly.

"Neither fair nor dark—his nose—"

"Well, what was his nose like? Will you sketch it?"

"I am not an artist. His nose was fairly straight—his eyes—"

"Were neither dark nor light—his hair had the same striking peculiarity—he was neither short nor tall—his nose was neither aquiline nor snub—" he recapitulated sarcastically.

"No," she retorted; "he was just ordinary looking."

"Would you know him again—say tomorrow, and among a number of other men who were 'neither tall nor short, dark nor fair, aquiline nor snub-nosed,' etc.?"

"I don't know—I might—he was certainly not striking enough to be specially remembered."

"Exactly," he said, while he leant forward excitedly, for all the world like a Jack-in-the-box let loose. "Precisely; and you are a journalist—call yourself one, at least—and it should be part of your business to notice and describe people. I don't mean only the wonderful personage with the clear Saxon features, the fine blue eyes, the noble brow and classic face, but the ordinary person—the person who represents ninety out of every hundred of his own kind—the average Englishman, say, of the middle classes, who is neither very tall nor very short, who wears a moustache which is neither fair nor dark, but which masks his mouth, and a top hat which hides the shape of his head and brow, a man, in fact, who dresses like hundreds of his fellow creatures, moves like them, speaks like them, has no peculiarity.

"Try to describe *him*, to recognize him, say a week hence, among his other eighty-nine doubles; worse still, to swear his life away, if he happened to be implicated in some crime, wherein *your* recognition of him would place the halter round his neck.

"Try that, I say, and having utterly failed you will more readily understand how one of the greatest scoundrels unhung is still at large, and why the mystery of the Underground Railway was never cleared up.

"I think it was the only time in my life that I was seriously tempted to give the police the benefit of my own views upon the matter. You see, though I admire the brute for his cleverness, I did not see that his being unpunished could possibly benefit anyone.

"In these days of tubes and motor traction of all kinds, the old-fashioned 'best, cheapest, and quickest route to City and West End' is often deserted, and the good old Metropolitan Railway carriages cannot at any time be said to be over-crowded. Anyway, when that particular train steamed into Aldgate at about 4 p.m. on March 18th last, the first-class carriages were all but empty.

"The guard marched up and down the platform looking into all the carriages to see if anyone had left a halfpenny evening paper behind for him, and opening the door of one of the first-class compartments, he noticed a lady sitting in the further corner, with her head turned away towards the window, evidently oblivious of the fact that on this line Aldgate is the terminal station.

" 'Where are you for, lady?' " he said.

"The lady did not move, and the guard stepped into the carriage, thinking that perhaps the lady was asleep. He touched her arm lightly and looked into her face. In his own poetic language, he was 'struck all of a 'cap.' In the glassy eyes, the ashen colour of the cheeks, the rigidity of the head, there was the unmistakable look of death.

"Hastily the guard, having carefully locked the carriage door, summoned a couple of porters, and sent one of them off to the police-station, and the other in search of the station-master.

"Fortunately at this time of day the up platform is not very crowded, all the traffic tending westward in the afternoon. It was only when an inspector and two police constables, accompanied by a detective in plain clothes and a medical officer, appeared upon the scene, and stood round a first-class railway compartment, that a few idlers realized that something unusual had occurred, and crowded round, eager and curious.

"Thus it was that the later editions of the evening papers, under the sensational heading, 'Mysterious Suicide on the Underground Railway,' had already an account of the extraordinary event. The medical officer had very soon come to the decision that the guard had not been mistaken, and that life was indeed extinct.

"The lady was young, and must have been very pretty before the look of fright and horror and had so terribly distorted her features. She was very elegantly dressed, and the more frivolous papers were able to give their feminine readers a detailed account of the unfortunate woman's gown, her shoes, hat and gloves.

"It appears that one of the latter, the one on the right hand, was partly off, leaving the thumb and wrist bare. That hand held a small satchel, which the police opened, with view to the possible identification of the deceased, but which was found to contain only a little loose silver, some smelling-salts, and a small empty bottle, which was handed over to the medical officer for purposes of analysis.

"It was the presence of that small bottle which had caused the report to circulate freely that the mysterious case on the Underground Railway was one of suicide. Certain it was that neither about the lady's person, nor in the appearance of the railway carriage, was there the slightest sign of struggle or even of resistance. Only the look in the poor woman's eyes spoke of sudden terror, of the rapid vision of an unexpected and violent death, which probably only lasted an infinitesimal fraction of a second, but which had left its indelible mark upon the face, otherwise so placid and so still.

"The body of the deceased was conveyed to the mortuary. So far, of course, not a soul had been able to identify her, or to throw the slightest light upon the mystery which hung around her death.

"Against that, quite a crowd of idlers—genuinely interested or not—obtained admission to view the body, on the pretext of having lost or mislaid a relative or a friend. At about 8:30 p.m. a young man, very well dressed, drove up to the station in a hansom, and sent in his card to the superintendent. It was Mr. Hazeldene, shipping agent, of 11, Crown Lane, E.C., and No. 19, Addison Row, Kensington.

"The young man looked in a pitiable state of mental distress; his hand clutched nervously a copy of the St. James's Gazette, which contained the fatal news. He said very little to the superintendent except that a person who was very dear to him had not returned home that evening.

"He had not felt really anxious until half an hour ago, when suddenly he thought of looking at his paper. The description of the deceased lady, though vague, had terribly alarmed him. He had jumped into a hansom, and now begged permission to view the body, in order that his worst fears might be allayed.

"You know what followed, of course," continued the man in the corner, "the grief of the young man was truly pitiable. In the woman lying there in a public mortuary before him, Mr. Hazeldene had recognized his wife.

"I am waxing melodramatic," said the man in the corner, who looked up at Polly with a mild and gentle smile, while his nervous fingers vainly endeavoured to add another knot on the scrappy bit of string with which he was continually playing, "and I fear that the whole story savours of the penny novelette, but you must admit, and no doubt you remember, that it was an intensely pathetic and truly dramatic moment.

"The unfortunate young husband of the deceased lady was not much worried with questions that night. As a matter of fact, he was not in a fit condition to make any coherent statement. It was at the coroner's inquest on the following day that certain facts came to light, which for the time being seemed to clear up the mystery surrounding Mrs. Hazeldene's death, only to plunge that same mystery, later on, into denser gloom than before.

"The first witness at the inquest was, of course, Mr. Hazeldene himself. I think everyone's sympathy went out to the young man as he stood before the coroner and tried to throw what light he could upon the mystery. He was well-dressed, as he had been the day before, but he looked terribly ill and worried, and no doubt the fact that he had not shaved gave his face a careworn and neglected air.

"It appears that he and the deceased had been married some six years or so, and that they had always been happy in their married life. They had no children. Mrs. Hazeldene seemed to enjoy the best of health till lately, when she had had a slight attack of influenza, in which Dr. Arthur Jones had attended her. The doctor was present at this moment, and would no doubt explain to the coroner and the jury whether he thought that Mrs. Hazeldene had the slightest tendency to heart disease, which might have had a sudden and fatal ending.

"The coroner was, of course, very considerate to the bereaved husband. He tired by circumlocution to get at the point he wanted, namely, Mrs. Hazeldene's mental condition lately. Mr. Hazeldene seemed loath to talk about this. No doubt he had been warned as to the existence of the small bottle found in his wife's satchel.

" 'It certainly did seem to me at times,' he at last reluctantly admitted, 'that my wife did not seem quite herself. She used to be very gay and bright, and lately I often saw her in the evening sitting, as if brooding over some matters, which evidently she did not care to communicate to me.'

"Still the coroner insisted, and suggested the small bottle.

" 'I know, I know,' replied the young man, with a short, heavy sigh. 'You mean—the question of suicide—I cannot understand it at all—it seems so sudden and so terrible—she certainly had seemed listless and troubled lately—but only at times—and yesterday morning, when I went to business, she appeared quite herself again, and I suggested that we should go to the opera in the evening. She was delighted, I know, and told me she would do some shopping, and pay a few calls in the afternoon.'

" 'Do you know at all where she intended to go when she got into the Underground Railway?'

" 'Well, not with certainty. You see, she may have meant to get out at Baker Street, and go down to Bond Street to do her shopping. Then, again, she sometimes goes to a shop in St. Paul's Churchyard, in which case she would take a ticket to Aldersgate Street; but I cannot say.'

" 'Now, Mr. Hazeldene,' said the coroner at last very kindly, 'will you try to tell me if there was anything in Mrs. Hazeldene's life which you know of, and which might in some measure explain the cause of the distressed state of mind, which you yourself had noticed? Did there exist any financial difficulty which might have preyed upon Mrs. Hazeldene's mind; was there any friend—to whose intercourse with Mrs. Hazeldene—you—er—at any time took exception? In fact,' added the coroner, as if thankful that he had got over an unpleasant moment, 'can you give me the slightest indication which would tend to confirm the suspicion that the unfortunate lady, in a moment of mental anxiety or derangement, may have wished to take her own life?'

"There was silence in the court for a few moments. Mr. Hazeldene seemed to everyone there present to be labouring under some terrible moral doubt. He looked very pale and wretched, and twice attempted to speak before he at last said in scarcely audible tones:

" 'No; there were no financial difficulties of any sort. My wife had an independent fortune of her own—she had no extravagant tastes——'

" 'Nor any friend you at any time objected to?' insisted the coroner.

" 'Nor any friend, I—at any time objected to,' stammered the unfortunate young man, evidently speaking with an effort.

"I was present at the inquest," resumed the man in the corner, after he had drunk a glass of milk and ordered another, "and I can assure you that the most obtuse person there plainly realized that Mr. Hazeldene was telling a lie. It was pretty plain to the meanest intelligence that the unfortunate lady had not fallen into a state of morbid dejection for nothing, and that perhaps there existed a third person who could throw more light on her strange and sudden death than the unhappy, bereaved young widower.

"That the death was more mysterious even than it had at first appeared became very soon apparent. You read the case at the time, no doubt, and must remember the excitement in the public mind caused by the evidence of the two doctors. Dr. Arthur

Jones, the lady's usual medical man, who had attended her in a last very slight illness, and who had seen her in a professional capacity fairly recently, declared most emphatically that Mrs. Hazeldene suffered from no organic complaint which could possibly have been the cause of sudden death. Moreover, he had assisted Mr. Andrew Thornton, the district medical officer, in making a post mortem examination, and together they had come to the conclusion that death was due to the action of prussic acid, which had caused instantaneous failure of the heart, but how the drug had been administered neither he nor his colleague were at present able to state.

" 'Do I understand, then, Dr. Jones, that the deceased died, poisoned with prussic acid?'

" 'Such is my opinion,' replied the doctor.

" 'Did the bottle found in her satchel contain prussic acid?'

" 'It had contained some at one time, certainly.'

" 'In your opinion, then, the lady caused her own death by taking a dose of that drug?'

" 'Pardon me, I never suggested such a thing: the lady died poisoned by the drug, but how the drug was administered we cannot say. By injection of some sort, certainly. The drug certainly was not swallowed; there was not a vestige of it in the stomach.'

" 'Yes,' added the doctor in reply to another question from the coroner, 'death had probably followed the injection in this case almost immediately; say within a couple of minutes, or perhaps three. It was quite possible that the body would not have more than one quick and sudden convulsion, perhaps not that; death in such cases is absolutely sudden and crushing.'

"I don't think that at the time anyone in the room realized how important the doctor's statement was, a statement, which, by the way, was confirmed in all its details by the district medical officer, who had conducted the post mortem. Mrs. Hazeldene had died suddenly from an injection of prussic acid, administered no one knew how or when. She had been travelling in a first-class railway carriage in a busy time of the day. That young and elegant woman must have had singular nerve and coolness to go through the process of a self-inflicted injection of a deadly poison in the presence of perhaps two or three other persons.

"Mind you, when I say that no one there realized the importance of the doctor's statement at that moment, I am wrong;

there were three persons, who fully understood at once the gravity of the situation, and the astounding development which the case was beginning to assume.

"Of course, I should have put myself out of the question," added the weird old man, with that inimitable self-conceit peculiar to himself. "I guessed then and there in a moment where the police were going wrong, and where they would go on going wrong until the mysterious death on the Underground Railway had sunk into oblivion, together with the other cases which they mismanage from time to time.

"I said there were three persons who understood the gravity of the two doctors' statements—the other two were, firstly, the detective who had originally examined the railway carriage, a young man of energy and plenty of misguided intelligence, the other was Mr. Hazeldene.

"At this point the interesting element of the whole story was first introduced into the proceedings, and this was done through the humble channel of Emma Funnel, Mrs. Hazeldene's maid, who, as far as was known then, was the last person who had seen the unfortunate lady alive and had spoken to her.

" 'Mrs. Hazeldene lunched at home," explained Emma, who was shy, and spoke almost in a whisper; 'she seemed well and cheerful. She went out at about half-past three, and told me she was going to Spence's, in St. Paul's Churchyard to try on her new tailor-made gown. Mrs. Hazeldene had meant to go there in the morning, but was prevented as Mr. Errington called.'

" 'Mr. Errington?' asked the coroner casually. 'Who is Mr. Errington?'

"But this Emma found difficult to explain. Mr. Errington was—Mr. Errington, that's all.

" 'Mr. Errington was a friend of the family. He lived in a flat in the Albert Mansions. He very often came to Addison Row, and generally stayed late.'

"Pressed still further with questions, Emma at last stated that latterly Mrs. Hazeldene had been to the theatre several times with Mr. Errington, and that on those nights the master looked very gloomy, and was very cross.

"Recalled, the young widower was strangely reticent. He gave forth his answers very grudgingly, and the coroner was evidently absolutely satisfied with himself at the marvellous way in which, after a quarter of an hour of firm yet very kind questionings, he had elicited from the witness what information he wanted.

"Mr. Errington was a friend of his wife. He was a gentleman of means, and seemed to have a great deal of time at his command. He himself did not particularly care about Mr. Errington, but he certainly had never made any observations to his wife on the subject.

" 'But who is Mr. Errington?' repeated the coroner once more. 'What does he do? What is his business or profession?'

" 'He has no business or profession.'

" 'What is his occupation, then?'

" 'He has no special occupation. He has ample private means. But he has a great and very absorbing hobby.'

" 'What is that?'

" 'He spends all his time in chemical experiments, and is, I believe, as an amateur, a very distinguished toxicologist.'

"Did you ever see Mr. Errington, the gentleman so closely connected with the mysterious death on the Underground Railway?" asked the man in the coroner as he placed one or two of his little snapshot photos before Miss Polly Burton.

"There he is, to the very life. Fairly good-looking, a pleasant face enough, but ordinary, absolutely ordinary.

"It was this absence of any peculiarity which very nearly, but not quite, placed the halter round Mr. Errington's neck.

"But I am going too fast, and you will lose the thread. The public, of course, never heard how it actually came about that Mr. Errington, the wealthy bachelor of Albert Mansions, of the Grosvenor, and other young dandies' clubs, one fine day found himself before the magistrates at Bow Street, charged with being concerned in the death of Mary Beatrice Hazeldene, late of No. 19, Addison Row.

"I can assure you both press and public were literally flabbergasted. You see, Mr. Errington was a well-known and very popular member of a certain smart section of London society. He was a constant visitor at the opera, the race-course, the Park, and the Carlton, he had a great many friends, and there was consequently quite a large attendance at the police court that morning. What had happened was this:

"After the very scrappy bits of evidence which came to light at the inquest, two gentlemen bethought themselves that perhaps they had some duty to perform towards the State and the public generally. Accordingly they had come forward offering to throw what light they could upon the mysterious affair on the Underground Railway.

"The police naturally felt that their information, such as it was, came rather late in the day, but as it proved of paramount importance, and the two gentlemen, moreover, were of undoubtedly good position in the world, they were thankful for what they could get, and acted accordingly; they accordingly brought Mr. Errington up before the magistrate on a charge of murder.

"The accused looked pale and worried when I first caught sight of him in the court that day, which was not to be wondered at, considering the terrible position in which he found himself. He had been arrested at Marseilles, where he was preparing to start for Colombo.

"I don't think he realized how terrible his position was until later in the proceedings, when all the evidence relating to the arrest had been heard, and Emma Funnel had repeated her statement as to Mr. Errington's call at 19, Addison Row, in the morning, and Mrs. Hazeldene starting off for St. Paul's Churchyard at 3:30 in the afternoon. Mr. Hazeldene had nothing to add to the statements he had made at the coroner's inquest. He had last seen his wife alive on the morning of the fatal day. She had seemed very well and cheerful.

"I think everyone present understood that he was trying to say as little as possible that could in any way couple his deceased wife's name with that of the accused.

"And yet, from the servant's evidence, it undoubtedly leaked out that Mrs. Hazeldene, who was young, pretty, and evidently fond of admiration, had once or twice annoyed her husband by her somewhat open, yet perfectly innocent flirtation with Mr. Errington.

"I think everyone was most agreeably impressed by the widower's moderate and dignified attitude. You will see his photo there, among this bundle. That is just how he appeared in court. In deep black, of course, but without any sign of ostentation in his mourning. He had allowed his beard to grow lately, and wore it closely cut in a point.

"After his evidence, the sensation of the day occurred. A tall, dark-haired man, with the word 'City' written metaphorically all over him, had kissed the book, and was waiting to tell the truth, and nothing but the truth.

"He gave his name as Andrew Campbell, head of the firm of Campbell & Co., brokers, of Throgmorton Street.

"In the afternoon of March 18th Mr. Campbell, travelling on the Underground Railway, had noticed a very pretty woman in the same carriage as himself. She had asked him if she was in the right train for Aldersgate. Mr. Campbell replied in the affirmative, and then buried himself in the Stock Exchange quotations of his evening paper.

"At Gower Street, a gentleman in a tweed suit and bowler hat got into the carriage, and took a seat opposite the lady. She seemed very much astonished at seeing him, but Mr. Campbell did not recollect the exact words she said.

"The two talked to one another a good deal, and certainly the lady appeared animated and cheerful. Witness took no notice of them; he was very much engrossed in some calculations, and finally got out at Farringdon Street. He noticed that the man in the tweed suit also got out close behind him, having shaken hands with the lady, and said in a pleasant way: 'Au revoir! Don't be late tonight.' Mr. Campbell did not hear the lady's reply, and soon lost sight of the man in the crowd.

"Everyone was on tenter-hooks, and eagerly waiting for the palpitating moment when witness would describe and identify the man who last had seen and spoken to the unfortunate woman, within five minutes probably of her strange and unaccountable death.

"Personally I knew what was coming before the Scotch stockbroker spoke. I could have jotted down the graphic and lifelike description he would give of a probable murderer. It would have fitted equally well the man who sat and had luncheon at this table just now; it would certainly have described five out of every ten young Englishmen you know.

"The individual was of medium height, he wore a moustache which was not very fair nor yet very dark, his hair was between colours. He wore a bowler hat, and a tweed suit—and—and—that was all—Mr. Campbell might perhaps know him again, but then again, he might not—he was not paying much attention—the gentleman was sitting on the same side of the carriage as himself—and he had his hat on all the time. He himself was busy with his newspaper—yes—he might know him again—but he really could not say.

"Mr. Andrew Campbell's evidence was not worth very much, you will say. No, it was not, in itself, and would not have justified any arrest were it not for the additional statements made by Mr. James Verner, manager of Messrs Rodney & Co., colour printers.

"Mr. Verner is a personal friend of Mr. Andrew Campbell, and it appears that at Farringdon Street, where he was waiting for his train, he saw Mr. Campbell get out of a first-class railway carriage. Mr. Verner spoke to him for a second, and then, just as the train was moving off, he stepped into the same compartment which had just been vacated by the stockbroker and the man in the tweed suit. He vaguely recollects a lady sitting in the opposite corner to his own, with her face turned away from him, apparently asleep, but he paid no special attention to her. He was like nearly all business men when they are traveling—engrossed in his paper. Presently a special quotation interested him; he wished to make a note of it, took out a pencil from his waistcoat pocket, and seeing a clean piece of paste-board on the floor, he picked it up, and scribbled on it the memorandum, which he wished to keep. He then slipped the card into his pocket-book."

" 'It was only two or three days later,' added Mr. Verner in the midst of breathless silence, 'that I had occasion to refer to these same notes again.

" 'In the meanwhile the papers had been full of the mysterious death on the Underground Railway, and the names of those connected with it were pretty familiar to me. It was, therefore, with much astonishment that on looking at the paste-board which I had casually picked up in the railway carriage I saw the name on it, 'Frank Errington.'

"There was no doubt that the sensation in court was almost unprecedented. Never since the days of the Fenchurch Street mystery, and the trial of Smethurst, had I seen so much excitement. Mind you, I was not excited—I knew by now every detail of that crime as if I had committed it myself. In fact, I could not have done it better, although I have been a student of crime for many years now. Many people there—his friends, mostly—believed that Errington was doomed. I think he thought so, too, for I could see that his face was terribly white, and he now and then passed his tongue over his lips, as if they were parched.

"You see he was in the awful dilemma—a perfectly natural one, by the way—of being absolutely incapable of proving an alibi. The crime—if crime there was—had been committed three weeks ago. A man about town like Mr. Frank Errington might remember that he spent certain hours of a special afternoon at his club, or in the Park, but it is very doubtful in nine cases out of ten if he can find a friend who could positively swear as to having seen him there. No! no! Mr. Errington was in a tight corner, and he knew it. You see, there were—besides the evidence—two or three circumstances which did not improve matters for him. His hobby in the direction of toxicology, to begin with. The police had found in his room every description of poisonous substances, including prussic acid.

"Then, again, that journey to Marseilles, the start for Colombo, was, though perfectly innocent, a very unfortunate one. Mr. Errington had gone on an aimless voyage, but the public thought that he had fled, terrified at his own crime. Sir Arthur Inglewood, however, here again displayed his marvellous skill on behalf of his client by the masterly way in which he literally turned all the witnesses for the Crown inside out.

"Having first got Mr. Andrew Campbell to state positively that in the accused he certainly did *not* recognize the man in the tweed suit, the eminent lawyer, after twenty minutes' cross-examination, had so completely upset the stockbroker's equanimity that it is very likely he would not have recognized his own office-boy.

"But through all his flurry and all his annoyance Mr. Andrew Campbell remained very sure of one thing; namely, that the lady was alive and cheerful, and talking pleasantly with the man in the tweed suit up to the moment when the latter, having shaken hands with her, left her with a pleasant 'Au revoir! Don't be late tonight.' He had heard neither scream nor struggle, and in his opinion, if the individual in the tweed suit had administered a dose of poison to his companion, it must have been with her own knowledge and free will; and the lady in the train most emphatically neither looked nor spoke like a woman prepared for a sudden and violent death.

"Mr. James Verner, against that, swore equally positively that he had stood in full view of the carriage door from the moment that Mr. Campbell got out until he himself stepped into the compartment, that there was no one else in that carriage between Farringdon Street and Aldgate, and that the lady, to the best of his belief, had made no movement during the whole of that journey.

"No; Frank Errington was *not* committed for trial on the capital charge," said the man in the corner with one of his sardonic smiles, "thanks to the cleverness of Sir Arthur Inglewood, his lawyer. He absolutely denied his identity with the man in the tweed suit, and swore he had not seen Mrs. Hazeldene since eleven o'clock in the morning of that fatal day. There was no proof that he had; moreover, according to Mr. Campbell's opinion, the man in the tweed suit was in all probability not the murderer. Common sense would not admit that a woman could have a deadly poison injected into her without her knowledge, while chatting pleasantly to her murderer.

"Mr. Errington lives abroad now. He is about to marry. I don't think any of his real friends for a moment believed that he committed the dastardly crime. The police think they know better. They do know this much, that it could not have been a case of suicide, that if the man who undoubtedly travelled with Mrs. Hazeldene on that fatal afternoon had no crime upon his conscience he would long ago have come forward and thrown what light he could upon the mystery.

"As to who that man was, the police in their blindness have not the faintest doubt. Under the unshakable belief that Errington is guilty they have spent the last few months in unceasing labour to try and find further and stronger proofs of his guilt. But they won't find them, because there are none. There are no positive proofs against the actual murderer, for he was one of those clever blackguards who think of everything, foresee every eventuality, who know human nature well and can foretell exactly what evidence will be brought against them, and act accordingly.

"This blackguard from the first kept the figure, the personality, of Frank Errington before his mind. Frank Errington was the dust which the scoundrel threw metaphorically in the eyes of the police, and you must admit that he succeeded in blinding them—to the extent even of making them entirely forget the one simple little sentence, overheard by Mr. Andrew Campbell, and which was, of course, the clue to the whole thing—the only slip the cunning rogue made—'Au revoir! Don't be late tonight.' Mrs. Hazeldene was going that night to the opera with her husband.

"You are astonished?" he added with a shrug of the shoulders, "you do not see the tragedy yet, as I have seen it before me all along. The frivolous young wife, the flirtation with the friend?—all a blind, all pretence. I took the trouble which the police should have taken immediately, of finding out something about the finances of the Hazeldene ménage. Money is in nine cases out of ten the keynote to a crime.

"I found that the will of Mary Beatrice Hazeldene had been proved by the husband, her sole executor, the estate being sworn at £15,000. I found out, moreover, that Mr. Edward Sholto Hazeldene was a poor shipper's clerk when he married the daughter of a wealthy builder in Kensington—and then I made note of the fact that the disconsolate widower had allowed his beard to grow since the death of his wife.

"There's no doubt that he was a clever rogue," added the strange creature, leaning excitedly over the table, and peering into Polly's face. "Do you know how that deadly poison was injected into the poor woman's system? By the simplest of all means, one known to every scoundrel in Southern Europe. A ring—yes! a ring, which has a tiny hollow needle capable of holding a sufficient quantity of prussic acid to have killed two persons instead of one. The man in the tweed suit shook hands with his fair companion—probably she hardly felt the prick, not sufficiently in any case to make her utter a scream. And, mind you, the scoundrel had every facility, through his friendship with Mr. Errington, of procuring what poison he required, not to mention his friend's visiting card. We cannot gauge how many months ago he began to try and copy Frank Errington in his style of dress, the cut of his moustache, his general appearance, making the change probably so gradual, that no one in his own entourage would notice it. He selected for his model a man his own height and build, with the same coloured hair."

"But there was the terrible risk of being identified by his fellow-traveller in the Underground," suggested Polly.

"Yes, there certainly was that risk; he chose to take it, and he was wise. He reckoned that several days would in any case elapse before that person, who, by the way, was a business man absorbed in his newspaper, would actually see him again. The great secret of successful crime is to study human nature," added the man in the corner, as he began looking for his hat and coat. "Edward Hazeldene knew it well."

"But the ring?"

"He may have bought that when he was on his honeymoon," he suggested with a grim chuckle; "the tragedy was not planned in a week, it may have taken years to mature. But you will own that there goes a frightful scoundrel unhung. I have left you his photograph as he was a year ago, and as he is now. You will see he has shaved his beard again, but also his moustache. I fancy he is a friend now of Mr. Andrew Campbell."

He left Miss Polly Burton wondering, not knowing what to believe.

And that is why she missed her appointment with Mr. Richard Frobisher (of the London Mail) to go and see Maud Allan dance at the Palace Theatre that afternoon.

AGATHA CHRISTIE

(1890–1976)

Agatha Christie began her career with a modest success, introducing Hercule Poirot in The Mysterious Affair at Styles *(1920). Prolific and unrelenting, she gradually rose to become the best-known mystery writer in the world, and certainly the best selling. Poirot and Miss Marple are among the most familiar detectives in fiction; yet Christie's greatest skill was not in characterization. Plotting was the skill she lived by, and by the end of her life, plot had come to be less valued as the linchpin of crime writing. Critics and writers derided her cleverness and insulted her middle-class values, yet her books continued to sell and her plays to be performed; and motion pictures of both continued to be made. Perhaps the simplicity of Christie's work with the exception of plot construction produces the kind of pleasure one finds also in Cycladic sculpture or in Picasso's line drawings. Our attention is devoted to the purity of form, rather than to the complexities of realism. Christie produces a surprise exactly where a reader anticipates one. The fact that it is expected requires her to be very clever to surprise at all. She rarely fails. Several of her solutions (in* The Murder of Roger Ackroyd; Murder on the Orient Express; *and* Witness for the Prosecution, *to name a few) are considered some of the cleverest ever written. Naturally, a writer interested in the puzzle would be attracted to armchair detection. Christie used it in several Poirot stories and parodied Orczy's "Man in the Corner" in a Beresford story. Odd, yet ordinary, the spinster detective Miss Jane Marple was created in a series of stories that had her solving crimes almost as a party game. So popular were the stories, she then became the heroine of twelve novels written between 1930 and 1976. In our selection, Miss Marple attends a dinner party, is presented with a locked room problem, and uses her armchair detective skills to solve it.*

THE BLUE GERANIUM

"When I was down here last year—" said Sir Henry Clithering, and stopped.

His hostess, Mrs. Bantry, looked at him curiously.

The ex-Commissioner of Scotland Yard was staying with old friends of his, Colonel and Mrs. Bantry, who lived near St. Mary Mead.

Mrs. Bantry, pen in hand, had just asked his advice as to who should be invited to make a sixth guest at dinner that evening.

"Yes?" said Mrs. Bantry encouragingly. "When you were here last year?"

"Tell me," said Sir Henry, "do you know a Miss Marple?"

Mrs. Bantry was surprised. It was the last thing she had expected.

"Know Miss Marple? Who doesn't! The typical old maid of fiction. Quite a dear, but hopelessly behind the times. Do you mean you would like to ask her to dinner?"

"You are surprised?"

"A little, I must confess. I should hardly have thought you—but perhaps there's an explanation?"

"The explanation is simple enough. When I was down here last year we got into the habit of discussing unsolved mysteries—there were five or six of us. We each supplied a story to which we knew the answer, but nobody else did. It was supposed to be an exercise in the deductive faculties—to see who could get nearest the truth."

"Well?"

"Like in the old story—we hardly realized that Miss Marple was playing; but we were very polite about it—didn't want to hurt the old dear's feelings. And now comes the cream of the jest. The old lady outdid us every time!"

"But how extraordinary! Why, dear old Miss Marple has hardly ever been out of St. Mary Mead."

"Ah! But according to her, that has given her unlimited opportunities of observing human nature—under the microscope, as it were."

"I suppose there's something in that," conceded Mrs. Bantry. "One would at least know the petty side of people. But I don't think we have any really exciting criminals in our midst. I think we must try her with Arthur's ghost story after dinner. I'd be thankful if she'd find a solution to that."

"I didn't know that Arthur believed in ghosts?"

"Oh, he doesn't. That's what worries him so. And it happened to a friend of his, George Pritchard—a most prosaic person. It's really rather tragic for poor George. Either this extraordinary story is true—or else—"

"Or else what?"

Mrs. Berry did not answer. After a minute or two she said irrelevantly:

"You know, I like George—everyone does. One can't believe that he—but people do such extraordinary things."

Sir Henry nodded. He knew, better than Mrs. Bantry, the extraordinary things that people did.

So it came about that that evening Mrs. Bantry looked around her dinner table (shivering a little as she did so, because the dining-room, like most English dining-rooms, was extremely cold) and fixed her gaze on the very upright old lady sitting on her husband's right. Miss Marple wore black lace mittens; an old lace fichu was draped round her shoulders and another piece of lace surmounted her white hair. She was talking animatedly to the elderly doctor, Dr. Lloyd, about the workhouse and the suspected shortcomings of the district nurse.

Mrs. Bantry marvelled anew. She even wondered whether Sir Henry had been making an elaborate joke—but there seemed no point in that. Incredible that what he had said could be really true.

Her glance went on and rested affectionately on her red-faced broad-shouldered husband as he sat talking horses to Jane Helier, the beautiful and popular actress. Jane, more beautiful (if that were possible) off the stage than on, opened enormous blue eyes and murmured at discreet intervals, "Really?" "Oh, Fancy!" "How extraordinary!" She knew nothing whatever about horses and cared less.

"Arthur," said Mrs. Bantry, "you're boring poor Jane to distraction. Leave your horses alone and tell her your ghost story instead. You know . . . George Pritchard."

"Eh, Dolly? Oh, but I don't know—"

"Sir Henry wants to hear it too. I was telling him something about it this morning. It would be interesting to hear what everyone has to say about it."

"Oh, do!" said Jane. "I love ghost stories."

"Well—" Colonel Bantry hesitated. "I've never believed much in the supernatural. But this . . .

"I don't think any of you know George Pritchard. He's one of the best. His wife—well, she's dead now, poor woman. I'll say just this much; she didn't give George any too easy a time when she was alive. She was one of those semi-invalids—I believe she really had something wrong with her, but whatever it was, she played it for all it was worth. She was capricious, exacting, unreasonable. She complained from morning to night. George was expected to wait on her hand and foot, and everything he did was always wrong."

"She was a dreadful woman," said Mrs. Bantry with conviction.

"I don't quite know how this business started. George was rather vague about it. I gather Mrs. Pritchard had always had a weakness for fortunetellers, palmists, clairvoyants—anything of that sort. George didn't mind. If she found amusement in it, well and good. But he refused to go into rhapsodies himself, and that was another grievance.

"A succession of hospital nurses was always passing through the house, Mrs. Pritchard usually becoming dissatisfied with them after a few weeks. One young nurse had been very keen on this fortunetelling stunt, and for a time Mrs. Pritchard had been fond of her. Then she suddenly fell out with her and insisted on her going. She had back another nurse who had been with her previously—an older woman, experienced and tactful in dealing with a neurotic patient. Nurse Copling, according to George, was a very good sort—a sensible woman to talk to. She put up with Mrs. Pritchard's tantrums and nerve storms with complete indifference.

"Mrs. Pritchard always lunched upstairs, and it was usual at lunch time for George and the nurse to come to some arrangement for the afternoon. Strictly speaking, the nurse went off from two to four, but 'to oblige,' as the phrase goes, she would sometimes take her time off after tea if George wanted to be free for the afternoon. On this occasion she mentioned that she was going to see a sister at Golders Green and might be a little late returning. George's face fell, for he had arranged to play a round of golf. Nurse Copling, however, reassured him.

" 'We'll neither of us be missed, Mr. Pritchard.' A twinkle came into her eye. 'Mrs. Pritchard's going to have more exciting company than ours.'

" 'Who's that?'

" 'Wait a minute.' Nurse Copling's eyes twinkled more than ever. 'Let me get it right, *Zarida, Psychic Reader of the Future.*'

" 'That's a new one, isn't it?" groaned George.

" 'Quite new. I believe my predecessor, Nurse Carstairs, sent her along. Mrs. Pritchard hasn't seen her yet. She made me write, fixing an appointment for this afternoon.'

" 'Well, at any rate, I shall get my golf,' said George, and he went off with the kindliest feelings toward Zarida, the reader of the future.

"On his return to the house, he found Mrs. Pritchard in a state of great agitation. She was, as usual, lying on her invalid couch, and she had a bottle of smelling salts in her hand which she sniffed at frequent intervals.

" 'George,' she exclaimed, 'what did I tell you about this house? The moment I came into it, I felt there was something wrong! Didn't I tell you so at the time?'

"Repressing his desire to reply, 'You always do,' George said, 'No, can't say I remember it.'

" 'You never do remember anything that has to do with me. Men are all extraordinarily callous—but I really believe that you are even more insensitive than most.'

" 'Oh, come now, Mary dear, that's not fair.'

" 'Well, as I was telling you, this woman knew at once! She—she actually blenched—if you know what I mean—as she came in at that door, and she said, "There is evil here—evil and danger. I feel it." '

"Very unwisely, George laughed.

" 'Well, you have had your money's worth this afternoon.'

"His wife closed her eyes and took a long sniff from her smelling bottle.

" 'How you hate me! You would jeer and laugh if I were dying.'

"George protested, and after a minute or two she went on.

" 'You may laugh, but I shall tell you the whole thing. This house is definitely dangerous to me—the woman said so.'

"George's formerly kind feeling toward Zarida underwent a change. He knew his wife was perfectly capable of insisting on moving to a new house if the caprice got hold of her.

" 'What else did she say?' he asked.

" 'She couldn't tell me very much. She was so upset. One thing she did say. I had some violets in a glass. She pointed at them and cried out:

" 'Take those away. No blue flowers—never have blue flowers. Blue flowers are fatal to you—remember that.'

" 'And you know,' added Mrs. Pritchard, "I always have told you that blue as a colour is repellent to me. I feel a natural instinctive sort of warning against it.'

"George was much too wise to remark that he had never heard her say so before. Instead he asked what the mysterious Zarida was like. Mrs. Pritchard entered with gusto upon a description.

" 'Black hair in coiled knobs over her ears—her eyes were half closed—great black rims round them—she had a black veil over her mouth and chin—she spoke in a kind of singing voice with a marked foreign accent—Spanish, I think—'

" 'In fact, all the usual stock in trade,' said George cheerfully.

"His wife immediately closed her eyes.

" 'I feel extremely ill,' she said. 'Ring for Nurse. Unkindness upsets me, as you know only too well.'

"It was two days later that Nurse Copling came to George with a grave face.

" 'Will you come to Mrs. Pritchard, please. She has had a letter which upsets her greatly.'

"He found his wife with the letter in her hand. She held it out to him.

" 'Read it,' she said.

"George read it. It was on heavily scented paper, and the writing was big and black.

> I have seen the Future. Be warned before it is too late. Beware of the full moon. The Blue Primrose means Warn-

ing; the Blue Hollyhock means Danger; the Blue Geranium means Death. . . .

"Just about to burst out laughing. George caught Nurse Copling's eye. She made a quick warning gesture. He said rather awkwardly, 'The woman's probably trying to frighten you, Mary. Anyway, there aren't such things as blue primroses and blue geraniums.'

"But Mrs. Pritchard began to cry and say her days were numbered. Nurse Copling came out with George upon the landing.

" 'Of all the silly tomfoolery,' he burst out.

" 'I suppose it is.'

"Something in the nurse's tone struck him, and he stared at her in amazement.

" 'Surely, Nurse, you don't believe—'

" 'No, no, Mr. Pritchard. I don't believe in reading the future—that's nonsense. What puzzles me is the meaning of this. Fortunetellers are usually out for what they can get. But this woman seems to be frightening Mrs. Pritchard with no advantage to herself. I can't see the point. There's another thing—'

" 'Yes?'

" 'Mrs. Pritchard says that something about Zarida was faintly familiar to her.'

" 'Well?'

" 'Well, I don't like it, Mr. Pritchard, that's all.'

" 'I didn't know you were so superstitious, Nurse.'

" 'I'm not superstitious, but I know when a thing is fishy.'

"It was about four days after this that the first incident happened. To explain it to you, I shall have to describe Mrs. Pritchard's room—"

"You'd better let me do that," interrupted Mrs. Bantry.

"It was papered with one of those new wallpapers where you apply clumps of flowers to make a kind of herbaceous border. The effect is almost like being in a garden—though, of course, the flowers are all wrong. I mean they simply couldn't be in bloom all at the same time—"

"Don't let a passion for horticultural accuracy run away with you, Dolly," said her husband. "We all know you're an enthusiastic gardener."

"Well, it is absurd," protested Mrs. Bantry. "To have bluebells and daffodils and lupins and hollyhocks and Michaelmas daises all grouped together."

"Most unscientific," said Sir Henry. "But to proceed with the story . . ."

"Well, among these named flowers were primroses, clumps of yellow and pink primroses, and—oh, go on, Arthur, this is your story."

Colonel Bantry took up the tale.

"Mrs. Pritchard rang her bell violently one morning. The household came running—thought she was in extremis; not at all. She was violently excited and pointing at the wallpaper, and there, sure enough, was one blue primrose in the midst of the others . . ."

"Oh!" said Miss Helier, "how creepy!"

"The question was: Hadn't the blue primrose always been there? That was George's suggestion and the nurse's. But Mrs. Pritchard wouldn't have it at any price. She had never noticed it till that very morning, and the night before had been full moon. She was very upset about it."

"I met George Pritchard that same day and he told me about it," said Mrs. Bantry. "I went to see Mrs. Pritchard and did my best to ridicule the whole thing, but without success. I came away really concerned, and I remember I met Jean Instow and told her about it. Jean is a queer girl. She said, 'So she's really upset about it? I told her that I thought the woman was perfectly capable of dying of fright—she was really abnormally superstitious.

"I remember Jean rather startled me with what she said next. She said, 'Well, that might be all for the best, mightn't it?' And she said it so coolly, in so matter-of-fact a tone, that I was really—well, shocked. Of course I know it's done nowadays—to be brutal and outspoken, but I never get used to it. Jean smiled at me rather oddly and said, 'You don't like my saying that—but it's true. What use is Mrs. Pritchard's life to her? None at all, and it's hell for George Pritchard. To have his wife frightened out of existence would be the best thing that could happen to him.' I said, 'George is most awfully good to her always.' And she said, 'Yes, he deserves a reward, poor dear. He's a very attractive person, George Pritchard. The last nurse thought so—the pretty one—what was her name? Carstairs. That was the cause of the row between her and Mrs. P.'

"Now I didn't like hearing Jean say that. Of course, one had wondered—"

Mrs. Bantry paused significantly.

"Yes, dear," said Miss Marple placidly. "One always does. Is Miss Instow a pretty girl? I suppose she plays golf?"

"Yes. She's good at all games. And she's nice-looking, attractive-looking, very fair with a healthy skin and nice steady blue eyes. Of course, we always have felt that she and George Pritchard—I mean, if things had been different—they are so well suited to one another."

"And they were friends?" asked Miss Marple.

"Oh yes. Great friends."

"Do you think, Dolly," said Colonel Bantry plaintively, "that I might be allowed to go on with my story?"

"Arthur," said Mrs. Bantry resignedly, "wants to get back to his ghosts."

"I had the rest of the story from George himself," went on the colonel. "There's no doubt that Mrs. Pritchard got the wind up badly toward the end of the next month. She marked off on a calendar the day when the moon would be full, and on that night she had both the nurse and then George into her room and made them study the wallpaper carefully. There were pink hollyhocks and red ones, but there were no blue among them. Then when George left the room she locked the door—"

"And in the morning there was a large blue hollyhock," said Miss Helier joyfully.

"Quite right," said Colonel Bantry. "Or at any rate, nearly right. One flower of a hollyhock just above her head had turned blue. It staggered George, and of course, the more it staggered him the more he refused to take the thing seriously. He insisted that the whole thing was some kind of a practical joke. He ignored the evidence of the locked door and the fact that Mrs. Pritchard discovered the change before anyone—even Nurse Copling—was admitted.

"It staggered George, and it made him unreasonable. His wife wanted to leave the house, and he wouldn't let her. He was inclined to believe in the supernatural for the first time, but he wasn't going to admit it. He usually gave in to his wife, but this time he wouldn't. Mary was not to make a fool of herself, he said. The whole thing was the most infernal nonsense.

"And so the next month sped away. Mrs. Pritchard made less protest than one would have imagined. I think she was superstitious enough to believe that she couldn't escape her fate. She repeated again and again: 'The blue primrose—warning. The blue hollyhock—danger. The blue geranium—death.' And she would lie looking at the clump of pinky-red geraniums nearest her bed.

"The whole business was pretty nervy. Even the nurse caught the infection. She came to George two days before full moon and begged him to take Mrs. Pritchard away. George was angry.

" 'If all the flowers on that wall turned into blue devils, it couldn't kill anyone!' he shouted.

" 'It might. Shock has killed people before now.'

" 'Nonsense,' said George.

"George has always been a shade pigheaded. You can't drive him. I believe he had a secret idea that his wife worked the changes herself and that it was all some morbid, hysterical plan of hers.

"Well, the fatal night came. Mrs. Pritchard locked her door as usual. She was very calm—in almost an exalted state of mind. The nurse was worried by her state—and wanted to give her a stimulant, an injection of strychnine, but Mrs. Pritchard refused. In a way, I believe, she was enjoying herself. George said she was."

"I think that's quite possible," said Mrs. Bantry. "There must have been a strange sort of glamour about the whole thing."

"There was no violent ringing of a bell the next morning. Mrs. Pritchard usually woke about eight. When, at eight-thirty, there was no sign from her, Nurse rapped loudly on the door. Getting no reply, she fetched George and insisted on the door being broken open. They did so with the help of a chisel.

"One look at the still figure on the bed was enough for Nurse Copling. She sent George to telephone for the doctor, but it was too late. Mrs. Pritchard, he said, must have been dead at least eight hours. Her smelling salts lay by her hand on the bed, and on the wall beside her one of the pinky-red geraniums was a bright deep blue."

"Horrible," said Miss Helier with a shiver.

Sir Henry was frowning.

"No additional details?"

Colonel Bantry shook his head, but Mrs. Bantry spoke quickly.

"The gas."

"What about the gas?" asked Sir Henry.

"When the doctor arrived there was a slight smell of gas, and sure enough, he found the gas ring in the fireplace very slightly turned on, but so little that it couldn't have mattered."

"Did Mr. Pritchard and the nurse not notice it when they first went in?"

"The nurse said she did notice a slight smell. George said he didn't notice gas, but something made him feel very queer and overcome; but he put that down to shock—and probably it was. At any rate, there was no question of gas poisoning. The smell was scarcely noticeable."

"And that's the end of the story?"

"No, it isn't. One way and another, there was a lot of talk. The servants, you see, had overheard things—had heard, for instance, Mrs. Pritchard telling her husband that he hated her and would jeer if she were dying. And also more recent remarks. She said one day, apropos of his refusing to leave the house, 'Very well. When I am dead, I hope everyone will realize that you have killed me.' And as ill luck would have it, he had been mixing some weed killer for the garden paths the very day before. One of the younger servants had seen him and had afterward seen him taking up a glass of hot milk to his wife.

"The talk spread and grew. The doctor had given a certificate—I don't know exactly in what terms—shock, syncope, heart failure, probably some medical term meaning nothing much. However, the poor lady had not been a month in her grave before an exhumation order was applied for and granted."

"And the result of the autopsy was nil, I remember," said Sir Henry gravely. "A case, for once, of smoke without fire."

"The whole thing is really very curious," said Mrs. Bantry. "That fortuneteller, for instance—Zarida. At the address where she was supposed to be, no one had ever heard of any such person!"

"She appeared once—out of the blue," said her husband, "and then utterly vanished. Out of the blue—that's rather good!"

"And what is more," continued Mrs. Bantry, "little Nurse Carstairs, who was supposed to have recommended her, had never even heard of her."

They looked at each other.

"It's a mysterious story," said Dr. Lloyd. "One can make guesses, but to guess—"

He shook his head.

"Has Mr. Pritchard married Miss Instow?" asked Miss Marple in her gentle voice.

"Now why do you ask that?" inquired Sir Henry.

Miss Marple opened gentle blue eyes.

"It seems to me so important," she said. "Have they married?"

Colonel Bantry shook his head.

"We—well, we expected something of the kind—but it's eighteen months now. I don't believe they even see much of each other."

"That is important," said Miss Marple. "Very important."

"Then you think the same as I do," said Mrs. Bantry. "You think—"

"Now, Dolly," said her husband. "It's unjustifiable—what you're going to say. You can't go about accusing people without a shadow of proof."

"Don't be so—so manly, Arthur. Men are always afraid to say anything. Anyway, this is all between ourselves. It's just a wild, fantastic idea of mine that possibly—only possibly—Jean Instow disguised herself as a fortuneteller. Mind you, she may have done it for a joke. I don't for a minute think that she meant any harm; but if she did do it, and if Mrs. Pritchard was foolish enough to die of fright—well, that's what Miss Marple meant, wasn't it?"

"No, dear, not quite," said Miss Marple. "You see, if I were going to kill anyone—which, of course, I wouldn't dream of doing for a minute, because it would be very wicked, and besides, I don't like killing—not even wasps, though I know it has to be, and I'm sure the gardener does it as humanely as possible. Let me see, what was I saying?"

"If you wished to kill anyone," prompted Sir Henry.

"Oh yes. Well, if I did, I shouldn't be at all satisfied to trust to fright. I know one reads of people dying of it, but it seems a very uncertain sort of thing, and the most nervous people are far more brave than one really thinks they are. I should like something definite and certain and make a thoroughly good plan about it."

"Miss Marple," said Sir Henry, "you frighten me. I hope you will never wish to remove me. Your plans would be too good."

Miss Marple looked at him reproachfully.

"I thought I had made it clear that I would never contemplate such wickedness," she said. "No, I was trying to put myself in the place of—er—a certain person."

"Do you mean George Pritchard?" asked Colonel Bantry. "I'll never believe it of George—though, mind you, even the nurse believes it. I went and saw her about a month afterward, at the time of the exhumation. She didn't know how it was done—in fact, she wouldn't say anything at all—but it was clear enough that she believed George to be in some way responsible for his wife's death. She was convinced of it."

"Well," said Dr. Lloyd, "perhaps she wasn't so far wrong. And mind you, a nurse often knows. She can't say—she's got no proof—but she knows."

Sir Henry leaned forward.

"Come now, Miss Marple," he said persuasively. "You're lost in a daydream. Won't you tell us all about it?"

Miss Marple started and turned pink.

"I beg your pardon," she said. "I was just thinking about our district nurse. A most difficult problem."

"More difficult than the problem of a blue geranium?"

"It really depends on the primroses," said Miss Marple. "I mean, Mrs. Bantry said they were yellow and pink. If it was a pink primrose that turned blue, of course, that fits in perfectly. But if it happened to be a yellow one—"

"It was a pink one," said Mrs. Bantry.

She stared. They all stared at Miss Marple.

"Then that seems to settle it," said Miss Marple. She shook her head regretfully. "And the wasp season and everything. And of course the gas."

"It reminds you, I suppose, of countless village tragedies?" said Sir Henry.

"Not tragedies," said Miss Marple. "And certainly nothing criminal. But it does remind me a little of the trouble we are having with the district nurse. After all, nurses are human beings, and what with having to be so correct in their behaviour and wearing those uncomfortable collars and being so thrown with the family—well, can you wonder that things sometimes happen?"

A glimmer of light broke upon Sir Henry.

"You mean Nurse Carstairs?"

"Oh no. Not Nurse Carstairs. Nurse Copling. You see, she had been there before and very much thrown with Mr. Pritchard, who you say is an attractive man. I daresay she thought, poor thing—well, we needn't go into that. I don't suppose she knew about Miss Instow, and of course afterward, when she found out, it turned her against him and she tried to do all the harm she could. Of course, the letter really gave her away, didn't it?"

"What letter?"

"Well, she wrote to the fortuneteller at Mrs. Pritchard's request, and the fortuneteller came, apparently in answer to the letter. But later it was discovered that there never had been such a person at that address. So that shows that Nurse Copling was in it. She only pretended to write—so what could be more likely than that she was the fortuneteller herself?"

"I never saw the point about the letter," said Sir Henry. "That's a most important point, of course."

"Rather a bold step to take," said Miss Marple, "because Mrs. Pritchard might have recognized her in spite of the disguise—though of course if she had, the nurse could have pretended it was a joke."

"What did you mean," said Sir Henry, "when you said that if you were a certain person, you would not have trusted to fright?"

"One couldn't be sure that way," said Miss Marple. "No, I think that the warnings and the blue flowers were, if I may use a military term"—she laughed self-consciously—"just camouflage."

"And the real thing?"

"I know," said Miss Marple apologetically, "that I've got wasps on the brain. Poor things, destroyed in their thousands—and usually on such a beautiful summer's day. But I remember thinking, when I saw the gardener shaking up the cyanide of potassium in a bottle with water, how like smelling salts it looked. And if it were put in a smelling-salt bottle and substituted for the real one—well, the poor lady was in the habit of using her smelling salts. Indeed, you said they were found by her hand. Then, of course, while Mr. Pritchard went to telephone to the doctor, the nurse would change it for the real bottle, and she'd just turn on the gas a little bit to mask any smell of almonds and in case anyone felt queer, and I always have heard the cyanide leaves no trace if you wait long enough. But, of course, I may be wrong, and it may have been something entirely different in the bottle, but that doesn't really matter, does it?"

Miss Marple paused, a little out of breath.

Jane Helier leaned forward and said, "But the blue geranium and the other flowers?"

"Nurses always have litmus paper, don't they?" said Miss Marple, "for—well, for testing. Not a very pleasant subject. We won't dwell on it. I have done a little nursing myself." She grew delicately pink. "Blue turns red with acids, and red turns blue with alkalies. So easy to paste some red litmus over a red flower—near the bed, of course. And then, when the poor lady used her smelling salts, the strong ammonia fumes would turn it blue. Really most ingenious. Of course, the geranium wasn't blue when they first broke into the room—nobody noticed it till afterward. When nurse changed the bottles, she held the sal ammoniac against the wallpaper for a minute, I expect."

"You might have been there, Miss Marple," said Sir Henry.

"What worries me," said Miss Marple, "is poor Mr. Pritchard and that nice girl, Miss Instow. Probably both suspecting each other and keeping apart—and life so very short."

She shook her head.

"You needn't worry," said Sir Henry. "As a matter of fact, I have something up my sleeve. A nurse has been arrested on a charge of murdering an elderly patient who had left her a legacy. It was done with cyanide of potassium substituted for smelling salts. Nurse Copling trying the same trick again. Miss Instow and Mr. Pritchard need have no doubts as to the truth."

"Now isn't that nice?" cried Miss Marple. "I don't mean about the new murder, of course. That's very sad and shows how much wickedness there is in the world and that if once you give away—which reminds me, I must finish my little conversation with Dr. Lloyd about the village nurse."

ELLERY QUEEN

(Frederic Dannay, 1905–1982; Manfred B. Lee, 1905–1971)

Born Daniel Nathan and Manfred Lepofsky, cousins Frederic Dannay and Manfred B. Lee were working in advertising when they read of a detective story contest. Using the gimmick that the author of the story, Ellery Queen, was also the detective, they won the contest. The magazine sponsoring the contest went broke, but another publisher released "The Roman Hat Mystery" (1929) as a novel and the cousins never looked back. Despite their success, they were far from amiable collaborators. They fought so viciously they eventually resorted to working over the telephone or by mail. Their creation, Ellery Queen, is the quintessential puzzle-solving detective. In the "fair play" tradition, all the clues are presented to the reader, often with an invitation to solve the case before the detective himself. As the reading public's taste in detective styles changed over time toward active, tough he-men, Dannay and Lee adapted their character. The authors maintained their interest in puzzle plotting but the effete, thinking machine became more "manly." Queen even developed a love interest, though when Dashiell Hammett once demanded to know whether Queen had a sex life or not, the cousins never answered. While Ellery Queen may not be the greatest American detective character, he is certainly the greatest American puzzle detective. Although Queen sometimes investigates on the site, the following adventure is almost purely intellectual and filled with armchair elements. The crucial scene consists of Queen free-associating, as the evidence is presented to him, using his impressive mind to solve a puzzle that a dead man has arranged. With little consequence in the solution and without even a serious crime to be exposed, the story provides pure puzzle pleasure.

THE ADVENTURE OF ABRAHAM LINCOLN'S CLUE

The case began on the outskirts of an upstate New York city with the dreadful name of Eulalia, behind the flaking shutters of a fat and curlicued house with architectural dandruff, recalling for all the world some blowsy ex-Bloomer Girl from the gay Nineties of its origin.

The owner, a formerly wealthy man named DiCampo, possessed a grandeur not shared by his property, although it was no less fallen into ruin. His falcon's face, more Florentine then Victorian, was—like the house—ravaged by time and the inclemencies of fortune; but haughtily so, and indeed DiCampo wore his scurfy purple velvet house jacket like the prince he was entitled to call himself, but did not. He was proud, and stubborn, and useless; and he had a lovely daughter named Bianca, who taught at a Eulalia grade school and, through marvels of economy, supported them both.

How Lorenzo San Marco Borghese-Ruffo DiCampo came to this decayed estate is no concern of ours. The presence there this day of a man named Harbidger and a man named Tungston, however, is to the point: they had come, Harbidger from Chicago, Tungston from Philadelphia, to buy something each wanted very much, and Di-

Campo had summoned them in order to sell it. The two visitors were collectors, Harbidger's passion being Lincoln, Tungston's Poe.

The Lincoln collector, an elderly man who looked like a migrant fruit picker, had plucked his fruits well: Harbidger was worth about $40,000,000, every dollar of which was at the beck of his mania for Lincolniana. Tungston, who was almost as rich, had the aging body of a poet and the eyes of a starving panther, armament that had served him well in the wars of Poeana.

"I must say, Mr. DiCampo," remarked Harbidger, "that your letter surprised me." He paused to savor the wine his host had poured from an ancient and honorable bottle (DiCampo had filled it with California claret before their arrival). "May I ask what has finally induced you to offer the book and document for sale?"

"To quote Lincoln in another context, Mr. Harbidger," said DiCampo with a shrug of his wasted shoulders, " 'the dogmas of the quiet past are inadequate to the stormy present.' In short, a hungry man sells his blood."

"Only if it's of the right type," said old Tungston, unmoved. "You've made that book and document less accessible to collectors and historians, DiCampo, than the gold in Fort Knox. Have you got them here? I'd like to examine them."

"No other hand will ever touch them except by right of ownership," Lorenzo DiCampo replied bitterly. He had taken a miser's glee in his lucky finds, vowing never to part with them; now forced by his need to sell them, he was like a suspicion-caked old prospector who, stumbling at last on pay dirt, draws cryptic maps to keep the world from stealing the secret of its location. "As I informed you gentlemen, I represent the book as bearing the signatures of Poe and Lincoln, and the document as being in Lincoln's hand; I am offering them with the customary proviso that they are returnable if they should prove to be not as represented; and if this does not satisfy you," and the old prince actually rose, "let us terminate our business here and now."

"Sit down, sit down, Mr. DiCampo," Harbidger said.

"No one is questioning your integrity," snapped old Tungston. "It's just that I'm not used to buying sight unseen. If there's a money-back guarantee, we'll do it your way."

Lorenzo DiCampo reseated himself stiffly. "Very well, gentlemen. Then I take it you are both prepared to buy?"

"Oh, yes!" said Harbidger. "What is your price?"

"Oh, no," said DiCampo. "What is your bid?"

The Lincoln collector cleared his throat, which was full of

slaver. "If the book and document are as represented, Mr. DiCampo, you might hope to get from a dealer or realize at auction—oh—$50,000. I offer you $55,000."

"$56,000," said Tungston.

"$57,000," said Harbidger.

"$58,000," said Tungston.

"$59,000," said Harbidger.

Tungston showed his fangs. "$60,000," he said.

Harbidger fell silent, and DiCampo waited. He did not expect miracles. To these men, five times $60,000 was of less moment than the undistinguished wine they were smacking their lips over; but they were veterans of many a hard auction-room campaign, and a collector's victory tasted very nearly as sweet for the price as for the prize.

So the impoverished prince was not surprised when the Lincoln collector suddenly said, "Would you be good enough to allow Mr. Tungston and me to talk privately for a moment?"

DiCampo rose and strolled out of the room, to gaze somberly through a cracked window at the jungle growth that had once been his Italian formal gardens.

It was the Poe collector who summoned him back. "Harbidger has convinced me that for the two of us to try to outbid each other would simply run the price up out of all reason. We're going to make you a sporting proposition."

"I've proposed to Mr. Tungston, and he has agreed," nodded Harbidger, "that our bid for the book and document be $65,000. Each of us is prepared to pay that sum, and not a penny more."

"So that is how the screws are turned," said DiCampo, smiling. "But I do not understand. If each of you makes the identical bid, which of you gets the book and document?"

"Ah," grinned the Poe man, "that's where the sporting proposition comes in."

"You see, Mr. DiCampo," said the Lincoln man, "we are going to leave that decision to you."

Even the old prince, who had seen more than his share of the astonishing, was astonished. He looked at the two rich men really for the first time. "I must confess," he murmured, "that your compact is an amusement. Permit me?" He sank into thought while the two collectors sat expectantly. When the old man looked up he was smiling like a fox. "The very thing, gentlemen! From the typewritten copies of the document I sent you, you both know that Lincoln himself left a clue to a theoretical hiding place for the book which he never explained. Some time ago I arrived at a possible solution to the President's little mystery. I propose to hide the book and document in accordance with it."

"You mean whichever of us figures out your interpretation of the Lincoln clue and finds the book and document where you will hide them, Mr. DiCampo, gets both for the agreed price?"

"That is it exactly."

The Lincoln collector looked dubious. "I don't know . . ."

"Oh, come, Harbidger," said Tungston, eyes glittering. "A deal is a deal. We accept, DiCampo! Now what?"

"You gentlemen will of course have to give me a little time. Shall we say three days?"

Ellery let himself into the Queen apartment, tossed his suitcase aside, and set about opening windows. He had been out of town for a week on a case, and Inspector Queen was in Atlantic City attending a police convention.

Breathable air having been restored, Ellery sat down to the week's accumulation of mail. One envelope made him pause. It had come by airmail special delivery, it was postmarked four days earlier, and in the lower left corner, in red, flamed the word *URGENT*. The printed return address on the flap said: L.S.M.B.-R DICAMPO, POST OFFICE BOX 69, SOUTHERN DISTRICT, EULALIA, N.Y. The initials of the name had been crossed out and "Bianca" written above them.

The enclosure, in a large agitated female hand on inexpensive notepaper, said:

> Dear Mr. Queen,
>
> The most important detective book in the world has disappeared. Will you please find it for me?
>
> Phone me on arrival at the Eulalia RR station or airport and I will pick you up.
>
> Bianca DiCampo

A yellow envelope then caught his eye. It was a telegram, dated the previous day:

> WHY HAVE I NOT HEARD FROM YOU STOP AM IN DESPERATE NEED YOUR SERVICES
>
> BIANCA DICAMPO

He had no sooner finished reading the telegram than the telephone on his desk trilled. It was a long-distance call.

"Mr. Queen?" throbbed a contralto voice. "Thank heaven I've finally got through to you! I've been calling all day—"

"I've been away," said Ellery, "and you would be Miss Bianca DiCampo of Eulalia. In two words, Miss DiCampo: Why me?"

"In two words, Mr. Queen: Abraham Lincoln."

Ellery was startled. "You plead a persuasive case," he chuckled. "It's true, I'm an incurable Lincoln addict. How did you find out? Well, never mind. Your letter refers to a book, Miss DiCampo. Which book?"

The husky voice told him, and certain other provocative things as well. "So will you come, Mr. Queen?"

"Tonight if I could! Suppose I drive up first thing in the morning. I ought to make Eulalia by noon. Harbidger and Tungston are still around, I take it?"

"Oh, yes. They're staying at a motel downtown."

"Would you ask them to be there?"

The moment he hung up, Ellery leaped to his bookshelves. He snatched out his volume of *Murder for Pleasure,* the historical work on detective stories by his good friend Howard Haycraft, and found what he was looking for on page 26:

> And . . . young William Dean Howells thought it significant praise to assert of a nominee for President of the United States:
>
> The bent of his mind is mathematical and metaphysical, and he is therefore pleased with the absolute and logical method of Poe's tales and sketches, in which the problem of mystery is given, and wrought out into everyday facts by processes of cunning analysis. It is said that he suffers no year to pass without a perusal of this author.
>
> Abraham Lincoln subsequently confirmed this statement, which appeared in his little-known "campaign biography" by Howells in 1860. . . . The instance is chiefly notable, of course, for its revelation of a little-suspected affinity between two great Americans. . . .

Very early the next morning Ellery gathered some papers from his files, stuffed them into his brief case, scribbled a note for his father, and ran for his car, Eulalia-bound.

* * *

He was enchanted by the DiCampo house, which looked like something out of Poe by Charles Addams; and, for other reasons, by Bianca, who turned out to be a genetic product supreme of northern Italy, with titian hair and Mediterranean blue eyes and a figure that needed only some solid steaks to qualify her for Miss Universe competition. Also, she was in deep mourning; so her conquest of the Queen heart was immediate and complete.

"He died of a cerebral hemorrhage, Mr. Queen," Bianca said, dabbing at her absurd little nose. "In the middle of the second night after his session with Mr. Harbidger and Mr. Tungston."

So Lorenzo San Marco Borghese-Ruffo DiCampo was unexpectedly dead, bequeathing the lovely Bianca near-destitution and a mystery.

"The only things of value Father really left me are that book and the Lincoln document. The $65,000 they now represent would pay off Father's debts and give me a fresh start. But I can't find them, Mr. Queen, and neither can Mr. Harbidger and Mr. Tungston—who'll be here soon, by the way. Father hid the two things, as he told them he would; but where? We've ransacked the place."

"Tell me more about the book, Miss DiCampo."

"As I said over the phone, it's called *The Gift: 1845*. The Christmas annual that contained the earliest appearance of Edgar Allan Poe's 'The Purloined Letter.' "

"Published in Philadelphia by Carey & Hart? Bound in red?" At Bianca's nod Ellery said, "You understand that an ordinary copy of *The Gift: 1845* isn't worth more than about $50. What makes your father's copy unique is that double autograph you mentioned."

"That's what he said, Mr. Queen. I wish I had the book here to show you—that beautifully handwritten *Edgar Allan Poe* on the flyleaf, and under Poe's signature the signature *Abraham Lincoln*."

"Poe's own copy, once owned, signed and read by Lincoln," Ellery said slowly. "Yes, that would be a collector's item for the ages. By the way, Miss DiCampo, what's the story behind the other piece—the Lincoln document?"

Bianca told him what her father had told her.

One morning in the spring of 1865, Abraham Lincoln opened the rosewood door of his bedroom in the southwest corner of the second floor of the White House and stepped out into the redcarpeted hall at the unusually late hour—for him—of 7:00 a.m.; he was more accustomed to beginning his workday at six.

But (as Lorenzo DiCampo had reconstructed events) Mr. Lincoln that morning had lingered in his bedchamber. He had awakened at his usual hour but, instead of leaving immediately on dressing for his office, he had pulled one of the cane chairs over to the round table, with its gas-fed reading lamp, and sat down to reread Poe's "The Purloined Letter" in his copy of the 1845 annual; it was a dreary morning, and the natural light was poor. The President was alone; the folding doors to Mrs. Lincoln's bedroom remained closed.

Impressed as always with Poe's tale, Mr. Lincoln on this occasion was struck by a whimsical thought; and, apparently finding no paper handy, he took an envelope from his pocket, discarded its enclosure, slit the two short edges so that the envelope opened out into a single sheet, and began to write on the blank side . . .

"Describe it to me, please."

"It's a long envelope, one that must have contained a bulky letter. It is addressed to the White House, but there is no return address, and Father was never able to identify the sender from the handwriting. We do know that the letter came through the regular mails, because there are two Lincoln stamps on it, lightly but unmistakably canceled."

"May I see your father's transcript of what Lincoln wrote out that morning on the inside of the envelope?"

Bianca handed him a typewritten copy and, in spite of himself, Ellery felt goose flesh rise as he read:

> *Apr. 14, 1865*
>
> Mr. Poe's The Purloined Letter is a work of singular originality. Its simplicity is a master-stroke of cunning, which never fails to arouse my wonder.
>
> Reading the tale over this morning has given me a "notion." Suppose I wished to hide a book, this very book, perhaps? Where best to do so? Well, as Mr. Poe in his tale hid a letter *among letters,* might not a book be hidden *among books?* Why, if this very copy of the tale were to be deposited in a library and on purpose not recorded—would not the Library of Congress make a prime depository!—well might it repose there, undiscovered, for a generation.
>
> On the other hand, let us regard Mr. Poe's "notion" turnabout: suppose the book were to be placed, not amongst

other books, but *where no book would reasonably be expected?* (I may follow the example of Mr. Poe, and, myself, compose a tale of "ratiocination"!)

The "notion" beguiles me, it is nearly seven o'clock. Later to-day, if the vultures and my appointments leave me a few moments of leisure, I may write further of my imagined hiding-place.

In self-reminder: the hiding place of the book is in 3od, which

Ellery looked up. "The document ends there?"

"Father said that Mr. Lincoln must have glanced again at his watch, and shamefacedly jumped up to go to his office, leaving the sentence unfinished. Evidently he never found the time to get back to it."

Ellery brooded. Evidently indeed. From the moment when Abraham Lincoln stepped from his bedroom that Good Friday morning, fingering his thick gold watch on its vest chain, to bid the still-unrelieved night guard his customary courteous "Good morning" and make for his office at the other end of the hall, his day was spoken for. The usual patient push through the clutching crowd of favor seekers, many of whom had bedded down all night on the hall carpet; sanctuary in his sprawling office, where he read official correspondence; by 8:00 a.m. having breakfast with his family—Mrs. Lincoln chattering away about plans for the evening, twelve-year-old Tad of the cleft palate lisping a complaint that "nobody asked me to go," and young Robert Lincoln, just returned from duty, bubbling with stories about his hero Ulysses Grant and the last days of the war; then back to the presidential office to look over the morning newspapers (which Lincoln had once remarked he "never" read, but these were happy days, with good news everywhere), sign two documents, and signal the soldier at the door to admit the morning's first caller, Speaker of the House Schuyler Colfax (who was angling for a Cabinet post and had to be tactfully handled); and so on throughout the day—the historic Cabinet meeting at 11:00 a.m., attended by General Grant himself, that stretched well into the afternoon; a hurried lunch at almost half past two with Mrs. Lincoln (had this forty-five-pounds-underweight man eaten his usual midday meal of a biscuit, a glass of milk, and an apple?); more visitors to see in his office (including the unscheduled Mrs. Nancy Bushrod, escaped slave and wife of an escaped slave and mother of three small children, weeping that Tom, a soldier in the Army of the Potomac, was no longer getting his pay: "You are entitled to your husband's pay. Come this time tomorrow," and the tall President escorted her to the door, bowing her out "like I was a natural-born lady"; the late afternoon drive in the barouche to the Navy Yard and back with Mrs. Lincoln; more work, more visitors, into the evening . . . until finally, at five minutes past 8:00 p.m., Abraham Lincoln stepped into the White House formal coach after his wife, waved, and sank back to be driven off to see a play he did not much want to see, *Our American Cousin*, at Ford's Theatre . . .

Ellery mused over the black day in silence. And, like a relative hanging on the specialist's yet undelivered diagnosis, Bianca DiCampo sat watching him with anxiety.

Harbidger and Tungston arrived in a taxi to greet Ellery with the fervor of castaways grasping at a smudge of smoke on the horizon.

"As I understand it, gentlemen," Ellery said when he had calmed them down, "neither of you has been able to solve Mr. DiCampo's interpretation of the Lincoln clue. If I succeed in finding the book and paper where DiCampo hid them, which of you gets them?"

"We intend to split the $65,000 payment to Miss DiCampo," said Harbidger, "and take joint ownership of the two pieces."

"An arrangement," growled old Tungston, "I'm against on principle, in practice, and by plain horse sense."

"So am I," sighed the Lincoln collector, "but what else can we do?"

"Well," and the Poe man regarded Bianca DiCampo with the icy intimacy of the cat that long ago marked the bird as its prey, "Miss DiCampo, who now owns the two pieces, is quite free to renegotiate a sale on her own terms."

"Miss DiCampo," said Miss DiCampo, giving Tungston stare for stare, "considers herself bound by her father's wishes. His terms stand."

"In all likelihood, then," said the other millionaire, "one of us will retain the book, the other the document, and we'll exchange them every year, or some such thing." Harbidger sounded unhappy.

"Only practical arrangement under the circumstances," grunted Tungston, and *he* sounded unhappy. "But all this is academic, Queen, unless and until the book and document are found."

Ellery nodded. "The problem, then, is to fathom DiCampo's interpretation of that 3*od* in the document. 3od . . . I notice, Miss DiCampo—or, may I? Bianca?—that your father's typewritten copy of the Lincoln holograph text runs the 3 and *o* and *d* together—no spacing in between. Is that the way it occurs in the longhand?"

"Yes."

"Hmm. Still . . . 3od . . . Could *d* stand for *days* . . . or the British *pence* . . . or *died,* as used in obituaries? Does any of these make sense to you, Bianca?"

"No."

"Did your father have any special interest in, say, pharmacology? chemistry? physics? algebra? electricity? Small *d* is an abbreviation used in all those." But Bianca shook her splendid head. "Banking? Small *d* for *dollars, dividends?*"

"Hardly," the girl said with a sad smile.

"How about theatricals? Was your father ever involved in a play production? Small *d* stands for *door* in playscript stage directions."

"Mr. Queen, I've gone through every darned abbreviation my dictionary lists, and I haven't found one that has a point of contact with any interest of my father's."

Ellery scowled. "At that—I assume the typewritten copy is accurate—the manuscript shows no period after the *d,* making an abbreviation unlikely. 3od . . . let's concentrate on the number. Does the number 30 have any significance for you?"

"Yes, indeed," said Bianca, making all three men sit up. But then they sank back. "In a few years it will represent my age, and that has enormous significance. But only for me, I'm afraid."

"You'll be drawing wolf whistles at twice thirty," quoth Ellery warmly. "However! Could the number have cross-referred to anything in your father's life or habits?"

"None that I can think of, Mr. Queen. And," Bianca said, having grown roses in her cheeks, "thank you."

"I think," said old Tungston testily, "we had better stick to the subject."

"Just the same, Bianca, let me run over some 'thirty' associations as they come to mind. Stop me if one of them hits a nerve. The Thirty Tyrants—was your father interested in classical Athens? Thirty Years' War—in seventeenth-century European history? Thirty all—did he play or follow tennis? Or . . . did he ever live at an address that included the number 30?" Ellery went on and on, but to each suggestion Bianca DiCampo could only shake her head.

"The lack of spacing, come to think of it, doesn't necessarily mean that Mr. DiCampo chose to view the clue that way," said Ellery thoughtfully. "He might have interpreted it arbitrarily as 3-space-*o-d*."

"Three od?" echoed old Tungston. "What the devil could that mean?"

"Od? Od is the hypothetical force or power claimed by Baron von Reichenbach—in 1850, wasn't it?—to pervade the whole of nature. Manifests itself in magnets, crystals and such, which according to the excited Baron explained animal magnetism and mesmerism. Was your father by any chance interested in hypnosis, Bianca? Or the occult?"

"Not in the slightest."

"Mr. Queen," exclaimed Harbidger, "are you serious about all this—this semantic sludge?"

"Why, I don't know," said Ellery. "I never know till I stumble over something. Od . . . the word was used with prefixes, too—*biod,* the force of animal life; *elod,* the force of electricity; and so forth. *Three* od . . . or *triod,* the triune force—it's all right, Mr. Harbidger, it's not ignorance on your part, I just coined the word. But it does rather suggest the Trinity, doesn't it? Bianca, did your father tie up to the Church in a personal, scholarly, or any other way? No? That's too bad, really, because Od—capitalized—has been a minced form of the word God since the sixteenth century. Or . . . you wouldn't happen to have three Bibles on the premises, would you? Because—"

Ellery stopped with the smashing abruptness of an ordinary force meeting an absolutely immovable object. The girl and the two collectors gawped. Bianca had idly picked up the typewritten copy of the Lincoln document. She was not reading it; she was simply holding it on her knees, but Ellery, sitting opposite her, had shot forward in a crouch, rather like a pointer, and he was regarding the paper in her lap with a glare of pure discovery.

"That's it!" he cried.

"What's it, Mr. Queen?" the girl asked, bewildered.

"Please—the transcript!" He plucked the paper from her. "Of course. Hear this: *'On the other hand, let us regard Mr. Poe's "notion" turn-about.' Turn-about.* Look at the 3od 'turn-about'—as I just saw it!"

He turned the Lincoln message upside down for their inspection. In that position the 3od became:

poɛ

"Poe!" exploded Tungston.

"Yes, crude but recognizable," Ellery said swiftly. "So now we read the Lincoln clue as *'The hiding-place of the book is in* Poe!' "

There was a silence.

"In Poe," said Harbidger blankly.

"In Poe?" muttered Tungston. "There are only a couple of trade editions of Poe in DiCampo's library, Harbidger, and we went through those. We looked in every book here."

"He might have meant among the Poe books in the *public* library. Miss DiCampo—"

"Wait." Bianca sped away. But when she came back she was drooping. "It isn't. We have two public libraries in Eulalia, and I know the head librarian in both. I just called them. Father didn't visit either library."

Ellery gnawed a fingernail. "Is there a bust of Poe in the house, Bianca? Or any other Poe-associated object, aside from books?"

"I'm afraid not."

"Queer," he mumbled. "Yet I'm positive your father interpreted *'the hiding-place of the book'* as being *'in Poe.'* So he'd have hidden it 'in Poe' . . ." Ellery's mumbling dribbled away into a tormented sort of silence: his eyebrows worked up and down, Groucho Marx fashion; he pinched the tip of his nose until it was scarlet; he yanked at his unoffending ears; he munched on his lip . . . until, all at once, his face cleared; and he sprang to his feet. "Bianca, may I use your phone?"

The girl could only nod, and Ellery dashed. They heard him telephoning in the entrance hall, although they could not make out the words. He was back in two minutes.

"One thing more," he said briskly, "and we're out of the woods. I suppose your father used a key ring or a key case, Bianca? May I have it, please?"

She fetched a key case. To the two millionaires it seemed the sorriest of objects, a scuffed and dirty tan leatherette case. But Ellery received it from the girl as if it were an artifact of historic importance from a newly discovered Fourth Dynasty tomb. He unsnapped it with concentrated love; he fingered its contents like a scientist. Finally he decided on a certain key.

"Wait here!" Thus Mr. Queen; and exit, running.

"I can't decide," old Tungston said after a while, "whether that fellow is a genius or an escaped lunatic."

Neither Harbidger nor Bianca replied. Apparently they could not decide, either.

They waited through twenty elongated minutes; at the twenty-first, they heard his car, champing. All three were in the front doorway as Ellery strode up the walk.

He was carrying a book with a red cover, and smiling. It was a compassionate smile, but none of them noticed.

"You—" said Bianca. "—found—" said Tungston. "—the book!" shouted Harbidger. "Is the Lincoln holograph in it?"

"It is," said Ellery. "Shall we all go into the house, where we may mourn in decent privacy?"

"Because," Ellery said to Bianca and the two quivering collectors as they sat across a refectory table from him. "I have foul news. Mr. Tungston, I believe you have never actually seen Mr. DiCampo's book. Will you now look at the Poe signature on the flyleaf?"

The panther claws leaped. There, toward the top of the flyleaf, in faded ink-script, ran the signature *Edgar Allan Poe.*

The claws curled, and old Tungston looked up sharply. "DiCampo never mentioned that it's a full autograph—he kept referring to it as 'the Poe signature.' Edgar *Allan* Poe . . . Why, I don't know of a single instance after his West Point days when Poe wrote out his middle name in an autograph! And the earliest he could have signed this 1845 edition is obviously when it was published, which was around the fall of 1844. In 1844 he'd surely have abbreviated the 'Allan,' signing 'Edgar A. Poe,' the way he signed everything! This is a forgery."

"My God," murmured Bianca, clearly intending no impiety; she was as pale as Poe's Lenore. "Is that true, Mr. Queen?"

"I'm afraid it is," Ellery said sadly. "I was suspicious the moment you told me the Poe signature on the flyleaf contained the 'Allan.' And if the Poe signature is a forgery, the book itself can hardly be considered Poe's own copy."

Harbidger was moaning. "And the Lincoln signature underneath the Poe, Mr. Queen! DiCampo never told me it reads

Abraham Lincoln—the full Christian name. Except on official documents, Lincoln practically always signed his name 'A. Lincoln.' Don't tell me this Lincoln autograph is a forgery, too?"

Ellery forbore to look at poor Bianca. "I was struck by the 'Abraham' as well, Mr. Harbidger, when Miss DiCampo mentioned it to me, and I came equipped to test it. I have here"—and Ellery tapped the pile of documents he had taken from his briefcase—"facsimiles of Lincoln signatures from the most frequently reproduced of the historical documents he signed. Now I'm going to make a precise tracing of the Lincoln signature on the flyleaf of the book"—he proceeded to do so—"and I shall superimpose the tracing on the various signatures of the authentic Lincoln documents. So." He worked rapidly. On his third superimposition Ellery looked up. "Yes. See here. The tracing of the purported Lincoln signature from the flyleaf fits in minutest detail over the authentic Lincoln signature on this facsimile of the Emancipation Proclamation. It's a fact of life that's tripped many a forger that *nobody ever writes his name exactly the same way twice.* There are always variations. If two signatures are identical, then one must be a tracing of the other. So the 'Abraham Lincoln' signed on the flyleaf can be dismissed without further consideration as a forgery also. It's a tracing of the Emancipation Proclamation signature.

"Not only was this book not Poe's own copy; it was never signed and therefore probably never owned—by Lincoln. However your father came into possession of the book, Bianca, he was swindled."

It was the measure of Bianca DiCampo's quality that she said quietly, "Poor, poor Father," nothing more.

Harbidger was poring over the worn old envelope on whose inside appeared the dearly beloved handscript of the Martyr President. "At least," he muttered, "We have *this.*"

"Do we?" asked Ellery gently. "Turn it over, Mr. Harbidger."

Harbidger looked up, scowling. "No! You're not going to deprive me of this, too!"

"Turn it over," Ellery repeated in the same gentle way. The Lincoln collector obeyed reluctantly. "What do you see?"

"An authentic envelope of the period! With two authentic Lincoln stamps!"

"Exactly. And the United States has never issued postage stamps depicting living Americans; you have to be dead to qualify. The earliest U.S. stamp showing a portrait of Lincoln went on sale April 15, 1866—a year to the day after his death. Then a living Lincoln could scarcely have used this envelope, with these stamps on it, as writing paper. The document is spurious, too. I am so very sorry, Bianca."

Incredibly, Lorenzo DiCampo's daughter managed a smile with her *"Non importa, signor."* He could have wept for her. As for the two collectors, Harbidger was in shock; but old Tungston managed to croak, "Where the devil did DiCampo hide the book, Queen? And how did you know?"

"Oh, that," said Ellery, wishing the two men would go away so that he might comfort this admirable creature. "I was convinced that DiCampo interpreted what we now know was the forger's, not Lincoln's, clue, as 3od read upside down; or, crudely, *Poe.* But *'the hiding-place of the book is in Poe'* led nowhere.

"So I reconsidered, P, o, e. If those three letters of the alphabet didn't mean Poe, what could they mean? Then I remembered something about the letter you wrote me, Bianca. You'd used one of your father's envelopes, on the flap of which appeared his address: *Post Office Box 69, Southern District, Eulalia, N.Y.* If there was a Southern District in Eulalia, it seemed reasonable to conclude that there were post offices for other points of the compass, too. As, for instance, an Eastern District. Post Office Eastern. P.O. East. P.O.E."

"Poe!" cried Bianca.

"To answer your question, Mr. Tungston: I phoned the main post office, confirmed the existence of a Post Office East, got directions as to how to get there, looked for a postal box key in Mr. DiCampo's key case, found the right one, located the box DiCampo had rented especially for the occasion, unlocked it—and there was the book." He added, hopefully, "And that is that."

"And that is that," Bianca said when she returned from seeing the two collectors off. "I'm not going to cry over an empty milk bottle, Mr. Queen. I'll straighten out Father's affairs somehow. Right now all I can think of is how glad I am he didn't live to see the signatures and documents declared forgeries publicly, as they would surely have been when they were expertized."

"I think you'll find there's still some milk in the bottle, Bianca."

"I beg your pardon?" said Bianca.

Ellery tapped the pseudo-Lincolnian envelope. "You know, you didn't do a very good job describing this envelope to me. All you said was that there were two canceled Lincoln stamps on it."

"Well, there are."

"I can see you misspent your childhood. No, little girls don't collect things, do they? Why, if you'll examine these 'two canceled Lincoln stamps,' you'll see that they're a great deal more than that. In the first place, they're not separate stamps. They're a vertical pair—that is, one stamp is joined to the other at the horizontal edges. Now look at this upper stamp of the pair."

The Mediterranean eyes widened. "It's upside down, isn't it!"

"Yes, it's upside down," said Ellery, "and what's more, while the pair have perforations all around, there are no perforations between them, where they're joined.

"What you have here, young lady—and what our unknown forger didn't realize when he fished around for an authentic White House cover of the period on which to perpetrate the Lincoln forgery is what's known to stamp collectors as a double printing error: a pair of 1866 black 15-cent Lincolns imperforate horizontally, with one of the pair printed upside down. No such error of the Lincoln issue has ever been reported. You're the owner, Bianca, of what may well be the rarest item in U.S. philately, and the most valuable."

The world will little note, nor long remember.

But don't try to prove it by Bianca DiCampo.

REX STOUT

(1886–1975)

Rex Stout, born in Danbury, Connecticut, began publishing before World War I, but the creation that would place him among the most commercially successful crime writers of all time, in the novel Fer-de-Lance, *was not introduced until 1934. More than forty books would follow featuring the 300-pound detective Nero Wolfe and his sidekick Archie Goodwin. In the 1930s the gentleman detective, popular since Poe, was losing ground to the hard-boiled detective. Stout, however, blended the two types. There is a Holmes-Watson–style relationship between Wolfe and Goodwin. The crimes are usually resolved by the solution of a puzzle, with the police frequently requiring Wolfe's eccentric, Holmes-like genius for observing the salient point that will make all things clear. Goodwin, however, is a man of action, a wisecracking tough guy with a shoulder holster who can duke it out with any gangster. Hybrids of such different formulas are not often successful, but Stout's dialogue crackles, and the collection of suspects is often brilliantly characterized. There is also Stout's playfulness. Nero (an emperor) is created by Rex (Latin for "king"). He has "wolfish" appetites and is very "stout." The implications of "Good-win" are obvious. Stout shares with his audience the understanding that one shouldn't take much of this too seriously, and the audience congratulates itself for being in the know. In Nero Wolfe stories, the great detective is most often kept safely at home among his orchids, a true armchair detective. The narrator, Goodwin, is free to roam the mean streets. In the following selection, Stout confines the possible suspects to Wolfe's brownstone.*

THE AFFAIR OF THE TWISTED SCARF

My problems hit a new high that day. What I really felt like doing was to go out for a walk but I wasn't quite desperate enough for that. So I merely beat it down to the office, shutting the door from the hall behind me, and went and sat at my desk with my feet up, leaned back and closed my eyes, and took a couple of deep breaths.

I had made two mistakes. When Bill McNab, garden editor of the *Gazette,* had suggested to Nero Wolfe that the members of the Manhattan Flower Club be invited to drop in some afternoon to look at the orchids, I should have fought it.

And when the date had been set and the invitations sent, and Wolfe had arranged that Fritz and Saul should do the receiving at the front door and I should stay up in the plant-rooms with him and Theodore, mingling with the guests, if I had had an ounce of brains I would have put my foot down. But I hadn't, and as a result I had been up there a good hour and a half, grinning around and acting pleased and happy. . . . "No, sir, that's not a brasso, it's a laelia." . . . "Quite all right, madam—your sleeve happened to hook it. It'll bloom again next year."

It wouldn't have been so bad if there had been something for the eyes. It was understood that the Manhattan Flower Club was choosy about whom it took in, but obviously its standards were totally different from mine. The men were just men; okay as men go. But the women! It was a darned good thing they had picked on flowers to love, because flowers don't have to love back.

There had, in fact, been one—just one. I had got a glimpse of her at the other end of the crowded aisle as I went through the door into the cool-room. From ten paces off she looked absolutely promising, and when I had maneuvered close enough to make her an offer to answer questions if she had any, there was simply no doubt about it—no doubt at all.

The first quick, slanting glance she gave me said plainly that she could tell the difference between a flower and a man, but she just smiled and shook her head, and moved on with her companions, an older female and two males. Later, I had made another try and got another brush-off, and still later, too long later, feeling that the grin might freeze on me for good if I didn't take a recess, I went AWOL by worming my way to the far end of the warm-room and sidling on out.

All the way down the three flights of stairs new guests were coming up, though it was then four o'clock. Nero Wolfe's old brownstone house on West 35th Street had seen no such throng as that within my memory, which is long and good. One flight down, I stopped off at my bedroom for a pack of cigarettes; and another flight down, I detoured to make sure the door of Wolfe's bedroom was locked.

In the main hall downstairs I halted a moment to watch Fritz Brenner, busy at the door with both departures and arrivals, and to see Saul Panzer emerge from the front room, which was being used as a cloakroom, with someone's hat and topcoat. Then, as aforesaid, I entered the office, shutting the door from the hall behind me, went and sat at my desk with my feet up, leaned back and closed my eyes, and took some deep breaths.

I had been there maybe eight or ten minutes, and was getting relaxed and a little less bitter, when the door opened and she came in. Her companions were not along. By the time she had closed the door and turned to me I had got to my feet, with a friendly leer, and had begun, "I was just sitting here thinking—"

The look on her face stopped me. There was nothing wrong with it basically, but something had got it out of kilter. She headed for me, got halfway, jerked to a stop, sank into one of the yellow chairs, and squeaked, "Could I have a drink?"

"Sure thing," I said. I went to the cupboard and got a hooker of old whiskey. Her hand was shaking as she took the glass, but she didn't spill any, and she got it down in two swallows.

"Did I need that!"

"More?"

She shook her head. Her bright brown eyes were moist, from the whiskey, as she gave me a full, straight look with her head tilted up.

"You're Archie Goodwin," she stated.

I nodded. "And you're the Queen of Egypt?"

"I'm a baboon," she declared. "I don't know how they ever taught me to talk." She looked around for something to put the glass on, and I moved a step and reached for it. "Look at my hand shake," she complained.

She kept her hand out, looking at it, so I took it in mine and gave it some friendly but gentle pressure. "You do seem a little upset," I conceded.

She jerked the hand away. "I want to see Nero Wolfe. I want to see him right away, before I change my mind." She was gazing up at me, with the moist brown eyes. "I'm in a fix now, all right! I've made up my mind. I'm going to get Nero Wolfe to get me out of this somehow."

I told her it couldn't be done until the party was over.

She looked around. "Are people coming in here?"

I told her no.

"May I have another drink, please?"

I told her she should give the first one time to settle, and instead of arguing she arose and helped herself. I sat down and frowned at her. Her line sounded fairly screwy for a member of the Manhattan Flower Club, or even for a daughter of one. She came back to her chair, sat, and met my eyes. Looking at her straight like that could have been a nice way to pass the time if there had been any chance for a meeting of minds.

"I could tell you," she said.

"Many people have," I said modestly.

"I'm going to."

"Good. Shoot."

"Okay. I'm a crook."

"It doesn't show," I objected. "What do you do—cheat at Canasta?"

"I didn't say I'm a cheat." She cleared her throat for the hoarseness. "I said I'm a crook. Remind me some day to tell you the story of my life—how my husband got killed in the war and I broke through the gate. Don't I sound interesting?"

"You sure do. What's your line—orchid-stealing?"

"No. I wouldn't be small and I wouldn't be dirty— That's what I used to think, but once you start it's not so easy. You meet people and you get involved. Two years ago four of us took over a hundred grand from a certain rich woman with a rich husband. I can tell you about that one, even names, because she couldn't move, anyhow."

I nodded. "Blackmailers' customers seldom can. What—?"

"I'm not a blackmailer!"

"Excuse me. Mr. Wolfe often says I jump to conclusions."

"You did that time." She was still indignant. "A blackmailer's not a crook; he's a snake! Not that it really matters. What's wrong with being a crook is the other crooks—they make it dirty whether you like it or not. It makes a coward of you, too—that's the worst. I had a friend once—as close as a crook ever comes to having a friend—and a man killed her, strangled her. If I had told what I knew about it they could have caught him, but I was afraid to go to the cops, so he's still loose. And she was my friend! That's getting down toward the bottom. Isn't it?"

"Fairly low," I agreed, eying her. "Of course, I don't know you any too well. I don't know how you react to two stiff drinks. Maybe your hobby is stringing private detectives."

She simply ignored it. "I realized long ago," she went on, as if it were a one-way conversation, "that I had made a mistake. About a year ago I decided to break loose. A good way to do it would have been to talk to someone the way I'm talking to you now, but I didn't have sense enough to see that."

I nodded. "Yeah, I know."

"So I kept putting it off. We got a good one in December and I went to Florida for a vacation, but down there I met a man with a lead, and we followed it up here just a week ago. That's what I'm working on now. That's what brought me here today. This man—" She stopped abruptly.

"Well?" I invited her.

She looked dead serious, not more serious, but a different kind. "I'm not putting anything on him," she declared. "I don't owe him anything, and I don't like him. But this is strictly about me and no one else—only, I had to explain why I'm here. I wish to heaven I'd never come!"

There was no question about that coming from her heart, unless she had done a lot of rehearsing in front of a mirror.

"It got you this talk with me," I reminded her.

She was looking straight through me and beyond. "If only I hadn't come! If only I hadn't seen him!"

She leaned toward me for emphasis. "I'm either too smart or not smart enough; that's my trouble. I should have looked away from him, turned away quick, when I realized I knew who he was, before he turned and saw it in my eyes. But I was so shocked I couldn't help it! I stood there staring at him, thinking I wouldn't have recognized him if he hadn't had a hat on, and then he looked at me and saw what was happening. But it was too late.

"I know how to manage my face with nearly anybody, anywhere, but that was too much for me. It showed so plain that Mrs. Orwin asked me what was the matter with me, and I had to try to pull myself together. Then, seeing Nero Wolfe gave me the idea of telling him; only of course I couldn't right there with the crowd. Then I saw you going out, and as soon as I could break away I came down to find you."

She tried smiling at me, but it didn't work so good. "Now I feel somewhat better," she said hopefully.

I nodded. "That's good whiskey. Is it a secret who you recognized?"

"No. I'm going to tell Nero Wolfe."

"You decided to tell me." I flipped a hand. "Suit yourself. Whoever you tell, what's the good?"

"Why—then he can't do anything to me."

"Why not?"

"Because he wouldn't dare. Nero Wolfe will tell him that I've told about him, so that if anything happened to me he would know it was him, and he'd know who he is—I mean, Nero Wolfe would know—and so would you."

"We would if we had his name and address." I was studying her. "He must be quite a specimen, to scare you that bad. And speaking of names, what's yours?"

She made a little noise that could have been meant for a laugh. "Do you like Marjorie?"

"Not bad. What are you using now?"

She hesitated, frowning.

"For Pete's sake," I protested, "you're not in a vacuum, and I'm a detective. They took the names down at the door."

"Cynthia Brown," she said.

"That's Mrs. Orwin you came with?"

"Yes."

"She's the current customer? The lead you picked up in Florida?"

"Yes. But that's—" She gestured. "That's finished. I'm through."

"I know. There's just one thing you haven't told me, though. Who was it you recognized?"

She turned her head for a glance at the door and then turned it still farther to look behind her.

"Can anyone hear us?" she asked.

"Nope. That other door goes to the front room—today, the cloakroom. Anyhow, this room's soundproofed."

She glanced at the hall door again, returned to me, and lowered her voice: "This has to be done the way I say."

"Sure; why not?"

"I wasn't being honest with you."

"I wouldn't expect it from a crook. Start over."

"I mean . . ." She used the teeth on the lip again. "I mean I'm not just scared about myself. I'm scared, all right, but I don't just want Nero Wolfe for what I said. I want him to get him for murder, but he has to keep me out of it. I don't want to have anything to do with any cops—not now I don't, especially. If he won't do it that way—Do you think he will?"

I was feeling a faint tingle at the base of my spine. I only get that on special occasions, but this was unquestionably something special. I gave her a hard look and didn't let the tingle get into my voice: "He might, for you, if you pay him. What kind of evidence have you got? Any?"

"I saw him."

"You mean today?"

"I mean I saw him then." She had her hands clasped tight. "I told you—I had a friend. I stopped in at her apartment that afternoon. I was just leaving—Doris was inside, in the bathroom—and as I got near the entrance door I heard a key turning in the lock, from the outside. I stopped, and the door came open and a man came in. When he saw me he just stood and stared. I had never met Doris's bank account, and I knew she didn't want me to. And since he had a key I supposed of course it was him, making an unexpected call; so I mumbled something about Doris being in the bathroom and went past him, through the door and on out."

She paused. Her clasped hands loosened and then tightened again.

"I'm burning my bridges," she said, "but I can deny all this if I have to. I went and kept a cocktail date, and then phoned Doris's number to ask if our dinner date was still on, considering the visit of the bank account. There was no answer, so I went back to her apartment and rang the bell, and there was no answer to that, either. It was a self-service-elevator place, no doorman or hallman, so there was no one to ask anything.

"Her maid found her body the next morning. The papers said she had been killed the day before. That man killed her. There wasn't a word about him—no one had seen him enter or leave. And I didn't open my mouth! I was a rotten coward!"

"And today, all of a sudden, there he is, looking at orchids?"

"Yes."

"Are you sure he knows you recognized him?"

"Yes. He looked straight at me, and his eyes—"

She was stopped by the house phone buzzing. Stepping to my desk, I picked it up and asked it, "Well?"

Nero Wolfe's voice, peevish, came: "Archie!"

"Yes, sir."

"What the devil are you doing? Come back up here!"

"Pretty soon. I'm talking with a prospective client—"

"This is no time for clients! Come at once!"

The connection went. He had slammed it down. I hung up and went back to the prospective client: "Mr. Wolfe wants me upstairs. Do you want to wait here?"

"Yes."

"If Mrs. Orwin asks about you?"

"I didn't feel well and went home."

"Okay. It shouldn't be long—the invitations said two thirty to five. If you want a drink, help yourself. . . . What name does this murderer use when he goes to look at orchids?"

She looked blank.

I got impatient: "What's his name? This bird you recognized."

"I don't know."

"Describe him."

She thought it over a little, gazing at me, and then shook her head. "Not now. I want to see what Nero Wolfe says first."

She must have seen something in my eyes, or thought she did, for suddenly she came up out of her chair and moved to me and put a hand on my arm. "That's all I mean," she said earnestly. "It's not you—I know you're all right. I might as well tell you—you'd never want any part of me anyhow—this is the first time in years, I don't know how long, that I've talked to a man straight—you know, just human. I—" She stopped for a word, and a little color showed in her cheeks. "I've enjoyed it very much."

"Good. Me, too. Call me Archie. I've got to go, but describe him."

But she hadn't enjoyed it that much. "Not until Nero Wolfe says he'll do it," she said firmly.

I had to leave it at that, knowing as I did that in three more minutes Wolfe might have a fit. Out in the hall I had the notion of passing the word to Saul and Fritz to give departing guests a good look, but rejected it because (a) they weren't there, both of them presumably being busy in the cloakroom, (b) he might have departed already, and (c) I had by no means swallowed a single word of Cynthia's story, let alone the whole works.

Up in the plant-rooms there were plenty left. When I came into Wolfe's range he darted me a glance of cold fury, and I turned on the grin. Anyway, it was a quarter to five, and if they took the hint on the invitation it wouldn't last much longer.

They didn't take the hint on the dot, but it didn't bother me because my mind was occupied. I was now really interested in them—or at least one of them, if he had actually been there and hadn't gone home.

First, there was a chore to get done. I found the three Cynthia had been with, a female and two males.

"Mrs. Orwin?" I asked politely.

She nodded at me and said, "Yes?" Not quite tall enough, but plenty plump enough, with a round, full face and narrow little eyes that might have been better if they had been wide open. She struck me as a lead worth following.

"I'm Archie Goodwin," I said. "I work here."

I would have gone on if I had known how, but I needed a lead myself.

Luckily one of the males horned in. "My sister?" he inquired anxiously.

So it was a brother-and-sister act. As far as looks went he wasn't a bad brother at all. Older than me maybe, but not much. He was tall and straight, with a strong mouth and jaw and keen gray eyes. "My sister?" he repeated.

"I guess so. You are—?"

"Colonel Brown. Percy Brown."

"Yeah." I switched back to Mrs. Orwin: "Miss Brown asked me to tell you that she went home. I gave her a little drink and it seemed to help, but she decided to leave. She asked me to apologize for her."

"She's perfectly healthy," the colonel asserted. He sounded a little hurt.

"Is she all right?" Mrs. Orwin asked.

"For her," the other male put in, "you should have made it three drinks. Or just hand her the bottle."

His tone was mean and his face was mean, and anyhow that was no way to talk in front of the help in a strange house, meaning me. He was a bit younger than Brown, but he already looked enough like Mrs. Orwin, especially the eyes, to make it more than a guess that they were mother and son.

That point was settled when she commanded him, "Be quiet, Gene!" She turned to the colonel: "Perhaps you should go and see about her?"

He shook his head, with a fond but manly smile at her. "It's not necessary, Mimi. Really."

"She's all right," I assured them, and pushed off, thinking there were a lot of names in this world that could stand a reshuffle. Calling that overweight, narrow-eyed, pearl-and-mink proprietor Mimi was a paradox.

I moved around among the guests, being gracious. Fully aware that I was not equipped with a Geiger counter that would flash a signal if and when I established contact with a strangler, the fact remained that I had been known to have hunches. It would be something for my scrapbook if I picked the killer of Doris Hatten.

Cynthia Brown hadn't given me the Hatten, only the Doris, but with the context that was enough. At the time it had happened, some five months ago, early in October, the papers had given it a big play, of course. She had been strangled with her own scarf, of white silk with the Declaration of Independence printed on it, in her cozy fifth-floor apartment in the West Seventies, and the scarf had been left around her neck, knotted at the back.

The cops had never got within a mile of charging anyone, and Sergeant Purley Stebbins of Homicide had told me that they had never even found out who was paying the rent.

I kept on the go through the plant-rooms, leaving all switches open for a hunch. Some of them were plainly preposterous, but with everyone else I made an opportunity to exchange some words, full face and close up. That took time, and it was no help to my current and chronic campaign for a raise in wages, since it was the women, not the men, that Wolfe wanted off his neck. I stuck at it, anyhow. It was true that if Cynthia was on the level, we would soon have specifications, but I had had that tingle at the bottom of my spine and I was stubborn.

As I say, it took time, and meanwhile five o'clock came and went and the crowd thinned out. Going on five-thirty, the remaining groups seemed to get the idea all at once that time was up and made for the entrance to the stairs.

I was in the moderate-room when it happened, and the first thing I knew I was alone there, except for a guy at the north bench studying a row of dowianas. He didn't interest me, as I had already canvassed him and crossed him off as the wrong type for a strangler; but as I glanced his way he suddenly bent forward to pick up a pot with a flowering plant, and as he did so I felt my back stiffening. The stiffening was a reflex, but I knew what had caused it; the way his fingers closed around the pot, especially the thumbs. No matter how careful you are of other people's property, you don't pick up a five-inch pot as if you were going to squeeze the life out of it.

I made my way around to him. When I got there he was holding the pot so that the flowers were only a few inches from his eyes.

"Nice flower," I said brightly.

He nodded.

He leaned to put the pot back, still choking it. I swiveled my head. The only people in sight, beyond the glass partition between us and the cool-room, were Nero Wolfe and a small group of guests, among whom were the Orwin trio and Bill McNab, the garden editor of the *Gazette*. As I turned my head back to my man he straightened up, pivoted on his heel, and marched off without a word.

I followed him out to the landing and down the three flights of stairs. Along the main hall I was courteous enough not to step on his heel, but a lengthened stride would have reached it. The hall was next to empty. A woman, ready for the street in a caracul coat, was standing there, and Saul Panzer was posted near the front door with nothing to do.

I followed my man on into the front room, now the cloakroom, where Fritz Brenner was helping a guest on with his coat. Of course, the racks were practically bare, and with one glance my man saw his property and went to get it. I stepped forward to help, but he ignored me without even bothering to shake his head. I was beginning to feel hurt.

When he emerged into the hall I was beside him, and as he moved to the front door I spoke: "Excuse me, but we're checking guests out as well as in. Your name, please?"

"Ridiculous," he said curtly, and reached for the knob, pulled the door open, and crossed the sill.

Saul, knowing I must have had a reason for wanting to check him out, was at my elbow, and we stood watching his back as he descended the seven steps of the stoop.

"Tail?" Saul muttered to me.

I shook my head and was parting my lips to mutter something back, when a sound came from behind us that made us both whirl around—a screech from a woman, not loud but full of feeling. As we whirled, Fritz and the guest he had been serving came out of the front room, and all four of us saw the woman in the caracul coat come running out of the office into the hall. She kept coming, gasping something, and the guest, making a noise like an alarmed male, moved to meet her. I moved faster, needing about eight jumps to the office door and two inside. There I stopped.

Of course, I knew the thing on the floor was Cynthia, but only because I had left her in there in those clothes. With the face blue and contorted, the tongue halfway out and the eyes popping, it could have been almost anybody. I knelt down and slipped my hand inside her dress front, kept it there ten seconds, and felt nothing.

Saul's voice came from behind: "I'm here."

I got up and went to the phone on my desk and started dialing, telling Saul "No one leaves. We'll keep what we've got. Have the door open for Doc Vollmer." After only two whirs the nurse answered and put Vollmer on, and I snapped it at him: "Doc, Archie Goodwin. Come on the run. Strangled woman . . . Yeah, strangled."

I pushed the phone back, reached for the house phone, and buzzed the plant-rooms, and after a wait had Wolfe's irritated bark in my ear: "Yes?"

"I'm in the office. You'd better come down. That prospective client I mentioned is here on the floor strangled. I think she's done, but I've sent for Vollmer."

"Is this flummery?" he roared.

"No, sir. Come down and look at her and then ask me."

The connection went. He had slammed it down. I got a sheet of thin tissue paper from a drawer, tore off a corner, and placed it carefully over Cynthia's mouth and nostrils.

Voices had been sounding from the hall. Now one of them entered the office. Its owner was the guest who had been in the cloakroom with Fritz when the screech came. He was a chunky, broad-shouldered guy with sharp, domineering dark eyes and arms like a gorilla's. His voice was going strong as he started toward me from the door, but it stopped when he had come far enough to get a good look at the object on the floor.

"Oh, no!" he said huskily.

"Yes, sir," I agreed.

"How did it happen?"

"Don't know."

"Who is it?"

"Don't know."

He made his eyes come away from it and up until they met mine, and I gave him an A for control. It really was a sight.

"The man at the door won't let us leave," he stated.

"No, sir. You can see why."

"I certainly can." His eyes stayed with me, however. "But we know nothing about it. My name is Carlisle, Homer N. Carlisle. I am the executive vice-president of the North American Foods Company. My wife was merely acting under impulse; she wanted to see the office of Nero Wolfe, and she opened the door and entered. She's sorry she did, and so am I. We have an appointment, and there's no reason why we should be detained."

"I'm sorry, too," I told him, "but for one thing if for nothing else; your wife discovered the body. We're stuck worse than you are, with a corpse here in our office. So I guess—Hello, Doc."

Vollmer, entering and nodding at me on the fly, was panting a little as he set his black case on the floor and knelt beside it. His house was down the street and he had had only two hundred yards to trot, but he was taking on weight. As he opened the case and got out the stethoscope, Homer Carlisle stood and watched with his lips pressed tight, and I did likewise until I heard the sound of Wolfe's elevator.

Crossing to the door and into the hall, I surveyed the terrain. Toward the front, Saul and Fritz were calming down the woman in the caracul coat, now Mrs. Carlisle to me. Nero Wolfe and

Mrs. Mimi Orwin were emerging from the elevator. Four guests were coming down the stairs: Gene Orwin, Colonel Percy Brown, Bill McNab, and a middle-aged male with a mop of black hair. I stayed by the office door to block the quartet on the stairs.

As Wolfe headed for me, Mrs. Carlisle darted to him and grabbed his arm: "I only wanted to see your office! I want to go! I'm not—"

As she pulled at him and sputtered, I noted a detail: the caracul coat was unfastened, and the ends of a silk scarf, figured and gaily colored, were flying loose. Since at least half of the female guests had sported scarfs, I mention it only to be honest and admit that I had got touchy on that subject.

Wolfe, who had already been too close to too many women that day to suit him, tried to jerk away, but she hung on. She was the big-boned, flat-chested, athletic type, and it could have been quite a tussle, with him weighing twice as much as her and four times as big around, if Saul hadn't rescued him by coming in between and prying her loose. That didn't stop her tongue, but Wolfe ignored it and came on toward me: "Has Dr. Vollmer come?"

"Yes, sir."

The executive vice-president emerged from the office, talking: "Mr. Wolfe, my name is Homer N. Carlisle and I insist—"

"Shut up," Wolfe growled. On the sill of the door to the office, he faced the audience. "Flower lovers," he said with bitter scorn. "You told me, Mr. McNab, a distinguished group of sincere and devoted gardeners. Pfui! . . . Saul!"

"Yes, sir."

"Put them all in the dining-room and keep them there. Let no one touch anything around this door, especially the knob . . . Archie, come with me."

He wheeled and entered the office. Following, I used my foot to swing the door neatly shut, leaving no crack but not latching it. When I turned, Vollmer was standing, facing Wolfe's scowl.

"Well?" Wolfe demanded.

"Dead," Vollmer told him. "With asphyxiation from strangling."

"How long ago?"

"I don't know, but no more than an hour or two. Two hours at the outside, probably less."

Wolfe looked at the thing on the floor with no change in his scowl, and back at Doc. "Finger marks?"

"No. A constricting band of something with pressure below the hyoid bone. Not a stiff or narrow band; something soft, like a strip of cloth—say, a scarf."

Wolfe switched to me: "You didn't notify the police?"

"No, sir." I glanced at Vollmer and back. "I need a word."

"I suppose so." He spoke to Doc: "If you will leave us for a moment? The front room?"

Vollmer hesitated, uncomfortable. "As a doctor called to a violent death I'd catch the devil. Of course, I could say—"

"Then go to a corner and cover your ears."

He did so. He went to the farthest corner, the angle made by the partition of the bathroom, pressed his palms to his ears, and stood facing us. I addressed Wolfe with a lowered voice:

"I was here and she came in. She was either scared good or putting on a very fine act. Apparently, it wasn't an act, and I now think I should have alerted Saul and Fritz, but it doesn't matter what I now think. Last October a woman named Doris Hatten was killed, strangled, in her apartment. No one got elected. Remember?"

"Yes."

"She said she was a friend of Doris Hatten's and was at her apartment that day, and saw the man that did the strangling, and that he was here this afternoon. She said he was aware that she had recognized him—that's why she was scared—and she wanted to get you to help by telling him that we were wise and he'd better lay off. No wonder I didn't gulp it down. I realize that you dislike complications and therefore might want me to scratch this out, but at the end she touched a soft spot by saying that she had enjoyed my company, so I prefer to open up to the cops."

"Then do so. Confound it!"

I went to the phone and started dialing WAtkins 9-8241. Doc Vollmer came out of his corner. Wolfe was pathetic. He moved around behind his desk and lowered himself into his own oversized custom-made number; but there smack in front of him was the object on the floor, so after a moment he made a face, got back onto his feet, grunted like an outraged boar, went across to the other side of the room, to the shelves, and inspected the backbones of books.

But even that pitiful diversion got interrupted. As I finished with my phone call and hung up, sudden sounds of commotion came from the hall. Dashing across, getting fingernails on the edge of the door and pulling it open, I saw trouble. A group was gathered in the open doorway of the dining-room, which was across the hall. Saul Panzer went bounding past me toward the front.

At the front door, Colonel Percy Brown was stiff-arming Fritz Brenner with one hand and reaching for the doorknob with the other. Fritz, who is chef and housekeeper, is not supposed to double in acrobatics, but he did fine. Dropping to the floor, he grabbed the colonel's ankles and jerked his feet out from under him.

Then I was there, and Saul, with his gun out; and there, with us, was the guest with the mop of black hair.

"You fool," I told the colonel as he sat up. "If you'd got outdoors Saul would have winged you."

"Guilt," said the black-haired guest emphatically. "The compression got unbearable and he exploded. I'm a psychiatrist."

"Good for you." I took his elbow and turned him. "Go back in and watch all of 'em. With that wall mirror you can include yourself."

"This is illegal," stated Colonel Brown, who had scrambled to his feet.

Saul herded them to the rear.

Fritz got hold of my sleeve: "Archie, I've got to ask Mr. Wolfe about dinner."

"Nuts," I said savagely. "By dinner-time this place will be more crowded than it was this afternoon."

"But he has to eat; you know that."

"Nuts," I said. I patted him on the shoulder. "Excuse my manners, Fritz; I'm upset. I've just strangled a young woman."

"Phooey," he said scornfully.

"I might as well have," I declared.

The doorbell rang. It was the first consignment of cops.

In my opinion, Inspector Cramer made a mistake. It is true that in a room where a murder has occurred the city scientists may shoot the works. And they do. But, except in rare circumstances, the job shouldn't take all week, and in the case of our office a couple of hours should have been ample. In fact, it was. By eight o'clock the scientists were through. But Cramer, like a sap, gave the order to seal it up until further notice, in Wolfe's hearing. He knew that Wolfe spent at least three hundred evenings a year in there, and that was why he did it.

It was a mistake. If he hadn't made it, Wolfe might have called his attention to a certain fact as soon as Wolfe saw it himself, and Cramer would have been saved a lot of trouble.

The two of them got the fact at the same time, from me. We

were in the dining-room—this was shortly after the scientists had got busy in the office, and the guests, under guard, had been shunted to the front room—and I was relating my conversation with Cynthia Brown. Whatever else my years as Wolfe's assistant may have done for me or to me, they have practically turned me into a tape recorder. I gave them the real thing, word for word. When I finished, Cramer had a slew of questions, but Wolfe not a one. Maybe he had already focused on the fact above referred to, but neither Cramer nor I had.

Cramer called a recess on the questions to take steps. He called men in and gave orders. Colonel Brown was to be photographed and fingerprinted, and headquarters records were to be checked for him and Cynthia. The file on the murder of Doris Hatten was to be brought to him at once. The lab reports were to be rushed. Saul Panzer and Fritz Brenner were to be brought in.

They came. Fritz stood like a soldier at attention, grim and grave. Saul, only five feet seven, with the sharpest eyes and one of the biggest noses I have ever seen, in his unpressed brown suit and his necktie crooked—he stood like Saul, not slouching and not stiff. Of course, Cramer knew both of them.

"You and Fritz were in the hall all afternoon?"

Saul nodded. "The hall and the front room, yes."

"Who did you see enter or leave the office?"

"I saw Archie go in about four o'clock—I was just coming out of the front room with someone's hat and coat. I saw Mrs. Carlisle come out just after she screamed. In between those two I saw no one either enter or leave. We were busy most of the time, either in the hall or the front room."

Cramer grunted. "How about you, Fritz?"

"I saw no one." Fritz spoke louder than usual. "I would like to say something."

"Go ahead."

"I think a great deal of all of this disturbance is unnecessary. My duties here are of the household and not professional, but I cannot help hearing what reaches my ears. Many times Mr. Wolfe has found the answer to problems that were too much for you. This happened here in his own house, and I think it should be left entirely to him."

I yooped, "Fritz, I didn't know you had it in you!"

Cramer was goggling at him. "Wolfe told you to say that, huh?"

"Bah." Wolfe was contemptuous. "It can't be helped, Fritz. Have we plenty of ham and sturgeon?"

"Yes, sir."

"Later, probably. For the guests in the front room, but not the police. . . . Are you through with them, Mr. Cramer?"

"No," Cramer went back to Saul: "How'd you check the guests in?"

"I had a list of the members of the Manhattan Flower Club. They had to show their membership cards. I checked on the list those who came. If they brought a wife or husband, or any other guest, I took the names."

"Then you have a record of everybody?"

"Yes."

"About how many names?"

"Two hundred and nineteen."

"This place wouldn't hold that many."

Saul nodded. "They came and went. There wasn't more than a hundred or so at any one time."

"That's a help." Cramer was getting more and more disgusted, and I didn't blame him. "Goodwin says he was there at the door with you when that woman screamed and came running out of the office, but that you hadn't seen her enter the office. Why not?"

"We had our backs turned. We were watching a man who had just left. Archie had asked him for his name and he had said that was ridiculous. If you want it, his name is Malcolm Vedder."

"How do you know?"

"I had checked him in with the rest."

Cramer stared. "Are you telling me that you could fit that many names to that many faces after seeing them once?"

Saul's shoulders went slightly up and down. "There's more to people than faces. I might go wrong on a few, but not many."

Cramer spoke to a dick standing by the door: "You heard that name, Levy—Malcolm Vedder. Tell Stebbins to check it on that list and send a man to bring him in."

Cramer returned to Saul: "Put it this way: Say I sit you here with that list, and a man or woman is brought in—"

"I could tell you positively whether the person had been here or not, especially if he was wearing the same clothes and hadn't been disguised. On fitting him to his name I might go wrong in a few cases, but I doubt it."

"I don't believe you."

"Mr. Wolfe does," Saul said complacently. "Archie does. I have developed my faculties."

"You sure have. All right; that's all for now. Stick around."

Saul and Fritz went. Wolfe, in his own chair at the end of the dining table, where ordinarily, at this hour, he sat for a quite different purpose, heaved a deep sigh and closed his eyes. I, seated beside Cramer at the side of the table which put us facing the door to the hall, was beginning to appreciate the problem we were up against.

"Goodwin's story," Cramer growled. "I mean her story. What do you think?"

Wolfe's eyes came open a little. "What followed seems to support it. I doubt if she would have arranged for that"—he flipped a hand in the direction of the office across the hall—"just to corroborate a tale. I accept it."

"Yeah. I don't need to remind you that I know you well and I know Goodwin well. So I wonder how much chance there is that in a day or so you'll suddenly remember that she had been here before, or one or more of the others had, and you've got a client, and there was something leading up to this."

"Bosh," Wolfe said dryly. "Even if it were like that—and it isn't—you would be wasting time, since you know us."

A dick came to relay a phone call from a deputy commissioner. Another dick came in to say that Homer Carlisle was raising the roof in the front room. Meanwhile, Wolfe sat with his eyes shut, but I got an idea of his state of mind from the fact that intermittently his forefinger was making little circles on the polished top of the table.

Cramer looked at him. "What do you know," he asked abruptly, "about the killing of that Doris Hatten?"

"Newspaper accounts," Wolfe muttered. "And what Mr. Stebbins has told Mr. Goodwin, casually."

"Casual is right." Cramer got out a cigar, conveyed it to his mouth, and sank his teeth in it. He never lit one. "Those houses with self-service elevators are worse than walk-ups for a checking job. No one ever sees anyone coming or going. Even so, the man who paid the rent for that apartment was lucky. He may have been clever and careful, but also he was lucky never to have anybody see him enough to give a description of him."

"Possibly Miss Hatten paid the rent herself."

"Sure," Cramer conceded, "she paid it all right, but where did she get it from? No, it was that kind of a set-up. She had only been living there two months, and when we found out how well the man who paid for it had kept himself covered, we decided that maybe he had installed her there just for that purpose. That was why we gave it all we had. Another reason was that the papers started hinting that we knew who he was and that he was such a big shot we were sitting on the lid."

Cramer shifted his cigar one tooth over to the left. "That kind of thing used to get me sore, but what the heck; for newspapers that's just routine. Big shot or not, he didn't need us to do any covering for him—he did too good a job himself. Now, if we're to take it the way this Cynthia Brown gave it to Goodwin, it was the man who paid the rent. I would hate to tell you what I think of the fact that Goodwin sat there in your office and was told he was right here on these premises, and all he did was—"

"You're irritated," I said charitably. "Not that he *was* on the premises, that he *had* been. Also, I was taking it with salt. Also, she was saving specifications for Mr. Wolfe. Also—"

"Also, I know you. How many of these two hundred and nineteen people were men?"

"I would say a little over half."

"Then how do *you* like it?"

"I hate it."

Wolfe grunted. "Judging from your attitude, Mr. Cramer, something that has occurred to me has not occurred to you."

"Naturally. You're a genius. What is it?"

"Something that Mr. Goodwin told us. I want to consider it a little."

"We could consider it together."

"Later. Those people in the front room are my guests. Can't you dispose of them?"

"One of your guests," Cramer rasped, "was a beaut, all right." He spoke to the dick by the door: "Bring in that woman—what's her name? Carlisle."

Mrs. Homer N. Carlisle came in with all her belongings: her caracul coat, her gaily colored scarf, and her husband. Perhaps I should say that her husband brought her. As soon as he was through the door he strode across to the dining table and delivered a harangue.

At the first opening Cramer, controlling himself, said he was sorry and asked them to sit down.

Mrs. Carlisle did. Mr. Carlisle didn't.

"We're nearly two hours late now,' he stated. "I know you have your duty to perform, but citizens have a few rights left, thank God. Our presence here is purely adventitious. I warn you that if my name is published in connection with this miserable affair,

I'll make trouble. Why should we be detained? What if we had left five or ten minutes earlier, as others did?"

"That's not quite logical," Cramer objected. "No matter when you left, it would have been the same if your wife had acted the same. She discovered the body."

"By accident!"

"May I say something, Homer?" the wife put in.

"It depends on what you say."

"Oh," Cramer said significantly.

"What do you mean, oh?" Carlisle demanded.

"I mean that I sent for your wife, not you, but you came with her, and that tells me why. You wanted to see to it that she wasn't indiscreet."

"What's she got to be indiscreet about?"

"I don't know. Apparently you do. If she hasn't, why don't you sit down and relax?"

"I would, sir," Wolfe advised him. "You came in here angry, and you blundered. An angry man is a jackass."

It was a struggle for the executive vice-president, but he made it.

Cramer went to the wife: "You wanted to say something, Mrs. Carlisle?"

"Only that I'm sorry." Her bony hands, the fingers twined, were on the table before her. "For the trouble I've caused."

"I wouldn't say you caused it exactly—except for yourself and your husband." Cramer was mild. "The woman was dead, whether you went in there or not. But if only as a matter of form, it was essential for me to see you, since you discovered the body. That's all there is to it as far as I know."

"How could there be anything else?" Carlisle blurted.

Cramer ignored him. "Goodwin, here, saw you standing in the hall not more than two minutes, probably less, prior to the moment you screamed and ran out of the office. How long had you then been downstairs?"

"We had just come down. I was waiting for my husband to get his things."

"Had you been downstairs before that?"

"No—only when we came in."

"What time did you arrive?"

"A little after three, I think."

"Were you and your husband together all the time?"

"Of course. Well—you know how it is . . . He would want to look longer at something, and I would—"

"Certainly we were," Carlisle said irritably. "You can see why I made that remark about it depending on what she said. She has a habit of being vague."

"I'm not actually vague," she protested. "It's just that everything is relative. Who would have thought my wish to see Nero Wolfe's office would link me with a crime?"

Carlisle exploded. "Hear that? *Link!*"

"Why did you want to see Wolfe's office?" Cramer inquired.

"Why, to see the globe."

I gawked at her. I had supposed that naturally she would say it was curiosity about the office of a great and famous detective. Apparently, Cramer reacted the same as me.

"The globe?" he demanded.

"Yes, I had read about it, and I wanted to see how it looked. I thought a globe that size, three feet in diameter, would be fantastic in an ordinary room—Oh!"

"Oh, what?"

"I didn't see it!"

Cramer nodded. "You saw something else, instead. By the way, I forgot to ask—Did you know her?"

"You mean—her?"

"We had never known her or seen her or heard of her," the husband declared.

"Had you, Mrs. Carlisle?"

"No."

"Of course. She wasn't a member of this flower club. Are you a member?"

"My husband is."

"We both are," Carlisle stated. "Vague again. It's a joint membership. Isn't this about enough?"

"Plenty," Cramer conceded. "Thank you, both of you. We won't bother you again unless we have to. . . . Levy, pass them out."

When the door had closed behind them Cramer glared at me and then at Wolfe. "This is sure a sweet one," he said grimly. "Say it's within the range of possibility that Carlisle is it, and the way it stands right now, why not? So we look into him. We check back on him for six months, and try doing it without getting roars out of him—a man like that in his position. However, it can be done—by three or four men in two or three weeks. Multiply that by what? How many men were here?"

"Around a hundred and twenty," I told him. "But you'll find

that at least half of them are disqualified one way or another. As I told you, I took a survey. Say sixty."

"All right, multiply it by sixty. Do you care for it?"

"No," I said.

"Neither do I." Cramer took the cigar from his mouth. "Of course," he said sarcastically, "when she sat in there telling you about him the situation was different. You wanted her to enjoy being with you. You couldn't reach for the phone and tell us you had a self-confessed crook who could put a quick finger on a murderer and let us come and take over. No! You had to save it for a fee for Wolfe!"

"Don't be vulgar," I said severely.

"You had to go upstairs and make a survey! You had to—Well?"

Lieutenant Rowcliff had opened the door and entered. There were some city employees I liked, some I admired, some I had no feeling about, some I could have done without easy—and one whose ears I was going to twist some day. That was Rowcliff. He was tall, strong, handsome, and a pain in the neck.

"We're all through in there, sir," he said importantly. "We've covered everything. Nothing is being taken away, and it is all in order. We were especially careful with the contents of the drawers of Wolfe's desk, and also we—"

"My desk!" Wolfe roared.

"Yes, your desk," Rowcliff said precisely, smirking.

The blood was rushing into Wolfe's face.

"She was killed there," Cramer said gruffly. "Did you get anything at all?"

"I don't think so," Rowcliff admitted. "Of course, the prints have to be sorted, and there'll be lab reports. How do we leave it?"

"Seal it up and we'll see tomorrow. You stay here and keep a photographer. The others can go. Tell Stebbins to send that woman in—Mrs. Irwin."

"Orwin, sir."

"Wait a minute," I objected. "Seal what up? The office?"

"Certainly," Rowcliff sneered.

I said firmly, to Cramer, not to him. "You don't mean it. We work there. We live there. All our stuff is there."

"Go ahead, Lieutenant," Cramer told Rowcliff, and he wheeled and went.

I was full of both feelings and words, but I knew they had to be held in. This was far and away the worst Cramer had ever pulled. It was up to Wolfe. I looked at him. He was white with fury, and his mouth was pressed to so tight a line that there were no lips.

"It's routine," Cramer said aggressively.

Wolfe said icily, "That's a lie. It is not routine."

"It's *my* routine—in a case like this. Your office is not just an office. It's the place where more fancy tricks have been played than any other spot in New York. When a woman is murdered there, soon after a talk with Goodwin, for which we have no word but his—I say sealing it is routine."

Wolfe's head came forward an inch, his chin out. "No, Mr. Cramer. I'll tell you what it is. It is the malefic spite of a sullen little soul and a crabbed and envious mind. It is the childish rancor of a primacy too often challenged and offended. It is the feeble wiggle—"

The door came open to let Mrs. Orwin in.

With Mrs. Carlisle, the husband had come along. With Mrs. Orwin, it was the son. His expression and manner were so different I would hardly have known him. Upstairs his tone had been mean and his face had been mean. Now his narrow little eyes were working overtime to look frank and cordial.

He leaned across the table at Cramer, extending a hand: "Inspector Cramer? I've been hearing about you for years! I'm Eugene Orwin." He glanced at his right. "I've already had the pleasure of meeting Mr. Wolfe and Mr. Goodwin—earlier today, before this terrible thing happened. It *is* terrible."

"Yes," Cramer agreed. "Sit down."

"I will in a moment. I do better with words standing up. I would like to make a statement on behalf of my mother and myself, and I hope you'll permit it. I'm a member of the bar. My mother is not feeling well. At the request of your men she went in with me to identify the body of Miss Brown, and it was a bad shock, and we've been detained now more than two hours."

His mother's appearance corroborated him. Sitting with her head propped on a hand and her eyes closed, obviously she didn't care as much about the impression they made on the inspector as her son did.

"A statement would be welcome," Cramer told him, "if it's relevant."

"I thought so," Gene said approvingly. "So many people have an entirely wrong idea of police methods! Of course, you know that Miss Brown came here today as my mother's guest, and therefore it might be supposed that my mother knows her. But actually she doesn't."

"Go ahead."

Gene glanced at the shorthand dick. "If it's taken down I would like to go over it when convenient."

"You may."

"Then here are the facts: In January my mother was in Florida. You meet all kinds in Florida. My mother met a man who called himself Colonel Percy Brown—a British colonel in the reserve, he said. Later on, he introduced his sister Cynthia to her. My mother saw a great deal of them. My father is dead, and the estate, a rather large one, is in her control. She lent Brown some money, not much—that was just an opener."

Mrs. Orwin's head jerked up. "It was only five thousand dollars and I didn't promise him anything," she said wearily.

"All right, Mother." Gene patted her shoulder. "A week ago she returned to New York and they came along. The first time I met them I thought they were impostors. They weren't very free with family details, but from them and Mother, chiefly Mother, I got enough to inquire about, and sent a cable to London. I got a reply Saturday and another one this morning and there was more than enough to confirm my suspicion, but not nearly enough to put it up to my mother. When she likes people she can be very stubborn about them.

"I was thinking it over, what step to take next. Meanwhile, I thought it best not to let them be alone with her if I could help it. That's why I came here with them today—my mother is a member of that flower club—I'm no gardener myself—"

He turned a palm up. "That's what brought me here. My mother came to see the orchids, and she invited Brown and his sister to come, simply because she is goodhearted. But actually she knows nothing about them."

He put his hands on the table and leaned on them, forward at Cramer. "I'm going to be quite frank, Inspector. Under the circumstances, I can't see that it would serve any useful purpose to let it be published that that woman came here with my mother. I want to make it perfectly clear that we have no desire to evade our responsibility as citizens. But how would it help to get my mother's name in the headlines?"

"Names in headlines aren't what I'm after," Cramer told him, "but I don't run the newspapers. If they've already got it I can't stop them. I'd like to say I appreciate your frankness. So you only met Miss Brown a week ago?"

Cramer had plenty of questions for both mother and son. It was in the middle of them that Wolfe passed me a slip of paper on which he had scribbled:

"Tell Fritz to bring sandwiches and coffee for you and me. Also for those left in the front room. No one else. Of course, Saul and Theodore."

I left the room, found Fritz in the kitchen, delivered the message, and returned.

Gene stayed cooperative to the end, and Mrs. Orwin tried, though it was an effort. They said they had been together all the time, which I happened to know wasn't so, having seen them separated at least twice during the afternoon, and Cramer did too, since I had told him.

They said a lot of other things, among them that they hadn't left the plant-rooms between their arrival and their departure with Wolfe; that they had stayed until most of the others were gone because Mrs. Orwin wanted to persuade Wolfe to sell her some plants; that Colonel Brown had wandered off by himself once or twice; that they had been only mildly concerned about Cynthia's absence, because of assurances from Colonel Brown and me; and so on.

Before they left, Gene made another try for a commitment to keep his mother's name out of it, and Cramer promised to do his best.

Fritz had brought trays for Wolfe and me, and we were making headway with them. In the silence that followed the departure of the Orwins, Wolfe could plainly be heard chewing a mouthful of mixed salad.

Cramer sat frowning at us. He turned his head: "Levy! Get that Colonel Brown in."

"Yes, sir. That man you wanted—Vedder—he's here."

"Then I'll take him first."

Up in the plant-room, Malcolm Vedder had caught my eye by the way he picked up a flowerpot and held it. As he took a chair across the dining table from Cramer and me, I still thought he was worth another good look, but after his answer to Cramer's third question I relaxed and concentrated on my sandwiches. He was an actor and had had parts in three Broadway plays. Of course, that explained it. No actor would pick up a flowerpot just normally, like you or me. He would have to dramatize it some way, and Vedder had happened to choose a way that looked to me like fingers closing around a throat.

Now he was dramatizing this by being wrought-up and indignant.

"Typical!" he told Cramer, his eyes flashing and his voice throaty with feeling. "Typical of police clumsiness! Pulling *me* into this!"

"Yeah," Cramer said sympathetically. "It'll be tough for an actor, having your picture in the paper. You a member of this flower club?"

No, Vedder said, he wasn't. He had come with a friend, a Mrs. Beauchamp, and when she had left to keep an appointment he had remained to look at more orchids. They had arrived about three-thirty and he had remained in the plant-rooms continuously until leaving.

Cramer went through all the regulation questions, and got all the expected negatives, until he suddenly asked, "Did you know Doris Hatten?"

Vedder frowned. "Who?"

"Doris Hatten. She was also—"

"Ah!" Vedder cried. "She was also strangled! I remember!"

"Right."

Vedder made fists of his hands, rested them on the table, and leaned forward. "You know," he said tensely, "that's the worst of all, strangling—especially a woman."

"Did you know Doris Hatten?"

"Othello," Vedder said in a deep, resonant tone. His eyes lifted to Cramer and his voice lifted, too: "No, I didn't know her; I only read about her." He shuddered all over, and then, abruptly, he was out of his chair and on his feet. "I only came here to look at orchids!"

He ran his fingers through his hair, turned, and made for the door.

Levy looked at Cramer with his brows raised, and Cramer shook his head.

The next one in was Bill McNab, garden editor of the *Gazette*.

"I can't tell you how much I regret this, Mr. Wolfe," he said miserably.

"Don't try," Wolfe growled.

"What a terrible thing! I wouldn't have dreamed such a thing could happen—the Manhattan Flower Club! Of course, she wasn't a member, but that only makes it worse, in a way." McNab turned to Cramer: "I'm responsible for this."

"You are?"

"Yes, it was my idea. I persuaded Mr. Wolfe to arrange it. He let me word the invitations. And I was congratulating myself on the great success! Then this! What can I do?"

"Sit down a minute," Cramer invited him.

McNab varied the monotony on one detail, at least. He admitted that he had left the plant-rooms three times during the afternoon, once to accompany a departing guest down to the ground floor, and twice to go down alone to check on who had come and who hadn't. Aside from that, he was more of the same. By now it was beginning to seem not only futile, but silly to spend time on seven or eight of them merely because they happened to be the last to go and so were at hand. Also, it was something new to me from a technical standpoint. I had never seen one stack up like that.

Any precinct dick knows that every question you ask of everybody is aimed at one of the three targets: motive, means, and opportunity. In this case there were no questions to ask, because those were already answered. Motive: the guy had followed her downstairs, knowing she had recognized him, had seen her enter Wolfe's office and thought she was doing exactly what she was doing, getting set to tell Wolfe, and had decided to prevent that the quickest and best way he knew. Means: any piece of cloth, even his handkerchief, would do. Opportunity: he was there—all of them on Saul's list were.

So, if you wanted to learn who strangled Cynthia Brown, first you had to find out who had strangled Doris Hatten.

As soon as Bill McNab had been sent on his way, Colonel Percy Brown was brought in. Brown was not exactly at ease, but he had himself well in hand. You would never have picked him for a con man, and neither would I. His mouth and jaw were strong and attractive, and as he sat down he leveled his keen gray eyes at Cramer and kept them there. He wasn't interested in Wolfe or me. He said his name was Colonel Percy Brown, and Cramer asked him which army he was a colonel in.

"I think," Brown said in a cool, even tone, "it will save time if I state my position: I will answer fully and freely all questions that relate to what I saw, heard, or did since I arrived here this afternoon. Answers to any other questions will have to wait until I consult my attorney."

Cramer nodded. "I expected that. The trouble is I'm pretty sure I don't give a hoot what you saw or heard this afternoon. We'll come back to that. I want to put something up to you. As you see, I'm not even wanting to know why you tried to break away before we got here."

"I merely wanted to phone—"

"Forget it. On information received, I think it's like this: The woman who called herself Cynthia Brown, murdered here today, was not your sister. You met her in Florida six or eight weeks ago. She went in with you on an operation of which Mrs. Orwin was the subject, and you introduced her to Mrs. Orwin as your sister. You two came to New York with Mrs. Orwin a week ago, with the operation well under way. As far as I'm concerned, that is only background. Otherwise, I'm not interested in it. My work is homicide.

"For me," Cramer went on, "the point is that for quite a period you have been closely connected with this Miss Brown, associating with her in a confidential operation. You must have had many intimate conversations with her. You were having her with you as your sister, and she wasn't, and she's been murdered. We could give you a merry time on that score alone.

"But I wanted to give you a chance first," Cramer continued. "For two months you've been on intimate terms with Cynthia Brown. She certainly must have mentioned that a friend of hers named Doris Hatten was murdered—strangled last October. Cynthia Brown had information about the murderer which she kept to herself. If she had come out with it she'd be alive now. She must have told you all about it. Now you can tell me. If you do, we can nail him for what he did here today, and it might even make things a little smoother for you. Well?"

Brown had pursed his lips. They straightened out again, and his hand came up for a finger to scratch his cheek.

"I'm sorry I can't help."

"Do you expect me to believe that during all those weeks she never mentioned the murder of her friend Doris Hatten?"

"I'm sorry I can't help." Brown's tone was firm and final.

Cramer said, "Okay. We'll move on to this afternoon. Do you remember a moment when something about Cynthia Brown's appearance—some movement she made or the expression on her face—caused Mrs. Orwin to ask her what was the matter with her?"

A crease was showing on Brown's forehead. "I'm sorry. I don't believe I do," he stated.

"I'm asking you to try. Try hard."

Silence. Brown pursed his lips and the crease in his forehead deepened. Finally he said, "I may not have been right there at the moment. In those aisles—in a crowd like that—we weren't rubbing elbows continuously."

"You do remember when she excused herself because she wasn't feeling well?"

"Yes, of course."

"Well, this moment I'm asking about came shortly before that. She exchanged looks with some man nearby, and it was her reaction to that that made Mrs. Orwin ask her what was the matter. What I'm interested in is that exchange of looks."

"I didn't see it."

Cramer banged his fist on the table so hard the trays danced. "Levy! Take him out and tell Stebbins to send him down and lock him up. Material witness. Put more men on him—he's got a record somewhere. Find it!"

As the door closed behind them, Cramer turned and said, "Gather up, Murphy. We're leaving."

Levy came back in and Cramer addressed him: "We're leaving. Tell Stebbins one man out front will be enough—No, I'll tell him—"

"There's one more, sir. His name is Nicholson Morley. He's a psychiatrist."

"Let him go. This is getting to be a joke."

Cramer looked at Wolfe. Wolfe looked back at him.

"A while ago," Cramer rasped, "you said something had occurred to you."

"Did I?" Wolfe inquired coldly.

Their eyes went on clashing until Cramer broke the connection by turning to go. I restrained an impulse to knock their heads together. They were both being childish. If Wolfe really had something, anything at all, he knew Cramer would gladly trade the seals on the office door for it, sight unseen. And Cramer knew he could make the deal himself with nothing to lose. But they were both too sore and stubborn to show any horse sense.

Cramer had circled the end of the table on his way out when Levy reentered to report: "That man Morley insists on seeing you. He says it's vital."

Cramer halted, glowering. "What is he, a screwball?"

"I don't know, sir. He may be."

"Oh, bring him in."

This was my first really good look at the middle-aged male

with the mop of black hair. His quick-darting eyes were fully as black as his hair.

Cramer nodded impatiently. "You have something to say, Dr. Morley?"

"I have. Something vital."

"Let's hear it."

Morley got better settled in his chair. "First, I assume that no arrest has been made. Is that correct?"

"Yes—if you mean an arrest with a charge of murder."

"Have you a definite object of suspicion, with or without evidence in support?"

"If you mean am I ready to name the murderer, no. Are you?"

"I think I may be."

Cramer's chin went up. "Well? I'm in charge here."

Dr. Morley smiled. "Not quite so fast. The suggestion I have to offer is sound only with certain assumptions." He placed the tip of his right forefinger on the tip of his left little finger. "One: that you have no idea who committed this murder, and apparently you haven't." He moved over a finger. "Two: that this was not a commonplace crime with a commonplace discoverable motive." To the middle finger. "Three: that nothing is known to discredit the hypothesis that this girl was strangled by the man who strangled Doris Hatten . . . May I make those assumptions?"

"You can try. Why do you want to?"

Morley shook his head. "Not that I want to. That if I am permitted to, I have a suggestion. I wish to make it clear that I have great respect for the competence of the police, within proper limits. If the man who murdered Doris Hatten had been vulnerable to police techniques and resources, he would almost certainly have been caught. But he wasn't. You failed. Why?

"Because he was out of bounds for you. Because your exploration of motive is restricted by your preconceptions." Morley's black eyes gleamed. "You're a layman, so I won't use technical terms. The most powerful motives on earth are motives of the personality, which cannot be exposed by any purely objective investigation. If the personality is twisted, distorted, as it is with a psychotic, then the motives are twisted, too. As a psychiatrist I was deeply interested in the published reports on the murder of Doris Hatten—especially the detail that she was strangled with her own scarf. When your efforts to find the culprit ended in complete failure, I would have been glad to come forward with a suggestion, but I was as helpless as you."

"Get down to it," Cramer muttered.

"Yes." Morley put his elbows on the table and paired all his fingertips. "Now, today. On the basis of the assumptions I began with, it is a tenable theory, worthy to be tested, that this was the same man. If so, it is no longer a question of finding him among thousands or millions; it's a mere hundred or so, and I am willing to contribute my services." The black eyes flashed. "I admit that for a psychiatrist this is a rare opportunity. Nothing could be more dramatic than a psychosis exploding into murder. All you have to do is to have them brought to my office, one at a time—"

"Wait a minute," Cramer put in. "Are you suggesting that we deliver everyone that was here today to your office for you to work on?"

"No, not everyone, only the men. When I have finished I may have nothing that can be used as evidence, but there's an excellent chance that I can tell you who the strangler is—"

"Excuse me," Cramer said. He was on his feet. "Sorry to cut you off, Doctor, but I must get downtown." He was on his way. "I'm afraid your suggestion wouldn't work—I'll let you know—"

He went, and Levy and Murphy with him.

Dr. Morley pivoted his head to watch them go, kept it that way a moment, and then he arose and walked out without a word.

"Twenty minutes to ten," I announced.

Wolfe muttered, "Go look at the office door."

"I just did, as I let Morley out. It's sealed. Malefic spite. But this isn't a bad room to sit in," I said brightly.

"Pfui! I want to ask you something."

"Shoot."

"I want your opinion of this. Assume that we accept without reservation the story Miss Brown told you. Assume also that the man she had recognized, knowing she had recognized him, followed her downstairs and saw her enter the office; that he surmised she intended to consult me; that he postponed joining her in the office, either because he knew you were in there with her or for some other reason; that he saw you come out and go upstairs; that he took an opportunity to enter the office unobserved, got her off guard, killed her, got out unobserved, and returned upstairs."

"I'll take it that way."

"Very well. Then we have significant indications of his character. Consider it. He has killed her and is back upstairs, knowing that she was in the office talking with you for some time. He would like to know what she said to you. Specifically, he would like to know whether she told you about him, and, if so, how much. Had she or had she not named or described him in his current guise? With that question unanswered, would a man of his character, as indicated, *leave the house?* Or would he prefer the challenge and risk of remaining until the body had been discovered, to see what you would do? And I, too, of course, after you had talked with me, and the police?"

"Yeah." I chewed my lip. There was a long silence. "So that's how your mind's working. I could offer a guess."

"I prefer a calculation to a guess. For that, a basis is needed, and we have it. We know the situation as we have assumed it, and we know something of his character."

"Okay," I conceded, "a calculation. The answer I get, he would stick around until the body was found, and if he did, then he is one of the bunch Cramer has been talking with. So that's what occurred to you, huh?"

"No. By no means. That's a different matter. This is merely a tentative calculation for a starting point. If it is sound, I *know* who the murderer is."

I gave him a look. Sometimes I can tell how much he is putting on and sometimes I can't tell. I decided to buy it.

"That's interesting," I said admiringly. "If you want me to get him on the phone I'll have to use the one in the kitchen."

"I want to test the calculation."

"So do I."

"But that's a difficulty. The best I have in mind, the only one I can contrive to my satisfaction—only you can make it. And in doing so you would have to expose yourself to great personal risk."

"For Pete's sake!" I gawked at him. "This is a brand-new one. The errands you've sent me on! Since when have you flinched or faltered in the face of danger to me?"

"This danger is extreme."

"Let's hear the test."

"Very well." He turned a hand over. "Is that old typewriter of yours in working order?"

"Fair."

"Bring it down here, and some sheets of blank paper—any kind. I'll need a blank envelope."

"I have some."

"Bring one. Also the telephone book, Manhattan, from my room."

When I returned to the dining-room and was placing the typewriter in position on the table, Wolfe spoke: "No, bring it here. I'll use it myself."

I lifted my brows at him. "A page will take you an hour."

"It won't be a page. Put a sheet of paper in it."

I did so, got the paper squared, lifted the machine, and put it in front of him. He sat and frowned at it for a long minute, and then started pecking. I turned my back on him to make it easier to withhold remarks about his two-finger technique, and passed the time by trying to figure his rate. All at once he pulled the paper out.

"I think that will do," he said.

I took it and read what he had typed:

"She told me enough this afternoon so that I know who to send this to, and more. I have kept it to myself because I haven't decided what is the right thing to do. I would like to have a talk with you first, and if you will phone me tomorrow, Tuesday, between nine o'clock and noon, we can make an appointment; please don't put it off or I will have to decide myself."

I read it over three times. I looked at Wolfe. He had put an envelope in the typewriter and was consulting the phone book. He began pecking, addressing the envelope. I waited until he had finished and rolled the envelope out.

"Just like this?" I asked. "No name or initials signed?"

"No."

"I admit it's nifty," I admitted. "We could forget the calculation and send this to every guy on that list and wait to see who phoned."

"I prefer to send it only to one person—the one indicated by your report of that conversation. That will test the calculation."

"And save postage." I glanced at the paper. "The extreme danger, I suppose, is that I'll get strangled."

"I don't want to minimize the risk of this, Archie."

"Neither do I. I'll have to borrow a gun from Saul—ours are in the office. . . . May I have that envelope? I'll have to go to Times Square to mail it."

"Yes. Before you do so, copy that note. Keep Saul here in the morning. If and when the phone call comes you will have to use your wits to arrange the appointment advantageously."

"Right. The envelope, please."

He handed it to me.

That Tuesday morning I was kept busy from eight o'clock on by the phone and the doorbell. After nine, Saul was there to help, but not with the phone, because the orders were that I was to answer all calls. They were mostly from newspapers, but there were a couple from Homicide and a few scattered ones. I took them on the extension in the kitchen.

Every time I lifted the thing and told the transmitter, "Nero Wolfe's office, Archie Goodwin speaking," my pulse went up a notch, and then had to level off again. I had one argument, with a bozo in the District Attorney's office who had the strange idea that he could order me to report for an interview at eleven-thirty sharp, which ended by my agreeing to call later to fix an hour.

A little before eleven I was in the kitchen with Saul, who, at Wolfe's direction, had been briefed to date, when the phone rang.

"Nero Wolfe's office, Archie Goodwin speaking."

"Mr. Goodwin?"

"Right."

"You sent me a note."

My hand wanted to grip the phone the way Vedder had gripped the flowerpot, but I wouldn't let it.

"Did I? What about?"

"You suggested that we make an appointment. Are you in a position to discuss it?"

"Sure. I'm alone and no extensions are on. But I don't recognize your voice. Who is this?"

"I have two voices. This is the other one. Have you made a decision yet?"

"No. I was waiting to hear from you."

"That's wise, I think. I'm willing to discuss the matter. Are you free this evening?"

"I can wiggle free."

"With a car to drive?"

"Yeah, I have a car."

"Drive to a lunchroom at the north-east corner of Fifty-first Street and Eleventh Avenue. Get there at eight o'clock. Park your car on Fifty-first Street, but not at the corner. You will be alone, of course. Go in the lunchroom and order something to eat. I won't be there, but you will get a message. You'll be there at eight?"

"Yes. I still don't recognize your voice. I don't think you're the person I sent the note to."

"I am. It's good, isn't it?"

The connection went. I hung up, told Fritz he could answer calls now, and hotfooted it to the stairs and up three flights.

Wolfe was in the cool-room. When I told him about the call he merely nodded.

"That call," he said, "validates our assumption and verifies our calculation, but that's all. Has anyone come to take those seals off?"

I told him no. "I asked Stebbins about it and he said he'd ask Cramer."

"Don't ask again," he snapped. "We'll go down to my room."

If the strangler had been in Wolfe's house the rest of that day he would have felt honored—or anyway he should. Even during Wolfe's afternoon hours in the plant-rooms, from four to six, his mind was on my appointment, as was proved by the crop of new slants and ideas that poured out of him when he came down to the kitchen. Except for a trip to Leonard Street to answer an hour's worth of questions by an assistant district attorney, my day was devoted to it, too. My most useful errand—though at the time it struck me as a waste of time and money—was one made to Doc Vollmer for a prescription and then to a drugstore, under instructions from Wolfe.

When I got back from the D.A.'s office Saul and I got in the sedan and went for a reconnaissance. We didn't stop at 51st Street and 11th Avenue but drove past it four times. The main idea was to find a place for Saul. He and Wolfe both insisted that he had to be there.

We finally settled for a filling station across the street from the lunchroom. Saul was to have a taxi drive in there at eight o'clock, and stay in the passenger's seat while the driver tried to get his carburetor adjusted. There were so many contingencies to be agreed on that if it had been anyone but Saul I wouldn't have expected him to remember more than half. For instance, in case I left the lunchroom and got in my car and drove off, Saul was not to follow unless I cranked my window down.

Trying to provide for contingencies was okay, in a way, but actually it was strictly up to me, since I had to let the other guy make the rules. And with the other guy making the rules no one gets very far, not even Nero Wolfe arranging for contingencies ahead of time.

Saul left before I did, to find a taxi driver that he liked the looks of. When I went to the hall for my hat and raincoat, Wolfe came along.

"I still don't like the idea," he insisted, "of your having that thing in your pocket. I think you should slip it inside your sock."

"I don't." I was putting the raincoat on. "If I get frisked, a sock is as easy to feel as a pocket."

"You're sure that gun is loaded?"

"I never saw you so anxious. Next you'll be telling me to put on my rubbers."

He even opened the door for me.

It wasn't actually raining, merely trying to make up its mind, but after a couple of blocks I reached to switch on the windshield wiper. As I turned uptown on 10th Avenue the dash clock said 7:47; as I turned left on 51st Street it had only got to 7:51. At that time of day in that district there was plenty of space, and I rolled to the curb and stopped about twenty yards short of the corner, stopped the engine and turned the window down for a good view of the filling station across the street. There was no taxi there. At 7:59 a taxi pulled in and stopped by the pumps, and the driver got out and lifted the hood and started peering. I put my window up, locked the doors, and entered the lunchroom.

There was one hash slinger behind the counter and five customers scattered along on the stools. I picked a stool that left me elbowroom, sat, and ordered ice cream and coffee. The counterman served me and I took my time. At 8:12 the ice cream was gone and my cup empty, and I ordered a refill.

I had about got to the end of that, too, when a male entered, looked along the line, came straight to me, and asked me what my name was. I told him, and he handed me a folded piece of paper and turned to go. He was barely old enough for high school and I made no effort to hold him, thinking that the bird I had a date with was not likely to be an absolute sap. Unfolding the paper, I saw, neatly printed in pencil:

"Go to your car and get a note under the windshield wiper. Sit in the car to read it."

I paid what I owed, walked to my car and got the note as I was told, unlocked the car and got in, turned on the light, and read, in the same print:

"Make no signal of any kind. Follow instructions precisely. Turn right on 11th Ave. and go slowly to 56th St. Turn right on 56th and go to 9th Ave. Turn right on 9th Ave. Right again on 45th. Left on 11th Ave. Left on 38th. Right on 7th Ave. Right on 27th St. Park on 27th between 9th and 10th Aves. Go to No. 814 and tap five times on the door. Give the man who opens the door this note and the other one. He will tell you where to go."

I didn't like it much, but I had to admit it was a handy arrangement for seeing to it that I went to the conference unattached.

It had now decided to rain. Starting the engine, I could see dimly through the misty window that Saul's taxi driver was still monkeying with his carburetor, but of course I had to resist the impulse to crank the window down to wave so-long. Keeping the instructions in my left hand, I rolled to the corner, waited for the light to change, and turned right on 11th Avenue.

Since I had not been forbidden to keep my eyes open I did so, and as I stopped at 52nd for the red light I saw a black or dark-blue sedan pull away from the curb behind me and creep in my direction. I took it for granted that that was my chaperon.

The guy in the sedan was not the strangler, as I soon learned. On 27th Street there was space smack in front of Number 814, and I saw no reason why I shouldn't use it. The sedan went to the curb right behind me. After locking my car I stood on the sidewalk a moment, but my chaperon just sat tight, so I kept to the instructions, mounted the steps to the stoop of the rundown old brownstone, entered the vestibule, and knocked five times on the door. Through the glass panel the dimly-lit hall looked empty. As I peered in, I heard footsteps behind and turned. It was my chaperon.

"Well, we got here," I said cheerfully.

"You almost lost me at one light," he said. "Give me them notes."

I handed them to him—all the evidence I had. As he unfolded them for a look, I took him in. He was around my age and height, skinny but with muscles, with outstanding ears and a purple mole on his right jaw.

"They look like it," he said, and stuffed the notes in a pocket. From another pocket he produced a key, unlocked the door, and pushed it open. "Follow me."

As we ascended two flights, with him in front, it would have been a cinch for me to reach and take a gun off his hip if there had been one there, but there wasn't. He may have preferred a shoulder holster, like me. The stair steps were bare, worn wood, the walls had needed plaster since at least Pearl Harbor, and the smell was a mixture I wouldn't want to analyze. On the second landing he went down the hall to a door at the rear and signaled me through.

There was another man there, but still it wasn't my date—anyway, I hoped not. It would be an overstatement to say the room was furnished, but I admit there was a table, a bed, and three chairs, one of them upholstered. The man, who was lying on the bed, pushed himself up as we entered, and as he swung around to sit, his feet barely reached the floor. He had shoulders and a torso like a heavyweight wrestler, and legs like an underweight jockey. His puffed eyes blinked in the light from the unshaded bulb as if he had been asleep.

"That him?" he demanded.

Skinny said it was.

The wrestler-jockey, W-J for short, got up and went to the table, picked up a ball of thick cord. "Take off your hat and coat and sit there." He pointed to one of the straight chairs.

"Hold it," Skinny commanded him. "I haven't explained yet." He faced me: "The idea is simple. This man that's coming to see you don't want any trouble. He just wants to talk. So we tie you in that chair and leave you, and he comes and you have a talk, and after he leaves we come back and cut you loose, and out you go. Is that plain enough?"

I grinned at him. "It sure is, brother. It's too plain. What if I won't sit down?"

"Then he don't come and you don't have a talk."

"What if I walk out now?"

"Go ahead. We get paid anyhow. If you want to see this guy there's only one way: We tie you in the chair."

"We get more if we tie him," W-J objected. "Let me persuade him."

"Lay off," Skinny commanded.

"I don't want any trouble either," I stated. "How about this? I sit in the chair and you fix the cord to look right, but so I'm free to move in case of fire. There's a hundred bucks in the wallet in my breast pocket. Before you leave, you help yourselves."

"A lousy C?" W-J sneered. "Shut up and sit down."

"He had his choice," Skinny said reprovingly.

I did, indeed. It was a swell illustration of how much good it does to try to consider contingencies in advance. In all our discussions that day none of us had put the question, what to do if a pair of smooks offered me my pick of being tied in a chair or going home to bed. As far as I could see, standing there looking them over, that was all there was to it, and it was too early to go home to bed.

"Okay," I told them, "but don't overdo it. I know my way around, and I can find you if I care enough."

They unrolled the cord, cutting pieces off, and went to work. W-J tied my left wrist to the rear left leg of the chair, while

Skinny did the right. They wanted to do my ankles the same way, to the bottoms of the front legs of the chair, but I claimed I would get cramps sitting like that. It would be just as good to tie my ankles together. They discussed it, and I had my way. Skinny made a final inspection of the knots and then went over me. He took the gun from my shoulder holster and tossed it on the bed, made sure I didn't have another one, and left the room.

W-J picked up the gun, and scowled at it. "These things," he muttered. "They make more trouble." He went to the table and put the gun down on it. Then he crossed to the bed and stretched out on it.

"How long do we have to wait?" I asked.

"Not long. I wasn't to bed last night." He closed his eyes.

He got no nap. His barrel chest couldn't have gone up and down more than a dozen times before the door opened and Skinny came in. With him was a man in a gray pinstripe suit and a dark-gray homburg, with a gray topcoat over his arm. He had gloves on. W-J got off the bed and onto his toothpick legs. Skinny stood by the open door. The man put his hat and coat on the bed, came and took a look at my fastenings, and told Skinny, "All right; I'll come for you." The two rummies departed, shutting the door. The man stood facing me.

He smiled. "Would you have known me?"

"Not from Adam," I said, both to humor him and because it was true.

I wouldn't want to exaggerate how brave I am. It wasn't that I was too fearless to be impressed by the fact that I was thoroughly tied up and the strangler was standing there smiling at me; I was simply astounded. It was an amazing disguise. The two main changes were the eyebrows and eyelashes; these eyes had bushy brows and long, thick lashes, whereas yesterday's guest hadn't had much of either one. The real change was from the inside. I had seen no smile on the face of yesterday's guest, but if I had it wouldn't have been like this one. The hair made a difference too, of course, parted on the side and slicked down.

He pulled the other straight chair around and sat. I admired the way he moved. That in itself could have been a dead giveaway, but the movements filled the get-up to a T.

"So she told you about me?" he said.

It was the voice he had used on the phone. It was actually different, pitched lower, for one thing, but with it, as with the face and movements, the big change was from the inside. The voice was stretched tight, and the palms of his gloved hands were pressed against his kneecaps with the fingers straight out.

I said, "Yes," and added conversationally, "When you saw her go in the office why didn't you follow her in?"

"I had seen you leave, upstairs, and I suspected you were in there."

"Why didn't she scream or fight?"

"I talked to her. I talked a little first." His head gave a quick jerk, as if a fly were bothering him and his hands were too occupied to attend to it. "What did she tell you?"

"About that day at Doris Hatten's apartment—you coming in and her going out. And of course her recognizing you there yesterday."

"She is dead. There is no evidence. You can't prove anything."

I grinned. "Then you're wasting a lot of time and energy and the best disguise I ever saw. Why didn't you just toss my note in the wastebasket? . . . Let me answer. You didn't dare. In getting evidence, knowing exactly what and who to look for makes all the difference. You knew I knew."

"And you haven't told the police?"

"No."

"Nor Nero Wolfe?"

"No."

"Why not?"

I shrugged. "I may not put it very well," I said, "because this is the first time I have ever talked with my hands and feet tied, and I find it cramps my style. But it strikes me as the kind of coincidence that doesn't happen very often. I'm fed up with the detective business, and I'd like to quit. I have something that's worth a good deal to you—say, fifty thousand dollars. It can be arranged so that you get what you pay for. I'll go the limit on that, but it has to be closed quick. If you don't buy, I'm going to have a tough time explaining why I didn't remember sooner what she told me. Twenty-four hours from now is the absolute limit."

"It couldn't be arranged so I could get what I paid for."

"Sure, it could. If you don't want me on your neck the rest of your life, believe me, I don't want you on mine, either."

"I suppose you don't. I suppose I'll have to pay."

There was a sudden noise in his throat as if he had started to choke. He stood up. "You're working your hand loose," he said huskily, and moved toward me.

It might have been guessed from his voice, thick and husky

from the blood rushing to his head, but it was plain as day in his eyes, suddenly fixed and glassy, like a blind man's eyes. Evidently he had come there fully intending to kill me, and had now worked himself up to it.

"Hold it!" I snapped at him.

He halted, muttering, "You're getting your hand loose," and moved again, passing me to get behind.

I jerked my body and the chair violently aside and around, and had him in front of me again.

"No good," I told him. "They only went down one flight. I heard 'em. It's no good, anyway. I've got another note for you—from Nero Wolfe—here in my breast pocket. Help yourself, but stay in front of me."

He was only two steps from me, but it took him four small, slow ones. His gloved hand went inside my coat to the breast pocket, and came out with a folded slip of yellow paper. From the way his eyes looked, I doubted if he would be able to read, but apparently he was. I watched his face as he took it in, in Wolfe's precise handwriting:

"If Mr. Goodwin is not home by midnight the information given him by Cynthia Brown will be communicated to the police, and I shall see that they act immediately. NERO WOLFE."

He looked at me, and slowly his eyes changed. No longer glassy, they began to let light in. Before, he had just been going to kill me. Now, he hated me.

I got voluble: "So it's no good, see? He did it this way because if you had known I had told him, you would have sat tight. He figured that you would think you could handle me, and I admit you tried your best. He wants fifty thousand dollars by tomorrow at six o'clock, no later. You say it can't be arranged so you'll get what you pay for, but we say it can and it's up to you. You say we have no evidence, but we can get it—don't think we can't. As for me, I wouldn't advise you even to pull my hair. It would make him sore at you, and he's not sore now, he just wants fifty thousand bucks."

He had started to tremble, and knew it, and was trying to stop.

"Maybe," I conceded, "you can't get that much that quick. In that case he'll take your I.O.U.—you can write it on the back of that note he sent you. My pen's here in my vest pocket. He'll be reasonable."

"I'm not such a fool," he said harshly.

"Who said you were?" I was sharp and urgent, and thought I

had loosened him. "Use your head, that's all. We've either got you cornered or we haven't. If we haven't, what are you doing here? If we have, a little thing like your name signed to an I.O.U. won't make it any worse. He won't press you too hard. Here, get my pen, right here."

I still think I had loosened him. It was in his eyes and the way he stood, sagging a little. If my hands had been free, so I could have got the pen myself, and uncapped it and put it between his fingers, I would have had him. I had him to the point of writing and signing, but not to the point of taking my pen out of my pocket. But, of course, if my hands had been free I wouldn't have been bothering about an I.O.U. and a pen.

So he slipped from under. He shook his head, and his shoulders stiffened. The hate that filled his eyes was in his voice, too: "You said twenty-four hours. That gives me tomorrow. I'll have to decide. Tell Nero Wolfe I'll decide."

He crossed to the door and pulled it open. He went out, closing the door, and I heard his steps descending the stairs; but he hadn't taken his hat and coat, and I nearly cracked my temples trying to use my brain. I hadn't got far when there were steps on the stairs again, coming up, and in they came, all three of them.

My host spoke to Skinny: "What time does your watch say?"

Skinny glanced at his wrist. "Nine thirty-two."

"At half-past ten untie his left hand. Leave him like that and go. It will take him five minutes or more to get his other hand and his feet free. Have you any objection to that?"

"Nah. He's got nothing on us."

The strangler took a roll of bills from his pocket, having a little difficulty on account of his gloves, peeled off two twenties, went to the table with them, and gave them a good rub on both sides with his handkerchief.

He held the bills out to Skinny. "I've got the agreed amount, as you know. This extra is so you won't get impatient and leave before half-past ten."

"Don't take it!" I called sharply.

Skinny, the bills in his hand, turned. "What's the matter—they got germs?"

"No, but they're peanuts, you sap! He's worth ten grand to you! As is!"

"Nonsense," the strangler said scornfully, and started for the bed to get his hat and coat.

"Gimme my twenty," W-J demanded.

Skinny stood with his head cocked, regarding me. He looked faintly interested but skeptical, and I saw it would take more than words. As the strangler picked up his hat and coat and turned, I jerked my body violently to the left, and over I went, chair and all. I have no idea how I got across the floor to the door. I couldn't simply roll, on account of the chair; I couldn't crawl without hands; and I didn't even try to jump. But I made it, and not slow, and was there down on my right side, the chair against the door and me against the chair, before any of them snapped out of it enough to reach me.

"You think," I yapped at Skinny, "it's just a job? Let him go and you'll find out! Do you want his name? Mrs. Carlisle—*Mrs.* Homer N. Carlisle. Do you want her address?"

The strangler, on his way to me, stopped and froze. He—or I should say, she—stood stiff as a bar of steel, the long-lashed eyes aimed at me.

"Missus?" Skinny demanded incredulously. "Did you say 'Missus'?"

"Yes. She's a woman. I'm tied up, but you've got her. I'm helpless, so you can have her. You might give me a cut of the ten grand." The strangler made a movement. "Watch her!"

W-J, who had started for me and stopped, turned to face her. I had banged my head and it hurt. Skinny stepped up to her, jerked both sides of her double-breasted coat open, released them, and backed up a step.

"It could be a woman," he said.

"We can find that out easy enough." W-J moved. "Dumb as I am, I can tell *that*."

"Go ahead," I urged. "That will check her and me both. Go ahead!"

W-J got to her and put out a hand.

She shrank away and screamed, "Don't touch me!"

"I'll be—" W-J said wonderingly.

"What's this gag," Skinny demanded, "about ten grand?"

"It's a long story," I told him, "but it's there if you want it. If you'll cut me in for a third, it's a cinch. If she gets out of here and gets safe home, we can't touch her. All we have to do is connect her as she is—here now, disguised—with Mrs. Homer N. Carlisle, which is what she'll be when she gets home. If we do that we've got her shirt. As she is here now, she's red-hot. As she is at home, you couldn't even get in."

"So what?" Skinny asked. "I didn't bring my camera."

"I've got something better. Get me loose and I'll show you."

Skinny didn't like that. He eyed me a moment and turned for a look at the others. Mrs. Carlisle was backed against the bed, and W-J stood studying her with his fists on his hips.

Skinny returned to me. "I'll do it. Maybe. What is it?"

I snapped, "At least, put me right side up. These cords are eating my wrists."

He came and got the back of the chair with one hand and my arm with the other, and I clamped my feet to the floor to give us leverage. He was stronger than he looked. Upright on the chair again, I was still blocking the door.

"Get a bottle," I told him, "out of my right-hand coat pocket. . . . No, here; the coat I've got on. I hope it didn't break."

He fished it out. It was intact. He held it to the light to read the label. "What is it?"

"Silver nitrate. It makes a black, indelible mark on most things, including skin. Pull up her pants leg and mark her with it."

"Then what?"

"Let her go. We'll have her. With the three of us able to explain how and when she got marked, she's sunk."

"How come you've got this stuff?"

"I was hoping for a chance to mark her myself."

"How much will it hurt her?"

"Not at all. Put some on me—anywhere you like, as long as it doesn't show."

He studied the label again. I watched his face, hoping he wouldn't ask if the mark would be permanent, because I didn't know what answer would suit him, and I had to sell him.

"A woman," he muttered. "A woman!"

"Yeah," I said sympathetically. "She sure made a monkey of you."

He swiveled his head and called, "Hey!"

W-J turned.

Skinny commanded him, "Pin her up! Don't hurt her."

W-J reached for her. But, as he did so, all of a sudden she was neither man nor woman, but a cyclone. Her first leap, away from his reaching hand, was sidewise, and by the time he had realized he didn't have her she had got to the table and grabbed the gun. He made for her, and she pulled the trigger, and down he went, tumbling right at her feet. By that time Skinny was almost to her, and she whirled and blazed away again. He kept going, and from the force of the blow on my left shoulder I might have calculated, if I had been in a mood for calculating, that the bullet had not gone through Skinny before it hit me. She pulled the trigger a third time, but by then Skinny had her wrist and was breaking her arm.

"She got me!" W-J was yelling indignantly. "She got me in the leg!"

Skinny had her down on her knees. "Come and cut me loose," I called to him, "and go find a phone."

Except for my wrists and ankles and shoulder and head, I felt fine.

"I hope you're satisfied," Inspector Cramer said sourly. "You and Goodwin have got your pictures in the paper again. You got no fee, but a lot of free publicity. I got my nose wiped."

Wolfe grunted comfortably.

The whole squad had been busy with chores: visiting W-J at the hospital; conversing with Mr. and Mrs. Carlisle at the D.A.'s office; starting to round up circumstantial evidence to show that Mr. Carlisle had furnished the necessary for Doris Hatten's rent and Mrs. Carlisle knew it; pestering Skinny; and other items. I had been glad to testify that Skinny, whose name was Herbert Marvel, was one-hundred-proof.

"What I chiefly came for," Cramer went on, "was to let you know that I realize there's nothing I can do. I know Cynthia Brown described her to Goodwin, and probably gave him her name, too, and Goodwin told you. And you wanted to hog it. I suppose you thought you could pry a fee out of somebody. Both of you suppressed evidence." He gestured. "Okay, I can't prove it. But I know it, and I want you to know I know it. And I'm not going to forget it."

"The trouble is," Wolfe murmured, "that if you can't prove you're right, and of course you can't, neither can I prove you're wrong."

"I would gladly try. How?"

Cramer leaned forward. "Like this: If she hadn't been described to Goodwin, how did you pick her for him to send that blackmail note to?"

Wolfe shrugged. "It was a calculation, as I told you. I concluded that the murderer was among those who remained until the body had been discovered. It was worth testing. If there had been no phone call in response to Mr. Goodwin's note, the calculation would have been discredited and I would—"

"Yeah, but why her?"

"There were only two women who remained. Obviously, it couldn't have been Mrs. Orwin; with her physique she would be hard put to pass as a man. Besides, she is a widow, and it was a sound presumption that Doris Hatten had been killed by a jealous wife, who—"

"But why a woman? Why not a man?"

"Oh, that." Wolfe picked up a glass of beer and drained it with more deliberation than usual. He was having a swell time. "I told you in my dining-room"—he pointed a finger—"that something had occurred to me and I wanted to consider it. Later, I would have been glad to tell you about it if you had not acted so irresponsibly and spitefully in sealing up this office. That made me doubt if you were capable of proceeding properly on any suggestion from me, so I decided to proceed, myself.

"What had occurred to me was simply this, that Miss Brown had told Mr. Goodwin that *she wouldn't have recognized 'him' if he hadn't had a hat on!* She used the masculine pronoun, naturally, throughout that conversation, because it had been a man who had called at Doris Hatten's apartment that October day, and he was fixed in her mind as a man. But it was in my plant-rooms that she had seen him that afternoon—*and no man wore his hat up there!* The men left their hats downstairs. Besides, I was there and saw them. *But nearly all the women had hats on.*"

Wolfe upturned a palm. "So it was a woman."

Cramer eyed him. "I don't believe it," he said flatly.

"You have a record of Mr. Goodwin's report of that conversation."

"I still wouldn't believe it."

"There were other little items." Wolfe wiggled a finger. "For example: The strangler of Doris Hatten had a key to the door. But surely the provider, who had so carefully avoided revealment, would not have marched in at an unexpected hour to risk encountering strangers. And who so likely to have found an opportunity, or contrived one, to secure a duplicate key as that provider's jealous wife?"

"Talk all day. I still don't believe it."

Well, I thought to myself, observing Wolfe's smirk and for once completely approving of it, Cramer the office-sealer has his choice of believing it or not.

As for me, I had no choice.

Come into My Parlor

"Come into my parlor" is among the many formulas shared by the mystery and horror genres. While horror fiction assumes that the supernatural exists and is central to understanding the world, in the mystery genre the supernatural does not exist, or, if it does, it does not actively interfere in the physical world. When Sherlock Holmes confronts the hound of the Baskervilles, he battles not a demon spirit but a hoax. Many detectives expose similar fake spectres. Ratiocination, the process of logically examining evidence, would be impossible if the laws of nature were suspended. However, a come into my parlor story comes close to the primary premise of horror fiction in that concealed human evil is revealed, sometimes motiveless, but nonetheless lurking like a hungry spider, ready to consume the unwary fly. Characters are drawn into attractive situations only to discover that they have badly misjudged and will be destroyed for their error. An early exemplar is Edgar Allan Poe's "The Cask of Amontillado," in which the narrator draws Fortunato to his entombment, exploiting both the oenophile's pride in his palate and his disdain for the man who will kill him. In most come into my parlor stories, we are not told initially of the evildoer's intention and we fully identify with the naivete of the victim. As we begin to sense that something is subtly wrong, we face the unhappy realization that we, too, would be likely to fall unwarily into a similar trap. The Prince of Darkness is a gentleman, Shakespeare warns us, and the Devil can quote Scripture. Furthermore, many of these stories suggest the victim's own responsibility in being attracted into the "spider's web." The victims are prideful, gluttonous, lecherous, greedy, or, more ironically, looking for a kindness that they should not expect. With this element, a come into my parlor story becomes a moral tale, reminiscent of early Renaissance dramas featuring the vice figure, who weakens and destroys people by exploiting their own longings and desires. The come into my parlor formula offers a cautionary warning about temptation, repeating the old saw that something too good to be true probably is.

ROALD DAHL

(1916–1990)

*One of the most inventive short story writers in the crime field, Roald Dahl was born of a Welsh mother and a Norwegian father. His father died when Dahl was four, and his mother honored his father's wishes by sending him to English schools, which his father thought were the best in the world. Instead of going to university, however, Dahl accompanied an exploratory expedition to Newfoundland, then worked for Shell Oil in London and East Africa. During World War II, he served with distinction in Africa in the Royal Air Force. Dahl's first book was a collection of stories about flying, but he made his mark in two areas of writing: fiction for children (*James and the Giant Peach *[1961] and* Charlie and the Chocolate Factory *[1964] are classics) and wicked stories involving the grotesque. Perhaps these two areas are not very far apart. There is a sense in all his work that people get what they deserve for their sins—or perhaps, comically, get a bit* more *than they deserve, whether it is exploding from stealing candy in Willy Wonka's chocolate factory or being caught in adultery. The child in us delights in the comeuppance of the arrogant. Dahl's tales also delight us with grotesqueries: a man preserved as a brain; a man who collects fingers; the hopeful birth of a child who turns out to be Hitler; a woman who commits murder with a frozen leg of lamb. The seemingly innocent exact a terrifying and horrific revenge when they are provoked, mocking the cleverness of those who have abused them. Sometimes they simply find revenge against the world for thinking them insignificant. A strong and satisfying morality underlies these comic oddities. In the following story, a hopeful and eager young man is misguided in his intent to be a successful businessman. Perhaps his is a healthy greed, but in Dahl's stories even healthy sins lead people into the spider's parlor.*

THE LANDLADY

Billy Weaver had traveled down from London on the slow afternoon train, with a change at Swindon on the way, and by the time he got to Bath it was about nine o'clock in the evening and the moon was coming up out of a clear starry sky over the houses opposite the station entrance. But the air was deadly cold and the wind was like a flat blade of ice on his cheeks.

"Excuse me," he said, "but is there a fairly cheap hotel not too far away from here?"

"Try the Bell and Dragon," the porter answered, pointing down the road. "They might take you in. It's about a quarter of a mile along on the other side."

Billy thanked him and picked up his suitcase and set out to walk the quarter-mile to The Bell and Dragon. He had never been to Bath before. He didn't know anyone who lived there. But Mr. Greenslade at the Head Office in London had told him it was a splendid city. "Find your own lodgings," he had said, "and then go along and report to the Branch Manager as soon as you've got yourself settled."

Billy was seventeen years old. He was wearing a new navy-blue overcoat, a new brown trilby hat, and a new brown suit, and he was feeling fine. He walked briskly down the street. He was trying to do everything briskly these days. Briskness, he had decided, was *the* one common characteristic of all successful businessmen. The big shots up at Head Office were absolutely fantastically brisk all the time. They were amazing.

There were no shops on this wide street that he was walking along, only a line of tall houses on each side, all of them identical. They had porches and pillars and four or five steps going up to their front doors, and it was obvious that once upon a time they had been very swanky residences. But now, even in the darkness, he could see that the paint was peeling from the woodwork on their doors and windows, and that the handsome white façades were cracked and blotchy from neglect.

Suddenly, in a downstairs window that was brilliantly illuminated by a street-lamp not six yards away, Billy caught sight of a printed notice propped up against the glass in one of the upper panes. It said BED AND BREAKFAST. There was a vase of pussy-willows, tall and beautiful, standing just underneath the notice.

He stopped walking. He moved a bit closer. Green curtains (some sort of velvety material) were hanging down on either side of the window. The pussy-willows looked wonderful beside them. He went right up and peered through the glass into the room, and the first thing he saw was a bright fire burning in the hearth. On the carpet in front of the fire, a pretty little dachshund was curled up asleep with its nose tucked into its belly. The room itself, so far as he could see in the half-darkness, was filled with pleasant furniture. There was a baby-grand piano and a big sofa and several plump armchairs; and in one corner he spotted a large parrot in a cage. Animals were usually a good sign in a place like this, Billy told himself; and all in all, it looked to him as though it would be a pretty decent house to stay in. Certainly it would be more comfortable than The Bell and Dragon.

On the other hand, a pub would be more congenial than a boarding-house. There would be beer and darts in the evenings, and lots of people to talk to, and it would probably be a good bit cheaper, too. He had stayed a couple of nights in a pub once before and he had liked it. He had never stayed in any boarding-houses, and, to be perfectly honest, he was a tiny bit frightened of them. The name itself conjured up images of watery cabbage, rapacious landladies, and a powerful smell of kippers in the living-room.

After dithering about like this in the cold for two or three minutes, Billy decided that he would walk on and take a look at The Bell and Dragon before making up his mind. He turned to go.

And now a queer thing happened to him. He was in the act of stepping back and turning away from the window when all at once his eye was caught and held in the most peculiar manner by the small notice that was there. BED AND BREAKFAST, it said, BED AND BREAKFAST, BED AND BREAKFAST, BED AND BREAKFAST. Each word was like a large black eye staring at him through the glass, holding him, compelling him, forcing him to stay where he was and not to walk away from that house, and the next thing he knew, he was actually moving across from the window to the front door of the house, climbing the steps that led up to it, and reaching for the bell.

He pressed the bell. Far away in the back room he heard it ringing, and then *at once*—it must have been at once because he hadn't even had time to take his finger from the bell-button—the door swung open and a woman was standing there.

Normally you ring the bell and you have at least a half-minute's wait before the door opens. But this dame was like a jack-in-the-box. He pressed the bell—and out she popped! It made him jump.

She was about forty-five or fifty years old, and the moment she saw him, she gave him a warm welcoming smile.

"*Please* come in," she said pleasantly. She stepped aside, holding the door wide open, and Billy found himself automatically starting forward into the house. The compulsion or, more accurately, the desire to follow after her into that house was extraordinarily strong.

"I saw the notice in the window," he said, holding himself back.

"Yes, I know."

"I was wondering about a room."

"It's *all* ready for you, my dear," she said. She had a round pink face and very gentle blue eyes.

"I was on my way to The Bell and Dragon," Billy told her. "But the notice in your window just happened to catch my eye."

"My dear boy," she said, "why don't you come in out of the cold?"

"How much do you charge?"

"Five and sixpence a night, including breakfast."

It was fantastically cheap. It was less than half of what he had been willing to pay.

"If that is too much," she added, "then perhaps I can reduce it just a tiny bit. Do you desire an egg for breakfast? Eggs are expensive at the moment. It would be sixpence less without the egg."

"Five and sixpence is fine," he answered. "I should like very much to stay here."

"I knew you would. Do come in."

She seemed terribly nice. She looked exactly like the mother of one's best school-friend welcoming one into the house to stay for the Christmas holidays. Billy took off his hat, and stepped over the threshold.

"Just hang it there," she said, "and let me help you with your coat."

There were no other hats or coats in the hall. There were no umbrellas, no walking-sticks—nothing.

"We have it *all* to ourselves," she said, smiling at him over her shoulder as she led the way upstairs. "You see, it isn't very often I have the pleasure of taking a visitor into my little nest."

The old girl was slightly dotty, Billy told himself. But at five and sixpence a night, who gives a damn about that? "I should've thought you'd be simply swamped with applicants," he said politely.

"Oh, I am, my dear, I am, of course I am. But the trouble is that I'm inclined to be just a teeny weeny bit choosy and particular—if you see what I mean."

"Ah, yes."

"But I'm always ready. Everything is always ready day and night in this house just on the off-chance that an acceptable young gentleman will come along. And it is such a pleasure, my dear, such a very great pleasure when now and again I open the door and I see someone standing there who is just *exactly* right." She was half-way up the stairs, and she paused with one hand on the stair-rail, turning her head and smiling down at him with pale lips. "Like you," she added, and her blue eyes traveled slowly all the way down the length of Billy's body, to his feet, and then up again.

On the first-floor landing she said to him, "This floor is mine."

They climbed up a second flight. "And this one is *all* yours," she said. "Here's your room. I do hope you'll like it." She took him into a small but charming front bedroom, switching on the light as she went in.

"The morning sun comes right in the window, Mr. Perkins. It *is* Mr. Perkins, isn't it?"

"No," he said. "It's Weaver."

"Mr. Weaver. How nice. I've put a water-bottle between the sheets to air them out, Mr. Weaver. It's such a comfort to have a hot water-bottle in a strange bed with clean sheets, don't you agree? And you may light the gas fire at any time if you feel chilly."

"Thank you," Billy said. "Thank you ever so much." He noticed that the bedspread had been taken off the bed, and that the bedclothes had been neatly turned back on one side, all ready for someone to get in.

"I'm so glad you appeared," she said, looking earnestly into his face. "I was beginning to get worried."

"That's all right," Billy answered brightly. "You mustn't worry about me." He put his suitcase on the chair and started to open it.

"And what about supper, my dear? Did you manage to get anything to eat before you came here?"

"I'm not a bit hungry, thank you," he said. "I think I'll just go to bed as soon as possible because tomorrow I've got to get up rather early and report to the office."

"Very well, then. I'll leave you now so that you can unpack. But before you go to bed, would you be kind enough to pop into the sitting-room on the ground floor and sign the book? Everyone has to do that because it's the law of the land, and we don't want to go breaking any laws at *this* stage of the proceedings, do we?" She gave him a little wave of the hand and went quickly out of the room and closed the door.

Now, the fact that his landlady appeared to be slightly off her rocker didn't worry Billy in the least. After all, she was not only harmless—there was no question about that—but she was also quite obviously a kind and generous soul. He guessed that she had probably lost a son in the war, or something like that, and had never got over it.

So a few minutes later, after unpacking his suitcase and washing his hands, he trotted downstairs to the ground floor and entered the living-room. His landlady wasn't there, but the fire was glowing in the hearth, and the little dachshund was still sleeping in front of it. The room was wonderfully warm and cosy. I'm a lucky fellow, he thought, rubbing his hands. This is a bit of all right.

He found the guest-book lying open on the piano, so he took out his pen and wrote down his name and address. There were only two other entries above his on the page, and, as one always does with guest-books, he started to read them. One was a Christopher Mulholland from Cardiff. The other was Gregory W. Temple from Bristol.

That's funny, he thought suddenly. Christopher Mulholland. It rings a bell.

Now where on earth had he heard that rather unusual name before?

Was he a boy at school? No. Was it one of his sister's numerous young men, perhaps, or a friend of his father's? No, no, it wasn't any of those. He glanced down again at the book.

Christopher Mulholland	*231 Cathedral Road, Cardiff*
Gregory W. Temple	*27 Sycamore Drive, Bristol*

As a matter of fact, now he came to think of it, he wasn't at all sure that the second name didn't have almost as much of a familiar ring about it as the first.

"Gregory Temple?" he said aloud, searching his memory. "Christopher Mulholland? . . ."

"Such charming boys," a voice behind him answered, and he turned and saw his landlady sailing into the room with a large silver tea-tray in her hands. She was holding it well out in front of her, and rather high up, as though the tray were a pair of reins on a frisky horse.

"They sound somehow familiar," he said.

"They do? How interesting."

"I'm almost positive I've heard those names before somewhere. Isn't that queer? Maybe it was in the newspapers. They weren't famous in any way, were they? I mean famous cricketers or footballers or something like that?"

"Famous," she said, setting the tea-tray down on the low table in front of the sofa. "Oh no, I don't think they were famous. But they were extraordinarily handsome, both of them, I can promise you that. They were tall and young and handsome, my dear, just exactly like you."

Once more, Billy glanced down at the book. "Look here," he said, noticing the dates. "This last entry is over two years old."

"It is?"

"Yes, indeed. And Christopher Mulholland's is nearly a year before that—more than *three years* ago."

"Dear me," she said, shaking her head and heaving a dainty little sigh. "I would never have thought it. How time does fly away from us all, doesn't it, Mr. Wilkins?"

"It's Weaver," Billy said. "W-e-a-v-e-r."

"Oh, of course it is!" she cried, sitting down on the sofa. "How silly of me. I do apologize. In one ear and out the other, that's me, Mr. Weaver."

"You know something?" Billy said. "Something that's really quite extraordinary about all this?"

"No, dear, I don't."

"Well, you see—both of these names, Mulholland and Temple, I not only seem to remember each one of them separately, so to speak, but somehow or other, in some peculiar way, they both appear to be sort of connected together as well. As though they were both famous for the same sort of thing, if you see what I mean—like . . . well . . . like Dempsey and Tunney, for example, or Churchill and Roosevelt."

"How amusing," she said. "But come over here now, dear, and sit down beside me on the sofa and I'll give you a nice cup of tea and a ginger biscuit before you go to bed."

"You really shouldn't bother," Billy said. "I didn't mean you to do anything like that." He stood by the piano, watching her as she fussed about with the cups and saucers. He noticed that she had small, white, quickly moving hands, and red finger-nails.

"I'm almost positive it was in the newspapers I saw them," Billy said. "I'll think of it in a second. I'm sure I will."

There is nothing more tantalizing than a thing like this which lingers just outside the borders of one's memory. He hated to give up.

"Now wait a minute," he said. "Wait just a minute. Mulholland . . . Christopher Mulholland . . . wasn't *that* the name of the Eton schoolboy who was on a walking-tour through the West Country, and then all of a sudden . . ."

"Milk?" she said. "And sugar?"

"Yes, please. And then all of a sudden . . ."

"Eton schoolboy?" she said. "Oh no, my dear, that can't possibly be right because *my* Mr. Mulholland was certainly not an Eton schoolboy when he came to me. He was a Cambridge undergraduate. Come over here now and sit next to me and warm yourself in front of this lovely fire. Come on. Your tea's all ready for you." She patted the empty place beside her on the sofa, and she sat there smiling at Billy and waiting for him to come over.

He crossed the room slowly, and sat down on the edge of the sofa. She placed his teacup on the table in front of him.

"*There* we are," she said. "How nice and cosy this is, isn't it?"

Billy started sipping his tea. She did the same. For half a minute or so, neither of them spoke. But Billy knew that she was looking at him. Her body was half-turned towards him, and he could feel her eyes resting on his face, watching him over the rim of her teacup. Now and again, he caught a whiff of a peculiar smell that seemed to emanate directly from her person. It was not in the least unpleasant, and it reminded him—well, he wasn't quite sure what it reminded him of. Pickled walnuts? New leather? Or was it the corridors of a hospital?

"Mr. Mulholland was a great one for his tea," she said at length. "Never in my life have I seen anyone drink as much tea as dear, sweet Mr. Mulholland."

"I suppose he left fairly recently," Billy said. He was still puzzling his head about the two names. He was positive now that he had seen them in the newspapers—in the headlines.

"Left?" she said, arching her brows. "But my dear boy, he never left. He's still here. Mr. Temple is also here. They're on the third floor, both of them together."

Billy set down his cup slowly on the table, and stared at his landlady. She smiled back at him, and then she put out one of her white hands and patted him comfortingly on the knee. "How old are you, my dear?" she asked.

"Seventeen."

"Seventeen!" she cried. "Oh, it's the perfect age! Mr. Mulholland was also seventeen. But I think he was a trifle shorter than you are, in fact I'm sure he was, and his teeth weren't *quite* so white. You have the most beautiful teeth, Mr. Weaver, did you know that?"

"They're not as good as they look," Billy said. "They've got simply masses of fillings in them at the back."

"Mr. Temple, of course, was a little older," she said, ignoring his remark. "He was actually twenty-eight. And yet I never would have guessed it if he hadn't told me, never in my whole life. There wasn't a *blemish* on his body."

"A what?" Billy said.

"His skin was *just* like a baby's."

There was a pause. Billy picked up his teacup and took another sip of his tea, then he set it down again gently in its saucer. He waited for her to say something else, but she seemed to have lapsed into another of her silences. He sat there staring straight ahead of him into the far corner of the room, biting his lower lip.

"That parrot," he said at last. "You know something? It had me completely fooled when I first saw it through the window from the street. I could have sworn it was alive."

"Alas, no longer."

"It's most terribly clever the way it's been done," he said. "It doesn't look in the least bit dead. Who did it?"

"I did."

"*You* did?"

"Of course," she said. "And you have met my little Basil as well?" She nodded towards the dachshund curled up so comfortably in front of the fire. Billy looked at it. And suddenly, he realized that this animal had all the time been just as silent and motionless as the parrot. He put out a hand and touched it gently on the top of its back. The back was hard and cold, and when he pushed the hair to one side with his fingers, he could see the skin underneath, greyish-black and dry and perfectly preserved.

"Good gracious me," he said. "How absolutely fascinating." He turned away from the dog and stared with deep admiration at the little woman beside him on the sofa. "It must be most awfully difficult to do a thing like that."

"Not in the least," she said. "I stuff *all* my little pets myself when they pass away. Will you have another cup of tea?"

"No, thank you," Billy said. The tea tasted faintly of bitter almonds, and he didn't much care for it.

"You did sign the book, didn't you?"

"Oh, yes."

"That's good. Because later on, if I happen to forget what you were called, then I can always come down here and look it up. I still do that almost every day with Mr. Mulholland and Mr. . . . Mr. . . ."

"Temple," Billy said. "Gregory Temple. Excuse my asking, but haven't there been *any* other guests here except them in the last two or three years?"

Holding her teacup high in one hand, inclining her head slightly to the left, she looked up at him out of the corners of her eyes and gave him another gentle little smile.

"No, my dear," she said. "Only you."

STANLEY ELLIN

(1916–1986)

Like Roald Dahl, Stanley Ellin is a master of the wicked story, the delightful yet dark tale in which the reader enjoys a character's horrible predicament. Ellin once said that the crime genre offered him an infinite diversity of theme and treatment. In fact, in his great creativity he rarely used the typical whodunit devices without reshaping them to his own purposes. His volume Mystery Stories *(1956) has been called one of the finest collections ever written in the genre. He set the tone with his first story, "The Specialty of the House" (1948), about a particularly delicious but hideous dish served at a gourmet restaurant. Frederick Dannay, editor of* Ellery Queen's Mystery Magazine, *immediately recognized the story's brilliance upon its arrival at the magazine, and he was instrumental in launching Ellin's career. Ellin won an Edgar Allan Poe award for "The House Party" in 1954, then again in 1956 for "The Blessington Method," a look at a future society in which the elderly are murdered at the behest of their relatives. Many of his stories became classic episodes of the television series* Alfred Hitchcock Presents. *Educated at Brooklyn College in New York, he served in the army in World War II, then worked as a dairyman, steelworker, and teacher. He became a full-time writer in 1948 and wrote many excellent novels including* The Eighth Circle *(1958) and* Mirror, Mirror on the Wall *(1972), but his reputation has always been strongest in the short story form. A methodical perfectionist, Ellin produced stories at the rate of only about one a year, yet he is credited by some with changing the emphasis of the mid-century crime story toward the imaginative and psychological. The following selection is another of Ellin's gems. In a clever reversal of plot the reader is drawn uncomfortably into sympathy for the seducer who is seduced, the predator who is trapped.*

THE ORDERLY WORLD OF MR. APPLEBY

Mr. Appleby was a small, prim man who wore rimless spectacles, parted his graying hair in the middle, and took sober pleasure in pointing out that there was no room in the properly organized life for the operations of Chance. Consequently, when he decided that the time had come to investigate the most efficient methods for disposing of his wife he knew where to look.

He found the book, a text on forensic medicine, on the shelf of a secondhand bookshop among several volumes of like topic, and since all but one were in a distressingly shabby and dog-eared state which offended him to his very core, he chose the only one in reasonably good condition. Most of the cases it presented, he discovered on closer examination, were horrid studies of the results (vividly illustrated) of madness and lust—enough to set any decent man wondering at the number of monsters inhabiting the earth. One case, however, seemed to be exactly what he was looking for, and this he made the object of his most intensive study.

It was the case of Mrs. X (the book was replete with Mrs. X's, and Mr. Y's, and Miss Z's), who died after what was presumably an accidental fall on a scatter rug in her home. However, a lawyer representing the interests of the late lamented charged her husband with murder, and at a coroner's investigation was attempting to prove his charge when the accused abruptly settled matters by dropping dead of a heart attack.

All this was of moderate interest to Mr. Appleby, whose motive, a desire to come into the immediate possession of his wife's estate, was strikingly similar to the alleged motive of Mrs. X's husband. But more important were the actual details of the case. Mrs. X had been in the act of bringing him a glass of water, said her husband, when the scatter rug, as scatter rugs will, had suddenly slipped from under her feet.

In rebuttal the indefatigable lawyer had produced a medical authority who made clear through a number of charts (all of which were handsomely reproduced in the book) that in the act of receiving the glass of water it would have been child's-play for the husband to lay one hand behind his wife's shoulder, another hand along her jaw, and with a sudden thrust produce the same drastic results as the fall on the scatter rug, without leaving any clues as to the nature of his crime.

It should be made clear now that in studying these charts and explanations relentlessly, Mr. Appleby was not acting the part of the greedy man going to any lengths to appease that greed. True, it was money he wanted, but it was money for the maintenance of what he regarded as a holy cause. And that was the Shop: *Appleby, Antiques and Curios.*

The Shop was the sun of Mr. Appleby's universe. He had bought it twenty years before with the pittance left by his father, and at best it provided him with a poor living. At worst—and it was usually at worst—it had forced him to draw on his mother's meager store of goodwill and capital. Since his mother was not one to give up a penny lightly, the Shop brought about a series of pitched battles which, however, always saw it the victor—since in the last analysis, the Shop was to Mr. Appleby what Mr. Appleby was to his mother.

This unhappy triangle was finally shattered by his mother's death, at which time Mr. Appleby discovered that she had played a far greater role in maintaining his orderly little world than he had hitherto realized. This concerned not only the money she occasionally gave him, but also his personal habits.

He ate lightly and warily. His mother had been adept at toasting and boiling his meals to perfection. His nerves were violently shaken if anything in the house was out of place, and she had been a living assurance he would be spared this. Her death, therefore, left a vast and uncomfortable gap in his life, and in studying methods to fill it he was led to contemplate marriage, and then to the act itself.

His wife was a pale, thin-lipped woman so much like his mother in appearance and gesture that sometimes on her entrance into a room he was taken aback by the resemblance. In only one respect did she fail him: she could not understand the significance of the Shop, nor his feelings about it. That was disclosed the first time he broached the subject of a small loan that would enable him to meet some business expenses.

Mrs. Appleby had been well in the process of withering on the vine when her husband-to-be had proposed to her, but to give her full due she was not won by the mere prospect of finally making a marriage. Actually, though she would have blushed at such a blunt statement of her secret thought, it was the large mournful eyes behind his rimless spectacles that turned the trick, promising, as they did, hidden depths of emotion neatly garbed in utter respectability. When she learned very soon after her wedding that the hidden depths were evidently too well hidden ever to be explored by her, she shrugged the matter off and turned to boiling and toasting his meals with good enough grace. The knowledge that the impressive *Appleby, Antiques and Curios* was a hollow shell she took in a different spirit.

She made some brisk investigations and then announced her findings to Mr. Appleby with some heat.

"Antiques and curios!" she said shrilly. "Why, that whole collection of stuff is nothing but a pile of junk. Just a bunch of worthless dust-catchers, that's all it is!"

What she did not understand was that these objects, which to the crass and commercial eye might seem worthless, were to Mr. Appleby the stuff of life itself. The Shop had grown directly from his childhood mania for collecting, assorting, labeling, and preserving anything he could lay his hands on. And the value of any item in the Shop increased proportionately with the length of time he possessed it; whether a cracked imitation of Sèvres, or clumsily faked Chippendale, or rusty saber made no difference. Each piece had won a place for itself, a permanent, immutable place, as far as Mr. Appleby was concerned; and strangely enough it was the sincere agony he suffered in giving up a piece that led to the few sales he made. The customer who was uncertain of values had only to get a glimpse of this agony to be convinced that he was getting a rare bargain. Fortunately, no customer could have imagined for a moment that it was the thought of the empty space left by the object's departure—the brief disorder which the emptiness made—and not a passion for the object itself that drew Mr. Appleby's pinched features into a mask of pain.

So, not understanding, Mrs. Appleby took an unsympathetic tack. "You'll get my mite when I'm dead and gone," she said, "and only when I'm dead and gone."

Thus unwittingly she tried herself, was found wanting, and it only remained for sentence to be executed. When the time came, Mr. Appleby applied the lessons he had gleaned from his invaluable textbook and found them accurate in every detail. It was over quickly, quietly, and outside of a splash of water on his trousers, neatly. The Medical Examiner growled something about those indescribable scatter rugs costing more lives than drunken motorists; the policeman in charge kindly offered to do whatever he could in the way of making funeral arrangements; and that was all there was to it.

It had been so easy—so undramatic, in fact—that it was not until a week later when a properly sympathetic lawyer was making him an accounting of his wife's estate that Mr. Appleby suddenly understood the whole, magnificent new world that had been opened up to him.

Discretion must sometimes outweigh sentiment, and Mr. Appleby was, if anything, a discreet man. After his wife's estate had been cleared, the Shop was moved to another location far from its original setting. It was moved again after the sudden demise of the second Mrs. Appleby, and by the time the sixth Mrs. Appleby had been disposed of, the removals were merely part of a fruitful pattern.

Because of their similarities—they were all pale, thin-featured women with pinched lips, adept at toasting and boiling, and adamant on the subjects of regularity and order—Mr. Appleby was inclined to remember his departed wives rather vaguely en masse. Only in one regard did he qualify them: the number of digits their bank accounts totaled up to. For that reason he thought of the first two Mrs. Applebys as Fours; the third as a Three (an unpleasant surprise); and the last three as Fives. The sum would have been a pretty penny by anyone else's standards, but since each succeeding portion of it had been snapped up by the insatiable *Appleby, Antiques and Curios*—in much the way a fly is snapped up by a hungry lizard—Mr. Appleby found himself soon after the burial of the sixth Mrs. Appleby in deeper and warmer financial waters than ever. So desperate were his circumstances that although he dreamed of another Five, he would have settled for a Four on the spot. It was at this opportune moment that Martha Sturgis entered his life, and after fifteen minutes' conversation with her he brushed all thoughts of Fours and Fives from his mind.

Martha Sturgis, it seemed, was a Six.

It was not only in the extent of her fortune that she broke the pattern established by the women of Mr. Appleby's previous experience. Unlike them, Martha Sturgis was a large, rather shapeless woman who in person, dress, and manner might almost be called (Mr. Appleby shuddered a little at the word) blowsy.

It was remotely possible that properly veneered, harnessed, coiffured, and appareled, she might have been made into something presentable, but from all indications Martha Sturgis was a woman who went out of her way to defy such conventions. Her hair, dyed a shocking orange-red, was piled carelessly on her head; her blobby features were recklessly powdered and painted entirely to their disadvantage; her clothes, obviously worn for comfort, were, at the same time, painfully garish; and her shoes gave evidence of long and pleasurable wear without corresponding care being given their upkeep.

Of all this and its effect on the beholder, Martha Sturgis seemed totally unaware. She strode through *Appleby, Antiques and Curios* with an energy that set movable objects dancing in their places; she smoked incessantly, lighting one cigarette from another, while Mr. Appleby fanned the air before his face and coughed suggestively; and she talked without pause, loudly and in a deep, hoarse voice that dinned strangely in a Shop so accustomed to the higher, thinner note.

In the first fourteen minutes of their acquaintance, the one quality she displayed that led Mr. Appleby to modify some of his immediate revulsion even a trifle was the care with which she priced each article. She examined, evaluated, and cross-examined in detail before moving on with obvious disapproval; and he moved along with her with mounting assurance that he could get her out of the Shop before any damage was done to the stock or his patience. And then in the fifteenth minute she spoke the Word.

"I've got half a million dollars in the bank," Martha Sturgis remarked with cheerful contempt, "but I never thought I'd get around to spending a nickel of it on this kind of stuff."

Mr. Appleby had his hand before his face preparatory to waving aside some of the tobacco smoke that eddied about him. In the time it took the hand to drop nervelessly to his side, his mind attacked an astonishing number of problems. One concerned the important finger on her left hand which was ringless; the others concerned certain mathematical problems largely dealing with short-term notes, long-term notes, and rates of interest. By the time the hand touched his side, the problems, as far as Mr. Appleby was concerned, were well on the way to solution.

And it may be noted, there was an added fillip given the matter by the very nature of Martha Sturgis's slovenly and strident being. Looking at her after she had spoken the Word, another man might perhaps have seen her through the sort of veil that a wise photographer casts over the lens of his camera in taking the picture of a prosperous but unprepossessing subject. Mr. Appleby, incapable of such self-deceit, girded himself instead with the example of the man who carried a heavy weight on his back for the pleasure it gave him in laying it down. Not only would the final act of a marriage to Martha Sturgis solve important mathematical problems, but it was an act he could play out with the gusto of a man ridding the world of an unpleasant object.

Therefore he turned his eyes, more melancholy and luminous than ever, on her and said, "It's a great pity, Mrs.—"

She told him her name, emphasizing the "Miss" before it, and Mr. Appleby smiled apologetically.

"Of course. As I was saying, it's a great pity when someone of refinement and culture—" (the "like yourself" floated delicately unsaid on the air) "—should never have known the joy in possession of fine works of art. But, as we all learn, it is never too late to begin, is it?"

Martha Sturgis looked at him sharply and then laughed a hearty bellow of laughter that stabbed his eardrums painfully. For a moment, Mr. Appleby, a man not much given to humor, wondered darkly if he had unwittingly uttered something so excruciatingly epigrammatic that it was bound to have this alarming effect.

"My dear man," said Martha Sturgis, "if it is your idea that I am here to start cluttering up my life with your monstrosities, perish the thought. What I'm here for is to buy a gift for a friend, a thoroughly infuriating and loathsome person who happens to have the nature and disposition of a bar of stainless steel. I can't think of a better way of showing my feelings toward her than by presenting her with almost anything displayed in your shop. If possible, I should also like delivery arranged so that I can be on the scene when she receives the package."

Mr. Appleby staggered under this, then rallied valiantly. "In that case," he said, and shook his head firmly, "it is out of the question. Completely out of the question."

"Nonsense," Martha Sturgis said. "I'll arrange for delivery myself if you can't handle it. Really, you ought to understand that there's no point in doing this sort of thing unless you're on hand to watch the results."

Mr. Appleby kept tight rein on his temper. "I am not alluding to the matter of delivery," he said. "What I am trying to make clear is that I cannot possibly permit anything in my Shop to be bought in such a spirit. Not for any price you could name."

Martha Sturgis's heavy jaw dropped. "What was that you said?" she asked blankly.

It was a perilous moment, and Mr. Appleby knew it. His next words could set her off into another spasm of that awful laughter that would devastate him completely; or, worse, could send her right out of the Shop forever; or could decide the issue in his favor then and there. But it was a moment that had to be met, and, thought Mr. Appleby desperately, whatever else Martha Sturgis might be, she was a Woman.

He took a deep breath. "It is the policy of this Shop," he said quietly, "never to sell anything unless the prospective purchaser shows full appreciation for the article to be bought and can assure it the care and devotion to which it is entitled. That has always been the policy, and always will be as long as I am here. Anything other than that I would regard as desecration."

He watched Martha Sturgis with bated breath. There was a chair nearby, and she dropped into it heavily so that her skirts were drawn tight by her widespread thighs and the obscene shoes were displayed mercilessly. She lit another cigarette, regarding him meanwhile with narrowed eyes through the flame of the match, and then fanned the air a little to dispel the cloud of smoke.

"You know," she said, "this is very interesting. I'd like to hear more about it."

To the inexperienced, the problem of drawing information of

the most personal nature from a total stranger would seem a perplexing one. To Mr. Appleby, whose interests had so often been dependent on such information, it was no problem at all. In very short time he had evidence that Martha Sturgis's estimate of her fortune was quite accurate; that she was apparently alone in the world without relatives or intimate friends; and—that she was not averse to the idea of marriage.

This last he drew from her during her now regular visits to the Shop where she would spread herself comfortably on a chair and talk to him endlessly. Much of her talk was about her father, to whom Mr. Appleby evidently bore a striking resemblance.

"He even dressed like you," Martha Sturgis said reflectively. "Neat as a pin, and not only about himself, either. He used to make an inspection of the house every day—march through and make sure everything was exactly where it had to be. And he kept it up right to the end. I remember an hour before he died how he went about straightening pictures on the wall."

Mr. Appleby, who had been peering with some irritation at a picture that hung slightly awry on the Shop wall, turned his attentions reluctantly from it.

"And you were with him to the end?" he asked sympathetically.

"Indeed I was."

"Well," Mr. Appleby said brightly, "one does deserve some reward for such sacrifice, doesn't one? Especially—and I hope this will not embarrass you, Miss Sturgis—when one considers that such a woman as yourself could undoubtedly have left the care of an aged father to enter matrimony almost at will. Isn't that so?"

Martha Sturgis sighed. "Maybe it is, and maybe it isn't," she said, "and I won't deny that I've had my dreams. But that's all they are, and I suppose that's all they ever will be."

"Why?" asked Mr. Appleby encouragingly.

"Because," said Martha Sturgis somberly, "I have never yet met the man who could fit those dreams. I am not a simpering schoolgirl, Mr. Appleby; I don't have to balance myself against my bank account to know why any man would devote himself to me, and frankly, his motives would be of no interest. But he must be a decent, respectable man who would spend every moment of his life worrying about me and caring for me; and he must be a man who would make the memory of my father a living thing."

Mr. Appleby rested a hand lightly on her shoulder.

"Miss Sturgis," he said gravely, "you may yet meet such a man."

She looked at him with features that were made even more blobby and unattractive by her emotion

"Do you mean that, Mr. Appleby?" she asked. "Do you really believe that?"

Faith glowed in Mr. Appleby's eyes as he smiled down at her. "He may be closer than you dare realize," he said warmly.

Experience had proved to Mr. Appleby that once the ice is broken, the best thing to do is take a deep breath and plunge in. Accordingly, he let very few days elapse before he made his proposal.

"Miss Sturgis," he said, "there comes a time to every lonely man when he can no longer bear his loneliness. If at such a time he is fortunate enough to meet the one woman to whom he could give unreservedly all his respect and tender feelings, he is a fortunate man indeed. Miss Sturgis—I am that man."

"Why, Mr. Appleby!" said Martha Sturgis, coloring a trifle. "That's really very good of you, but . . ."

At this note of indecision his heart sank. "Wait!" he interposed hastily. "If you have any doubts, Miss Sturgis, please speak them now so that I may answer them. Considering the state of my emotions, that would only be fair, wouldn't it?"

"Well, I suppose so," said Martha Sturgis. "You see, Mr. Appleby, I'd rather not get married at all than take the chance of getting someone who wasn't prepared to give me exactly what I'm looking for in marriage: absolute, single-minded devotion all the rest of my days."

"Miss Sturgis," said Mr. Appleby solemnly, "I am prepared to give you no less."

"Men say these things so easily," she sighed. "But—I shall certainly think about it, Mr. Appleby."

The dismal prospect of waiting an indefinite time for a woman of such careless habits to render a decision was not made any lighter by the sudden receipt a few days later of a note peremptorily requesting Mr. Appleby's presence at the offices of Gainsborough, Gainsborough, and Golding, attorneys-at-law. With his creditors closing in like a wolf pack, Mr. Appleby could only surmise the worst, and he was pleasantly surprised upon his arrival at Gainsborough, Gainsborough, and Golding to find that they represented, not his creditors, but Martha Sturgis herself.

The elder Gainsborough, obviously very much the guiding spirit of the firm, was a short, immensely fat man with pendulous dewlaps that almost concealed his collar, and large fishy eyes that goggled at Mr. Appleby. The younger Gainsborough was a duplicate of his brother—with jowls not quite so impressive—while Golding was an impassive young man with a hatchet face.

"This," said the elder Gainsborough, his eyes fixed glassily on Mr. Appleby, "is a delicate matter. Miss Sturgis, an esteemed client—" the younger Gainsborough nodded at this "—has mentioned entering matrimony with you, sir."

Mr. Appleby, sitting primly on his chair, was stirred by a pleased excitement. "Yes?" he said.

"And," continued the elder Gainsborough, "while Miss Sturgis is perfectly willing to concede that her fortune may be the object of attraction in any suitor's eyes—" he held up a pudgy hand to cut short Mr. Appleby's shocked protest "—she is also willing to dismiss that issue—"

"To ignore it, set it aside," said the younger Gainsborough sternly.

"—if the suitor is prepared to meet all other expectations in marriage."

"I am," said Mr. Appleby fervently.

"Mr. Appleby," said the elder Gainsborough abruptly, "have you been married before?"

Mr. Appleby thought swiftly. Denial would make any chance word about his past a deadly trap; admission, on the other hand, was a safeguard against that, and a thoroughly respectable one.

"Yes," he said.

"Divorced?"

"Good heavens, no!" said Mr. Appleby, genuinely shocked.

The Gainsboroughs looked at each other in approval. "Good," said the elder, "very good. Perhaps, Mr. Appleby, the question seemed impertinent, but in these days of moral laxity . . ."

"I should like it known in that case," said Mr. Appleby sturdily, "that I am as far from moral laxity as any human being can be. Tobacco, strong drink, and—ah—"

"Loose women," said the younger Gainsborough briskly.

"Yes," said Mr. Appleby, reddening, "are unknown to me."

The elder Gainsborough nodded. "Under any conditions," he said, "Miss Sturgis will not make any precipitate decision. She should have her answer for you within a month, however, and during that time, if you don't mind taking the advice of an old man, I suggest that you court her assiduously. She is a woman, Mr. Appleby, and I imagine that all women are much alike."

"I imagine they are," said Mr. Appleby.

"Devotion," said the younger Gainsborough. "Constancy. That's the ticket."

What he was being asked to do, Mr. Appleby reflected in one of his solitary moments, was to put aside the Shop and the orderly world it represented and to set the unappealing figure of Martha Sturgis in its place. It was a temporary measure, of course; it was one that would prove richly rewarding when Martha Sturgis had been properly wed and sent the way of the preceding Mrs. Applebys; but it was not made any easier by enforced familiarity with the woman. It was inevitable that since Mr. Appleby viewed matters not only as a prospective bridegroom but also as a prospective widower, so to speak, he found his teeth constantly set on edge by the unwitting irony which crept into so many of her tedious discussions on marriage.

"The way I see it," Martha Sturgis once remarked, "is that a man who would divorce his wife would divorce any other woman he ever married. You take a look at all these broken marriages today, and I'll bet that in practically every case you'll find a man who's always shopping around and never finding what he wants. Now, the man I marry," she said pointedly, "must be willing to settle down and stay settled."

"Of course," said Mr. Appleby.

"I have heard," Martha Sturgis told him on another, and particularly trying, occasion, "that a satisfactory marriage increases a woman's span of years. That's an excellent argument for marriage, don't you think?"

"Of course," said Mr. Appleby.

It seemed to him that during that month of trial, most of his conversation was restricted to the single phrase "of course," delivered with varying inflections; but the tactic must have been the proper one, since at the end of the month he was able to change the formula to "I do," in a wedding ceremony at which Gainsborough, Gainsborough, and Golding were the sole guests.

Immediately afterward, Mr. Appleby (to his discomfort) was borne off with his bride to a photographer's shop where innumerable pictures were made under the supervision of the dour Golding, following which, Mr. Appleby (to his delight) exchanged documents with his wife which made them each other's heirs to all properties, possessions, et cetera, whatsoever.

If Mr. Appleby had occasionally appeared rather abstracted during these festivities, it was only because his mind was neatly arranging the program of impending events. The rug (the very same one that had served so well in six previous episodes) had to be placed; and then there would come the moment when he would ask for a glass of water, when he would place one hand on her shoulder, and with the other . . . It could not be a moment that took place without due time passing; yet it could not be forestalled too long in view of the pressure exercised by the Shop's voracious creditors. Watching the pen in his wife's hand as she signed her will, he decided there would be time within a few weeks. With the will in his possession there would be no point in waiting longer than that.

Before the first of those weeks was up, however, Mr. Appleby knew that even this estimate would have to undergo drastic revision. There was no question about it: he was simply not equipped to cope with his marriage.

For one thing, her home (and now his), a brownstone cavern inherited from her mother, was a nightmare of disorder. On the principle, perhaps, that anything flung casually aside was not worth picking up since it would only be flung aside again, an amazing litter had accumulated in every room. The contents of brimming closets and drawers were recklessly exchanged, mislaid, or added to the general litter, and over all lay a thin film of dust. On Mr. Appleby's quivering nervous system all this had the effect of a fingernail dragging along an endless blackboard.

The one task to which Mrs. Appleby devoted herself, as it happened, was the one which her husband prayerfully wished she would spare herself. She doted on cookery, and during mealtimes would trudge back and forth endlessly between kitchen and dining room laden with dishes outside any of Mr. Appleby's experience.

At his first feeble protests, his wife had taken pains to explain in precise terms that she was sensitive to any criticism of her cooking, even the implied criticism of a partly emptied plate; and, thereafter, Mr. Appleby, plunging hopelessly through rare meats, rich sauces, and heavy pastries, found added to his tribulations the incessant pangs of dyspepsia. Nor were his pains eased by his wife's insistence that he prove himself a trencherman of her mettle. She would thrust plates heaped high with indigestibles under his quivering nose; and, bracing himself like a martyr facing the lions, Mr. Appleby would empty his portion into a digestive tract that cried for simple fare properly boiled or toasted.

It became one of his fondest waking dreams, that scene where he returned from his wife's burial to dine on hot tea and toast and, perhaps, a medium-boiled egg. But even that dream and its sequel—where he proceeded to set the house in order—were not sufficient to buoy him up each day when he awoke and reflected on what lay ahead of him.

Each day found his wife more insistent in her demands for his attentions. And on that day when she openly reproved him for devoting more of those attentions to the Shop than to herself, Mr. Appleby knew the time had come to prepare for the final act. He brought home the rug that evening and carefully laid it in place between the living room and the hallway that led to the kitchen. Martha Appleby watched him without any great enthusiasm.

"That's a shabby-looking thing, all right," she said. "What is it, Appie, an antique or something?"

She had taken to calling him by that atrocious name and seemed cheerfully oblivious to the way he winced under it. He winced now.

"It is not an antique," Mr. Appleby admitted, "but I hold it dear for many reasons. It has a great deal of sentimental value to me."

Mrs. Appleby smiled fondly at him. "And you brought it for me, didn't you?"

"Yes," said Mr. Appleby, "I did."

"You're a dear," said Mrs. Appleby. "You really are."

Watching her cross the rug on slipshod feet to use the telephone, which stood on a small table the other side of the hallway, Mr. Appleby toyed with the idea that since she used the telephone at about the same time every evening, he could schedule the accident for that time. The advantages were obvious: since those calls seemed to be the only routine she observed with any fidelity, she would cross the rug at a certain time, and he would be in a position to settle matters then and there.

However, thought Mr. Appleby as he polished his spectacles, that brought up the problem of how best to approach her under such circumstances. Clearly the tried and tested methods were best, but if the telephone call and the glass of water could be synchronized . . .

"A penny for your thoughts, Appie," said Mrs. Appleby brightly. She had laid down the telephone and crossed the hallway so that she stood squarely on the rug. Mr. Appleby replaced his spectacles and peered at her through them.

"I wish," he said querulously, "you would not address me by that horrid name. You know I detest it."

"Nonsense," his wife said briefly. "I think it's cute."

"I do not."

"Well, I like it," said Mrs. Appleby with the air of one who has settled a matter once and for all. "Anyhow," she pouted, "that couldn't have been what you were thinking about before I started talking to you, could it?"

It struck Mr. Appleby that when this stout, unkempt woman pouted, she resembled nothing so much as a wax doll badly worn by time and handling. He pushed away the thought to frame some suitable answer.

"As it happens," he said, "my mind was on the disgraceful state of my clothes. Need I remind you again that there are buttons missing from practically every garment I own?"

Mrs. Appleby yawned broadly. "I'll get to it sooner or later."

"Tomorrow perhaps?"

"I doubt it," said Mrs. Appleby. She turned toward the stairs. "Come to sleep, Appie. I'm dead tired."

Mr. Appleby followed her thoughtfully. Tomorrow, he knew, he would have to get one of his suits to the tailor if he wanted to have anything fit to wear at the funeral.

He had brought home the suit and hung it neatly away; he had eaten his dinner; and he had sat in the living room listening to his wife's hoarse voice go on for what seemed interminable hours, although the clock was not yet at nine.

Now, with rising excitement, he saw her lift herself slowly from her chair and cross the room to the hallway. As she reached for the telephone Mr. Appleby cleared his throat sharply. "If you don't mind," he said, "I'd like a glass of water."

Mrs. Appleby turned to look at him. "A glass of water?"

"If you don't mind," said Mr. Appleby, and waited as she hesitated, then set down the telephone, and turned toward the kitchen. There was the sound of a glass being rinsed in the kitchen, and then Mrs. Appleby came up to him holding it out. He laid one hand appreciatively on her plump shoulder, and then lifted the other as if to brush back a strand of untidy hair at her cheek.

"Is that what happened to all the others?" said Mrs. Appleby quietly.

Mr. Appleby felt his hand freeze in midair and the chill from it run down into his marrow. "Others?" he managed to say. "What others?"

His wife smiled grimly at him, and he saw that the glass of water in her hand was perfectly steady. "Six others," she said. "That is, six by my count. Why? Were there any more?"

"No," he said, then caught wildly at himself. "I don't understand what you're talking about!"

"Dear Appie. Surely you couldn't forget six wives just like that. Unless, of course, I've come to mean so much to you that you can't bear to think of the others. That would be a lovely thing to happen, wouldn't it?"

"I was married before," Mr. Appleby said loudly. "I made that quite clear myself. But this talk about six wives!"

"Of course you were married before, Appie. And it was quite easy to find out to whom—and it was just as easy to find out about the one before that—and all the others. Or even about your mother, or where you went to school, or where you were born. You see, Appie, Mr. Gainsborough is really a very clever man."

"Then it was Gainsborough who put you up to this!"

"Not at all, you foolish little man," his wife said contemptuously. "All the time you were making your plans I was unmaking them. From the moment I laid eyes on you I knew you for what you are. Does that surprise you?"

Mr. Appleby struggled with the emotions of a man who had picked up a twig to find a viper in his hand. "How could you know?" he gasped.

"Because you were the image of my father. Because in everything—the way you dress, your insufferable neatness, your priggish arrogance, the little moral lectures you dote on—you are what he was. And all my life I hated him for what he was, and what it did to my mother. He married her for her money, made her every day a nightmare, and then killed her for what was left of her fortune."

"Killed her?" said Mr. Appleby, stupefied.

"Oh, come," his wife said sharply. "Do you think you're the only man who was ever capable of that? Yes, he killed her—murdered her, if you prefer—by asking for a glass of water and then breaking her neck when she offered it to him. A method strangely similar to yours, isn't it?"

Mr. Appleby found the incredible answer rising to his mind, but refused to accept it. "What happened to him?" he demanded. "Tell me, what happened! Was he caught?"

"No, he was never caught. There were no witnesses to what he did, but Mr. Gainsborough had been my mother's lawyer, a dear friend of hers. He had suspicions and demanded a hearing. He brought a doctor to the hearing who made it plain how my father could have killed her and made it look as if she had slipped on a rug, but before there was any decision my father died of a heart attack."

"That was the case—the case I read!" Mr. Appleby groaned, and then was silent under his wife's sardonic regard.

"When he was gone," she went on inexorably, "I swore I would someday find a man exactly like that, and I would make that man live the life my father should have lived. I would know his every habit and every taste, and none of them should go satisfied. I would know he married me for my money, and he would never get a penny of it until I was dead and gone. And that would be a long, long time, because he would spend his life taking care that I should live out my life to the last possible breath."

Mr. Appleby pulled his wits together, and saw that despite her emotion, she had remained in the same position. "How can you make him do that?" he asked softly, and moved an inch closer.

"It does sound strange, doesn't it, Appie?" she observed. "But hardly as strange as the fact that your six wives died by slipping on a rug—very much like this one—while bringing you a glass of water—very much like this one. So strange that Mr. Gainsborough was led to remark that too many coincidences will certainly hang a man. Especially if there is reason to bring them to light in a trial for murder."

Mr. Appleby suddenly found the constriction of his collar unbearable. "That doesn't answer my question," he said craftily. "How can you make sure that I would devote my life to prolonging yours?"

"A man whose wife is in a position to have him hanged should be able to see that clearly."

"No," said Mr. Appleby in a stifled voice, "I only see that such a man is forced to rid himself of his wife as quickly as possible."

"Ah, but that's where the arrangements come in."

"Arrangements? What arrangements?" demanded Mr. Appleby.

"I'd like very much to explain them," his wife said. "In fact, I see the time has come when it's imperative to do so. But I do find it uncomfortable standing here like this."

"Never mind that," said Mr. Appleby impatiently, and his wife shrugged.

"Well, then," she said coolly, "Mr. Gainsborough now has all the documents about your marriages—the way the previous deaths took place, the way you always happened to get the bequests at just the right moment to pay your shop's debts.

"Besides this, he has a letter from me, explaining that in the event of my death an investigation be made immediately and all necessary action be taken. Mr. Gainsborough is really very efficient. The fingerprints and photographs . . ."

"Fingerprints and photographs!" cried Mr. Appleby.

"Of course. After my father's death it was found that he had made all preparations for a quick trip abroad. Mr. Gainsborough has assured me that in case you had such ideas in mind you should get rid of them. No matter where you are, he said, it will be quite easy to bring you back again."

"What do you want of me?" asked Mr. Appleby numbly. "Surely you don't expect me to stay now, and—"

"Oh, yes, I do. And since we've come to this point, I may as well tell you I expect you to give up your useless shop once and for all, and make it a point to be at home with me the entire day."

"Give up the Shop!" he exclaimed.

"You must remember, Appie, that in my letter asking for a full investigation at my death, I did not specify death by any particular means. I look forward to a long and pleasant life with you always at my side, and perhaps—mind you, I only say perhaps—someday I shall turn over that letter and all the evidence to you. You can see how much it is to your interest, therefore, to watch over me very carefully."

The telephone rang with abrupt violence, and Mrs. Appleby nodded toward it. "Almost as carefully," she said softly, "as Mr. Gainsborough. Unless I call him every evening at nine to report I am well and happy, it seems he will jump to the most shocking conclusions."

"Wait," said Mr. Appleby. He lifted the telephone, and there was no mistaking the voice that spoke.

"Hello," said the elder Gainsborough. "Hello, Mrs. Appleby?"

Mr. Appleby essayed a cunning move. "No," he said, "I'm afraid she can't speak to you now. What is it?"

The voice in his ear took on an unmistakable cold menace. "This is Gainsborough, Mr. Appleby, and I wish to speak to your wife immediately. I will give you ten seconds to have her at this telephone, Mr. Appleby. Do you understand?"

Mr. Appleby turned dully toward his wife and held out the telephone. "It's for you," he said, and then saw with a start of terror that as she turned to set down the glass of water, the rug skidded slightly under her feet. Her arms flailed the air as she fought for balance; the glass smashed at his feet, drenching his neat trousers; and her face twisted into a silent scream. Then her body struck the floor and lay inertly in the position with which he was so familiar.

Watching her, he was barely conscious of the voice emerging tinnily from the telephone in his hand.

"The ten seconds are up, Mr. Appleby," it said shrilly. "Do you understand? *Your time is up!*"

CHRISTIANNA BRAND

(1909–1988)

*Born in Malaya (now Malaysia), Christianna Brand (Mary Christianna Milne) spent her childhood in India, then was sent to England to be educated in a Franciscan convent. She worked in a variety of occupations—as model, governess, dancer, salesperson, and secretary—all providing material for her writing. A versatile author, she published screenplays, short stories, and crime, juvenile, and mainstream novels under several pseudonyms. Although she said she wrote simply to entertain, she was a careful editor of her own work and intended that her novels would also be of interest purely as novels, to general readers who were not mystery fans. Nonetheless, Brand was renowned for her inventive use of the conventions of the mystery, cleverly employing intricate plotting, false clues, surprise endings, and an engaging group of least likely suspects. Her series character, Inspector Cockrill of the Kent County Police, is a traditional oddball detective, cranky and shabby but able to sniff out the significant clue from numerous red herrings. She was very concerned to make the "regulation puzzle" scrupulously fair to the reader. As might be expected from a writer whose first novel (*Death in High Heels, *1941) appeared as the golden age was fading, her work provides the pleasures we associate with such writers as Agatha Christie and Dorothy L. Sayers. What keeps her work from appearing to be a nostalgic survival, however, is her ironic sense of humor. It winks to the reader as if author and audience share the secret of a guilty pleasure. In the following story, we see Brand breathing new vitality into the conventional pattern of the character drawn into destruction. An elderly woman invites a homeless couple into her life. It all sounds familiar and creates familiar expectations; Brand, however, has some unusual surprises in store.*

BLESS THIS HOUSE

They were beautiful; and even in that first moment, the old woman was to think later, she should have known; should have recognised them for what they were. Standing there so still and quiet in face of her own strident aggression, the boy in the skin-tight blue jeans, with his mac held over his head against the fine drizzle of the evening rain—held over his head like a mantle; the girl with her long hair falling straight as a veil down to the pear-shaped bulge of her pregnancy. But though suspicion died in her, she would not be done out of her grievance. "What you doing here? You got no right here, parking outside my window."

They did not reply that after all the street did not belong to her. The girl said only, apologetically: "We got nowhere else to sleep."

"Nowhere to sleep?" She glanced at the ringless hand holding together the edges of the skimpy coat. "Can't you go home?"

"Our homes aren't in London," said the boy.

"You slept somewhere last night."

"We had to leave. The landlady—Mrs. Mace—she went away and her nephew was coming home and wanted the place. We've been hunting and hunting for days. No one else will take us in."

"Because of the baby," said the girl. "In case it comes, you see."

Suspicion gleamed again. "Well, don't look at me. I got nothing, only my one bed-sit, here in the basement—the other rooms are used for storage, all locked up and bolted. And upstairs—well, that's full."

"Oh, of course," said the girl. "We didn't mean that at all. We were sleeping in the car."

"In the car?" she stood at the top of the area steps peering at them in the light of the street lamp, shawled, also against the rain. She said to the boy: "You can't let her sleep in that thing. Not like she is."

"Well, I know," he said. "But what else? That's why we came to this quiet part."

"We'll move along of course," said the girl, "if you mind our being here."

"It's a public street," she said illogically. But it was pitiful, poor young thing; and there was about them this—something: so beautiful, so still and quiet, expressionless, almost colourless, like figures in some dim old church, candle-lit at—yes, at Christmas time. Like figures in a Christmas crèche. She said uncertainly: "If a few bob would help—"

But they disclaimed at once. "No, no, we've got money; well, enough, anyway. And he can get work in the morning, it's nothing like that. It's only . . . Well," said the girl, spreading slow, explanatory hands, "it's like we told you. The baby's coming and no one will take us in. They just say, sorry—no room."

Was it then that she had known?—when she heard herself saying, almost without her own volition: "Out in the back garden—there's a sort of shed . . ."

It was the strain, perhaps, the uncertainty, the long day's search for accommodation, the fading hope; but the baby came that night. No time for doctor or midwife; but Mrs. Vaughan was experienced in such matters, delivered the child safely, dealt with the young mother—unexpectedly resilient despite her fragile look, calm, uncomplaining, apparently impervious to the pain—settled her comfortably at last on the old mattress in the shed, covered over with clean bedclothes. "When you're fit to be moved—we'll see." And to the boy she said sharply "What you got there?"

He had employed the waiting time in knocking together a sort of cradle out of a wooden box; padded it round and fitted it with a couple of down-filled cushions from their car. Taken nothing of hers; all the things were their own. "Look, Marilyn—for the baby."

"Oh, Jo," she said, "you always were a bit of a carpenter! You always were good with your hands!"

Joseph. And Marilyn. And Joseph a bit of a carpenter, clever with his hands. And a boy child born in an outhouse because there was no room elsewhere for his coming . . . She got down slowly on to her thick, arthritic knees beside the mattress and, with something like awe in her heart, gathered the baby from his mother's arms. "I'll lay him in the box. It'll do for him lovely." And under her breath: "He won't be the first," she said.

The boy left money with her next day for necessities and went out and duly returned that evening with news of a job on a building site; and carrying in one scarred hand a small, dropping bunch of flowers which he carefully divided between them, half for Marilyn, half for Mrs. Vaughan—"till I can get you something better"—and one violet left over to place in the baby's tiny mottled fist. "And till I can get *you* something better," he said.

They gave him no name . . . Other young couples, she thought, would have spent the idle hours trying to think up "something different" or christened him after a pop-star, some loose-mouthed, long-haired little good-for-nothing shrieking out nonsense, thin legs kept jerking by drugs in an obscene capering. But no—it was "the baby," "the little one." Perhaps, she thought, they dared not name him; dared not acknowledge, even to themselves . . .

For the huge question in her mind was: how much do they know?

For that matter—how much did she herself know? And what?—what in fact did she know? The Holy Child had been born already, had been born long ago. Vague thoughts of a Second Coming wandered through her brain, but was that not to be a major, a clearly recognizable event, something terrible, presaging the end of all things? The End. And the other had been the Beginning. Perhaps, she thought, there could be a Beginning-Again? Perhaps with everything having gone wrong with the world, there was going to be a second chance . . . ?

It was a long time since she had been to church. In the old days, yes; brought up the two girls to be good Catholics, washed and spruced-up for Mass every Sunday, convents, Catechism, the lot. And much good it had done her—married a couple of heathen GIs in the war and gone off to America for good—for good or ill, she did not know and could no longer care; for years she had heard not a word from either of them. But now . . . She put on her crumpled old hat and, arthritically stumping, went off to St. Stephen's.

It was like being a schoolgirl again, all one's childhood closing in about one; to be kneeling there in the stuffy, curtained darkness, to see the outlined profile crowned by the black hump of the biretta with its pom-pom a-top, leaning against the little iron-work grille that was all that separated them. "In the name of the Father and of the Son and of the Holy Ghost . . . Yes, my child?"

He talked to her quietly and kindly, while waiting penitents shifted restlessly outside, and thought, among their Firm Purposes of Amendment, that the old girl must be having a right old load of sins to cough up. About chance, he spoke, and about coincidence, about having the Holy Child in one's heart and not trying to—well, rationalise things . . . She thanked him, made of old habit the sign of the cross and left. "Them others—*they* didn't recognise Him either," she said to herself.

And she came to her room and saw the quiet face bent over the sleeping baby lying in its wooden cradle; and surely—surely—there was a light about its head?

On pay day, Jo brought in flowers again. But the vase got knocked over almost at once and the flowers and water spilt—there was no room for even the smallest extras in the close little room, now that Marilyn was up and sitting in the armchair with the wooden box beside her and the increasing paraphernalia of babyhood taking up so much of the scanty space. The car was being used as a sort of storage dump for anything not in daily use. "During the week-end," said Jo. "I'll find us a place."

"A place?" she said, as though the idea came freshly to her. But she had dreaded it. "Marilyn can't be moved yet."

"By the end of the week?" he said.

"You've been so good," said Marilyn. "We can't go on taking up your room. We'll have to get somewhere."

But it wasn't so easy. He spent all his evenings, after that, tramping round, searching; but as soon as he mentioned the baby, hearts and doors closed against him. She protested: "But I don't want you to go. I got none of my own now. I like having you here," and she knelt, as so often she did, by the improvised wooden-box cradle and said, worshipping: "And I couldn't lose—Him." And she went out and bought a second-hand bed and fixed that up in the shed, brought Marilyn in to her own bed, was happy to sleep on a mattress on the floor, the box-cradle close to her so that if the child stirred in the night, it was she who could hush it and croon to it and soothe it to sleep again. Is He all-knowing, she would wonder to herself in the dark, does He understand, even though He's so small, does the God-head in Him understand that it's I who hold Him? Will I one day sit at the right hand of the Father because on this earth I nursed His only begotten Son . . . ? (Well, His—second begotten Son . . . ? It was all so difficult. And she dared not ask.)

She had no close friends these days, but at last, one night, a little in her cups, she whispered it to Nellie down at the Dog.

"You'll never guess who I got at my place."

Nellie knocked back her fifth brown ale and volunteered a bawdy suggestion. "A boy and a girl," said Mrs. Vaughan, ignoring it. "And a Baby." And she thought of him lying there in his wooden bed. "His little head," she said. "Behind His little head, you can see, like—a light. Shining in the darkness—a kind of a ring of light."

"You'll see a ring of light round me," said Nellie, robustly, "if you put back another of them barley wines." And to the landlord she confided, when Mrs. Vaughan, a little bit tottery, had gone off home, "I believe she's going off her rocker, honestly I do."

"She looked all right to me," said the landlord, who did not care for his regulars going off their rockers.

"They're after her stocking," said Nellie to the pub at large. "You'll see. Them and their Baby Jesus! They're after what she's got."

And she set a little trap. "Hey, Billy, you work on the same site as this Jo of hers. Give him a knock some day about the old girl's money. Got it in a stocking, saving it up for her funeral. Worried, she is, about being put in the common grave. Well, who isn't? But she, she's proper scared of it."

So Billy strolled up to Jo on the site, next break-time. "I hear you're holed up with old Mother Vaughan, down near the Dog. After her stocking then, are you?" And he pretended knowledge of its place of concealment. "Fill it up with something; she'll never twig till after you've gone. Split me a third to two-thirds if I tell you where it's hid?"

And he looked up for the first time into Jo's face and saw the look that Jo gave him: a look almost—terrible. "He come straight home," Mrs. Vaughan told Nellie in the pub that night, "and—'they're saying you got money, Mrs. V,' he says. 'If you have, you should stash it away somewhere,' he says, 'and let everyone know you've done it. Living here on your tod, it isn't safe for you, people thinking you're worth robbing.' " And he had explained to her how to pay it into the post office so that no one but herself could ever touch it. Only a few quid it was, scrimped and saved for her funeral. "I couldn't a-bear to go into the common grave, not with all them strangers . . ."

"'Never mind the common grave, it'll be the common bin for *you*, if you don't watch out," said Nellie. "You and your Mary and Joseph—they come in a car, didn't they, not on a donkey?"

"You haven't got eyes to see. You don't live with them."

"They've lived other places before you. Did them other landladies have eyes to see?"

What was the name—Mrs. Mace? Had Mrs. Mace had eyes to see, had she recognised, even before the baby came—? "Course not," said Nellie, crossly. "She chucked 'em out, didn't she?"

"No, she never. She was moving out herself to the country, her son or someone needed the flat." But if one could have seen Mrs. Mace, consulted with her . . . "Don't you ever visit your last landlady?" she asked them casually. "Does she live too far?"

"No, not far; but with the baby and all . . . All the same, Marilyn," said Jo, "we ought to go some day soon, just to see she's all right. Take you along," he suggested to Mrs. Vaughan. "You'd enjoy the drive and it's a lovely place, all flowers and trees and a little stream."

"Oh, I wouldn't half like that. I dare say," said Mrs. Vaughan, craftily, "she thought a lot of you, that Mrs. Mace?"

"She was very kind to us," said Marilyn. "Very kind."

"And the baby? She wasn't, like—shocked?"

"Shocked? She was thrilled," said Jo. And he used an odd expression: "Quietly thrilled."

So she *had* known. Mrs. Mace had known. The desire grew strong within Mrs. Vaughan's anxious breast to see Mrs. Mace, to discuss, to question, to talk it all over. With familiarity, with the lessening of the first impact of her own incredulous wonder, it became more difficult to understand that others should not share her faith. "I tell you, I see the light shining behind His head!"

She confided it to strangers on buses, to casual acquaintances on their way to the little local shops. They pretended interest and hastily detached themselves. "Poor thing—another of them loonies," they said with the mirthless sniggers of those who find themselves outside normal experience, beyond their depths. She was becoming notorious, a figure of fun.

The news reached the ears of the landlord, a local man. He came round to the house and afterwards spoke to the boy. "I've told her—you can't all go on living in that one little room, it's not decent."

"There's the shed," said Jo. "I sleep out in the shed."

"You won't like that for long," said the man with a leer.

Billy had seen that look, on the building site. But the boy only said quietly: "You couldn't let us have another room? She says they're only used for storage."

"They're let—storage or not, no business of mine. For that matter," said the man, growing cunning, "it's no business of mine how you live or what you do. Only . . . Well, three and a kid for the price of one—"

"I'll pay extra if that's it," said Jo. "I could manage that. It's only that I can't find anywhere else, not at the price I could afford."

"Just between the two of us, then. Though how you put up with it," he said, as the boy sorted through his pocket book, "I don't know. The old girl's round the bend. What's this about your kid got a light around its head?—and your girl's a—" But the look came once more. A strange look almost—frightening. "Well, like that other lot, Jesus and all. She's mad."

"She has some ideas," said the boy. "That doesn't make her mad."

But not everyone agreed with him. The greengrocer's wife tackled Marilyn one day when she went out for the shopping, Mrs. Vaughan left worshipping the baby at home. "They're all saying she's going off her rocker. You shouldn't be there, what with the baby and all. It could be dangerous."

So still and beautiful, the quiet face framed in its veil of long, straight hair. "Mrs. Vaughan—dangerous? She's kind. She'd do us no harm, she loves us."

"She told us last time that the baby lies with its arms stretched out like a—well, like a cross. She said it knows how it's going to die. Well, I *mean*! It's blasphemous."

"He does lie with his arms stretched out."

"Any baby does, sometimes. And she says he shines. She says there's always a light around his head."

"I put the lamp on the floor once to keep the brightness out of his eyes. It did sort of gleam through a crack in the wood. We explained it to her."

"Well, she never listened then. And I say it's not right. Everyone's talking. They say . . ." It took a little courage to persist, in face of that quiet calm. "They're saying you ought to fetch a doctor to her."

Mrs. Vaughan rebelled, predictably, against any suggestion of seeing a doctor. "What for? I'm not ill. Never better." But it alarmed her. "You don't think there's something wrong with me?"

"We just thought you looked a bit pale, that's all."

"I'm not pale, I'm fine, never been better in my life. Even them arthritics nearly gone, hardly any pain these days at all." And she knew why. Alone with Him, she had taken the little hand and with it touched her swollen knees, had moved it, soft and firm, across her own gnarled fingers. "Look at 'em," she had insisted to Nellie next evening in the pub. "Half the size. All them swollen joints gone down."

"They look the same to me," said Nellie and suddenly saw Mrs. Hoskins through in the Private and had to hurry off and join her. "Barmy!" she said to Mrs. Hoskins. "I don't feel safe with her. How do I know she won't suddenly do her nut and start bashing me? It should be put a stop to."

Only one thing seemed to threaten Mrs. Vaughan with any suggestion of doing her nut and that was mention of her precious little family going away. If Jo searched for rooms now, he kept very quiet about it. To outside representations that she ought to let them go, that young people should be together in a place of their own, she replied that it wasn't "like that" between them; that Marilyn was "different." All the same, they were young and shouldn't always be cooped up with an old woman, and she fought to be allowed to move out to the shed and let them have her room; there was the bed out there now and in this weather it was warm and dry—she'd like it. In other days, she would have gone off to the pub in the evenings and left them free, but the Dog wasn't what it had been, people didn't seem so friendly, they looked at her funny and sometimes, she suspected, made mock behind her back of her claim to be housing God. Not that that worried her too much. In them old days, no one had believed in Him then, either. And I'll prove it to them, she thought, and she would watch the children playing in the street and when she saw a tumble, bring in the poor victim with its bruises and scratches and cajole it into letting the baby touch the sore places with its little hand. "Now you feel better, love, don't you?" she would anxiously say. "Now it's stopped bleeding, hasn't it?—when the Baby touched you, it was all better in a minute? Now you tell me—wasn't it?" "Yes," the children would declare, wriggling in her grasp, intent only upon getting away. "It's dangerous," said their mothers, gathering outside the shops in anxious gossip. "You don't know what she might do, luring them inside like that." And a deputation at last sought out Jo. "You ought to clear out, you two, and leave her alone. You're driving her up the wall with these ideas."

"That's just what we can't do now," said Jo. "She gets upset if we even mention it."

"It could be the last straw," admitted Mrs. Hoskins, who knew all about it from Nellie at the Dog. "Properly finish her off."

"And then she'd be there without us to look after her."

"You can't spend your whole lives in that one room."

"If we could get a place and take her with us . . . but we can't find anywhere, not that we could possibly afford; let alone where she could come too."

"What?—you two kids, saddle yourselves for ever with a mad old woman? You couldn't do that."

"She saddled herself with us," said Jo. "Where'd we be now, but for her?"

All the same, clearly something must be done. With every day of her life with them, Mrs. Vaughan's obsession increased. She could not bear the baby out of her sight, would walk with Marilyn when she carried it out for a breath of fresh air and almost threateningly warn off the curious who tried for a glimpse of the now quite famous child. If they came to worship, well and good. If not . . . "If you don't make some arrangement about her," said the greengrocer's wife at last to Jo, "I will. She's terrorising the whole neighbourhood."

"She wouldn't hurt a fly. She believes our baby's—something special. What harm does that do anyone else?"

"You never know," said the greengrocer, supporting the missis, though in fact he was fond of Mrs. Vaughan—as indeed everyone had been in easier days. "They do turn queer, sometimes. Why not just take her to the doctor and ask him, or take her to the hospital?"

"She won't go to any hospital, she won't go to any doctor."

"They can be forced," said the wife. "Straitjackets and that.

They come and fetch them in a padded van." But anyway, she repeated, if something were not done and soon, she herself would ring up the police and let *them* deal with it. "She's keeping custom from the shop. It can't go on."

He promised hastily and later convened a little meeting of the malcontents. "Well, I've done what you said. I went to the hospital and they sent me to some special doctor and I told him all about it. They're going to send her to a place where she won't be too suspicious and they'll have her under observation there, that's what they call it, and then there'll be psychiatrists and that, and she can have treatment. He says it's probably only a temporary thing, she can be cured all right."

"Well, there you are! You and Marilyn can be finding somewhere else in the meantime and when she gets back and you're not there, she'll just settle down again."

"We'll go anyway even if we don't find anywhere. We couldn't let it start all over again."

"These things aren't as quick as all that. You'll have time to look around."

"It's not very nice," he said, "us there in her room and her in the bin."

"If you ever get her there. How'll you persuade her to go?"

"I've thought of that," he said. "Our last landlady—"

"Oh, yes, that Mrs. Mace she's always talking about! Mrs. Mace would understand, she keeps saying, Mrs. Mace knew all about it . . . You tell her she's going to see Mrs. Mace."

"That's what I thought. Mrs. Mace is out in the country now and so's this place, fifteen, twenty miles. I can drive her there in the car. She'll go if she thinks Mrs. Mace is there. I think it'll work."

And it worked. Mrs. Vaughan was prepared to leave even the precious Baby for a while, if she could go and talk to Mrs. Mace. So many puzzling things that Mrs. Mace might be able to help her with. That about the Second Coming, for example, and then no Kings had arrived, not even a shepherd carrying a woolly lamb; and what about Herod killing off all them boy babies? Of course these were modern days, what would they have done with a live lamb, anyway?—and people didn't go around killing babies any more. But you'd think there'd be something to take the place of these events, something—well, sybollick or whatever the word was, and it might be important to recognise it. Mrs. Mace would understand, would at least be sympathetic and talk it all over; she had known them since before the baby even started, had been brushed by the very wings of Gabriel, bringing the message: Hail Mary, full of grace, the Lord is with thee . . . She could hardly wait to gather up her few shabby clothes and pack them into the cardboard box that must do for a suitcase. "You'll look after things, Marilyn, love, just the couple of days? I'd like to have some good long talks with Mrs. Mace. You do think she'll let me stay?"

"It's a big place; like, sort of, a hotel," said Jo. "But lovely, all them trees and flowers. And lots of nice people," he added, cautiously.

"I thought it was a cottage? It's only Mrs. Mace I want to see. I can be with her?"

"Oh, yes, of course. We've written and told her," fibbed Jo, "how good you've been to us."

"Me—good?" she said. "When you think what you've done for *me*. Me being chosen. But still, there—the last time it was only a pub-keeper, wasn't it?" The thought struck her that perhaps in fact it had been meant that they should park outside the Dog that night, only a few doors down—that only through an error had they come to her. "Well, never mind, even if I wasn't worthy to be chosen, fact remains it was me that got you—and reckernised you. First minute I saw you. I'll never forget it." So beautiful, so quiet and undemanding, standing out there in the drizzle of the evening rain. Mary and Joseph and the promise of the Holy Child. And as they had been then, so they had remained: quiet, considerate, gentle; reserved, unemotional as she was emotional and out-giving; almost colourless, almost impersonal—a little apart from other human beings, from ordinary people like herself; and yet living with herself, close together in that little place with her for their only friend—the Mother and the Guardian of the Son of God; and the Word made flesh. She knelt and kissed the tiny hand. "I'll come back to you, my little Lord. I'll always love You and serve You, You know that. It's only just that I want to know everything about You, I want to get things right, I want to ask Mrs. Mace." And all unaware of eyes watching from behind window curtains, balefully or pityingly or only with relief, she climbed into the battered little old car with Jo and drove away.

* * *

Marilyn was nursing the baby when he got home. "You've got the place all cleared up," he said, astonished at the change in it. "You must have been slaving."

"It kept my mind off things," she said. But still she did not ask what must be uppermost there. "Without Mrs. Vaughan here, I must say there's more room. Not as much as we had at Mrs. Mace's—"

"We couldn't stay at Mrs. Mace's once the nephew was coming home."

"No, I know. I was only saying." And now she did ask at last: "Did it go all right?"

"Yes, not a murmur. A bit surprised when we got there, of course, but I kept urging her on, saying she'd be with Mrs. Mace."

"You found the place again, no trouble?"

"Yes, I found it. A lovely spot, perfect, in the middle of all those woods."

"And Mrs. Mace?"

"Still there, quite OK. A bit lonely, I daresay. She'll be glad of company."

"They should get on fine." She smiled her own cool, quiet, impersonal little smile, shifting the baby on her shoulder so that its fluffy head pressed, warm and sweet, against her cheek. "Well, she got her wish. You couldn't call that a common grave."

"No, just her and Mrs. Mace; and right in the middle of them lovely woods like I told her, and all them flowers and the stream and all." He came across and ran a bent forefinger up the little channel at the back of the baby's tender neck. "A shame to have to bash her. She was a kind old thing. But there you are, it's so hard to find anywhere—we had to have the place."

"Yes," she said. "Especially now we got the kid."

LAWRENCE BLOCK

(b.1938)

*Born in Buffalo, New York, Lawrence Block attended Antioch College in Ohio, then almost immediately set out to make a living as a writer. He wrote both under his own name and under the pseudonyms of Chip Harrison and Paul Kavanaugh, primarily publishing paperback originals. Initially, Block exploited the sensibilities of the 1960s. The Chip Harrison novels began as ribald adolescent adventures, but by the third—*Make Out With Murder *(1974)—Block's character Chip becomes assistant to a Nero Wolfe type named Leo Haig. With* The Thief Who Couldn't Sleep *(1966), Block began a spy series with the insomniac hero Evan Tanner. By far his greatest successes have been with the characters of Matthew Scudder and Bernie Rhodenbarr. The first Matt Scudder novel,* In the Midst of Death, *appeared in 1976. Scudder is a recovering alcoholic ex-cop working as a private eye. He moves through an urban world of cruelty and heartbreak with sensitivity, sadness, and empathy. The first Bernie Rhodenbarr novel,* Burglars Can't Be Choosers *(1977), reveals quite a different character. The novels are lighter, using Block's considerable comic talents. Rhodenbarr is a thief who solves crimes—a modern, lower-class descendant of Raffles. Block is also an extremely talented short story writer, with a series featuring the shady attorney Martin Ehrengraf. In 1994, Block was the youngest writer ever to become a Grandmaster of the Mystery Writers of America. In the following story, which involves none of his series characters, Block reveals his powerful sympathy for the human condition in a tale of spousal abuse. The female narrator is firmly under the violent thumb of her husband, who traps her in her own love for him until a hidden world of women's secret alternatives is revealed to her.*

SOMEDAY I'LL PLANT MORE WALNUT TREES

There is a silence that is just stillness, just the absence of sound, and there is a deeper silence that is more than that. It is the antithesis, the aggressive opposite, of sound. It is to sound as antimatter is to matter, an auditory black hole that reaches out to swallow up and nullify the sounds of others.

My mother can give off such a silence. She is a master at it. That morning at breakfast she was thus silent, silent as she cooked eggs and made coffee, silent while I spooned baby oatmeal into Livia's little mouth, silent while Dan fed himself and while he smoked the day's first cigarette along with his coffee. He had his own silence, sitting there behind his newspaper, but all it did was insulate him. It couldn't reach out beyond that paper shield to snatch other sound out of the air.

He finished and put out his cigarette, folded his paper. He said it was supposed to be hot today, with rain forecast for late afternoon. He patted Livia's head, and with his forefinger drew aside a strand of hair that had fallen across her forehead.

I can see that now, his hand so gentle, and her beaming up at him, wide-eyed, gurgling.

Then he turned to me, and with the same finger and the same

softness he reached to touch the side of my face. I did not draw away. His finger touched me, ever so lightly, and then he reached to draw me into the circle of his arms. I smelled his shirt, freshly washed and sun-dried, and under it the clean male scent of him.

We looked at each other, both of us silent, the whole room silent. And then Livia cooed and he smiled quickly and chucked me under the chin and left. I heard the screen door slam, and then the sounds of the car as he drove to town. When I could not hear it anymore I went over to the radio and switched it on. They were playing a Tammy Wynette song. "Stand by your man," Tammy urged, and my mother's silence swallowed up the words.

While the radio played unheard I changed Livia and put her in for her nap. I came back to the kitchen and cleared the table. My mother waved a hand at the air in front of her face.

"He smokes," I said.

"I didn't say anything," she said.

We did the dishes together. There is a dishwasher but we never use it for the breakfast dishes. She prefers to run it only once a day, after the evening meal. It could hold all the day's dishes, they would not amount to more than one load in the machine, but she does not like to let the breakfast and lunch dishes stand. It seems wasteful to me, of time and effort, and even of water, although our well furnishes more than we ever need. But it is her house, after all, and her dishwasher, and hers the decision as to when it is to be used.

Silently she washed the dishes, silently I wiped them. As I reached to stack plates in a cupboard I caught her looking at me. Her eyes were on my cheek, and I could feel her gaze right where I had felt Dan's finger. His touch had been light. Hers was firmer.

I said, "It's nothing."

"All right."

"Dammit, Mama!"

"I didn't say anything, Tildie."

I was named Matilda for my father's mother. I never knew her, she died before I was born, before my parents met. I was never called Matilda. It was the name on my college diploma, on my driver's license, on Livia's birth certificate, but no one every used it.

"He can't help it," I said. "It's not his fault."

Her silence devoured my words. On the radio Tammy Wynette sang a song about divorce, spelling out the word. Why were they playing all her records this morning? Was it her birthday? Or an anniversary of some failed romance?

"It's not," I said. I moved to her right so that I could talk to her good ear. "It's a pattern. His father was abusive to his mother. Dan grew up around that. His father drank and was free with his hands. Dan swore he would never be like that, but patterns like that are almost impossible to throw off. It's what he knows, can you understand that? On a deep level, deeper than intellect, bone deep, that's how he knows to behave as a man, as a husband."

"He marked your face. He hasn't done that before, Tildie."

My hand flew to the spot. "You knew that—"

"Sounds travel. Even with my door closed, even with my good ear on the pillow. I've heard things."

"You never said anything."

"I didn't say anything today," she reminded me.

"He can't help it," I said. "You have to understand that. Didn't you see him this morning?"

"I saw him."

"It hurts him more than it hurts me. And it's my fault as much as it's his."

"For allowing it?"

"For provoking him."

She looked at me. Her eyes are a pale blue, like mine, and at times there is accusation in them. My gaze must have the same quality. I have been told that it is penetrating. "Don't look at me like that," my husband has said, raising a hand as much to ward off my gaze as to threaten me. "Damn you, don't you look at me like that!"

Like what? I'd wondered. How was I looking at him? What was I doing wrong?

"I do provoke him," I told her. "I make him hit me."

"How?"

"By saying the wrong thing."

"What sort of thing?"

"Things that upset him."

"And then he has to hit you, Tildie? Because of what you say?"

"It's a *pattern*," I said. "It's the way he grew up. Men who drink have sons who drink. Men who beat their wives have sons who beat their wives. It's passed on over the generations like a genetic illness. Mama, Dan's a good man. You see how he is with Livia, how he loves her, how she loves him."

"Yes."

"And he loves me, Mama. Don't you think it tears him up when something like this happens? Don't you think it eats at him?"

"It must."

"It does!" I thought how he'd cried last night, how he'd held me and touched the mark on my cheek and cried. "And we're going to try to do something about it," I said. "To break the pattern. There's a clinic in Fulton City where you can go for counseling. It's not expensive, either."

"And you're going?"

"We've talked about it. We're considering it."

She looked at me and I made myself meet her eyes. After a moment she looked away. "Well, you would know more about this sort of thing than I do," she said. "You went to college, you studied, you learned things."

I studied art history. I can tell you about the Italian Renaissance, although I have already forgotten much of what I learned. I took one psychology course in my freshman year and we observed the behavior of white rats in mazes.

"Mama," I said, "I know you disapprove."

"Oh, no," she said. "Tildie, that's not so."

"It's not?"

She shook her head. "I just hurt for you," she said. "That's all."

We live on 220 acres, only a third of them level. The farm has been in our family since the land was cleared early in the last century. It has been years since we farmed it. The MacNaughtons run sheep in our north pastures, and Mr. Parkhill leases forty acres, planting alfalfa one year and field corn the next. Mama has some bank stock and some utilities, and the dividends plus what she's paid for the land rent are enough to keep her. There's no mortgage on the land and the taxes have stayed low. And she has a big kitchen garden. We eat out of it all summer long and put up enough in the fall to carry us through the winter.

Dan studied comparative lit while I studied art history. He got a master's and did half the course work for a doctorate and then knew he couldn't do it anymore. He got a job driving a taxi and I worked waiting tables at Paddy Mac's, where we used to come for beer and hamburgers when we were students. When I got pregnant with Livia he didn't want me on my feet all day but we couldn't make ends meet on his earnings as a cabdriver. Rents were high in that city, and everything cost a fortune.

And we both loved country living, and knew the city was no

place to bring up Livia. So we moved here, and Dan got work right away with a construction company in Caldwell. That's the nearest town, just six miles from us on county roads, and Fulton City is only twenty-two miles.

After that conversation with Mama I went outside and walked back beyond the garden and the pear and apple orchard. There's a stream runs diagonally across our land, and just beyond it is the spot I always liked the best, where the walnut trees are. We have a whole grove of black walnuts, twenty-six trees in all. I know because Dan counted them. He was trying to estimate what they'd bring.

Walnut is valuable. People will pay thousands of dollars for a mature tree. They make veneer from it, because it's too costly to use as solid wood.

"We ought to sell these off," Dan said. "Your mama's got an untapped resource here. Somebody could come in, cut 'em down, and steal 'em. Like poachers in Kenya, killing the elephants for their ivory."

"No one's going to come onto our land."

"You never know. Anyway, it's a waste. You can't even see this spot from the house. And nobody does anything with the nuts."

When I was a girl my mama and I used to gather the walnuts after they fell in early autumn. Thousands fell from the trees. We would just gather a basketful and crack them with a hammer and pick the meat out. My hands always got black from the husks and stayed that way for weeks.

We only did this a few times. It was after Daddy left, but while Grandma Yount was still alive. I don't remember Grandma bothering with the walnuts, but she did lots of other things. When the cherries came in we would all pick them and she would bake pies and put up jars of the rest, and she'd boil the pits to clean them and sew scraps of cloth to make beanbags. There are still beanbags in the attic that Grandma Yount made. I'd brought one down for Livia and fancied I could still smell cherries through the cloth.

"We could harvest the walnuts," I told Dan. "If you want."

"What for? You can't get anything for them. Too much trouble to open and hardly any meat in them. I'd sooner harvest the trees."

"Mama likes having them here."

"They're worth a fortune. And they're a renewable resource. You could cut them and plant more and someday they'd put your grandchildren through college."

"You don't need to cut them to plant more. There's other land we could use."

"No point planting more if you're not going to cut these, is there? What do we need them for?"

"What do our grandchildren need college for?"

"What's that supposed to mean?"

"Nothing," I'd said, backing away.

And hours later he'd taken it up again. "You meant I wasted my education," he said. "That's what you meant by that crack, isn't it?"

"No."

"Then what did you mean? What do I need a master's for to hammer a nail? That's what you meant."

"It's not, but evidently that's how you'd rather hear it."

He hit me for that. I guess I had it coming. I don't know if I deserved it, I don't know if a woman deserves to get hit, but I guess I provoked it. Something makes me say things I shouldn't, things he'll take amiss. I don't know why.

Except I do know why, and I'd walked out of the kitchen and across to the walnut grove to keep from talking about it to Mama. Because he had his pattern and I had mine.

His was what he'd learned from his daddy, which was to abuse a woman, to slap her, to strike her with his fists. And mine was a pattern I'd learned from my mama, which was to make a man leave you, to taunt him with your mouth until one day he put his clothes in a suitcase and walked out the door.

In the mornings it tore at me to hear the screen door slam. Because I thought, Tildie, one day you'll hear that sound and it'll be for the last time. One day you'll do what your mother managed to do, and he'll do like your father did and you'll never see him again. And Livia will grow up as you did, in a house with her mother and her grandmother, and she'll have cherry-pit beanbags to play with and she'll pick the meat out of black walnuts, but what will she do for a daddy? And what will you do for a man?

All the rest of that week he never raised his hand to me. One night Mama stayed with Livia while Dan and I went to a movie in Fulton City. Afterward we went to a place that reminded us both of Paddy Mac's, and we drank beer and got silly. Driving home, we rolled down the car windows and sang songs at the top of our lungs. By the time we got home the beer had worn off but we were still happy and we hurried upstairs to our room.

Mama didn't say anything next morning but I caught her looking at me and knew she'd heard the old iron bedstead. I thought, *You hear a lot, even with your good ear pressed against the pillow.* Well, if she had to hear the fighting, let her hear the loving, too.

She could have heard the bed that night, too, although it was a quieter and gentler lovemaking than the night before. There were no knowing glances the next day, but after the screen door closed behind Dan and after Livia was in for her nap, there was a nice easiness between us as we stood side by side doing the breakfast dishes.

Afterward she said, "I'm so glad you're back home, Tildie."

"So you don't have to do the dishes all by yourself."

She smiled. "I knew you'd be back," she said.

"Did you? I wonder if I knew. I don't think so. I thought I wanted to live in a city, or in a college town. I thought I wanted to be a professor's wife and have earnest conversations about literature and politics and art. I guess I was just a country girl all along."

"You always loved it here," she said. "Of course it will be yours when I'm gone, and I had it in mind that you'd come back to it then. But I hoped you wouldn't wait that long."

She had never left. She and her mother lived here, and when she married my father he just moved in. It's a big old house, with different wings added over the years. He moved in, and then he left, and she just stayed on.

I remembered something. "I don't know if I thought I'd live here again," I said, "but I always thought I would die here." She looked at me, and I said, "Not so much die here as be buried here. When we buried Grandma I thought, *Well, this is where they'll bury me someday.* And I always thought that."

Grandma Yount's grave is on our land, just to the east of the pear and apple orchard. There are graves there dating back to when our people first lived here. The two children Mama lost are laid to rest there, and Grandma Yount's mother, and a great many children. It wasn't that long ago that people would have four or five children to raise one. You can't read what's cut into most of the stones, it's worn away with time, and it wears faster now that we have the acid rain, but the stones are there, the graves are there, and I always knew I'd be there, too.

"Well, I'll be there, too," Mama said. "But not too soon, I hope."

"No, not soon at all," I said. "Let's live a long time. Let's be old ladies together."

I thought it was a sweet conversation, a beautiful conversation. But when I told Dan about it we wound up fighting.

"When she goes," he said, "that's when those walnuts go to market."

"That's all you can think about," I said. "Turning a beautiful grove into dollars."

"That timber's money in the bank," he said, "except it's not in the bank because anybody could come in and haul it out of there behind our backs."

"Nobody's going to do that."

"And other things could happen. It's no good for a tree to let it grow beyond its prime. Insects can get it, or disease. There's one tree already that was struck by lightning."

"It didn't hurt it much."

"When they're my trees," he said, "they're coming down."

"They won't be your trees."

"What's that supposed to mean?"

"Mama's not leaving the place to you, Dan."

"I thought what's mine is yours and what's yours is mine."

"I love those trees," I said. "I'm not going to see them cut." His face darkened, and a muscle worked in his jaw. This was a warning sign, and I knew it as such, but I was stuck in a pattern, God help me, and I couldn't leave it alone. "First you'd sell off the timber," I said, "and then you'd sell off the acreage."

"I wouldn't do that."

"Why? Your daddy did."

Dan grew up on a farm that came down through his father's father. Unable to make a living farming, first his grandfather and then his father had sold off parcels of land little by little, whittling away at their holdings and each time reducing the potential income of what remained. After Dan's mother died his father had stopped farming altogether and drank full time, and the farm was auctioned for back taxes while Dan was still in high school.

I knew what it would do to him and yet I threw that in his face all the same. I couldn't seem to help it, any more than he could help what followed.

At breakfast the next day the silence made me want to scream. Dan read the paper while he ate, then hurried out the door without a word. I couldn't hear the screen door when it banged shut or the car engine when it started up. Mama's silence—and his, and mine—drowned out everything else.

I thought I'd burst when we were doing the dishes. She didn't say a word and neither did I. Afterward she turned to me and said, "I didn't go to college so I don't know about patterns, or what you do and what it makes him do."

The *quattrocento* and rats in a maze, that's all I learned in college. What I know about patterns and family violence I learned watching Oprah and Phil Donahue, and she watched the same programs I did. ("He blacked your eye and broke your nose. He kicked you in the stomach while you were pregnant. How can you stay with a brute like this?" "But I love him, Geraldo. And I knew he loves me.")

"I just know one thing," she said. "It won't get better. And it will get worse."

"No."

"Yes. And you know it, Tildie."

"No."

He hadn't blacked my eye or broken my nose, but he had hammered my face with his fists and it was swollen and discolored. He hadn't kicked me in the stomach but he had shoved me from him. I had been clinging to his arm. That was stupid, I knew better than to do that, it drove him crazy to have me hang on him like that. He had shoved me and I'd gone sprawling, wrenching my leg when I fell on it. My knee ached now, and the muscles in the front of that thigh were sore. And my rib cage was sore where he'd punched me.

But I love him, Geraldo, Oprah, Phil. And I know he loves me.

That night he didn't come home.

I couldn't sit still, couldn't catch my breath. Livia caught my anxiety and wouldn't sleep, couldn't sleep. I held her in my arms and paced the floor in front of the television set. Back and forth, back and forth.

At midnight finally I put her in her crib and she slept. Mama was playing solitaire at the pine table. Only the top is pine, the base is maple. An antique, Dan pronounced it when he first saw it, and better than the ones in the shops. I suppose he had it priced in his mind, along with the walnut trees.

I pointed out a move. Mama said, "I know about that. I just haven't decided whether I want to do it, that's all." But she always says that. I don't believe she saw it.

At one I heard our car turn off the road and onto the gravel. She heard it, too, and gathered up the cards and said she was tired now, she'd just turn in. She was out of the room and up the stairs before he came in the door.

He was drunk. He lurched into the room, his shirt open halfway to his waist, his eyes unfocused. He said, "Oh, Jesus, Tildie, what's happening to us?"

"Shhh," I said. "You'll wake the baby."

"I'm sorry, Tildie," he said. "I'm sorry, I'm so goddam sorry."

Going up the stairs, he spun away from me and staggered into the railing. It held. I got him upstairs and into our room, but he passed out the minute he lay down on our bed. I got his shoes off, and his shirt and pants, and let him sleep in his socks and underwear.

In the morning he was still sleeping when I got up to take care of Livia. Mama had his breakfast on the table, his coffee poured, the newspaper at his place. He rushed through the kitchen without a word to anybody, tore out the door and was gone. I moved toward the door but Mama was in my path.

I cried, "Mama, he's leaving! He'll never be back!"

She glanced meaningfully at Livia. I stepped back, lowered my voice. "He's leaving," I said, helpless. He had started the car, he was driving away. "I'll never see him again."

"He'll be back."

"Just like my daddy," I said. "Livvy, your father's gone, we'll never see him again."

"Stop that," Mama said. "You don't know how much sticks in their minds. You mind what you say in front of her."

"But it's true."

"It's not," she said. "You won't lose him that easy. He'll be back."

In the afternoon I took Livia with me while I picked pole beans and summer squash. Then we went back to the pear and apple orchard and played in the shade. After a while I took her over to Grandma Yount's grave. We'll all be here someday, I wanted to say, your grandma and your daddy and your mama, too. And you'll be here when your time comes. This is our land, this is where we all end up.

I might have said this, it wouldn't hurt for her to hear it, but for what Mama said. I guess it's true you don't know what sticks in their minds, or what they'll make of it.

She liked it out there, Livia did. She crawled right up to Grandma Yount's stone and ran her hand over it. You'd have thought she was trying to read it that way, like a blind person with Braille.

* * *

He didn't come home for dinner. It was going on ten when I heard the car on the gravel. Mama and I were watching television. I got up and went into the kitchen to be there when he came in.

He was sober. He stood in the doorway and looked at me. Every emotion a man could have was there on his face.

"Look at you," he said. "I did that to you."

My face was worse than the day before. Bruises and swellings are like that, taking their time to ripen.

"You missed dinner," I said, "but I saved some for you. I'll heat up a plate for you."

"I already ate. Tildie, I don't know what to say."

"You don't have to say anything."

"No," he said. "That's not right. We have to talk."

We slipped up to our room, leaving Mama to the television set. With our door closed we talked about the patterns we were caught in and how we seemed to have no control, like actors in a play with all their lines written for them by someone else. We could improvise, we could invent movements and gestures, we could read our lines in any of a number of ways, but the script was all written down and we couldn't get away from it.

I mentioned counseling. He said, "I called that place in Fulton City. I wouldn't tell them my name. Can you feature that? I called them for help but I was too ashamed to tell them my name."

"What did they say?"

"They would want to see us once a week as a couple, and each of us individually once a week. Total price for the three sessions would be eighty dollars."

"For how long?"

"I asked. They couldn't say. They said it's not the sort of change you can expect to make overnight."

I said, "Eighty dollars a week. We can't afford that."

"I had the feeling they might reduce it some."

"Did you make an appointment?"

"No. I thought I'd call tomorrow."

"I don't want to cut the trees," I said. He looked at me. "To pay for it. I don't want to cut Mama's walnut trees."

"Tildie, who brought up the damn trees?"

"We could sell the table," I said.

"What are you talking about?"

"In the kitchen. The pine-top table, didn't you say it was an antique? We could sell that."

"Why would I want to sell the table?"

"You want to sell those trees bad enough. You as much as said that as soon as my mama dies you'll be out back with a chain saw."

"Don't start with me," he said. "Don't you start with me, Tildie."

"Or what? Or you'll hit me? Oh, God, Dan, what are we doing? Fighting over how to pay for the counseling to keep from fighting. Dan, what's the matter with us?"

I went to embrace him but he backed away from me. "Honey," he said, "we better be real careful with this. They were telling me about escalating patterns of violence. I'm afraid of what could happen. I'm going to do what they said to do."

"What's that?"

"I want to pack some things," he said. "That's what I came home to do. There's that Welcome Inn Motel outside of Caldwell, they say it's not so bad and I believe they have weekly rates."

"No," I said. "No."

"They said it's best. Especially if we're going to start counseling, because that brings everything up and out into the open, and it threatens the part of us that wants to be in this pattern. Tildie, from what they said it'd be dangerous for us to be together right now."

"You can't leave," I said.

"I wouldn't be five miles away. I'd be coming for dinner some nights, we'd be going to a movie now and then. It's not like—"

"We can't afford it," I said. "Dan, how can we afford it? Eighty dollars a week for the counseling and God knows how much for the motel, and you'd be having most of your meals out, and how can we afford it? You've got a decent job but you don't make that kind of money."

His eyes hardened but he breathed in and out, in and out, and said, "Tildie, just talking like this is a strain, don't you see that? We can afford it, we'll find a way to afford it. Tildie, don't grab on to my arm like that, you know what it does to me. Tildie, stop it, will you for God's sake stop it?"

I put my arms around my own self and hugged myself. I was

shaking. My hands just wanted to take hold of his arm. What was so bad about holding on to your husband's arm? What was wrong with that?

"Don't go," I said.

"I have to."

"Not now. It's late, they won't have any rooms left anyhow. Wait until morning. Can't you wait until morning?"

"I was just going to get some of my things and go."

"Go in the morning. Don't you want to see Livvy before you go? She's your daughter, don't you want to say good-bye to her?"

"I'm not leaving, Tildie. I'm just staying a few miles from here so we'll have a chance to keep from destroying ourselves. My God, Tildie, I don't want to leave you. That's the whole point, don't you see that?"

"Stay until morning," I said. "Please?"

"And will we go through this again in the morning?"

"No," I said. "I promise."

We were both restless, but then we made love and that settled him, and soon he was sleeping. I couldn't sleep, though. I lay there for a time, and then I put a robe on and went down to the kitchen and sat there for a long time, thinking of patterns, thinking of ways to escape them. And then I went back up the stairs to the bedroom again.

I was in the kitchen the next morning before Livia woke up. I was there when Mama came down, and her eyes widened at the sight of me. She started to say something but then I guess she saw something in my eyes and she stayed silent.

I said, "Mama, we have to call the police. You'll mind the baby when they come for me. Will you do that?"

"Oh, Tildie," she said.

I led her up the stairs again and into our bedroom. Dan lay facedown, the way he always slept. I drew the sheet down and showed her where I'd stabbed him, slipping the kitchen knife between two ribs and into the heart. The knife lay on the table beside the bed. I had wiped the blood from it. There had not been very much blood to wipe.

"He was going to leave," I said, "and I couldn't bear it, Mama. And I thought, Now he won't leave, now he'll never leave me. I thought, This is a way to break the pattern. Isn't that crazy, Mama? It doesn't make any sense, does it?"

"My poor Tildie."

"Do you want to know something? I feel safe now, Mama. He won't hit me anymore and I never have to worry about him leaving me. He can't leave me, can he?" Something caught in my throat. "Oh, and he'll never hold me again, either. In the circle of his arms."

I broke then, and it was Mama who held me, stroking my forehead, soothing me. I was all right then, and I stood up straight and told her she had better call the police.

"Livia'll be up any minute now," she said. "I think she's awake, I think I heard her fussing a minute ago. Change her and bring her down and feed her her breakfast."

"And then?"

"And then put her in for her nap."

After I put Livia back in her crib for her nap Mama told me that we weren't going to call the police. "Now that you're back where you belong," she said, "I'm not about to see them take you away. Your baby needs her mama and I need you, too."

"But Dan—"

"Bring the big wheelbarrow around to the kitchen door. Between the two of us we can get him down the stairs. We'll dig his grave in the back, we'll bury him here on our land. People won't suspect anything. They'll just think he went off, the way men do."

"The way my daddy did," I said.

Somehow we got him down the stairs and out through the kitchen. The hardest part was getting him into the old wheelbarrow. I checked Livia and made sure she was sleeping soundly, and then we took turns with the barrow, wheeling it out beyond the kitchen garden.

"What I keep thinking," I said, "is at least I broke the pattern."

She didn't say anything, and what she didn't say became one of her famous silences, sucking up all the sound around us. The barrow's wheel squeaked, the birds sang in the trees, but now I couldn't hear any of that.

Suddenly she said, "Patterns." Then she didn't say anything more, and I tried to hear the squeak of the wheel.

Then she said, "He never would have left you. If he left he'd only come back again. And he never would have quit hitting you. And each time would be a little worse than the last."

"It's not always like it is on *Oprah,* Mama."

"There's things you don't know," she said.

"Like what?"

The squeaking of the wheel, the song of birds. She said, "You know how I lost the hearing in the one ear?"

"You had an infection."

"That's what I always told you. It's not true. Your daddy cupped his hands and boxed my ears. He deafened me on the one side. I was lucky, nothing happened to the other ear. I still hear as good as ever out of it."

"I don't believe it," I said.

"It's the truth, Tildie."

"Daddy never hit you."

"Your daddy hit me all the time," she said. "All the time. He used his hands, he used his feet. He used his belt."

I felt a tightening in my throat. "I don't remember," I said.

"You didn't know. You were little. What do you think Livia knows? What do you think she'll remember?"

We walked on a ways. I said, "I just remember the two of you hollering. I thought you hollered and finally he left. That's what I always thought."

"That's what I let you think. It's what I wanted you to think. I had a broken jaw, I had broken ribs, I had to keep telling the doctor I was clumsy, I kept falling down. He believed me, too. I guess he had lots of women told him the same thing." We switched, and I took over the wheelbarrow. She said, "Dan would have done the same to you, if you hadn't done what you did."

"He wanted to stop."

"They can't stop, Tildie. No, not that way. To your left."

"Aren't we going to bury him alongside Grandma Yount?"

"No," she said. "That's too near the house. We'll dig his grave across the stream, where the walnut grove is."

"It's beautiful there."

"You always liked it."

"So did Dan," I said. I felt so funny, so light-headed. My world was turned upside down and yet it felt safe, it felt solid. I thought how Dan had itched to cut down those walnut trees. Now he'd lie forever at their feet, and I could come back here whenever I wanted to feel close to him.

"But he'll be lonely here," I said. "Won't he? Mama, won't he?"

I Confess!

WHILE MANY THUGS IN THE REAL WORLD SEEM TO FEEL LITTLE OR nothing about their crimes and victims, the idea of consciousness of guilt is a part of law and is almost always assumed in mysteries. The thriller genre often offers up conscienceless (and often characterless) evildoers who bomb, rape, mutilate, and murder, but stories of detection usually presume that criminals are aware of violating human, if not divine, laws, and therefore reveal themselves by their symptoms of guilt. Mafiosi are said to have loved *Perry Mason* because of the confession produced in the last few moments of the popular TV show; they couldn't imagine anything more comically implausible. Yet, strangely, most real murderers do confess with little coercion. Often they call the police themselves and wait patiently for the detectives to arrive. A recurring pattern in mystery stories has the investigator, because of his or her psychological insight, detecting guilty behavior, which does not seem to a casual observer to be guilty, and using that guilty behavior to coerce a confession out of the evildoer. In fiction, the reader's pleasure derives largely from this contest of wills. The investigator must understand the psychology of the criminal opponent and find exactly the right device to destroy his resistance. A legion of fictional detectives and attorneys have tangled malefactors in their own lies to break them down. Sometimes confronting the criminal with overlooked evidence produces a confession. Other times the tried-and-true device of a cheap trick nets the criminal. Hamlet uses a play to catch the conscience of the king. How many times in stories are criminals tricked into returning to the scene of the crime? We might ask why we enjoy the spectacle of justice relying on trickery. There is something comical about weighty matters being resolved through prestidigitation. Perhaps there is also appeal in great schemes being undone by the smallest mistakes. A more potent reason might be the hopeful assumption that "murder will out," that the truth cannot be concealed because the balance of the universe cannot be restored until justice is served. Another perhaps unrealistic assumption is that criminals cannot help feeling the heavy weight of the crime upon their souls, no matter how rationalized, or that criminals are vain about their crimes and cannot resist bragging about them. Their torment can only end with confession, when investigators use psychology to tempt or trick the criminals into revealing themselves.

EDGAR ALLAN POE

(1809–1849)

Born in Boston, Massachusetts, and educated at the University of Virginia and at West Point in New York, Edgar Allan Poe achieved literary immortality through his haunting poetry, intense fiction, and brilliant criticism. Although many of his stories focus on crime, only a handful of them contain elements that define the mystery and detective story. Most of these ingredients may be found in the works of earlier writers, but no one consolidated them in the way Poe did, and thus he is generally honored as the inventor of the mystery. He used the term "ratiocination" to describe the process of deduction based upon detailed examination of empirical evidence; it is his depiction of this process that makes five of his stories the progenitors of the genre. Three of his stories—"The Murders in the Rue Morgue" (1841), "The Mystery of Marie Rogêt" (1842), and "The Purloined Letter" (1844)—feature C. Auguste Dupin, the genius of analysis who would later inspire the creation of many intellectual detectives with worshipful sidekicks. These stories offer a panoply of devices on which later writers have drawn, including the locked room and the armchair analysis of a true crime. "The Gold Bug" (1843) is a puzzle story revolving around the breaking of a mysterious code. Our selection, " 'Thou Art the Man' " (1844), is often neglected because of its crude comedy, but black humor in itself is a recurring element in the crime writing tradition. This story also features murder in a small town, the framing of a likely suspect with false clues, the guilt of the least likely suspect, ballistic evidence, the amateur detective, and the narrator as detective, without which it is impossible to imagine Marlowe, Milhone, and a host of more recent private eyes. Finally, the story employs the device of the investigator tricking a confession out of the guilty party. When an evildoer is clever, an investigator may require unorthodox, unusual, even incredibly grotesque methods to elicit the truth.

"THOU ART THE MAN"

I will now play the Œdipus to the Rattleborough enigma. I will expound to you—as I alone can—the secret of the enginery that effected the Rattelborough miracle—the one, the true, the admitted, the undisputed, the indisputable miracle, which put a definite end to infidelity among the Rattleburghers and converted to the orthodoxy of the grandames all the carnal-minded who had ventured to be sceptical before.

This event—which I should be sorry to discuss in a tone of unsuitable levity—occurred in the summer of 18–. Mr. Barnabas Shuttleworthy—one of the wealthiest and most respectable citizens of the borough—had been missing for several days under circumstances which gave rise to suspicion of foul play. Mr. Shuttleworthy had set out from Rattleborough very early one Saturday morning, on horseback, with the avowed intention of proceeding to the city of ——, about fifteen miles distant, and of returning the night of the same day. Two hours after his departure, however, his horse returned without him, and without the saddle-bags which had been strapped on his back at starting. The animal was wounded, too, and covered with mud. These circumstances naturally gave rise to much alarm among the friends of the missing man; and when it was found, on Sunday morning, that he had not yet made his appearance, the whole borough arose *en masse* to go and look for his body.

The foremost and most energetic in instituting this search was the bosom friend of Mr. Shuttleworthy—a Mr. Charles Goodfellow, or, as he was universally called, "Charley Goodfellow," or "Old Charley Goodfellow." Now, whether it is a marvellous coincidence, or whether it is that the name itself has an imperceptible effect upon the character, I have never yet been able to ascertain; but the fact is unquestionable, that there never yet was any person named Charles who was not an open, manly, honest, good-natured, and frank-hearted fellow, with a rich, clear voice, that did you good to hear it, and an eye that looked you always straight in the face, as much as to say: "I have a clear conscience myself, am afraid of no man, and am altogether above doing a mean action." And thus all the hearty, careless, "walking gentlemen" of the stage are very certain to be called Charles.

Now, "Old Charley Goodfellow," although he had been in Rattleborough not longer than six months or thereabouts, and although nobody knew anything about him before he came to settle in the neighborhood, had experienced no difficulty in the world in making the acquaintance of all the respectable people in the borough. Not a man of them but would have taken his bare word for a thousand at any moment; and as for the women, there is no saying what they would not have done to oblige him. And all this came of his having been christened Charles, and of his possessing, in consequence, that ingenuous face which is proverbially the very "best letter of recommendation."

I have already said that Mr. Shuttleworthy was one of the most respectable and, undoubtedly, he was the most wealthy man in Rattleborough, while "Old Charley Goodfellow" was upon as intimate terms with him as if he had been his own brother. The two old gentlemen were next-door neighbours, and, although Mr. Shuttleworthy seldom, if ever, visited "Old Charley," and never was known to take a meal in his house, still this did not prevent the two friends from being exceedingly intimate, as I have just observed; for "Old Charley" never let a day pass without stepping in three or four times to see how his neighbour came on, and very often he would stay to breakfast or tea, and almost always to dinner; and then the amount of wine that was made way with by the two cronies at a sitting, it would really be a difficult thing to ascertain. "Old Charley's" favorite beverage was *Chateau-Margaux,* and it appeared to do Mr. Shuttleworthy's heart good to see the old fellow swallow it, as he did, quart after quart; so that, one day, when the wine was *in* and the wit, as a natural consequence, somewhat *out,* he said to his crony, as he slapped him upon the back—"I tell you what it is, 'Old Charley,' you are, by all odds, the heartiest old fellow I ever came across in all my born days; and, since you love to guzzle the wine at that fashion, I'll be darned if I don't have to make thee a present of a big box of the Chateau-Margaux. Od rot me,"—(Mr. Shuttleworthy had a sad habit of swearing, although he seldom went beyond "Od rot me," or "By gosh," or "By the jolly golly,")—"Od rot me," says he, "if I don't send an order to town this very afternoon for a double box of the best that can be got, and I'll make ye a present of it, I will!—ye needn't say a word now—I *will,* I tell ye, and there's an end of it; so look out for it—it will come to hand some of these fine days, precisely when ye are looking for it the least!" I mention this little bit of liberality on the part of Mr. Shuttleworthy, just by way of showing you how *very* intimate an understanding existed between the two friends."

Well, on the Sunday morning in question, when it came to be fairly understood that Mr. Shuttleworthy had met with foul play, I never saw any one so profoundly affected as "Old Charley Goodfellow." When he first heard that the horse had come home without his master, and without his master's saddle-bags, and all bloody from a pistol-shot, that had gone clean through and through the poor animal's chest without quite killing him; when he heard all this, he turned as pale as if the missing man had been his own dear brother or father, and shivered and shook all over as if he had had a fit of the ague.

At first he was too much overpowered with grief to be able to do any thing at all, or to concert upon any plan of action; so that for a long time he endeavoured to dissuade Mr. Shuttleworthy's other friends from making a stir about the matter, thinking it best to wait awhile—say for a week or two, or a month, or two—to see if something wouldn't turn up, or if Mr. Shuttleworthy wouldn't come in the natural way, and explain his reasons for sending his horse on before. I dare say you have often observed this disposition to temporize, or to procrastinate, in people who are labouring under any very poignant sorrow. Their powers of mind seem to be rendered torpid, so that they have a horror of any thing like action, and like nothing in the world so well as to lie quietly in bed and "nurse their grief," as the old ladies express it—that is to say, ruminate over the trouble.

The people of Rattleborough had, indeed, so high an opinion

of the wisdom and discretion of "Old Charley," that the greater part of them felt disposed to agree with him, and not to make a stir in the business "until something should turn up," as the honest old gentleman worded it; and I believe that, after all, this would have been the general determination, but for the very suspicious interference of Mr. Shuttleworthy's nephew, a young man of very dissipated habits, and otherwise of rather bad character. This nephew, whose name was Pennifeather, would listen to nothing like reason in the matter of "lying quiet," but insisted upon making immediate search for the "corpse of the murdered man." This was the expression he employed; and Mr. Goodfellow acutely marked at the time, that it was "a *singular* expression, to say no more." This remark of "Old Charley's," too, had great effect upon the crowd; and one of the party was heard to ask, very impressively, "how it happened that young Mr. Pennifeather was so intimately cognizant of all the circumstances connected with his wealthy uncle's disappearance, as to feel authorized to assert, distinctly and unequivocally, that his uncle *was* 'a murdered man.' " Hereupon some little squibbing and bickering occurred among various members of the crowd, and especially between "Old Charley" and Mr. Pennifeather—although this latter occurrence was, indeed, by no means a novelty, for no good will had subsisted between the parties for the last three or four months; and matters had even gone so far that Mr. Pennifeather had actually knocked down his uncle's friend for some alleged excess of liberty that the latter had taken in the uncle's house, of which the nephew was an inmate. Upon this occasion "Old Charley" is said to have behaved with exemplary moderation and Christian charity. He arose from the blow, adjusted his clothes, and made no attempt at retaliation at all—merely muttering a few words about "taking summary vengeance at the first convenient opportunity,"—a natural and very justifiable ebullition of anger, which meant nothing, however, and, beyond doubt, was no sooner given vent to than forgotten.

However these matters may be (which have no reference to the point now at issue), it is quite certain that the people of Rattleborough, principally through the persuasion of Mr. Pennifeather, came at length to the determination of dispersion over the adjacent country in search of the missing Mr. Shuttleworthy. I say they came to this determination in the first instance. After it had been fully resolved that a search should be made, it was considered almost a matter of course that the seekers should disperse—that is to say, distribute themselves in parties—for the more thorough examination of the region round about. I forget, however, by what ingenious train of reasoning it was that "Old Charley" finally convinced the assembly that this was the most injudicious plan that could be pursued. Convince them, however, he did—all except Mr. Pennifeather; and, in the end, it was arranged that a search should be instituted, carefully and very thoroughly, by the burghers *en masse,* "Old Charley" himself leading the way.

As for the matter of that, there could have been no better pioneer than "Old Charley," whom everybody knew to have the eye of a lynx; but, although he led them into all manner of out-of-the-way holes and corners, by routes that nobody had ever suspected of existing in the neighbourhood, and although the search was incessantly kept up day and night for nearly a week, still no trace of Mr. Shuttleworthy could be discovered. When I say no trace, however, I must not be understood to speak literally; for trace, to some extent, there certainly was. The poor gentleman had been tracked, by his horse's shoes (which were peculiar), to a spot about three miles to the east of the borough, on the main road leading to the city. Here the track made off into a by-path through a piece of woodland—the path coming out again into the main road, and cutting off about half a mile of the regular distance. Following the shoemarks down this lane, the party came at length to a pool of stagnant water, half hidden by the brambles, to the right of the lane, and opposite this pool all vestige of the track was lost sight of. It appeared, however, that a struggle of some nature had here taken place, and it seemed as if some large and heavy body, much larger and heavier than a man, had been drawn from the by-path to the pool. This latter was carefully dragged twice, but nothing was found; and the party was upon the point of going away, in despair of coming to any result, when Providence suggested to Mr. Goodfellow the expediency of draining the water off altogether. This project was received with cheers, and many high compliments to "Old Charley" upon his sagacity and consideration. As many of the burghers had brought spades with them, supposing that they might possibly be called upon to disinter a corpse, the drain was easily and speedily effected; and no sooner was the bottom visible, than right in the middle of the mud that remained was discovered a black silk velvet waistcoat, which nearly every one present immediately recognized as the property of Mr. Pennifeather. This waistcoat was much torn and stained with blood, and there were several persons among the party who had a distinct remembrance of its having been worn by its owner on the very morning of Mr. Shuttleworthy's departure for the city; while there were others, again, ready to testify upon oath, if required, that Mr. P. did *not* wear the garment in question at any period during the *remainder* of that memorable day; nor could any one be found to say that he had seen it upon Mr. P.'s person at any period at all subsequent to Mr. Shuttleworthy's disappearance.

Matters now wore a very serious aspect for Mr. Pennifeather, and it was observed, as an indubitable confirmation of the suspicions which were excited against him, that he grew exceedingly pale, and when asked what he had to say for himself, was utterly incapable of saying a word. Hereupon, the few friends his riotous mode of living had left him, deserted him at once to a man, and were even more clamorous than his ancient and avowed enemies for his instantaneous arrest. But, on the other hand, the magnanimity of Mr. Goodfellow shone forth with only the more brilliant lustre through contrast. He made a warm and intensely eloquent defence of Mr. Pennifeather, in which he alluded more than once to his own sincere forgiveness of that wild young gentleman—"the heir of the worthy Mr. Shuttleworthy,"—for the insult which he (the young gentleman) had, no doubt in the heat of passion, thought proper to put upon him (Mr. Goodfellow). "He forgave him for it," he said, "from the very bottom of his heart; and for himself (Mr. Goodfellow), so far from pushing the suspicious circumstances to extremity, which he was sorry to say, really *had* arisen against Mr. Pennifeather, he (Mr. Goodfellow) would make every exertion in his power, would employ all the little eloquence in his possession to—to—to—soften down, as much as he could conscientiously do so, the worst features of this really exceedingly perplexing piece of business."

Mr. Goodfellow went on for some half hour longer in this strain, very much to the credit both of his head and of his heart; but your warm-hearted people are seldom apposite in their observations—they run into all sorts of blunders, *contretemps* and *mal apropos-isms,* in the hot-headedness of their zeal to serve a friend—thus, often with the kindest intentions in the world, doing infinitely more to prejudice his cause than to advance it.

So, in the present instance, it turned out with all the eloquence of "Old Charley"; for, although he laboured earnestly in behalf of the suspected, yet it so happened, somehow or other, that every syllable he uttered of which the direct but unwitting tendency was not to exalt the speaker in the good opinion of his audience, had the effect to deepen the suspicion already attached to the individual whose cause he pleaded, and to arouse against him the fury of the mob.

One of the most unaccountable errors committed by the orator was his allusion to the suspected as "the heir of the worthy old gentleman Mr. Shuttleworthy." The people had really never thought of this before. They had only remembered certain threats of disinheritance uttered a year or two previously by the uncle (who had no living relative except the nephew), and they had, therefore, always looked upon this disinheritance as a matter that was settled—so single-minded a race of beings were the Rattleburghers; but the remark of "Old Charley" brought them at once to a consideration of this point, and thus gave them to see the possibility of the threats having been nothing *more* than a threat. And straightway hereupon, arose the natural question of *cui bono?*—a question that tended even more than the waistcoat to fasten the terrible crime upon the young man. And here, lest I may be misunderstood, permit me to digress for one moment merely to observe that the exceedingly brief and simple Latin phrase which I have employed, is invariably mistranslated and misconceived. "*Cui bono?*" in all the crack novels and elsewhere,—in those of Mrs. Gore, for example, (the author of "Cecil,") a lady who quotes all tongues from the Chaldæan to Chickasaw, and is helped to her learning, "as needed," upon a systematic plan, by Mr. Beckford,—in *all* the crack novels, I say, from those of Bulwer and Dickens to those of Turnapenny and Ainsworth, the two little Latin words *cui bono* are rendered "to what purpose?" or, (as if *quo bono,*) "to what good." Their true meaning, nevertheless, is "for whose advantage." *Cui,* to whom; *bono,* is it for a benefit. It is a purely legal phrase, and applicable precisely in cases such as we have now under consideration, where the probability of the doer of a deed hinges upon the probability of the benefit accruing to this individual or to that from the deed's accomplishment. Now in the present instance, the question *cui bono?* very pointedly implicated Mr. Pennifeather. His uncle had threatened him, after making a will in his favour, with disinheritance. But the threat had not been actually kept; the original will, it appeared, had not been altered. *Had* it been altered, the only supposable motive for murder on the part of the suspected would have been the ordinary one of revenge; and even this would have been counteracted by the hope of reinstation into the good graces of the uncle. But the will being unaltered, while the threat to alter remained suspended over the nephew's head, there appears at once the very strongest possible inducement for the atrocity; and so concluded, very sagaciously, the worthy citizens of the borough of Rattle.

Mr. Pennifeather was, accordingly, arrested upon the spot, and the crowd, after some further search, proceeded homeward, having him in custody. On the route, however, another circumstance occurred tending to confirm the suspicion entertained. Mr. Goodfellow, whose zeal led him to be always a little in advance of the party, was seen suddenly to run forward a few paces, stoop, and then apparently to pick up some small object from the grass. Having quickly examined it, he was observed, too, to make a sort of half attempt at concealing it in his coat pocket; but this action was noticed, as I say, and consequently prevented, when the object picked up was found to be a Spanish knife which a dozen persons at once recognized as belonging to Mr. Pennifeather. Moreover, his initials were engraved upon the handle. The blade of this knife was open and bloody.

No doubt now remained of the guilt of the nephew, and immediately upon reaching Rattleborough he was taken before a magistrate for examination.

Here matters again took a most unfavourable turn. The prisoner, being questioned as to his whereabouts on the morning of Mr. Shuttleworthy's disappearance, had absolutely the audacity to acknowledge that on that very morning he had been out with his rifle deer-stalking, in the immediate neighbourhood of the pool where the blood-stained waistcoat had been discovered through the sagacity of Mr. Goodfellow.

This latter now came forward, and, with tears in his eyes, asked permission to be examined. He said that a stern sense of the duty he owed his Maker, not less than his fellow-men, would permit him no longer to remain silent. Hitherto, the sincerest affection for the young man (not-withstanding the latter's ill-treatment of himself, Mr. Goodfellow) had induced him to make every hypothesis which imagination could suggest, by way of endeavouring to account for what appeared suspicious in the circumstances that told so seriously against Mr. Pennifeather; but these circumstances were now altogether *too* convincing—*too* damning; he would hesitate no longer—he would tell all he knew, although his heart (Mr. Goodfellow's) should absolutely burst asunder in the effort. He then went on to state that, on the afternoon of the day previous to Mr. Shuttleworthy's departure for the city, that worthy old gentleman had mentioned to his nephew, in *his* hearing (Mr. Goodfellow's), that his object in going to town on the morrow was to make a deposit of an unusually large sum of money in the "Farmers and Mechanics' Bank," and that, then and there, the said Mr. Shuttleworthy had distinctly avowed to the said nephew his irrevocable determination of rescinding the will originally made, and of cutting him off with a shilling. He (the witness) now solemnly called upon the accused to state whether what he (the witness) had just stated was or was not the truth in every substantial particular. Much to the astonishment of every one present, Mr. Pennifeather frankly admitted that *it was.*

The magistrate now considered it his duty to send a couple of constables to search the chamber of the accused in the house of his uncle. From this search they almost immediately returned with the well-known steel-bound, russet leather pocket-book which the old gentleman had been in the habit of carrying for years. Its valuable contents, however, had been abstracted, and the magistrate in vain endeavoured to extort from the prisoner the use which had been made of them, or the place of their concealment. Indeed, he obstinately denied all knowledge of the matter. The constables, also, discovered, between the bed and sacking of the unhappy man, a shirt and neck-handkerchief both marked with the initials of his name, and both hideously besmeared with the blood of the victim.

At this juncture, it was announced that the horse of the murdered man had just expired in the stable from the effects of the wound he had received, and it was proposed by Mr. Goodfellow that a *post mortem* examination of the beast should be immediately made, with the view, if possible, of discovering the ball. This was accordingly done; and, as if to demonstrate beyond a question the guilt of the accused, Mr. Goodfellow, after considerable searching in the cavity of the chest, was enabled to detect and to pull forth a bullet of very extraordinary size, which, upon trial, was found to be exactly adapted to the bore of Mr. Pennifeather's rifle, while it was far too large for that of any other person in the borough or its vicinity. To render the matter even surer yet, however, this bullet was discovered to have a flaw or seam at right angles to the usual suture, and upon examination, this seam corresponded precisely with an accidental ridge or elevation in a pair of moulds acknowledged by the accused himself to be his own property. Upon finding of this bullet, the examining magistrate refused to listen to any farther testimony, and immediately committed the prisoner for trial—declining resolutely to take any bail in the case, although against this severity Mr. Goodfellow very warmly remonstrated, and offered to become surety in whatever amount might be required. This generosity on the part of "Old Charley" was only in accordance with the whole tenour of his amiable and chivalrous conduct during the entire period of his sojourn in the borough of Rattle. In the present instance the worthy man was so entirely carried away by the excessive warmth of his sympathy, that he seemed to have quite forgotten, when he offered to go bail for his young friend, that he himself (Mr. Goodfellow) did not possess a single dollar's worth of property upon the face of the earth.

The result of the committal may be readily foreseen. Mr. Pennifeather, amid the loud execrations of all Rattleborough, was brought to trial at the next criminal sessions, when the chain of circumstantial evidence (strengthened as it was by some additional damning facts, which Mr. Goodfellow's sensitive conscientiousness forbade him to withhold from the court) was considered so unbroken and so thoroughly conclusive, that the jury, without leaving their seats, returned an immediate verdict of *"Guilty of murder in the first degree."* Soon afterward the unhappy wretch received sentence of death, and was remanded to the county jail to await the inexorable vengeance of the law.

In the meantime, the noble behavior of "Old Charley Goodfellow" had doubly endeared him to the honest citizens of the borough. He became ten times a greater favorite than ever; and, as a natural result of the hospitality with which he was treated, he relaxed, as it were, perforce, the extremely parsimonious habits which his poverty had hitherto impelled him to observe, and very frequently had little *réunions* at his own house, when wit and jollity reigned supreme—dampened a little, *of course,* by the occasional remembrance of the untoward and melancholy fate which impended over the nephew of the late lamented bosom friend of the generous host.

One fine day, this magnanimous old gentleman was agreeably surprised at the receipt of the following letter:—

Chat. Mar. A—No. 1.—
6 doz. bottles (½ Gross)
From H. F. B. & Co.
Charles Goodfellow, Esq., Rattleborough

"Charles Goodfellow, Esquire:

"Dear Sir—In conformity with an order transmitted to our firm about two months since, by our esteemed correspondent, Mr. Barnabus Shuttleworthy, we have the honour of forwarding this morning, to your address, a double box of Chateau-Margaux, of the antelope brand, violet seal. Box numbered and marked as per margin.

"We remain, sir,
"Your most ob'nt ser'ts,
Hoggs, Frogs, Bogs, & Co.

"City of ——, June 21, 18—.

"P.S.—The box will reach you by wagon, on the day after your receipt of this letter. Our respects to Mr. Shuttleworthy.

"H., F., B., & Co."

The fact is, that Mr. Goodfellow had, since the death of Mr. Shuttleworthy, given over all expectation of ever receiving the promised Chateau-Margaux; and he, therefore, looked upon it *now* as a sort of especial dispensation of Providence in his behalf. He was highly delighted, of course, and in the exuberance of his joy invited a large party of friends to a *petit souper* on the morrow, for the purpose of broaching the good old Mr. Shuttleworthy's present. Not that he *said* anything about "the good old Mr. Shuttleworthy" when he issued the invitations. The fact is, he thought much and concluded to say nothing at all. He did *not* mention to anyone—if I remember aright—that he had received a *present* of Chateau-Margaux. He merely asked his friends to come and help him drink some, of a remarkable fine quality and rich flavour, that he had ordered up from the city a couple of months ago, and of which he would be in the receipt upon the morrow. I have often puzzled myself to imagine *why* it was that "Old Charley" came to the conclusion to say nothing about having received the wine from his old friend, but I could never precisely understand his reason for the silence, although he had *some* excellent and very magnanimous reason, no doubt.

The morrow at length arrived, and with it a very large and highly respectable company at Mr. Goodfellow's house. Indeed, half the borough was there,—I myself among the number,—but, much to the vexation of the host, the Chateau-Margaux did not arrive until a late hour, and when the sumptuous supper supplied by "Old

Charley" had been done very ample justice by the guests. It came at length, however—a monstrously big box of it there was, too—and as the whole party were in excessively good humor, it was decided, *nem. con.*, that it should be lifted upon the table and its contents disembowelled forthwith.

No sooner said than done. I lent a helping hand; and, in a trice we had the box upon the table, in the midst of all the bottles and glasses, not a few of which were demolished in the scuffle. "Old Charley," who was pretty much intoxicated, and excessively red in the face, now took a seat, with an air of mock dignity, at the head of the board, and thumped furiously upon it with a decanter, calling upon the company to keep order "during the ceremony of disinterring the treasure."

After some vociferation, quiet was at length fully restored, and, as very often happens in similar cases, a profound and remarkable silence ensued. Being then requested to force open the lid, I complied, of course, "with an infinite deal of pleasure." I inserted a chisel, and giving it a few slight taps with a hammer, the top of the box flew suddenly off, and at the same instant, there sprang up into a sitting position, directly facing the host, the bruised, bloody, and nearly putrid corpse of the murdered Mr. Shuttleworthy himself. It gazed for a few seconds, fixedly and sorrowfully, with its decaying and lack-lustre eyes, full into the countenance of Mr. Goodfellow; uttered slowly, but clearly and impressively, the words—"Thou art the man!" and then, falling over the side of the chest as it thoroughly satisfied, stretched out its limbs quiveringly upon the table.

The scene that ensued is altogether beyond description. The rush for the doors and windows was terrific, and many of the most robust *men* in the room fainted outright through sheer horror. But after the first wild, shrieking burst of affright, all eyes were directed to Mr. Goodfellow. If I live a thousand years, I can never forget the more than mortal agony which was depicted in that ghastly face of his, so lately rubicund with triumph and wine. For several minutes he sat rigidly as a statue of marble; his eyes seeming, in the intense vacancy of their gaze, to be turned inward and absorbed in the contemplation of his own miserable, murderous soul. At length their expression appeared to flash suddenly out into the external world, when, with a quick leap, he sprang from his chair, and falling heavily with his head and shoulders upon the table, and in contact with the corpse, poured out rapidly and vehemently a detailed confession of the hideous crime for which Mr. Pennifeather was then imprisoned and doomed to die.

What he recounted was in substance this:—He followed his victim to the vicinity of the pool; there shot his horse with a pistol; despatched its rider with the butt end; possessed himself of the pocket-book; and, supposing the horse dead, dragged it with great labour to the brambles by the pond. Upon his own beast he slung the corpse of Mr. Shuttleworthy, and thus bore it to a secure place of concealment a long distance off through the woods.

The waistcoat, the knife, the pocket-book, and bullet, had been placed by himself where found, with the view of avenging himself upon Mr. Pennifeather. He had also contrived the discovery of the stained handkerchief and shirt.

Towards the end of the blood-chilling recital, the words of the guilty wretch faltered and grew hollow. When the record was finally exhausted, he arose, staggered backward from the table, and fell—*dead*.

The means by which this happily-timed confession was extorted, although efficient, were simple indeed. Mr. Goodfellow's excess of frankness had disgusted me, and excited my suspicions from the first. I was present when Mr. Pennifeather had struck him, and the fiendish expression which then rose upon his countenance, although momentary, assured me that his threat of vengeance would, if possible, be rigidly fulfilled. I was thus prepared to view the *manœuvring* of "Old Charley" in a very different light from that in which it was regarded by the good citizens of Rattleborough. I saw at once that all the criminating discoveries arose, either directly or indirectly, from himself. But the fact which clearly opened my eyes to the true state of the case, was the affair of the bullet, *found* by Mr. G. in the carcass of the horse. *I* had not forgotten, although the Rattleburghers *had*, that there was a hole where the ball had entered the horse, and another where it *went out*. If it were found in the animal then, after having made its exit, I saw clearly that it must have been deposited by the person who found it. The bloody shirt and handkerchief confirmed the idea suggested by the bullet; for the blood on examination proved to be capital claret, and no more. When I came to think of these things, and also of the late increase of liberality and expenditure on the part of Mr. Goodfellow, I entertained a suspicion which was none the less strong because I kept it altogether to myself.

In the meantime, I instituted a rigorous private search for the corpse of Mr. Shuttleworthy, and, for good reasons, searched in quarters as divergent as possible from those to which Mr. Goodfellow conducted his party. The result was that, after some days, I came across an old dry well, the mouth of which was nearly hidden by brambles; and here, at the bottom, I discovered what I sought.

Now it so happened that I had overheard the colloquy between the two cronies, when Mr. Goodfellow had contrived to cajole his host into the promise of a box of Chateaux-Margaux. Upon this hint I acted. I procured a stiff piece of whalebone, thrust it down the throat of the corpse, and deposited the latter in an old wine box—taking care so to double the body up as to double the whalebone with it. In this manner I had to press forcibly upon the lid to keep it down while I secured it with nails; and I anticipated, of course, that as soon as these latter were removed, the top would fly *off* and the body *up*.

Having thus arranged the box, I marked, numbered, and addressed it as already told; and then writing a letter in the name of the wine merchants with whom Mr. Shuttleworthy dealt, I gave instructions to my servant to wheel the box to Mr. Goodfellow's door, in a barrow, at a given signal from myself. For the words which I intended the corpse to speak, I confidently depended upon my ventriloquial abilities; for their effect, I counted upon the conscience of the murderous wretch.

I believe there is nothing more to be explained. Mr. Pennifeather was released upon the spot, inherited the fortune of his uncle, profited by the lessons of experience, turned over a new leaf, and led happily ever afterward a new life.

SIR ARTHUR CONAN DOYLE

(1859–1930)

Sir Arthur Conan Doyle was a complicated man. Born in Edinburgh, he was educated by the Jesuits, though he later gave up Catholicism. Trained as a physician, he created the world's most famous rational, intellectual detective, Sherlock Holmes, yet became fascinated with spiritualism after his son's death from a wound received in World War I. Conan Doyle believed his literary reputation would be secured in the historical romances he wrote, which in fact go virtually unread today. In 1887, two years after receiving his M.D. degree, he published A Study in Scarlet, *the first novel to feature his famous detective, to supplement the meager income from his medical practice in Southsea. Within a few years, Sherlock Holmes was so popular that a throng of imitators filled the popular magazines. Conan Doyle tired of Holmes, however, and famously killed him off, only to revive him later at popular demand. Devotees have searched for sources for the detective in Conan Doyle's life and acquaintances. Though Conan Doyle said that many traits of Holmes were based upon a medical professor, Dr. Joseph Bell, Conan Doyle's debt to Edgar Allan Poe was so enormous that he worried about being accused of plagiarism. The Holmes storyline clearly echoes Poe's three Dupin stories, not just in characterization but also in the use of a worshipful sidekick. Conan Doyle, however, manages to make Holmes less forbidding than Dupin, establishing genuine subtle affection between Holmes and his narrator, rather than the pure adulation evinced by Dupin's unnamed friend. In our selection, Holmes uses a methodology similar to that of the narrator in Poe's "'Thou Art the Man,'" extracting the truth by accusing a dead man.*

THE ADVENTURE OF THE DYING DETECTIVE

Mrs. Hudson, the landlady of Sherlock Holmes, was a long-suffering woman. Not only was her first-floor flat invaded at all hours by throngs of singular and often undesirable characters but her remarkable lodger showed an eccentricity and irregularity in his life which must have sorely tried her patience. His incredible untidiness, his addiction to music at strange hours, his occasional revolver practice within doors, his weird and often malodorous scientific experiments, and the atmosphere of violence and danger which hung around him made him the very worst tenant in London. On the other hand, his payments were princely. I have no doubt that the house might have been purchased at the price which Holmes paid for his rooms during the years that I was with him.

The landlady stood in the deepest awe of him and never dared to interfere with him, however outrageous his proceedings might seem. She was fond of him, too, for he had a remarkable gentleness and courtesy in his dealings with women. He disliked and distrusted the sex, but he was always a chivalrous opponent. Knowing how genuine was her regard for him, I listened earnestly to her story when she came to my rooms in the second year of my married life and told me of the sad condition to which my poor friend was reduced.

"He's dying, Mr. Watson," said she. "For three days he has been sinking, and I doubt if he will last the day. He would not let me get a doctor. This morning when I saw his bones sticking out of his face and his great bright eyes looking at me I could stand no more of it. 'With your leave or without it, Mr. Holmes, I am going for a doctor this very hour,' said I. 'Let it be Watson, then,' said he. I wouldn't waste an hour in coming to him, sir, or you may not see him alive."

I was horrified for I had heard nothing of his illness. I need not say that I rushed for my coat and my hat. As we drove back I asked for the details.

"There is little I can tell you, sir. He has been working at a case down at Rotherhithe, in an alley near the river, and he has brought this illness back with him. He took to his bed on Wednesday afternoon and has never moved since. For these three days neither food nor drink has passed his lips."

"Good God! Why did you not call in a doctor?"

"He wouldn't have it, sir. You know how masterful he is. I didn't dare to disobey him. But he's not long for this world, as you'll see for yourself the moment that you set eyes on him."

He was indeed a deplorable spectacle. In the dim light of a foggy November day the sick room was a gloomy spot, but it was that gaunt, wasted face staring at me from the bed which sent a chill to my heart. His eyes had the brightness of fever, there was a hectic flush upon either cheek, and dark crusts clung to his lips; the thin hands upon the coverlet twitched incessantly, his voice was croaking and spasmodic. He lay listlessly as I entered the room, but the sight of me brought a gleam of recognition to his eyes.

"Well, Watson, we seem to have fallen upon evil days," said he in a feeble voice, but with something of his old carelessness of manner.

"My dear fellow!" I cried, approaching him.

"Stand back! Stand right back!" said he with the sharp imperiousness which I had associated only with moments of crisis. "If you approach me, Watson, I shall order you out of the house."

"But why?"

"Because it is my desire. Is that not enough?"

Yes, Mrs. Hudson was right. He was more masterful than ever. It was pitiful, however, to see his exhaustion.

"I only wished to help," I explained.

"Exactly! You will help best by doing what you are told."

"Certainly, Holmes."

He relaxed the austerity of his manner.

"You are not angry?" he asked, gasping for breath.

Poor devil, how could I be angry when I saw him lying in such a plight before me?"

"It's for your own sake, Watson," he croaked.

"For *my* sake?"

"I know what is the matter with me. It is a coolie disease from Sumatra—a thing that the Dutch know more about than we, though they have made little of it up to date. One thing only is certain. It is infallibly deadly, and it is horribly contagious."

He spoke now with a feverish energy, the long hands twitching and jerking as he motioned me away.

"Contagious by touch, Watson—that's it, by touch. Keep your distance and all is well."

"Good heavens, Holmes! Do you suppose that such a consideration weighs with me for an instant? It would not affect me in the case of a stranger. Do you imagine it would prevent me from doing my duty to so old a friend?"

Again I advanced, but he repulsed me with a look of furious anger.

"If you will stand there I will talk. If you do not you must leave the room."

I have so deep a respect for the extraordinary qualities of Holmes that I have always deferred to his wishes, even when I least understood them. But now all my professional instincts were aroused. Let him be my master elsewhere, I at least was his in a sick room.

"Holmes," said I, "you are not yourself. A sick man is but a child, and so I will treat you. Whether you like it or not, I will examine your symptoms and treat you for them."

He looked at me with venomous eyes.

"If I am to have a doctor whether I will or not, let me at least have someone in whom I have confidence," said he.

"Then you have none in me?"

"In your friendship, certainly. But facts are facts. Watson, and, after all, you are only a general practitioner with very limited experience and mediocre qualifications. It is painful to have to say these things, but you leave me no choice."

I was bitterly hurt.

"Such a remark is unworthy of you, Holmes. It shows me very clearly the state of your own nerves. But if you have no confidence in me I would not intrude my services. Let me bring Sir Jasper Meek or Penrose Fisher, or any of the best men in London. But someone you *must* have, and that is final. If you think that I am going to stand here and see you die without either helping you myself or bringing anyone else to help you, then you have mistaken your man."

"You mean well," Watson," said the sick man with something between a sob and a groan. "Shall I demonstrate your own ignorance? What do you know, pray, of Tapanuli fever? What do you know of the black Formosa corruption?"

"I have never heard of either."

"There are many problems of disease, many strange pathological possibilities, in the East, Watson." He paused after each sentence to collect his failing strength. "I have learned so much during some recent researches which have a medico-criminal aspect. It was in the course of them that I contracted this complaint. You can do nothing."

"Possibly not. But I happen to know that Dr. Ainstree, the greatest living authority upon tropical disease, is now in London. All remonstrance is useless, Holmes, I am going this instant to fetch him." I turned resolutely to the door.

Never have I had such a shock! In an instant, with a tiger spring, the dying man had intercepted me. I heard the sharp snap of a twisted key. The next moment he had staggered back to his bed, exhausted and panting after his one tremendous outflame of energy.

"You won't take the key from me by force, Watson. I've got you, may friend. Here you are, and here you will stay until I will otherwise. But I'll humour you." (All this in little gasps, with terrible struggles for breath between.) "You've only my own good at heart. Of course I know that very well. You shall have your way, but give me time to get my strength. Not now, Watson, not now. It's four o'clock. At six you can go."

"This is insanity, Holmes."

"Only two hours, Watson. I promise you will go at six. Are you content to wait?"

"I seem to have no choice."

"None in the world, Watson. Thank you, I need no help in arranging the clothes. You will please keep your distance. Now, Watson, there is one other condition that I would make. You will seek help, not from the man you mention, but from the one that I choose."

"By all means."

"The first three sensible words that you have uttered since you entered this room, Watson. You will find some books over there. I am somewhat exhausted; I wonder how a battery feels when it pours electricity into a non-conductor? At six, Watson, we resume our conversation."

But it was destined to be resumed long before that hour, and in circumstances which gave me a shock hardly second to that cause by his spring to the door. I had stood for some minutes looking at the silent figure in the bed. His face was almost covered by the clothes and he appeared to be asleep. Then, unable to settle down to reading, I walked slowly round the room, examining the pictures of celebrated criminals with which every wall was adorned. Finally, in my aimless perambulation, I came to the mantelpiece. A litter of pipes, tobacco-pouches, syringes, penknives, revolver-cartridges, and other debris was scattered over it. In the midst of these was a small black and white ivory box with a sliding lid. It was a neat little thing, and I had stretched out my hand to examine it more closely when—

It was a dreadful cry that he gave—a yell which might have been heard down the street. My skin went cold and my hair bristled at that horrible scream. As I turned I caught a glimpse of a convulsed face and frantic eyes. I stood paralyzed, with the little box in my hand.

"Put it down! Down, this instant, Watson—this instant, I say!" His head sank back upon the pillow and he gave a deep sigh of relief as I replaced the box upon the mantelpiece. "I hate to have my things touched, Watson. You know that I hate it. You fidget me beyond endurance. You, a doctor—you are enough to drive a patient into an asylum. Sit down, man, and let me have my rest!"

The incident left a most unpleasant impression upon my mind. The violent and causeless excitement, followed by this brutality of speech, so far removed from his usual suavity, showed me how deep was the disorganization of his mind. Of all ruins, that of a noble mind is the most deplorable. I sat in silent dejection until the stipulated time had passed. He seemed to have been watching the clock as well as I, for it was hardly six before he began to talk with the same feverish animation as before.

"Now, Watson," said he. "Have you any change in your pocket?"

"Yes."

"Any silver?"

"A good deal."

"How many half-crowns?"

"I have five."

"Ah, too few! Too few! How very unfortunate. Watson! However, such as they are you can put them in your watchpocket. And all the rest of your money in your left trouserpocket. Thank you. It will balance you so much better like that."

This was raving insanity. He shuddered, and again made a sound between a cough and a sob.

"You will now light the gas, Watson, but you will be very careful that not for one instant shall it be more than half on. I implore you to be careful, Watson. Thank you, that is excellent. No, you need not draw the blind. Now you will have the kindness to place some letters and papers upon this table within my reach. Thank you. Now some of that litter from the mantelpiece. Excellent, Watson! There is a sugar-tongs there. Kindly raise that small ivory box with its assistance. Place it here among the papers. Good! You can now go and fetch Mr. Culverton Smith, of 13 Lower Burke Street."

To tell the truth, my desire to fetch a doctor had somewhat weakened, for poor Holmes was so obviously delirious that it seemed dangerous to leave him. However, he was as eager now to consult the person named as he had been obstinate in refusing.

"I never heard the name," said I.

"Possibly not, my good Watson. It may surprise you to know that the man upon earth who is best versed in this disease is not a medical man, but a planter. Mr. Culverton Smith is a well-known resident of Sumatra, now visiting London. An outbreak of the disease upon his plantation, which was distant from medical aid, caused him to study it himself, with some rather far-reaching consequences. He is a very methodical person, and I did not desire you to start before six, because I was well aware that you would not find him in his study. If you could persuade him to come here and give us the benefit of his unique experience of this disease, the investigation of which has been his dearest hobby, I cannot doubt that he could help me."

I give Holmes's remarks as a consecutive whole and will not attempt to indicate how they were interrupted by gasping for breath and those clutchings of his hands which indicated the pain from which he was suffering. His appearance had changed for the worse during the few hours that I had been with him. Those hectic spots were more pronounced, the eyes shone more brightly out of darker hollows, and a cold sweat glimmered upon his brow. He still retained, however, the jaunty gallantry of his speech. To the last gasp he would always be the master.

"You will tell him exactly how you have left me," said he. "You will convey the very impression which is in your own mind—a dying man—a dying and delirious man. Indeed, I cannot think why the whole bed of the ocean is not one solid mass of oysters, so prolific the creatures seem. Ah, I am wandering! Strange how the brain controls the brain! What was I saying, Watson?"

"My directions for Mr. Culverton Smith."

"Ah, yes, I remember. My life depends upon it. Plead with him, Watson. There is no good feeling between us. His nephew, Watson—I had suspicions of foul play and I allowed him to see it. The boy died horribly. He has a grudge against me. You will soften him, Watson. Beg him, pray him, get him here by any means. He can save me—only he!"

"I will bring him in a cab, if I have to carry him down to it."

"You will do nothing of the sort. You will persuade him to come. And then you will return in front of him. Make any excuse so as not to come with him. Don't forget, Watson. You won't fail me. You never did fail me. No doubt there are natural enemies which limit the increase of the creatures. You and I, Watson, we have done our part. Shall the world, then, be overrun by oysters? No, no; horrible! You'll convey all that is in your mind."

I left him full of the image of this magnificent intellect babbling like a foolish child. He had handed me the key, and with a happy thought I took it with me lest he should lock himself in. Mrs. Hudson was waiting, trembling and weeping, in the passage. Behind me as I passed from the flat I heard Holmes's high, thin voice in some delirious chant. Below, as I stood whistling for a cab, a man came on me through the fog.

"How is Mr. Holmes, sir?" he asked.

It was an old acquaintance, Inspector Morton, of Scotland Yard, dressed in unofficial tweeds.

"He is very ill," I answered.

He looked at me in a most singular fashion. Had it not been too fiendish, I could have imagined that the gleam of the fanlight showed exultation in his face.

"I heard some rumour of it," said he.

The cab had driven up, and I left him.

Lower Burke Street proved to be a line of fine houses lying in the vague borderland between Notting Hill and Kensington. The particular one at which my cabman pulled up had an air of smug and demure respectability in its old-fashioned iron railings, its massive folding-door, and its shining brasswork. All was in keeping with a solemn butler who appeared framed in the pink radiance of a tinted electric light behind him.

"Yes, Mr. Culverton Smith is in. Dr. Watson! Very good, sir, I will take up your card."

My humble name and title did not appear to impress Mr. Culverton Smith. Through the half-open door I heard a high, petulant, penetrating voice.

"Who is this person? What does he want? Dear me, Staples, how often have I said that I am not to be disturbed in my hours of study?"

There came a gentle flow of soothing explanation from the butler.

"Well, I won't see him, Staples. I can't have my work interrupted like this. I am not at home. Say so. Tell him to come in the morning if he really must see me."

Again the gentle murmur.

"Well, well, give him that message. He can come in the morning, or he can stay away. My work must not be hindered."

I thought of Holmes tossing upon his bed of sickness and counting the minutes, perhaps, until I could bring help to him. It was not a time to stand upon ceremony. His life depended upon my promptness. Before the apologetic butler had delivered his message I had pushed past him and was in the room.

With a shrill cry of anger a man rose from a reclining chair beside the fire. I saw a great yellow face, coarse-grained and greasy, with heavy, double-chin, and two sullen, menacing gray eyes which glared at me from under tufted and sandy brows. A high bald head had a small velvet smoking-cap poised coquettishly upon one side of its pink curve. The skull was of enormous capacity, and yet as I looked down I saw to my amazement that the figure of the man was small and frail, twisted in the shoulders and back like one who has suffered from rickets in his childhood.

"What's this?" he cried in a high, screaming voice. "What is the meaning of this intrusion? Didn't I send you word that I would see you tomorrow morning?"

"I am sorry," said I, "but the matter cannot be delayed. Mr. Sherlock Holmes—"

The mention of my friend's name had an extraordinary effect upon the little man. The look of anger passed in an instant from his face. His features became tense and alert.

"Have you come from Holmes?" he asked.

"I have just left him."

"What about Holmes? How is he?"

"He is desperately ill. That is why I have come."

The man motioned me to a chair, and turned to resume his own. As he did so I caught a glimpse of his face in the mirror over the mantelpiece. I could have sworn that it was set in a malicious and abominable smile. Yet I persuaded myself that it must have been some nervous contraction which I had surprised, for he turned to me an instant later with genuine concern upon his features.

"I am sorry to hear this," said he. "I only know Mr. Holmes through some business dealings which we have had, but I have every respect for his talents and his character. He is an amateur of crime, as I am of disease. For him the villain, for me the microbe. There are my prisons," he continued, pointing to a row of bottles and jars which stood upon a side table. "Among those gelatine cultivations some of the very worst offenders in the world are now doing time."

"It was on account of your special knowledge that Mr. Holmes desired to see you. He has a high opinion of you and thought that you were the one man in London who could help him."

The little man started, and the jaunty smoking-cap slid to the floor.

"Why?" he asked. "Why should Mr. Holmes think that I could help him in his trouble?"

"Because of your knowledge of Eastern diseases."

"But why should he think that this disease which he has contracted is Eastern?"

"Because, in some professional inquiry, he has been working among Chinese sailors down on the docks."

Mr. Culverton Smith smiled pleasantly and picked up his smoking-cap.

"Oh, that's it—is it?" said he. "I trust the matter is not so grave as you suppose. How long has he been ill?"

"About three days."

"Is he delirious?"

"Occasionally."

"Tut, tut! This sounds serious. It would be inhuman not to answer his call. I very much resent any interruption to my work, Dr. Watson, but this case is certainly exceptional. I will come with you at once."

I remembered Holmes's injunction.

"I have another appointment," said I.

"Very good. I will go alone. I have a note of Mr. Holmes's address. You can rely upon my being there within half an hour at most."

It was with a sinking heart that I reentered Holmes's bedroom. For all that I knew the worst might have happened in my absence. To my enormous relief, he had improved greatly in the interval. His appearance was as ghastly as ever, but all trace of delirium had left him and he spoke in a feeble voice, it is true, but with even more than his usual crispness and lucidity.

"Well, did you see him, Watson?"

"Yes; he is coming."

"Admirable, Watson! Admirable! You are the best of messengers."

"He wished to return with me."

"That would never do, Watson. That would be obviously impossible. Did he ask what ailed me?"

"I told him about the Chinese in the East End."

"Exactly! Well, Watson, you have done all that a good friend could. You can now disappear from the scene."

"I must wait and hear his opinion, Holmes."

"Of course you must. But I have reasons to suppose that this opinion would be very much more frank and valuable if he imagines that we are alone. There is just room behind the head of my bed, Watson."

"My dear Holmes!"

"I fear there is no alternative, Watson. The room does not lend itself to concealment, which is as well, as it is the less likely to arouse suspicion. But just there, Watson, I fancy that it could be done." Suddenly he sat up with a rigid intentness upon his haggard face. "There are the wheels, Watson. Quick, man, if you love me! And don't budge, whatever happens—whatever happens, do you hear? Don't speak! Don't move! Just listen with all your ears." Then in an instant his sudden access of strength departed, and his masterful, purposeful talk droned away into the low, vague murmurings of a semi-delirious man.

From the hiding-place into which I had been so swiftly hustled I heard the footfalls upon the stair, with the opening and the closing of the bedroom door. Then, to my surprise, there came a long silence, broken only by the heavy breathings and gaspings of the sick man. I could imagine that our visitor was standing by the bedside and looking down at the sufferer. At last that strange hush was broken.

"Holmes!" he cried. "Holmes!" in the insistent tone of one who awakens a sleeper. "Can't you hear me, Holmes?" There was a rustling, as if he had shaken the sick man roughly by the shoulder.

"Is that you, Mr. Smith?" Holmes whispered. "I hardly dared hope that you would come."

The other laughed.

"I should imagine not," he said. "And yet, you see, I am here. Coals of fire, Holmes—coals of fire!"

"It is very good of you—very noble of you. I appreciate your special knowledge."

Our visitor sniggered.

"You do. You are, fortunately, the only man in London who does. Do you know what is the matter with you?"

"The same," said Holmes.

"Ah! You recognize the symptoms?"

"Only too well."

"Well, I shouldn't be surprised, Holmes. I shouldn't be surprised if it *were* the same. A bad lookout for you if it is. Poor Victor was a dead man on the fourth day—a strong, hearty young fellow. It was certainly, as you said, very surprising that he should have contacted an out-of-the-way Asiatic disease in the heart of London—a disease, too, of which I had made such a very special study. Singular coincidence, Holmes. Very smart of you to notice it, but rather uncharitable to suggest that it was cause and effect."

"I knew that you did it."

"Oh, you did, did you? Well, you couldn't prove it, anyhow. But what do you think of yourself spreading reports about me like that, and then crawling to me for help the moment you are in trouble? What sort of a game is that—eh?"

I heard the rasping, laboured breathing of the sick man. "Give me the water!" he gasped.

"You're precious near your end, my friend, but I don't want you to go till I have had a word with you. That's why I gave you water. There, don't slop it about! That's right. Can you understand what I say?"

Holmes groaned.

"Do what you can for me, Let bygones be bygones," he whispered. "I'll put the words out of my head—I swear I will. Only cure me, and I'll forget it."

"Forget what?"

"Well, about Victor Savage's death. You as good as admitted just now that you had done it. I'll forget it."

"You can forget it or remember it, just as you like. I don't see you in the witness-box. Quite another shaped box, my good Holmes, I assure you. It matters nothing to me that you should know how my nephew died. It's not him we are talking about. It's you."

"Yes, yes."

"The fellow who came for me—I've forgotten his name—said that you contracted it down in the East End among the sailors."

"I could only account for it so."

"You are proud of your brains, Holmes, are you not? Think yourself smart, don't you? You came across someone who was smarter this time. Now cast your mind back, Holmes. Can you think of no other way you could have got this thing?"

"I can't think. My mind is gone. For heaven's sake help me!"

"Yes, I will help you. I'll help you to understand just where you are and how you got here. I'd like you to know before you die."

"Give me something to ease my pain."

"Painful, is it? Yes, the coolies used to do some squealing towards the end. Takes you as cramp, I fancy."

"Yes, yes; it is cramp."

"Well, you can hear what I say, anyhow. Listen now! Can you remember any unusual incident in your life just about the time your symptoms began?"

"No, no: nothing."

"Think again."

"I'm too ill to think."

"Well, then, I'll help you. Did anything come by post?"

"By post?"

"A box by chance?"

"I'm fainting—I'm gone!"

"Listen, Holmes!" There was a sound as if he was shaking the dying man, and it was all that I could do to hold myself quiet in my hiding-place. "You must hear me. You *shall* hear me. Do you remember a box—an ivory box? It came on Wednesday. You opened it—do you remember?"

"Yes, yes, I opened it. There was a sharp spring inside it. Some joke—"

"It was no joke, as you will find to your cost. You fool, you would have it and you have got it. Who asked you to cross my path? If you had left me alone I would not have hurt you."

"I remember," Holmes gasped. "The spring! It drew blood. This box—this on the table."

"The very one, by George! And it may as well leave the room in my pocket. There goes your last shred of evidence. But you have the truth now, Holmes, and you can die with the knowledge that I killed you. You knew too much of the fate of Victor Savage, so I have sent you to share it. You are very near your end, Holmes. I will sit here and I will watch you die."

Holmes's voice had sunk to an almost inaudible whisper.

"What is that?" said Smith. "Turn up the gas? Ah, the shadows begin to fall, do they? Yes, I will turn it up, that I may see you the better." He crossed the room and the light suddenly brightened. "Is there any other little service that I can do you, my friend?"

"A match and a cigarette."

I nearly called out in my joy and my amazement. He was speaking in his natural voice—a little weak, perhaps, but the very voice I knew. There was a long pause, and I felt that Culverton Smith was standing in silent amazement looking down at his companion.

"What's the meaning of this?" I heard him say at last in a dry, rasping tone.

"The best way of successfully acting a part is to be it," said Holmes. "I give you my word that for three days I have tasted neither food nor drink until you were good enough to pour me out that glass of water. But it is the tobacco which I find most irksome. Ah, here *are* some cigarettes." I heard the striking of a match. "That is very much better. Halloa! halloa! Do I hear the step of a friend?"

There were footfalls outside, the door opened, and Inspector Morton appeared.

"All is in order and this is your man," said Holmes.

The officer gave the usual cautions.

"I arrest you on the charge of murder of one Victor Savage," he concluded.

"And you might add of the attempted murder of one Sherlock Holmes," remarked my friend with a chuckle. "To save an invalid trouble, Inspector, Mr. Culverton Smith was good enough to give our signal by turning up the gas. By the way, the prisoner has a small box in the right-hand pocket of his coat which it would be as well to remove. Thank you. I would handle it gingerly if I were you. Put it down here. It may play its part in the trial."

There was a sudden rush and a scuffle, followed by the clash of iron and a cry of pain.

"You'll only get yourself hurt," said the inspector. "Stand still, will you?" There was the click of the closing handcuffs.

"A nice trap!" cried the high, snarling voice. "It will bring *you* into the dock, Holmes, not me. He asked me to come here to cure him. I was sorry for him and I came. Now he will pretend, no doubt, that I have said anything which he may invent which will corroborate his insane suspicions. You can lie as you like, Holmes. My word is always as good as yours."

"Good heavens!" cried Holmes. "I had totally forgotten him. My dear Watson, I owe you a thousand apologies. To think that I should have overlooked you! I need not introduce you to Mr. Culverton Smith, since I understand that you met somewhat earlier in the evening. Have you the cab below? I will follow you when I am dressed, for I may be of some use at the station."

"I never needed it more," said Holmes as he refreshed himself with a glass of claret and some biscuits in the intervals of his toilet. "However, as you know, my habits are irregular, and such a feat means less to me than to most men. It was very essential that I should impress Mrs. Hudson with the reality of my condition, since she was to convey it to you, and you in turn to him. You won't be offended, Watson? You will realize that among your many talents dissimulation finds no place, and that if you had shared my secret you would never have been able to impress Smith with the urgent necessity of his presence, which was the vital point of the whole scheme. Knowing his vindictive nature, I was perfectly certain that he would come to look upon his handiwork."

"But your appearance, Holmes—your ghastly face?"

"Three days of absolute fast does not improve one's beauty, Watson. For the rest, there is nothing which a sponge may not cure. With vaseline upon one's forehead, belladonna in one's eyes, rouge over the cheekbones, and crusts of beeswax round one's lips, a very satisfying effect can be produced. Malingering is a subject upon which I have sometimes thought of writing a monograph. A little occasional talk about half-crowns, oysters, or any other extraneous subject produces a pleasing effect of delirium."

"But why would you not let me near you, since there was in truth no infection?"

"Can you ask, my dear Watson? Do you imagine that I have no respect for your medical talents? Could I fancy that your astute judgment would pass a dying man who, however weak, had no rise of pulse or temperature? At four yards, I could deceive you. If I failed to do so, who would bring my Smith within my grasp? No, Watson, I would not touch that box. You can just see if you look at it sideways where the sharp spring like a viper's tooth emerges as you open it. I dare say it was by some such device that poor Savage, who stood between this monster and a reversion, was done to death. My correspondence, however, is, as you know, a varied one, and I am somewhat upon my guard against any packages which reach me. It was clear to me, however, that by pretending that he had really succeeded in his design I might surprise a confession. That pretence I have carried out with the thoroughness of the true artist. Thank you, Watson, you must help me on with my coat. When we have finished at the police-station I think that something nutritious at Simpson's would not be out of place."

JACK LONDON

(1876–1916)

Much of John Griffith London's life is the stuff of legend. Born in San Francisco, he was the son of an unmarried middle-class woman from Ohio; his father was an astrologer. By age fifteen, he was working in a cannery, fighting, drinking, and reading adventure stories. To escape the life of crime he seemed destined for, he became a sailor, participated in Coxey's march on Washington to protest unemployment, and joined in the Klondike gold rush in the Yukon Territory in 1897. Somehow during all these excursions, he managed to win a newspaper story contest and attend the University of California at Berkeley. His rough-and-tumble experiences lent a brilliant, if sometimes brutal, authenticity to such classics as The Call of The Wild *(1903),* The Sea Wolf *(1904), and* White Fang *(1906). His empathy with people on the lower levels of society, coupled with his reading of Marx, Engels, Darwin, and Shaw, made him a believer in socialism, which is reflected in many of his tracts and several stories and novels. He made a million dollars on some fifty books, money he frittered away. He had become a celebrity, but his increasing problems with alcoholism and debt caused him to commit suicide at Wolf House, his ranch, cutting short the life of one of the most promising talents of the early twentieth century. London is not usually thought of as a crime writer, but his work frequently touches upon crime in an authentic way, foreshadowing later realistic trends. In the following selection, set among the Tlingit (spelled Thlinket by London) tribe of the northwest, we see London using the device of a forced confession in connection with a crime that might seem trivial in our world, but that was shocking among these Pacific coast tribespeople.*

THE MASTER OF MYSTERY

There was complaint in the village. The women chattered together with shrill, high-pitched voices. The men were glum and doubtful of aspect, and the very dogs wandered dubiously about, alarmed in vague ways by the unrest of the camp and ready to take to the woods on the first outbreak of trouble. The air was filled with suspicion. No man was sure of his neighbor, and each was conscious that he stood in like unsureness with his fellows. Even the children were oppressed and solemn, and little Di Ya, the cause of it all, had been soundly thrashed, first by Hooniah, his mother, and then by his father, Bawn, and was now whimpering and looking pessimistically out upon the world from the shelter of the big overturned canoe on the beach.

And to make the matter worse Scundoo, the shaman, was in disgrace and his known magic could not be called upon to seek out the evildoer. Forsooth, a month gone, he had promised a fair south wind so that the tribe might journey to the *potlatch* at Tonkin, where Taku Jim was giving away the savings of twenty years; and when the day came, lo, a grievous north wind blew, and of the first three canoes to venture forth, one was swamped in the big seas, and two were pounded to pieces on the rocks, and a child was drowned. He had pulled the string of the wrong bag, he explained—a mistake. But the people refused to listen; the offerings of meat and fish and fur ceased to come to his door; and he sulked within—so they thought—fasting in bitter penance; in reality, eating generously from his well-stored cache and meditating upon the fickleness of the mob.

The blankets of Hooniah were missing. They were good blankets, of most marvelous thickness and warmth, and her pride in them was greatened in that they had been come by so cheaply. Ty-Kwan, of the next village but one, was a fool to have so easily parted with them. But then, she did not know they were the blankets of the murdered Englishman, because of whose take-off the United States cutter nosed along the coast for a time, while its launches puffed and snorted among the secret inlets. And not knowing that Ty-Kwan had disposed of them in haste so that his own people might not have to render account to the Government, Hooniah's pride was unshaken. And because the women envied her, her pride was without end and boundless, till it filled the village and spilled over along the Alaskan shore from Dutch Harbor to St. Mary's. Her totem had become justly celebrated, and her name known on the lips of men wherever men fished and feasted, what of the blankets and their marvelous thickness and warmth. It was a most mysterious happening, the manner of their going.

"I but stretched them up in the sun by the sidewall of the house," Hooniah disclaimed for the thousandth time to her Thlinket sisters. "I but stretched them up and turned my back; for Di Ya, dough-thief and eater of raw flour that he is, with head into the big iron pot, overturned and stuck there, his legs waving like the branches of a forest tree in the wind. And I did but drag him out and twice knock his head against the door for riper understanding, and behold, the blankets were not!"

"The blankets were not!" the women repeated in awed whispers.

"A great loss," one added. A second, "Never were there such blankets." And a third, "We be sorry, Hooniah, for thy loss." Yet each woman was glad in her heart that the odious, dissension-breeding blankets were gone.

"I but stretched them up in the sun," Hooniah began again.

"Yea, yea," Bawn spoke up, wearied. "But there were no gossips in the village from other places. Wherefore it be plain that some of our own tribespeople have laid unlawful hand upon the blankets."

"How can that be, O Bawn?" the women chorused indignantly. "Who should there be?"

"Then has there been witchcraft," Bawn continued stolidly enough, though he stole a sly glance at their faces.

"*Witchcraft!*" And at the dread word their voices hushed and they looked fearfully at each other.

"Ay," Hooniah affirmed, the latent malignancy of her nature flashing into a moment's exultation. "And word has been sent to Klok-No-Ton, and strong paddles. Truly shall he be here with the afternoon tide."

The little groups broke up and fear descended upon the village. Of all misfortune, witchcraft was the most appalling. With the intangible and unseen things only the shamans could cope, and neither man, woman, nor child could know until the moment of ordeal whether devils possessed their souls or not. And of all shamans Klok-No-Ton, who dwelt in the next village, was the most terrible. None found more evil spirits than he, none visited his victims with more frightful tortures. Even had he found, once, a devil residing within the body of a three-months babe—a most obstinate devil which could only be driven out when the babe had lain for a week on thorns and briers. The body was thrown into the sea after that, but the waves tossed it back again and again as a curse upon the village, nor did it finally go away till two strong men were staked out at low tide and drowned.

And Hooniah had sent for this Klok-No-Ton. Better had it been if Scundoo, their own shaman, were undisgraced. For he had ever a gentler way, and he had been known to drive forth two devils from a man who afterward begat seven healthy children. But Klok-No-Ton! They shuddered with dire foreboding at thought of him, and each one felt himself the center of accusing eyes, and looked accusingly upon his fellows—each one and all, save Sime, and Sime was a scoffer whose evil end was destined with a certitude his success could not shake.

"Hoh! Hoh!" he laughed. "Devils and Klok-No-Ton!—than whom no greater devil can be found in Thlinket Land."

"Thou fool! Even now he cometh with witcheries and sorceries; so beware thy tongue, lest evil befall thee and thy days be short in the land!"

So spoke La-lah, otherwise the Cheater, and Sime laughed scornfully.

"I am Sime, unused to fear, unafraid of the dark. I am a strong man, as my father before me, and my head is clear. Nor you nor I have seen with our eyes the unseen evil things—"

"But Scundoo hath," La-lah made answer. "And likewise Klok-No-Ton. This we know."

"How dost thou know, son of a fool?" Sime thundered, the choleric blood darkening his thick bull neck.

"By the word of their mouths—even so."

Sime snorted. "A shaman is only a man. May not his words be crooked, even as thine and mine? Bah! Bah! And once more, bah! And this for thy shamans and thy shamans' devils! and this! and this!"

And Sime snapped his fingers to right and left.

When Klok-No-Ton arrived on the afternoon tide, Sime's defiant laugh was unabated; nor did he forebear to make a joke when the shaman tripped on the sand in the landing. Klok-No-Ton looked at him sourly, and without greeting stalked straight through their midst to the house of Scundoo.

Of the meeting with Scundoo none of the tribespeople might know, for they clustered reverently in the distance and spoke in whispers while the masters of mystery were together.

"Greeting, O Scundoo!" Klok-No-Ton rumbled, wavering perceptibly from doubt of his reception.

He was a giant in stature and towered massively above little Scundoo, whose thin voice floated upward like the faint far rasping of a cricket.

"Greeting, Klok-No-Ton," Scundoo returned. "The day is fair with thy coming."

"Yes it would seem . . ." Klok-No-Ton hesitated.

"Yea, yea," the little shaman put in impatiently, "that I have fallen on ill days, else would I not stand in gratitude to you in that you do my work."

"It grieves me, friend Scundoo . . ."

"Nay, I am made glad, Klok-No-Ton."

"But will I give thee half of that which be given me."

"Not so, good Klok-No-Ton," murmured Scundoo, with a deprecatory wave of the hand. "It is I who am thy slave, and my days shall be filled with desire to befriend thee."

"As I—"

"As thou now befriendest me."

"That being so, it is then a bad business, these blankets of the woman Hooniah?"

The big shaman blundered tentatively in his quest, and Scundoo smiled a wan, gray smile, for he was used to reading men, and all men seemed very small to him.

"Ever hast thou dealt in strong medicine," he said. "Doubtless the evildoer will be briefly known to thee."

"Ay, briefly known when I set eyes upon him." Again Klok-No-Ton hesitated. "Have there been gossips from other places?" he asked.

Scundoo shook his head. "Behold! Is this not a most excellent mucluc?"

He held up the foot-covering of sealskin and walrus hide, and his visitor examined it with interest.

"It did come to me by a close-driven bargain."

Klok-No-Ton nodded attentively.

"I got it from the man La-lah. He is a remarkable man, and often have I thought . . ."

"So?" Klok-No-Ton ventured impatiently.

"Often have I thought," Scundoo concluded, his voice falling as he came to a full pause. "It is a fair day, and thy medicine be strong, Klok-No-Ton."

Klok-No-Ton's face brightened. "Thou art a great man, Scundoo, a shaman of shamans. I go now. I shall remember thee always. And the man La-lah, as you say, is remarkable."

Scundoo smiled yet more wan and gray, closed the door on the heels of his departing visitor, and barred and double-barred it.

Sime was mending his canoe when Klok-No-Ton came down the beach, and he broke off from his work only long enough to load his rifle ostentatiously and place it near him.

The shaman noted the action and called out: "Let all the people come together on this spot! It is the word of Klok-No-Ton, devil-seeker and driver of devils!"

He had been minded to assemble them at Hooniah's house, but it was necessary that all should be present, and he was doubtful of Sime's obedience and did not wish trouble. Sime was a good man to let alone, his judgement ran, and a bad one for the health of any shaman.

"Let the woman Hooniah be brought," Klok-No-Ton commanded, glaring ferociously about the circle and sending chills up and down the spines of those he looked upon.

Hooniah waddled forward, head bent and gaze averted.

"Where be thy blankets?"

"I but stretched them up in the sun, and behold, they were not!" she whined.

"So?"

"It was because of Di Ya."

"So?"

"Him have I beaten sore, and he shall yet be beaten, for that he brought trouble upon us who be poor people."

"The blankets!" Klok-No-Ton bellowed hoarsely, foreseeing her desire to lower the price to be paid. "The blankets, woman! Thy wealth is known."

"I but stretched them up in the sun," she sniffled, "and we be poor people and have nothing."

He stiffened suddenly, with a hideous distortion of the face, and Hooniah shrank back. But so swiftly did he spring forward, with inturned eye-balls and loosened jaw, that she stumbled and fell groveling at his feet. He waved his arms about, wildly flagellating the air, his body writhing and twisting in torment. An epilepsy seemed to come upon him. A white froth flecked his lips, and his body was convulsed with shiverings and tremblings.

The women broke into a wailing chant, swaying backward and forward in abandonment, while one by one the men succumbed to the excitement. Only Sime remained. He, perched upon his canoe, looked on in mockery; yet the ancestors whose seed he bore pressed heavily upon him, and he swore his strongest oaths that his courage might be cheered. Klok-No-Ton was horrible to behold. He had cast off his blanket and torn his clothes from him, so that he was quite naked, save for a girdle of eagle-claws about his thighs. Shrieking and yelling, his long black hair flying like a blot of night, he leaped frantically about the circle. A certain rude rhythm characterized his frenzy, and when all were under its sway, swinging their bodies in accord with his and venting their cries in unison, he sat bolt upright, with arm outstretched and long, talon-like finger extended. A low moaning, as of the dead, greeted this, and the people cowered with shaking knees as the dread finger passed them slowly by. For death went with it, and life remained with those who watched it go; and being rejected, they watched with eager intentness.

Finally, with a tremendous cry, the fateful finger rested upon La-lah. He shook like an aspen, seeing himself already dead, his household goods divided, and his widow married to his brother. He strove to speak, to deny, but his tongue clove to his mouth and his throat was sanded with an intolerable thirst. Klok-No-Ton seemed half to swoon away, now that his work was done; but he waited with closed eyes, listening for the great blood-cry to go up—the great blood-cry, familiar to his ear from a thousand conjurations, when the tribespeople flung themselves like wolves upon the trembling victim. But there was only silence, then a low tittering from nowhere in particular which spread and spread until a vast laughter welled up to the sky.

"Wherefore?" he cried.

"Na! Na!" the people laughed. "Thy medicine be ill, O Klok-No-Ton!"

"It be known to all," La-lah stuttered. "For eight weary months have I been gone afar with the Siwash sealers, and but this day am I come back to find the blankets of Hooniah gone ere I came!"

"It be true!" they cried with one accord. "The blankets of Hooniah were gone ere he came!"

"And thou shalt be paid nothing for thy medicine which is of no avail," announced Hooniah, on her feet once more and smarting from a sense of ridiculousness.

But Klok-No-Ton saw only the face of Scundoo and its wan, gray smile, heard only the faint far cricket's rasping. "I got it from the man La-lah, and often have I thought," and, "It is a fair day and thy medicine be strong."

He brushed by Hooniah, and the circle instinctively gave way for him to pass. Sime flung a jeer from the top of the canoe, the women snickered in his face, cries of derision rose in his wake, but he took no notice, pressing onward to the house of Scundoo. He hammered on the door, beat it with his fists, and howled vile imprecations. Yet there was no response, save that in the lulls Scundoo's voice rose eerily in incantation. Klok-No-Ton raged about like a madman, but when he attempted to break in the door with a huge stone, murmurs arose from the men and women. And he, Klok-No-Ton, knew that he stood shorn of his strength and authority before an alien people. He saw a man stoop for a stone, and a second, and a bodily fear ran through him.

'Harm not Scundoo, who is a master!" a woman cried out.

"Better you return to your own village," a man advised menacingly.

Klok-No-Ton turned on his heel and went down among them to the beach, a bitter rage at his heart, and in his head a just apprehension for his defenseless back. But no stones were cast. The children swarmed mockingly about his feet, and the air was wild with laughter and derision, but that was all. Yet he did not breathe freely until his canoe was well out upon the water, when he rose up and laid a futile curse upon the village and its people, not forgetting to specify Scundoo who had made a mock of him.

Ashore there was a clamor for Scundoo and the whole population crowded his door, entreating and imploring in confused babel till he came forth and raised his hand.

"In that ye are my children I pardon freely," he said. "But never again. For the last time thy foolishness goes unpunished. That which ye wish shall be granted, and it be already known to me. This night, when the moon has gone behind the world to look upon the mighty dead, let all the people gather in the blackness before the house of Hooniah. Then shall the evildoer stand forth and take his merited reward. I have spoken."

"It shall be death!" Bawn vociferated, "for that it hath brought worry upon us, and shame."

"So be it," Scundoo replied, and shut his door.

"Now shall all be made clear and plain, and content rest upon us once again," La-lah declaimed oracularly.

"Because of Scundoo, the little man," Sime sneered.

"Because of the medicine of Scundoo, the little man," La-lah corrected.

"Children of foolishness, these Thlinket people!" Sime smote his thigh a resounding blow. "It passeth understanding that grown women and strong men should get down in the dirt to dream-things and wonder tales."

"I am a traveled man," La-lah answered. "I have journeyed on the deep seas and seen signs and wonders, and I know that these things be so. I am La-lah—"

"The Cheater—"

"So called, but the Far-Journeyer right-named."

"I am not so great a traveler—" Sime began.

"Then hold thy tongue," Bawn cut in, and they separated in anger.

When the last silver moonlight had vanished beyond the world, Scundoo came among the people huddled about the house of Hooniah. He walked with a quick, alert step, and those who saw him in the light of Hooniah's slush-lamp noticed that he came empty-handed, without rattles, masks, or shaman's paraphernalia, save for a great sleepy raven carried under one arm.

"Is there wood gathered for a fire, so that all may see when the work be done?" he demanded.

"Yea," Bawn answered. "There be wood in plenty."

"Then let all listen, for my words be few. With me have I brought Jelchs, the Raven, diviner of mystery and seer of things. Him, in his blackness, shall I place under the big black pot of Hooniah, in the blackest corner of her house. The slush-lamp shall cease to burn, and all remain in outer darkness. It is very simple. One by one shall ye go into the house, lay hand upon the pot for the space of one long intake of the breath, and withdraw again. Doubtless Jelchs will make outcry when the hand of the evildoer is nigh him. Or who knows but otherwise he may manifest his wisdom. Are ye ready?"

"We be ready," came the multivoiced response.

"Then will I call the name aloud, each in his turn and hers, till all are called."

La-lah was first chosen, and he passed in at once. Every ear strained, and through the silence they could hear his footsteps creaking across the rickety floor. But that was all. Jelchs made no outcry, gave no sign. Bawn was next chosen, for it well might be that a man should steal his own blankets with intent to cast shame upon his neighbors. Hooniah followed, and other women and children, but without result.

"Sime!" Scundoo called out.

"Sime!" he repeated.

But Sime did not stir.

"Art thou afraid of the dark?" La-lah, his own integrity being proved, demanded fiercely.

Sime chuckled. "I laugh at it all, for it is a great foolishness. Yet will I go in, not in belief in wonders, but in token that I am unafraid."

And he passed in boldly, and came out still mocking.

"Some day shalt thou die with great suddenness," La-lah whispered, righteously indignant.

"I doubt not," the scoffer answered airily. "Few men of us die in our beds, what with the shamans and the deep sea."

When half the villagers had safely undergone the ordeal, the excitement, because of its repression, became painfully intense. When two-thirds had gone through, a young woman, close on her first child-bed, broke down, and in nervous shrieks and laughter gave form to her terror.

Finally the turn came for the last of all to go in—and nothing had yet happened. And Di Ya was the last of all. It must surely be he. Hooniah let out a lament to the stars, while the rest drew back from the luckless lad. He was half dead from fright, and his legs gave under him so that he staggered on the threshold and nearly fell. Scundoo shoved him inside and closed the door. A long time went by, during which could be heard only the boy's weeping. Then, very slowly, came the creak of his steps to the far corner, a pause, and the creaking of his return. The door opened and he came forth. Nothing had happened and he was the last.

"Let the fire be lighted," Scundoo commanded.

"Surely the thing has failed," Hooniah whispered hoarsely.

"Yea," Bawn answered complacently. "Scundoo groweth old, and we stand in need of a new shaman."

Sime threw his chest out arrogantly and strutted up to the little shaman. "Hoh! Hoh! As I said, nothing has come of it!"

"So it would seem, so it would seem," Scundoo answered meekly. "And it would seem strange to those unskilled in the affair of mystery."

"As thou?" Sime queried.

"Mayhap even as I." Scundoo spoke quite softly, his eyelids dropping, slowly drooping, down, down, till his eyes were all but hidden. "So I am minded of another test. *Let every man, woman, and child, now and at once, hold their hands up above their heads!*"

So unexpected was the order, and so imperatively was it given, that it was obeyed without question. Every hand was in the air.

"Let each look on the other's hands, and let all look," Scundoo commanded, "so that—"

But a noise of laughter, which was more of wrath, drowned his voice. All eyes had come to rest upon Sime. Every hand but his was black with soot, and his was guiltless of the smirch of Hooniah's pot.

A stone hurtled through the air and struck him on the cheek.

"It is a lie!" he yelled. "A lie! I know naught of Hooniah's blankets!"

A second stone gashed his brow, a third whistled past his head, the great blood-cry went up, and everywhere were people groping for missiles.

"Where hast thou hidden them?" Scundoo's shrill, sharp voice cut through the tumult like a knife.

"In the large skin-bale in my house, the one slung by the ridge-pole," came the answer. "But it was a joke—"

Scundoo nodded his head, and the air went thick with flying

stones. Sime's wife was crying, but his little boy, with shrieks and laughter, was flinging stones with the rest.

Hooniah came waddling back with the precious blankets. Scundoo stopped her.

"We be poor people and have little," she whimpered. "So be not hard upon us, O Scundoo."

The people ceased from the quivering stone pile they had builded, and looked on.

"Nay, it was never my way, good Hooniah," Scundoo made answer, reaching for the blankets. "In token that I am not hard, these only shall I take. Am I not wise, my children?"

"Thou art indeed wise, O Scundoo!" they cried in one voice.

And Scundoo, the Master of Mystery, went away into the darkness, the blankets around him and Jelchs nodding sleepily under his arm.

ISAK DINESEN

(1885–1962)

Karen Christence Dinesen was born in Rungsted, Denmark, of an aristocratic background. After studying art at the Academy of Fine Arts in Copenhagen and in various European cities, she moved to British East Africa in 1914 to marry her cousin Baron Bror Blixen-Finecke. They raised coffee and hunted big game, but the marriage was very unhappy. When they separated in 1921 she continued to operate the plantation until coffee prices collapsed in 1931. She sold the plantation, returned to Denmark, and began to write under the name Isak Dinesen, publishing Seven Gothic Tales *(1934), a collection with romantic and supernatural elements. She would continue to work in this vein throughout her career, publishing the collections* Winter's Tales *(1943),* Last Tales *(1957),* Anecdotes of Destiny *(1958), and the posthumous* Carnival *(1977). Her only novel,* The Angelic Avengers *(1944, published under the pseudonym of Pierre Andrézel), was a satire of Denmark under Nazi occupation. Her most famous work,* Out of Africa *(1937), was an autobiographical account of her life in Kenya. The latter provided the basis for a major motion picture in 1986, starring Meryl Streep as Dinesen, which increased public interest in her work.* Shadows on the Grass *(1960) also consisted of sketches inspired by Africa. Dinesen strove very hard in both Danish and English to achieve a highly polished prose style, which, though stark at times, is more modern in its tone than many other writers in the supernatural genre. The following superb story, "The Fat Man," does not rely on supernatural elements, though its atmosphere is dark, moody, and expressionistic. The feeling of director Fritz Lang's great film about a child murderer,* M *(1931), is evoked and was likely an inspiration. In Dinesen's tale, the bartender finds an unusual way of coercing an admission of guilt, proving that sometimes a confession consists not of what is said but of what is unsaid.*

THE FAT MAN

On one November evening a horrible crime was committed in Oslo, the capital of Norway. A child was murdered in an uninhabited house on the outskirts of the town.

The newspapers brought long and detailed accounts of the murder. In the short, raw November days people stood in the street outside the house and stared up at it. The victim had been a workman's child, resentment of ancient wrongs stirred in the minds of the crowd.

The police had got but one single clue. A shopkeeper in the street told them that as he was closing up his shop on the evening of the murder he saw the murdered child walk by, her hand in the hand of a fat man.

The police had arrested some tramps and vagabonds and shady persons, but such people as a rule are not fat. So they looked elsewhere, among tradesmen and clerks of the neighborhood. Fat men were stared at in the streets. But the murderer had not been found.

In this same month of November a young student named Kristoffer Lovunden in Oslo was cramming for his examination. He had come down to the town from the north of Norway, where it is day half the year and night the other half and where people are different from other Norwegians. In a world of stone and concrete Kristoffer was sick with longing for the hills and the salt sea.

His people up in Norland were poor and could have no idea of what it cost to live in Oslo, he did not want to worry them for money. To be able to finish his studies he had taken a job as bartender at the Grand Hotel, and worked there every night from eight o'clock till midnight. He was a good-looking boy with gentle and polite manners, conscientious in the performance of his duties, and he did well as a bartender. He was abstinent himself, but took a kind of scientific interest in the composition of other people's drinks.

In this way he managed to keep alive and to go on with his lessons. But he got too little sleep and too little time for ordinary human intercourse. He read no books outside his textbooks, and not even the newspapers, so that he did not know what was happening in the world around him. He was aware himself that this was not a healthy life, but the more he disliked it the harder he worked to get it over.

In the bar he was always tired, and he sometimes fell asleep standing up, with open eyes. The brilliant light and the noises made his head swim. But as he walked home from the Grand Hotel after midnight the cold air revived him so that he entered his small room wide awake. This he knew to be a dangerous hour. If now a thing caught his mind it would stick in it with unnatural vividness and keep him from sleep, and he would be no good for his books the next day. He had promised himself not to read at this time, and while he undressed to go to bed he closed his eyes.

All the same, one night his glance fell on a newspaper wrapped round a sausage that he had brought home with him. Here he read of the murder. The paper was two days old, people would have been talking about the crime around him all the time, but he had not heard what they said. The paper was torn, the ends of the lines were missing, he had to make them up from his own imagination. After that the thing would not leave him. The words "a fat man" set his mind running from one to another of the fat men he had ever known till at last it stopped at one of them.

There was an elegant fat gentleman who often visited the bar. Kristoffer knew him to be a writer, a poet of a particular, refined, half-mystical school. Kristoffer had read a few of his poems and had himself been fascinated by their queer, exquisite choice of words and symbols. They seemed to be filled with the colors of old precious stained glass. He often wrote about medieval legends and mysteries. This winter the theater was doing a play by him named *The Werewolf,* which was in parts macabre, according to its subject, but more remarkable still for its strange beauty and sweetness. The man's appearance too was striking. He was fat, with wavy dark hair, a large white face, a small red mouth, and curiously pale eyes. Kristoffer had been told that he had lived much abroad. It was the habit of this man to sit with his back to the bar, developing his exotic theories to a circle of young admirers. His name was Oswald Senjen.

Now the poet's picture took hold of the student. All night he seemed to see the big face close to his, with all kinds of expressions. He drank much cold water but was as hot as before. This fat man of the Grand Hotel, he thought, was the fat man of the newspaper.

It did not occur to him, in the morning, to play the part of a detective. If he went to the police they would send him away, since he had no facts whatever, no argument or reason even, to put before them. The fat man would have an alibi. He and his friends would laugh, they would think him mad or they would be indignant and complain to the manager of the hotel, and Kristoffer would lose his job.

So for three weeks the odd drama was played between the two actors only: the grave young bartender behind the bar and the smiling poet before it. The one was trying hard all the time to get out of it, the other knew nothing about it. Only once did the parties look each other in the face.

A few nights after Kristoffer had read about the murder, Oswald Senjen came into the bar with a friend. Kristoffer had no wish to spy upon them—it was against his own will that he moved to the side of the bar where they sat.

They were discussing fiction and reality. The friend held that to a poet the two must be one, and that therefore his existence must be mysteriously happy. The poet contradicted him. A poet's mission in life, he said, was to make others confound fiction with reality in order to render them, for an hour, mysteriously happy. But he himself must, more carefully than the crowd, hold the two apart. "Not as far as enjoyment of them is concerned," he added, "I enjoy fiction, I enjoy reality too. But I am happy because I have an unfailing instinct for distinguishing one from the other. I know fiction where I meet it. I know reality where I meet it."

This fragment of conversation stuck in Kristoffer's mind, he went over it many times. He himself had often before pondered on the idea of happiness and tried to find out whether such a thing really existed. He had asked himself if anybody was happy and, if so, who was happy. The two men at the bar had repeated the word more than once—they were probably happy. The fat man, who knew reality when he saw it, had said that he was happy.

Kristoffer remembered the shopkeeper's evidence. The face of the little girl Mattea, he had explained, when she passed him in the rainy street, had looked happy, as if, he said, she had been promised something, or was looking forward to something, and was skipping along toward it. Kristoffer thought: "And the man by her side?" Would his face have had an expression of happiness as well? Would he too have been looking forward to something? The shopkeeper had not had time to look the man in the face, he had seen only his back.

Night after night Kristoffer watched the fat man. At first he felt it to be a grim jest of fate that he must have this man with him wherever he went, while the man himself should hardly be aware of his existence. But after a time he began to believe that his unceasing observation had an effect on the observed, and that he was somehow changing under it. He grew fatter and whiter, his eyes grew paler. At moments he was as absent-minded as Kristoffer himself. His pleasing flow of speech would run slower, with sudden unneeded pauses, as if the skilled talker could not find his words.

If Oswald Senjen stayed in the bar till it closed, Kristoffer would slip out while he was being helped into his furred coat in the hall, and wait for him outside. Most often Oswald Senjen's large car would be there, and he would get into it and glide off. But twice he slowly walked along the street, and Kristoffer followed him. The boy felt himself to be a mean, wild figure in the town and the night, sneaking after a man who had done him no harm, and about whom he knew nothing, and he hated the figure who was dragging him after it. The first time it seemed to him that the fat man turned his head a little to one side and the other as if to make sure that there was nobody close behind him. But the second time he walked on looking straight ahead, and Kristoffer then wondered if that first slight nervous movement had not been a creation of his own imagination.

One evening in the bar the poet turned in his deep chair and looked at the bartender.

Toward the end of November Kristoffer suddenly remembered that his examination was to begin within a week. He was dismayed and seized with pangs of conscience, he thought of his future and of his people up in Norland. The deep fear within him grew stronger. He must shake off his obsession or he would be ruined by it.

At this time an unexpected thing happened. One evening Oswald Senjen got up to leave early, his friends tried to hold him back but he would not stay. "Nay," he said, "I want a rest. I want to rest." When he had gone, one of his friends said: "He was looking bad tonight. He is much changed. Surely he has got something the matter with him." One of the others answered: "It is that old matter from when he was out in China. But he ought to look after himself. Tonight one might think that he would not last till the end of the year."

As Kristoffer listened to these assertions from an outside and real world he felt a sudden, profound relief. To this world the man himself, at least, was a reality. People talked about him.

"It might be a good thing," he thought, "it might be a way out if I could talk about the whole matter to somebody else."

He did not choose a fellow student for his confidant. He could imagine the kind of discussion this would bring about and his mind shrank from it. He turned for help to a simple soul, a boy two or three years younger than himself, who washed up at the bar and who was named Hjalmar.

Hjalmar was born and bred in Oslo, he knew all that could be known about the town and very little about anything outside it. He and Kristoffer had always been on friendly terms, and Hjalmar enjoyed a short chat with Kristoffer in the scullery, after working hours, because he knew that Kristoffer would not interrupt him. Hjalmar was a revolutionary spirit, and would hold forth on the worthless rich customers of the bar, who rolled home in big cars with gorgeous women with red lips and nails, while underpaid sailors hauled tarred ropes, and tired laborers led their plowhorses to the stable. Kristoffer wished that he would not do so, for at such times his nostalgia for boats and tar, and for the smell of a sweaty horse, grew so strong that it became a physical pain. And the deadly horror that he felt at the idea of driving home with one of the women Hjalmar described proved to him that his nervous system was out of order.

As soon as Kristoffer mentioned the murder to Hjalmar he found that the scullery boy knew everything about it. Hjalmar had his pockets filled with newspaper cuttings, from which he read reports of the crime and of the arrests, and angry letters about the slowness of the police.

Kristoffer was uncertain how to explain his theory to Hjalmar. In the end he said: "Do you know, Hjalmar, I believe that the fat gentleman in the bar is the murderer." Hjalmar stared at him, his mouth open. The next moment he had caught the idea, and his eyes shone.

After a short while Hjalmar proposed that they should go to the police, or again to a private detective. It took Kristoffer some time to convince his friend, as he had convinced himself, that their case was too weak, and that people would think them mad.

Then Hjalmar, more eager even than before, decided that they must be detectives themselves.

To Kristoffer it was a strange experience, both steadying and alarming, to face his own nightmare in the sharp white light of the scullery, and to hear it discussed by another live person. He felt that he was holding on to the scullery boy like a drowning man to a swimmer; every moment he feared to drag his rescuer down with him, into the dark sea of madness.

The next evening Hjalmar told Kristoffer that they would find some scheme by which to surprise the murderer and make him give himself away.

Kristoffer listened to his various suggestions for some time, then smiled a little. He said: "Hjalmar, thou art even such a man . . ." He stopped. "Nay," he said, "you will not know this piece, Hjalmar. But let me go on a little, all the same—!

I have heard
that guilty creatures sitting at a play
have by the very cunning of the scene
been struck so to the soul that presently
they have proclaim'd their malefactions.
For murder, though it have no tongue, will speak.

"I understand that very well," said Hjalmar.

"Do you, Hjalmar?" asked Kristoffer. "Then I shall tell you one thing more:

the plays's the thing
wherein we'll catch the conscience of the king.

"Where have you got that from?" asked Hjalmar. "From a play

called *Hamlet,*" said Kristoffer. "And how do you mean to go and do it?" asked Hjalmar again. Kristoffer was silent for some time.

"Look here, Hjalmar," he said at last, "you told me that you have got a sister."

"Yes," said Hjalmar, "I have got five of them."

"But you have got one sister of nine," said Kristoffer, "the same age as Mattea?"

"Yes," said Hjalmar.

"And she has got," Kristoffer went on, "a school mackintosh with a hood to it, like the one Mattea had on that night?"

"Yes," said Hjalmar.

Kristoffer began to tremble. There was something blasphemous in the comedy which they meant to act. He could not have gone on with it if he had not felt that somehow his reason hung upon it.

"Listen, Hjalmar," he said, "we will choose an evening when the man is in the bar. Then make your little sister put on her mackintosh, and make one of your big sisters bring her here. Tell her to walk straight from the door, through all the room, up to the bar, to me, and to give me something—a letter or what you will. I shall give her a shilling for doing it, and she will take it from the counter when she has put the letter there. Then tell her to walk back again, through the room."

"Yes," said Hjalmar.

"If the manager complains," Kristoffer added after a while, "we will explain that it was all a misunderstanding."

"Yes," said Hjalmar.

"I myself," said Kristoffer, "must stay at the bar. I shall not see his face, for he generally sits with his back to me, talking to people. But you will leave the washing up for a short time, and go round and keep guard by the door. You will watch his face from there."

"There will be no need to watch his face," said Hjalmar, "he will scream or faint, or jump up and run away, you know."

"You must never tell your sister, Hjalmar," said Kristoffer, "why we made her come here."

"No, no," said Hjalmar.

On the evening decided upon for the experiment, Hjalmar was silent, set on his purpose. But Kristoffer was in two minds. Once or twice he came near to giving up the whole thing. But if he did so, and even if he could make Hjalmar understand and forgive—what would become of himself afterwards?

Oswald Senjen was in his chair in his usual position, with his back to the bar. Kristoffer was behind the bar, Hjalmar was at the swinging door of the hall, to receive his sister.

Through the glass door Kristoffer saw the child arrive in the hall, accompanied by an elder sister with a red feather in her hat, for in these winter months people did not let children walk alone in the streets at night. At the same time he became aware of something in the room that he had not noticed before. "I can never, till tonight," he told himself, "have been quite awake in this place, or I should have noticed it." To each side of the glass door there was a tall looking glass, in which he could see the faces turned away from him. In both of them he now saw Oswald Senjen's face.

The little girl in her mackintosh and hood had some difficulty opening the door, and was assisted by her brother. She walked straight up to the bar, neither fast nor slow, placed the letter on the counter, and collected her shilling. As she did so she lifted her small pale face in the hood slightly, and gave her brother's friend a little pert, gentle grin of acquittal—now that the matter was done with. Then she turned and walked back and out of the door, neither fast nor slow.

"Was it right?" she asked her brother who had been waiting for her by the door. Hjalmar nodded, but the child was puzzled at the expression of his face and looked at her big sister for an explanation. Hjalmar remained in the hall till he had seen the two girls disappear in the rainy street. Then the porter asked him what he was doing there, and he ran round to the back entrance and to his tub and glasses.

The next guest who ordered a drink at the bar looked at the bartender and said: "Hello, are you ill?" The bartender did not answer a word. He did not say a word either when, an hour later, as the bar closed, he joined his friend in the scullery.

"Well, Kristoffer," said Hjalmar, "he did not scream or faint, did he?"

"No," said Kristoffer.

Hjalmar waited a little. "If it is him," he said, "he is tough."

Kristoffer stood quite still for a long time, looking at the glasses. At last he said: "Do you know why he did not scream or faint?"

"No," said Hjalmar, "why was it?"

Kristoffer said: "Because he saw the only thing he expected to see. The only thing he ever sees now. All the other men in the bar gave some sign of surprise at the sight of a little girl in a mackintosh walking in here. I watched the fat man's face in the mirror, and saw that he looked straight at her as she came in, and that his eyes followed her as she walked out, but that his face did not change at all."

"What?" said Hjalmar. After a few moments he repeated very low: "What?"

"Yes, it is so," said Kristoffer. "A little girl in a mackintosh is the only thing he sees wherever he looks. She has been with him here in the bar before. And in the streets. And in his own house. For three weeks."

There was a long silence.

"Are we to go to the police now, Kristoffer?" Hjalmar asked.

"We need not go to the police," said Kristoffer. "We need not do anything in the matter. You and I are too heavy, or too grown up, for that. Mattea does it as it ought to be done. It is her small light step that has followed close on his own all the time. She looks at him, just as your sister looked at me, an hour ago. He wanted rest, he said. She will get it for him before the end of the year."

Hoist on Their Own Petards

The petard was a particularly notorious form of early cannon that often blew up its own cannoneer; the term has survived in our language to mean a device that turns against its user. In crime stories many authors use such ironic reversals to enthrall us. Just as an evil deed so carefully calculated and perfectly planned is about to triumph, something blasts the weapon back upon its creator. Often, the exact source of this reversal, this poetic justice, is not clear. Sometimes it might seem like the plotter's bad luck, but the best writers avoid this implication. Other times, a flaw in the criminal's reasoning is often stated or implied. A criminal mind capable of such plots may overlook an obvious, but essential, detail because of its own skewed perspective. (Consider William Brittain's story earlier in this volume.) The most important implication, however, is that there is a moral order, and that occasionally a godlike force intervenes to preserve that moral order. This adherence to The Golden Rule makes the petard story enduringly popular: If you do unto others, the same shall be done unto you. Ironically, to be successful, a petard story (like a caper story) requires that the reader become involved in, even revel in, the criminal's scheme. The reader enjoys a guilty pleasure because the victim of the scheme deserves some punishment, but usually it is the contrivance of the scheme that delights the reader. As in the assembly of a clockwork mechanism, each part of the machinery (be it mechanical or a series of social occurrences) is carefully put into action. Often it is not clear as the story progresses how these parts will work together, but as they move into action the evildoer seems to have created the perfect instrument of crime. In the traditional whodunit, the crime has already been committed and the significance of the details, the crucial clues, may not be clear until the solution is revealed. In a petard story, the crime has yet to be committed, and among the details is a significant flaw (analogous to a crucial clue) that will cause the whole crime to blow up on its creator. At the conclusion, as the flaw is identified, much of the reader's delight comes from the fact that the flaw was in plain sight all along. The reader is allowed to enjoy the creation of the theoretically perfect crime—and even to admire it—but then is reassured that there is no such thing.

ANNA KATHARINE GREEN

(1846–1935)

Anna Katharine Green is one of the most important pioneers of the mystery genre. Critics argue that she may have been the first woman to write a detective novel, and she appears to have been the first writer to use the term "detective story." Born in Brooklyn, New York, she attended Ripley Female College in Poultney, Vermont, graduating in 1867 with a degree in English. At first she wrote poetry, earning praise from Ralph Waldo Emerson, but with the publication of The Leavenworth Case *(1878) she became one of the most popular prose writers in America for several decades. The novel, an authentic look at criminal justice, was based on elements of her father's career as a noted criminal attorney. The hero, Ebenezer Gryce, was a portly police detective with the capacity for building a case out of minute observations. Agatha Christie's character Hercule Poirot was inspired partly by a number of Gryce novels, though Gryce is not a gentleman but more of a working policeman. In addition to a number of Gryce novels, Green also wrote several novels featuring Amelia Butterworth, who is a prototype for Agatha Christie's Miss Marple. Green also created a young woman who solved crimes, Violet Strange, a precursor to Nancy Drew. Despite Green's prominence as a founder of the mystery genre, the novelty of a woman writing crime novels faded rapidly as more women took up the pen. By the 1920s the sentimental quality of much of Green's work seemed dated in comparison to the writing style of the day. Nonetheless, she remained for nearly forty years as a major figure. The ingredients of her mysteries are still in regular use. In "Midnight in Beauchamp Row," Green uses the standard ingredients of a woman in jeopardy and the least likely suspect as she explores the contemporaneous racial prejudices about criminals. For our purposes, the story provides an excellent example of how a criminal may be "hoist on his own petard."*

MIDNIGHT IN BEAUCHAMP ROW

It was the last house in Beauchamp Row, and it stood several rods away from its nearest neighbor. It was a pretty house in the daytime, but owing to its deep, sloping roof and small bediamonded windows it had a lonesome look at night, notwithstanding the crimson hall-light which shone through the leaves of its vine-covered doorway.

Ned Chivers lived in it with his six months' married bride, and as he was both a busy fellow and a gay one there were many evenings when pretty Letty Chivers sat alone until near midnight.

She was of an uncomplaining spirit, however, and said little, though there were times when both the day and evening seemed very long and married life not altogether the paradise she had expected.

On this evening—a memorable evening for her, the twenty-fourth of December, 1894—she had expected her husband to remain with her, for it was not only Christmas eve, but the night when, as manager of a large manufacturing concern, he brought up from New York the money with which to pay off the men on the next working day, and he never left her when there was any unusual amount of money in the house. But from the first glimpse she had of him coming up the road she knew she was to be disappointed in this hope, and, indignant, alarmed almost, at the prospect of a lonesome evening under these circumstances, she ran hastily down to the gate to meet him, crying:

"Oh, Ned, you look so troubled I know you have only come home for a hurried supper. But you cannot leave me to-night. Tennie" (their only maid) "has gone for a holiday, and I never can stay in this house alone with all that." She pointed to the small bag he carried, which, as she knew, was filled to bursting with bank notes.

He certainly looked troubled. It is hard to resist the entreaty in a young bride's uplifted face. But this time he could not help himself, and he said:

"I am dreadful sorry, but I must ride over to Fairbanks to-night. Mr. Pierson has given me an imperative order to conclude a matter of business there, and it is very important that it should be done. I should lose my position if I neglected the matter, and no one but Hasbrouck and Suffren knows that we keep the money in the house. I have always given out that I intrusted it to Hale's safe over night."

"But I cannot stand it," she persisted. "You have never left me on these nights. That is why I let Tennie go. I will spend the evening at The Larches, or, better still, call in Mr. and Mrs. Talcott to keep me company."

But her husband did not approve of her going out or of her having company. The Larches was too far away, and as for Mr. and Mrs. Talcott, they were meddlesome people, whom he had never liked; besides, Mrs. Talcott was delicate, and the night threatened storm. It seemed hard to subject her to this ordeal, and he showed that he thought so by his manner, but, as circumstances were, she would have to stay alone, and he only hoped she would be brave and go to bed like a good girl, and think nothing about the money, which he would take care to put away in a very safe place.

"Or," said he, kissing her downcast face, "perhaps you would rather hide it yourself; women always have curious ideas about such things."

"Yes, let me hide it," she murmured. "The money, I mean, not the bag. Every one knows the bag. I should never dare to leave it in that." And begging him to unlock it, she began to empty it with a feverish haste that rather alarmed him, for he surveyed her anxiously and shook his head as if he dreaded the effects of this excitement upon her.

But as he saw no way of averting it he confined himself to using such soothing words as were at his command, and then, humoring her weakness, helped her to arrange the bills in the place she had chosen, and restuffing the bag with old receipts till it acquired its former dimensions, he put a few bills on top to make the whole look natural, and, laughing at her white face, relocked the bag and put the key back in his pocket.

"There, dear; a notable scheme and one that should relieve your mind entirely!" he cried. "If any one should attempt burglary in my absence and should succeed in getting into a house as safely locked as this will be when I leave it, then trust to their being satisfied when they see this booty, which I shall hide where I always hide it—in the cupboard over my desk."

"And when will you be back?" she murmured, trembling in spite of herself at these preparations.

"By one o'clock if possible. Certainly by two."

"And our neighbors go to bed at ten," she murmured. But the words were low, and she was glad he did not hear them, for if it was his duty to obey the orders he had received, then it was her duty to meet the position in which it left her as bravely as she could.

At supper she was so natural that his face rapidly brightened, and it was with quite an air of cheerfulness that he rose at last to lock up the house and make such preparations as were necessary for his dismal ride over the mountains to Fairbanks. She had the supper dishes to wash up in Tennie's absence, and as she was a busy little housewife she found herself singing a snatch of song as she passed back and forth from dining-room to kitchen. He heard it, too, and smiled to himself as he bolted the windows on the ground floor and examined the locks of the three lower doors, and when he finally came into the kitchen with his great-coat on to give her his final kiss, he had but one parting injunction to urge, and that was that she should lock the front door after him and then forget the whole matter till she heard his double knock at midnight.

She smiled and held up her ingenuous face.

"Be careful of yourself," she murmured. "I hate this dark ride for you, and on such a night too." And she ran with him to the door to look out.

"It is certainly very dark," he responded, "but I'm to have one of Brown's safest horses. Do not worry about me. I shall do well enough, and so will you, too, or you are not the plucky little woman I have always thought you."

She laughed, but there was a choking sound in her voice that made him look at her again. But at sight of his anxiety she recovered herself, and pointing to the clouds said earnestly:

"It is going to snow. Be careful as you ride by the gorge, Ned; it is very deceptive there in a snowstorm."

But he vowed that it would not snow before morning, and giving her one final embrace he dashed down the path toward Brown's livery stable. "Oh, what is the matter with me?" she murmured to herself as his steps died out in the distance. "I never knew I was such a coward." And she paused for a moment, looking up and down the road, as if in despite of her husband's command she had the desperate idea of running away to some neighbor.

But she was too loyal for that, and smothering a sigh she retreated into the house. As she did so the first flakes fell of the storm that was not to have come till morning.

It took her an hour to get her kitchen in order, and nine o'clock struck before she was ready to sit down. She had been so busy she had not noticed how the wind had increased or how rapidly the snow was falling. But when she went to the front door for another glance up and down the road she started back, appalled at the fierceness of the gale and at the great pile of snow that had already accumulated on the doorstep.

Too delicate to breast such a wind, she saw herself robbed of her last hope of any companionship, and sighing heavily she locked and bolted the door for the night and went back into her little sitting-room, where a great fire was burning. Here she sat down, and determined, now that she must pass the evening alone, to do it as cheerfully as possible, and so began to sew. "Oh, what a Christmas eve!" she thought, and a picture of other homes rose before her eyes, homes in which husbands sat by wives and brothers by sisters, and a great wave of regret poured over her and a longing for something, she hardly dared say what, lest her unhappiness should acquire a sting that would leave traces beyond the passing moment.

The room in which she sat was the only one on the ground floor except the dining-room and kitchen. It therefore was used both as parlor and sitting-room, and held not only her piano, but her husband's desk.

Communicating with it was the tiny dining-room. Between the two, however, was an entry leading to a side entrance. A lamp was in this entry, and she had left it burning, as well as the one in the kitchen, that the house might look cheerful and as if all the family were at home.

She was looking toward this entry and wondering whether it was the mist made by her tears that made it look so dismally dark to her when there came a faint sound from the door as its further end.

Knowing that her husband must have taken peculiar pains with the fastenings of this door, as it was the one toward the woods and therefore most accessible to wayfarers, she sat where she was, with all her faculties strained to listen. But no further sound came from that direction, and after a few minutes of silent terror she was allowing herself to believe that she had been deceived by her fears when she suddenly heard the same sound at the kitchen door, followed by a muffled knock.

Frightened now in good earnest, but still alive to the fact that the intruder was as likely to be a friend as a foe, she stepped to the door, and with her hand on the lock stooped and asked boldly enough who was there. But she received no answer, and more affected by this unexpected silence than by the knock she had heard she recoiled farther and farther till not only the width of the kitchen, but the dining-room also, lay between her and the scene of her alarm, when to her utter confusion the noise shifted again to the side of the house, and the door she thought so securely fastened, swung violently open as if blown in by a fierce gust, and she saw precipitated into the entry the burly figure of a man covered with snow and shaking with the violence of the storm that seemed at once to fill the house.

Her first thought was that it was her husband come back, but before she could clear her eyes from the cloud of snow which had entered with him he had thrown off his outer covering and she found herself face to face with a man in whose powerful frame and cynical visage she saw little to comfort her and much to surprise and alarm.

"Ugh!" was his coarse and rather familiar greeting. "A hard night, missus! Enough to drive any man indoors. Pardon the liberty, but I couldn't wait for you to lift the latch; the wind drove me right in."

"Was—was not the door locked?" she feebly asked, thinking he must have staved it in with his foot, that looked only too well fitted for such a task.

"Not much," he chuckled. "I s'pose you're too hospitable for that." And his eyes passed from her face to the comfortable fire-light shining through the sitting-room.

"Is it refuge you want?" she demanded, suppressing as much as possible all signs of fear.

"Sure, missus—what else! A man can't live in a gale like that, specially after a tramp of twenty miles or more. Shall I shut the door for you?" he asked, with a mixture of bravado and good nature that frightened her more and more.

"I will shut it," she replied, with a half notion of escaping this sinister stranger by a flight through the night.

But one glance into the swirling snow-storm deterred her, and making the best of the alarming situation, she closed the door, but did not lock it, being more afraid now of what was inside the house than of anything left to threaten her from without.

The man, whose clothes were dripping with water, watched her with a cynical smile, and then, without any invitation, entered the dining-room, crossed it and moved toward the kitchen fire.

"Ugh! ugh! But it is warm here!" he cried, his nostrils dilating with an animal-like enjoyment that in itself was repugnant to her womanly delicacy. "Do you know, missus, I shall have to stay here all night? Can't go out in that gale again; not such a fool." Then with a sly look at her trembling form and white face he insinuatingly added, "All alone, missus?"

The suddenness with which this was put, together with the leer that accompanied it, made her start. Alone? Yes, but should she acknowledge it? Would it not be better to say that her husband was up-stairs. The man evidently saw the struggle going on in her mind, for he chuckled to himself and called out quite boldly:

"Never mind, missus; it's all right. Just give me a bit of cold meat and a cup of tea or something, and we'll be very comfortable together. You're a slender slip of a woman to be minding a house like this. I'll keep you company if you don't mind, leastwise until the storm lets up a bit, which ain't likely for some hours to come. Rough night, missus, rough night."

"I expect my husband home at any time," she hastened to say. And thinking she saw a change in the man's countenance at this she put on quite an air of sudden satisfaction and bounded toward the front of the house. "There! I think I hear him now," she cried.

Her motive was to gain time, and if possible to obtain the opportunity of shifting the money from the place where she had first put it into another and safer one. "I want to be able," she thought, "of swearing that I have no money with me in this house. If I can only get it into my apron I will drop it outside the door into the snowbank. It will be as safe there as in the bank it came from." And dashing into the sitting-room she made a feint of dragging down a shawl from a screen, while she secretly filled her skirt with the bills which had been put between some old pamphlets on the bookshelves.

She could hear the man grumbling in the kitchen, but he did not follow her front, and taking advantage of the moment's respite from his none too encouraging presence she unbarred the door and cheerfully called out her husband's name.

The ruse was successful. She was enabled to fling the notes where the falling flakes would soon cover them from sight, and feeling more courageous, now that the money was out of the house, she went slowly back, saying she had made a mistake, and that it was the wind she had heard.

The man gave a gruff but knowing guffaw and then resumed his watch over her, following her steps as she proceeded to set him out a meal, with a persistency that reminded her of a tiger just on the point of springing. But the inviting look of the viands with which she was rapidly setting the table soon distracted his attention, and allowing himself one grunt of satisfaction, he drew up a chair and set himself down to what to him was evidently a most savory repast.

"No beer? No ale? Nothing o' that sort, eh? Don't keep a bar?" he growled, as his teeth closed on a huge hunk of bread.

She shook her head, wishing she had a little cold poison bottled up in a tight-looking jug.

"Nothing but tea," she smiled, astonished at her own ease of manner in the presence of this alarming guest.

"Then let's have that," he grumbled, taking the bowl she handed him, with an odd look that made her glad to retreat to the other side of the room.

"Jest listen to the howling wind," he went on between the huge mouthfuls of bread and cheese with which he was gorging himself. "But we're very comfortable, we two! We don't mind the storm, do we?"

Shocked by his familiarity and still more moved by the look of mingled inquiry and curiosity with which his eyes now began to wander over the walls and cupboards, she took an anxious step toward the side of the house looking toward her neighbors, and lifting one of the shades, which had all been religiously pulled down, she looked out. A swirl of snowflakes alone confronted her. She could neither see her neighbors, nor could she be seen by them. A shout from her to them would not be heard. She was as completely isolated as if the house stood in the center of a desolate western plain.

"I have no trust but in God," she murmured as she came from the window. And, nerved to meet her fate, she crossed to the kitchen.

It was now half-past ten. Two hours and a half must elapse before her husband could possibly arrive.

She set her teeth at the thought and walked resolutely into the room.

"Are you done?" she asked.

"I am, ma'am," he leered. "Do you want me to wash the dishes? I kin, and I will." And he actually carried his plate and cup to the sink, where he turned the water upon them with another loud guffaw.

"If only his fancy would take him into the pantry," she thought, "I could shut and lock the door upon him and hold him prisoner till Ned gets back."

But his fancy ended its flight at the sink, and before her hopes had fully subsided he was standing on the threshold of the sitting-room door.

"It's pretty here," he exclaimed, allowing his eye to rove again over every hiding-place within sight. "I wonder now"—He stopped. His glance had fallen on the cupboard over her husband's desk.

"Well?" she asked, anxious to break the thread of his thought, which was only too plainly mirrored in his eager countenance.

He started, dropped his eyes, and turning looked at her with a momentary fierceness. But, as she did not let her own glance quail, but continued to look at him with what she meant for a smile on her pale lips, he subdued this outward manifestation of passion, and, chuckling to hide his embarrassment, began backing into the entry, leering in evident enjoyment of the fears he caused, with what she felt was a most horrible smile. Once in the hall, he hesitated, however, for a long time; then he slowly went toward the garment he had dropped on entering and stooping, drew from underneath its folds a wicked-looking stick. Giving a kick to the coat, which sent it into a remote corner, he bestowed upon her another smile, and still carrying the stick went slowly and reluctantly away into the kitchen.

"Oh, God Almighty, help me!" was her prayer.

There was nothing for her to do now but endure, so throwing herself into a chair, she tried to calm the beating of her heart and summon up courage for the struggle which she felt was before her. That he had come to rob and only waited to take her off her guard she now felt certain, and rapidly running over in her mind all the expedients of self-defense possible to one in her situation, she suddenly remembered the pistol which Ned kept in his desk. Oh, why had she not thought of it before! Why had she let herself grow mad with terror when here, within reach of her hand, lay such a means of self-defense? With a feeling of joy (she had always hated pistols before and scolded Ned when he bought this one) she started to her feet and slid her hand into the drawer. But it came back empty. Ned had taken the weapon away with him.

For a moment, a surge of the bitterest feeling she had ever experienced passed over her; then she called reason to her aid and was obliged to acknowledge that the act was but natural, and that from his standpoint he was much more likely to need it than herself. But the disappointment, coming so soon after hope, unnerved her, and she sank back in her chair, giving herself up for lost.

How long she sat there with her eyes on the door, through which she momentarily expected her assailant to reappear, she never knew. She was conscious only of a sort of apathy that made movement difficult and even breathing a task. In vain she tried to change her thoughts. In vain she tried to follow her husband in fancy over the snow-covered roads and into the gorge of the mountains. Imagination failed her at this point. Do what she would, all was misty in her mind's eye, and she could not see that wandering image. There was blankness between his form and her, and no life or movement anywhere but here in the scene of her terror.

Her eyes were on a strip of rug that covered the entry floor, and so strange was the condition of her mind that she found herself mechanically counting the tassels that finished its edge, growing wroth over one that was worn, till she hated that sixth tassel and mentally determined that if she ever outlived this night she would strip them all off and be done with them.

The wind had lessened, but the air had grown cooler and the snow made a sharp sound where it struck the panes. She felt it falling, though she had cut off all view of it. It seemed to her that a pall was settling over the world and that she would soon be smothered under its folds. Meanwhile no sound came from the kitchen, only that dreadful sense of a doom creeping upon her—a sense that grew in intensity till she found herself watching for the shadow of that lifted stick on the wall of the entry, and almost imagined she saw the tip of it appearing, when without any premonition, that fatal side door again blew in and admitted another man of so threatening an aspect that she succumbed instantly before him and forgot all her former fears in this new terror.

The second intruder was a negro of powerful frame and lowering aspect, and as he came forward and stood in the doorway there was observable in his fierce and desperate countenance no attempt at the insinuation of the other, only a fearful resolution that made her feel like a puppet before him, and drove her, almost without her volition, to her knees.

"Money? Is it money you want?" was her desperate greeting. "If so, here's my purse and here are my rings and watch. Take them and go."

But the stolid wretch did not even stretch out his hands. His eyes went beyond her, and the mingled anxiety and resolve which he displayed would have cowed a stouter heart than that of this poor woman.

"Keep de trash," he growled. "I want de company's money. You've got it—two thousand dollars. Show me where it is, that's all, and I won't trouble you long after I close on it."

"But it's not in the house," she cried. "I swear it is not in the house. Do you think Mr. Chivers would leave me here alone with two thousand dollars to guard?"

But the negro, swearing that she lied, leaped into the room, and tearing open the cupboard above her husband's desk, seized the bag from the corner where they had put it.

"He brought it in this," he muttered, and tried to force the bag open, but finding this impossible he took out a heavy knife and cut a big hole in its side. Instantly there fell out the pile of old receipts with which they had stuffed it, and seeing these he stamped with rage, and flinging them in one great handful at her rushed to the drawers below, emptied them, and, finding nothing, attacked the bookcase.

"The money is somewhere here. You can't fool me," he yelled. "I saw the spot your eyes lit on when I first came into the room. Is it behind these books?" he growled, pulling them out and throwing them helter-shelter over the floor. "Women is smart in the hiding business. Is it behind these books, I say?"

They had been, or rather had been placed between the books, but she had taken them away, as we know, and he soon began to realize that his search was bringing him nothing, for leaving the bookcase he gave the books one kick, and seizing her by the arm, shook her with a murderous glare on his strange and distorted features.

"Where's the money?" he hissed. "Tell me, or you are a goner."

He raised his heavy fist. She crouched and all seemed over, when, with a rush and a cry, a figure dashed between them and he fell, struck down by the very stick she had so long been expecting to see fall upon her own head. The man who had been her terror for hours had at the moment of need acted as her protector.

She must have fainted, but if so, her unconscious was but momentary, for when she again recognized her surroundings she found the tramp still standing over her adversary.

"I hope you don't mind, ma'am," he said, with an air of humbleness she certainly had not seen in him before, "but I think the man's dead." And he stirred with his foot the heavy figure before him.

"Oh, no, no, no!" she cried. "That would be too fearful. He's shocked, stunned; you cannot have killed him."

But the tramp was persistent. "I'm 'fraid I have," he said. "I done it before, and it's been the same every time. But I couldn't see a man of that color frighten a lady like you. My supper was too warm in me, ma'am. Shall I throw him outside the house?"

"Yes," she said, and then, "No; let us first be sure there is no life in him." And, hardly knowing what she did, she stooped down and peered into the glassy eyes of the prostrate man.

Suddenly she turned pale—no, not pale, but ghastly, and cowering back, shook so that the tramp, into whose features a certain refinement had passed since he had acted as her protector, thought she had discovered life in those set orbs, and was stooping down to make sure that this was so, when he saw her suddenly lean forward and, impetuously plunging her hand into the negro's throat, tear open the shirt and give one look at his bared breast.

It was white.

"O God! O God!" she moaned, and lifting the head in her two hands she gave the motionless features a long and searching look. "Water!" she cried. "Bring water." But before the now obedient tramp could respond, she had torn off the woolly wig disfiguring the dead man's head, and seeing the blond curls beneath had uttered such a shriek that it rose above the gale and was heard by her distant neighbors.

It was the head and hair of her husband.

They found out afterwards that he had contemplated this theft for months, that each and every precaution possible to a successful issue to this most daring undertaking had been made use of and that but for the unexpected presence in the house of the tramp, he would doubtless have not only extorted the money from his wife, but have so covered up the deed by a plausible *alibi* as to have retained her confidence and that of his employers.

Whether the tramp killed him out of sympathy for the defenseless woman or in rage at being disappointed in his own plans has never been determined. Mrs. Chivers herself thinks he was actuated by a rude sort of gratitude.

RAYMOND CHANDLER

(1888–1959)

Raymond Chandler wandered through many jobs before taking up a career as a writer. Born in Chicago, he was taken to England as a child by his mother. He was educated at Dulwich College and in Europe. Chandler served in the Canadian army and in the Royal Air Force during World War I. Later he worked for the Admiralty and as a reporter. Chandler returned to the United States to work on a ranch, in a sporting goods firm, for a creamery, a bank, a Los Angeles newspaper, then an oil firm. In 1933 he finally became a full-time writer. His seven novels and his short stories are easily among the most influential that the genre has produced. Recent polls of published crime writers in England and the United States place The Big Sleep *(1939),* Farewell, My Lovely *(1940), and* The Long Goodbye *(1954) among the top crime novels of all time; Chandler's stature in the rest of the world may be even greater. His brilliant essay, "The Simple Art of Murder" (1944), has become the starting point for anyone wishing to consider the style, logic, and meaning of the modern crime novel. What sets Chandler apart is not only his brilliant characterization, or even his moral view, but his unique and powerful style. Through the voice of a stoic, sympathetic hero (usually Philip Marlowe), he portrays the hero's seemingly futile battle against societal corruption. By the dark days of the Great Depression, readers rejoiced in any tiny victory over the overwhelming evil their hero faced while retaining a sense of how small that victory was. In Chandler's view, a tiny victory is perhaps the best people can do in our time. This tragic irony is something of which Chandler's heroes are very aware. Yet, they cannot refuse to act or they will cease to be human. "Down these mean streets a man must go," Chandler wrote. This existentialist view is an outgrowth of its time, but even today remains a profound statement about the human condition, like the story that follows, one that reflects the repercussions of a man's actions.*

I'LL BE WAITING

At one o'clock in the morning, Carl, the night porter, turned down the last of three table lamps in the main lobby of the Windermere Hotel. The blue carpet darkened a shade or two and the walls drew back into remoteness. The chairs filled with shadowy loungers. In the corners were memories like cobwebs.

Tony Reseck yawned. He put his head on one side and listened to the frail, twittery music from the radio room beyond a dim arch at the far side of the lobby. He frowned. That should be his radio room after one A.M. Nobody should be in it. That red-haired girl was spoiling his nights.

The frown passed and a miniature of a smile quirked at the corners of his lips. He sat relaxed, a short, pale, paunchy, middle-aged man with long, delicate fingers clasped on the elk's tooth on his watch chain; the long delicate fingers of a sleight-of-hand artist, fingers with shiny, molded nails and tapering first joints, fingers a little spatulate at the ends. Handsome fingers. Tony Reseck rubbed them gently together and there was peace in his quiet sea-gray eyes.

The frown came back on his face. The music annoyed him. He got up with a curious litheness, all in one piece, without moving his clasped hands from the watch chain. At one moment he was leaning back relaxed, and the next he was standing balanced on his feet, perfectly still, so that the movement of rising seemed to be a thing perfectly perceived, an error of vision. . . .

He walked with small, polished shoes delicately across the blue carpet and under the arch. The music was louder. It contained the hot, acid blare, the frenetic, jittering runs of a jam session. It was too loud. The red-haired girl sat there and stared silently at the fretted part of the big radio cabinet as though she could see the band with its fixed professional grin and the sweat running down its back. She was curled up with her feet under her on a davenport which seemed to contain most of the cushions in the room. She was tucked among them carefully, like a corsage in the florist's tissue paper.

She didn't turn her head. She leaned there, one hand in a small fist on her peach-colored knee. She was wearing lounging pajamas of heavy ribbed silk embroidered with black lotus buds.

"You like Goodman, Miss Cressy?" Tony Reseck asked.

The girl moved her eyes slowly. The light in there was dim, but the violet of her eyes almost hurt. They were large, deep eyes without a trace of thought in them. Her face was classical and without expression.

She said nothing.

Tony smiled and moved his fingers at his sides, one by one, feeling them move. "You like Goodman, Miss Cressy?" he repeated gently.

"Not to cry over," the girl said tonelessly.

Tony rocked back on his heels and looked at her eyes. Large, deep, empty eyes. Or were they? He reached down and muted the radio.

"Don't get me wrong," the girl said. "Goodman makes money, and a lad that makes legitimate money these days is a lad you have to respect. But this jitterbug music gives me the backdrop of a beer flat. I like something with roses in it."

"Maybe you like Mozart," Tony said.

"Go on, kid me," the girl said.

"I wasn't kidding you, Miss Cressy. I think Mozart was the greatest man that ever lived—and Toscanini is his prophet."

"I thought you were the house dick." She put her head back on a pillow and stared at him through her lashes.

"Make me some of that Mozart," she added.

"It's too late," Tony sighed. "You can't get it now."

She gave him another long lucid glance. "Got the eye on me,

haven't you, flatfoot?" She laughed a little, almost under her breath. "What did I do wrong?"

Tony smiled his toy smile. "Nothing, Miss Cressy. Nothing at all. But you need some fresh air. You've been five days in this hotel and you haven't been outdoors. And you have a tower room."

She laughed again. "Make me a story about it. I'm bored."

"There was a girl here once had your suite. She stayed in the hotel a whole week, like you. Without going out at all, I mean. She didn't speak to anybody hardly. What do you think she did then?"

The girl eyed him gravely. "She jumped her bill."

He put his long delicate hand out and turned it slowly, fluttering the fingers, with an effect almost like a lazy wave breaking. "Unh-uh. She sent down for her bill and paid it. Then she told the hop to be back in half an hour for her suitcases. Then she went out on her balcony."

The girl leaned forward a little, her eyes still grave, one hand capping her peach-colored knee. "What did you say your name was?"

"Tony Reseck."

"Sounds like a hunky."

"Yeah," Tony said. "Polish."

"Go on, Tony."

"All the tower suites have private balconies, Miss Cressy. The walls of them are too low for fourteen stories above the street. It was a dark night, that night, high clouds." He dropped his hand with a final gesture, a farewell gesture. "Nobody saw her jump. But when she hit, it was like a big gun going off."

"You're making it up, Tony." Her voice was a clean dry whisper of sound.

He smiled his toy smile. His quiet sea-gray eyes seemed almost to be smoothing the long waves of her hair. "Eve Cressy," he said musingly. "A name waiting for lights to be in."

"Waiting for a tall dark guy that's no good, Tony. You wouldn't care why. I was married to him once. I might be married to him again. You can make a lot of mistakes in just one lifetime." The hand on her knee opened slowly until the fingers were strained back as far as they would go. Then they closed quickly and tightly, and even in that dim light the knuckles shone like the little polished bones. "I played him a low trick once. I put him in a bad place—without meaning to. You wouldn't care about that either. It's just that I owe him something."

He leaned over softly and turned the knob on the radio. A

waltz formed itself dimly on the warm air. A tinsel waltz, but a waltz. He turned the volume up. The music gushed from the loudspeaker in a swirl of shadowed melody. Since Vienna died, all waltzes are shadowed.

The girl put her hand on one side and hummed three or four bars and stopped with a sudden tightening of her mouth.

"Eve Cressy," she said. "It was in lights once. At a bum night club. A dive. They raided it and the lights went out."

He smiled at her almost mockingly. "It was no dive while you were there, Miss Cressy . . . That's the waltz the orchestra always played when the old porter walked up and down in front of the hotel entrance, all swelled up with his medals on his chest. *The Last Laugh.* Emil Jannings. You wouldn't remember that one, Miss Cressy."

" 'Spring, Beautiful Spring,' " she said. "No, I never saw it."

He walked three steps away from her and turned. "I have to go upstairs and palm doorknobs. I hope I didn't bother you. You ought to go to bed now. It's pretty late."

The tinsel waltz stopped and a voice began to talk. The girl spoke through the voice. "You really thought something like that—about the balcony?"

He nodded. "I might have," he said softly. "I don't any more."

"No chance, Tony." Her smile was a dim lost leaf. "Come and talk to me some more. Redheads don't jump, Tony. They hang on—and wither."

He looked at her gravely for a moment and then moved away over the carpet. The porter was standing in the archway that led to the main lobby. Tony hadn't looked that way yet, but he knew somebody was there. He always knew if anybody was close to him. He could hear the grass grow, like the donkey in *The Blue Bird.*

The porter jerked his chin at him urgently. His broad face above the uniform collar looked sweaty and excited. Tony stepped up close to him and they went together through the arch and out to the middle of the dim lobby.

"Trouble?" Tony asked wearily.

"There's a guy outside to see you, Tony. He won't come in. I'm doing a wipe-off on the plate glass of the doors and he comes up beside me, a tall guy. 'Get Tony,' he says, out of the side of his mouth.

Tony said: "Uh-huh," and looked at the porter's pale blue eyes. "Who was it?"

"Al, he said to say he was."

Tony's face became as expressionless as dough. "Okey." He started to move off.

The porter caught his sleeve. "Listen, Tony. You got any enemies?"

Tony laughed politely, his face still like dough.

"Listen, Tony." The porter held his sleeve tightly. "There's a big black car down the block, the other way from the hacks. There's a guy standing beside it with his foot on the running board. This guy that spoke to me, he wears a dark-colored, wrap-around overcoat with a high collar turned up against his ears. His hat's way low. You can't hardly see his face. He says, 'Get Tony,' out of the side of his mouth. You ain't got any enemies, have you, Tony?"

"Only the finance company," Tony said. "Beat it."

He walked slowly and a little stiffly across the blue carpet, up the three shallow steps to the entrance lobby with the three elevators on one side and the desk on the other. Only one elevator was working. Beside the open doors, his arms folded, the night operator stood silent in a neat blue uniform with silver facings. A lean, dark Mexican named Gomez. A new boy, breaking in on the night shift.

The other side was the desk, rose marble, with the night clerk leaning on it delicately. A small neat man with a wispy reddish mustache and cheeks so rosy they looked roughed. He stared at Tony and poked a nail at his mustache.

Tony pointed a stiff index finger at him, folded the other three fingers tight to his palm, and flicked his thumb up and down on the stiff finger. The clerk touched the other side of his mustache and looked bored.

Tony went on past the closed and darkened newsstand and the side entrance to the drugstore, out to the brassbound plate-glass doors. He stopped just inside them and took a deep, hard breath. He squared his shoulders, pushed the doors open and stepped out into the cold damp night air.

The street was dark, silent. The rumble of traffic on Wilshire, two blocks away, had no body, no meaning. To the left were two taxis. Their drivers leaned against a fender, side by side, smoking. Tony walked the other way. The big dark car was a third of a block from the hotel entrance. Its lights were dimmed and it was only when he was almost up to it that he heard the gentle sound of its engine turning over.

A tall figure detached itself from the body of the car and strolled toward him, both hands in the pockets of the dark overcoat with the high collar. From the man's mouth a cigarette tip glowed faintly, a rusty pearl.

They stopped two feet from each other.

The tall man said, "Hi, Tony. Long time no see."

"Hello, Al. How's it going?"

"Can't complain." The tall man started to take his right hand out of his overcoat pocket, then stopped and laughed quietly. "I forgot. Guess you don't want to shake hands."

"That don't mean anything," Tony said. "Shaking hands. Monkeys can shake hands. What's on your mind, Al?"

"Still the funny little fat guy, eh, Tony?"

"I guess." Tony winked his eyes tight. His throat felt tight.

"You like your job back there?"

"It's a job."

Al laughed his quiet laugh again. "You take it slow, Tony. I'll take it fast. So it's a job and you want to hold it. Okey. There's a girl named Eve Cressy flopping in your quiet hotel. Get her out. Fast and right now."

"What's the trouble?"

The tall man looked up and down the street. A man behind in the car coughed lightly. "She's hooked with a wrong number. Nothing against her personal, but she'll lead trouble to you. Get her out, Tony. You got maybe an hour."

"Sure," Tony said aimlessly, without meaning.

Al took his hand out of his pocket and stretched it against Tony's chest. He gave him a light lazy push. "I wouldn't be telling you just for the hell of it, little fat brother. Get her out of there."

"Okey," Tony said, without any tone in his voice.

The tall man took back his hand and reached for the car door. He opened it and started to slip in like a lean black shadow.

Then he stopped and said something to the men in the car and got out again. He came back to where Tony stood silent, his pale eyes catching a little dim light from the street.

"Listen, Tony. You always kept your nose clean. You're a good brother, Tony."

Tony didn't speak.

Al leaned toward him, a long urgent shadow, the high collar almost touching his ears. "It's trouble business, Tony. The boys won't like it, but I'm telling you just the same. This Cressy was married to a lad named Johnny Ralls. Ralls is out of Quentin two, three days, or a week. He did a three-spot for manslaughter. The girl put him there. He ran down an old man one night when he was drunk, and she was with him. He wouldn't stop. She told him to go in and tell it, or else. He didn't go in. So the Johns come for him."

Tony said, "That's too bad."

"It's kosher, kid. It's my business to know. This Ralls flapped his mouth in stir about how the girl would be waiting for him when he got out, all set to forgive and forget, and he was going straight to her."

Tony said, "What's he to you?" His voice had a dry, stiff crackle, like thick paper.

Al laughed. "The trouble boys want to see him. He ran a table at a spot on the Strip and figured out a scheme. He and another guy took the house for fifty grand. The other lad coughed up, but we still need Johnny's twenty-five. The trouble boys don't get paid to forget."

Tony looked up and down the dark street. One of the taxi drivers flicked a cigarette stub in a long arc over the top of one of the cabs. Tony watched it fall and spark on the pavement. He listened to the quiet sound of the big car's motor.

"I don't want any part of it," he said, "I'll get her out."

Al backed away from him, nodding. "Wise kid. How's mom these days?"

"Okey," Tony said.

"Tell her I was asking for her."

"Asking for her isn't anything," Tony said.

Al turned quickly and got into the car. The car curved lazily in the middle of the block and drifted back toward the corner. Its lights went up and sprayed on a wall. It turned a corner and was gone. The lingering smell of its exhaust drifted past Tony's nose. He turned and walked back to the hotel and into it. He went along to the radio room.

The radio still muttered, but the girl was gone from the davenport in front of it. The pressed cushions were hollowed out by her body. Tony reached down and touched them. He thought they were still warm. He turned the radio off and stood there, turning a thumb slowly in front of his body, his hand flat against his stomach. Then he went back through the lobby toward the elevator bank and stood beside a majolica jar of white sand. The clerk fussed behind a pebbled-glass screen at one end of the desk. The air was dead.

The elevator bank was dark. Tony looked at the indicator of the middle car and saw that it was at 14.

"Gone to bed," he said under his breath.

The door of the porter's room beside the elevators opened and the little Mexican night operator came out in street clothes. He looked at Tony with a quiet sidewise look out of eyes the color of dried-out chestnuts.

"Good night, boss."

"Yeah," Tony said absently.

He took a thin dappled cigar out of his vest pocket and smelled it. He examined it slowly, turning it around in his neat fingers. There was a small tear along the side. He frowned at that and put the cigar away.

There was a distant sound and the hand on the indicator began to steal around the bronze dial. Light glittered up in the shaft and the straight line of the car floor dissolved the darkness below. The car stopped and the doors opened, and Carl came out of it.

His eyes caught Tony's with a kind of jump and he walked over to him, his head on one side, a thin shine along his pink upper lip.

"Listen, Tony."

Tony took his arm in a hard swift hand and turned him. He pushed him quickly, yet somehow casually, down the steps to the dim main lobby and steered him into a corner. He let go of the arm. His throat tightened again, for no reason he could think of.

"Well?" he said darkly. "Listen to what?"

The porter reached into a pocket and hauled out a dollar bill. "He gimme this," he said loosely. His glittering eyes looked past Tony's shoulder at nothing. They winked rapidly. "Ice and ginger ale."

"Don't stall," Tony growled.

"Guy in Fourteen-B," the porter said.

"Lemme smell your breath."

The porter leaned toward him obediently.

"Liquor," Tony said harshly.

"He gimme a drink."

Tony looked down at the dollar bill. "Nobody's in Fourteen-B. Not on my list," he said.

"Yeah. There is." The porter licked his lips and his eyes opened and shut several times. "Tall dark guy."

"All right," Tony said crossly. "All right. There's a tall dark guy in Fourteen-B and he gave you a buck and a drink. Then what?"

"Gat under his arm," Carl said, and blinked.

Tony smiled, but his eyes had taken on the lifeless glitter of thick ice. "You take Miss Cressy up to her room?"

Carl shook his head. "Gomez. I saw her go up."

"Get away from me," Tony said between his teeth. "And don't accept any more drinks from the guests."

He didn't move until Carl had gone back into his cubbyhole by the elevators and shut the door. Then he moved silently up the three steps and stood in front of the desk, looking at the veined rose marble, the onyx pen set, the fresh registration card in its leather frame. He lifted a hand and smacked it down hard on the marble. The clerk popped out from behind the glass screen like a chipmunk coming out of its hole.

Tony took a flimsy out of his breast pocket and spread it on the desk. "No Fourteen-B on this," he said in a bitter voice.

The clerk wisped politely at his mustache. "So sorry. You must have been out to supper when he checked in."

"Who?"

"Registered as James Watterson, San Diego." The clerk yawned.

"Ask for anybody?"

The clerk stopped in the middle of the yawn and looked at the top of Tony's head. "Why yes. He asked for a swing band. Why?"

"Smart, fast and funny," Tony said. "If you like 'em that way." He wrote on his flimsy and stuffed it back into his pocket. "I'm going upstairs and palm doorknobs. There's four tower rooms you ain't rented yet. Get up on your toes, son. You're slipping."

"I made out," the clerk drawled, and completed his yawn. "Hurry back, pop. I don't know how I'll get through the time."

"You could shave that pink fuzz off your lip," Tony said, and went across to the elevators.

He opened up a dark one and lit the dome light and shot the car up to fourteen. He darkened it again, stepped out and closed the doors. This lobby was smaller than any other, except the one immediately below it. It had a single blue-paneled door in each of the walls other than the elevator wall. On each door was a gold number and letter with a gold wreath around it. Tony walked over to 14A and put his ear to the panel. He heard nothing. Eve Cressy might be in bed asleep, or in the bathroom, or out on the balcony. Or she might be sitting there in the room, a few feet from the door, looking at the wall. Well, he wouldn't expect to be able to hear her sit and look at the wall. He went over to 14B and put his ear to that panel. This was different. There was a sound in there. A man coughed. It sounded somehow like a solitary cough. There were no voices. Tony pressed the small nacre button beside the door.

Steps came without hurry. A thickened voice spoke through the panel. Tony made no answer, no sound. The thickened voice repeated the question. Lightly, maliciously, Tony pressed the bell again.

Mr. James Watterson, of San Diego, should now open the door and give forth noise. He didn't. A silence fell beyond that door that was like the silence of a glacier. Once more Tony put his ear to the wood. Silence utterly.

He got out a master key on a chain and pushed it delicately into the lock of the door. He turned it, pushed the door inward three inches and withdrew the key. Then he waited.

"All right," the voice said harshly. "Come in and get it."

Tony pushed the door wide and stood there, framed against the light from the lobby. The man was tall, black-haired, angular and white-faced. He held a gun. He held it as though he knew about guns.

"Step right in," he drawled.

Tony went in through the door and pushed it shut with his shoulder. He kept his hands a little out from his sides, the clever fingers curled and slack. He smiled his quiet little smile.

"Mr. Watterson?"

"And after that what?"

"I'm the house detective here."

"It slays me."

The tall, white-faced, somehow handsome and somehow not handsome man backed slowly into the room. It was a large room with a low balcony around two sides of it. French doors opened out on the little private open-air balcony that each of the tower rooms had. There was a grate set for a log fire behind a paneled screen in front of a cheerful davenport. A tall misted glass stood on a hotel tray beside a deep, cozy chair. The man backed toward this and stood in front of it. The large, glistening gun drooped and pointed at the floor.

"It slays me," he said. "I'm in the dump an hour and the house copper gives me the bus. Okey, sweetheart, look in the closet and bathroom. But she just left."

"You didn't see her yet," Tony said.

The man's bleached face filled with unexpected lines. His thickened voice edged toward a snarl. "Yeah? Who didn't I see yet?"

"A girl named Eve Cressy."

The man swallowed. He put his gun down on the table beside

the tray. He let himself down into the chair backwards, stiffly, like a man with a touch of lumbago. Then he leaned forward and put his hands on his kneecaps and smiled brightly between his teeth. "So she got here, huh? I didn't ask about her yet. I'm a careful guy. I didn't ask yet."

"She's been here five days," Tony said. "Waiting for you. She hasn't left the hotel a minute."

The man's mouth worked a little. His smile had a knowing tilt to it. "I got delayed a little up north," he said smoothly. "You know how it is. Visiting old friends. You seem to know a lot about my business, copper."

"That's right, Mr. Ralls."

The man lunged to his feet and his hand snapped at the gun. He stood leaning over, holding it on the table, staring. "Dames talk too much," he said with a muffled sound in his voice as though he held something soft between his teeth and talked through it.

"Not dames, Mr. Ralls."

"Huh?" The gun slithered on the hard wood of the table. "Talk it up, copper. My mind reader just quit."

"Not dames, guys. Guys with guns."

The glacier silence fell between them again. The man straightened his body out slowly. His face was washed clean of expression, but his eyes were haunted. Tony leaned in front of him, a shortish plump man with a quiet, pale, friendly face and eyes as simple as forest water.

"They never run out of gas—those boys," Johnny Ralls said, and licked at his lip. "Early and late, they work. The old firm never sleeps."

"You know who they are?" Tony said softly.

"I could maybe give nine guesses. And twelve of them would be right."

"The trouble boys," Tony said, and smiled a brittle smile.

"Where is she?" Johnny Ralls asked harshly.

"Right next door to you."

The man walked to the wall and left his gun lying on the table. He stood in front of the wall, studying it. He reached up and gripped the grillwork of the balcony railing. When he dropped his hand and turned, his face had lost some of its lines. His eyes had a quieter glint. He moved back to Tony and stood over him.

"I've got a stake," he said. "Eve sent me some dough and I built it up with a touch I made up north. Case dough, what I mean. The trouble boys talk about twenty-five grand." He smiled crookedly. "Five C's I can count. I'd have a lot of fun making them believe that, I would."

"What did you do with it?" Tony asked indifferently.

"I never had it, copper. Leave that lay. I'm the only guy in the world that believes it. It was a little deal that I got suckered on."

"I'll believe it," Tony said.

"They don't kill often. But they can be awful tough."

"Mugs," Tony said with a sudden bitter contempt. "Guys with guns. Just mugs."

Johnny Ralls reached for his glass and drained it empty. The ice cubes tinkled softly as he put it down. He picked his gun up, danced it on his palm, then tucked it, nose down, into an inner breast pocket. He stared at the carpet.

"How come you're telling me this, copper?"

"I thought maybe you'd give her a break."

"And if I wouldn't?"

"I kind of think you will," Tony said.

Johnny Ralls nodded quietly. "Can I get out of here?"

"You could take the service elevator to the garage. You could rent a car. I can give you a card to the garage man."

"You're a funny little guy," Johnny Ralls said.

Tony took out a worn ostrich-skin billfold and scribbled on a printed card. Johnny Ralls read it, and stood holding it, tapping it against a thumbnail.

"I could take her with me," he said, his eyes narrow.

"You could take a ride in a basket too," Tony said. "She's been here five days, I told you. She's been spotted. A guy I know called me up and told me to get her out of here. Told me what it was all about. So I'm getting you out instead."

"They'll love that," Johnny Ralls said. "They'll send you violets."

"I'll weep about it on my day off."

Johnny Ralls turned his hand over and stared at the palm. "I could see her, anyway. Before I blow. Next door to here, you said?"

Tony turned on his heel and started for the door. He said over his shoulder, "Don't waste a lot of time, handsome. I might change my mind."

The man said, almost gently: "You might be spotting me right now, for all I know."

Tony didn't turn his head. "That's a chance you have to take."

He went on to the door and passed out of the room. He shut it carefully, silently, looked once at the door of 14-A and got into his dark elevator. He rode it down to the linen-room floor and got out to remove the basket that held the service elevator open at that floor. The door slid quietly shut. He held it so that it made no noise. Down the corridor, light came from the open door of the housekeeper's office. Tony got back into his elevator and went on down to the lobby.

The little clerk was out of sight behind his pebbled-glass screen, auditing accounts. Tony went through the main lobby and turned into the radio room. The radio was on again, soft. She was there, curled on the davenport again. The speaker hummed to her, a vague sound so low that what it said was as wordless as the murmur of trees. She turned her head slowly and smiled at him.

"Finished palming doorknobs? I couldn't sleep worth a nickel. So I came down again. Okey?"

He smiled and nodded. He sat down in a green chair and patted the plump brocade arms of it. "Sure, Miss Cressy."

"Waiting is the hardest kind of work, isn't it? I wish you'd talk to that radio. It sounds like a pretzel being bent."

Tony fiddled with it, got nothing he liked, set it back where it had been.

"Beer-parlor drunks are all the customers now."

She smiled at him again.

"I don't bother you being here, Miss Cressy?"

"I like it. You're a sweet little guy, Tony."

He looked stiffly at the floor and a ripple touched his spine. He waited for it to go away. It went slowly. Then he sat back, relaxed again, his neat fingers clasped on his elk's tooth. He listened. Not to the radio—to far-off, uncertain things, menacing things. And perhaps to just the safe whir of wheels going away into a strange night.

"Nobody's all bad," he said out loud.

The girl looked at him lazily. "I've met two or three I was wrong on, then."

He nodded. "Yeah," he admitted judiciously. "I guess there's some that are."

The girl yawned and her deep violet eyes half closed. She nestled back into the cushions. "Sit there for a while, Tony. Maybe I could nap."

"Sure. Not a thing for me to do. Don't know why they pay me."

She slept quickly and with complete stillness, like a child. Tony hardly breathed for ten minutes. He just watched her, his mouth a little open. There was a quiet fascination in his limpid eyes, as if he was looking at an altar.

Then he stood up with infinite care and padded away under the arch to the entrance lobby and the desk. He stood at the desk listening for a little while. He heard a pen rustling out of sight. He went around the corner to the row of house phones in little glass cubbyholes. He lifted one and asked the night operator for the garage.

It rang three or four times and then a boyish voice answered: "Windermere Hotel. Garage speaking."

"This is Tony Reseck. That guy Watterson I gave a card to. He leave?"

"Sure, Tony. Half an hour almost. Is it your charge?"

"Yeah," Tony said. "My party. Thanks. Be seein' you."

He hung up and scratched his neck. He went back to the desk and slapped a hand on it. The clerk wafted himself around the screen with his greeter's smile in place. It dropped when he saw Tony.

"Can't a guy catch up on his work?" he grumbled.

"What's the professional rate on Fourteen-B?"

The clerk stared morosely. "There's no professional rate in the tower."

"Make one. The fellow left already. Was there only an hour."

"Well, well," the clerk said airily. "So the personality didn't click tonight. We get a skip-out."

"Will five bucks satisfy you?"

"Friend of yours?"

"No. Just a drunk with delusions of grandeur and no dough."

"Guess we'll have to let it ride, Tony. How did he get out?"

"I took him down the service elevator. You was asleep. Will five bucks satisfy you?"

"Why?"

The worn ostrich-skin wallet came out and a weedy five slipped across the marble. "All I could shake him for," Tony said loosely.

The clerk took the five and looked puzzled. "You're the boss," he said, and shrugged. The phone shrilled on the desk and he reached for it. He listened and then pushed it toward Tony. "For you."

Tony took the phone and cuddled it close to his chest. He put his mouth close to the transmitter. The voice was strange to him. It had a metallic sound. Its syllables were meticulously anonymous.

"Tony? Tony Reseck?"

"Talking."

"A message from Al. Shoot?"

Tony looked at the clerk. "Be a pal," he said over the mouthpiece. The clerk flicked a narrow smile at him and went away. "Shoot," Tony said into the phone.

"We had a little business with a guy in your place. Picked him up scramming. Al had a hunch you'd run him out. Tailed him and took him to the curb. Not so good. Backfire."

Tony held the phone very tight and his temples chilled with the evaporation of moisture. "Go on," he said. "I guess there's more."

"A little. The guy stopped the big one. Cold. Al—Al said to tell you goodbye."

Tony leaned hard against the desk. His mouth made a sound that was not speech.

"Get it?" The metallic voice sounded impatient, a little bored. "This guy had him a rod. He used it. Al won't be phoning anybody any more."

Tony lurched at the phone, and the base of it shook on the rose marble. His mouth was a hard dry knot.

The voice said: "That's as far as we go, bub. G'night." The phone clicked dryly, like a pebble hitting a wall.

Tony put the phone down in its cradle very carefully, so as not to make any sound. He looked at the clenched palm of his left hand. He took a handkerchief out and rubbed the palm softly and straightened the fingers out with his other hand. Then he wiped his forehead. The clerk came around the screen again and looked at him with glinting eyes.

"I'm off Friday. How about lending me that phone number?"

Tony nodded at the clerk and smiled a minute frail smile. He put his handkerchief away and patted the pocket he had put it in. He turned and walked away from the desk, across the entrance lobby, down the three shallow steps, along the shadowy reaches of the main lobby, and so in through the arch to the radio room once more. He walked softly, like man moving in a room where somebody is very sick. He reached the chair he had sat in before and lowered himself into it inch by inch. The girl slept on, motionless, in that curled-up looseness achieved by some women and all cats. Her breath made no slightest sound against the vague murmur of the radio.

Tony Reseck leaned back in the chair and clasped his hands on his elk's tooth and quietly closed his eyes.

SHIRLEY JACKSON

(1919–1965)

Shirley Jackson is one of those writers whose fame, like that of Thomas Burke or Susan Glaspell, is based primarily upon a single, remarkable short story that has captured widespread public attention. No matter how often anthologized and taught in high schools, "The Lottery," with its strange ritualistic killing, is far from the limit of her versatile talent. She was born in San Francisco, grew up in Rochester, New York, and attended Syracuse University, where she established, edited, and wrote for the student literary magazine. After her marriage to literary critic Stanley Edgar Hyman she moved to Vermont, where Hyman taught at Bennington College, famous for its writing workshops. She published stories in The New Yorker, Harper's, Vogue, *and other periodicals and also published several novels, including* The Road Through the Wall *(1948),* Hangsaman *(1951), and* We Have Always Lived in the Castle *(1962), among others.* The Haunting of Hill House *(1959) was adapted into a minor fright classic,* The Haunting *(1963), directed by Robert Wise and starring Julie Harris and Claire Bloom. She also wrote humorous books about raising her children and living in Vermont, and a children's book on the Salem witch trials. Jackson's sense of the evil in ordinary life is the most memorable element of her work. She uses apparently realistic settings and pushes them to a Gothic feel, often incorporating the supernatural. These dimensions of Jackson's work were described by Stanley Hyman as a metaphorical way of expressing the real terrors of day-to-day existence. In the following selection, Jackson is at her best, revealing the texture of evil in a small community, creating a parable about how malice begins in an excessive sincerity and, like Frankenstein's monster, grows to consume its earnest creator.*

THE POSSIBILITY OF EVIL

Miss Adela Strangeworth came daintily along Main Street on her way to the grocery. The sun was shining, the air was fresh and clear after the night's heavy rain, and everything in Miss Strangeworth's little town looked washed and bright. Miss Strangeworth took deep breaths and thought that there was nothing in the world like a fragrant summer day.

She knew everyone in town, of course; she was fond of telling strangers—tourists who sometimes passed through the town and stopped to admire Miss Strangeworth's roses—that she had never spent more than a day outside this town in all her long life. She was seventy-one, Miss Strangeworth told the tourists, with a pretty little dimple showing by her lip, and she sometimes found herself thinking that the town belonged to her. "My grandfather built the first house on Pleasant Street," she would say, opening her blue eyes wide with the wonder of it. "This house, right here. My family has lived here for better than a hundred years. My grandmother planted these roses, and my mother tended them, just as I do. I've watched my town grow; I can remember when Mr. Lewis, Senior, opened the grocery store, and the year the river flooded out the shanties on the low road, and the excitement when some young folks wanted to move the park over to the space in front of where the new post office is today. They wanted to put up a statue of Ethan Allen"—Miss Strangeworth would frown a little and sound stern—"but it should have been a statue of my grandfather. There wouldn't have been a town here at all if it hadn't been for my grandfather and the lumber mill."

Miss Strangeworth never gave away any of her roses, although the tourists often asked her. The roses belonged on Pleasant Street, and it bothered Miss Strangeworth to think of people wanting to carry them away, to take them into strange towns and down strange streets. When the new minister came, and the ladies were gathering flowers to decorate the church, Miss Strangeworth sent over a great basket of gladioli; when she picked the roses at all, she set them in bowls and vases around the inside of the house her grandfather had built.

Walking down Main Street on a summer morning, Miss Strangeworth had to stop every minute or so to say good morning to someone or to ask after someone's health. When she came into the grocery, half a dozen people turned away from the shelves and the counters to wave at her or call out good morning.

"And good morning to you, too, Mr. Lewis," Miss Strangeworth said at last. The Lewis family had been in the town almost as long as the Strangeworths; but the day young Lewis left high school and went to work in the grocery, Miss Strangeworth had stopped calling him Tommy and started calling him Mr. Lewis, and he had stopped calling her Addie and started calling her Miss Strangeworth. They had been in high school together, and had gone to picnics together, and to high-school dances and basketballs games; but now Mr. Lewis was behind the counter in the grocery, and Miss Strangeworth was living alone in the Strangeworth house on Pleasant Street.

"Good morning," Mr. Lewis said, and added politely, "Lovely day."

"It is a very nice day," Miss Strangeworth said, as though she had only just decided that it would do after all. "I would like a chop, please, Mr. Lewis, a small, lean veal chop. Are those strawberries from Arthur Parker's garden? They're early this year."

"He brought them in this morning," Mr. Lewis said.

"I shall have a box," Miss Strangeworth said. Mr. Lewis looked worried, she thought, and for a minute she hesitated, but then she decided that he surely could not be worried over the strawberries. He looked very tired indeed. He was usually so chipper, Miss Strangeworth thought, and almost commented, but it was far too personal a subject to be introduced to Mr. Lewis, the grocer, so she only said, "and a can of cat food and, I think, a tomato."

Silently, Mr. Lewis assembled her order on the counter, and waited. Miss Strangeworth looked at him curiously and then said, "It's Tuesday, Mr. Lewis. You forgot to remind me."

"Did I? Sorry."

"Imagine your forgetting that I always buy my tea on Tuesday," Miss Strangeworth said gently. "A quarter pound of tea, please, Mr. Lewis."

"Is that all, Miss Strangeworth?"

"Yes, thank you, Mr. Lewis. Such a lovely day, isn't it?"

"Lovely," Mr. Lewis said.

Miss Strangeworth moved slightly to make room for Mrs. Harper at the counter. "Morning, Adela," Mrs. Harper said, and Miss Strangeworth said, "Good morning, Martha."

"Lovely day," Mrs. Harper said, and Miss Strangeworth said, "Yes, lovely," and Mr. Lewis, under Mrs. Harper's glance, nodded.

"Ran out of sugar for my cake frosting," Mrs. Harper explained. Her hand shook slightly as she opened her pocketbook. Miss Strangeworth wondered, glancing at her quickly, if she had been taking proper care of herself. Martha Harper was not as young as she used to be, Miss Strangeworth thought. She probably could use a good strong tonic.

"Martha," she said, "you don't look well."

"I'm perfectly all right," Mrs. Harper said shortly. She handed her money to Mr. Lewis, took her change and her sugar, and went out without speaking again. Looking after her, Miss Strangeworth shook her head slightly. Martha definitely did *not* look well.

Carrying her little bag of groceries, Miss Strangeworth came out of the store into the bright sunlight and stopped to smile down on the Crane baby. Don and Helen Crane were really the two most infatuated young parents she had ever known, she thought indulgently, looking at the delicately embroidered baby cap and the lace-edged carriage cover.

"That little girl is going to grow up expecting luxury all her life," she said to Helen Crane.

Helen laughed. "That's the way we want her to feel," she said. "Like a princess."

"A princess can see a lot of trouble sometimes," Miss Strangeworth said dryly. "How old is Her Highness now?"

"Six months next Tuesday," Helen Crane said, looking down

with rapt wonder at her child. "I've been worrying, though, about her. Don't you think she ought to move around more? Try to sit up, for instance?"

"For plain and fancy worrying," Miss Strangeworth said, amused, "give me a new mother every time."

"She just seems—slow," Helen Crane said.

"Nonsense. All babies are different. Some of them develop much more quickly than others."

"That's what my mother says." Helen Crane laughed, looking a little bit ashamed.

"I suppose you've got young Don all upset about the fact that his daughter is already six months old and hasn't yet begun to learn to dance?"

"I haven't mentioned it to him. I suppose she's just so precious that I worry about her all the time."

"Well, apologize to her right now," Miss Strangeworth said. "*She* is probably worrying about why you keep jumping around all the time." Smiling to herself and shaking her old head, she went on down the sunny street, stopping once to ask little Billy Moore why he wasn't out riding in his daddy's shiny new car, and talking for a few minutes outside the library with Miss Chandler, the librarian, about the new novels to be ordered and paid for by the annual library appropriation. Miss Chandler seemed absentminded and very much as though she were thinking about something else. Miss Strangeworth noticed that Miss Chandler had not taken much trouble with her hair that morning, and sighed. Miss Strangeworth hated sloppiness.

Many people seemed disturbed recently, Miss Strangeworth thought. Only yesterday the Stewarts' fifteen-year-old Linda had run crying down her own front walk and all the way to school, not caring who saw her. People around town thought she might have had a fight with the Harris boy, but they showed up together at the soda shop after school as usual, both of them looking grim and bleak. Trouble at home, people concluded, and sighed over the problems of trying to raise kids right these days.

From halfway down the block Miss Strangeworth could catch the heavy scent of her roses, and she moved a little more quickly. The perfume of roses meant home, and home meant the Strangeworth House on Pleasant Street. Miss Strangeworth stopped at her own front gate, as she always did, and looked with deep pleasure at her house, with the red and pink and white roses massed along the narrow lawn, and the rambler going up along the porch; and the neat, the unbelievably trim lines of the house itself, with its slimness and its washed white look. Every window sparkled, every curtain hung stiff and straight, and even the stones of the front walk were swept and clear. People around town wondered how old Miss Strangeworth managed to keep the house looking the way it did, and there was a legend about a tourist once mistaking it for the local museum and going all through the place without finding out about his mistake. But the town was proud of Miss Strangeworth and her roses and her house. They had all grown together.

Miss Strangeworth went up her front steps, unlocked her front door with her key, and went into the kitchen to put away her groceries. She debated about having a cup of tea and then decided that it was too close to midday dinnertime; she would not have the appetite for her little chop if she had tea now. Instead she went into the light, lovely sitting room, which still glowed from the hands of her mother and her grandmother, who had covered the chairs with bright chintz and hung the curtains. All the furniture was spare and shining, and the round hooked rugs on the floor had been the work of Miss Strangeworth's grandmother and her mother. Miss Strangeworth had put a bowl of her red roses on the low table before the window, and the room was full of their scent.

Miss Strangeworth went to the narrow desk in the corner and unlocked it with a key. She never knew when she might feel like writing letters, so she kept her notepaper inside and the desk locked. Miss Strangeworth's usual stationery was heavy and cream-colored, with STRANGEWORTH HOUSE engraved across the top, but, when she felt like writing her other letters, Miss Strangeworth used a pad of various-colored paper bought from the local newspaper shop. It was almost a town joke, that colored paper, layered in pink and green and blue and yellow; everyone in town bought it and used it for odd, informal notes and shopping lists. It was usual to remark, upon receiving a note written on a blue page, that so-and-so would be needing a new pad soon—here she was, down to the blue already. Everyone used the matching envelopes for tucking away recipes, or keeping odd little things in, or even to hold cookies in the school lunchboxes. Mr. Lewis sometimes gave them to the children for carrying home penny candy.

Although Miss Strangeworth's desk held a trimmed quill pen which had belonged to her grandfather, and a gold-frosted fountain pen which had belonged to her father, Miss Strangeworth always used a dull stub of pencil when she wrote her letters, and she printed them in a childish block print. After thinking for a minute, although she had been phrasing the letter in the back of her mind all the way home, she wrote on a pink sheet: DIDN'T YOU EVER SEE AN IDIOT CHILD BEFORE? SOME PEOPLE JUST SHOULDN'T HAVE CHILDREN SHOULD THEY?

She was pleased with the letter. She was fond of doing things exactly right. When she made a mistake, as she sometimes did, or when the letters were not spaced nicely on the page, she had to take the discarded page to the kitchen stove and burn it at once. Miss Strangeworth never delayed when things had to be done.

After thinking for a minute, she decided that she would like to write another letter, perhaps to go to Mrs. Harper, to follow up the ones she had already mailed. She selected a green sheet this time and wrote quickly: HAVE YOU FOUND OUT YET WHAT THEY WERE ALL LAUGHING ABOUT AFTER YOU LEFT THE BRIDGE CLUB ON THURSDAY? OR IS THE WIFE REALLY ALWAYS THE LAST ONE TO KNOW?

Miss Strangeworth never concerned herself with facts; her letters all dealt with the more negotiable stuff of suspicion. Mr. Lewis would never have imagined for a minute that his grandson might be lifting petty cash from the store register if he had not had one of Miss Strangeworth's letters. Miss Chandler, the librarian, and Linda Stewart's parents would have gone unsuspectingly ahead with their lives, never aware of possible evil lurking nearby, if Miss Strangeworth had not sent letters opening their eyes. Miss Strangeworth would have been genuinely shocked if there *had* been anything between Linda Stewart and the Harris boy, but, as long as evil existed unchecked in the world, it was Miss Strangeworth's duty to keep her town alert to it. It was far more sensible for Miss Chandler to wonder what Mr. Shelley's first wife had really died of than to take a chance on not knowing. There were so many wicked people in the world and only one Strangeworth left in the town. Besides, Miss Strangeworth liked writing her letters.

She addressed an envelope to Don Crane after a moment's thought, wondering curiously if he would show the letter to his wife, and using a pink envelope to match the pink paper. Then she addressed a second envelope, green, to Mrs. Harper. Then an idea came to her and she selected a blue sheet and wrote: YOU NEVER KNOW ABOUT DOCTORS. REMEMBER THEY'RE ONLY

HUMAN AND NEED MONEY LIKE THE REST OF US. SUPPOSE THE KNIFE SLIPPED ACCIDENTALLY. WOULD DR. BURNS GET HIS FEE AND A LITTLE EXTRA FROM THAT NEPHEW OF YOURS?

She addressed the blue envelope to old Mrs. Foster, who was having an operation next month. She had thought of writing one more letter, to the head of the school board, asking how a chemistry teacher like Billy Moore's father could afford a new convertible, but, all at once, she was tired of writing letters. The three she had done would do for one day. She could write more tomorrow; it was not as though they all had to be done at once.

She had been writing her letters—sometimes two or three every day for a week, sometimes no more than one in a month—for the past year. She never got any answers, of course, because she never signed her name. If she had been asked, she would have said that her name, Adela Strangeworth, a name honored in the town for so many years, did not belong on such trash. The town where she lived had to be kept clean and sweet, but people everywhere were lustful and evil and degraded, and needed to be watched; the world was so large, and there was only one Strangeworth left in it. Miss Strangeworth sighed, locked her desk, and put the letters into her big black leather pocketbook, to be mailed when she took her evening walk.

She broiled her little chop nicely, and had a sliced tomato and a good cup of tea ready when she sat down to her midday dinner at the table in her dining room, which could be opened to seat twenty-two, with a second table, if necessary, in the hall. Sitting in the warm sunlight that came through the tall windows of the dining room, seeing her roses massed outside, handling the heavy, old silverware and the fine, translucent china, Miss Strangeworth was pleased; she would not have cared to be doing anything else. People must live graciously, after all, she thought, and sipped her tea. Afterward, when her plate and cup and saucer were washed and dried and put back onto the shelves where they belonged, and her silverware was back in the mahogany silver chest, Miss Strangeworth went up the graceful staircase and into her bedroom, which was the front room overlooking the roses, and had been her mother's and her grandmother's. Their Crown Derby dresser set and furs had been kept here, their fans and silver-backed brushes and their own bowls of roses; Miss Strangeworth kept a bowl of white roses on the bed table.

She drew the shades, took the rose satin spread from the bed, slipped out of her dress and her shoes, and lay down tiredly. She knew that no doorbell or phone would ring; no one in town would dare to disturb Miss Strangeworth during her afternoon nap. She slept, deep the rich smell of roses.

After her nap she worked in her garden for a little while, sparing herself because of the heat; then she came in to her supper. She ate asparagus from her own garden, with sweet-butter sauce and a soft-boiled egg, and, while she had her supper, she listened to a late-evening news broadcast and then to a program of classical music on her small radio. After her dishes were done and her kitchen set in order, she took up her hat—Miss Strangeworth's hats were proverbial in the town; people believed that she had inherited them from her mother and her grandmother—and, locking the front door of her house behind her, set off on her evening walk, pocketbook under her arm. She nodded to Linda Stewart's father, who was washing his car in the pleasantly cool evening. She thought that he looked troubled.

There was only one place in town where she could mail her letters, and that was the new post office, shiny with red brick and silver letters. Although Miss Strangeworth had never given the matter any particular thought, she had always made a point of mailing her letters very secretly; it would, of course, not have been wise to let anyone see her mail them. Consequently, she timed her walk so she could reach the post office just as darkness was starting to dim the outlines of the trees and the shapes of people's faces, although no one could ever mistake Miss Strangeworth, with her dainty walk and her rustling skirts.

There was always a group of young people around the post office, the very youngest roller-skating upon its driveway, which went all the way around the building and was the only smooth road in town; and the slightly older ones already knowing how to gather in small groups and chatter and laugh and make great, excited plans for going across the street to the soda shop in a minute or two. Miss Strangeworth had never had any self-consciousness before the children. She did not feel that any of them were staring at her unduly or longing to laugh at her; it would have been most reprehensible for their parents to permit their children to mock Miss Strangeworth of Pleasant Street. Most of the children stood back respectfully as Miss Strangeworth passed, silenced briefly in her presence, and some of the older children greeted her, saying soberly, "Hello, Miss Strangeworth."

Miss Strangeworth smiled at them and quickly went on. It had been a long time since she had known the name of every child in town. The mail slot was in the door of the post office. The children stood away as Miss Strangeworth approached it, seemingly surprised that anyone should want to use the post office after it had been officially closed up for the night and turned over to the children. Miss Strangeworth stood by the door, opening her black pocketbook to take out the letters, and heard a voice which she knew at once to be Linda Stewart's. Poor little Linda was crying again, and Miss Strangeworth listened carefully. This was, after all, her town, and these were her people; if one of them was in trouble she ought to know about it.

"I can't tell you, Dave," Linda was saying—so she *was* talking to the Harris boy, as Miss Strangeworth had supposed—"I just *can't*. It's just *nasty*."

"But why won't your father let me come around anymore? What on earth did I do?"

"I can't tell you. I just wouldn't tell you for *any*thing. You've got to have a dirty, dirty mind for things like that."

"But something's happened. You've been crying and crying, and your father is all upset. Why can't *I* know about it, too? Aren't I like one of the family?"

"Not anymore, Dave, not anymore. You're not to come near our house again; my father said so. He said he'd horse-whip you. That's all I can tell you: You're not to come near our house anymore."

"But I didn't *do* anything."

"Just the same, my father said . . ."

Miss Strangeworth sighed and turned away. There was so much evil in people. Even in a charming little town like this one, there was still so much evil in people.

She slipped her letters into the slot, and two of them fell inside. The third caught on the edge and fell outside, onto the ground at Miss Strangeworth's feet. She did not notice it because she was wondering whether a letter to the Harris boy's father might not be of some service in wiping out this potential badness. Wearily Miss Strangeworth turned to go home to her quiet bed in her lovely house, and never heard the Harris boy calling to her to say that she had dropped something.

"Old lady Strangeworth's getting deaf," he said, looking after her and holding in his hand the letter he had picked up.

"Well, who cares?" Linda said. "Who cares anymore, anyway?"

"It's for Don Crane," the Harris boy said, "this letter. She dropped a letter addressed to Don Crane. Might as well take it on over. We pass his house anyway." He laughed. "Maybe it's got a check or something in it and he'd be just as glad to get it tonight instead of tomorrow."

"Catch old lady Strangeworth sending anybody a check," Linda said. "Throw it in the post office. Why do anyone a favor?" She sniffled. "Doesn't seem to me anybody around here cares about us," she said. "Why should we care about them?"

"I'll take it over anyway," the Harris boy said. "Maybe it's good news for them. Maybe they need something happy tonight, too. Like us."

Sadly, holding hands, they wandered off down the dark street, the Harris boy carrying Miss Strangeworth's pink envelope in his hand.

Miss Strangeworth awakened the next morning with a feeling of intense happiness, and for a minute wondered why, and then remembered that this morning three people would open her letters. Harsh, perhaps, at first, but wickedness was never easily banished, and a clean heart was a scoured heart. She washed her soft old face and brushed her teeth, still sound in spite of her seventy-one years, and dressed herself carefully in her sweet, soft clothes and buttoned shoes. Then, coming downstairs and reflecting that perhaps a little waffle would be agreeable for breakfast in the sunny dining room, she found the mail on the hall floor and bent to pick it up. A bill, the morning paper, a letter in a green envelope that looked oddly familiar. Miss Strangeworth stood perfectly still for a minute, looking down at the green envelope with the penciled printing, and thought: It looks like one of my letters. Was one of my letters sent back? No, because no one would know where to send it. How did this get here?

Miss Strangeworth was a Strangeworth of Pleasant Street. Her hand did not shake as she opened the envelope and unfolded the sheet of green paper inside. She began to cry silently for the wickedness of the world when she read the words: LOOK OUT AT WHAT USED TO BE YOUR ROSES.

PETER LOVESEY

(b.1936)

Witty and ingenious, Peter Lovesey's first novel, Wobble to Death *(1970), was written as a contest entry and was inspired by his discovery of a peculiar entertainment of the Victorian period—marathon walking races. The charm of his novel made it an immediate success and led to the reprise of his characters—Sergeant Cribb, Constable Thackeray, and Inspector Jowett—in a series of historical mysteries centered around common aspects of Victorian life, such as seaside holidays, art collecting, and popular theater. Lovesey describes the Sergeant Cribb novels as Victorian police procedurals. His vivid re-creation of the tone and atmosphere of the period is very original and has inspired a host of imitators. Several of Sergeant Cribb's cases were filmed for television in England and were aired in the United States on the PBS* Mystery! *series. Before inventing Sergeant Cribb, Lovesey attended the University of Reading, where he graduated in 1958 with honors in English. Most of his non-writing work has been related to education; even when he served in the Royal Air Force he was an education officer. He has published books on track and field, as well as other fiction not limited to the Victorian period. He published* Goldengirl *(1977) under the pseudonym Peter Lear, and has written many superb short stories. In our selection he displays his skill in dealing cleverly with the details of contemporary life. He uses the classic irony of turning the crime back upon the criminal in the context of a love triangle to unveil a powerful, though understated, surprise. A love triangle is a simple notion, yet there are so many possibilities for love, hate, revenge, and murder in its minimal architecture.*

THE SECRET LOVER

"Pam."

"Yes?"

"Will you see him this weekend?"

Pam Meredith drew a long breath and stifled the impulse to scream. She knew exactly what was coming. "See who?"

"Your secret lover."

She summoned a coy smile, said "Give over!" and everyone giggled.

For some reason, that last session of the working week regularly turned three efficient medical receptionists into overgrown schoolgirls. They were all over thirty, too. As soon as they arrived at the health center on Saturday morning, they were into their routine. After flexing their imaginations with stories of what the doctors had been getting up to with the patients, they started on each other. Then it was never long before Pam's secret lover came up.

He was an inoffensive, harassed-looking man in his late thirties who happened to walk into the center one afternoon to ask for help. A piece of grit had lodged under his left eyelid. Not one of the doctors or the district nurse had been in the building at the time, so Pam had dealt with it herself. From her own experiences with contact lenses, she had a fair idea how to persuade the eye to eject a foreign body, and she had succeeded very quickly, without causing the patient any serious discomfort. He had thanked her and left in a rush, as if the episode had embarrassed him. Pam had thought no more about him until a fortnight later, when she came on duty and was told that a man had been asking for her personally and would be calling back at lunchtime. This, understandably, created some lively interest in reception, particularly when he arrived at five minutes to one carrying a bunch of daffodils.

At thirty-three, Pam was the second youngest of the medical receptionists. She exercised, dieted, and tinted her hair blond and she was popular with many of the men who came in to collect their prescriptions, but she was not used to floral tributes. In her white overall she thought of herself as clinical and efficient. She had a pale, oval face with brown eyes and a small, neat mouth that she had been told projected refinement rather than sensuality. Lately, she had noticed some incipient wrinkles on her neck and taken to wearing polo sweaters.

Under the amused and frankly envious observation of her colleagues, Pam had blushingly accepted the flowers, trying to explain that such a tribute was not necessary, charming as it was. However, when the giver followed it up by asking her to allow him to buy her a drink at the Green Dragon, she had found him difficult to refuse. She had stuttered something about being on duty after lunch, so he had suggested tomato juice or bitter lemon, and one of the other girls had given her an unseen nudge and planted her handbag in her hand.

That was the start of the long-running joke about Pam's secret lover.

Really the joke was on the others. They hadn't guessed it in their wildest fantasies, but things had developed to the extent that Pam now slept with him regularly.

Do not assume too much about the relationship. In the common understanding of the word, he was not her lover. Sleeping together and making love are not of necessity the same thing. The possibility was not excluded, yet it was not taken as the automatic consequence of sharing a bed, and that accorded well with Pam's innate refinement.

So it wasn't entirely as the girls in the health center might have imagined it. Pam had learned over that first tomato juice in the Green Dragon that Cliff had a job in the cider industry which entailed calling on various producers in the West Midlands and South-West, and visiting Hereford for an overnight stay once a fortnight. He liked traveling, yet he admitted that the nights away from home had been instrumental in the failure of his marriage. He had not been unfaithful, but, as he altruistically put it, anyone who read the accounts of rapes and muggings in the papers couldn't really blame a wife who sought companionship elsewhere when her husband spent every other week away on business.

Responding to his candor, Pam had found herself admitting that she, too, was divorced. The nights, she agreed, were the worst. Even in the old cathedral city of Hereford, which had no reputation for violence, she avoided going out alone after dark and she often lay awake listening acutely in case someone was tampering with the locks downstairs.

The first lunchtime drink had led to another when Cliff was next in the city. The fortnight after, Pam had invited him to the house for a "spot of supper," explaining that it was no trouble, because you could do much more interesting things cooking for two than alone. Cliff had heaped praise on her chicken *cordon bleu,* and after that the evening meal had become a fortnightly fixture. On the first occasion, he had quite properly returned to his hotel at the end of the evening, but the following time he had introduced Pam to the old-fashioned game of cribbage, and they had both got so engrossed that neither of them had noticed the time until it was well after midnight. By then, Pam felt so relaxed and safe with Cliff that it had seemed the most natural thing in the world to make up the spare bed for him and invite him to stay the night. There had been no suggestion on either side of a more intimate arrangement. That was what she liked about Cliff. He wasn't one of those predatory males. He was enough of a gentleman to suppress his natural physical instincts. And one night six weeks after in a thunderstorm, when she had tapped on his bedroom door and said she was feeling frightened, he had offered in the same gentlemanly spirit to come to her room until the storm abated. As it happened, Pam still slept in the king-sized double bed she had got used to when she was married, so there was room for Cliff without any embarrassment about inadvertent touching. They had fallen asleep listening for the thunder. By then it was the season of summer storms, so next time he had come to the house, they had agreed that it was a sensible precaution to sleep together even when the sky was clear. You could never be certain when a storm might blow up during the night. And when the first chill nights of autumn arrived, neither of them liked the prospect of sleeping apart between cool sheets. Besides, as Cliff considerately mentioned, using one bed was less expensive on the laundry.

Speaking of laundry, Pam took to washing out his shirts, underclothes and pyjamas. She had bought him a special pair of bottlegreen French pajamas without buttons and with an elasticized waistband. They were waiting on his pillow, washed and ironed, each time he came. He was very appreciative. He never failed to arrive with a bottle of cider that they drank with the meal. Once or twice he mentioned that he would have taken her out to a restaurant if her cooking had not been so excellent that it would have shown up the cook. He particularly relished the cooked breakfast on a large oval plate that she supplied before he went on his way in the morning.

So Pam staunchly tolerated the teasing in the health center, encouraged by the certainty that it was all fantasy on their part; she had been careful never to let them know that she had invited Cliff home. She was in a better frame of mind as she walked home that lunchtime. It was always a relief to get through Saturday morning.

As she turned the corner of her street, she saw a small car, a red Mini, outside her house, with someone sitting inside it. She wasn't expecting a visitor. She strolled towards her gate, noticing that it was a woman who made no move to get out, and whom she didn't recognize, so she passed the car and let herself indoors.

There was a letter on the floor, a greetings card by the look of it. She had quite forgotten that her birthday was on Sunday. Living alone, with no family to speak of, she tended to ignore such occasions. However, someone had evidently decided that this one should not go by unremarked. She didn't recognize the handwriting, and the postmark was too faint to read. She opened it and smiled. A print of a single daffodil, and inside, under the printed birthday greeting, the handwritten letter C.

The reason why she hadn't recognized Cliff's writing was that this was the first time she had seen it. He wasn't one for sending letters. And the postmark wouldn't have given Pam a clue, even if she had deciphered it, because she didn't know where he lived. He was vague or dismissive when it came to personal information, so she hadn't pressed him. He was entitled to his privacy. She couldn't help wondering sometimes, and her best guess was that since the failure of his marriage he had tended to neglect himself and his home and devote himself to his job. He lived for the traveling, and, Pam was encouraged to believe, his fortnightly visit to Hereford.

Presently the doorbell chimed. Pam opened the door to the woman she had seen in the car, dark-haired, about her own age or a little older, good-looking, with one of those long, elegant faces with high cheekbones that you see in foreign films. She was wearing a dark blue suit and white blouse buttoned to the neck as if she were attending an interview for a job. Mainly, Pam was made aware of the woman's gray-green eyes that scrutinized her with an interest unusual in people who called casually at the door.

"Hello," said Pam.

"Mrs. Pamela Meredith?"

"Yes."

The look became even more intense. "We haven't met. You may not even know that I exist. I'm Tracey Gibbons." She paused for a reaction.

Pam smiled faintly. "You're right. I haven't heard your name before."

Tracey Gibbons sighed and shook her head. "I'm not surprised. I don't know what you're going to think of me, coming to your house like this, but it's reached the point when something has to be done. It's about your husband."

Pam frowned. "My husband?" She hadn't heard from David in six years.

"May I come in?"

"I suppose you'd better."

As she showed the woman into her front room, Pam couldn't help wondering if this was a confidence trick. The woman's eyes blatantly surveyed the room, the furniture, the ornaments, everything.

Pam said sharply, "I think you'd better come to the point, Miss Gibbons."

"Mrs., actually. Not that it matters. I'm waiting for my divorce to come through." Suddenly the woman sounded nervous and defensive. "I'm not promiscuous. I want you to understand that, Mrs. Meredith, whatever you may think of me. And I'm not deceitful, either, or I wouldn't be here. I want to get things straight between us. I've driven over from Worcester this morning to talk to you."

Pam was beginning to fathom what this was about. Mrs. Gibbons was having an affair with David, and for some obscure reason she felt obliged to confess it to his ex-wife. Clearly the poor woman was in a state of nerves, so it was kindest to let her say her piece before gently showing her the door.

"You probably wonder how I got your address," Mrs. Gibbons went on. "He doesn't know I'm here, I promise you. It's only over the last few weeks that I began to suspect he had a wife. Certain things you notice, like his freshly ironed shirts. He left his suitcase open the last time he came, and I happened to see the birthday card he addressed to you. That's how I got your address."

Pam's skin prickled. "Which card?"

"The daffodil. I looked inside, I'm ashamed to admit. I had to know."

Pam closed her eyes. The woman wasn't talking about David at all. It was Cliff, *her* Cliff. Her head was spinning. She thought she was going to faint. She said, "I think I need some brandy."

Mrs. Gibbons nodded. "I'll join you, if I may."

When she handed over the glass, Pam said in a subdued voice, "You *are* talking about a man named Cliff?"

"Of course."

"He is not my husband."

"What?" Mrs. Gibbons stared at her in disbelief.

"He visits me sometimes."

"And you wash his shirts?"

"Usually."

"The bastard!" said Mrs. Gibbons, her eyes brimming. "The rotten, two-timing bastard! I knew there was someone else, but I thought it was his wife he was so secretive about. I persuaded myself he was unhappily married and I came here to plead with you to let him go. I could kill him!"

"How do you think I feel?" Pam blurted out. "I didn't even know there was anyone else in his life."

"Does he keep a toothbrush and razor in your bathroom?"

"A face flannel as well."

"And I suppose you bought him some expensive aftershave?"

Pam confirmed it bitterly. In her outraged state, she needed to talk, and sharing the trouble seemed likely to dull the pain. She related how she and Cliff had met and how she had invited him home.

"And one thing led to another?" speculated Mrs. Gibbons. "When I think of what I was induced to do in the belief that I was the love of his life . . ." She finished her brandy in a gulp.

Pam nodded. "It was expensive, too."

"Expensive?"

"Preparing three-course dinners and large cooked breakfasts."

"I wasn't talking about cooking," said Mrs. Gibbons, giving Pam a penetrating look.

"Ah," said Pam, with a slow dip of the head, in an attempt to convey that she understood exactly what Mrs. Gibbons *was* talking about.

"Things I didn't get up to in ten years of marriage to a very athletic man," Mrs. Gibbons further confided, looking modestly away. "But you know all about it. Casanova was a boy scout compared to Cliff. God, I feel so humiliated."

"Would you like a spot more brandy, Mrs. Gibbons?"

"Why don't you call me Tracey?" suggested Mrs. Gibbons, holding out her glass. "We're just his playthings, you and I. How many others are there, do you suppose?"

"Who knows?" said Pam, seizing on the appalling possibility and speaking her thoughts aloud. "There are plenty of divorced women like you and me, living in relative comfort in what was once the marital home, pathetically grateful for any attention that comes our way. Let's face it: we're second-hand goods."

After a sobering interval, Tracey Gibbons pushed her empty glass towards the brandy bottle again, and asked, "What are we going to do about him?"

"Kick him out with his toothbrush and face flannel, I suppose," Pam answered inadequately.

"So that he finds other deluded women to prey one?" said Tracey. "That's not the treatment for the kind of animal we're dealing with. Personally, I feel so angry and abused that I could kill him if I knew how to get away with it. Wouldn't you?"

Pam stared at her. "Are you serious?"

"Totally. He's ruined my hopes and every atom of self-respect I had left. What was I to him? His bit in Worcester, his Monday night amusement."

"And I was Tuesday night in Hereford," Pam added bleakly, suddenly given a cruel and vivid understanding of the way she had been used. Sex was Monday, supper Tuesday. In her own way, she felt as violated as Tracey. An arrangement that had seemed to be considerate and beautiful was revealed as cynically expedient. The reason why he had never touched her was that he was always sated after his night of unbridled passion in Worcester. "Tracey, if you know of a way to kill him," she stated with the calm that comes when a crucial decision is made, "I know how to get away with it."

Tracey's eyes opened very wide.

Pam made black coffee and sandwiches and explained her plan. To describe it as a plan is perhaps misleading, because it had only leapt to mind as they were talking. She wasn't given to thinking much about murder. Yet as she spoke, she sensed excitedly that it could work. It was simple, tidy, and within her capability.

The two women talked until late in the afternoon. For the plan to work, they had to devise a way of killing without mess. The body should not be marked by violence. They solemnly debated various methods of dispatching a man. Whether the intention was serious or not, Pam found that just talking about it was a balm for the pain that Cliff had inflicted on her. She and Tracey sensibly agreed to take no action until they had each had time to adjust to the shock, but they were adamant that they would meet again.

On the following Monday evening, Pam received a phone call from Tracey. "Have you thought any more about what we were discussing?"

"On and off, yes," Pam answered guardedly.

"Well, I've been doing some research," Tracey told her with the excitement obvious in her voice. "I'd better not be too specific over the phone, but I know where to get some stuff that will do the job. Do you understand me?"

"I think so."

"It's simple, quick, and very effective, and the best thing about it is that I can get it at work."

Pam recalled that Tracey had said she worked for a firm that manufactured agricultural fertilizers. She supposed she was talking about some chemical substance.

Poison.

"The thing is," Tracey was saying, "if I get some, are you willing to do your part? You said it would be no problem."

"That's true, but—"

"By the weekend? He's due to visit me on Monday."

The reminder of Cliff's Monday assignations in Worcester was like a stab of pain to Pam. "By the weekend," she confirmed emphatically. "Come over about the same time on Saturday. I'll do my part, I promise you, Tracey."

The part Pam had to play in the killing of Cliff was to obtain a blank death certificate from one of the doctors at the center. She had often noticed how careless Dr. Holt-Wagstaff was with his paperwork. He was the oldest of the five practitioners and his desk was always in disorder. She waited for her opportunity for most of the week. On Friday morning she had to go into his surgery to ask him to clarify his handwriting on a prescription form. The death certificate pad was there on the desk. At twelve-fifteen, when he went out on his rounds, and Pam was on duty with one other girl, she slipped back into the surgery. No one saw her.

Saturday was a testing morning for Pam. The time dragged and the teasing about her secret lover was difficult to take without snapping back at the others. She kept wondering whether Dr. Holt-Wagstaff had noticed anything. She need not have worried. He left at noon, wishing everyone a pleasant weekend. At twelve-thirty, the girls locked up and left.

When Pam got home, Tracey was waiting on her doorstep. "I came by train," she explained. "Didn't want to leave my car outside again. It's surprising how much people notice."

"Sensible," said Pam, with approval, as she opened the door. "Now I want to hear about the stuff you've got. Is it really going to work?"

Tracey put her hand on Pam's arm. "Darling, it's foolproof. Do you want to see it?" She opened her handbag and took out a small brown glass bottle. "Pure nicotine. We use it at work."

Pam held the bottle in her palm. "Nicotine? Is it a poison?"

"Deadly."

"There isn't much here."

"The fatal dose is measured in milligrams, Pam. A few drops will do the trick."

"How can we get him to take it?"

"I've thought of that." Tracey smiled. "You're going to like this. In a glass of his own buckshee cider. Nicotine goes yellow on exposure to light and air, and there's a bitter taste which the sweet cider will mask."

"How does it work?"

"It acts as a massive stimulant. The vital organs simply can't withstand it. He'll die of cardiac arrest in a very short time. Did you get the death certificate?"

Pam placed the poison bottle on the kitchen table and opened one of her cookbooks. The certificate was inside.

"You're careful, too," Tracey said with a conspiratorial smile. She delved into her handbag again. "I brought a prescription from my doctor to copy the signature, as you suggested. What else do we have to fill in here? *Name of deceased.* What shall we call him?"

"Anything but Cliff," said Pam. "How about Clive? Clive Jones."

"All right. Clive Jones it is. *Date of death.* I'd better fill that in after the event. What shall we put as the cause of death? Cardiac failure?"

"No, that's likely to be a sudden death," said Pam, thinking of post-mortems. "Broncho-pneumonia is better."

"Suits me," said Tracey, writing it down. "After he's dead, I take this to the Registry of Births, Marriages, and Deaths in Worcester, and tell them that Clive Jones was my brother, is that right?"

"Yes, it's very straightforward. They'll want his date of birth and one or two other details that you can invent. Then they issue you with another certificate that you show to the undertaker. He takes over after that."

"I ask for a cremation, of course. Will it cost much?"

"Don't worry," said Pam. "He can afford it."

"Too true!" said Tracey. "His wallet is always stuffed with notes."

"He never has to spend much," Pam pointed out. "The way he runs his life, he gets everything he wants for nothing."

"The bastard," said Tracey with a shudder.

"You really mean to do it, don't you?"

Tracey stood up and looked steadily at Pam with her gray-green eyes. "On Monday evening when he comes to me. I'll phone you when it's done."

Pam linked her arm in Tracey's. "The first thing I'm going to do is burn those pyjamas."

Tracey remarked, "He never wore pyjamas with me."

"Really?" Pam hesitated, her curiosity aroused. "What exactly did he do with you? Are you table to talk about it?"

"I don't believe I could," answered Tracey with eyes lowered.

"If I poured you a brandy? We *are* in this together now."

"All right," said Tracey with a sigh.

Sunday seemed like the longest day of Pam's life, but she finally got through it. On Monday she didn't go in to work. That evening, she waited nervously by the phone from six-thirty onwards.

The call came at a few minutes after seven. Pam snatched up the phone.

"Hello, darling." *The voice was Cliff's.*

"Cliff?"

"Yes. Not like me to call you on a Monday, is it? The fact is, I happen to be in Worcester on my travels, and it occurred to me that I could get over to you in Hereford in half an hour if you're free this evening."

"Has something happened?" asked Pam.

"No, my darling. Just a change of plans. I won't expect much of a meal."

"That's good, because I haven't got one for you," Pam candidly told him.

There was a moment's hesitation before he said, "Are you all right, dear? You don't sound quite yourself."

"Don't I?" said Pam flatly. "Well, I've had a bit of a shock. My sister died here on Saturday. It wasn't entirely unexpected. Broncho-pneumonia. I've had to do everything myself. She's being cremated on Wednesday."

"Your sister? Pam, darling, I'm terribly sorry. I didn't even know you had a sister."

"Her name was Olive. Olive Jones," said Pam, and she couldn't help smiling at her own resourcefulness. After she had poisoned Tracey with a drop of nicotine in her brandy, all it had wanted on the death certificate was a touch of the pen. "We weren't close. I'm not too distressed. Yes, why don't you come over?"

"You're sure you want me?"

"Oh, I want you," answered Pam. "Yes, I definitely want you."

When she had put down the phone, she didn't go to the fridge to see what food she had in there. She went upstairs to the bedroom and changed into a black negligée.

Over the Edge

From King David's lust for Bathsheba and his grief at the death of Absalom to Ajax's suicidal rage to Medea's slaughter of her children, exaggerated states of mind have been a staple of dramatic stories throughout history. In Shakespeare's time the revenge tragedy, exploring the madness of Hieronimo, Ophelia, and Lear, was a popular theatrical spectacle. The Enlightenment's emphasis on reason discouraged such entertainment as unhealthy, leading to the passionate rebellion of younger artists that we call Romanticism. The mystery, of course, had its beginnings in this rebellion and combines the Enlightenment's scientific rationalism with the Romantic interest in madness and abnormality. Poe's short stories come immediately to mind, particularly his "Tell-Tale Heart," "The Fall of the House of Usher," and "The Black Cat," but dozens of writers and artists of the period mined the mother lode of passion and madness so enthusiastically that their works are still enjoyed in great numbers. Hearts are broken, homes are invaded for a thrill, greed overpowers the once content, and the serial killer coldly goes on trying to feed his appetite for murder. Over the edge stories examine what drives people to go outside the bounds of normal behavior. Somewhere hidden deep in each person is a vulnerable spot, a place that if touched may unhinge all the values the person has carefully held. To paraphrase author John Barth, murder ticks in your spouse's loving heart like a bomb. But what is it that will send an individual over the edge? the tenth insulting comment?

a burnt meat loaf? a cold look? the photograph of a clean beach in the Bahamas? Each of us is different, yet we each suspect that there is such a spot within us and we fear it. An essential element in the following stories is, if not sympathy, understanding. The character is developed in such a way that the reader recognizes the push, gentle or stiff, as a sufficient impetus for the character's tumble into madness. In these stories we accept the delicateness of our own psyches and the humbling realization that we are indeed lucky if we manage during our tempestuous lives to escape going over the edge.

SUSAN GLASPELL

(1876–1948)

After a small-town upbringing in Davenport, Iowa, Susan Glaspell attended Drake University, where she wrote her first stories and received a doctoral degree in 1899. Following a stint as a legislative reporter in Des Moines, she returned to Davenport and pursued her dream of becoming a writer. In 1909, she published a first novel, Glory of the Conquered. *She moved to Europe, then to Chicago, and then to Greenwich Village. She came to embrace socialism and turned her writing increasingly toward the problems of society. In 1913, she married George Cram Cook, a writer who in 1915 founded the Provincetown Playhouse on Cape Cod, Massachusetts. Most famous as the first venue for playwright Eugene O'Neill, the playhouse inspired Glaspell to turn to drama. She wrote eleven plays for the company, one of which,* Trifles *(1916), is the source of the work for which she is most remembered, "A Jury of Her Peers" (1917). Though she published many novels and short stories, Glaspell never produced anything equal to "A Jury of Her Peers," one of the all-time classic crime stories. There are several dimensions to the story. Even with the meticulous attention to the "trifles" of the original title (the details that reveal the crime), the investigation is far from an ordinary whodunit. The story offers up a hidden world (the world of women) and a sense of the mystery concealed in the things we take for granted, things visible only to an eye that knows not just where to look but how to see. The story also implies that justice frequently lies outside the law. Finally, it points up the fragility of the human mind. What may be a trifle to one person is sufficient to drive another to the ultimate crime—murder.*

A JURY OF HER PEERS

When Martha Hale opened the storm-door and got a cut of the north wind, she ran back for her big woolen scarf. As she hurriedly wound that round her head her eye made a scandalized sweep of her kitchen. It was no ordinary thing that called her away—it was probably farther from ordinary than anything that had ever happened in Dickson County. But what her eye took in was that her kitchen was in no shape for leaving: her bread all ready for mixing, half the flour sifted and half unsifted.

She hated to see things half done; but she had been at that when the team from town stopped to get Mr. Hale, and then the sheriff came running in to say his wife wished Mrs. Hale would come too—adding, with a grin, that he guessed she was getting scarey and wanted another woman along. So she had dropped everything right where it was.

"Martha!" now came her husband's impatient voice. "Don't keep folks waiting out here in the cold."

She again opened the storm-door, and this time joined the three men and the one woman waiting for her in the big two-seated buggy.

After she had the robes tucked around her she took another look at the woman who sat beside her on the back seat. She had met Mrs. Peters the year before at the county fair, and the thing she remembered about her was that she didn't seem like a sheriff's wife. She was small and thin and didn't have a strong voice. Mrs. Gorman, sheriff's wife before Gorman went out and Peters came in, had a voice that somehow seemed to be backing up the law with every word. But if Mrs. Peters didn't look like a sheriff's wife, Peters made it up in looking like a sheriff. He was to a dot the kind of man who could get himself elected sheriff—a heavy man with a big voice, who was particularly genial with the law-abiding, as if to make it plain that he knew the difference between criminals and non-criminals. And right there it came into Mrs. Hale's mind, with a stab, that this man who was so pleasant and lively with all of them was going to the Wrights' now as a sheriff.

"The country's not very pleasant this time of year," Mrs. Peters at last ventured, as if she felt they ought to be talking as well as the men.

Mrs. Hale scarcely finished her reply, for they had gone up a little hill and could see the Wright place now, and seeing it did not make her feel like talking. It looked very lonesome this cold March morning. It had always been a lonesome-looking place. It was down in a hollow, and the poplar trees around it were lonesome-looking trees. The men were looking at it and talking about what had happened. The county attorney was bending to one side of the buggy, and kept looking steadily at the place as they drew up to it.

"I'm glad you came with me," Mrs. Peters said nervously, as the two women were about to follow the men in through the kitchen door.

Even after she had her foot on the door-step, her hand on the knob, Martha Hale had a moment of feeling she could not cross that threshold. And the reason it seemed she couldn't cross it now was simply because she hadn't crossed it before. Time and time again it had been in her mind, "I ought to go over and see Minnie Foster"—she still thought of her as Minnie Foster, though for twenty years she had been Mrs. Wright. And then there was always something to do and Minnie Foster would go from her mind. But *now* she could come.

The men went over to the stove. The women stood close together by the door. Young Henderson, the county attorney, turned around and said, "Come up to the fire, ladies."

Mrs. Peters took a step forward, then stopped. "I'm not—cold," she said.

And so the two women stood by the door, at first not even so much as looking around the kitchen.

The men talked for a minute about what a good thing it was the sheriff had sent his deputy out that morning to make a fire for them, and then Sheriff Peters stepped back from the stove, unbuttoned his outer coat, and leaned his hands on the kitchen table in a way that seemed to mark the beginning of official business. "Now, Mr. Hale," he said in a sort of semi-official voice, "before we move things about, you tell Mr. Henderson just what it was you saw when you came here yesterday morning."

The county attorney was looking around the kitchen.

"By the way," he said, "has anything been moved?" He turned to the sheriff. "Are things just as you left them yesterday?"

Peters looked from cupboard to sink; from that to a small worn rocker a little to one side of the kitchen table.

"It's just the same."

"Somebody should have been left here yesterday," said the county attorney.

"Oh—yesterday," returned the sheriff, with a little gesture as of yesterday having been more than he could bear to think of. "When I had to send Frank to Morris Center for that man who went crazy—let me tell you, I had my hands full *yesterday*. I knew you could get back from Omaha by to-day, George, and as long as I went over everything here myself—"

"Well, Mr. Hale," said the county attorney, in a way of letting what was past and gone go, "tell just what happened when you came here yesterday morning."

Mrs. Hale, still leaning against the door, had that sinking feeling of the mother whose child is about to speak a piece. Lewis often wandered along and got things mixed up in a story. She hoped he would tell this straight and plain, and not say unnecessary things that would just make things harder for Minnie Foster. He didn't begin at once, and she noticed that he looked queer—as if standing in that kitchen and having to tell what he had seen there yesterday morning made him almost sick.

"Yes, Mr. Hale?" the county attorney reminded.

"Harry and I had started to town with a load of potatoes," Mrs. Hale's husband began.

Harry was Mrs. Hale's oldest boy. He wasn't with them now, for the very good reason that those potatoes never got to town yesterday and he was taking them this morning, so he hadn't been home when the sheriff stopped to say he wanted Mr. Hale to come over to the Wright place and tell the county attorney his story there, where he could point it all out. With all Mrs.

Hale's other emotions came the fear that maybe Harry wasn't dressed warm enough—they hadn't any of them realized how that north wind did bite.

"We come along this road," Hale was going on, with a motion of his hand to the road over which they had just come, "and as we got in sight of the house I says to Harry, 'I'm goin' to see if I can't get John Wright to take a telephone.' You see," he explained to Henderson, "unless I can get somebody to go in with me they won't come out this branch road except for a price *I* can't pay. I'd spoke to Wright about it once before; but he put me off, saying folks talked too much anyway, and all he asked was peace and quiet—guess you know about how much he talked himself. But I thought maybe if I went to the house and talked about it before his wife, and said all the women-folks liked the telephones, and that in this lonesome stretch of road it would be a good thing—well, I said to Harry that that was what I was going to say—though I said at the same time that I didn't know as what his wife wanted made much difference to John—"

Now, there he was!—saying things he didn't need to say. Mrs. Hale tried to catch her husband's eye, but fortunately the county attorney interrupted with:

"Let's talk about that a little later, Mr. Hale. I do want to talk about that, but I'm anxious now to get along to just what happened when you got here."

When he began this time, it was very deliberately and carefully:

"I didn't see or hear anything. I knocked at the door. And still it was all quiet inside. I knew they must be up—it was past eight o'clock. So I knocked again, louder, and I thought I heard somebody say 'Come in.' I wasn't sure—I'm not sure yet. But I opened the door—this door," jerking a hand toward the door by which the two women stood, "and there, in that rocker"—pointing to it—"sat Mrs. Wright."

Every one in the kitchen looked at the rocker. It came into Mrs. Hale's mind that that rocker didn't look in the least like Minnie Foster—the Minnie Foster of twenty years before. It was a dingy red, with wooden rungs up the back, and the middle rung was gone, and the chair sagged to one side.

"How did she—look?" the county attorney was inquiring.

"Well," said Hale, "she looked—queer."

"How do you mean—queer?"

As he asked it he took out a note-book and pencil. Mrs. Hale did not like the sight of that pencil. She kept her eye fixed on her husband, as if to keep him from saying unnecessary things that would go into that note-book and make trouble.

Hale did speak guardedly, as if the pencil had affected him too. "Well, as if she didn't know what she was going to do next. And kind of—done up."

"How did she seem to feel about your coming?"

"Why, I don't think she minded—one way or other. She didn't pay much attention. I said, 'Ho' do, Mrs. Wright? It's cold, ain't it?' And she said, 'Is it?'—and went on pleatin' at her apron.

"Well, I was surprised. She didn't ask me to come up to the stove, or to sit down, but just set there, not even lookin' at me. And so I said: 'I want to see John.'

"And then she—laughed. I guess you would call it a laugh.

"I thought of Harry and the team outside, so I said, a little sharp, 'Can I see John?' 'No,' says she—kind of dull like. 'Ain't he home?' says I. Then she looked at me. 'Yes,' says she, 'he's home.' 'Then why can't I see him?' I asked her, out of patience with her now. 'Cause he's dead,' says she, just as quiet and dull—and fell to pleatin' her apron. 'Dead?' says I, like you do when you can't take in what you've heard.

"She just nodded her head, not getting a bit excited, but rockin' back and forth.

" 'Why—where is he?' says I, not knowing *what* to say.

"She just pointed upstairs—like this"—pointing to the room above.

"I got up, with the idea of going up there myself. By this time I—didn't know what to do. I walked from there to here; then I says: 'Why, what did he die of?'

" 'He died of a rope around his neck,' says she; and just went on pleatin' at her apron."

Hale stopped speaking, and stood staring at the rocker, as if he were still seeing the woman who had sat there the morning before. Nobody spoke; it was as if every one were seeing the woman who had sat there the morning before.

"And what did you do then?" the county attorney at last broke the silence.

"I went out and called Harry. I thought I might—need help. I got Harry in, and we went upstairs." His voice fell almost to a whisper. "There he was—lying over the—"

"I think I'd rather have you go into that upstairs," the county attorney interrupted, "where you can point it all out. Just go on now with the rest of the story."

"Well, my first thought was to get that rope off. It looked—"

He stopped, his face twitching.

"But Harry, he went up to him, and he said, 'No, he's dead all right, and we'd better not touch anything.' So we went downstairs.

"She was still sitting that same way. 'Has anybody been notified?' I asked. 'No,' says she, unconcerned.

" 'Who did this, Mrs. Wright?' said Harry. He said it businesslike, and she stopped pleatin' at her apron. 'I don't know,' she says. 'You don't *know?*' says Harry. 'Weren't you sleepin' in the bed with him?' 'Yes,' says she, 'but I was on the inside.' 'Somebody slipped a rope round his neck and strangled him, and you didn't wake up?' says Harry. 'I didn't wake up,' she said after him.

"We may have looked as if we didn't see how that could be, for after a minute she said, 'I sleep sound.'

"Harry was going to ask her more questions, but I said maybe that weren't our business; maybe we ought to let her tell her story first to the coroner or the sheriff. So Harry went fast as he could over to High Road—the Rivers' place, where there's a telephone."

"And what did she do when she knew you had gone for the coroner?" The attorney got his pencil in his hand all ready for writing.

"She moved from that chair to this one over here"—Hale pointed to a small chair in the corner—"and just sat there with her hands held together and looking down. I got a feeling that I ought to make some conversation, so I said I had come in to see if John wanted to put in a telephone; and at that she started to laugh, and then she stopped and looked at me—scared."

At the sound of a moving pencil the man who was telling the story looked up.

"I dunno—maybe it wasn't scared," he hastened; "I wouldn't like to say it was. Soon Harry got back, and then Dr. Lloyd came, and you, Mr. Peters, and so I guess that's all I know that you don't."

He said that last with relief, and moved a little, as if relaxing. Every one moved a little. The county attorney walked toward the stair door.

"I guess we'll go upstairs first—then out to the barn and around there."

He paused and looked around the kitchen.

"You're convinced there was nothing important here?" he asked the sheriff. "Nothing that would—point to any motive?"

The sheriff too looked all around, as if to re-convince himself.

"Nothing here but kitchen things," he said, with a little laugh for the insignificance of kitchen things.

The county attorney was looking at the cupboard—a peculiar, ungainly structure, half closet and half cupboard, the upper part of it being built in the wall, and the lower part just the old-fashioned kitchen cupboard. As if its queerness attracted him, he got a chair and opened the upper part and looked in. After a moment he drew his hand away sticky.

"Here's a nice mess," he said resentfully.

The two women had drawn nearer, and now the sheriff's wife spoke.

"Oh—her fruit," she said, looking to Mrs. Hale for sympathetic understanding. She turned back to the county attorney and explained: "She worried about that when it turned so cold last night. She said the fire would go out and her jars might burst."

Mrs. Peters' husband broke into a laugh.

"Well, can you beat the women! Held for murder, and worrying about her preserves!"

The young attorney set his lips.

"I guess before we're through with her she may have something more serious than preserves to worry about."

"Oh, well," said Mrs. Hale's husband, with good-natured superiority, "women are used to worrying over trifles."

The two women moved a little closer together. Neither of them spoke. The county attorney seemed suddenly to remember his manners—and think of his future.

"And yet," said he, with the gallantry of a young politician, "for all their worries, what would we do without the ladies?"

The women did not speak, did not unbend. He went to the sink and began washing his hands. He turned to wipe them on the roller towel—whirled it for a cleaner place.

"Dirty towels! Not much of a housekeeper, would you say, ladies?"

He kicked his foot against some dirty pans under the sink.

"There's a great deal of work to be done on a farm," said Mrs. Hale stiffly.

"To be sure. And yet"—with a little bow to her—"I know there are some Dickson County farm-houses that do not have such roller towels." He gave it a pull to expose its full length again.

"Those towels get dirty awful quick. Men's hands aren't always as clean as they might be."

"Ah, loyal to your sex, I see," he laughed. He stopped and gave her a keen look. "But you and Mrs. Wright were neighbors. I suppose you were friends, too."

Martha Hale shook her head.

"I've seen little enough of her of late years. I've not been in this house—it's more than a year."

"And why was that? You didn't like her?"

"I liked her well enough," she replied with spirit. "Farmers' wives have their hands full, Mr. Henderson. And then"—She looked around the kitchen.

"Yes?" he encouraged.

"It never seemed a very cheerful place," said she, more to herself than to him.

"No," he agreed; "I don't think any one would call it cheerful. I shouldn't say she had the home-making instinct."

"Well, I don't know as Wright had, either," she muttered.

"You mean they didn't get on very well?" he was quick to ask.

"No; I don't mean anything," she answered, with decision. As she turned a little away from him, she added: "But I don't think a place would be any the cheerfuler for John Wright's bein' in it."

"I'd like to talk to you about that a little later, Mrs. Hale," he said. "I'm anxious to get the lay of things upstairs now."

He moved toward the stair door, followed by the two men.

"I suppose anything Mrs. Peters does'll be all right?" the sheriff inquired. "She was to take in some clothes for her, you know—and a few little things. We left in such a hurry yesterday."

The county attorney looked at the two women whom they were leaving alone there among the kitchen things.

"Yes—Mrs. Peters," he said, his glance resting on the woman who was not Mrs. Peters, the big farmer woman who stood behind the sheriff's wife. "Of course Mrs. Peters is one of us," he said, in a manner of entrusting responsibility. "And keep your eye out, Mrs. Peters, for anything that might be of use. No telling; you women might come upon a clue to the motive—and that's the thing we need."

Mr. Hale rubbed his face after the fashion of a show man getting ready for a pleasantry.

"But would the women know a clue if they did come upon it?" he said; and, having delivered himself of this, he followed the others through the stair door.

The women stood motionless and silent, listening to the footsteps, first upon the stairs, then in the room above them.

Then, as if releasing herself from something strange, Mrs. Hale began to arrange the dirty pans under the sink, which the county attorney's disdainful push of the foot had deranged.

"I'd hate to have men comin' into my kitchen," she said testily—"snoopin' round and criticizin'."

"Of course it's no more than their duty," said the sheriff's wife, in her manner of timid acquiescence.

"Duty's all right," replied Mrs. Hale bluffly; "but I guess that deputy sheriff that come out to make the fire might have got a little of this on." She gave the roller towel a pull. "Wish I'd thought of that sooner! Seems mean to talk about her for not having things slicked up, when she had to come away in such a hurry."

She looked around the kitchen. Certainly it was not "slicked up." Her eye was held by a bucket of sugar on a low shelf. The cover was off the wooden bucket, and beside it was a paper bag—half full.

Mrs. Hale moved toward it.

"She was putting this in there," she said to herself—slowly.

She thought of the flour in her kitchen at home—half sifted, half not sifted. She had been interrupted and had left things half done. What had interrupted Minnie Foster? Why had that work been left half done? She made a move as if to finish it,—unfinished things always bothered her,—and then she glanced around and saw that Mrs. Peters was watching her—and she didn't want Mrs. Peters to get that feeling she had got of work begun and then—for some reason—not finished.

"It's a shame about her fruit," she said, and walked toward the cupboard that the county attorney had opened, and got on the chair, murmuring: "I wonder if it's all gone."

It was a sorry enough looking sight, but "Here's one that's all right," she said at last. She held it toward the light. "This is cherries, too." She looked again. "I declare I believe that's the only one."

With a sigh, she got down from the chair, went to the sink and wiped off the bottle.

"She'll feel awful bad, after all her hard work in the hot weather. I remember the afternoon I put up my cherries last summer."

She set the bottle on the table, and, with another sigh, started to sit down in the rocker. But she did not sit down. Something kept her from sitting down in that chair. She straightened—

stepped back, and, half turned away, stood looking at it, seeing the woman who sat there "pleatin' at her apron."

The thin voice of the sheriff's wife broke in upon her: "I must be getting those things from the front room closet." She opened the door into the other room, started in, stepped back. "You coming with me, Mrs. Hale?" she asked nervously. "You—you could help me get them."

They were soon back—the stark coldness of that shut-up room was not a thing to linger in.

"My!" said Mrs. Peters, dropping the things on the table and hurrying to the stove.

Mrs. Hale stood examining the clothes the woman who was being detained in town had said she wanted.

"Wright was close!" she exclaimed, holding up a shabby black skirt that bore the marks of much making over. "I think maybe that's why she kept so much to herself. I s'pose she felt she couldn't do her part; and then, you don't enjoy things when you feel shabby. She used to wear pretty clothes and be lively—when she was Minnie Foster, one of the town girls, singing in the choir. But that—oh, that was twenty years ago."

With a carefulness in which there was something tender, she folded the shabby clothes and piled them at one corner of the table. She looked at Mrs. Peters, and there was something in the other woman's look that irritated her.

"She don't care," she said to herself. "Much difference it makes to her whether Minnie Foster had pretty clothes when she was a girl."

Then she looked again, and she wasn't so sure; in fact, she hadn't at any time been perfectly sure about Mrs. Peters. She had that shrinking manner, and yet her eyes looked as if they could see a long way into things.

"This all you was to take in?" asked Mrs. Hale.

"No," said the sheriff's wife; "she said she wanted an apron. Funny thing to want," she ventured in her nervous little way, "for there's not much to get you dirty in jail, goodness knows. But I suppose just to make her feel more natural. If you're used to wearing an apron—. She said they were in the bottom drawer of this cupboard. Yes—here they are. And then her little shawl that always hung on the stair door."

She took the small gray shawl from behind the door leading upstairs, and stood a minute looking at it.

Suddenly Mrs. Hale took a quick step toward the other woman.

"Mrs. Peters!"

"Yes, Mrs. Hale?"

"Do you think she—did it?"

A frightened look blurred the other things in Mrs. Peters' eyes.

"Oh, I don't know," she said, in a voice that seemed to shrink away from the subject.

"Well, I don't think she did," affirmed Mrs. Hale stoutly. "Asking for an apron, and her little shawl. Worryin' about her fruit."

"Mr. Peters says—" Footsteps were heard in the room above; she stopped, looked up, then went on in a lowered voice: "Mr. Peters says—it looks bad for her. Mr. Henderson is awful sarcastic in a speech, and he's going to make fun of her saying she didn't—wake up."

For a moment Mrs. Hale had no answer. Then, "Well, I guess John Wright didn't wake up—when they was slippin' that rope under his neck," she muttered.

"No, it's *strange,*" breathed Mrs. Peters. "They think it was such a—funny way to kill a man."

She began to laugh; at sound of the laugh, abruptly stopped.

"That's just what Mr. Hale said," said Mrs. Hale, in a resolutely natural voice. "There was a gun in the house. He says that's what he can't understand."

"Mr. Henderson said, coming out, that what was needed for the case was a motive. Something to show anger—or sudden feeling."

"Well, I don't see any signs of anger around here," said Mrs. Hale. "I don't—"

She stopped. It was as if her mind tripped on something. Her eye was caught by a dish-towel in the middle of the kitchen table. Slowly she moved toward the table. One half of it was wiped clean, the other half messy. Her eyes made a slow, almost unwilling turn to the bucket of sugar and the half empty bag beside it. Things begun—and not finished.

After a moment she stepped back, and said, in that manner of releasing herself:

"Wonder how they're finding things upstairs? I hope she had it a little more red up there. You know,"—she paused, and feeling gathered,—"it seems kind of *sneaking;* locking her up in town and coming out here to get her own house to turn against her!"

"But, Mrs. Hale," said the sheriff's wife, "the law is the law."

"I s'pose 'tis," answered Mrs. Hale shortly.

She turned to the stove, saying something about that fire not being much to brag of. She worked with it a minute, and when she straightened up she said aggressively:

"The law is the law—and a bad stove is a bad stove. How'd you like to cook on this?"—pointing with the poker to the broken lining. She opened the oven door and started to express her opinion of the oven; but she was swept into her own thoughts, thinking of what it would mean, year after year, to have that stove to wrestle with. The thought of Minnie Foster trying to bake in that oven—and the thought of her never going over to see Minnie Foster—.

She was startled by hearing Mrs. Peters say: "A person gets discouraged—and loses heart."

The sheriff's wife had looked from the stove to the sink—to the pail of water which had been carried in from outside. The two women stood there silent, above them the footsteps of the men who were looking for evidence against the woman who had worked in that kitchen. That look of seeing into things, of seeing through a thing to something else, was in the eyes of the sheriff's wife now. When Mrs. Hale next spoke to her, it was gently:

"Better loosen up your things, Mrs. Peters. We'll not feel them when we go out."

Mrs. Peters went to the back of the room to hang up the fur tippet she was wearing. A moment later she exclaimed, "Why, she was piecing a quilt," and held up a large sewing basket piled high with quilt pieces.

Mrs. Hale spread some of the blocks on the table.

"It's log-cabin pattern," she said, putting several of them together. "Pretty, isn't it?"

They were so engaged with the quilt that they did not hear the footsteps on the stairs. Just as the stair door opened Mrs. Hale was saying:

"Do you suppose she was going to quilt it or just knot it?"

The sheriff threw up his hands.

"They wonder whether she was going to quilt it or just knot it!"

There was a laugh for the ways of women, a warming of hands over the stove, and then the county attorney said briskly:

"Well, let's go right out to the barn and get that cleared up."

"I don't see as there's anything so strange," Mrs. Hale said resentfully, after the outside door had closed on the three men—"our taking up our time with little things while we're waiting for them to get the evidence. I don't see as it's anything to laugh about."

"Of course they've got awful important things on their minds," said the sheriff's wife apologetically.

They returned to an inspection of the blocks for the quilt. Mrs. Hale was looking at the fine, even sewing, and preoccupied with thoughts of the woman who had done that sewing, when she heard the sheriff's wife say, in a queer tone:

"Why, look at this one."

She turned to take the block held out to her.

"The sewing," said Mrs. Peters, in a troubled way. "All the rest of them have been so nice and even—but—this one. Why, it looks as if she didn't know what she was about!"

Their eyes met—something flashed to life, passed between them; then, as if with an effort, they seemed to pull away from each other. A moment Mrs. Hale sat there, her hands folded over that sewing which was so unlike all the rest of the sewing. Then she had pulled a knot and drawn the threads.

"Oh, what are you doing, Mrs. Hale?" asked the sheriff's wife, startled.

"Just pulling out a stitch or two that's not sewed very good," said Mrs. Hale mildly.

"I don't think we ought to touch things," Mrs. Peters said, a little helplessly.

"I'd just finish up this end," answered Mrs. Hale, still in that mild, matter-of-fact fashion.

She threaded a needle and started to replace bad sewing with good. For a little while she sewed in silence. Then, in that thin, timid voice, she heard:

"Mrs. Hale!"

"Yes, Mrs. Peters?"

"What do you suppose she was so—nervous about?"

"Oh, *I* don't know," said Mrs. Hale, as if dismissing a thing not important enough to spend much time on. "I don't know as she was—nervous. I sew awful queer sometimes when I'm just tired."

She cut a thread, and out of the corner of her eye looked up at Mrs. Peters. The small, lean face of the sheriff's wife seemed to have tightened up. Her eyes had that look of peering into something. But the next moment she moved, and said in her thin, indecisive way:

"Well, I must get those clothes wrapped. They may be through sooner than we think. I wonder where I could find a piece of paper—and string."

"In that cupboard, maybe," suggested Mrs. Hale, after a glance around.

One piece of the crazy sewing remained unripped. Mrs. Peters' back turned, Martha Hale now scrutinized that piece, compared it with the dainty, accurate sewing of the other blocks. The difference was startling. Holding this block made her feel queer, as if the distracted thoughts of the woman who had perhaps turned to it to try and quiet herself were communicating themselves to her.

Mrs. Peters' voice roused her.

"Here's a bird-cage," she said. "Did she have a bird, Mrs. Hale?"

"Why, I don't know whether she did or not." She turned to look at the cage Mrs. Peters was holding up. "I've not been here in so long." She sighed. "There was a man round last year selling canaries cheap—but I don't know as she took one. Maybe she did. She used to sing real pretty herself."

Mrs. Peters looked around the kitchen.

"Seems kind of funny to think of a bird here." She half laughed—an attempt to put up a barrier. "But she must have had one—or why would she have a cage? I wonder what happened to it."

"I suppose maybe the cat got it," suggested Mrs. Hale, resuming her sewing.

"No; she didn't have a cat. She's got that feeling some people have about cats—being afraid of them. When they brought her to our house yesterday, my cat got in the room, and she was real upset and asked me to take it out."

"My sister Bessie was like that," laughed Mrs. Hale.

The sheriff's wife did not reply. The silence made Mrs. Hale turn round. Mrs. Peters was examining the bird-cage.

"Look at this door," she said slowly. "It's broke. One hinge has been pulled apart."

Mrs. Hale came nearer.

"Looks as if some one must have been—rough with it."

Again their eyes met—startled, questioning, apprehensive. For a moment neither spoke nor stirred. Then Mrs. Hale, turning away, said brusquely:

"If they're going to find any evidence, I wish they'd be about it. I don't like this place."

"But I'm awful glad you came with me, Mrs. Hale." Mrs. Peters put the bird-cage on the table and sat down. "It would be lonesome for me—sitting here alone."

"Yes, it would, wouldn't it?" agreed Mrs. Hale, a certain determined naturalness in her voice. She picked up the sewing, but now it dropped in her lap, and she murmured in a different voice: "But I tell you what I *do* wish, Mrs. Peters. I wish I had come over sometimes when she was here. I wish—I had."

"But of course you were awful busy, Mrs. Hale. Your house—and your children."

"I could've come," retorted Mrs. Hale shortly. "I stayed away because it weren't cheerful—and that's why I ought to have come. I"—she looked around—"I've never liked this place. Maybe because it's down in a hollow and you don't see the road. I don't know what it is, but it's a lonesome place, and always was. I wish I had come over to see Minnie Foster sometimes. I can see now—" She did not put it into words.

"Well, you mustn't reproach yourself," counseled Mrs. Peters. "Somehow, we just don't see how it is with other folks till—something comes up."

"Not having children makes less work," mused Mrs. Hale, after a silence, "but it makes a quiet house—and Wright out to work all day—and no company when he did come in. Did you know John Wright, Mrs. Peters?"

"Not to know him. I've seen him in town. They say he was a good man."

"Yes—good," conceded John Wright's neighbor grimly. "He didn't drink, and kept his word as well as most, I guess, and paid his debts. But he was a hard man, Mrs. Peters. Just to pass the time of day with him—." She stopped, shivered a little. "Like a raw wind that gets to the bone." Her eye fell upon the cage on the table before her, and she added, almost bitterly: "I should think she would've wanted a bird!"

Suddenly she leaned forward, looking intently at the cage. "But what do you s'pose went wrong with it?"

"I don't know," returned Mrs. Peters; "unless it got sick and died."

But after she said it she reached over and swung the broken door. Both women watched it as if somehow held by it.

"You didn't know—her?" Mrs. Hale asked, a gentler note in her voice.

"Not till they brought her yesterday," said the sheriff's wife.

"She—come to think of it, she was kind of like a bird herself. Real sweet and pretty, but kind of timid and—fluttery. How—she—did—change."

That held her for a long time. Finally, as if struck with a happy thought and relieved to get back to everyday things, she exclaimed:

"Tell you what, Mrs. Peters, why don't you take the quilt in with you? It might take up her mind."

"Why, I think that's a real nice idea, Mrs. Hale," agreed the sheriff's wife, as if she too were glad to come into the atmosphere of a simple kindness. "There couldn't possibly be any objection to that, could there? Now, just what will I take? I wonder if her patches are in here—and her things."

They turned to the sewing basket.

"Here's some red," said Mrs. Hale, bringing out a roll of cloth. Underneath that was a box. "Here, maybe her scissors are in here—and her things." She held it up. "What a pretty box! I'll warrant that was something she had a long time ago—when she was a girl."

She held it in her hand a moment; then, with a little sigh, opened it.

Instantly her hand went to her nose.

"Why—!"

Mrs. Peters drew nearer—then turned away.

"There's something wrapped up in this piece of silk," faltered Mrs. Hale.

"This isn't her scissors," said Mrs. Peters in a shrinking voice.

Her hand not steady, Mrs. Hale raised the piece of silk. "Oh, Mrs. Peters!" she cried. "It's—"

Mrs. Peters bent closer.

"It's the bird," she whispered.

"But, Mrs. Peters!" cried Mrs. Hale. "*Look* at it! Its neck—look at its neck! It's all—other side *to.*"

She held the box away from her.

The sheriff's wife again bent closer.

"Somebody wrung its neck," said she, in a voice that was slow and deep.

And then again the eyes of the two women met—this time

clung together in a look of dawning comprehension, of growing horror. Mrs. Peters looked from the dead bird to the broken door of the cage. Again their eyes met. And just then there was a sound at the outside door.

Mrs. Hale slipped the box under the quilt pieces in the basket, and sank into the chair before it. Mrs. Peters stood holding to the table. The county attorney and the sheriff came in from outside.

"Well, ladies," said the county attorney, as one turning from serious things to little pleasantries, "have you decided whether she was going to quilt it or knot it?"

"We think," began the sheriff's wife in a flurried voice, "that she was going to—knot it."

He was too preoccupied to notice the change that came in her voice on that last.

"Well, that's very interesting, I'm sure," he said tolerantly. He caught sight of the bird-cage. "Has the bird flown!"

"We think the cat got it," said Mrs. Hale in a voice curiously even.

He was walking up and down, as if thinking something out.

"Is there a cat?" he asked absently.

Mrs. Hale shot a look up at the sheriff's wife.

"Well, not *now*," said Mrs. Peters. "They're superstitious, you know; they leave."

She sank into her chair.

The county attorney did not heed her. "No sign at all of any one having come in from the outside," he said to Peters, in the manner of continuing an interrupted conversation. "Their own rope. Now let's go upstairs again and go over it, piece by piece. It would have to have been some one who knew just the—"

The stair door closed behind them and their voices were lost.

The two women sat motionless, not looking at each other, but as if peering into something and at the same time holding back. When they spoke now it was as if they were afraid of what they were saying, but as if they could not help saying it.

"She liked the bird," said Martha Hale, low and slowly. "She was going to bury it in that pretty box."

"When I was a girl," said Mrs. Peters, under her breath, "my kitten—there was a boy took a hatchet, and before my eyes—before I could get there—" She covered her face an instant. "If they hadn't held me back I would have"—she caught herself, looked upstairs where footsteps were heard, and finished weakly—"hurt him."

Then they sat without speaking or moving.

"I wonder how it would seem," Mrs. Hale at last began, as if feeling her way over strange ground—"never to have had any children around?" Her eyes made a slow sweep of the kitchen, as if seeing what that kitchen had meant through all the years. "No, Wright wouldn't like the bird," she said after that—"a thing that sang. She used to sing. He killed that too." Her voice tightened.

Mrs. Peters moved uneasily.

"Of course we don't know who killed the bird."

"I knew John Wright," was Mrs. Hale's answer.

"It was an awful thing was done in this house that night, Mrs. Hale," said the sheriff's wife. "Killing a man while he slept—slipping a thing round his neck that choked the life out of him."

Mrs. Hale's hand went out to the bird-cage.

"His neck. Choked the life out of him."

"We don't *know* who killed him." whispered Mrs. Peters wildly. "We don't *know*."

Mrs. Hale had not moved. "If there had been years and years of—nothing, then a bird to sing to you, it would be awful—still—after the bird was still."

It was as if something within her not herself had spoken, and it found in Mrs. Peters something she did not know as herself.

"I know what stillness is," she said, in a queer, monotonous voice. "When we homesteaded in Dakota, and my first baby died—after he was two years old—and me with no other then—"

Mrs. Hale stirred.

"How soon do you suppose they'll be through looking for evidence?"

"I know what stillness is," repeated Mrs. Peters, in just the same way. Then she too pulled back. "The law has got to punish crime, Mrs. Hale," she said in her tight little way.

"I wish you'd seen Minnie Foster," was the answer, "when she wore a white dress with blue ribbons, and stood up there in the choir and sang."

The picture of that girl, the fact that she had lived neighbor to that girl for twenty years, and had let her die for lack of life, was suddenly more than she could bear.

"Oh, I *wish* I'd come over here once in a while!" she cried. "That was a crime! That was a crime! Who's going to punish that?"

"We mustn't take on," said Mrs. Peters, with a frightened look toward the stairs.

"I might 'a' *known* she needed help! I tell you, it's *queer*, Mrs.

Peters. We live close together, and we live far apart. We all go through the same things—its all just a different kind of the same thing! If it weren't—why do you and I *understand*? Why do we *know*— what we know this minute?"

She dashed her hand across her eyes. Then, seeing the jar of fruit on the table, she reached for it and choked out:

"If I was you I wouldn't *tell* her her fruit was gone! Tell her it *ain't*. Tell her it's all right—all of it. Here—take this in to prove it to her! She—she may never know whether it was broke or not."

She turned away.

Mrs. Peters reached out for the bottle of fruit as if she were glad to take it—as if touching a familiar thing, having something to do, could keep her from something else. She got up, looked about for something to wrap the fruit in, took a petticoat from the pile of clothes she had brought from the front room, and nervously started winding that round the bottle.

"My!" she began, in a high, false voice, "it's a good thing the men couldn't hear us! Getting all stirred up over a little thing like a—dead canary." She hurried over that. "As if that could have anything to do with—with—My, wouldn't they *laugh*?"

Footsteps were heard on the stairs.

"Maybe they would," muttered Mrs. Hale—"maybe they wouldn't."

"No, Peters," said the county attorney incisively; "it's all perfectly clear, except the reason for doing it. But you know juries when it comes to women. If there was some definite thing—something to show. Something to make a story about. A thing that would connect up with this clumsy way of doing it."

In a covert way Mrs. Hale looked at Mrs. Peters. Mrs. Peters was looking at her. Quickly they looked away from each other. The outer door opened and Mr. Hale came in.

"I've got the team round now," he said. "Pretty cold out there."

"I'm going to stay here awhile by myself," the county attorney suddenly announced. "You can send Frank out for me, can't you?" he asked the sheriff. "I want to go over everything. I'm not satisfied we can't do better."

Again, for one brief moment, the two women's eyes found one another.

The sheriff came up to the table.

"Did you want to see what Mrs. Peters was going to take in?"

The county attorney picked up the apron. He laughed.

"Oh, I guess they're not very dangerous things the ladies have picked out."

Mrs. Hale's hand was on the sewing basket in which the box was concealed. She felt that she ought to take her hand off the basket. She did not seem able to. He picked up one of the quilt blocks which she had piled on to cover the box. Her eyes felt like fire. She had a feeling that if he took up the basket she would snatch it from him.

But he did not take it up. With another little laugh, he turned away, saying:

"No; Mrs. Peters doesn't need supervising. For that matter, a sheriff's wife is married to the law. Ever think of it that way, Mrs. Peters?"

Mrs. Peters was standing beside the table. Mrs. Hale shot a look up at her; but she could not see her face. Mrs. Peters had turned away. When she spoke, her voice was muffled.

"Not—just that way," she said.

"Married to the law!" chuckled Mrs. Peters' husband. He moved toward the door into the front room, and said to the county attorney:

"I just want you to come in here a minute, George. We ought to take a look at these windows.

"Oh—windows," said the county attorney scoffingly.

"We'll be right out, Mr. Hale," said the sheriff to the farmer, who was still waiting by the door.

Hale went to look after the horses. The sheriff followed the county attorney into the other room. Again—for one moment—the two women were alone in that kitchen.

Martha Hale sprang up, her hands tight together, looking at that other woman, with whom it rested. At first she could not see her eyes, for the sheriff's wife had not turned back, since she turned away at that suggestion of being married to the law. But now Mrs. Hale made her turn back. Her eyes made her turn back. Slowly, unwillingly, Mrs. Peters turned her head until her eyes met the eyes of the other woman. There was a moment when they held each other in a steady, burning look in which there was no evasion nor flinching. Then Martha Hale's eyes pointed the way to the basket in which was hidden the thing that would make certain the conviction of the other woman—that woman who was not there and yet who had been there with them all through the hour.

For a moment Mrs. Peters did not move. And then she did it.

With a rush forward, she threw back the quilt pieces, got the box, tried to put it in her handbag. It was too big. Desperately she opened it, started to take the bird out. But there she broke—she could not touch the bird. She stood helpless, foolish.

There was the sound of a knob turning in the inner door. Martha Hale snatched the box from the sheriff's wife, and got it in the pocket of her big coat just as the sheriff and the county attorney came back into the kitchen.

THOMAS BURKE

(1886–1945)

Thomas Burke has held a special distinction in the world of detective fiction ever since the publication of "The Hands of Mr. Ottermole," an imaginative reworking of the search for Jack the Ripper, who terrorized London in 1888. In 1949, a board of eminent mystery critics and writers (including Anthony Boucher, John Dickson Carr, and Ellery Queen) voted it the greatest mystery story of all time. Burke's early background, however, promised nothing in the way of literary distinction. He was orphaned as a baby and lived with an uncle in a working-class neighborhood of London until he was nine. Placed in an orphanage, he left at age fourteen to work at a boarding house, then in an office. Yet, his early life shaped his literary career. He developed an intimate knowledge of Limehouse and London's seedy East End, where the Ripper committed his crimes. He developed a friendship with an elderly and kindly Chinese man who owned a tea shop and gave young Burke pieces of ginger and fascinated him with stories of what Burke described as the peculiarly Oriental mixture of cruelty, beauty, evil, and wisdom. Burke published a book of verse and some essays about London, but after his friend was deported for operating an opium den, Burke wrote a series of stories about the area he knew so well. Limehouse Nights: Tales of Chinatown *(1916) was an international success, especially when part of it became the source for D. W. Griffith's film* Broken Blossoms *(1919), with Lillian Gish. Burke went on to write many books in several genres and dozens of short stories, but he was always at his best when recreating the atmosphere of mystery and menace in the poor streets of the East End. "The Hands of Mr. Ottermole" combines this foggy atmosphere, a least likely suspect, a vivid insight into the compulsion of a serial killer, and an understanding that being fascinated with a killer's compulsion can be as dangerous as possessing the compulsion oneself.*

THE HANDS OF MR. OTTERMOLE

Murder (said old Quong)—oblige me by passing my pipe—murder is one of the simplest things in the world to do. Killing a man is a much simpler matter than killing a duck. Not always so safe, perhaps, but simpler. But to certain gifted people it is both simple and entirely safe. Many minds of finer complexion than my own have discolored themselves in seeking to name the identity of the author of those wholesale murders which took place last year. Who that man or woman really was, I know no more than you do, but I have a theory of the person it could have been; and if you are not pressed for time I will elaborate that theory into a little tale."

As I had the rest of that evening and the whole of the next day for dalliance in my ivory tower, I desired that he would tell me the story; and, having reckoned up his cash register and closed the ivory gate, he told me—between then and the dawn—his story of the Mallon End murders. Paraphrased and condensed, it came out something like this.

At six o'clock of a January evening Mr. Whybrow was walking home through the cobweb alleys of London's East End. He had left the golden clamor of the great High Street to which the tram had brought him from the river and his daily work, and was now in the chessboard of byways that is called Mallon End. None of the rush and gleam of the High Street trickled into these byways.

A few paces south—a flood tide of life, foaming and beating. Here—only slow shuffling figures and muffled pulses. He was in the sink of London, the last refuge of European vagrants.

As though in tune with the street's spirit, he too walked slowly, with head down. It seemed that he was pondering some pressing trouble, but he was not. He had no trouble. He was walking slowly because he had been on his feet all day; and he was bent in abstraction because he was wondering whether the Missis would have herrings for his tea, or haddock; and he was trying to decide which would be the more tasty on a night like this. A wretched night it was, of damp and mist, and the mist wandered into his throat and his eyes, and the damp had settled on pavement and roadway, and where the sparse lamplight fell it sent up a greasy sparkle that chilled one to look at. By contrast it made his speculations more agreeable, and made him ready for that tea—whether herring or haddock. His eye turned from the glum bricks that made his horizon, and went forward half a mile. He saw a gas-lit kitchen, a flamy fire, and a spread tea table. There was toast in the hearth and a singing kettle on the side and a piquant effusion of herrings, or maybe of haddock, or perhaps sausages. The vision gave his aching feet a throb of energy. He shook imperceptible damp from his shoulders, and hastened toward its reality.

But Mr. Whybrow wasn't going to get any tea that evening—or any other evening. Mr. Whybrow was going to die. Somewhere within a hundred yards of him, another man was walking: a man much like Mr. Whybrow and much like any other man, but without the only quality that enables mankind to live peaceably together and not as madmen in a jungle. A man with a dead heart eating into itself and bringing forth the foul organisms that arise from death and corruption. And that thing in man's shape, on a whim or a settled idea—one cannot know—had said within himself that Mr. Whybrow should never taste another herring. Not that Mr. Whybrow had injured him. Not that he had any dislike of Mr. Whybrow. Indeed, he knew nothing of him save as a familiar figure about the streets. But, moved by a force that had taken possession of his empty cells, he had picked on Mr. Whybrow with that blind choice that makes us pick one restaurant table that has nothing to mark it from four or five other tables, or one apple from a dish of half-a-dozen equal apples; or that drives nature to send a cyclone upon one corner of this planet and destroy five hundred lives in that corner, and leave another five hundred in the same corner unharmed. So this man had picked on Mr. Whybrow as he might have picked on you or me, had we been within his daily observation; and even now he was creeping through the blue-toned streets, nursing his large white hands, moving ever closer to Mr. Whybrow's tea table, and so closer to Mr. Whybrow himself.

He wasn't, this man, a bad man. Indeed, he had many of the social and amiable qualities, and passed as a respectable man, as most successful criminals do. But the thought had come into his moldering mind that he would like to murder somebody, and as he held no fear of God or man, he was going to do it, and would then go home to *his* tea. I don't say that flippantly, but as a statement of fact. Strange as it may seem to the humane, murderers must and do sit down to meals after a murder. There is no reason why they shouldn't, and many reasons why they should. For one thing, they need to keep their physical and mental vitality at full beat for the business of covering their crime. For another, the strain of their effort makes them hungry, and satisfaction at the accomplishment of a desired thing brings a feeling of relaxation toward human pleasures. It is accepted among non-murderers that the murderer is always overcome by fear for his safety and horror at his act; but this type is rare. His own safety is, of course, his immediate concern, but vanity is a marked quality of most murderers, and that, together with the thrill of conquest, makes him confident that he can secure it; and when he has restored his strength with food, he goes about securing it as a young hostess goes about the arranging of her first big dinner—a little anxious, but no more. Criminologists and detectives tell us that *every* murderer, however intelligent or cunning, always makes one slip in his tactics—one little slip that brings the affair home to him. But that is only half-true. It is true only of the murderers who are caught. Scores of murderers are not caught: therefore, scores of murderers do not make any mistake at all. This man didn't.

As for horror or remorse, prison chaplains, doctors, and lawyers have told us that of murderers they have interviewed under condemnation and the shadow of death, only one here and there has expressed any contrition for his act or shown any sign of mental misery. Most of them display only exasperation at having been caught when so many have gone undiscovered, or indignation at being condemned for a perfectly reasonable act. However normal and humane they may have been before the murder, they are utterly without conscience after it. For what is conscience? Simply a polite nickname for superstition, which is a polite nickname for fear. Those who associate remorse with murder are, no doubt, basing their ideas on the world-legend of the remorse of Cain, or are projecting their own frail minds into the mind of the murderer, and getting false reactions. Peaceable folk cannot hope to make contact with this mind, for they are not merely different in mental type from the murderer; they are different in their personal chemistry and construction. Some men can and do kill—not one man, but two or three—and go calmly about their daily affairs. Other men could not, under the most agonizing provocation, bring themselves even to wound. It is men of this sort who imagine the murderer in torments of remorse and fear of the law, whereas he is actually sitting down to his tea.

The man with the large white hands was as ready for his tea as Mr. Whybrow was, but he had something to do before he went to it. When he had done that something, and made no mistake about it, he would be even more ready for it, and would go to it as comfortably as he went to it the day before, when his hands were stainless.

Walk on, then, Mr. Whybrow, walk on; and as you walk, look your last upon the familiar features of your nightly journey. Follow your jack-o'-lantern tea table. Look well upon its warmth and color and kindness; feed your eyes with it and tease your nose with its gentle domestic odors, for you will never sit down to it. Within ten minutes' pacing of you, a pursuing phantom has spoken in his heart, and you are doomed. There you go—you and phantom—two nebulous dabs of mortality moving through green air along pavements of powder-blue, the one to kill, the other to be killed. Walk on. Don't annoy your burning feet by hurrying, for the more slowly you walk, the longer you will breathe the green air of this January dusk, and see the dreamy lamplight and the little shops, and hear the agreeable commerce of the London crowd and the haunting pathos of the street organ. These things are dear to you, Mr. Whybrow. You don't know it now, but in fifteen minutes you will have two seconds in which to realize how inexpressibly dear they are.

Walk on, then, across this crazy chessboard. You are in Lagos Street now, among the tents of the wanderers of Eastern Europe. A minute or so, and you are in Loyal Lane, among the lodging houses that shelter the useless and the beaten of London's camp followers. The lane holds the smell of them, and its soft darkness seems heavy with the wail of the futile. But you are not sensitive to impalpable things, and you plod through it, unseeing, as you do every evening, and come to Blean Street, and plod through that. From basement to sky rise the tenements of an alien colony. Their windows slot the ebony of their walls with lemon. Behind those windows, strange life is moving, dressed with forms that are not of London or of England, yet, in essence, the same agreeable life that you have been living, and tonight will live no more. From high above you comes a voice crooning *The Song of Katta.* Through a window you see a family keeping a religious rite. Through another you see a woman pouring out tea for her husband. You see a man mending a pair of boots; a mother bathing her baby. You have seen all these things before, and never noticed them. You do not notice them now, but if you knew that you were never going to see them again, you would notice them. You never *will* see them again, not because your life has run its natural course, but because a man whom you have often passed in the street has at his own solitary pleasure decided to usurp the awful authority of nature, and destroy you. So perhaps it's as well that you don't notice them, for your part in them is ended. No more for you these pretty moments of our earthly travail: only one moment of terror, and then a plunging darkness.

Closer to you this shadow of massacre moves, and now he is twenty yards behind you. You can hear his footfall, but you do not turn your head. You are familiar with footfalls. You are in London, in the easy security of your daily territory, and footfalls behind you, your instinct tells you, are no more than a message of human company.

But can't you hear something in those footfalls—something that goes with a widdershins beat? Something that says: *Look out, look out. Beware, beware.* Can't you hear the very syllables of *murd-er-er, murd-er-er*? No; there is nothing in footfalls. They are neutral. The foot of villainy falls with the same quiet note as the foot of honesty. But those footfalls, Mr. Whybrow, are bearing on to you a pair of hands, and there *is* something in hands. Behind you that pair of hands is even now stretching its muscles in preparation for your end. Every minute of your days, you have been seeing human hands. Have you ever realized the sheer horror of hands—those appendages that are a symbol of our moments of trust and affection and salutation? Have you thought of the sickening potentialities that lie within the scope of that five-tentacled member? No, you never have; for all the human hands that you have seen have been stretched to you in kindness or fellowship. Yet, though the eyes can hate and the lips can sting, it is only that dangling member that can gather the accumulated essence of evil and electrify it into currents of destruction. Satan may enter into man by many doors, but in the hands alone can he find the servants of his will.

Another minute, Mr. Whybrow, and you will know all about the horror of human hands.

You are nearly home now. You have turned into your street—Caspar Street—and you are in the center of the chessboard. You can see the front window of your little four-roomed house. The street is dark, and its three lamps give only a smut of light that is more confusing than darkness. It is dark—empty, too. Nobody about; no lights in the front parlors of the houses, for the families are at tea in their kitchens; and only a random glow in a few upper rooms occupied by lodgers. Nobody about but you and your following companion, and you don't notice him. You see him so often that he is never seen. Even if you turned your head and saw him, you would only say "Good evening" to him, and walk on. A suggestion that he was a possible murderer would not even make you laugh. It would be too silly.

And now you are at your gate. And now you have found your door key. And now you are in, and hanging up your hat and coat. The Missis has just called a greeting from the kitchen, whose smell is an echo of that greeting (herrings!), and you have answered it, when the door shakes under a sharp knock.

Go away, Mr. Whybrow. Go away from that door. Don't touch it. Get right away from it. Get out of the house. Run with the Missis to the back garden, and over the fence. Or call the neighbors. But don't touch that door. Don't, Mr. Whybrow, don't open. . . .

Mr. Whybrow opened the door.

That was the beginning of what became known as London's Strangling Horrors. Horrors they were called because they were something more than murders: they were motiveless, and there was an air of black magic about them. Each murder was committed at a time when the street where the bodies were found was empty of any perceptible or possible murderer. There would be an empty alley. There would be a policeman at its end. He would turn his back on the empty alley for less than a minute. Then he would look round and run into the night with news of another strangling. And in any direction he looked, nobody to be seen and no report to be had of anybody being seen. Or he would be on duty in a long-quiet street, and suddenly be called to a house of dead people whom a few seconds earlier he had seen alive. And, again, whichever way he looked nobody to be seen; and although police whistles put an immediate cordon around the area and searched all houses, no possible murderer to be found.

The first news of the murder of Mr. and Mrs. Whybrow was brought by the station sergeant. He had been walking through Caspar Street on his way to the station for duty, when he noticed the open door of No. 98. Glancing in, he saw by the gaslight of the passage a motionless body on the floor. After a second look he blew his whistle; and when the constables answered him, he took one to join him in search of the house, and sent others to watch all neighboring streets and make inquiries at adjoining houses. But neither in the house nor in the streets was anything found to indicate the murderer. Neighbors on either side, and opposite, were questioned, but they had seen nobody about, and had heard nothing. One had heard Mr. Whybrow come home—the scrape of his latchkey in the door was so regular an evening sound, he said, that you could set your watch by it for half-past six—but he had heard nothing more than the sound of the opening door until the sergeant's whistle. Nobody had been seen to enter the house or leave it, by front or back, and the necks of the dead people carried no fingerprints or other traces. A nephew was called in to go over the house, but he could find nothing missing; and anyway his uncle possessed nothing worth stealing. The little money in the house was untouched, and there were no signs of any disturbance of the property, or even of struggle. No signs of anything but brutal and wanton murder.

Mr. Whybrow was known to neighbors and workmates as a quiet, likable, home-loving man; such a man as could not have any enemies. But, then, murdered men seldom have. A relentless enemy who hates a man to the point of wanting to hurt him seldom wants to murder him, since to do that puts him beyond suffering. So the police were left with an impossible situation: no clue to the murderer and no motive for the murders, only that they had been done.

The first news of the affair sent a tremor through London generally, and an electric thrill through all Mallon End. Here was a murder of two inoffensive people, not for gain and not for revenge; and the murderer, to whom, apparently, killing was a casual impulse, was at large. He had left no traces, and provided he had no companions, there seemed no reason why he should not remain at large. Any clearheaded man who stands alone and has no fear of God or man, can, if he chooses, hold a city, even a nation, in subjection; but your everyday criminal is seldom clearheaded and dislikes being lonely. He needs, if not the support of confederates, at least somebody to talk to; his vanity needs the satisfaction of perceiving at first hand the effect of his work. For this he will frequent bars and coffee shops and other public places. Then, sooner or later, in a glow of comradeship, he will utter the one word too much; and the nark, who is everywhere, has an easy job.

But though the doss-houses and saloons and other places were "combed" and set with watches, and it was made known by whispers that good money and protection were assured to those with information, nothing attaching to the Whybrow case could be found. The murderer clearly had no friends and kept no company. Known men of this type were called up and questioned, but each was able to give a good account of himself; and in a few days the police were at a dead end. Against the constant public gibe that the thing had been done almost under their noses, they became restive, and for four days each man of the force was working his daily beat under a strain. On the fifth day they became still more restive.

It was the season of annual teas and entertainments for the children of the Sunday Schools; and on an evening of fog, when London was a world of groping phantoms, a small girl, in the bravery of best Sunday frock and shoes, shining face and new-washed hair, set out from Logan Passage for St. Michael's Parish Hall. She never got there. She was not actually dead until half-past six, but she was as good as dead from the moment she left her mother's door. Somebody like a man, pacing the street from which the passage led, saw her come out; and from that moment she was dead. Through the fog somebody's large white hands reached after her, and in fifteen minutes they were about her.

At half-past six a whistle screamed trouble, and those answering it found the body of little Nellie Vrinoff in a warehouse entry in Minnow Street. The sergeant was first among them, and he posted his men to useful points, ordering them here and there in the tart tones of repressed rage, and berating the officer whose beat the street was. "I saw you, Magson, at the end of the lane. What were you up to there? You were there ten minutes before you turned." Magson began an explanation about keeping an eye on a suspicious-looking character at that end, but the sergeant cut him short: "Suspicious characters be damned. You don't want to look for suspicious characters. You want to look for *murderers*. Messing about . . . and then this happens right where you ought to be. Now think what they'll say."

With the speed of ill news came the crowd, pale and perturbed; and on the story that the unknown monster had appeared again, and this time to a child, their faces streaked the fog with spots of hate and horror. But then came the ambulance and more police, and swiftly they broke up the crowd; and as it broke, the sergeant's thought was thickened into words, and from all sides came low murmurs of "Right under their noses." Later inquiries showed that four people of the district, above suspicion, had passed that entry at intervals of seconds before the murder, and seen nothing and heard nothing. None of them had passed the child alive or seen her dead. None of them had seen anybody in the street except themselves. Again the police were left with no motive and with no clue.

And now the district, as you will remember, was given over, not to panic, for the London public never yields to that, but to apprehension and dismay. If these things were happening in their familiar streets, then anything might happen. Wherever people met—in the streets, the markets, and the shops—they debated the one topic. Women took to bolting their windows and doors at the first fall of dusk. They kept their children closely under their eye. They did their shopping before dark, and watched anxiously—while pretending they weren't watching—for the return of their husbands from work. Under the cockney's semi-humorous resignation to disaster, they hid an hourly foreboding. By the whim of one man with a pair of hands, the structure and tenor of their daily life were shaken, as they always can be shaken by any man contemptuous of humanity and fearless of its laws. They began to realize that the pillars that supported the peaceable society in which they lived were mere straws that anybody could snap; that laws were powerful only so long as they were obeyed; that the police were potent only so long as they were feared. By the power of his hands this one man had made a whole community do something new: he had made it think, and left it gasping at the obvious.

And then, while it was yet gasping under his first two strokes, he made his third. Conscious of the horror that his hands had created, and hungry as an actor who has once tasted the thrill of the multitude, he made fresh advertisement of his presence; and on Wednesday morning, three days after the murder of the child, the papers carried to the breakfast tables of England the story of a still more shocking outrage.

At 9:32 on Tuesday night a constable was on duty in Jarnigan Road, and at that time spoke to a fellow officer named Petersen at the top of Clemming Street. He had seen this officer walk down that street. He could swear that the street was empty at that time, except for a lame bootblack whom he knew by sight, and who passed him and entered a tenement on the side opposite that on which his fellow officer was walking. He had the habit, as all constables had just then, of looking constantly behind him and around him, whichever way he was walking, and he was certain that the street was empty. He passed his sergeant at 9:33, saluted him, and answered his inquiry for anything seen. He reported that he had seen nothing, and passed on. His beat ended at a short distance from Clemming Street, and having paced it, he turned and came again at 9:34 to the top of the street. He had scarcely reached it before he heard the hoarse voice of the sergeant: "Gregory! You there? Quick. Here's another. My God, it's Petersen! Garroted. Quick, call 'em up!"

That was the third of the Strangling Horrors, of which there were to be a fourth and a fifth; and the five horrors were to pass into the unknown and unknowable. That is, unknown as far as authority and the public were concerned. The identity of the murderer *was* known, but to two men only. One was the murderer himself; the other was a young journalist.

This young man, who was covering the affairs for his paper, the *Daily Torch,* was no smarter than the other zealous newspapermen who were hanging about these byways in the hope of a sudden story. But he was patient, and he hung a little closer to the case than the other fellows, and by continually staring at it he at last raised the figure of the murderer like a genie from the stones on which he had stood to do his murders.

After the first few days the men had given up any attempt at exclusive stories, for there were none to be had. They met regularly at the police station, and what little information there was they shared. The officials were agreeable to them, but no more. The sergeant discussed with them the details of each murder; suggested possible explanations of the man's methods; recalled from the past those cases that had some similarity; and on the matter of motive reminded them of the motiveless Neil Cream and the wanton John Williams, and hinted that work was being done which would soon bring the business to an end; but about that work he would not say a word. The Inspector, too, was gracefully garrulous on the thesis of Murder, but whenever one of the party edged the talk toward what was being done in this immediate matter, he glided past it. Whatever the officials knew, they were not giving it to newspapermen. The business had fallen heavily upon them, and only by a capture made by their own efforts could they rehabilitate themselves in official and public esteem. Scotland Yard, of course, was at work, and had all the station's material; but the station's hope was that they themselves would have the honor of settling the affair; and however useful the cooperation of the press might be in other cases, they did not want to risk a defeat by a premature disclosure of their theories and plans.

So the sergeant talked at large, and propounded one interesting theory after another, all of which the newspapermen had thought of themselves.

The young man soon gave up these morning lectures on the philosophy of crime, and took to wandering about the streets and making bright stories out of the effect of the murders on the normal life of the people. A melancholy job made more melancholy by the district. The littered roadways, the crestfallen houses, the bleared windows—all held the acid misery that evokes no sympathy: the misery of the frustrated poet. The misery was the creation of the aliens, who were living in this makeshift fashion because they had no settled homes, and would neither take the trouble to make a home where they *could* settle, nor get on with their wandering.

There was little to be picked up. All he saw and heard were indignant faces, and wild conjectures of the murderer's identity and of the secret of his trick of appearing and disappearing unseen. Since a policeman himself had fallen a victim, denunciations of the force had ceased, and the unknown was now invested with a cloak of legend. Men eyed other men as though thinking: It might be *him*. It might be *him*. They were no longer looking for a man who had the air of a Madame Tussaud murderer; they were looking for a man, or perhaps some harridan woman, who had done these particular murders. Their thoughts ran mainly on the foreign set. Such ruffianism could scarcely belong to England, nor could the bewildering cleverness of the thing. So they turned to Rumanian gypsies and Turkish carpet-sellers. There, clearly, would be found the "warm" spot. These Eastern fellows—they knew all sorts of tricks, and they had no real religion—nothing to hold them within bounds. Sailors returning from those parts had told tales of conjurors who made themselves invisible; and there were tales of Egyptian and Arab potions that were used for abysmally queer purposes. Perhaps it *was* possible to them; you never knew. They were so slick and cunning, and they had such gliding movements; no Englishman could melt away as they could. Almost certainly the murderer would be found to be one of that sort—with some dark trick of his own—and just because they were sure that he *was* a magician, they felt that it was useless to look for him. He was a power, able to hold them in subjection and to hold himself untouchable. Superstition, which so easily cracks the frail shell of reason, had got into them. He could do anything he chose; he would never be discovered. These two points they settled, and they went about the streets in a mood of resentful fatalism.

They talked of their ideas to the journalist in half-tones, looking right and left, as though *HE* might overhear them and visit them. And though all the district was thinking of him and ready to pounce upon him, yet, so strongly had he worked upon them, that if any man in the street—say, a small man of commonplace features and form—had cried "*I* am the Monster!" would their stifled fury have broken into flood and have borne him down and engulfed him? Or would they not suddenly have seen something unearthly in that everyday face and figure, something unearthly in his everyday boots, something unearthly about his hat, something that marked him as one whom none of their weapons could alarm or pierce? And would they not momentarily have fallen back from this devil, as the devil fell back from the cross made by the sword of Faust, and so have given him time to escape? I do not know; but so fixed was their belief in his invincibility that it is at least likely that they would have made this hesitation, had such an occasion arisen. But it never did. Today this commonplace fellow, his murder lust glutted, is still seen and observed among them as he was seen and observed all the time; but because nobody then dreamt, or now dreams, that he was what he was, they observed him then, and observe him now, as people observe a lamppost.

Almost was their belief in his invincibility justified; for, five days after the murder of the policeman Petersen, when the experience and inspiration of the whole detective force of London were turned toward his identification and capture, he made his fourth and fifth strokes.

At nine o'clock that evening, the young newspaperman, who hung about every night until his paper was away, was strolling along Richards Lane. Richards Lane is a narrow street, partly a stall-market, and partly residential. The young man was in the residential section, which carries on one side small working-class cottages, and on the other the wall of a railway goods-yard. The great wall hung a blanket of shadow over the lane, and the shadow and the cadaverous outline of the now deserted market stalls gave it the appearance of a living lane that had been turned to frost in the moment between breath and death. The very lamps, that elsewhere were nimbuses of gold, had here the rigidity of gems. The journalist, feeling this message of frozen eternity, was telling himself that he was tired of the whole thing, when in one stroke the frost was broken. In the moment between one pace and another, silence and darkness were racked by a high scream and through the scream a voice: "Help! help! *He's here!*"

Before he could think what movement to make, the lane came to life. As though its invisible populace had been waiting on that cry, the door of every cottage was flung open, and from them and from the alleys poured shadowy figures bent in question-mark form. For a second or so they stood as rigid as the lamps; then a police whistle gave them direction, and the flock of shadows sloped up the street. The journalist followed them, and others followed him. From the main street and from surrounding streets they came, some risen from unfinished suppers, some disturbed in their ease of slippers and shirtsleeves, some stumbling on infirm limbs, and some upright and armed with pokers or the tools of their trade. Here and there above the wavering cloud of heads moved the bold helmets of policemen. In one dim mass they surged upon a cottage whose doorway was marked by the sergeant and two constables; and voices of those behind urged them on with "Get in! Find him! Run round the back! Over the wall!" And those in front cried, "Keep back! Keep back!"

And now the fury of a mob held in thrall by unknown peril broke loose. He was here—on the spot. Surely this time he *could not* escape. All minds were bent upon the cottage; all energies thrust toward its doors and windows and roof; all thought was turned upon one unknown man and his extermination. So that no one man saw any other man. No man saw the narrow, packed lane and the mass of struggling shadows, and all forgot to look among themselves for the monster who never lingered upon his victims. All forgot, indeed, that they, by their mass crusade of vengeance, were affording him the perfect hiding place. They saw only the house, and they heard only the rending of woodwork and the smash of glass at back and front, and the police giving orders or crying with the chase; and they pressed on.

But they found no murderer. All they found was news of murder and a glimpse of the ambulance, and for their fury there was no other object than the police themselves, who fought against this hampering of their work.

The journalist managed to struggle through to the cottage door, and to get the story from the constable stationed there. The cottage was the home of a pensioned sailor and his wife and daughter. They had been at supper, and at first it appeared that some noxious gas had smitten all three in mid-action. The daughter lay dead on the hearth rug, with a piece of bread and butter in her hand. The father had fallen sideways from his chair, leaving on his plate a filled spoon of rice pudding. The mother lay half under the table, her lap filled with the pieces of a broken cup and splashes of cocoa. But in three seconds the idea of gas was dismissed. One glance at their necks showed that this was the Strangler again; and the police stood and looked at the room and momentarily shared the fatalism of the public. They were helpless.

This was his fourth visit, making seven murders in all. He was to do, as you know, one more—and to do it that night; and then he was to pass into history as the unknown London horror, and return to the decent life that he had always led, remembering little of what he had done and worried not at all by the memory. Why did he stop? Impossible to say. Why did he begin? Impossible again. It just happened like that; and if he thinks at all of those days and nights, I surmise that he thinks of them as we think of foolish or dirty little sins that we committed in childhood. We say that they were not really sins because we were not then consciously ourselves: we had not come to realization; and we look back at that foolish little creature that we once were and forgive him because he didn't know. So, I think, with this man.

There are plenty like him. Eugene Aram, after the murder of Daniel Clarke, lived a quiet, contented life for fourteen years, unhaunted by his crime and unshaken in his self-esteem. Dr. Crippen murdered his wife, and then lived pleasantly with his mistress in the house under whose floor he had buried the wife.

Constance Kent, found Not Guilty of the murder of her young brother, led a peaceful life for five years before she confessed. George Joseph Smith and William Palmer lived amiably among their fellows untroubled by fear or by remorse for their poisonings and drownings. Charles Peace, at the time he made his one unfortunate essay, had settled down into a respectable citizen with an interest in antiques. It happened that, after a lapse of time, these men were discovered; but more murderers than we guess are living decent lives today, and will die in decency, undiscovered and unsuspected. As this man will.

But he had a narrow escape, and it was perhaps this narrow escape that brought him to a stop. The escape was due to an error of judgment on the part of the journalist.

As soon as he had the full story of the affair, which took some time, he spent fifteen minutes on the telephone, sending the story through, and at the end of the fifteen minutes, when the stimulus of the business had left him, he felt physically tired and mentally disheveled. He was not yet free to go home; the paper would not go away for another hour; so he turned into a bar for a drink and some sandwiches.

It was then, when he had dismissed the whole business from his mind and was looking about the bar and admiring the landlord's taste in watch chains and his air of domination, and was thinking that the landlord of a well-conducted tavern had a more comfortable life than a newspaperman, that his mind received from nowhere a spark of light. He was not thinking about the Strangling Horrors; his mind was on his sandwich. As a public-house sandwich, it was a curiosity. The bread had been thinly cut, it was buttered, and the ham was not two months stale; it was ham as it should be. His mind turned to the inventor of this refreshment, the Earl of Sandwich, and then to George the Fourth, and then to the Georges, and to the legend of that George who was worried to know how the apple got into the apple dumpling. He wondered whether George would have been equally puzzled to know how the ham got into the ham sandwich, and how long it would have been before it occurred to him that the ham could not have got there unless somebody had put it there. He got up to order another sandwich, and in that moment a little active corner of his mind settled the affair. If there was ham in his sandwich, somebody must have put it there. If seven people had been murdered, somebody must have been there to murder them. There was no aeroplane or automobile that would go into a man's pocket; therefore, that somebody must have escaped either by running away or standing still; and again therefore—

He was visualizing the front-page story that his paper would carry if his theory was correct, and if—a matter of conjecture—his editor had the necessary nerve to make a bold stroke, when a cry of "Time, gentlemen, please! All out!" reminded him of the hour. He got up and went out into a world of mist, broken by the ragged discs of roadside puddles and the streaming lightning of motor buses. He was certain that he had *the* story, but even if it was proved, he was doubtful whether the policy of his paper would permit him to print it. It had one great fault. It was truth, but it was impossible truth. It rocked the foundations of everything that newspaper readers believed and that newspaper editors helped them to believe. They might believe that Turkish carpet-sellers had the gift of making themselves invisible. They would not believe this.

As it happened, they were not asked to, for the story was never written. As his paper had by now gone away, and as he was nourished by his refreshment and stimulated by his theory, he thought he might put in an extra half hour by testing that theory. So he began to look about for the man he had in mind—a man with white hair and large white hands; otherwise an everyday figure whom nobody would look twice at. He wanted to spring his idea on this man without warning, and he was going to place himself within reach of a man armored in legends of dreadfulness and grue. This might appear to be an act of supreme courage—that one man, with no hope of immediate outside support, should place himself at the mercy of one who was holding a whole parish in terror. But it wasn't. He didn't think about the risk. He didn't think about his duty to his employers or loyalty to his paper. He was moved simply by an instinct to follow a story to its end.

He walked slowly from the tavern and crossed into Fingal Street, making for Deever Market, where he had hope of finding his man. But his journey was shortened. At the corner of Lotus Street he saw him—or a man who looked like him. This street was poorly lit, and he could see little of the man: but he *could* see white hands. For some twenty paces he stalked him; then drew level with him; and at a point where the arch of a railway crossed the street, he saw that this was his man. He approached him with the current conversational phrase of the district: "Well, seen anything of the murderer?" The man stopped to look sharply at him; then, satisfied that the journalist was not the murderer, said:

"Eh? No, nor's anybody else, curse it. Doubt if they ever will."

"I don't know. I've been thinking about them, and I've got an idea."

"So?"

"Yes. Came to me all of a sudden. Quarter of an hour ago. And I'd felt that we'd all been blind. It's been staring us in the face."

The man turned again to look at him, and the look and the movement held suspicion of this man who seemed to know so much. "Oh? Has it? Well, if you're so sure, why not give us the benefit of it?"

"I'm going to." They walked level, and were nearly at the end of the little street where it meets Deever Market when the journalist turned casually to the man. He put a finger on his arm. "Yes, it seems to me quite simple now. But there's still one point I don't understand. One little thing I'd like to clear up. I mean the motive. Now, as man to man, tell me, Sergeant Ottermole, just *why* did you kill all those inoffensive people?"

The sergeant stopped, and the journalist stopped. There was just enough light from the sky, which held the reflected light of the continent of London, to give him a sight of the sergeant's face, and the sergeant's face was turned to him with a wide smile of such urbanity and charm that the journalist's eyes were frozen as they met it. The smile stayed for some seconds. Then said the sergeant, "Well, to tell you the truth, Mister Newspaperman, I don't know. I really don't know. In fact, I've been worried about it myself. But I've got an idea—just like you. Everybody knows that we can't control the workings of our minds. Don't they? Ideas come into our minds without asking. But everybody's supposed to be able to control his body. Why? Eh? We get our minds from lord-knows-where—from people who were dead hundreds of years before we were born. Mayn't we get our bodies in the same way? Our faces—our legs—our heads—they aren't completely ours. We don't make 'em. They come to us. And couldn't ideas come into our bodies like ideas come into our minds? Eh? Can't ideas live in nerve and muscle as well as in brain? Couldn't it be that parts of our bodies aren't really us, and couldn't ideas come into those parts all of a sudden, like ideas come into . . . into"—he shot his arms out, showing the great white-gloved hands and hairy wrists; shot them out so swiftly to the journalist's throat that his eyes never saw them—"into *my hands!*"

CHESTER HIMES

(1909–1984)

Chester Himes's career spanned an extraordinary period of social change, not just for African Americans but also for society as a whole. After attending Ohio State University, he served seven years, from 1928 to 1936, in the penitentiary for jewel theft. He wrote in his autobiography The Quality of Hurt *(1971) that he spent much time in prison reading stories in the mystery magazine* Black Mask, *particularly stories by Dashiell Hammett, and he thought he could do as well. He bought himself a typewriter while incarcerated and began writing under the assumption that all a writer had to do was "tell it like it is." Though he published his first short story in 1933, telling the truth would cause him a lifetime of trouble and snatch out of his grasp what success he could gather. In Europe he was regarded as a sociological writer and respected for it, but in America his novel* If He Hollers Let Him Go *(1945) had its print run cut short because it offended a staff member at his own publisher. The hard truths he portrayed in subsequent novels did not enhance his career. He ended up broke in Paris, where Marcel Duhamel at Librairie Gallimard urged him to write a hard-boiled novel noir.* La Reine des Pommes *(published as* For Love of Imabelle, *in 1959; and as* A Rage in Harlem, *in 1965) began a series of violent crime novels featuring Coffin Ed Johnson and Grave Digger Jones, black policemen. These works revived his moribund career and brought him money from movie versions, though he died with not much more than he'd ever had. Himes once remarked that the violence he wrote about shocked him. In our selection from 1967, Himes reveals his disturbing ability to expose the unvarnished horror of reality. A man, T-bone Smith, hungry and willing to send his wife hooking for him, is trapped by poverty and unable to reshape himself into anything other than what his societal oppressors wish him to be. When faced with the possibility of fighting back, T-bone is overwhelmed and goes over the edge.*

TANG

A man called T-bone Smith sat in a cold-water slum flat on 113th Street east of Eighth Avenue in Harlem, looking at television with his old lady, Tang. They had a television set but they didn't have anything to eat. It was after ten o'clock at night and the stores were closed, but that didn't make any difference because they didn't have any money. It was a two-room flat so the television was in the kitchen with the table and the stove. Because it was summertime, the stove was cold and the windows were open.

T-bone was clad only in a pair of greasy black pants and his bare black torso was ropy with lean hard muscles and decorated with an elaborate variety of scars. His long narrow face was hinged on a mouth with lips the size of automobile tires and the corner of his sloe-shaped eyes were sticky with matter. The short hard burrs on his watermelon head were the color of half-burnt ashes. He had his bare black feet propped up on the kitchen table with the white soles toward the television screen. He was white-mouthed from hunger but was laughing like an idiot at two blackfaced white minstrels on the television screen who earned more money every week by blackening their faces and acting foolish than T-bone had earned in all his life.

In between laughing he was trying to get his old lady, Tang, to go down into Central Park and trick with some white man so they could eat.

"Go on, baby, you can be back in an hour with 'nuff bread so we can scoff."

"I'se tired as you are," she said evilly. "Go sell yo' own ass to whitey, you luvs him so much."

She had once been a beautiful jet-black woman with a broad flat face and softly rounded features which looked as though they had been made by a child at play; her figure had been something to invoke instant visions of sex contortions and black ecstasy. But both face and figure had been corroded by vice and hunger and now she was a lean, angular crone with burnt red hair and flat black features which looked like they had been molded by a stamping machine. Only her eyes looked alive; they were red, mean, disillusioned and defiant. She was clad in a faded green mother hubbard which looked at though it had never been laundered and her big, buniony feet trod restlessly about the dirty, rotting kitchen linoleum. The soles were unseen but the tops had wrinkled black skin streaked with dirt.

Suddenly, above the sound of the gibbering of the blackface white minstrels, they heard an impatient hammering on the door. Both knew instantly someone had first tried the doorbell, which had never worked. They looked suspiciously at one another. Neither could imagine anyone it could be except the police, so they quickly scanned the room to see if there were any incriminating evidence in sight; although, aside from her hustling about the lagoon in Central Park, neither had committed any crime recently enough to interest the police. Finally she stuck her bare feet into some old felt slippers and rubbed red lipstick over her rusty lips while he got up and shambled across the floor in his bare feet to open the door.

A young black uniformed messenger with smooth skin and bright intelligent eyes asked, "Mister Smith?"

"Dass me," T-bone admitted.

The messenger extended a long cardboard box wrapped in white paper tied with red ribbon. Conspicuous on the white wrapping paper was the green and white label of a florist, decorated with pink and yellow flowers, and on the lines for the name and address were the typed words: *Mr. T. Smith, West 113th Street, 4th floor.* The messenger placed the box directly into T-bone's outstretched hands and waited until T-bone had a firm grip before releasing it.

"Flowers for you, sir," he trilled.

T-bone was so startled he almost let go of the box, but the

messenger was already hurtling down the stairs and T-bone was too slow-witted to react in any fashion. He simply stood there holding the box in his outstretched hands, his mouth hanging open, not a thought in his head; he just looked stupid and stunned.

But Tang's thoughts were working like a black IBM. "Who sending you flowers, black and ugly as you is?" she demanded suspiciously from across the room. And the fact of it was, she really meant it. Still he was her man, simple-minded or not, and it made her jealous for him to get flowers, other than for his funeral, which hadn't happened yet.

"Dese ain't flowers," he said, sounding just as suspicious as she had. "Lessen they be flowers of lead."

"Maybe it's some scoff from the government's thing for the poor folks," she perked hopefully.

"Not unless it's pig-iron knuckles," he said.

She bent over beside him and gingerly fingered the white wrapped box. "It's got your name on it," she said. "And your address. What would anybody be sending to your name and your address?"

"We gonna soon see," he said and stepped across the room to lay the box atop the table. It made a clunking sound. The two blackfaced comedians danced merrily on the television screen until interrupted by a beautiful blonde reading a commercial for Nu-cream, which made dirty skin so fresh and white.

She stood back and watched him break the ribbon and tear off the white wrapping paper. She was practically holding her breath when he opened the gray cardboard carton, but he was too unimaginative to have any thoughts one way or another. If God had sent him down a trunk full of gold bricks from heaven he would have wondered if he was expected to brick up a wall which wasn't his.

Inside the cardboard box they saw a long object wrapped in brown oiled paper and packed in paper excelsior in the way they had seen machine tools packed when they had worked in a shipyard in Newark before she had listened to his sweet talk and had come to Harlem to be his whore. She couldn't imagine anybody sending him a machine tool unless he had been engaged in activities which she didn't know anything about. Which wasn't likely, she thought, as long as she made enough to feed him. He just stared at it stupidly, wondering why anybody would send him something which looked like something he couldn't use even if he wanted to use it.

"Pick it up," she said sharply. "It ain't gonna bite you."

"I ain't scaird of nuttin bitin' me," he said, fearlessly lifting the object from its bed of excelsior. "It ain't heavy as I thought," he said stupidly, although he had given no indication of what he had thought.

She noticed a typewritten sheet which had been lying underneath the object which she instantly suspected was a letter. Quickly she snatched it up.

"Wuss dat?" he asked with the automatic suspicion of one who can't read.

She knew he couldn't read and instinctive jealousy provoked her to needle him. "Writing! That's what."

"What's it say?" he demanded, panic-stricken.

First she read the typed words to herself: WARNING!!! DO NOT INFORM POLICE!!! LEARN YOUR WEAPON AND WAIT FOR INSTRUCTIONS!!! LEARN YOUR WEAPON AND WAIT FOR INSTRUCTIONS!!! WARNING!!! DO NOT INFORM POLICE!!! FREEDOM IS NEAR!!!

Then she read them aloud. They alarmed him so much that sweat broke out over his face and his eyes stretched until they were completely round. Frantically he began tearing off the oiled wrapping paper. The dull gleam of an automatic rifle came into sight. She gasped. She had never seen a rifle that looked as dangerous as that. But he had seen and handled the M-14 used by the United States Army when he had served in the Korean War.

"Iss a M-14," he said. "Iss uh army gun."

He was terrified. His skin dried and appeared dusty.

"I done served my time," he continued, adding "Effen iss stolen I don't want it. Wuss anybody wanna send me a stolen gun for?"

Her eyes blazed in a face contorted with excitement. "It's the uprising, nigger!" she cried. "We gonna be free!"

"Uprising?" He shied away from the thought as though it were a rattlesnake. *"Free?"* He jumped as though the snake had bit him. "Ise already free. All someun wants to do is gat my ass in jail." He held the rifle as though it were a bomb which might go off in his hand.

But she looked at the gun with awe and love. "That'll chop a white policeman two ways sides and flat. That'll blow the shit out of whitey's asshole."

"Wut?" He put the gun down onto the table and pushed it

away from him. "Shoot the white police? Someun 'spects me tuh shoot de white police?"

"Why not? You wanna uprise, don't you?"

"Uprise? Whore, is you crazy? Uprise where?"

"Uprise here, nigger. Is you that stupid? Here we is and here we is gonna uprise."

"Now me! I ain't gonna get my ass blown off waving that thing around. We had them things in Korea and them cats kilt us niggers like flies."

"You got shit in your blood," she said contemptuously. "Let me feel that thing."

She picked the rifle up from the table and held it as though she were shooting rabbits about the room. "Baby," she said directly to the gun. "You and me can make it, baby."

"Wuss de matter wid you? You crazy?" he shouted. "Put that thing down. I'm gonna go tell de man 'fo we gets both our ass in jail."

"You going to tell whitey?" she asked in surprise. "You going run tell the man 'bout this secret that'll make us free?"

"Shut yo' mouth, whore, Ise doin it much for you as I is for me."

At first she didn't take him seriously. "For me, nigger? You think I wanna sell my pussy to whitey all my life?" But, with the gun in her hand, the question was rhetorical. She kept shooting at imaginary rabbits about the room, thinking she could go hunting and kill her a whitey or two. Hell, give her enough time and bullets she could kill them all.

Her words caused him to frown in bewilderment. "You wanna stop being a whore, whore?" he asked in amazement. "Hell, whore, we gotta live."

"You call this living?" She drew the gun tight to her breast as though it were a lover. "This is the only thing what made me feel alive since I met you."

He looked outraged. "You been lissenin to that black power shit, them Black Panthers 'n that shit," he accused. "Ain't I always done what's best?"

"Yeah, put me on the block to sell my black pussy to poor white trash."

"I ain' gonna argy wid you," he said in exasperation. "Ise goan 'n get de cops 'fore we both winds up daid."

Slowly and deliberately, she aimed the gun at him. "You call whitey and I'll waste you," she threatened.

He was moving toward the door but the sound of her voice

stopped him. He turned about and looked at her. It was more the sight of her than the meaning of her words which made him hesitate. He wasn't a man to dare anyone and she had sounded as though she would blow him away. But he knew she was tender-hearted and wouldn't hurt him as long as he didn't cross her. So he decided to kid her along until he could grab the gun, then he'd whip her ass. With this in mind he began shuffling around the table in her direction, grinning obsequiously, playing the part of the forgiving lover. "Baby, I were jes playin—"

"Maybe you are but I ain't," she warned him.

"I weren't gonna call the cops, I were jes gonna see if the door is locked."

"You see and you won't know it."

She talking too much, he thought, shuffling closer to her. Suddenly he grabbed for the gun. She pulled the trigger. Nothing happened. Both froze in shock. It had never occurred to either that the gun was not loaded.

He was the first to react. He burst out laughing. "Haw-haw-haw."

"Wouldn't have been so funny if this thing had been loaded," she said sourly.

Suddenly his face contorted with rage. It was as though the relief felt by the dissipation of his fear had been replaced by fury. He whipped out a springblade knife. "I teach you, whore," he raved. "You try to kill me."

She looked from the knife to his face and said stoically, "I shoulda known, you are whitey's slave; you'll never be free."

"Free of you," he shouted and began slashing at her.

She tried to protect herself with the rifle but shortly he had cut it out of her grasp. She backed around the table trying to keep away from the slashing blade. But soon the blade began reaching her flesh and the floor became covered with blood; she crumpled and fell and died, as she had known she would after the first look at his enraged face.

FREDRIC BROWN

(1906–1972)

Born in Cincinnati, Fredric Brown attended the University of Cincinnati and Hanover College in Indiana. An office worker from 1924 to 1936, he later became a writer on the staff of the Milwaukee Journal. *He began working as a freelancer after 1947, the same year he published* The Fabulous Clipjoint, *the first of seven novels featuring the amateur detective team of Ed and Am Hunter. Brown was a restless talent, however, and wrote many other novels and short stories. Much of his work was in the science fiction field, which he claimed allowed him to be free of the realistic aspect of detective writing with its attention to physical facts and strict probabilities. His only "straight" novel,* The Office *(1958), is based upon work experiences before 1936. He also wrote a juvenile novel,* Mitkey Astromouse *(1971), and teleplays for* Alfred Hitchcock Presents. *Brown is often a disturbing writer who relishes paradox and confronts his readers with a dark vision of life. Much of his work veers so close to horror that the crime element becomes obscured by the bloodshed.* The Screaming Mimi *(1949) featured a mutilating serial killer long before such characters became fashionable, but other works, like* The Far Cry *and* Knock Three One Two *provoked accusations of sordidness. What was once considered to be the hyperbole of Brown's imagination seems less exaggerated today; much of his work speaks loudly to our time. He provides no easy answers, no clean sense of justice that redeems. As in our featured story "Little Apple Hard to Peel," even the justice has an unsettling, operatic excess as a character is driven to revenge.*

LITTLE APPLE HARD TO PEEL

The Appel family moved to our part of the county when John Appel was ten or eleven years old. He was the only kid.

New kids didn't move in very often and, naturally, some of us took considerable interest in finding out whether we could lick him. He liked to fight, we found, and he was good at it.

His name being John Appel, Jonathan Apple was the nickname we picked at first. For some reason, it made him mad, and there wasn't any trouble getting him to fight. He fought with a cold calmness that was unusual for a boy. He never seemed to see red, like the rest of us.

He was small for his age, but tough and muscular. He could lick, we soon learned, any kid his own size. And he could lick most kids who were bigger. He licked me twice, and Les Willis three or four times.

Les Willis, my best pal, was a little slow on the up-take. It took him that many lickings to find out that the Appel kid was too much for him.

It was one of the bigger kids, a few grades above us in school, that first called him "Little Apple Hard to Peel." Appel liked that nickname. He used to brag about it, in fact. Of course nobody called him that much, because it was too long.

The first incident occurred when he'd been around only a week. He knocked a chip off Nick Burton's shoulder. Nick was only a few months older than Appel, but Nick was big for his age. Appel fought like a devil but he just couldn't handle Nick. After the fight was over, he got up and we dusted him off and he wanted to shake hands with Nick. That shaking hands after a fight was new to us; usually we kids stayed mad a few hours and tapered off, sort of.

It was the next day at school that Nick sat on the nail and had to go home. He was in bed three days, and limped quite a while. Somebody'd driven a long, thin nail up through the bottom of his seat, so it stuck out almost two inches.

We kids had often played tricks like that with thumb tacks, but this was something else again. It wasn't any joke. It was obviously meant to hurt badly, and it succeeded. There was quite an inquisition about it. but no one ever found out who had put it there. Somebody, though, had made a secret trip to the schoolhouse at night. Nick sat on it first thing in the morning after the bell rang.

Those of us who knew about the fight Nick had had with Appel wondered a little, but that was all. It didn't seem possible a kid would do something as cruel as that.

Then there was that dirty drawing on the blackboard. Not the usual comic caricature of a teacher that kids draw, but something pretty smutty. There wasn't any name sighed to it, but it was done in yellow chalk, and Les Willis was the only one in the class who had any yellow chalk. The teacher believed Les' denial, finally, or at least she said she did.

But Les failed that year in school and it put him a year behind the rest of us. He'd been sort of on the borderline of keeping up before; he might have made it, if it hadn't been for that. The drawing on the board happened a couple days after Les beat Appel in the tryouts for pitcher for our class team. Appel played second base. But next term he pitched, because Les was still back in the same grade and the rest of us had moved on.

There was another thing. Appel never liked dogs, and dogs didn't take to him at all. There was the time Bud Sherry's little fox terrier, Sport, bit Appel in the leg. Two weeks later Sport died. He died in one of the most painful ways a dog can die. Someone had fed him, not poison, but a sponge pressed tight and coated with meat grease to make a dog gobble it quick. Then that sponge swells up inside the dog. Bud Sperry's uncle was a vet, and when Sport's agony started, Bud took him to his uncle. His uncle chloroformed the dog, and then cut him open—on a hunch—and found the sponge.

Bud Sperry would have killed whoever gave Sport that sponge, if he'd *known* for sure. But there wasn't ever any proof. Not then, or later.

I think it would have been a good thing if Bud Sperry had killed Appel then, proof or no proof. That's a hell of a thing for a sheriff to say. But other things happened, after that, and not always to dogs.

Appel was a good-looking kid about the time we graduated from high school. He was still small, but he was stocky. Despite his size, he'd made a good football player, and he had curly hair, and the girls were crazy about him.

Les Willis had quit high school in his second year and was helping his folks on their farm, just outside of town. The Appel place was just down the road. John Appel wasn't doing anything then, just living with his folks and "looking around." You got the idea, from the way he put it, that there wasn't anything in town good enough for him to do, but that he was looking anyway.

And I was running errands for the sheriff's office, as sort of quasi-deputy with the promise of a deputy's badge when I got "a couple years older and a little less fat in the head."

We were all about eighteen then. Les Willis and John Appel were both in love with Lucinda Howard. She seemed to prefer Les at first, although I wouldn't go so far as to say that she was ever really in love with him.

But Les was starry-eyed about Lucinda. It was serious with Les all right, the kind of love that happens only once in a lifetime and then only to someone who is as fine and clean a fellow as Les. He was the best friend I ever had, and he was a prince of a chap. But he didn't have any glamour. He didn't have curly hair and he wasn't a football player, and he worked pretty hard and didn't have as much time off to take her places.

And besides, after the accident to his foot, he limped. And that meant he couldn't dance, and Lucinda loved to dance. Appel took her out after that and had the field pretty much to himself. Lucinda fell in love with him.

Les' foot—well, it could have been an accident. He was in the habit of taking a morning plunge in good weather, in a creek half a mile back of the Willis farmhouse. He always ran along the path, both ways, barefoot and in just his swimming trunks, and one morning he stepped into a trap along the path. Just a small trap, but barefoot as he was, it cost him two toes and laid him up for quite a while. It was during that time that John Appel made the most progress with Lucinda.

Lucinda fell for him hard. I know that she thought of herself as being engaged to him, although the engagement was never announced.

Then, suddenly, John Appel wasn't around any more, and we learned that he'd taken the night train and bought a ticket for Chicago, and had taken all his clothes and things with him. All but Lucinda; he hadn't even said good-by to her. And he hadn't left a forwarding address, even with his folks. We didn't know that till later, though.

It didn't make a splash. Nobody thought much about it except maybe to wonder whether Lucinda was telling the truth. She said, with her head up and her chin firm, that she'd heard from him by mail and he'd been offered a job that was too good to turn down. Bud Sperry's father was postmaster then and he didn't remember that Lucinda Howard had got any letter from Chicago. And he'd have noticed.

A week later they fished Lucinda Howard's body out of the river. Yes, she'd been going to have a child. She didn't leave a note or anything blaming anybody. There still wasn't any provable charge against Appel.

Les took it hard. Seemed to break him all up inside. He was just back from the hospital then; an infection had set in after his toes were amputated and almost healed. He'd been waiting a decent time for Lucinda to get over John and for him to be able to get around again, before he called on her. Yes, Les would have wanted to marry her anyway. He was that kind of guy. And Lucinda had meant the whole world to him, and now there wasn't any world left. If he hadn't had a good strong religion, he might have followed Lucinda.

Nobody in town heard of John Appel for a long time after that. Twelve years, in fact. I was sheriff then; at thirty I was about the youngest sheriff in the state. Couple of plainclothes men were down from Chicago, checking up on a pennyweighter who'd been down our way and gypped old Angstrom, our jeweler, out of some rings.

I said to them, "Ever hear of a guy named Appel, John Appel? Local boy moved up your way. I was wondering if he made good in the big city."

One of them whistled and shoved his hat back on his head. "Don't tell me Appel came from this freckle on the map."

"I've watched the circulars," I told him. "Never saw his name or his mug. Tell me about him."

"Runs a chunk of the north side of Chi. If it's the same Appel. Short, stocky, about your age?"

I nodded.

The Chicago detective grinned. "They call him Little Apple Hard to Peel."

"Harry Weston gave him that nickname," I told him. "Nearly twenty years ago. He liked it, and I reckon he started it himself where he is now. Used to kind of brag about it."

The Chicago man's eyes narrowed. "Ain't no charge from back here we could make stick, is there? My God, if there is—"

I shook my head slowly.

He sighed. "That was hoping for too much. Listen, there ain't a charge on the blotter against him. Just if there's somebody he don't like or that double-crosses him, something happens to them, that's all. Something not nice. They don't even die clean, mostly, if you understand what I mean."

"That's the guy," I assured him.

"He's too smart. Even makes out his income tax returns right. Or right enough so they can't prove otherwise. He's a legitimate business man. Runs a chain of laundries!" He snorted.

"Officially," I said. "Outside of that?"

His face wasn't nice to look at. There are square cops even from Chicago. "When someone thinks of something dirtier than peddling dope to school kids," he said, "John Appel will back them. But if there's trouble they'll take the rap, not him."

"That his line?"

"I couldn't prove it, but I'd say it was one of them."

The Chi men left town an hour or so later. I didn't say anything about that conversation to Les because it would have opened an old wound.

One thing did occur to me though. Lucinda Howard might have been worse off than she was. Appel might have taken her with him.

Les Willis had, in a way, gathered up the pieces of his life. He'd been pretty no-count for a couple of years, and then he had the full responsibility of the farm put on his shoulders when his pa got sick, and he plunged in and worked like a horse and the work seemed to do him good.

He got to looking all right again, and he acted and thought all right, too, except there was a sort of blank in one part of his mind, as though he'd built up a wall there to shut off one corner.

His love for Lucinda Howard was still there, I guess, in that walled-off corner.

I think Mary Burton understood that part of him better than any of the rest of us. Mary was Nick Burton's kid sister, and she'd loved Les in a quiet sort of way, all through school. He'd dated her a few times when Lucinda had turned him down, but he'd never taken her seriously.

But after his parents died, I guess it was lonesomeness made Les turn to her again. As a friend, at first. But Mary was wise, and she understood him.

For a couple of years she was just a good pal to him. Then Les discovered that she was more than that and they were married. He was twenty-five, then, and Lucinda had been dead six years. Mary was twenty-two.

After their honeymoon Les fixed up the old farmhouse until you wouldn't have known it was the same place, and pretty soon he was painting one room light blue for a nursery. They had twins a year after they were married. A boy and a girl, Dottie and Bill. For Les and Mary the sun rose and set in those kids.

The years rolled along, and the twins were in school, then in high school. No one here thought of John Appel much, except when his parents died, almost at the same time, and our local lawyer sent a routine advertisement for him to the Chicago papers.

A lawyer from Chicago came down, then, with a power of attorney from John, and took over the farm. It wasn't put up for sale, nor was it used. A check for taxes came each year, and the fields lay fallow and the yard was choked with weeks. Plow and harrow rusted in a rotting barn.

Occasionally a bit of news would reach us from Chicago. Appel was tangling in this racket or that. Then there was a rumor that he was dipping into politics; another that he'd sold out all but his gambling interests and was concentrating on that and extending his territory.

Then, utterly without warning, John Appel returned. He dropped off the afternoon train, alone, as casually as though he were returning after a week-end trip. It had been twenty years.

He walked over to where I was standing talking to the station master and said, "Hello, Barney," just as casually as that.

He still had the same curly blond hair, and he looked scarcely any older than when I'd seen him last. He was heavier, but he hadn't picked up a paunch. His skin was tanned, and he looked as fit as an athlete.

Then he noticed the badge I was wearing and grinned. "Glad to see you've made good," he said. He was wearing a suit that had cost at least two hundred dollars, and there was a three-carat diamond ring on his left hand.

"Coming back to show off to the home folks?" I asked casually. "Or hiding out from someone?"

"You name it."

"For long?" I asked. "And if you feel that way about it, consider the question official."

But I'd noticed that the boys were unloading several trunks from the baggage car, and Appel was the only passenger who'd got off the train, so I didn't need the answer to my question.

He took out a platinum cigarette case. I refused, but he lighted one himself. He blew a long exhalation of smoke through his nostrils before he answered, if one could call it an answer. He said, "Do you always welcome people so enthusiastically? Don't tell me you've been hearing stories about me."

"We don't want you here," I told him.

He grinned again, apparently genuinely amused this time.

"Don't tell me *that's* official, Barney. If it is, I'd be curious to know the charge."

He turned away before I could reply. Which was just as well, because there wasn't any answer. He was a property-holder, and there wasn't a legal reason I could think of for taking official action. There wasn't a proven charge against him here; probably none in Chicago or elsewhere. But I'd let him know where he stood with me, and I wasn't sorry.

Then I heard footsteps coming around the wooden platform from the other side of the station, and for a moment my heart slowed. For those footsteps limped; they were made by Les Willis.

I thought for a moment he knew that Appel was here and that this was why he had come. Then I saw his clear eyes as he walked toward me and I realized he'd come to the station on some other errand.

I put my hand on his arm and said, "Take it easy, Les."

He looked at me, puzzled, and then before I could explain he turned and flashed a glance up and down the platform as though he'd guessed. And he saw John Appel.

I was holding tightly to his arm and I felt him start to tremble. I didn't look at his face; I thought it best not to, just then. That tremble wasn't because of fear.

I spoke softly. "Take it easy, Les, I know how you feel, but there's nothing we can do. Nothing. There's not a scrap of evidence against him on any charge."

He didn't answer. I don't know whether he heard me or not. I said, "Go home, Les. Keep away from him. He won't stay long. Keep clear of him—for Dottie and Bill's sake! He's a killer now, Les!"

I guess it was the mention of the twins that brought him back. But he said, "He was a killer even when he was a kid, Barney."

I knew what Les meant. To me, too, those things that had happened more than twenty years ago seemed worse to us than the real murders Appel had undoubtedly committed since. Possibly because we were closer to them. Those things had happened to people we knew and loved. They weren't gangster stuff.

I heard Appel crossing toward where we stood. I could tell by Les' face that he was coming too. I said, "Les, for God's sake, go—"

He said, quietly, "I'm all right, Barney. Don't worry."

His voice was so calm that I took my hand off his arm.

Appel said smoothly. "If it isn't Willis. You look older, Les. Golly, you look twenty years older'n Barney here. Been misbehaving?"

Les Willis showed better sense than I'd dared to hope he would show. He didn't answer, but turned on his heel and started off.

Appel's face got ugly at that. I think if Les had gotten mad and cussed him out, it would have amused him, but not speaking at all managed to get under his hide. He said, loud enough so Les would hear it, "Barney, there's gratitude for you. I go off and leave him a clear field to get that little tramp he was in love with—what was her name? Lucinda something—and here he—"

Thinking it over afterward, I guess Appel had never heard what had happened to Lucinda Howard. He was merely trying to bait Les into an argument. Otherwise he would have been prepared for what happened.

Les was a few steps beyond me. He whirled and was back past me almost in a single leap, so suddenly that I wasn't able to stop him. His fist caught Appel flush on the mouth, and Appel went down—not knocked out, but simply carried over backward by the momentum of the blow.

He started to scramble to his feet. Les, his face filled with cold fury, stood over him, fists clenched. I got between them.

"Les," I said sharply, and took him by the arm and shook him. "Get out of here. Remember Dottie and Bill—your kids. You can't start trouble! For their sakes!"

I shook him harder. He didn't answer, but he turned and walked off like a man in a daze. His footsteps limped across the platform toward the steps.

I whirled on Appel. And I had my hand on the butt of the gun in my pocket as I whirled. He'd just got to his feet. His face was a gargoyle mask. He took a step as though to push past me, but I stopped him. I said, "Cut it out. This isn't Chicago."

His face returned to normal so suddenly that I thought I had misread the expression that had been on it before. His fists unclenched. He said, "That's right. This isn't Chicago."

I said, "You had that coming; you know it. The matter's over, unless you want to bring an assault charge. If you do—"

He grinned. "Maybe I had it coming. Nope, I won't bring any charge, sheriff. I won't hurt your little boy, Les, *if* he stays away from me from now on."

Yes, I was fool enough to believe him. I sighed with relief. I knew I could talk Les out of ever going near him again, and I thought I'd avoided trouble. Sure, I remembered the way Appel had held grudges before, but that was when he was younger. He'd grown up now, he was interested in bigger game and bigger money. Besides he'd admitted he was in the wrong.

I even relented enough to walk with him to the hotel, although I refused a drink. I heard him order the best room they had.

The next day a dozen workmen went out to the old Appel place. Carpenters, painters, decorators, gardeners. They worked three days putting the place in shape. His orders, I learned, had been to repair and restore—not to change anything. To make it as nearly as possible like the place it had been twenty years ago when he'd known it last. I've never understood that. A strange sentimental streak in a man who hadn't come back for the funerals of his own parents.

But he insisted that same furniture be retained, placed just as it was, except that it should be refinished and repaired.

No, I never understood that about John Appel, any more than I understood why he came back at all or for how long he had originally intended to stay.

I was fool enough to think that maybe it meant that he was

tired of crime, that he was coming back to try to find himself. I gave him the benefit of the doubt. Having no legal excuse for ordering him out of the county, I made a virtue of a necessity by telling myself that possibly it was for the best.

I saw him but a few times—and then only casually—before the end of the week when the work on the old Appel farm was done, and he moved his trunks out there from the hotel. He took no servants to live with him, and said he was going to do his own cooking, but he made arrangements with a woman to come in three times a week to do cleaning and laundering.

Meanwhile, of course, I'd talked to Les Willis. He'd listened to all I had to say, and had answered, "All right, Barney." But I could see that he'd changed, almost over night. That wall across one section of his mind had broken down again. He was remembering. I don't mean that he'd ever forgotten, actually, but he'd managed not to think about certain things. Now those memories were back with him.

It was two weeks and four days after Appel had stepped off the train that Les Willis' house burned down.

The fire must have started about midnight. Les had driven Mary over to her mother's to spend the evening. The twins were in high school then and they'd been left at home to study, as they had final exams the next day.

As it happened, the Burtons' mare was foaling that evening. Les was a good hand with animals and knew quite a bit about vetting. He'd stayed to help, and that was why he and Mary didn't leave until after twelve o'clock.

It was a bright moonlit night. As they drove their car out of the Burtons' driveway they saw the red glow against the sky.

Right away they knew it was a fire somewhere near their place, and for a minute they were going back in to the Burton house to phone town for the fire apparatus. Then, through the still night, they heard its clanging bell and knew that someone else had phoned already.

Les put the accelerator to the floor and held it there. When they got home the fire department was already on the scene. And there wasn't much left of the house.

It had been an old, weathered frame building that had gone up like tinder. The twins, Dottie and Bill, slept in bedrooms that had been partitioned off in the attic. Apparently smoke had smothered them in their sleep and they'd never awakened.

I got there rather late.

Chet Harrington, the fire chief, called me over. He said, "Barney, maybe this is a case for you. Looks like this fire was *set.*"

He pointed toward where a shapeless piece of candle-stub lay in a puddle of water alongside one corner of the house.

"My guess," he said, "is that that could be the joker. Someone could'a splashed some gasoline on this side of the house—it went first—and stuck that piece of candle against the house and lit it. Look, what's left of that candle is gutted along one side like it burned horizontally, and then dropped off. It rolled out from the house then when it hit, and—"

"Where's Les?" I interrupted.

"Mary sorted collapsed. They took her into town. Guess Les went along."

"Les see that candle? Did you tell him about it, Chet?"

He nodded. "I didn't show him, but I saw him looking queerly at it once."

I ran over to the people by the gate. "Did Les go into town with Mary?"

There were conflicting answers at first. Then it was decided Les hadn't gone in that car. But Les' own car was gone . . . No, there it was, still on the road. Who'd seen Les last?

While they were arguing about that, I started running across the fields to the Appel farm.

From some distance away I could see that there was a light on downstairs, and I tried to run faster.

Then I saw Les Willis coming across the porch, from inside the house. It was dark in the shadows of the porch, but I knew him by his slight figure, and by the limp. I knew, of course, that he'd killed Appel, and that was bad enough, but I'd figured it would be the other way. That Appel would have had another self-defense killing to his credit.

No, I hadn't expected to see Les Willis alive again. He came down the porch steps into the bright moonlight, holding onto the rail. And I saw that he wasn't alive, really. He stood there holding onto the post of the railing to keep from falling. I saw that he was covered with blood. I could see where at least two bullets had hit him. And with bullets in those places, he had no reason to be alive. But all that blood couldn't have come from those wounds.

I said, "Les?"

I wouldn't have known his voice. I had to strain my ears to catch the words. He said, "He wasn't too hard to peel. But he died . . . too soon."

His knees buckled, and as he crumpled slowly something fell from his hand. It was a knife—the kind used for skinning game.

It was minutes before I got up the nerve to enter the house, to see what was in that lighted room.

Les' funeral was one of the biggest our town had ever seen, but only the coroner and I attended the other one. I imagine, though, that we could have had a tremendous gate for the funeral of Little Apple Hard to Peel if I hadn't announced that the coffin was nailed shut and would stay that way.

ACKNOWLEDGMENTS

Block, Lawrence: "Someday I'll Plant More Walnut Trees." Copyright © 1993 by Lawrence Block.

Brand, Christianna: "Bless This House." Copyright © 1993. The late Christianna Brand. Reprinted by permission of AM Heath & Company Limited.

Brett, Simon: "Don't Know Much About Art." Copyright © 1984 by Simon Brett. First published in *Winter's Crimes* 16. Reprinted by permission of the author and Michael Motley Ltd.

Brittain, William: "The Man Who Read John Dickson Carr." Copyright © 1965 by Davis Publications, Inc., reprinted by permission of the author. First appeared in *Ellery Queen's Mystery Magazine*.

Brown, Fredric: "Little Apple Hard to Peel." First published in *Detective Tales,* February 1942; published in collection of Fredric Brown stories *Mostly Murder,* E.P. Dutton. Copyright © 1953 by Fredric Brown.

Burke, Thomas: "The Hands of Mr. Ottermole." Copyright © 1931 by Richard Sezler. Reprinted by permission of John Hawkins & Associates, Inc.

Carr, John Dickson: "The Shadow of the Goat." Copyright © 1980 by Clarice M. Carr. Reprinted by permission of Harold Ober Associates, Incorporated.

Chandler, Raymond: "I'll Be Waiting," from *The Simple Art of Murder.* Copyright © 1934, 1935, 1936, 1938, 1939, 1944, 1950 by Raymond Chandler. Copyright © 1978 by Helga Greene. Reprinted by permission of Houghton Mifflin Company. All rights reserved.

Christie, Agatha: "The Blue Geranium." Copyright © 1928, 1929, 1930, 1933 by Agatha Christie. Renewed 1956, 1960 by Agatha Christie Mallowan. Reprinted by permission of Harold Ober Associates, Incorporated.

Dahl, Roald: "The Landlady." From *Kiss Kiss* by Roald Dahl. Copyright © 1959 by Roald Dahl. Reprinted by permission of Alfred A. Knopf, Inc. Originally appeared in *The New Yorker.*

Dinesen, Isak: "The Fat Man." Copyright © 1977 by University of Chicago. All rights reserved.

Doyle, Arthur Conan: "The Adventure of the Dying Detective." Copyright © 1921 by International Magazine Company. Reprinted by permission of the copyright owner.

Ellin, Stanley: "The Orderly World of Mr. Appleby." Copyright © 1950 by Mercury Publications, renewed 1977 by Stanley Ellin. Reprinted by permission of Curtis Brown Ltd.

Glaspell, Susan: "A Jury of Her Peers." Copyright © 1917 by Susan Glaspell. Reprinted by permission of Curtis Brown Ltd. First appeared in *Everyweek.*

Hammett, Dashiell: "They Can Only Hang You Once." Copyright © renewed 1960 by Dashiell Hammett. Reprinted by permission of the Literary Property Trustees.

Himes, Chester: "Tang." From the book *The Collected Stories of Chester Himes* by Chester Himes. Copyright © 1990 by Lesley Himes. Reprinted by permission of the publisher, Thunder's Mouth Press.

Hoch, Edward D.: "The Leopold Locked Room." Copyright © 1971 by Edward D. Hoch. First published in *Ellery Queen's Mystery Magazine.*

Jackson, Shirley: "The Possibility of Evil." From *Just an Ordinary Day: The Uncollected Stories* by Shirley Jackson. Copyright ©

1997 by The Estate of Shirley Jackson. Reprinted by permission of Bantam Books, a division of Bantam Doubleday Dell Publishing Group, Inc.

Kaminsky, Stuart M.: "Busted Blossoms." Copyright © 1986 by Stuart Kaminsky. First published in *Mean Streets,* edited by Robert J. Randisi, published by Mysterious Press.

Lovesy, Peter: "The Secret Lover." Copyright © 1985. Reprinted by permission of the author.

Queen, Ellery: "The Adventure of Abraham Lincoln's Clue." Copyright © 1965 by Ellery Queen, renewed. Reprinted by permission of the author's estate and its agents, Scott Meredith Literary Agency, L.P., New York, NY.

Runyon, Damon: "What, No Butler?" Copyright renewed © 1961 by Damon Runyon, Jr. and Mary Runyon McCann, Children of the Author. Copyright assigned to Sheldon Abend in 1992.

Sayers, Dorothy L. : "The Necklace of Pearls." Copyright © 1972 by Harper & Row Publishers, Inc. Reprinted by permission of the estate of Anthony Fleming and Watkins/Loomis Agency, Inc.

Stout, Rex: "Disguise for Murder," Copyright © 1950 by Rex Stout, renewed. Original title "The Twisted Scarf," from *Curtains for Three* by Rex Stout. Reprinted by permission of Viking Penguin, a division of Penguin Books USA, Inc.

Suter, John F.: "The Impossible Theft." Copyright © 1964 by John F. Suter. First published by Davis Publications, Inc. Reprinted by permission of the author.

Westlake, Donald E.: "The Ultimate Caper." Copyright © 1975 by Donald E. Westlake. Reprinted by permission of Knox Burger Associates.

CPSIA information can be obtained
at www.ICGtesting.com
Printed in the USA
BVHW080713290323
661185BV00001B/1

9 780195 104875